THE KING

August Trello: He founded a massive company that produced cheap wine—and made him dangerously rich.

THE PRINCELINGS

Gus Jr.: A weak-willed playboy, he had been broken by his father's uncompromising demands.
Frank: Cowed, submissive, he tragically sought to please the father who openly despised him.
Jules: An amoral, manipulating schemer, he was determined to make it big without his father's help—whatever the cost.

THE PRINCESS

Audra Trello Mancini: Trello's daughter, she married Robert Mancini, who broke away from the family dynasty to produce a finer wine—and broke away from his rocky marriage when journalist Barbara Turner entered the picture.

Books by Jack M. Bickham

Twister
The Winemakers

Published by POCKET BOOKS

THE WINE MAKERS

JACK BICKHAM

PUBLISHED BY POCKET BOOKS NEW YORK

POCKET BOOKS, a Simon & Schuster division of
GULF & WESTERN CORPORATION
1230 Avenue of the Americas, New York, N.Y. 10020

Copyright © 1977 by Jack M. Bickham

Published by arrangement with Doubleday & Company, Inc.
Library of Congress Catalog Card Number: 76-56265

ISBN: 0-671-82136-9

First Pocket Books printing December, 1978

Trademarks registered in the United States and other countries.

Printed in the U.S.A.

For Bob, Dan, Steve, and Lisè

The author gratefully acknowledges the help provided during research by the California Wine Institute; Charles Carpy, of Freemark Abbey; Robert Mondavi, president of Robert Mondavi Vineyards; Jerry Gleeson, of the Christian Brothers; Mr. and Mrs. Richard T. Kessler, Napa Valley growers, and others who helped in lesser but significant ways. They will find that I have taken fictional liberties with their valley, but not—I hope—with winemaking technique.

Part One

1

The first hint of serious trouble came shortly after ten o'clock on a Tuesday night early in May.

Susan Knight, alone in the quiet, wood-paneled blending room beside her laboratory in the winery, had no warning.

A tall, lithe young woman with long blond hair and remarkable green eyes, Susan wore a white lab smock over her colorful spring dress, and had her lustrous hair tied back in a utilitarian bun. Even though she usually looked like this at work, visitors to the winery were fond of telling her that she looked more like a fashion model or a California beach girl than the chief winemaker at one of America's most respected new vineyards. Susan usually smiled at such comments and took them as compliments; the people who made them would have been shocked by an expletive.

There were no visitors in the winery at this hour, however. The entire complex was almost deserted. Susan wanted it that way. She intended to remain working until she had found precisely the right blend for the new Robert Mancini Vineyards wine, and she wanted no interruptions.

Arranged along the back edge of the spotless blending table, in a single row from Susan's left to right, were twenty-five six-ounce bottles. Each bottle, of dark-green glass and stoppered with a cork, contained red wine. Each bore on its side a white three-digit number, written there by Susan with a fluid-marking stylus. Each represented a wine presently in cooperage—oak barrel storage—within the Man-

3

cini winery. Most were different lots of wine fermented totally from the Cabernet Sauvignon, the noble black grape which produced the great reds of the Bordeaux in France. Others represented lots of Merlot, a Cabernet-like wine with slightly different characteristics. Others were Zinfandel, another dark grape of mysterious California origins which was closely related to the Cabernet. Two bottles represented small cooperage quantities of Petite Sirah, a fruity, brightly red wine usually consumed quite young.

Some of the wines represented by the sample bottles had been fermented more quickly than others, using temperature management to control the rate of fermentation. Some were very young, while others had mellowed in the finest French oak barrels for three years. Some had come from the finest old vineyards, others from younger fields of great promise. While one small blending bottle represented more than fifty thousand gallons of red wine waiting for use, others represented less than a tenth of that amount in cooperage.

California law required only that a wine contain at least 51 per cent of a certain grape to be labeled as the product of that grape. To be vintage dated, a wine had to be at least 95 per cent from the stated year. Robert Mancini, however, like many of California's top winemakers, refused to use these minimums; his top "varietal" wines—those labeled with grape names such as Cabernet Sauvignon, Sauvignon Blanc, Zinfandel, Pinot Chardonnay, and the like—were always 100 per cent of that varietal, or very close to it. And there was no mixing of one year with another in these premium wines.

The wine Susan Knight was trying to blend properly tonight was not, then, one of these top labels. But lesser wines, given only a general descriptive title on the label, were not treated lightly either. Susan's goal tonight was to find the finest possible blending to produce the finest possible lower-priced wine. Combining her knowledge of each wine's characteristics with hard-headed realities of costs and inventory levels, she must find precisely the right blend for the best color, bouquet and complex of tastes sought in the new product, while at the same time best managing inventories and holding a certain price line.

In front of each blending bottle was a standard wine glass. Nearby were beakers and pipettes of various bores and capacities, and a steel-jacketed notebook.

Her eyebrows knit slightly with concentration, Susan Knight opened a bottle numbered 218. Using a cylindrical glass tube, she measured a precise amount of this wine into a glass, flipped open the notebook, and recorded what she had done. She held the wine glass to the light and assured herself that it was perfectly clear, with the rich, deep, slightly bluish red of a Cabernet Sauvignon.

Because she had planned this blending, she then moved swiftly. Moving seven other bottles slightly forward of the line, she measured varying amounts from each into the glass. She recorded each step.

"Now," she said softly, raising the glass of blended wine.

The tasting procedure was one she had learned, with slight variations, in years of study at a university. There she had tasted wines and learned to evaluate them hour after hour, day after day, month in and month out. She held the glass in her hands, allowing her body heat to warm the contents slightly as she swirled the liquid gently. She noted the distant bouquet, slightly dry, fruity, with overtones of both the Cabernet and the Zinfandel.

She held the glass to the light, examining it critically. The color was good, but with a slightly undesirable purple quality which she tended to identify with a very young wine. An ordinary connoisseur would not have noticed this cast.

Raising the glass slowly, she again swirled the contents and dipped her nose in well over the rim. The liberated vapors surrounded her, and at close range were good: no hint of off-odors of any kind, with the dominant impression of a clean, dry Cabernet. There was the tiniest hint of the Merlot, and perhaps a suggestion of strawberry-like fruit, the Zinfandel.

Susan repeated the swirling, taking quick, full sniffs.

Satisfied, she then raised the glass again in a sort of silent ritual toast to whatever happy gods had looked down on winemaking for all the centuries.

"Now," she said softly, raising the glass toward her lips.

But she did not get to taste the wine. Somewhere beyond the closed door of the lab, an alarm-system bell began clamoring at shattering volume.

The bell signified either fire or some other extreme emergency. Susan Knight had never heard it before, and its loudness—and implications—jarred her to the quick. Quickly placing the wine glass back on the table, she assured herself with a glance that all the bottles were stoppered. Then she ran to the door.

It opened into a darkened, paneled corridor. The old winery building, remodeled less than a decade ago, had retained its high ceilings and dark wood, so that the effect now, with an alarm bell clamoring less than a dozen paces away, was eerie. Susan ran under the bell and to the far staircase, which led down toward the first floor.

There was no one in the first-floor hallway, but the bells were hammering there too. Susan burst through glass doors into the main foyer, its handful of security lights aglow against the ornate scroll-work of old high ceilings and the deep reds and blues of stained-glass windows. This area, mainly for winery visitors, was also deserted. She could detect no hint of smoke, only the familiar yeasty odors of fermentation.

Across the vast foyer were the double oak doors that led to the production areas one floor below. Susan hurried toward them. She had to find out what was happening before she could notify anyone—and she had to learn how much help there was now in the winery.

It was the worst possible time for a crisis. Regular workers left at 5 or 6 P.M. During the peak times of fermentation or bottling, many employees might be on hand around the clock. But this was the slackest period, and she knew that only the smallest caretaker force might be on duty at this hour. *My God,* she thought, *I can't handle a fire.* And then for an instant she saw in her imagination how a major conflagration could leap through this old winery, destroying everything all of them had worked so hard to build.

She opened the doors into the production area stairwell. Thicker wine odors enveloped her. She stepped forward, intent on watching the wooden stairs, and collided with someone coming up. She staggered and felt an instant of unreasoning fear before she recognized lanky, bald, overall-clad Henry Hover, the maintenance foreman.

Hover looked as startled as she, but recovered faster. Grasping her arms, he shook her as if to assure himself she was there. "Is you, Miz Knight?" he panted in his thick Scandinavian accent. "Is any peoples vit you?"

"I'm alone, Henry. What's happening?"

"Tank good Lord *sawmbody* here! I vas on way oopstairs—"

"Henry, what's happening? Is it a fire?"

"No—no fire. I set off de alarm myself."

"Why?"

"Come. I show you." Greatly agitated, Hover turned and started back down the stairs at a reckless pace.

Following, Susan descended the spiraling stairs into an atmosphere that was unusually warm and redolent of fermentation fumes. The past several days had been unseasonally warm and sunny, and the production rooms were in a new wing that extended from the thick walls of the main winery structure. The cooperage buildings would never have been allowed to get this warm—over 80 degrees—but because all the fermentation tanks were individually temperature-controlled, the temperature of the air had been allowed to rise while the central air conditioning was being re-engineered and improved.

Susan followed Hover now into a long, steel-roofed structure that looked like the set for a science-fiction movie. Rows of huge stainless-steel tanks, each with a capacity of 1,250 gallons, stood like gleaming silos one after another. Overhead fluorescent lights gleamed on racks, metal stairs, metal fittings and miles of glittering pipe. Thick white hoses extended and interlaced all over bare concrete floors studded with drains. Dials and control valves jutted from the sides of tanks festooned with thick white frost around their midsections, where coils containing ethylene glycol provided constant cooling to desired temperature. It was down these rows that the elderly custodian led Susan Knight at breakneck pace.

"Here," he said finally, pausing at a spot where the tanks loomed over them on all sides. He was badly out of breath.

Susan stared at him, confused. "Here . . . *what?*"

Hover put a knobby hand to the side of the nearest tank. "Dese tanks. Dey are broke."

Susan's breath caught as she looked up at the cooling coils on the midsection of the nearest tank. There was no frost. She ran to the gauge which recorded interior temperature, and received a worse shock.

She knew without having to consult any records that these tanks contained Sauvignon Blanc being fermented by the relatively new cold fermentation process. The juice, or *must*, was being held at a steady 40 degrees, providing fermentation that required a full nine months for its fruition.

Other white wines nearby had already completed fermentation, and many tanks had already been emptied and sterilized again. The normal process called for crushing, inoculation with the proper yeast, fermentation for fifteen days at 55 degrees, vacuum filtration to remove undesirable downstream activity, and three weeks in stainless steel. The longer cold process, however, yielded a different sort of wine, the colder fermentation locking in more flavor and aroma esters. Ethylene glycol cooling made it possible, and Robert Mancini had high hopes for this wine—ten thousand gallons in a row of eight tanks, the yield of some sixty-four tons of fine grapes which had been coaxed, watched and babied for more than seven months already.

But Henry Hover was obviously right: something had gone wrong. The temperature on this tank was already above 41 degrees.

Susan ran to the next tank, and the next. Shocked, she saw that the cooling system had failed on all eight of them. Temperatures, driven by the warmth of the area and the processes of fermentation, were on the steady, accelerating rise. The entire batch—all the wine of this type to be made in the year—was on the brink of ruin.

As Susan hurried back to where the custodian waited, she saw three other workers hurry in from the cooperage area. None was expert; she had no sign of skilled help in whatever she had to do. But she knew that delay was impossible. She had to act.

Hover mopped sweat from his brow with a bandana. "You see? All temperatures is oop, yah?"

"Yes," Susan muttered, glancing around at available equipment, trying to form a plan.

"I do right, ringing bell?" Hover insisted worriedly.

"You did right," Susan assured him. "Now we have to do something about it."

"I call Mr. Mancini?"

Susan hesitated an instant. There was not even time for that. Every minute might count now. As the immense quantities of wine in each tank began rising in temperature at some kind of exponential rate, all calculations about quality would be thrown out of kilter: new molecules would form, new esters thrown. Temperature control had to be regained *now*.

"We'll call later, Henry," she decided. "Help me." She strode to a nearby control panel beside the row of empty, sterilized tanks facing those that were mysteriously mal-functioning. Throwing switches, she was rewarded to hear the hum of compressors as they began to feed coolant to this unused row. With Hover's help, she adjusted temperature settings.

"But dese ain't de tanks with the wine in," Hover protested.

"They will be, Henry," Susan snapped, leading him back to the aisle.

Scanning the thick hoses arrayed on the floor, she directed one of the other men to fit it to the valve on the side of a malfunctioning tank. As he did this, she manhandled the other end of the hose to a spot near a floor drain.

"Do you know the big portable racking pump?" she asked another worker.

"The one on the orange dolly? Sure."

"You two go get it here, quick."

As they scurried off, Susan made certain the fitting at the side of the endangered tank was secure, then threw a valve. A slight stream of water or condensate spewed from the far end of the hose into the drain, and then a crystalline stream of cool wine from the tank's innards.

Satisfied that this hose was thoroughly flushed out, she hurried to repeat the process with another, attached to the next tank. Henry Hover and the remaining cooperage worker got the idea and went ahead of her to the next tank in the row.

The tanks on the right, disabled, were quickly being hooked to drain hoses. Those on the right, still empty, now wore frosty collars from refrigeration.

The next minutes were a blur. Drenched with her own sweat and the fluids gushing from hoses as they were flushed, Susan got her small makeshift crew to position the electrically operated pumping unit between the first two tanks. More hoses were flushed and connected between the pump and the empty, cooled tanks. In a little while, the endangered wine from No. 24 tank—the first connected—was gushing into its neighbor across the aisle, which had its refrigerating system intact.

"You can take a rest, ma'am," one of the workers told Susan. "We got the hang of it. As soon as this one is empty, we'll move to the next."

Exhausted, Susan sank to the rung of a steel ladder and

mopped her face with a towel. She did not believe damage had been done. She tried to catch her breath.

Henry Hover squatted beside her, gray-faced. "I call Mr. Mancini now?"

"Yes," Susan said. "I'd better stay right here—just in case. Tell him what's happened and what we're doing. Tell him I'm staying right here until he arrives."

Hover nodded and got stiffly to his feet. He limped down the wine-flooded concrete aisle toward the far stairs.

Susan watched him with intense admiration. If he had not been diligent, the wine might have been changed drastically within a few hours. Even when they had caught it, the chances were that refrigeration had been off for some time, perhaps since shortly after six o'clock.

How had an entire bank of tanks been disabled? How much damage had been done to the wine?

Only time would answer the latter question. But now a new and even more puzzling one formed in her fatigued mind.

Only last year Robert Mancini had installed a small computer, designed expressly to maintain constant surveillance on such matters as fermentation temperatures. The computer should have sounded its own alarm the moment cooling equipment failed.

Why hadn't the computer done its job?

Her legs aching sharply, Susan got up and walked away from the tank row. She cut between other tanks rows and past the one-hundred-thousand-dollar stainless-steel centrifuge that could take three hundred to six thousand gallons of wine per hour through its sight glass. Beyond this area was a doorway into the computer room.

Susan entered, and immediately recoiled.

Ordinarily, even with the overhead lights shut off, the far wall was like a Christmas tree of blinking panel displays as the freezer-sized mini-computer continued its constant operations. Now, however, the room was perfectly dark.

Susan flicked the light switch. Nothing happened.

A power failure in the computer room, then. This explained why automatic monitoring had not been going on. But it struck her immediately that bad luck could only be just so incredible before some other cause had to be considered. An unseasonal heat wave . . . work on the air conditioning . . . failure of cooling units . . . failure of power to the computer. *Wasn't this a little too much bad luck to be accidental?*

There was nothing she could do here. She retraced her steps to the tank line, where the workers were busier than ever. More wine was being transferred.

Going behind one of the inoperable tanks, Susan found the compressor connections. Although she knew little about the mechanical aspects of the cooling equipment, she could not immediately see what might have caused the shutdown; the valves were all turned properly, and there was pressure in the lines.

Tracing the lines to the electric motor which drove the unit, however, she immediately saw the problem. A pair of wires, red and blue, fed electricity to the motor. But the two wires were not connected. They hung onto the concrete, completely disconnected.

Susan picked up the wire ends and examined them. They had not merely slipped off and they had not broken. Their points of termination were too neat for that. They had been cut.

She stood there, shock trickling through her bloodstream. She could never have anticipated it, but she felt certain of her theory. This was sabotage.

What Susan Knight could not know, standing there then, was that she had just witnessed the first in a sequence of events destined to threaten the very existence of Robert Mancini Vineyards, bring death and violence to unsuspecting people, take the California wine industry to the brink of ruinous scandal, and reverberate even into the misty valleys of the Bordeaux.

2

Susan Knight had never felt any hesitation about going to work for Robert Mancini. She had felt very lucky to be offered the job when she finished college "for the second time"—adding a degree in enology to her earlier degree in journalism—because even in 1971, only three years after Robert had crushed his first grapes in his own winery, he was recognized as one of the leading young winemakers in America.

In 1973, when Robert Mancini's chief winemaker, Timothy Crocker, departed to found his own nearby Crocker Vineyards, Susan had again been surprised to be offered the top post, not only because she was a woman but because another assistant had been on the job a year longer than she. Again, however, she had felt no hesitancy; it was an unparalleled opportunity.

In the few years of their association, Susan had learned that Robert Mancini, in addition to being profoundly dedicated to the making of the finest possible wine, was a man of great kindness and courage. So it was with concern for his latest trouble, as well as fatigue and shaky knees in the aftermath of the sabotage, that she faced her employer across his desk well after midnight.

They both had plastic cups of coffee before them, and Robert was smoking a cigarette, something he did only when pressure overcame his continuing struggle to quit. A tall and craggily handsome man of forty-five, he wore

12

baggy corduroy trousers and a red sweatshirt that he evidently had thrown on at home when called about the emergency. The clothing was in sharp contrast to the continental suits and open-collared shirts he usually wore in impeccable taste, and his compactly curly hair was slightly rumpled, another unusual sign of his tension.

"You did exactly the right thing, Susan," Robert Mancini told her now. "It was just so lucky for us that you happened to be here."

"I'm sure I wasn't supposed to be," Susan replied.

Robert frowned at the tip of his cigarette. "While I was checking out the computer and getting it set again, I thought about what you said at the door. The compressors fail, the computer power switch just happens to slip—and both when it's unseasonably warm and the air conditioning is being worked on and we have our slackest period on employees in the winery. I don't see how there's any doubt: your guess has to be correct."

"Sabotage?" Susan said.

"I'm afraid so."

"I still can't believe it."

Robert's face set. "We have to believe it. I've contacted Mike. He'll have a half-dozen extra men on the grounds within the hour. They'll make extra checks on everything and maintain maximum security."

At the mention of Mike DeFrates, the hard-working chief of production, Susan felt another twinge of concern. "Poor Mike will take this hard. He's hand-picked practically every man who works in production."

"It doesn't have to be someone in production."

"You don't think someone on the office force—!"

Robert's face set into lines even more grim. "The computer printed out at five. By five-thirty it had been shut down. Anyone could have slipped the switch. Anyone."

"But *why?*"

Robert sipped his coffee, looked at his cigarette with distaste, and put it out in the seldom-used bronze ashtray on his large walnut desk. The desk, like his large, spartan office, and like the rest of his life, was very neat and well organized: the ashtray, a few pieces of correspondence in a leather-bound tray at one corner, a pen holder, a memo pad, a clear plastic paperweight laminated around the label from a priceless bottle of Burgundy he had enjoyed with a memorable meal in Paris in 1966. He said, "Of course we can't predict what this violence will do to that wine."

Eager to reassure him, Susan spoke with more confidence than she felt: "I don't think any harm at all has been done."

"I hope you're right. Certainly there's some reason to hope so. Which is my point. Whoever pulled this trick had no assurance that he—or she—would really do any damage to us. Yet that person ran considerable risk. Why would someone take such a risk just to cause us worry and misery?"

"I don't have any idea," Susan admitted.

"Neither do I. And that's what really worries me."

Susan thought about it. Robert Mancini had bought the historic old winery more than a decade ago, not long after the celebrated but mysterious dissolution of his partnership with his brother-in-law, Jules Trello. After a year of travel and intensive new study in Europe, Robert had then begun the massive job of rebuilding the old plant, acquiring additional vineyards, and installing new equipment. With the fervor of a missionary, he had told anyone who would listen that the future of this valley north of San Francisco had to be in the highest-quality wine, that the valley's marvelous climate and unique soils were being wasted by those producing cheap jug wines, and that the huge new irrigated vineyards in southern California would take over mass production of cheap wines within a few years anyway. Robert Mancini had quickly become known not only as a spokesman for changing ways, but as a leader; he had been among those pioneering new methods of cold fermentation in stainless steel, more extended cooperage of the best wines in small barrels of the finest oak from the Nevers Forest in France, use of the centrifuge and computer, and more rigorous standards for all grapes, with quality bonuses to outside growers who wished to sell to him.

Susan had never heard criticism of Robert Mancini for any of this. There were many other fine wineries in the valley, and Robert had not been alone in pioneering and upgrading. Yet now, faced with this evident sabotage, a sure sign that *someone* harbored serious animosity, Susan found herself wondering if there might not be jealousies she was not aware of. There might be growers, bitter because their grapes did not meet the Mancini standards. There might be former employees, dismissed because they did not demonstrate enough devotion to Robert's brand of fanatical quality control. Although she did not know the details (no one did, seemingly), it was said that the split between Robert and Jules Trello had been partially over the question of whether their winery of that time, known by its traditional name of Schreck Brothers, should continue in the jug wine business, or begin upgrading. Relations between Robert and Jules were cool to this day. So even Jules, or some of his associates, might have some hidden motive . . .

"Of course," she said without much force, "it could be a prankster—a total outsider."

"I doubt that," Robert said, draining his coffee cup. "But anything is possible. The thing to do now is get those tanks repaired, try to make sure it doesn't happen again, and keep a close eye on that wine."

"As I said, it probably wasn't harmed."

Robert's scowl—the one that showed his deepest concentration and commitment—deepened. "We'll taste it tomorrow morning. I'll want lab testing as well."

"I planned that."

"I hate to think we'd have to market all that wine as unnamed house wine after all the love we've given it."

"I don't think there can possibly be much change in it, Robert."

"We won't sell it as our finest Sauvignon Blanc unless it's perfect, unless it meets our highest standards. You know that."

Susan hesitated, seeing the near anger in his dark eyes. It occurred to her that the enemy, whoever it might be, had already achieved a purpose if the goal was to upset and worry Robert Mancini. Any deviation from the norm could upset this man with his fierce devotion to excellence.

It also occurred to Susan, as it had more than once before, that there should be limits even to this kind of devotion. She knew that Robert drove himself too hard, and seldom had time to laugh. But how could she say this to him? How, in a time when "good enough" was the label slapped on any kind of slipshod work, could she fault a man for demanding the very best? There were not enough men like Robert Mancini in this business . . . or in any business.

She said, "We can hope the wine shows no damage whatsoever."

Robert nodded. "In the meantime, we won't be notifying the authorities, as I told you before. I don't see what they could do, and with this important meeting coming up, we don't need any kind of publicity that will shake anyone up."

"Is there any objection if I let Rod know about it informally? In confidence?"

Robert looked at her, and his eyes warmed, became friendly again. "I assumed that. You and Deputy Poole are still—as we old folks say—keeping company, aren't you?"

"We are," Susan said, and felt her face warm.

"Rod is a good man. He won't say anything. Besides, it would be pretty difficult to keep from discussing something of this magnitude with him, wouldn't it?"

Susan had the feeling she was being teased a little. She had the terrible added feeling that she was blushing. "Yes. It would."

"Well, then, no problem. Just make sure Rod understands our motives for not calling the sheriff in on it in the first place."

"I will," Susan promised.

They talked a while longer, but seemed to be going back over the same ground. They left the office shortly after 1 A.M., Robert heading down to the fermenting room, Susan back to the lab. Robert's final words were assurance that she needn't try to come in before noon tomorrow; he practically insisted on this.

Walking toward the lab, Susan thought about this evidence of his consideration for her. Despite his intensity, he had a very great capacity for this kind of human warmth, and she admired him for it. Under the present circumstances, it was nothing short of amazing.

The sabotage could hardly have come at a worse time. Everything in Robert Mancini's life, personal and business, seemed already on the brink of serious readjustment, if not outright crisis. The wine industry itself faced serious trouble due to overplanting and slumping sales. Year after year since his first grape crushing, Robert had traded stock in his winery to the largest outside shareholder, the conglomerate known as Timmons Corporation, and each year's new influx of cash meant diminished control by Robert over his own winery as the Timmons stock portfolio grew. In another week, Robert would present to the Timmons representatives his plan to acquire a nearby defunct winery for expansion purposes, and it was by no means sure that Timmons would approve.

In Robert's personal life, which he never discussed, things were hardly more placid. It was an open secret that his marriage of twenty-five years to the still beautiful but erratic Audra Trello was in some kind of trouble. There had been whispers as long as Susan had been in the valley to hear them. But now the whispers were more insistent: Robert had appeared at the annual Vintners' Ball alone, without his wife; Audra was no longer seen around the country club; they still shared the house in the mountains, but were never seen in public together.

Old August Trello, founder of the massive cheap wine company which bore his name and dominated the market from its headquarters one hundred and fifty miles south of San Francisco, was now said to be terminally ill. Father of Robert's wife, Audra, and also of Robert's former partner, Jules Trello, the old man had, it was said, always exerted enormous influence on all members of his family. There was no way to predict how his passing might complicate life for everyone who survived him.

With all of this, Susan thought, Robert Mancini had had time to worry whether she had enough sleep tonight.

She re-entered her blending room. The wine glass remained where she had left it. With a sigh, she swirled the contents again and tasted, letting a small portion of the wine trickle over her tongue slowly, tasting it with various areas of her mouth. The taste buds for astringency, at the back of her tongue, were not pleased.

Rinsing out the glass, she decided to postpone another test. Fatigue pulled at her muscles, and she had the beginning of a headache. She shut down the lab and left it. Going downstairs, she let herself out through a side door and walked to her car, a Firebird, parked under the spreading old elms beside the lot. The car started promptly and she drove down the long, curving driveway, under more huge old trees, through the grounds to the rocked front gates.

The night was beautiful and clear, with a full moon. As she drove away from the winery, Susan glanced back at it for an instant, seeing the Victorian turrets, the multiple rooflines, the bulky production buildings scattered along the side hill beyond, the rolling vineyards, their great old vines still wintry and gaunt in this starting of the season. It was a scene she loved, but she looked away more quickly than usual this night because she was so tired and puzzled . . . and worried.

3

When he left the winery, Robert Mancini drove slowly, in
deep thought. He crossed the floor of the valley to the
intersection of the road that led into the mountains. This
road, much narrower than the highway, turned back and
forth upon itself, climbing through vineyard after vineyard
in the moonlight. After a while the fields were left behind,
and Robert shifted the Alfa Romeo to a lower gear as the
grade steepened and trees and boulders pressed in close on
either side.

There was nothing more to be done tonight at the
winery. He was baffled by what had happened. He had no
workable theories.

The damage had been done deliberately. He tended to
believe that it was the work of a disgruntled employee, but
even this idea shocked him because no one at the winery
had been there less than a year. He picked his people carefully and rewarded them well. It had always been his boast
that everyone at Robert Mancini Vineyards had a part in
the wine and took satisfaction in it. Now, perhaps, that
theory was destroyed.

In the morning, he thought, he would discuss it with
Mike DeFrates. There was also a great amount of other
work to be done, work having nothing to do with this latest
problem. In the next week or ten days, the 1975 Zinfandel
would be ready for bottling, and that would involve beehive activity, including relocation of thousands of barrels,

19

rearrangement of most of the cooperage to a more efficient stacking system. The figures for the proposed acquisition of the old Elmhurst Winery had to be pored over once more, and careful arguments planned for the two representatives of Timmons Corporation, John Endicott and the obsequious E. Z. Simms. Final spring inspections were scheduled for almost all the fields.

Thinking of it, Robert allowed the car to slow even more. He thought of turning around and heading back to the winery—perhaps checking over the Elmhurst figures again tonight.

The sports car, in a gear too high for its speed, shuddered and almost stalled.

Shifting down and accelerating a bit, Robert realized that he was loath to get home. This, too, struck him forcefully. It was a beautiful night, spring . . . the time of all the great promise and excitement of the new season. In years gone by, if he had had *any* of a dozen of his present thoughts in mind, he would have been rushing up the mountain at high speed, recklessly intent on getting back to Audra, to tell her about everything, discuss it with her.

Tonight he felt no such eagerness. He examined his feelings with care and realized that he was dreading the moment of return to her. He had been avoiding her as much as possible lately, since the news of her father's illness had worsened the tensions between them.

Not that the trouble was new.

For almost as long as he could remember now, there had been times of tension. He did not entirely understand it. The disintegration of their relationship had been the work of years, if not decades. Audra liked to blame his refusal to work for Gus Trello, and his dedication to the ideal of his own winery, making the best possible wine. But that was a simplistic explanation. It went deeper, this trouble, and he viewed it as the central problem and tragedy of his life.

Driving along, nearing the house he did not want to reach, Rober did as he often did. He tried to examine the causes.

It was not, surely (he began by telling himself), the winery or his work to build it. There had never been a time in his life when he had not been involved with wine. His father, Ernest Mancini, had operated a small winery in Sonoma for decades, and Robert had grown up in it. His father and mother had died in an automobile accident in 1950, and Robert had been operating the winery on his own for more than a year when he married Audra late in 1951. She had not complained then.

In 1952, after the disastrous fire that finished the Mancini Winery in Sonoma, Robert had come to this valley, working for Beaulieu. August Trello had made the first of several overtures to him at that time, and Audra had hinted that she wanted Robert to accept. But there had been no outright fight. Not with Audra.

The fights had been with old Gus. Had they begun the deterioration of the marriage? Audra had witnessed some of them, certainly, including one of the last ones.

Robert remembered that scene. It was sometime in 1954. Jules was old Gus's manager in those days, but Gus called Robert and Audra to the mansion in the south and said point-blank that Jules was not the kind of manager he wanted. He said he wanted Robert to have the job. Seeing Audra's eyes light for a moment, Robert nevertheless had to decline.

He remembered old Gus, an aging bull, wearing baggy overalls and flannel shirt, pacing back and forth the length of his white-carpeted office, waving his arms, raging: "How much money you want, eh? Hell with amount! I give it to you! How much?"

"It isn't the money, Gus," Robert had explained patiently, keenly aware of Audra's luminous eyes upon him. "The money is fine."

"What is it then, eh?"

"I have a job. And I'm not coming here and stealing the job Jules has."

"Jules is my own son, like Frank, like Gus junior! Shit on my own sons! They are not men I want! I want you for this job!"

"Gus, I have the job I want right now. I'm acquiring vineyard land in that valley. When I'm ready . . . when the time is right . . . I want a winery of my own again. A truly fine winery."

"Come in with me! Manage for me! Then, in five, ten year, maybe I set you up in that valley up there, let you have your own winery. Why not? Hell, I got plenty money. Do what I say, I will make you rich one day. You want to be rich for my Audra?"

"I want to make my own way. I want to *do* things my own way."

The old man bent, looked up at him, cocked his head. "What more could you want than what I got? I make more wine than almost anybody! I got more capacity in a day than most wineries got in a year! I am so rich I lend money to banks overnight, you know that? Is true! Come manage for me. One day, I set up big operation up there, too. You run it for me."

"That's not the kind of operation I want, Gus. I want a smaller winery, one that pays attention to every detail—"

"You think I don't? That's why I want you here, now! I need manager help me look after detail!"

"Your own sons are here. Jules is managing. Frank is in production. Young Gus, in marketing—"

"Don't talk to me my own sons!" Gus roared. "They are fools, fools! Jules knows nothing, he only wants to scheme to cheat people. Frank could not go bathroom if I don't tell him. Gus is lazy . . . lazy. I offer you what I never offer my own sons, a limited partnership."

"Gus, I'm sorry."

"Sorry? You think my wine is not good enough, is that it? What you want to do? Make wine from turds or something? You are bigger fool than my own sons! Get out! Get out!"

Robert believed the trouble had had its inception at that time. He and Gus had patched it up uneasily later, but then there had been other fights. Gus Trello was one of the five largest wine producers in California, but his mass-production methods would never produce fine wines, only very large quantities of consistent, mediocre wine at low prices. There was nothing wrong with this: it was simply not what Robert wanted to do with his life.

In 1959, after Jules had also left Gus to move to the valley and work for another wine company, what Robert always thought of as the great experiment had been tried. With Gus's financial help, he and Jules had purchased the old Schreck Brothers Winery. The five years of partnership had seen constant turmoil and increasing tension over the direction the winery should take. Finally, after Jules manipulated a meeting of three other shareholders, Robert had been forced out.

Certainly by this time, relations between himself and Audra had been strained. August Trello had raised his children sternly, and they felt fanatical loyalty to one another. Robert had never tried to explain to his wife just how underhanded Jules's maneuverings had been, because any word against her brother sent Audra into the deep freeze.

With the money he received from the Schreck buy-out, Robert acquired the old winery he now owned. Then, in 1965, seeking firsthand knowledge of Europe's best wine-making methods, he took Audra to the Continent for more than a year.

If he hoped the working vacation would patch up the rifts that now had begun to appear between them, however, he was disappointed. The time in Europe created new problems. While Robert visited the great vineyards of France and Germany, adding greatly to his storehouse of information, Audra drifted with another current. As time passed, she skipped side trips with him more and more frequently, falling in instead with fringes of the international jet set. By the time they returned to the United States late in 1966, they were further apart.

The rebuilding of the old winery brought new conflict over help from Gus Trello:

"Borrow from my father, Robert."

"No."

"Because of your stupid pride?"

"Because I want to be my own man."

"Are you any kind of man at all?"

The savage sexual innuendo was the latest development in the erosion. Robert tried to pretend things would improve. He began the long and costly renovation of the winery. He built a new home in the mountains overlooking the valley, a fine contemporary structure of glass and steel. Because he was Catholic, and had been raised traditionally, he believed the marriage must be forever. He trusted time.

Time, however, had brought only a prolonged truce. He had the all-involving burden of his work. Audra found outlets in her own social activities. They assured each other they were satisfied. Then, with the news that her father had incurable cancer, Audra had changed again. The flashes of bitterness and anger came more frequently, as if she were trying to blame Robert both for the sickness and perhaps the lack of real love that characterized old Gus's relationship with all his hard-driven children. Robert was hanging on. But driving home now was no joy.

When he reached the house, he found it ablaze with lights from top to bottom, the high, inverted vee of the central section glowing above the pines. He drove up the steep driveway and parked beside Audra's Oldsmobile in the helical carport. Mentally he braced himself. She had been off alone, at some country club function, and he had been at home alone, idly cleaning the roosting house occupied by his pet pigeons, when the emergency call came. Now she was back and would have been drinking, probably, and he was tired, with the faint suggestion of a headache. There would, if she ran true to form, be a scene.

He went into the house, entering by way of the two-story entranceway with two walls of natural rock, another of sheer glass vaulting upward to the parabolic redwood beams of the roof. Lights glowed in the living room to the right, the kitchen to the rear, the dining and game rooms to the left. More lights shone overhead, on the upstairs balcony, and on the curving white metal staircase near the top stood Audra.

Had she staged herself here for his arrival? Her position and appearance were dramatic, as she liked. Tall, graceful in a white floor-length gown, she stood unmoving, looking down at him. Her close-cropped red hair formed a blaze around her tapered cat's face, and her wide eyes were alive with resentment. Robert was struck by how beautiful she remained.

He smiled up at her, trying. "You're home. Good. We've had some excitement."

She came down the staircase, her slight swaying betraying the fact that she had indeed been drinking too much. "You have such an exciting life, Robert, while I have to face our friends alone, and make excuses."

He took this. It was not unusual, although she had a seemingly infinite capacity to sting him anew. "We had a complete failure on a row of tanks. You know the experiment on the Sauvignon Blanc? It was a close call—"

"I'm not interested," she murmured, smiling her sweet smile of hate as she came toward him. "But shall I pretend I am? Shall I be a good wife?" She put her arms around his neck. At close range, the lines were there, the marks of time.

"It was sabotage," he told her. "Someone—"

"When are we going to see my father?"

The change of pace did not catch him off guard as it once

might have done. It was one of her ways of fighting him now—sudden changes of topic, a cruel ignoring of whatever he wanted to discuss and a parallel insistence on her topic, whatever it might be. And she had been on the subject of her father for weeks.

He tried again. "This weekend. We'll drive down."

"I don't want to wait until the weekend."

"I just told you, we had trouble at the winery. There's no way I can get away before the weekend."

"I want to go now. My father is *dying!*"

"You can drive yourself, Audra. Then I can join you this weekend."

She stepped back from him, petulant. "You'd find some excuse not to come. It's always been this way. You still think you're better than me or anyone in my family."

"Gus and I don't get along very well, but you know I've always gone down to see him regularly. You can drive down tomorrow—"

"And leave you here to screw some little whore?"

"Audra, Jesus!"

"Do you deny it? Do you deny that's why you hired Susan Knight?"

"*Yes*, I deny it! You know there's never been anyone else!"

"But you never have any time for me, no time for my father, even when he's dying. What makes you think you're so superior to everyone else?"

"I don't, Audra. You know that. Why do we have to fight?"

Her face twisted, and for an instant the other Audra came out: the woman he seldom saw now . . . the woman he had married.

"Ah, Robert," she moued, "*I* don't want to fight."

"I don't either, babe," he said carefully.

"I don't know what's the matter with me any more. I'm so worried about Daddy . . . and that reception tonight was just awful. I didn't like anyone there. I missed you. Then I came home. This empty house is a tomb. I *hate* being alone. Tell me about your excitement tonight."

"Someone disconnected the cooling apparatus. And the computer. It was a very near thing."

She leaned back in his arms to look at his face. "But you fixed it?"

"I think so. We can't be sure of the effects—"

"Then, you can take me to see my father tomorrow."

"No, Audra. I'm sorry. I told you—"

"Do you love me?" It was said dangerously, and the other Audra was out again.

"Yes," he said.

"How do you love me?"

He struggled. Love as he had once known the meaning of the term was long since gone. But he had to convince her and himself that what remained was enough. "We've been together a long time," he said slowly. "We . . . care for each other. We live together and—"

"That isn't love. That's habit."

"It's love. I love you."

"Then come upstairs. Now. I want fucking."

Explicit language had never been a stimulant for him. The contrary was true, and Audra knew it. The challenge was clear in her eyes. He felt deepening dismay, knowing she would not let it alone now, that she had to vent this love-turned-hate which was the cement of whatever their relationship had become.

He said, "I left lights on everywhere. I'll be up later."

"Now, God damn you, Robert."

If he faced her another minute, he knew he would strike her. Shaken, he turned and strode into the living room. She screamed an obscenity after him and then ran up the stairs.

He went through the house, extinguishing lights. He stalled a while out in the pigeon building behind the garage, the White Kings fluttering and moving around nervously on their shelves, making their loud, combative cooing noises at one another as they prepared to fuss over food if he fed them at this hour. He had not flown them for over a week. There didn't seem to be time for anything any more.

Leaving the pigeons in darkness, he re-entered the house. It was still and dim, with all the lights still on upstairs. He thought about Audra's accusations about Susan Knight, and felt a stab of desire that it was true—that he had Susan, or *someone*. But he was proud of Susan's work. He could never do anything to jeopardize that. There would be no office hanky-panky. Nor could he seek out some illicit relationship that required sneaking . . . lying.

Perhaps, he thought, he would never feel the gladness of giving sex again. He could not really imagine divorce. He no longer attended Mass regularly, but what had his immigrant grandmother told him once, with pride, speaking for the Church? *"Give them to us for the first ten years of their lives, and they are ours forever."*

And she was right, Robert thought. In the gut, in the blood and sinew, he was a Catholic, and no matter how much experience might indicate otherwise, he accepted what he had been taught: *The marriage vows are promises made before God; they are forever; an honorable man does not break a vow; his marriage must endure; a man owes this to his woman and to his own integrity . . . and to God.*

He had to get through this, and endure.

Audra's voice shrilled from upstairs: "Robert?"

It was her combat tone and he steeled himself. "Yes?"

"Are you coming up now?"

"In a little while, Audra."

"Robert, I'm waiting."

He said nothing. *Love act out of hate, joining to despise one another.* He could not face this tonight. He turned and walked into the darkened living room, going to the back wall of glass which looked down the rolling mountainside to the valley floor. Lights twinkled across the expanse of miles. It looked very serene. Upstairs, now, Audra was weeping.

She did not understand any more than he could, he thought, what had happened to their marriage. They had slowly become almost enemies.

He remained at the windows, looking down at the valley.

4

The valley's sixty thousand acres of producing vineyards had begun to "push"—leaf out—in April. Now, in May, in the week following the attempt at sabotage in Robert Mancini's winery, the vines came into bloom. The tiny clusters of blossoms, emerging from new shoots, would soon set small, hard, acid berries; the year's grape crop would have begun its slow progress toward harvest in September or October.

Barring disaster with the weather, the harvest was predicted to be by far the largest in history. The total of productive acres had increased fivefold in the last three years as new vineyards, planted in the optimistic late sixties and early seventies, became mature enough to produce usable grapes. The predicted bountiful harvest, however, was by no means an unmixed blessing. Business conditions had actually shrunk the valley's capacity to ferment grapes, by causing three winery failures, at the same time the size of the crop increased tremendously each year. Prices exceeding one thousand dollars per ton for premium grapes had fallen to less than half that figure, and there had been vineyard failures, too. Here and there in the lush valley, two- and three-year-old fields lay untended and weedy. It was said things could get worse. The situation prevailed throughout California, and the French and Italian winemakers had problems of their own, including recent annual

28

wine surpluses exceeding two billion gallons. Many people were frightened.

Robert Mancini was not among them.

"All right," he told Susan Knight on the morning of the meeting. "Tasting shows no deleterious effects on the Sauvignon Blanc. So our saboteur failed. And there haven't been any more attempts. Whatever may be going on here, there's no reason why we shouldn't go ahead today and spring this proposed Elmhurst purchase on Endicott and Simms."

"Everything Timmons Corporation has done recently has been supercautious," Susan worried aloud. "They're worried about the effects of overplanting and slumping national sales of all California wines; we know that. As well prepared as we are, I'm still concerned about their acceptance of this idea."

Robert frowned, showing her that he was also concerned. When he spoke, however, it was with confidence. "You know the situation as well as I do, Susan. Each year since we went public with our stock in 1969, Timmons has bought parcels of my own stock in exchange for cash we needed for improvements. In 1970 it was new vineyard acquisitions. In 1971 it was new cooperage. In 1972 it was the new fermenters, the centrifuge and the first piece of the computer system."

"With the result," Susan agreed, "that you no longer own clearcut majority control of your own winery."

"Correct. But enough stock is scattered that Timmons doesn't have clear-cut control either. And they don't want any kind of show-down any more than we do. We have the contract: I operate the winery program, and they advise and consent. They've always gone along with our plans, and I believe we can convince them to go along on Elmhurst, too."

"I hope you're right. I hope this won't be the time they balk."

Robert tapped his index finger on the six file folders on his desk. "This proposal is solid. Those fine old vineyards that are part of the transaction are worth more than the price being asked by the creditors, alone. As far as we know, no one else knows the place is even for sale. When they came to me first, I got their assurance that they wouldn't broadcast the offer until we could give this proposal to the board. I think Endicott and Simms will jump at this chance. I think Timmons Corporation will approve before the end of the week, and we'll have those old vineyards and the Elmhurst buildings to expand our production of top-quality Cabernet and Pinot Noir. Count on it."

As she walked into the meeting room an hour later however, Susan still felt an intuitive worry. She had read an item in a recent *Fortune* about setbacks within several wings of the Timmons conglomerate. Endicott and Simms, two bureaucrats she would not have much liked under any circumstances, had muttered about retrenchment at every recent meeting.

The board room was on the second floor of the castle-like old building. By changing window openings, Robert's architect had provided the room with a fine view down the mossy side wall, past a shaded courtyard ablaze with blooming roses and geraniums, and to a side hill of one of the prized forty-year-old Cabernet Sauvignon fields nearby. The day was sunny and warm.

The carpeted room was dominated by a long walnut table of contemporary design. Everyone entered together. Robert walked to the far end, carrying the closely guarded file folders on the Elmhurst proposal. Susan walked to one side, to sit on his left. Mike DeFrates, the swarthy, khaki-clad production chief, slouched to a chair facing Susan. Next came Robert's secretary, a girl named Nancy, who took a chair back from the table with her notebook and pencils. Jim Young, the youthful, sandy-haired sales chief, entered next with his usual buoyant step and broad grin of optimism.

John C. Endicott, bluff, red-faced, portly vice president for Timmons, was next into the room. Grinning, with coffee cup in hand, he made a big thing of holding Susan's chair for her and managed to pat her arm in the process. Following him came E. Z. Simms, the efficiency expert. The sunlight slanting through the windows glinted off Simms's high-heeled black shoes as he carried his twin attaché cases to the table and placed them down almost reverently. Then Simms paused, hands on hips, his face twisting into the grimace that passed for his smile. He bobbed up and down on his toes, a characteristic mannerism.

"It appears we are all ready," he said. Balding, he stood five feet four inches, and looked like a precocious child inside his high-backed chair.

"We can get right to work," Robert said, his faint frown showing how he detested formal meetings.

Everyone sat down. Pads were pushed forward or back, coffee cups drained, pencils examined. Endicott lighted a large black cigar, puffing expansively. The meeting began routinely.

After a reading of the minutes, a question from a previous meeting was taken up again. E. Z. Simms, scowling over long computer printouts he had taken from one of his cases, reported in somewhat surprised tones that a thorough cost analysis had verified what Mike DeFrates had suggested in March—that local offset printing of labels was cheaper than any work available elsewhere. Purchase of a resupply of labels was routinely approved without a formal vote.

Robert provided a new update on acres in production within the valley and the early outlook for fall prices. He made note of the upcoming Zinfandel bottling, and set a tentative date of December 10 for release of the vintage after six months' bottle rest. That portion of the vintage that would bear the top "Estate Bottled" notation, he pointed out, would mellow in the bottle an additional full year.

"Talk to us about the seventy-five Pinot Noir," Endicott suggested at this point.

"We tasted the Pinot Noir again yesterday," Robert replied. "It's our judgment that it needs another six months in the wood."

"And how about the red house wine?"

"Also yesterday, we approved Susan's latest blending on that. We'll bottle within the next two weeks, rest it, and have it ready for sales about the same time as the Zinfandel."

"Gawwwd damn," Endicott breathed irritably with a glance at Simms. "Don't your figures show that red house wine is really selling?"

"Precisely," Simms chirped, looking over wire-framed glasses. "And further, your inventory is very low."

"Any chance," Endicott asked, "of cutting that bottle-aging time to get this stuff on the market faster?"

"People seldom shelf-age their wine after they buy it," Robert replied. "You know we like to put a little time on every bottle, even our cheaper wines, the blends."

"Not many other people age a general house wine, though, Bobby," Endicott said.

Robert smiled thinly. "Right. And maybe that's why ours is selling."

"Gawwwd damn," Endicott grumbled, and then shrugged. "Okay! Have it your way!"

The next item was a report from Mike DeFrates. He glowered at careful notes and rumbled through a concise report on winery activities, including the switchover in progress to pallet storage in the cooperage buildings. Almost always dour and of few words, DeFrates shared Robert Mancini's all-out dedication, and Susan liked him despite his gruff ways.

When DeFrates was finished, there were no questions.

Several other routine items were taken up briefly, including a discussion from E. Z. Simms on computer projections which showed ways to "actualize" sales and "maximize the parameters of margin" by increasing the emphasis on the cheaper wines. When he finished, there was no discussion. Secretly Susan wondered if groundwork were being laid in case the day ever came when some sort of showdown decided who really and ultimately controlled Robert Mancini Vineyards.

By now, however, the meeting had been in progress for more than an hour. The space on the agenda for "new business" was at hand, and Susan saw Robert reaching for the all-important Elmhurst folders.

"Bobby," John Endicott interrupted, "I don't know what you've got next there, but I wonder if I could bring up a matter."

"Of course," Robert said with a questioning look.

"Actually," Endicott said, standing, "I've got a visitor I want us to hear from. This proposition is his idea, and I think we ought to get it right from the horse's mouth."

Robert closed his hands over the Elmhurst folders. His eyes showed Susan that he was as mystified as she was. "You have someone outside?"

Endicott started toward the closed door. "I asked him to be here by eleven, and it's after that now, so I expect he is. Hang on a second and I'll bring him right in."

He went out, leaving the door ajar. Susan exchanged glances with Robert and then with DeFrates, who shrugged. E. Z. Simms had his nose buried in a sheaf of computer printouts, and Jim Young smiled blankly when Susan asked him, with another glance, if he knew what was going on.

In a moment Endicott walked back into the room, his

grin wide. Behind him came a youthful-looking, athletic kind of man with curly dark hair and a wide mouth. He wore gleaming Gucci loafers, tightly cut western-style pants, and a flamingly colorful body shirt. He walked jauntily, a broad grin on his lips, and of course Susan recognized him instantly.

Recognized him—and was shocked.

She turned to look at Robert. She had heard expressions such as "a face draining of color," but until this instant she had never really seen it happen.

Robert looked like he had been shot.

"You all know Jules Trello," Endicott said.

In the instant of silence, before anyone could react, Jules went into his act. Bounding to the head of the table, he grabbed Robert's hand. "Bob, damn! It's been too long! You're looking fine!" He turned. "Hey! Mike DeFrates! Good old Michael! Big as life and twice as. You look good, Mike! Put 'er there! Hey, Jim, how's the boy? Susie, you get prettier every day! I can't stand it if you get much prettier! How about coming over to work for me at Schreck Brothers?" He paused, hands on hips, and turned all the way around. The expression on his face was boyish; only the eyes were like ice. "Gosh, this is some layout! You know I've never been in here before? It's really great to be here." He did a comic double take. "Where am I?"

Susan had seen it all before, and as stunned as she was to see Jules Trello here and in this meeting, she was equally surprised that he would go into his act.

It was his public face, the one many people knew him by exclusively. At parties or banquets he was unquestionably a highlight, joking, bounding from spotlight to spotlight, keeping up a continuous barrage of gags. At the first dinner she had ever seen him in action, she had been amused and fascinated. The second time, her pleasure had been diminished. As time passed, she had slowly come to learn the incredible coldness and cruelty that lay behind the façade.

Most people had never penetrated the façade.

But now she could not ponder either Jules Trello's complex personality or the surprise of his appearance. John Endicott was pulling a chair out beside his own and motioning to it. "Sit down, Jules, sit down. I'm sure everyone is eager to hear this idea of yours."

"Durn right!" Jules grinned, leaping toward the assigned

place. "I've got no notes, but I'll do my best. That's a quote. Lincoln at Gettysburg."

Endicott turned back to Robert, who still sat white-faced, his eyes clearly betraying his shock. "Okay if Jules launches right in, Bobby?"

"You know I don't do business with Jules," Robert said hoarsely.

"I know that, Bob," Jules replied with a ferociously sincere frown. "But this is such a good deal, I just have to give you a shot at it anyway. Let bygones be basketballs, right?"

Endicott added, "After all, this is business. We can hear Jules out."

Robert leaned back in his chair. His face was sternly composed. The anger flashed only in his eyes.

"Go ahead, Jules," Endicott said.

Jules smiled, pulled a folded envelope from his pocket, and glanced at the handwritten notes on it. "Well, Schreck Brothers has two basic propositions, one that I'm taking to many winemakers in the area, and the other for Mancini Vineyards alone. I'll just go ahead and state them.

"The suggestion I'm carrying to as many winemakers as I can reach is very simple. We've had overplanting for several years running. We all know that there probably will be many more grapes this fall than we can possibly process. That can result in several bad things happening. Number one, some growers may not sell their grapes at all, and be ruined. Number two, the finest grapes could demand a higher price than the total tonnage would ordinarily dictate, because the best growers might try to hold us up, force strenuous bidding if they aren't locked into contracts. Number three, we could get into all sorts of bitternesses and rivalries over the thing."

Watching him as he paused, Susan marveled at the way the good-guy image had vanished and the hard-nosed businessman had surfaced. But she had no time to think about this because he continued:

"Here's what we suggest. First. All grapes should be purchased at a prearranged price, on continuing contract; that will eliminate uncertainty for the grower, and unfairly high prices for the winemaker. Two. The winemakers should work with the growers to secure eastern markets for grapes that can't be processed locally. Third. All quality bonuses should be discontinued. That way we have a healthy, stable situation. And everyone knows where he stands."

Robert leaned forward, his face showing amazement. "That sounds like price-fixing to me, Jules. How many people have you discussed this with?"

"You're the first," Jules said without hesitation.

"Why?" Robert shot back.

"You have a lot of influence, Bob. If you accept the package, a lot of people will tend to fall in line."

Susan could not stay quiet. "And also," she suggested, "you would be surer of keeping prices as low as possible if we weren't offering our usual top-quality bonus payments?"

Jules grinned broadly at her. "The little lady is right on the ball."

Endicott said slowly, "I wanted to get reactions, since the idea sounds so good to E.Z. and me."

"It's collusion," Robert said. "I seriously doubt that it's possible to carry off such a scheme without running into trouble with the law."

Jules replied smoothly, "No one is suggesting collusion or anything like it. With the overplanting, the price paid per ton is bound to sag. We've already seen that trend. All I suggest is that we stay in touch with one another, very informally, to assure that everyone pays fair prices."

"Fair to whom?" Robert snapped.

"Fair to everyone." Jules's neck began to get pink.

"We won't eliminate premium-quality bonuses," Robert said.

"I had hoped you would consider the matter. It would be a terrible thing, Bob, if you were out of line with the majority on this."

"Terrible for whom?" Robert came back. "Terrible for you, because your reputation for bottom-dollar bids might get you only inferior grapes, so your cost-cutting would show in your wine?"

"Think of the industry and not just your own operation!"

"I *am* thinking of the industry. We'll buy some of our grapes from independent growers this fall, as we have in the past. If prices go too low, there won't even be enough market in the East for all the grapes. People will be ruined. If there's really an effort to organize the field workers this summer—and God knows it's a miracle we haven't had labor troubles long before this—then the growers will face additional costs. Any concerted effort by us or anyone to drive prices below their normal market value could result in a lot of small growers simply going bankrupt."

"Dog eat dog," Jules said.

"Maybe," Robert grunted, implying he disagreed.

"Your quality bonuses are notoriously high. They inflate the market."

"They buy better grapes."

"Gentlemen," Endicott said nervously. "We need to discuss this in private. But can't we move on to your second offer, Jules?"

Jules Trello reshaped his face into a bland smile with what seemed a major effort. "Of course. The second offer is even simpler, folks. Before long, Schreck Brothers is going to have control of a considerable quantity of bulk wine. Now, frankly, we could market this wine. But I know that some wineries are rather low on their cheaper wine inventories." He paused and smiled at Robert.

"How do you know that?" Robert asked.

"Well, let's just say a little bird told me."

"It's no big secret," Endicott muttered. "Anyone might look at our shelves and know we're almost out of the house red and house white labels."

"Anyway," Jules said, "my proposal is simple enough. Once Schreck Brothers has this wine, we'd be willing to sell it at a good price—a real steal. If you're interested. You can buy it in bulk, bottle it, and resell it at a nice, quick profit."

E. Z. Simms leaned forward, a pocket calculator appearing in his hands. "Please conceptualize this in quantities and dollars."

"Before we get to that," Robert cut in, "let's hear what kind of wine it is."

"A very nice little Cabernet," Jules said. "A Seventy-four. Also seventy-four Pinot Chardonnay, and probably some Riesling."

"We don't need any," Robert said.

E. Z. Simms looked up from his unused calculator. "We haven't even heard the prices yet!"

"We don't need it," Robert said. His face was very pale again with anger.

Jules Trello got to his feet. "Well, let me put it to you this way. I've made my pitch, so now I'll get out of your way. Talk it over. Whatever you decide, you sure know where to find me." He shook hands with Jim Young, with

Mike DeFrates, with Robert. On the way around the other side of the table to shake hands with Endicott and Simms, he patted Susan on the shoulder. "I know you'll need some time. Shucks. No problem."

John Endicott rose. "We want to thank you for coming to us with this proposal, Jules."

"Pleasure is all mine," Jules said. With a jaunty wave, he moved quickly to the door and left, closing it loudly behind him.

For a moment the meeting room was silent.

"That," Endicott said at last, "was an interesting visit."

"We can't seriously consider either idea," Robert said.

Endicott raised bushy eyebrows. "Bobby, you know as well as anyone that we have always allowed you to operate this winery pretty much your own way. But by golly, I'm not sure in this case but that you've made a hasty mistake."

Robert started to reply, but Endicott raised his hand. "Furthermore, I think I ought to tell you that I intend to report to the top on what's been said here today. The last thing in the world I would want is some kind of confrontation on this. You know that. So what would you say to just sort of tabling the entire matter for right now until I can get a reading up top?"

"If any report goes to Timmons," Robert replied, "it must contain the statement that I'm dead set against both proposals."

"Well, I understand that," Endicott said sadly. "I certainly do. But you have to consider, too, Bobby, that there's been a lot of retrenchment throughout the organization in the last year. I see no harm that could come from getting some figures together for E.Z. here—letting him talk to those old computers awhile—see what sort of effect a little co-operation might have on grape prices . . . and what sort of price structure we might work out if we were able to buy some of that bulk wine from Jules."

Robert scowled. His fingers moved over the Elmhurst folders, and Susan guessed that he was wondering how strongly he could argue right now without ruining any chance of a favorable report on the acquisition proposal.

She tried to cut in to give him time to think. "What I don't understand," she said, "is where Jules thinks he has much extra wine. I happen to know Schreck's capacity. There isn't that much wine there."

"Oh, they have plenty of wine now, Miss Knight," E. Z. Simms said.

"Now?" Susan echoed, puzzled.

"Yes." Simms smiled. "Mr. Trello told us about it this morning when he called us at the motel. He has just concluded negotiations to buy the old Elmhurst winery, and I understand the cellars over there are full to overflowing."

5

When the meeting broke up shortly before noon, nothing had been decided. John Endicott said smilingly that it was his duty to take Jules Trello's proposals back to Timmons Corporation. Robert Mancini picked up his unused Elmhurst folders and carried them back toward his office. Susan and Mike DeFrates, exchanging alarmed looks, walked as far as the front door with Endicott and Simms, and watched them walk out to their car in a parking lot now crowded with a few of the one hundred thousand visitors who toured the winery each year.

"Who in the *hell* told Jules about Elmhurst?" DeFrates demanded then.

"I think we'd better get to Robert's office," Susan said.

They found him standing at the window, looking down on the interior garden and its flowers. He turned as they entered, and his smile was as thin as water.

"Well," he said, "it looks like we've had a little setback."

"Who," DeFrates growled, "told that son of a bitch about Elmhurst?"

"I don't know. It wasn't any kind of state secret, I guess."

"I thought we had first shot at it!"

"I did too. Obviously we were both wrong."

"What does he want it for?" DeFrates insisted. "He can't even *use* it."

"The price was good. The creditors wanted out, and fast. I'm sure Jules can use the grapes, and as for the wine in cooperage, he obviously plans to sell it off in bulk as quickly as possible. We hoped to do much the same thing, remember."

Susan said, "Did he really think we would buy it? I don't think so. I think he just came here today to gloat."

Robert put his hands deeper into his pockets and puffed out his cheeks in an expression of perplexity. "One thing you can say about Jules. He never does anything for exactly the stated reason. Whatever he has up his sleeve, my guess is that we haven't heard the last of it."

"He'll turn around," DeFrates said, "and try to resell Elmhurst for a profit."

"Maybe. He might not get far. I know we won't pay any more than we planned. We can't."

Susan sat on the edge of a chair. "We've lost it, then," she said, the full impact of the defeat just sinking in. "I *wanted* that old winery. It's historic in this valley. And those old stone cooperage buildings! Those fine old vines!"

"We can forget it."

"I think Jules probably just bought it to spite us!"

"No. He's capable of that, I suppose. But he has deeper plans in mind."

"Look," DeFrates said, pacing. "Everybody knows Jules has expanded and expanded and expanded over there at Schreck. There's no *way* he could have swung this Elmhurst deal without a big loan. He's already in debt up to his pistol pockets already. *Why?*"

Robert sighed. "Maybe he plans to move the bulk wine quickly and recoup part of the initial outlay."

"At least," Susan said with angry satisfaction, "you made it clear that we won't buy the stuff."

"I'm not sure we've heard the last of that either, though."

"You made it clear enough!"

Robert looked at her with eyes that betrayed his worry. "You heard what Endicott said. He's going to report it back to the Timmons board."

"They've never tried to dictate."

"There's always a first time."

"They wouldn't!"

"What we have to face here," Robert scowled, "is the fact that Endicott and Simms have spoken increasingly of tightening up, trying to build profit, all through the recent months. You don't see some of the Timmons reports that I see. Several operations have sustained heavy losses this year. If this looked like a sure way to turn a quick buck, I know there are people up there who wouldn't hesitate."

"But they know that if they tried to pressure you, it would force a showdown on stock holdings. They wouldn't risk that."

"Not," Robert said after a pause, "unless they feel very confident that they have the firepower."

"Oh, Robert."

"It's possible."

No one spoke. Susan saw the angry, troubled expression on Mike DeFrates's face, and knew she shared it. She didn't know what to say. She was both angry and depressed. This latest setback, so unexpected, had thrown her.

"It's even possible," Robert went on, "that something like this is designed as the opening gambit in a test of strength."

"I don't understand," Susan admitted.

"Suppose Timmons is in trouble—not really serious, but bothersome. Suppose further that management up there is confident of stock control in case of showdown. All right. Isn't it logical under those circumstances to start applying the screws to us, seeing how far we can be pushed toward quicker, easier profit? After all, we can only dig in our heels, and if we get too recalcitrant, that provides the excuse for the showdown and even a change of management."

"Change of management!" Susan gasped.

"I haven't been a very good businessman. I was too eager to get the money for our improvements. I didn't think Timmons could gather up enough stock. But I've been talking to a couple of friends I have up there, and my attorneys have been doing some checking. It is possible . . . not probable, but possible . . . that Timmons could control if a showdown vote came."

"Why," DeFrates asked angrily, "would they want to change anything? Who the hell knows as much about making wine as we do?"

Robert shrugged. After a moment he added, "We also have to face the fact that the Elmhurst deal might not have leaked accidentally." He saw their astonished looks and smiled again, without pleasure. "It could have been leaked."

"Not more than a handful of people knew about it here!" DeFrates said.

"I know that."

Again there was a silence. Susan realized that they were

all thinking exactly the same thing. The idea that someone within Robert Mancini Vineyards would leak the Elmhurst information to Jules Trello made no sense. But the idea that someone here would commit the act of intended sabotage against the Sauvignon Blanc did not make any sense either.

Quite suddenly there was more here than bad luck, or intended treachery by Jules Trello. There was the suggestion of a pattern, and if it was a reality, it was as threatening as it was mysterious.

As if reading her thoughts, Robert nodded and sat down behind the desk. "I think I'd better call my friends at the Timmons headquarters in Portland. I just have the feeling that we haven't heard the last of Jules's wine, or his wild idea to fix prices. We'll just have to do everything we can to head him off. In the meantime, we have that Zinfandel to handle, the cooperage work, the field inspections. Let's not let this thing throw us off schedule. It may not amount to anything in the long run."

Susan dutifully left the office and returned to work. It was not the first time Jules Trello had interfered in some way with someone else's operations. Thinking how many innocents considered him a *bon vivant*, a hail-fellow-well-met, a civic leader, she murmured an expletive. How she detested him!

6

Driving back to Schreck Brothers Winery, Jules Trello had seldom been in better spirits. Gently rubbing the slight protrusion of his belly over his belt, he held the Continental on a steady 55 *mph* and considered the ramifications of his achievement.

It would not take Robert Mancini long to learn about the Elmhurst buy, Jules thought, and this put icing on the cake. Jules expected Robert to be baffled and furious. Thwarting Robert Mancini was in itself a reward. But Jules's quick action, once he had been tipped off about the deal, had sprung from more than simple vengeance.

The new situation was sure to make things more difficult for Robert in several ways, Jules thought with pleasure. And Schreck Brothers, constantly expanding despite the severe financial worries this inevitably caused, would be boosted again by the acquisition.

Jules did not know how successful he would be in the long run on affecting prices this season. He had hopes. On quickly selling the bulk wine in the Elmhurst cooperage, he had more than hopes. This he simply had to do, because the loan for the purchase was of very short duration. As usual, he had put himself under grave pressures by moving swiftly. But he had had to move swiftly.

Now he had to work himself out of the hole he had dug. Well, he had always gotten out of holes before, and he would again.

Elmhurst had been closed for a number of months, but when his associate at Mancini's had tipped him off about a possible immediate sale, Jules had been caught by surprise. The creditors, seeking to recoup as much as they could after Elmhurst went out of business, had also been surprised by Jules's quick offer, but had been willing to accept instantly.

Elmhurst had been closed, ultimately, because it violated the law. Through inspection of records showing grape purchases and wines shipped, both federal and state inspectors had determined that approximately twelve thousand cases of Elmhurst Pinot Noir were in fact only about 40 per cent from that grape—below the legal minimum of 51 per cent for varietal labeling.

If the suspect wine had been Zinfandel or Merlot, the penalties would have been the same in the courts. But even casual wine drinkers knew that Pinot Noir, the grape of the great French Burgundies, was one of the two noblest in the world. A transgression with Pinot Noir was a sin in the very sacristy of the wine world.

So when Elmhurst was prosecuted first by the United States for violations of paragraphs 4.23, 4.31 (a) and (c), and 4.34 (b) of Part 4, Code of Federal Regulations 27, and then by California for violations under Sections 17001, 17015 (a) (2), and 17075, the media had latched onto the story with considerable enthusiasm. The case was branded the biggest since the celebrated Bordeaux scandal earlier in the decade, and sales dropped to nothing.

Financial difficulties which had led to the mislabeling scandal, the first in the history of the California wine industry, were escalated by customer resistance to all wines in the line. In the celebrated French case, fines exceeded two million dollars, and closed an old-line company. Elmhurst's fines were roughly eight hundred thousand dollars, and had the same terminal effect.

The penalties were harsh, and might be considered too harsh by the occasional consumer who wanders into a grocery store and looks for something sweet, preferably under two dollars a bottle. Wine codes were written by serious wine drinkers.

Bad luck for Elmhurst. Good luck for Jules Trello.

Near his own winery, Jules continued to think about Elmhurst. Little of its equipment was worth salvage, but its oak cooperage was in fine condition. So were its vineyards. Jules anticipated selling the grapes from Elmhurst at as high a price as possible, and buying other grapes for his own jug wines much more cheaply. Once the thousands of cases of wines now in storage were bottled and sold, he would use the added cooperage capacity for his own products. There was no reason why the deal should not turn out very well indeed . . . just as soon as he sold the wine on hand and repaid portions of his latest debts.

Schreck Brothers was a long, low, buff-colored building in the central section of the valley. Driving through its gates, Jules noted that workers were in the fields, inspecting and treating the vines. The scene of routine activity calmed him, and when he walked into his spacious contemporary office a few minutes later, he felt confident and happy.

He was surprised to find Carole, his wife, waiting for him. Elegant bare legs crossed, she smiled brightly as he entered. Her silver-blond hair flowed smoothly over her shoulders, tanned and bared by the low neckline of the pale-pink frock. Her sensuous mouth curving, she made large, childish eyes at him as he bent to kiss her on the cheek.

"Baby is here," she cooed in her tiny, baby-talk voice.

"Hello, Baby," Jules murmured.

"Is Daddy mad at Baby for visiting him at work?" Carole asked with a little-girl pout.

"Daddy is delighted," Jules told her, going around his desk. "The Elmhurst papers were signed at eight this morning, and I've just had the pleasure of going over to Robert's and setting it up so he finds out about it right away."

Carole, a faultless porcelain doll, wriggled her shoulders and heavy breasts. "Ooh!" She thickened the baby talk. "Was Wobert angwy with Daddy?"

"I don't know," Jules grinned. "But he'll shit one when he gets the details."

Carole wriggled again, setting up multiple tintinnabulations from a half-dozen ornate bracelets. "Ooh! I bet Gus is impressed when he hears it, too!"

Mention of his father soured Jules's mood at once. "I don't care what the old son of a bitch thinks. Baby, I told you: all these family rumors about possibly changing his will—that's all they are, rumors. Don't imagine I can do anything at this late date to get him to treat me fair. He started out screwing me and he's never stopped screwing me. This deal is not to impress my father." Jules licked his lips with pleasure. "This deal is strictly for the pleasure of sticking it in Robert."

For an instant Carole forgot her act. Out of her brilliant blue eyes shone a quick intelligence, and the curl of her perfect mouth was bitter. "You still hate him that much?"

"Who was it that almost took my job when I was managing for the old bastard?" Jules snapped. "Who has always been the favorite, even though he isn't really a member of the family? All my life my father has screwed me. Ever since he married into the family, who has been the one being offered all the help and favors? Robert has always tried to show me up. I'm Gus Trello's oldest son, but will I inherit? No. No chance. I've never been good enough. But I'll tell you one thing. Before that old man dies, there's time yet. He'll live to see Robert ruined, and me—*me!*—riding high."

Carole's eyes were like ice. "Wouldn't it be ironic," she said softly, "if Gus died before you accomplished it. Then it would all be wasted."

Jules, so intent upon his hate that he wasn't listening, blinked as he realized she had said something. "What? What, Baby?"

"Baby said," Carole preened, "won't it be *funny* when it happens!"

"It'll be funny, Baby. It'll be hysterical. Now, what the hell are you doing here?"

"Baby thought she would dwive to San Francisco, and buy a nice wittle dwess. Is that all wight with Daddy?"

"Sure," Jules grinned. "Anything. But, uh, listen, Baby. Take it just a little bit easy, all right?"

Carole pouted prettily.

"I'm not shutting you off," Jules added quickly, because it was an imperative for his ego to let this woman spend all the money she wished. "But you understand, Baby. Buying Elmhurst sort of . . . uh . . . extended us right now. Until I sell some wine I got as part of the deal, we'll be . . . just a little short of cash. You understand, Baby?"

Carole stood, her elegant hips swaying, light glinting off magnificent legs. "Baby undewstands. Daddy is nice to Baby."

"Sure he is," Jules smiled, patting her lush hip. "Run along now, Baby."

Carole ran along, beautifully. Jules watched her departure from his west window. There, he thought, went one fantastic piece of ass. Taking her places, showing her off, was among his greatest pleasures. If he sometimes felt impatient with her moronic talk . . . if sometimes late at night he was haunted by recurrent dreams of her with another man, spurning him now that he had "his trouble" . . . it was a small price to pay. She was his proudest possession, and nothing made him feel better than to know how many other men envied him.

Returning to his desk, he examined his personal checkbooks and worried about how much she might spend in San Francisco. He was terrifically overextended . . . it would not do for anyone to know how overextended. If anything went wrong with his hastily but well-conceived plan to unload the Elmhurst wine, the situation could become serious very fast.

But nothing would go wrong, he assured himself. He had already won Round 1.

7

With the deepening of the month of May, the vines progressed. Workers were in the fields regularly, but most of their work was toward prevention of disease or parasites. Pruning, designed to make sure that the vines did not produce more grape clusters than they could properly ripen, had been done much earlier. The vines were ready and bore their young fruit. Each vine would produce five to ten pounds of grapes, and there were about five hundred and forty vines per acre. Across the valley, more than one hundred thousand tons of wine grapes were moving toward the fall harvest.

At Robert Mancini Vineyards, the Zinfandel preparation was completed and everything was on normal schedule. There had been no more incidents of sabotage, and no new word from the Timmons Corporation representatives about possible follow-up on the proposals by Jules Trello.

Things had begun to seem so normal again, in fact, that Susan Knight put on her public-relations hat this Thursday, as she sometimes did, to spot-check the tour guides. She did not know that the tour would lead her to a new realization of how much trouble had already descended.

Many California wineries conducted guided tours of their premises, usually ending with free tasting of two or three of the firm's more pedestrian wines. Some wineries had discontinued the practice in recent years, but it was a tradition, and Robert Mancini believed in traditions. Maintaining tradition was made easier by the fact that the average visitor spent almost two dollars on wine following the tour; this allowed the operation to almost break even.

Susan Knight played no favorites in her periodic spot-checking of the performance of the tour guides. She felt that her occasional presence kept them on their toes, aware of the importance of their duties. On this day she decided to go with a group led by Charles Scarletti, an old-time wine company employee and guide.

Walking from her lab to the front of the main building, Susan joined about forty tourists clustered around the stone alcove near the front steps. There were a few more women than men in the group, and perhaps more young people than was usual. She quickly picked out some personality types: the young couples from someplace like Cleveland or Oshkosh who probably had a few wines in a closet and knew a little of what they were about; some older couples who gawked as they had at Disneyland, and wouldn't know a Lambrusco from a Chianti; the church lady who feared that this all might be a little sinful; the teen-ager near the back, already nervous about whether he would be allowed to taste. A normal group, then.

The doors at the back of the alcove opened and Charles Scarletti entered. A short man with a generous belly, he had curly gray hair, a small goatee, rakish sideburns. His olive skin glowed with good health and good humor. He wore a black silk body shirt, a bright green neckerchief, and red plaid trousers with black patent-leather boots.

"Good morning!" he said, his voice properly accented somewhere between French and Italian. "My name is Jacques La Tour, and what are you doing here in my winery?"

A few of the guests tittered.

"My little joke," Scarletti grinned, waving to Susan. "My name is Scarletti. All winemakers should have good Italian names, no?" He rolled his eyes. "Northern Italy—very near France! So. You come to take a tour? Good. You have a copy of our brochure?" He raised the small fact-filled pamphlet.

"Good," Scarletti said after a few latecomers received the brochure. "All right. You are standing now in the entry to Robert Mancini Vineyards, which is the oldest vineyard in the valley. It is also the youngest vineyard in the valley. How could that be so? I will tell you.

"One hundred years ago, a century ago, two brothers came to this valley and started this winery. Their name was Hoffman, so naturally they called their new winery—what? —Right. They called it the Nathan Brothers Winery. Why? Read your brochure. I cannot take time to explain everything, for if I did, I could not give you the extra-special tour and still get us back in time to taste many wines. Are you interested in tasting the wines? Good.

"This winery, as old as it is, did not invent making wine in the area. There was winemaking here as early as 1850. A man from North Carolina came, planted grapes. Probably Mission grapes. Mission grapes are still around, and do not shun them, they started the California wine business. But today maybe they are better for eating, because we have all the finest grapes of Europe growing here. And they do just fine.

"Mr. Robert Mancini took over his winery about ten years ago. It had been closed for a while. The historic aspects have all been preserved, but everything inside is modernized to make the best wine. You know what it takes to make the best wine? Okay. I tell you. You need, first, the finest grapevines, those from *Vitis vinifera*. That is the family of Europe's finest grapes. Sure, you can make wine from *Vitis Labrusca*—that's native American wines. But most people think it is not as good. In the eastern United States, where *Vitis vinifera* has trouble with the cold, they make wine from the other. But they buy a lot of California wine to ship back there and mix with theirs, to take off what we call the foxy flavor of the native grape.

"Okay. So you take fine grapevines. You find good soil for grapes, maybe chalky, maybe rocky sometimes, but the kind your type of grape is happy in. Then you find good climate: not too hot, not too cold; not too wet, because grapes like dry feet.

"Then, if you got these things, like we have in this valley, you take good care of your vines. You harvest carefully, at just the right time. You control your fermentation, you don't let wild yeasts, crazies that might taste bad, get in. You ferment just right, you age it in finest oak barrels.

"You know about barrels? Oak gives character to a wine, especially red wines. But all oak is not alike. Mr. Robert Mancini has experimented with many kinds of oak, small barrels, fifty imperial gallons each. You can take Yugoslavian oak; that is good, but . . . uh . . . maybe not the best.

Then you got French limousin oak. *Very* fine oak. But there is one better: French oak from the Nevers Forest. This is the very best. This is mostly what we use. It gives smoothness, body, just right quality. Oh, you can use American oak, from Arkansas, some too. But for most wines it gives taste that is *too* oaky. So you got to know what you are doing.

"That is why when we go inside you will see lots of barrels. Red wines stay in oak longer than white wines. Don't ask me why, I'm getting thirsty and it's a long story. Ask them that question at Christian Brothers or Robert Mondavi's or Montelana or Charles Krug; they will be impressed that you know so much already, eh?"

The tour moved inside, past the rows of stainless-steel tanks, including those where Susan had faced near-disaster so recently In the cooperage area, the air chill, Scarletti held the group again and lectured them more about the need to age wines for smoothness and body. After a little while, they reached the case-storage area, where tens of thousands of bottles of wine received their last resting before being offered for sale.

Scarletti turned and produced a bottle of red wine from a bin. "Okay, now. Next lesson. What is this? A bottle of wine, right? Did anyone say it was an Easter egg? Go to the back of the class. Here is how you read the label on a bottle of California wine."

Grinning as he held the bottle up for all to see, Scarletti continued the education that was part of any tour.

"Here is what our label says. 'Robert Mancini Vineyards. Estate Bottled. Napa Valley Cabernet Sauvignon. Produced and Bottled by Robert Mancini Vineyards. Alcohol 12.5 per cent by volume. 1972.'

"Okay. First says 'Robert Mancini Vineyards.' That's us—that's the name of the brand. Now. 'Estate Bottled' is a term used only for a wine produced from grapes in vineyards either owned or controlled by the winery, and in the vicinity of the winery. No grapes grown two hundred miles away and brought in on a donkey, right?

"The label tells you the general area where the winery is, too. You couldn't put the name of the valley on the label unless at least seventy-five per cent of the grapes used were grown right here in this valley.

" 'Cabernet Sauvignon.' That's the name of the grape. It makes the great reds of Bordeaux. You could have only fifty-one per cent Cabernet Sauvignon in there and call it

Cabernet Sauvignon. But we don't do it that way. This wine is one hundred per cent Cabernet Sauvignon. That's the way we do business."

Scarletti paused and rolled his eyes. "Side lecture. All blending of wines is not bad. You can have a more consistent product—completely the same—by blending a little, maybe. If you make your wine all from one grape, what happens if the weather is not so good for that grape some year? Answer: the wine isn't so good that year, either. Okay. We take this chance. We think we might have ups and downs, but most years will be very good, and some years will be magnificent—better by being a hundred per cent than anyone could produce by shooting for averages with blending. Right? Right.

"Back to the label. 'Produced and Bottled by' means exactly that. *We* did it, nobody else. Then, finally, we list amount of alcohol. Federal laws allow a table wine to be from ten to fourteen per cent alcohol by volume, but most just naturally falls right around twelve. That's because growers pick when the sugar is just right, and when it is just right, we get that much alcohol. Happy wine, happy growers."

While Scarletti chuckled at his joke, Susan thought about the growers. She wondered how much happiness there would be before this season was over. Much of the overplanting trend would be coming home to roost this year, as new vineyards reached their fourth year and began producing. Prices were sure to fall below last year's levels, continuing a trend. That was certain whether someone like Jules Trello had any effect or not.

Prices would not be the only problems, however. It seemed sure that this would be the year Alfredo Rodriques and his Workers United moved in. Their effort to organize the largely Chicano field workers was sure to cause problems . . .

Scarletti was saying, "—of course, some make wines with what we call generic names like 'Chablis' or 'Burgundy.' We don't do that. We think a Burgundy is a red wine from the Pinot Noir grape that is made in the Burgundy region of France, under strict controls. We don't use those general names, they mean little. We give you the name of the grape. You know us, you know the grape. You know what you will be getting.

"Now, one more thing. Robert Mancini wine is not for

everybody. It costs money to make wine slowly, carefully, like we do. You want a nice bottle of Estate Bottled Cabernet Sauvignon? Fine. Ten dollars, eighty cents. Too much? Sorry. That's what you pay for the best."

The tour proceeded again, passing the old "wine sipping oak" while Scarletti engagingly told that story. He then led the group past the stemmer-crushers, explaining how red wines were fermented with their skins for the color, how rosés stayed with their skins a few hours, how whites were fermented without their skins. He explained how gently the crushers worked, exerting maximum force, yet so carefully that not a single seed might be crushed, adding bitterness to the *must*.

In a little while, the tour turned toward the tasting rooms. Susan broke off and cut across the grounds, headed back for her lab.

Scarletti had performed well enough. There was nothing to be depressed about. And yet she felt downcast and worried over nothing . . . everything. It was, she decided, because nothing had happened since the meeting and the bad news. She knew things were not settled, that the saboteur must strike again, that none of the questions had been answered. The waiting in uncertainty was depressing her.

She reached her lab, went through it to her office beyond. There was a note on her desk from the pool secretary. Susan picked up the telephone and called the woman, whose desk was in the adjacent corridor.

"Helen? Susan Knight. Someone is waiting to see me?"

"Yes, Miss Knight. His name is Ned Henderson. He says he's a contract grower for Schreck Brothers, but he wants to talk to someone here who knows about grapes."

"Do you know the guy, Helen?"

"No." Helen lowered her voice. "He's fairly young and not too bad looking. But he must have a problem because he sure looks worried."

"I'd better see him, then," Susan decided.

When Ned Henderson was escorted in moments later, Susan knew at once that she was going to like him. She also saw that Helen had been right. Henderson was worried.

A tall man with unusually broad, straight shoulders and the long, skinny legs of a former basketball player, Henderson limped slightly as he entered, but his grin was wide and genuine. His face, square and boyish, was topped by wavy blond hair that looked like it had been lopped off in the kitchen with shears. He had candid blue eyes. He wore faded Levi's and a lumberjack shirt that had seen better days.

"I understand you're a grower for Schreck Brothers?" Susan prodded gently after they were seated facing each other across her desk.

"Well, that's right," Henderson said, linking his hands over a bony knee. "At least I've got a contract that's effective next year."

"You're a new grower."

Henderson appeared startled. "Cripes, does it show that much? How new I am?"

Susan smiled at him. "Grapes bear profitably in their fourth year. If your contract becomes effective next season, it stands to reason your grapes will start bearing well at that time."

"You've got it figured right," Henderson said. "I hope to get maybe a couple of tons per acre this year . . . if I have any vines left by harvest."

"What's the problem?"

"That's just what I don't know. Half the vines don't seem to be coming out right, and they look sort of puny. I can't find anything to match it in my books, and I've talked to the county, but they might not be able to get out for a few days yet. I keep thinking that might be too late."

"Have you asked Schreck Brothers for help? If you have a contract with them, they should be glad to give you advice."

Ned Henderson's face twisted. "Right. They said they'd be glad to come right out. Fifty dollars a day minimum charge, three days minimum time."

Susan felt a pulse of anger. "I hope you told them that's a little steep."

"I did," Henderson said, his thirty-ish features suddenly looking older as he stared at bony-knuckled hands. "Mr. Redman, their foreman, told me that the way prices are slumping, they couldn't really encourage me to continue anyhow."

"That was certainly very sweet of Mr. Redman."

"Yeah. He also said, if I decided to give it up, Schreck would like to have first bid on my land."

Susan murmured under her breath, "Those bastards."

"Ma'am?"

"Nothing. How many acres do you have, Mr. Henderson?"

"Nine."

"What kind of grapes?"

"Pinot Chardonnay."

"Where are you located?"

"South of here about three miles."

"The east side or the west side?"

"East."

Susan nodded and thought about it. She understood why Henderson was worried. His small vineyard contained five hundred and forty vines per acre. Newly grafted plants cost a dollar each, and had to be nurtured for four years before they paid much of anything in return. If Henderson lost three or four acres of plants, he lost not only his cash investment and his time; he also lost income from production during the years new plants had to mature.

"You're in a good area for Pinot Chardonnay," she said. "A little farther north and I might disagree with your choice."

"I studied it before making up my mind," Henderson told her. "I've worked hard. You know, I almost came here last year to try to get a grower contract, but those people at Schreck talked me out of it. They said you buy such fine grapes, I might not qualify. So I signed with them. Now I damned sure wish I hadn't."

It was not the first time Susan had run across signs of Schreck interference. She felt her anger bubbling. She also wanted to find a way to help this earnest, baffled young grower.

"I think we just ought to go out and look at your plants," she said. "But let me go talk to Mr. Mancini a moment first."

"Anything you could suggest would be great," Henderson said, getting to his feet.

Susan left the office, found Robert Mancini, and explained the problem. He listened with interest, and then went back to her office with her.

"We'll follow you out there in my car," Robert told the astonished young grower.

"*You're* coming to *my* place?" Henderson gasped.

Robert smiled. "I need some air. Besides. I like grapes, too."

8

With Robert Mancini driving, he and Susan Knight followed Ned Henderson's battered green Chevrolet pickup truck south from the winery until the highway intersected a dirt road. The fields on both sides of the highway here were all small vineyards, pale green under the cloudy sunlight. Henderson drove down dirt roads between small vineyards, each with its own small house, passing through a brushy area and crossing a creek.

"I hope we can help the guy," Susan said.

"From what he told us, I have some idea of what the problem may be," Robert told her. "I don't think we'll need more than a look."

"I suppose you could have sent me alone."

Robert smiled, at ease as he always seemed to be when he was away from the office and out in the fields he loved. "I haven't been out in this area since they planted all these small vineyards. I'll be interested to see what he has back here."

"Your schedule is crowded today."

"I don't have anything I have to do until that new reporter comes to the office at two. We ought to be back long before then. There we are; he's turning in."

Ahead, Ned Henderson had driven past a small field of about nine acres. At its rear was a small, pale-green frame house with two smaller outbuildings alongside. Henderson parked his truck between the outbuildings and stood beside it, waiting for them. The house was neat, freshly painted, with flowerbeds around the foundation. In a new vegetable garden plot off to the far side, a Chicano was working with his vineyard hoe in freshly turned earth. On the gently sloping shingle roof, a number of fat gray-blue pigeons strutted around.

Robert's face wrinkled in a smile. "I knew he was all right. He has pigeons."

"But you keep yours penned up," Susan pointed out. "Won't those birds damage the grapes?"

"They might eat one or two," Robert admitted, turning into the bare-earth parking area. "But they won't rival the wild birds and rabbits."

They got out of the car. Ned Henderson, nervous and excited, pointed toward the grapevines neatly stacked in long rows in front of the house. Here and there the vines appeared stunted in growth and too pale for the season, although they were in partial leaf. "There's the problem," he said.

Susan started toward the vines.

"No sense getting yourself muddy, Susan," Robert called to her, pulling a pair of knee-length rubber boots from the back seat of his tiny car. "Let me walk over and take a look."

Susan returned to the side of the car. She waited while Robert and Henderson made a brief walk through portions of the field. She could see that the plants were well staked and neatly tied, and the pruning had been done properly. A small garden tractor had been operated between the rows, loosening the earth after the winter rains, and removing weeds. Here and there a plastic milk carton was wrapped around the base of a plant to protect against rabbits, and there were signs that Henderson had used his sulfur properly, too.

Waiting, Susan indulged in some web-spinning. She was thinking of Rod Poole. Although Rod now had several years with the sheriff's department, and was among the top deputies, he made no secret of the fact that a small acreage like this was his long-term goal. Imagining it, Susan saw what a good life it could be, working the vines, seeing the annual harvest, growing a garden, having a small home isolated from the hurry of the towns.

The trouble was Rod's old-fashioned ideas about the role

of a wife in such a setting. This was the only thing they had ever really argued about.

"My God, Susan, you'd have plenty to do at home!"

"Rod, I'm good at what I do. I won't give up my career."

"Look. I know I may be ten years behind the times, but I just don't want a working wife!"

"Rod, you're not ten years behind the times."

"Huh?"

"You're fifty years behind the times, darling."

"Then marry me right away and modernize my outlook."

"And end up barefooted and pregnant? Rod, that just isn't *me*."

Susan smiled to herself, waiting. She knew she was right. But at times like this she was tugged in the other direction. Even as she knew she would never give up her own hard-won working respect, she was very feminine; and this part of her yearned for all the silly frills that Rod Poole seemed to imagine were mandatory in a continuing relationship.

She was wondering how it would turn out when Robert and Henderson came back out of the vineyard. Both men were smiling.

"I would have never figured it out," Henderson said, "and it's the simplest thing in the world!"

"You can't really see it at ground level," Robert explained to Susan, "but the roll of the land is uneven. Whoever deep-plowed before the planting didn't do a very good job of smoothing, or else there was once some sort of natural wash through here. The natural depressions dry on the surface, but hold too much moisture underneath."

"Grapes like dry feet," Henderson grimaced. "The first thing you're told."

"What can be done about it?" Susan asked, relieved.

"In another week or two, the ground will have dried out enough so there'll be little problem. In the meantime, I've suggested to Ned that he can use his garden tractor and try to move some dirt around here and there to fill slightly in a couple of the worst areas."

Susan nodded. "Aerial photographs would show the depressions very clearly. At this time of year they would photograph darker."

Ned Henderson shook his head. "Aerial photographs cost money."

"No problem," Robert said, pulling out a small notebook and pencil.

"What do you mean?" Henderson asked.

"I've got a plane going up soon to shoot some things. I'll have the pilot drift by here and pop a couple of quick ones for you."

Henderson's boyish forehead wrinkled. "That's awfully nice of you, but those things do cost money."

"The film is a dollar a sheet," Robert told him. "Four shots, four bucks. Okay?"

"God," Henderson said with something like awe. "The difference between you and Jules Trello."

"Jules loves grapes too," Robert said. "He just gets preoccupied with making money."

"I don't know how to thank you. Can I offer you some pretty good coffee or some pretty bad wine?"

Robert grinned. "At this time of day I'll settle for the coffee."

They walked to the rear of the small house. Robert asked about the pigeons, which flocked down off the roof and walked around the brick patio underfoot as they spied Henderson.

"I was always a city boy," Henderson explained, unlocking the back door. "When we got this place, I found a man who had some of these homers and I bought ten. Three of them have flown away, but I've got these, and two of the females are sitting on eggs right now over by the toolshed." Before opening the door, he reached into a plastic garbage can by the entry, took out a plastic cup of grain, and tossed it onto the bricks. The fat blue pigeons began pecking happily.

"If you'd like some White Kings," Robert said, "remind me sometime and I'll give you a few young."

"That would be great, if you could spare them."

"I've got so many I don't know what to do with them."

Susan said, "I keep telling you squab would be nice."

Both men grimaced as Henderson led the way into the house.

It was small, freshly painted and papered, with white tile ceilings and indoor-outdoor carpet on the floor. The back entry led into the kitchen area, which was pale yellow and spotless. A wide doorway looked into a small living room with low-cost contemporary furniture and a surprising number of books.

"My wife, Johnelle, is a teacher," Henderson explained, bustling around with cups and saucers. "She reads like a maniac."

"Did you teach before you got the farm?" Susan asked.

"No. I sold securities. And before that, I was in real estate. That was in Iowa. And before that, insurance." Henderson paused in front of his Mr. Coffee on the counter, making a pained face. "I'd better make it as a grape grower. I've already failed at just about everything else."

"How did you come to the valley?" Robert asked as the coffee was served.

"Johnelle got the teaching job. I always wanted a farm or some sort of outdoor work. Also, the doctors said I needed physical activity."

Seeing their questioning looks, Henderson explained. "I shouldn't have said I was always a failure. I was great at collecting shrapnel in Vietnam. I've got a lot of it in my legs."

"That's why you limp slightly?" Susan said.

"Yeah, although I'm a lot better than I used to be. I'm still carrying a lot of metal. It works out little by little. I've got a couple of tiny fragments coming out around the right kneecap at the moment."

Robert nodded toward a red motorcycle helmet on the sideboard. "Is a bike part of the therapy too?"

Henderson grimaced. "That's Jamie, my kid. He's fourteen. I suppose if he didn't have that damned little motorcycle, it'd be something else."

"At least you make him wear a helmet."

"I *try* to make him wear the helmet. I'm learning that when a boy is his age, you have hell trying to make him do anything: wear his helmet, stay off the main road, get a haircut, bathe—"

"He sounds normal," Susan laughed.

Henderson glanced sharply at her for the merest instant, and the look spoke clearly of real conflicts and genuine anguish. It was a look Susan had encountered once or twice before when parents of rebellious teen-agers were caught momentarily off guard. It told her that all was not idyllic in the Henderson household.

"I suppose he's normal," Henderson conceded.

The conversation switched to other, perhaps safer, topics. Henderson worried aloud about the trend toward slumping prices for fine grapes. Robert was encouraging, and Susan

THE WINEMAKERS / 61

secretly thought how ironic it was that one man with problems should reassure another whose problems were only of a different kind.

In another little while, Robert looked at his watch. "We'd better be getting back, Susan."

They walked outside. As they did so, the Chicano laborer was just coming across the far side of the back yard toward them. Small and slender, he wore a pink tee shirt under his bib overalls, with heavy workboots and a frayed straw hat. He carried two hoes over his shoulder. He was young, in his early twenties, and Susan saw that his dark face was not only handsome but quickly intelligent.

"Sir," he said to Henderson, "two friends have come. I will return in less than one hour." His English was stilted but perfect.

Ned Henderson glanced toward the side driveway, where a black Oldsmobile sedan was parked beside the pickup, Robert's sports car, and the ancient green Rambler that was somewhat back from the others. "What's the trouble, Homero? Can't you get the green machine to start?"

Homero smiled, but it was only a quick reflex, as quickly gone. "I have business with these men, sir."

"Homero Artiz, this is Robert Mancini, and this is Susan Knight."

Homero Artiz hesitated, then shook hands after Robert and Susan offered.

"It is a great honor, sir," he told Robert. "I know of your wines."

"Have you ever done any work for us?" Robert asked.

"No, sir. I work for small growers only."

"Which is a break for me," Henderson said with evident feeling. "This man is one stud horse for work."

Homero smiled. "I had better leave now, sir."

Susan and the others watched the wiry youth walk toward the black Oldsmobile. A rear door popped open. There were two young white men in front. Homero got in and closed the door. The cloud-faded sunlight glinted on the windows, making it impossible to make out the faces of the two whites. The car pulled away slowly and proceeded up the dirt road.

"I'll tell you what," Henderson said softly, shaking his head. "I wish those two guys wouldn't show up around here."

"Who are they?" Susan asked.

"I don't know. I've just seen them from a distance. They look like rough types to me, though. I don't like them hanging around."

"Hanging around?"

"Well, I shouldn't say that. But Homero has done odd-job work for me for more than a year. Just every now and then those two jokers show up. It's always the same. They drive off, and after a while they drop Homero off again. There's nothing I can put my finger on. I just don't like them. Somehow I think Homero doesn't, either."

Susan thought about it as they walked toward the car. "Do you think it could be drugs . . . something like that?"

"Oh, hell no!" Henderson was certain. "Homero is clean as a whistle. Listen, you don't *know* the guy. He's decent, hard-working, totally honest. That's what bugs me about those guys coming around. They're not the type you would expect Homero to mess with. He has a lovely wife and two little kids, and he works night and day to support them. What does he need a couple of creeps like those two guys for?"

9

Homero Artiz needed Dave and Phil for his survival.

It was a symbiosis he hated with every fiber of his being.

Homero had spent his life trying to find a way to become secure. In school as a child, in Mexico, he had worked hard at his studies as a way of working toward liberation. He was intelligent and he had learned well. Later he had taught himself English, studying the books and then practically giving away his services as a guide to American tourists, in order to speak with them and practice his accent.

He had taken his biggest step toward security and a better life when he illegally entered the United States near San Diego at the age of seventeen.

Now he was twenty-four. He had a wife and two children. His life was hard, but the wages were good enough. He had hope . . . but it was a hope that Dave and Phil could crush at any time they chose.

It was Dave, his long blond hair whipped by the warm wind from the slightly opened side window, who did the driving. Phil, a casual smile splitting his cruel dark face, leaned over the back of the seat to face Homero and do the talking. They had driven to the highway and were proceeding south at a cautious speed.

Phil said, "You just can't skip payments, Homero. We've got our expenses too, man."

"I do not have any money until Saturday," Homero said.

"I mean," Phil went on as if Homero had not spoken, "it jacks up our expenses to have to come hunt you up like this. We don't want to hassle you. We don't want to hassle anybody. But you've just got to understand our point of view as businessmen."

"I cannot pay before Saturday!"

"We were very considerate all winter, man. I mean, we understand how your work slacks off. We're not out to depress your standard of living or anything like that. We're reasonable. But this having to come look you up—that tends to piss us off."

"I will pay you Saturday," Homero said miserably.

"That's too *late,* man. You'll just have to dip into your savings."

"Savings? We have no savings! We have no money. We are in debt."

"Oh, come on, man. You can dig it up. You have to."

"Give me until Saturday," Homero pleaded, hearing and despising the wheedling tone of his voice. "By Saturday Mr. Henderson will have paid me. Mr. Romero will pay me, too. I can give you the money then."

Phil sighed. "You know we'd like to let you wait, man, but if we did it for you, we'd have to do it for everybody. Then where would we be? That wouldn't be fair. You're just going to have to come up with the money by six tonight."

"But I cannot!" Homero cried.

"Fifty dollars," Phil said. "Tonight."

"But I have no fifty dollars!"

Phil looked at the driver. "Dave, what about Homero's old car? Don't you think Homero could sell that heap for at least fifty dollars?"

"I'm sure he could, Phil. He could get more than that."

"I cannot sell the car! I would have no way to get to my jobs!"

"That's your problem, buster. After all, we're helping you out, right? I mean, did *we* cause your problem? No. We're the ones who are helping you out. Right?"

Homero fought an urge to cry out of sheer frustration. "I do not know how you learned I am in this country illegally. But for two years, every month, you take this money from me. You say you are 'helping' me. You are not helping me!"

"We aren't telling the Immigration Service," Phil grinned.

"I'd say that's been a hell of a help to you. But of course, if you don't think so, why, we can just drop them a post-card at any time."

Dave added, "I'd hate that, though. Have you ever seen pictures of illegal immigrants being sent back home, Homero? I mean, man, they put them in trucks sometimes with cages on them. Those poor people in there look like they're in a dogcatcher truck or something. It's real sad."

Homero fought for self-control, although his desperation racketed. "I will pay you. By Saturday I can pay. You must see that I have always paid. It is only because you have raised the amount I must pay that I am late this month."

"It's inflation, man," Phil said. "That old inflation is eating us all alive."

Dave added, "Just putting gas in this car is a fantastic expense."

Homero's bitterness welled up and closed his throat.

Phil said, "Your wife knows about these payments, doesn't she?"

"Of course. It is part of my shame."

"Maybe she could help you out."

"Her job at the cafe pays forty-six dollars a week. How could she—"

"I didn't mean cash money, Homero," Phil cut in, smiling.

Homero stared at him, aware of the lazy smile, the long, tangled blond hair.

"Your old lady is a nice-looking woman," Phil said. "Now don't blow up; just consider this. We've got a connection. If your Dolores would like to put on her best dress, and fix her face and hair real nice, we know a man she could contact. All she has to do is go to some club, and wait near a telephone. Our friend calls her and tells her where to go. She goes in a cab, real nice. Then all she has to do is meet this guy, this friend of our friend, whoever he is, and play with him in the sack. She can make . . . her share . . . twenty or twenty-five a date. Saying she does only four dates a night, that's still—"

With a hoarse shout, Homero launched himself at Phil.

"*Jesus*—!" Phil yelled, covering up. "Get off me, you crazy—!" With that, Phil managed to catch Homero's hands and hurl him back into the rear seat. Homero lunged forward again. The car swerved. Phil ducked for an instant, and when his head showed over the seat again, he had a different expression, one of desperation. And there was a small knife in his hand.

"Try it and I'll cut you, man. I mean it."

Seeing the blade and the equally deadly look in Phil's frightened eyes, Homero controlled himself, shaking. "Do not talk of my wife, ever!"

Phil took a deep breath. "Dave, turn around. Let's take this crazy back where we picked him up." He turned back to Homero. "You just won't listen to reason, man."

Nothing more was said as the car turned and they drove back. Homero, his heart crashing sickly, watched other cars pass them. He looked at workers in fields and tourist-shoppers in the street of a little town they passed through. Everything appeared normal for everyone else, and he wondered if he would ever have a life like theirs, without the fear and torture.

As the car neared the Henderson farm, Phil turned to face Homero again. He was pale and his voice was soft with suppressed emotion. "Homero, we'll give you one more chance. We'll give you till Saturday. But that's just because we're nice guys. Don't ever expect a favor like this again, you understand?"

"I understand," Homero said thickly.

"I hope you understand, man, because if you insist on giving us any more trouble, we are just going to have to get rough. We don't want that, and you don't want that. Believe me. You don't want that any more than we do. So co-operate, man. It's for your own good."

Homero said nothing. The car turned onto the dirt road that led back to the Henderson farm.

10

Robert Mancini's wife Audra was waiting in his office when he returned. She looked lovely in a pale slacksuit and she smiled as he entered the room. He was surprised to see her, but thought everything would be all right this time.

"What a nice surprise," he said, kissing her.

"Am I interrupting anything?"

"I have an interview with some reporter after a while, but there's nothing pressing before that. I've been out to a new small vineyard. A young grower named Henderson."

"Do they belong to the club?"

"Oh, I'm sure they don't."

"I thought they must be poor. I've never heard of them."

"Well, *we* were poor once, Audra."

"And may be again?"

He was puzzled because it was said with a sudden combative tone. "I certainly hope not."

Audra crossed her legs and lit a cigarette. "I've decided you were right, Robert."

"Right? About what?"

"There's no earthly reason why I should wait for those rare times when you have sufficient leisure to take me to see my father. I plan to drive down there in a little while. I may stay a few days."

"Has anything new developed? I mean, this seems a sudden decision."

"I talked to him this morning on the telephone." Audra's

face tightened, bitterness surfacing. "Jules had been there. They had some sort of a row. And now my darling sister Loretta has arrived, with her latest husband. She brought her three brats along, and Tony—that's her latest husband—brought along his eighteen-year-old daughter and the daughter's boyfriend."

"The clan is gathering," Robert said without pleasure.

"Yes," Audra snapped. "They're all coming home. Loretta, Jules, even Gus Junior and his brood. They'll be obvious about it. He'll know he's dying."

Robert looked sharply at her. She was still a very beautiful woman. Her stubborn naïveté surprised him. "Gus already knew, Audra."

"He didn't. No one had told him. But now he has guessed."

"Did he say that?"

"He didn't have to. I could tell."

"I'm sorry, Audra."

Her eyes glistened with sudden tears, and as if in response to this weakness, the other personality began to come out. "Will you go down there with me now?"

"I can't. Maybe I can get down next weekend again."

"You can't go with me now even though he's dying?"

"Audra, you know I can't just walk away anytime I wish. We agreed not to discuss that any more."

"I think we *should* discuss it. After all, you owe a great deal to my father. Our wedding was designed to link two wine families. We owe all these years of delirious happiness to the foresight of your father and mine."

"My father is dead," Robert said, controlling himself. "Yours is dying. If we have to fight, there must be better things to fight about."

"Robert, what's wrong with us? Why do we always fight?"

"We don't always fight," he lied, forcing a smile. "It's just a rough time right now. We'll . . . get through it."

"Will we?" And now he could not tell which Audra was out.

"Yes," he said.

"Robert, do you want a divorce?"

"Oh, Christ!"

"Do you?"

"No!"

"Why? Are you sure? Have you thought about it?"

"Audra, are you saying *you* want a divorce?"

"I don't know," she said, her eyes luminous with pain. "We don't seem to have anything left."

"We just have to try harder," he said carefully, groping for the words he felt. "We have to . . . learn to talk again. We can do it. We can get through this thing with Gus. Then we can work on it. It's just that our whole . . . relationship has suffered so slowly over the years. Maybe we were in trouble before we ever realized it, I don't know. But I know we have to work it out."

"Because you want to?"

"Because I want to—and because marriage is for life."

She got jerkily to her feet. "Spare me any Old World morality!"

"It's what I believe."

She strode to a small framed clipping behind the office-door space, usually hidden when the door was open. It was a small article published about him by *Time* in 1973.

She read from it with vicious sarcasm, " 'Robert Mancini carries into his everyday activities a tremendous enthusiasm, almost a fervor, and the frightening demeanor of innocence. A man of considerable power and sophistication, he yet manages to convey a sense that every proof of original sin shocks and saddens him, as if he were born all over again, fresh and innocent, each morning about 6 A.M.' "

"Audra—"

"Maybe we're too far gone, Robert. Maybe there's no turning back. Maybe the only way either of us can ever hope to have anything like happiness again is by first going through the pain of a divorce."

"I don't believe that and neither do you. You're just upset about your father's call."

"You are so superior in every way, Robert."

"Audra, what are we fighting about? What do you want?"

"I want you to go with me now to see my father."

"I can't! You know I can't! My God, stop making impossible demands, as if you're constantly testing to see if I love you! I can't pass all these tests. Maybe it worked with your father. Maybe, as he rejected his sons to try to make them tougher and harder, he allowed his love to be bought by his daughters, and even played this game with them. But I—"

"My father is twice the man you'll ever be, Robert. You were a fool not to work for him when he asked you to."

"We're *not* going over that ground again."

"If you had done it, we would be rich now. We would be happy."

"You might be, Audra. I would be overseeing vineyards so huge that they're laid out with laser transits, and supervising the making of wines out of strawberries and pears for dopeheads to sip at Disneyland."

"Don't dare talk against my father! My father is a great man!"

The argument was so old, and so irritating, that he felt his caution and patience sliding away. In their place was anger. "Your father is—or was, until he got sick—a ruthless bastard who would do anything to have his own way, even breaking his children."

"God! You were always so good at pointing out the faults of lesser mortals!"

"Audra, what do you want? What do you *want?*"

She stiffened and changed the subject dizzyingly. "I was at the club this morning. Would it interest you to know that two of Alfredo Rodriques' organizers are already at work in the valley? That means there will be a full-scale attempt to organize the field workers this summer."

"I'm not surprised," Robert said grimly. "I've heard rumors that Rodriques himself will come."

"You may wish *then* that you had taken a job with Trello Industries!"

"I may. But I doubt it."

"You may wish you had some of my father's courage when you have to face pickets and strikers!"

"I won't have them beaten up," Robert flared. "I won't have them sprayed by cropdusters. I won't try to trump up morals charges against them. I won't—as your father finally did—go to bed with the Teamsters in a last-ditch effort to spite Rodriques."

"You'll collapse," Audra said triumphantly. "My father never collapsed. My brother will never collapse. But you will."

Robert stared at her, wondering how such a love could become hate. He said nothing. The effort to retain control sent a sharp pain through his clenched teeth and jaw.

Audra walked to the chair and picked up her purse. She went to the windows and peered out for a moment. She turned back to him.

She was crying. "Do you suppose children would have made any difference, Robert?"

He had had more violent mood shifts than he could take. He knew that he had lost control of himself before he spoke, but he said it anyway, slowly, in a tone designed to inflict the maximum damage.

"I'm reminded of an old football yarn, Audra. The Washington Redskins were playing somebody for the NFL title. Sammy Baugh, the quarterback for the Redskins, threw a long ball early in the game and his end dropped it in the clear. The other team then went on to win by a score of something like fifty to nothing. Afterward, a reporter asked Baugh if it might have changed the outcome if that early pass had been caught for a touchdown. Baugh said yes, instead of the score being fifty to nothing, it would have been fifty to six."

"You are a bastard, Robert," Audra said, and walked out of the office.

His pulse thumping in his ears, Robert sat very still at his desk. The door was ajar after his wife's departure, and he heard her make a pleasant, normal-sounding comment to Nancy, the secretary, as she went past the reception desk.

Their voices had not been raised. They had been very civilized in that regard. No one would know.

He felt sick and desperately lonely. The visit with Ned Henderson had bolstered his spirits and he would have liked to tell Audra about it. Once they would have shared such things. He could not understand what was happening. He only knew that Gus Trello's illness had somehow accelerated the change sweeping into their lives. The tension had brought all his wife's hostilities more into the open than ever before.

Even in a terminal illness, Gus Trello cast a shadow over them.

Robert did not understand it. He was seldom with the old man for long before some argument broke out. Gus had raised his children in a stern way, making them feel that nothing they ever did was quite good enough. He had explained this once to Robert, revealing that it was a conscious tactic. Children did not become good enough, tough enough, wily enough, if they won approval easily, Gus had said. Children had to be handled like wine: very carefully, with very strong controls. And they must never be praised too highly lest they fail in a later test.

It was a harsh, loveless code. Robert did not envy Audra or Jules or the others this kind of early life. It had . . . damaged them in some fundamental way. There was some coldness in them which they felt, yet denied, wanted filled up, yet fought against.

Robert dug around in the desk for a cigarette, his first in a week. The smoke going deep into his lungs felt good, relaxing him. He watched the smoke rise and swirl in the room.

She would go to the house where the Trellos were gathering, he thought. He would not interfere. This weekend, if at all possible, he would drive south himself, pretending if possible that nothing had happened between them.

It was all he could think to do.

Turning to his desk, he frowned at the few papers strewn across its surface. Included were the brief penciled notes he had made during the earlier telephone conversation with Jed Witchley, one of the two men at Timmons Corporation he felt certain were friendly.

He concentrated on the notes, trying to get his mind off Audra.

Witchley had had little hard information, but the things he had said, while not new, were disquieting. Timmons had gone through fast expansion in the early seventies. Among its acquisitions were a stereo amplifier manufacturing firm, a chain of motels in the South, and a company that made bearings and control rods for a jet-engine manufacturer. But the company's studies had been faulty in all three cases, or victimized by circumstance. Quadraphonic sound was on the upswing, meaning that the stereo company's basic product would soon have to be re-engineered or completely replaced to meet the new demand for four-channel sound. The motel chain, first hit by the gasoline shortage, now had serious deficits as many Americans took shorter vacation trips, leaving the chain's units empty in city after city. The aircraft-parts company had counted on a sister firm to win a large government contract, but the order for two hundred big jets had been canceled, and the slump in airline business meant a lack of orders for those jets, too.

At least two other companies with loose working relationships similar to Robert's were also in trouble, his informant had said. A cracker company allied with Timmons for many years had staked everything on selling a new sandwich cookie supposed to be superior to the Oreo. As it usually did, the Oreo won. Another firm bet everything on desk-sized calculators only weeks before price breakthroughs put pocket calculators—which could do all the desk model's functions—in everyone's pocket at a fourth the price.

Timmons Corporation had a number of other firms in its control or under its wing, and many were doing outstandingly well. But the corporation had the word out: it was a time for belt-tightening. It was also a time to look for legitimate ways—in the language of an E. Z. Simms—to maximize profits.

Robert had told Witchley about Jules Trello's proposal to sell him the bulk wine.

"If Endicott and Simms conclude that you can make some money at it, Bob," Witchley had said, "I'll bet you haven't heard the last of it."

"I don't want to be a part of dumping that wine on the market."

"Could you sell it?"

"I imagine," Robert admitted.

"Then you'd better have your arguments ready. It hasn't come up here yet that I know about. But I'd bet somebody will want to pressure you on it."

Now, recalling the conversation, Robert wondered what steps he could take to try to block the transaction. The fact that even the winery's low-priced house wines were usually in short supply made it popular and in demand. Great pains were taken even with these lesser wines. Dumping the Elmhurst bulk on the market could only damage the Mancini label and sales strategy. He did not want that.

It would, of course, help Jules Trello out of a possible financial squeeze. It would also, probably, make Endicott and Simms look good at Timmons. Did the fact that both of them might profit indicate how Jules could have gotten word of the Elmhurst availability?

Robert did not have time to speculate further. His telephone intercom button flashed. He picked up the telephone. "Yes, Nancy?"

"Sir, Mrs. Turner is here."

"Mrs. Turner?" He was drawing a blank.

"The reporter from downtown."

He glanced at his watch. "Send her right in."

Barbara Turner entered moments later. She was rather tall, with dark hair in short-cropped rings that framed a wide, friendly face lighted by vivid gray eyes and a wide mouth. She wore a lightweight plastic jacket, red, over a white jersey blouse and dark knit slacks. She moved without pretense but with grace.

They shook hands. Her smile was genuine and lively. "I hope I'm not late."

"As a matter of fact, you're very prompt. Won't you sit down?"

She took the chair facing his desk and produced a notebook and ballpoint from her small purse. There was a cool competence in the way she faced him, and there was no hint of fear in her remarkable eyes. "Mr. Mancini, I don't think my editor has given me an easy assignment here."

Robert had already decided he liked her. She was very attractive, and showed no tendency toward cheap feminine tricks. He guessed her age at between twenty-eight and thirty.

"I'll be glad to try to help in any way I can," he told her. "Is Mike still the city editor downtown, by the way?"

"Yes. He's the one who gave me this assignment."

"How long have you worked in the valley?"

"Only a month."

"I noticed your byline on the story about the highway contracts. That was a good piece."

Barbara Turner colored very slightly. "Thanks. I fell into that one."

She had a very nice voice, low and steady. Robert liked the sound of it. He found himself noticing the subtle curve of her breasts under the loose jersey blouse and the line of thigh betrayed by her crossed legs. He wanted to make the meeting last . . . wanted to know her. "You're on a regular beat at the paper, or doing assignments directly for Mike?"

"I moved to the valley only six weeks ago. I may work full time later if things work out, but right now I'm just working the hours when my son is in school."

Inadvertently he glanced at her hands. There were no rings on the long, tapering fingers of her left hand.

She caught the glance. "I'm a widow. My husband died in Vietnam in 1970."

"I'm sorry."

She smiled too brightly. "So am I. My son is twelve now, and he's at the age when he could use his father's guiding hand. I moved here, as a matter of fact, partly because of Jimmy. We were in Los Angeles. I thought this environment might be just a little better for him. There were a lot of drugs in the schools he attended there."

"From what I understand, the problem exists everywhere. But I think you made a good choice anyway. This is a great place to raise kids."

Barbara Turner tilted her head. "You have no children." It was a statement.

"You've done some homework on me?"

"Just what's in our files. I thought it might help with the assignment."

Robert nodded, somewhat sorry that she had managed to turn the conversation back to the subject of her story. He had been enjoying learning about her. It was not unusual for his loneliness to reach out toward an attractive woman, but it was unique for him to feel a real impulse toward acting on the attraction. The more he looked at her and talked with her, the better he liked what he discovered.

"So what," he asked reluctantly, "did Mike ask you to see me about?"

"My city editor has heard a rumor of . . . difficulties."

"Difficulties?" Internal alarms began to sound.

"Some suggestion that office security has been breached. Also a rumor, I'm sorry to tell you, of some kind of industrial sabotage."

It was bad news. "Where did Mike hear these rumors?"

"I have no idea."

"I see. And if you did know, you wouldn't divulge a source?"

"I wouldn't. But I would say *that*. When I say I don't know, it means I honestly don't know."

"Sorry. You know . . . if we had had some trouble here, and had tried to keep it quiet, the leaking of the news to a newspaper editor would probably be a new act of sabotage in itself, wouldn't you say?"

Her bright eyes were sympathetic but probing. "Are you saying you have had sabotage, then?" The ballpoint was poised.

Robert hesitated. He wanted to help. He knew, however, that he could not provide verification that would hurt the winery. "Can I discuss this with you in strictest confidence?"

"No. I'm sorry. I've had the experience of someone giving

information off the record in such a way that I could never print a story, even using what I had already known."

"I wasn't trying to trick you, Mrs. Turner. I was actually trying to be helpful and co-operative in the only way I can."

"Then you won't comment for the record?"

"I'm sorry. No."

She took it well. Showing no pique, she closed the notebook and placed both it and the pen back in her purse. "Thanks for your time." She rose.

And suddenly Robert knew he would do practically anything to keep her with him another few minutes.

"Look," he said, "would you like some coffee or something before you have to run off?"

She smiled. "Does information come with the coffee?"

"Not about the topic you want to discuss, I'm afraid."

She faced him squarely, the question clear in her fine eyes. "Then why should I stay, Mr. Mancini?"

"Robert," he said. "Or Bob. All right?"

She looked wary. "There are things I learned about you that weren't in the files. You aren't a womanizer. Everyone agrees on that."

For the second time he felt his face redden. "Damn it, I'd just like to talk with you some more. Are we going to send out for a polygraph?"

She laughed softly then at his evident discomfort. "No. But you could send for the coffee, Mr. Mancini."

"Robert. Or Bob."

She said nothing as she resumed her seat.

Robert pressed the intercom button to order coffee, and wondered why his heart had suddenly come alive.

11

For almost two weeks following his introduction to Barbara Turner, Robert Mancini heard no more from her. Audra remained in the south, at her father's mansion, and called only twice with brief comments each time. As well as Robert could determine, there had been no new changes in Gus Trello's condition. He had lost weight and was somewhat weakened. He no longer visited his production areas daily, but stayed most of the time at the remote, castle-like home where members of his family and hangers-on had begun to gather. Audra was increasingly cold on the telephone as, first, a series of production meetings and, then, bottling of a Riesling kept Robert in the valley, unable to make the lengthy drive well south of San Jose.

Robert tried not to think about either Audra or Barbara Turner. He was less than successful both ways. He was troubled and amazed that one brief visit with the young widow could have so affected him. Late at night, alone, he thought of her often. He admired her courage in making her own life after her tragedy. He found himself looking for her bylines in the newspaper, and reading the stories eagerly, as if he imagined the reading was real contact with her. At times his fantasies became sexual. He was a virile man and it had been a long time since he had had outlet.

He stubbornly did not even seriously consider calling her, however, and buried himself in work. There was plenty of that. Despite earlier excellent sales reports from Jim

Young, the sales manager's latest figures showed a sharp and alarming decline in sales across the country, with few new orders. Robert held a series of meetings with Young, and telephoned distributors in several states. It developed that a number of orders sent to the winery had not been processed, and this was a very uncharacteristic oversight for a man like Young. The shipments were made promptly, but even so, the latest reports were not encouraging. Knowing that the figures were likely to cause unpleasant repercussions from the Timmons people, Robert authorized placement of several one-time ads in prestige publications. This, he knew, would further reduce the profit margin immediately, but he was banking on sales stimulus to show itself before anyone might complain.

The advertising nudge was done against Jim Young's advice.

"This is seasonal, Bob," Young argued. "It will pass."

"We're going to hear from Endicott and Simms about that proposal from Jules on his bulk wine," Robert replied. "My information is that there's a difference of opinion in Portland about what should be done, but my informant is betting Endicott will win and we'll be pressured to go ahead with it. Slumping sales now will only give them more ammunition, and we can't afford to give them any more."

"Would it be so bad to sell that wine of Jules's?" Young asked blankly.

"Hell, yes!" Robert snapped. "We sell our own wine. Our reputation has been built on that. I won't change policy now for a quick buck."

"The implication being," Young snapped, "that I don't have the character to make correct decisions?"

Robert paused and looked sharply at his associate. He realized in this instant that Young had often seemed distant . . . preoccupied . . . in recent months. "Jim, we've been together in this business for a long time now. Have I ever criticized your judgment?"

"You changed my sales plans," Young said darkly.

"A difference of opinion. But that doesn't imply any basic criticism. That's one of the reasons we've always worked together so well—we always understood each other."

Young stared at him, obviously troubled. Then, however, he moved his eyes away. "I'm just a little tense. Forget it."

Nothing more was said at that time, and when Robert noted an immediate small rise in sales as a result of his personal calls and the few ads, he assumed that Young also would forget any momentary pique. Young had always been an intensely proud and hard-working man. He had always identified the fate of the winery with his personal happiness. There was no serious problem involving Jim Young, Robert decided, and forgot about it.

His lawyers both locally and in San Francisco, meanwhile, were continuing to make discreet inquiries into the stock situation. Their information was hardly reassuring. When Robert had gone public in 1969, he had held back a clear majority of the stock. But in 1970, 1971 and 1972, seeking large sums for additions and improvements, he had sold off more than a million dollars' worth. Timmons Corporation, which had been a big buyer on the original sale, had bought most of the later offerings. Robert now owned more than a third of the stock, and much of the remainder was scattered.

"But some of it is privately held by Timmons executives," a San Francisco lawyer told him soberly. "I wouldn't be at all surprised if Timmons couldn't muster enough stock to take control right now, if they wanted to."

"Things have always operated to their benefit the way they stand," Robert pointed out.

"Then I'd say your job is to make sure those people stay happy. Frankly, you don't appear to be in any position to force a showdown."

On the face of it, it seemed highly unlikely that something like Jules Trello's bulk-wine proposal could become the basis for a showdown. But Robert knew that things might not be as they seemed. There was still the puzzling sabotage, still the leak of the Elmhurst information. If there was a pattern behind events, and Jules was playing some of the cards, then everything possible would be done to force any vote which might damage Robert Mancini. Jules's pathological hatred had been demonstrated often enough before.

The hate, like so many other aspects of the situation, went back in devious ways to Gus Trello, the man whose personality so dominated his children. Robert knew that Jules, as the oldest son, had never gotten over being shunted aside as general manager for Trello Industries. Jules knew—probably had been cruelly told by Gus himself—that the job had been offered to Robert. The fact that Robert had turned it down only seemed to make matters worse. Jules's hate, the hate of a son rejected by his own father, had begun at that time.

But Jules Trello was complex. It had been after this sequence of events that he had, with seeming eagerness, joined Robert in buying and operating Schreck Brothers. For a while they had seemed to work well together; no one had ever accused Jules of not working hard. It had only been when they clashed over Jules's tendency to cut corners on quality and costs that the hate revealed itself. And it had only been when Robert began to insist on turning Schreck toward higher-quality production that Jules cautiously and cleverly laid the groundwork for the coup which forced Robert out entirely.

By the time Robert had realized what Jules was setting up with the five other men who at that time held financial power in the Schreck hierarchy, it was probably too late. But Robert had been so sickened by the treachery, he had not put up much of a fight, preferring to leave, taking less than a fair price for his investment. The money he did receive was enough to allow him to start again, assuming he was willing to take the risks he subsequently did take.

Jules's hatred, however, had not been satisfied. Maintaining a façade of outgoing friendliness, he had tried to hire several of Robert's key personnel, and had succeeded with a production chief and one enologist. Once before the Elmhurst deal, Jules had gotten wind of a plan by Robert to make a much more modest acquisition—a thirty-acre vineyard of mature French Colombard—and had managed to ruin the purchase by arranging for an outside investor to buy the land before Robert was ready.

Robert knew now that he could not overlook the possibility that Jules was somehow behind more than just the bulk-wine proposal. And that idea, Robert knew, also had to have a hidden clinker in it somewhere. Jules was a grim joke to some who knew him in the valley. It was said that when Jules Trello gave you a really good deal, you were lucky to come away with your clothes on your back.

Late in the third week in June, however, a new development momentarily distracted most of the growers and winemakers of the area. In Los Angeles, Alfredo Rodriques announced that his Workers United organization had voted to make the valley its prime target for organizing this summer.

Rodriques, the charismatic leader of the powerful Chicano fieldworker organization, which had fought a long and bitter battle with such giants as Trello Industries and J&E Wines, told the press that he would personally go to the valley later in the summer. He said the valley was one of the last areas where field workers had no representation and few if any rights. He said a "maximum effort" would be made to change this situation prior to the fall harvest.

An informal response began to form locally at once. Within twenty-four hours, a meeting of growers and wine-makers had been set for the banquet room of the largest downtown motel. The session was announced as a meeting on an informal basis to exchange information about the local planting situation and marketing techniques, but even the friendly local newspaper speculated that the real reason was the Rodriques announcement.

The Sunday afternoon meeting forced Robert to call Audra at the Trello mansion and cancel yet another planned journey there. She accepted the news with icy apparent in-difference, proving how much she was hurt.

When Robert reached the motel, more than fifty familiar faces were already in the long, low-ceilinged room. Linen-covered tables had been set in long rows, and coffee was being served. At the front, Timothy Crocker, president of the fine Crocker Vineyards, stood beside the podium. He was chatting with Barbara Turner.

His heart pounding, Robert made his way to the front of the room. On the way he was stopped a dozen times by friendly voices, but he replied distractedly.

"Bob!" Timothy Crocker said. "Good to see you." He was a tall man, handsome, with longish gray hair and aquiline features. "Have you met Mrs. Turner?"

"Yes," Robert said, extending his hand to her. "I'm glad to see you again."

She smiled, and was there some message in her eyes? "Hello, Mr. Mancini." She wore her hair as before, and it struck him again as youthful and lovely. There was not a pantsuit today, but a pale-yellow doubleknit dress with a high neckline and medium-cut sleeves. The hemline was to the knee and she wore low-heeled white shoes. She looked young and beautiful and thoroughly cool and competent.

"It looks like we're going to have a good turnout, Bob," Crocker said.

"Do you have an agenda?"

Crocker frowned. "I thought I would make a few general

remarks and throw it open to general discussion. Of course"—he glanced at Barbara Turner—"this lady has presented us with a problem before we get that far."

Robert looked at her. "Problem?"

Crocker responded. "We want to have an open discussion. The general feeling is that we shouldn't have the press in the thing."

Barbara Turner said, "I've already agreed, contrary to my usual policy, not to make any notes or report anything any individual might say."

"Won't that be good enough, Tim?" Robert asked.

"I don't know," Crocker said in his scholarly way. "No one has complained. I don't want to make an issue of it. But—"

"Look," Barbara Turner cut in. "Mike, my editor, wants me here to get background. If Alfredo Rodriques is coming here this summer we need to understand everyone's position just as clearly as possible. I'm here on that basis, strictly for background. I assure you that I won't report anything that might be said. I can do a little routine item that says you met and talked about a variety of topics. But the information I gather—the understanding I gain— might help provide fair coverage later."

Robert, watching her lips as she spoke, found himself wanting to kiss her. It shook him. "I think the lady should stay, Tim. I know her word is good."

"The trouble is," Crocker said, "someone is going to ask what she's doing here. You weren't invited, Mrs. Turner."

"Well," Robert said quickly, "that's not true."

"It isn't?" Crocker said, as Barbara Turner's lovely eyes turned to Robert's in silent question.

"*I* asked her to come," Robert said. "She's my guest."

Crocker's forehead wrinkled. "That puts a little different light on things, I suppose. If she stays with you, and sits with you—and if you *assure* me on the story, Mrs. Turner—"

"I do," Barbara said promptly.

There was a slight commotion toward the rear of the room. Jules Trello had just entered, and was making his way up an aisle, pumping hands and leaving outbursts of laughter behind in the wake of his one-liners.

"Well," Crocker said, still frowning, "I guess it will be all right."

Surprised by his own actions, Robert took Barbara Turner's arm. "Let's go back and find a place to sit, shall we?"

She moved with him, her touch electric. "Yes."

They walked back down one of the long tables, passing other growers and winemakers, and found two chairs together. Robert introduced her by name only to several men nearby. A few of them had brought their wives, so Barbara was not particularly conspicuous, although Robert was aware of more than one sharp glance.

"Your friends are wondering who I am," Barbara said as they sat down.

"Good."

"Why did you help me?"

"I like you."

"What if I double-cross you and write every word?"

"You won't."

"How do you know?"

"I already told you: I like you."

"And your friends can do no wrong?"

"Of course."

Near the front of the room, Jules had gathered a coterie. He was at one of the coffee urns, and was pouring coffee and handing out filled cups. He wore crimson golf slacks and a white shirt trimmed in the same crimson. He looked youthful and vibrant, as if he had just walked in off the eighteenth green. He said something, and the men around him burst into laughter.

"Who is that man?" Barbara asked.

"Jules Trello."

"Your former partner."

"Yes. Is that observation the proof of new homework?"

Her eyes smiled. "It might be."

Within a few minutes the rear doors of the room were closed. Timothy Crocker, as informal spokesman, went to the podium, its inverted lights shining whitely into his serious face. He called the meeting to order, pointing out that it was designed to exchange views and information, and was both off the record and confidential. He briefly reviewed what all of them already knew, the contents of the Rodriques press release about coming to the valley. He said it was unlikely any action could be taken today, but open talk and exchange of information and views might help everyone prepare for whatever tests might lie ahead.

It was a neatly organized introduction, in just the right

judicial tone. Robert, however, was unable to appreciate it properly. Barbara Turner was seated on his right, between him and the front of the room, and he watched and listened past her. He became uncomfortably aware of the sheen of her eyes, the quickly intelligent changes of her expression as Crocker made his points, the glint of light off her lips as she thoughtlessly moistened them with her tongue. The gentle thrust of her ample breasts and the valley of her thighs were maddeningly near; he was aware of the fine down of pale hair on her arms, and the way she moved her pale, sweetly unadorned hands. He ached to touch her.

While Crocker spoke, however, there was another diversion as well. Jules Trello was into his act. He had appointed himself coffee waiter, and as Crocker went on, Jules hurried back and forth along the aisles, whispering to various individuals, rushing their empty coffee cups to the urn and hurrying the filled ones back again. Grinning all the while, he served a few doughnuts as well and carried sugar bowls and creamers around on order. He looked like a grownup boy who was having a whale of a good time, showing off.

"—so I think we can open it up at this point," Crocker said.

Jules, ignoring several hands raised for recognition, bounded to the platform. "Can I say a few words, Tim?" He was still off to one side, so he called the question loudly.

"Of course," Crocker said, his smile thin.

Jules went to the microphone, nudging Crocker aside. His voice boomed through the system as he waved his arms and grinned broadly. "Okay! I knew if I served enough coffee you'd let me talk! Let's hear it for the coffee and doughnuts, guys!" He struck a posture like a cheerleader and some of the crowd good-naturedly cheered.

Barbara Turner leaned toward Robert, allowing him to catch her light scent. "What a remarkable man!"

Robert said nothing.

"I'll tell you what," Jules yelled through the microphone, "I'm real glad to be here." He did a double take. "Where am I? No. Seriously. It's always a great experience to be with old friends." He frowned at Crocker, standing silent beside him. "Have we been introduced?"

Each line brought a rumble of laughter. Some of them had heard it all before, but Robert heard someone nearby murmur, "Good old Jules; always ready to make you laugh." Barbara Turner, too, was enjoying the performance.

"I just want to say a couple of things," Jules announced, "and then I'll go back to serving coffee." There was a scattered cheer and he did another double take. "Listen. We've just begun to fight. Napoleon at Waterloo. But no, seriously." He glanced at Crocker again. "Cheer *up*, Tim! You've got a great future behind you. No. Really. Whatever happens this summer, or at any other time, I think the winemakers and the growers of this valley can handle it. If we stick together, we can lick anybody." He rolled his eyes. "Just remember the old saying." He minced. "When the going gets tough, the tough get going. Truman Capote."

Barbara Turner was laughing. There was some scattered applause around the room. Jules, grinning from ear to ear, held up his hand for silence, but his other hand was doing the old Milton Berle gag of signaling for more.

It was all old to Robert. He had to admit, grudgingly, that it was still effective for people who did not know Jules well. The jokes were ancient, the delivery all wrong. He was obviously spoiling the start of a serious session. But the boyish good nature of his expression, the way he jiggled and grinned and rolled his eyes, gave a luster to the performance. He seemed really *to be having a wonderful time*. Sincerity sang out of every glance. It was quite remarkable.

"I just want to say this and I'll shut up," Jules said, his smile fading a bit. "I've spent several years here now. I'm proud of this valley and I'm proud of my winery and my friends, many of whom I see here today. Now. Maybe I'm old-fashioned, but here's what I believe. If you distributed all the money in the world equally, inside a month it would all be back right where it is today. I believe there are leaders and there are followers. I believe there are employers and employees. I believe the American way of life works just the way it stands."

He paused, the light shining up into his earnest face. The room had suddenly quieted.

"There are people around who just want to tear down," he continued, serious now. "Now, I'm not saying their motives are impure. I'm not calling them Communists or anything else. All I'm saying is, they're always negative. And you never gained anything by being negative.

"Maybe it's time the field workers formed a union and we all recognized them. I don't know. When I picked grapes as a kid, *I* wasn't in any union. And I didn't have Blue Cross or anything else. I noticed, though, that I felt pretty good at the end of the day, knowing I had earned my money with my own hard work, and nobody had bargained it for me or given it to me.

"But as I say, maybe it's time the Chicanos did get organized. I want to say right here and now, Schreck Brothers will never stand in the way of legitimate social progress. But I also want to say right now, Schreck Brothers is not going to be panicked by anybody—*anybody*."

Jules paused. His voice was so persuasive, and he looked so boyishly sincere and well-meaning, that a few people in the room gave him a smattering of applause. Robert, studying Barbara Turner's face, saw that the smile was gone and her eyes were studious . . . and troubled.

"Just this one more thing," Jules added, leaning forward so the light was golden in his eyebrows. "A lot of meetings start with a prayer. A lot start with a song. If you don't mind, I think, as official coffee waiter, I ought to be allowed to lead a song."

He paused an instant and then began to sing, directly into the microphone, slightly off-key: "Oh, beautiful . . . for spacious skies—"

Near the front, a grower named James Higgins came to his feet, singing too. Then others joined, rising. Quickly Jules's voice became only one of many as the spirit moved. It was corny, it was outrageous, it should have been embarrassing. But there was Jules at the front, singing unabashedly, and most of the people in the room were singing their love for their country and their valley right with him. Robert wanted to cringe.

Even before the song had ended, Barbara Turner turned to Robert, leaning close to say something in confidence. There was no longer any amusement in her expression.

She said, "I think he is a very dangerous man."

12

The meeting lasted through the afternoon but accomplished nothing concrete. Even so, when he left the motel and drove north again into the valley, Jules Trello was satisfied.

Everyone was worried. Jules had planted the ideas he wanted considered. No Rodriques organizer would have an easy time of it this summer.

In Jules's view, it was imperative to head Alfredo Rodriques off. Jules had tangled with the Chicano leader at Trello Industries. There were those who called Rodriques "Vietnam for Gus Trello." The years-old stalemate, with continued picketing and boycott of Trello products, was still under way even though Rodriques was concentrating elsewhere. Trello wines had been damaged. But Jules would not concede any major damage, because you just did not concede anything to Communists.

When Rodriques and his people arrived in the valley, Jules thought, the struggle would not be easy for them. Jules had learned how to fight in the earlier war. Profit-cutting raises, insurance, and the like would not be granted easily, if at all. Here, with Jules quietly leading, Alfredo Rodriques would be beaten.

Jules was dedicated to this.

In the meantime, he had other work to do. The drive to town gave him his first genuine opportunity to make a leisurely inspection of Elmhurst Winery, which on his orders had been under padlock ever since the purchase.

He had been too busy to return after his original inspection, but his route homeward took him right by the historic old mission buildings and he could afford the time for a brief stop.

His earlier visit, made with frantic haste, had revealed little equipment of great value in the ramshackle stone buildings. In its last years before the government trouble, Elmhurst had been in long decline, making less than thirty thousand cases of wine each year with antiquated machinery. Only the cooperage, mostly Limousin oak, was in good shape. While bottling apparatus and the old assembly line for labeling might be used, Jules had no intention of using them.

Driving into the winery grounds now, however, passing through a tall, rusty gate, Jules was struck by the beauty of the rolling vineyards and the fine old vines, maintained in good order by a skeleton crew. Jules understood imperfectly why Robert had wanted the property. Being an incurable romantic, Robert probably would have rhapsodized over the mature vines and the chalky soil, as well as the location in the heart of the most desirable of the valley's five identified mini-climate zones. The history of the old location would also have appealed. But Jules knew Robert would never have made plans to utilize the property with any of the efficiency Jules now had.

First, of course, he had to sell the wine in cooperage. He hoped to press the proposal that Robert should buy it in bulk and resell it as his own, because Robert was certain to resist this idea and it would lead to conflict, which fit very well into the other plans for his demise. Even if that failed, however, the wine was mostly the good Cabernet, and Jules knew he could always bottle it and sell it under his own label if worst came to worst. The important thing was to get rid of the wine and have the money from it as soon as possible.

Once the cooperage was cleared, Jules would use it for storage of his Schreck wines. The main Elmhurst building would be turned into a tourist attraction. Although he could hardly install a ski lift and charge visitors for the ride in, as one clever winemaker had once done, there were plenty of other things he could do. The smaller building, once a chapel, would become a souvenir shop and snack bar. The larger building would become a dummy winery, with mocked-up equipment continuously crushing the same plastic grapes and pumping the same colored water through glass pipes.

Jules was anticipating a clear $100,000 per year profit from the operation in the long run.

Parking in the stone courtyard between the moss-covered old buildings, he let himself into the main area. Power had been off a long time, and only the faintest odor of wine came from the old production area. Mouse droppings littered the floor. The creditors had claimed some of the furniture, and dusty windows let in gauze-colored light over dust, mildew, and bare, cracked walls.

Jules visited the production area first, using a flashlight to examine the machinery more closely. He planned to salvage the German-made plastic tanks and some of the cooling equipment, which was in good condition. He quickly tired of examining the other equipment, however, and proceeded to the cooperage rooms underground.

Here, in cobwebbed silence, rested rows of small oak barrels. Jules saw wet spots on the floor here and there, indication that his workers had been keeping the barrels topped off after evaporation, as ordered. He walked among the barrels, touching the rough wood here and there with fondness.

The bulk Cabernet Sauvignon would make more than eight thousand cases. The bulk Riesling and Pinot Chardonnay would make about fifty-five hundred. Even at a low bulk price, Jules expected to enjoy a quick return of more than one hundred and twenty-five thousand dollars. This would provide him enough cash to satisfy his own creditors for a little while . . . long enough to allow him to wheel and deal through some longer-term note arrangements.

It would still be risky, Jules reflected, continuing his inspection into the old office area in the adjacent building. He had, however, lived on the brink of financial disaster before. He would manage. In the meantime he had had the pleasure of thwarting Robert again, and by this time his father would have heard of the transaction, and must again (old bastard!) be wondering how he had managed such an expansion of his holdings.

In the office area, Jules found two ancient desks, some broken chairs, and the huge old winery safe as they had been when he last visited. The government had taken all original winery records during its investigations, but the safe contained true copies of everything, certified by the investigators. Jules intended to remove the records and take them to Schreck for more careful examination.

Using a pair of keys, he opened the heavy door of the old safe. It was as tall as he was and a foot thick. Swinging it open, he was assailed by the odor of book mold.

The inside was a labyrinth of heavy shelving and compartments. A glance showed that the bracing struts and shelves of the thick door were empty, but several shelves in the main section of the safe were crammed with papers and ledgers. Using his flashlight, Jules quickly went through for the items he considered most important, piling these on a dusty desk nearby.

As he turned for the last time with a load of ledgers, he bumped heavily into the internal door bracing with his shoulder. It stung him and he cursed. As he did so, something fell out of the innards of the door and clunked to the floor. Jules looked down and saw that it was another long, narrow ledger book.

Putting the other items on the desk, he bent to retrieve the one that had fallen. It was dusty, and smeared with rust on its cover. In examining it, he saw indented marks on its cardboard front and back, and then he understood that it had been jammed behind struts in the doors, perhaps for easy access, perhaps to keep from getting it mixed up with other records.

When he opened it and saw that it contained grape-purchase records—was clearly an original—his heart thumped. The government had complained about incomplete records. This ledger had been overlooked. Covering at least four years of grape purchases, it would have been priceless to any investigator, for one of the ways the "purity" of a claimed varietal was established was by comparing the tonnage of a particular grape purchased against the claimed production of wine from such a grape; if more wine was claimed than could possibly have been made from the amount of grapes purchased, for example, something was very obviously amiss.

Dusting off an old packing crate, Jules sat near a window and began examining the ledger. He quickly made out the method behind the records system, for this was not a formal ledger, but the book in which someone had jotted notations at the very moment of purchases; a more formal record probably had been made later from this book.

The more formal record had been lost . . . or destroyed.

The fact that Jules now held this document was strictly accident.

In a way, it was the story of the wine below him in cooperage.

He took a pencil from his pocket and began making notes. Within a few minutes, beginning to be worried, he went out to the car and returned with a pocket calculator. His skin began to prickle and he started sweating.

The figures were not adding up as they should on the Cabernet Sauvignon.

But it was a legal 51 per cent varietal—it had to be!

Jules hurriedly turned pages, punching totals into the calculator. Within thirty minutes he was muttering to himself, and by the end of an hour, all his earlier sense of well-being had vanished.

Examining his hastily computed totals, he felt sick and helpless.

The formal records might show that the wine now in oak was a legitimate Cabernet Sauvignon. But the grape-purchase records indicated that the winery had simply not bought enough Cabernet Sauvignon grapes to make that much wine, even at the low 51 per cent blending.

The red wine he had below in cooperage was not legal Cabernet.

At best it was a cheap jug wine.

Jules mopped sweat from his face. If this came out, he would not receive anything like what he had hoped for the wine. He would not have anywhere else to turn. With a feeling like strangulation, he thought of his creditors.

If this information got out, he was simply ruined. He *had to* sell the red wine as higher-quality stuff than this ledger proved it to be.

Darkness was coming on as Jules left the winery again. He carefully loaded the records into his car—all but the ledger book. This he kept inside until the end, when the sun was partially behind the western rim of mountains.

By searching, Jules found a can of gasoline for an outside motor. There were matches in his glove box. The ledger book was very old and dry, and soaked up a lot of gasoline, and when he lit it, it burned with a bright, hot flame. He stood beside the little fire and watched it until the ledger book had been reduced to ashes, and then he kicked these around carefully and watched the evening breeze carry fragments of them across the yard, across the driveway, into the dark vineyard.

Shaken by what he had learned, he drove home in darkness. It would be all right, he told himself. There were no other records. He still had plenty of time to sell the wine, and no one would ever know what it was now. He would be all right.

He found Carole waiting for him. She wore a transparent white robe over a wisp of red bikini, and had just come from the lighted pool beyond the wall of glass at the rear of the living room.

"Daddy is late," she whispered, offering him her mouth.

Jules brushed his lips over hers. "Daddy was busy."

"Daddy had two telephone calls."

"Oh?"

"Baby wrote nice man's name down. He wants to speak to you vewy badly, Daddy."

Jules walked into the hall of the huge house and glanced at the notepad beside the telephone. The name was of a banker, a very important one because it was his institution which had advanced most of the money for the Elmhurst transaction.

Concerned, Jules dialed the number. The banker answered.

"Thanks for calling back," said the banker, whose name was Slater. "Hate to bother a man at home on the weekend, but you're hard to catch."

"What's on your mind?"

"Jules, I'm afraid I have some bad news."

"Oh?" Jules felt his pulse thump.

"Yes. The loan we made to you on the Elmhurst property."

"What about it?"

"Jules, we authorized that loan on a contingency basis, as you know. You needed the money quickly, and we understood that. Our preliminary investigations certainly indicated everything was all right—"

"Everything *is* all right!" Jules snapped, aware that Carole, her thumb at the corner of her mouth, had sidled in from the next room.

"There are two problems," Slater told him. "Nothing serious . . . at least we certainly hope not."

"I don't know what you're talking about."

"In the first place, Jules, we've learned that your Schreck

Brothers financial situation is not exactly as you portrayed it to us. We understood that you had only the equipment loan for one hundred twenty thousand dollars and the one small loan covering vehicles and repairs, about fifty thousand dollars. Now we discover a note for ninety thousand outstanding at City National, plus an unpaid balance of almost seventy-one thousand on another loan with First Federal."

"Those last two are personal notes," Jules said, trying to ignore Carole as she stole up beside him and began insinuating her pelvis against his thigh. "They have nothing to do with the Schreck situation."

"That's true, Jules, but we find that Schreck Brothers assets are pledged as collateral in both cases."

Jules began to sweat. "It's only a technicality. You know I'm good for those loans, Jim!"

"I know you are, Jules. But it puts us in a very peculiar position. We seem to have made a loan against insufficient collateral in this case, and frankly the board is damned unhappy about it."

Carole began teasing ribald fingers down the front of Jules's shirt and fly. Her baby expression had become sultry and preoccupied.

"Listen," Jules said thickly. "This Elmhurst property itself is worth enough to cover my loan. You *have* collateral."

"We assumed that too, for a while," Slater said unhappily. "But then we found out about those liens."

"Liens?" Jules's midsection trembled. "I don't know what you're talking about!"

"They've just been filed at the courthouse. A new roof was put on both main buildings at Elmhurst two years ago, and the contractor claims he was never paid. A heating and air-conditioning company has also just filed, and our lawyers understand there are going to be more."

"That's impossible!" Jules cried. "I was assured everything was clear!"

"It appeared to be. But now, suddenly, it isn't."

"How much . . . is involved here?"

"More than fifty thousand dollars so far. And it will go higher."

Jules felt the words like a physical blow. His mouth went dry and he was speechless. Carole, murmuring obscenely, continued her game with him: her left hand stole down to his crotch, kneading gently, and with a little smile she nuzzled at his chest, trying to find his nipple with her teeth.

Jules put one hand over the telephone and hurled her backward. "Get *away* from me, God damn you!"

Carole was flung against the far wall, bumping her head. Her eyes filled instantly.

"Leave me alone!" Jules told her. "Can't you see this is important?"

She fled into the living room.

Jules uncovered the telephone. "You've taken me by surprise here, old buddy. You know, gosh." He faked a laugh. "It's a real pleasure to be talking with you. Have we been introduced? But seriously—"

"Seriously, Jules," Slater broke in grimly, "the board is very upset about this. If it should get out, we would look very bad indeed. The board believes we must have some quick action on this loan we made to you. I'm sorry to tell you this on the telephone like this, but it's urgent, you see, and—"

"What you're doing," Jules said, "is demanding payment. Is that it?"

"In a nutshell, Jules, yes. I'm sorry."

Jules closed his eyes. The rows of other debts marched before his mind. Slater knew only a few of them. All were carefully balanced, one against another. Suddenly the house of cards was trying to slide down.

He said, "And how long do I have to make repayment, old friend?"

"Jules, please don't think this is personal. It's unfortunate—"

"How *long?*"

"The board has suggested repayment by August first."

"That's not enough time!"

"Jules, the board is very upset. Quite frankly, some of the members have openly suggested that you falsified your loan application. I consider it a personal victory for me to get you that long to repay."

Jules's mouth had become sandpapery again. Everything had been predicated on sale of the wine in bulk. But Jules had expected that to take at least another month, perhaps two months before delivery and payment. Now everything was accelerated, a noose was tightening around his neck. It was no longer necessary to sell the cooperage wine at the best possible price. It was now mandatory for his business survival.

"I know you understand our position, Jules," Slater was saying.

"Of course," Jules snapped. "You'll hear from me. Thanks for the notification." He hung up.

In the silence, he heard the sound of Carole in the next room. She was crying. He felt an urge to rush in and throttle her. Did he need her stupidity at a time like this?

With effort, he controlled himself. His hands shook as he picked up the personal telephone directory on the table and looked for John C. Endicott's home telephone number.

If the pressure had escalated for Jules, it would escalate all the way down the line. For him, now, it was fast becoming life or death.

13

Shortly before noon on the day following the motel meeting concerning Alfredo Rodriques' announced plans, Susan Knight was summoned to Robert Mancini's office, where she found Robert and Mike DeFrates waiting for her. One look at their expressions told her something else had gone wrong.

"I had a call a few minutes ago from one of my friends at Portland," Robert told her. "As I just explained to Mike, it's going to be a day or two before we're officially notified. But Endicott is going to call and ask for a meeting next week; they want to reopen the question of buying that bulk wine from Jules."

"I can't believe it," Susan said in dismay. "We made it clear to them that the Elmhurst wine shouldn't be sold under *any* of our labels!"

Robert looked grim. "Our assurances weren't sufficient. Timmons Corporation has just had some new bad news about its home-building operations and a frozen-food company that has an arrangement with them much like ours. The pressure is on to tighten up and turn any profits possible in the remainder of the calendar year. That includes us."

"We've always been highly profitable for them, haven't we?"

"Yes. But the way my friend explained it to me, they're scouring the corporate closets to find additional money to try to offset all the bad news that's going to be in the year-end reports."

"Don't they realize a winery has to have a consistent, predictable product in order to build loyal consumer relations?"

Mike DeFrates, his massive shoulders hunched up in sullen anger, spoke for the first time. "They're stupid. They don't know anything about us. They never have."

"That's not quite true," Robert said. "There has been some resistance to the idea of asking us to deviate from our normal procedures. But Endicott, and E. Z. Simms, too, to a lesser degree, have been persuasive. They've apparently argued that we can slightly alter the appearance of our house wine label, push distribution into grocery stores, and actually use a substandard product to broaden awareness of our better lines."

"Bullshit!" DeFrates rumbled.

Robert smiled thinly. "My sentiments exactly."

"What do we do?" Susan asked, more worried than ever.

"Well, they're not going to come down here and start twisting arms. Jed Witchley—my friend at Timmons—says the support isn't clear-cut enough for that. It looks like they'll ask for another meeting, come in, and say, in effect, 'Look. We need some quick profit. Either buy this bulk wine and resell it, or suggest something better right here and now.' "

"Is there anything we *can* offer as an alternative?"

Robert tugged his ear thoughtfully. "We need to give that a lot of consideration. In the meantime, though, I intend to fire off a long letter immediately. It won't be hostile, but it will go beyond the memo on the last meeting in detailing our reasons for not wanting any part of Jules's proposition."

"I don't know if it could do any good," Susan said, "but I could give you a written report on the Elmhurst wines. I'm the only one here who has tasted them, remember."

"I have your original notes, along with all the work Mike did on the physical plant. The research you two did over there was to be the basis of our proposal to buy, you'll remember."

"Yes," Susan said. "But you'll also remember that we kept my section on the wines in cooperage very brief, because I couldn't honestly say much good about them. Our intent was to find someone in the East who might use them for blending one of their own bottom-drawer products."

Robert looked dubious. "I wouldn't want you to lie just to make this new letter look stronger. That kind of tactic could backfire anyway."

"Robert, remember when I told you about the Elmhurst wines after Mike and I spent the afternoon over there? The whites are all right—ordinary and rather thin, but passable. The Cabernet, though, was really very poor: thin, high in acid, too tart, with a pronounced aftertaste, as if they had inadvertently crushed a few seeds. I also suggested that some of the barrels might have gone a little sour and Elmhurst had tried to reuse them anyway, with predictable results."

Robert studied her face. "The Cabernet is really *that* bad, and you could honestly say so in a letter?"

"Robert, if you put out a hundred Cabernets, I know I could pick that Elmhurst stuff out on a first tasting. It's not only bad; it has that very unusual seedy aftertaste that brands it clearly. If we sold that wine and someone accidentally liked it a little bit, there's no way they would ever find a bottle of our own wines that was anything like it. We couldn't make a Cabernet that bad if we tried."

"Okay, write me a brief memo, and we'll add it to the letter as an exhibit. But don't exaggerate. If anything, understate your case. I'm not going to use Endicott-type tactics."

"I'd give a lot," DeFrates said, "to know why Endicott and Simms are pushing so hard on this."

"There's no use even trying to speculate," Robert said.

"They're in cahoots with Jules Trello. That's what I think."

"They could be merely ambitious for advancement inside Timmons Corporation. If they could force us into some big profit figure, it would probably make them look awfully good. And nobody would likely notice the kind of slow flattening of our growth curve that would result in the next couple of years following."

"*God*, I wish this damned stock question didn't exist!" Susan exclaimed.

"Welcome to the club."

"Isn't there some way we can just buy back enough stock to make sure they couldn't win in a showdown?"

"To be *sure*, that would be quite a lot of stock. We don't

know their exact holdings, and some of it is veiled by private ownership by Timmons executives. I doubt Timmons would sell any stock it holds, and the rest of it is scattered. We have no idea who most of the stockholders are, although most of them are quite small. The only way we could buy back sufficient stock would be by making a public offering well above the current price. And *that* would take a lot of money."

"Do we have that kind of money?" Susan asked bluntly.

"No," Robert said.

"If there's a real crisis, Robert, can you raise it?"

"Susan, we're talking about well over a half-million dollars. The winery and grounds are worth far more than that, of course. On paper, *I'm* worth a lot more than that. But everything is tied up. There's no spare cash."

Susan did not reply at once. The prospects appeared bleak, and for the first time she saw clearly that the issue here could be much more than buying the bulk wine—and more even than the question of who held the top cards in setting policy. It was quite possible that Robert Mancini, who had built back this winery and its surrounding vineyards, and now began to enjoy an international reputation, had bartered away his very freedom to do his building. In an ultimate showdown, there was every chance, apparently, to believe that he would lose—everything.

"—and in the meantime," Robert was telling DeFrates, "an up-to-the-minute report on everything in cooperage. Simplified. With options."

"I'll get it," DeFrates grumbled, heading for the door. "But what I'd rather give them is a kick in the—"

"Right!"

DeFrates went out, leaving the door ajar.

"I'll get on that memorandum at once," Susan said, starting for the door as well.

"There's one other thing," Robert said.

She turned back to face him, and saw an additional sign of pressure . . . almost mortification . . . in his expression.

"Yes?" she said when he remained silent.

"That tasting Saturday at Christian Brothers. You haven't forgotten it."

Susan smiled. "Not likely!" Top winemakers from Napa, Sonoma, Mendocino and nearby areas would be gathered. This did not mean, however, that the number would be large; only the fifteen top people would attend for a tasting of two dozen fine Traminers. Winemakers learned endlessly from comparative blind tastings, and in this case a top wine magazine would publish the results. Susan would attend as an observer.

"I'm going to make arrangements for you to take part in my place," Robert surprisingly told her now. "I won't be there."

"But I know you've been looking forward to it!"

"I'm going to be out of town." He hesitated, and then added as if the words were dragged from him, "I'll be down at Gus Trello's place for the Fourth of July weekend."

Susan said nothing. Her curiosity, knowing the long-standing tensions between Robert Mancini and members of his wife's family, was very strong. But she knew she could not pry.

"Mr. Trello must be worsening," she said.

"He may be," Robert said. Then he hesitated, seemed to make some decision, and faced her with an almost angry expression. "I don't want this to go any further. But the real reason I'm going is that . . . well, Audra is already down there."

"I see," Susan said. She did not see at all.

"I don't know if I can say she has *left* me," Robert added, jamming his hands in his pockets. "But there's . . . trouble." He looked up at her, his eyes suddenly revealing some of his pain. "I wouldn't ask you to go to that tasting alone unless I thought it was necessary. But I've been putting off the trip south. Audra called last night, late. We had a long talk. I—have to go. We have to . . . try to settle some things."

Susan was acutely embarrassed and filled with concern for him. "I'll do my best at the tasting. And if there's anything else I can do—"

"I hate to dump my problems on someone else. Maybe I'll be able to iron everything out."

"Yes." Susan did not know what more to say. She knew of the rumors of trouble between Robert Mancini and his still beautiful wife. The fact that the problem had deepened—changed into a separation of some kind—saddened her. She looked at him, trying to think of words.

"Maybe I've been too proud with old Gus," Robert told her. "In his own way he's a great man. A very great man . . .

I guess I always fought his ruthlessness with Audra, with Jules, with everyone. I had to break with him or be steamrollered like everyone else. But now he's dying, you know. If I can make a visit and try to patch things up, maybe it will give Audra what she wants . . . needs . . . right now."

Susan felt a stab of pity and resentment. The last thing this man needed was selfish demands being made upon him. But Audra had always had an indefinable quality, and Robert had just put his finger on it in terms of the family characteristic: ruthlessness. It was the trait that made all the Trellos what they were.

"I'll handle the tasting," she said, "and try to do the very best job I can. And I'll be around all weekend. I'll keep an eye on things here."

"Mike will be around too. But he doesn't know why I'm going south."

"I understand. I won't say a word."

The meeting was concluded. Susan, preoccupied and upset, went back to her own office. She made three false starts before finally writing her memorandum about the Elmhurst wine. When she finished the draft and took it to the secretarial room for final typing, she found the area deserted. It was the lunch hour.

As she went back into her office, having left the memorandum with a note of instructions, her telephone blinked, signaling a call.

"Susan Knight," she answered crisply.

"Miss Knight?" a shaky feminine voice said. "This is Johnelle Henderson. Ned Henderson's wife."

"Yes," Susan said, surprised. "How are you today?"

"We haven't met, but Ned told me how you and Mr. Mancini helped him. Right now I don't know where Ned is. I don't know what to do. I need help real bad, right away!"

There was stark fear in Johnelle Henderson's voice. Susan tried to be calming. "Tell me what's happened, Mrs. Henderson."

"I can't," Johnelle Henderson said, and she sounded like she was crying. "Not on the phone. I came home for lunch and I'm home now, and please *please*—can you come out here? Please! I don't know what to do!" She began sobbing.

"Are you hurt?" Susan demanded. "Is it your boy?"

"No! No! Please! Can you come?"

The sheer fright and anxiety in Johnelle Henderson's voice spoke louder than any words she might have uttered. Susan made an instant decision.

"I can be there within fifteen minutes," she said.

14

The last of the morning fog had burned away and it was hot as Susan turned off the highway, found the dirt road leading back to the Henderson property, and drove eastward at reckless speed. Great plumes of yellow dust billowed behind her Firebird, and she knew the people in the houses she passed would hardly appreciate the mini-duststorm she was creating. No matter. Johnelle Henderson had sounded too upset to allow for delay.

When she drove into the area beside the Henderson house, Susan saw nothing unusual for a moment. A white Vega was parked near the ancient green Rambler, which Susan remembered as the property of part-time field worker Homero Artiz. There was no one in sight. The house, green garden plot, and vineyard lay silent and slightly dusty under the intense sun.

Susan stopped her car abruptly and got out. Ned Henderson's pigeons strutted on the house roof. It was silent.

Then a youthful blond woman wearing a simple olive sundress appeared on the far side of the old Rambler. She was pretty and she looked scared.

"Susan Knight?" she called.

"Yes," Susan said.

"Here—he's—over on this side."

Not understanding, Susan started around the old green Rambler. It was dirty and very beaten up, sitting slightly lopsided on its worn tires as if some of its springs were broken underneath. Rust splotched the broad fenders and hood. Susan was surprised to see both headlights were broken out, and so was the windshield. She wondered for an instant how Homero Artiz ever avoided being stopped by the highway patrol, and then she saw all the bright shards of newly broken glass around the car on the bare ground. *The headlights and windows had just been broken.*

On the far side of the car she met a worse surprise. Johnelle Henderson was on her knees beside someone— Homero Artiz—who was stretched out on his back. She had a small first-aid kit beside her, and a basin and some towels. She was sponging carefully at the Chicano's face, which was covered with bright blood.

With a cry, Susan knelt beside Johnelle Henderson. She saw that Homero Artiz's shirt had been torn nearly off his slender body, and dark bruises had already begun to show on his chest, shoulders and arms. His eyes were closed, but he winced as Johnelle Henderson dabbed at some of the cuts around his mouth. His breathing seemed strong but spasmodic as he reacted to the pain of being touched.

"What *happened?*" Susan demanded.

"I don't know," Johnelle Henderson replied, continuing to work. She had regained much of her self-control now, perhaps because she had help. Her chin was firm with resolve, although her clear blue eyes betrayed her anxiety. Susan's immediate impression was of an intelligent and resourceful young woman, a good match for the Ned Henderson she liked so much.

"How did this happen to him?" Susan asked.

"I came home for lunch because I had forgotten some papers we needed at work. When I got here, I found him this way." Johnelle looked up for an instant. "I'm sorry to bother you. I didn't know who else to call. We don't know many people—"

"It's all right," Susan assured her. "You did the right thing. I know a doctor we can call. We'd better do that right away."

Homero's eyes shot open. "No!" he said huskily. "No doctor! Do not call anyone else, please!"

"Somebody beat him up," Johnelle said. "Nothing else could explain this—the way he's hurt, all the awful damage to his car. But he begged me not to call a doctor or the police."

"Some of these cuts are going to require stitches." Susan

bent over Homero, meeting his pain-filled eyes. "You *must* have medical attention."

"No!" Homero tried weakly to sit up in protest.

Johnelle competently pushed him back down. "You just be quiet, Homero. I don't know why you're so afraid, but we're not going to get you into any trouble."

"No doctor," Homero repeated, and then closed his eyes and lay still.

"Has he passed out?" Susan asked, alarmed.

Homero opened his eyes again. "It . . . hurts."

"Of course it does," Susan told him. "You just lie still." Getting to her feet, she motioned Johnelle Henderson a few steps away. "Now, is there anything more about this that you couldn't say in front of him?"

"I came home," Johnelle said. "As I turned onto the road, a brown car—a Buick, I think—was coming out, fast. It sprayed a lot of dust around and I remember being irritated about it. Maybe it was the man who did this to Homero."

"Did you see him?"

"No, not really. I wasn't paying that much attention, and the car went by so fast, and there was so much dust. I think there might have been two men in the car. The driver was wearing a red baseball cap."

Susan hesitated a moment. Her impressions of Johnelle Henderson were all favorable. Whatever instant hysteria the young woman might have experienced, she was in control of herself now. Still, Johnelle was clearly allowing Susan to make the decisions.

"He has to have medical attention," Susan said.

"I hate to call a doctor or an ambulance when he begs us not to!"

"I know," Susan said grimly. "But he needs treatment. He could have serious injuries we don't know about." She thought about it. "And we have to notify the authorities," she added in a near-whisper.

Johnelle glanced toward Homero, who lay still. "He's frightened. He doesn't want that."

"I know someone we can trust," Susan said. "Let me use the telephone."

"Inside—in the kitchen."

Leaving Johnelle to return to Homero's side, Susan entered the house. It was not necessary to look up the number because she had called it often, although never before in an emergency.

"Sheriff's office," a man answered.

"Rod Poole, please," Susan said. *Be there, Rod.*

"Moment, please."

Susan waited, her nerves racketing.

"Rod Poole speaking."

"Rod? Susan."

His voice changed from the brisk businesslike tone. "Hey, how nice. You couldn't last till this evening without hearing my voice, right?"

"Rod, listen to me."

His voice had a lazy grin in it. "I knew you couldn't resist me, and all that, but with dinner set this evening, I thought—"

"Rod!"

This time the tension crackled in her voice and he reacted instantly, cool. "What is it, Susan?"

She told him what she had found at the Henderson place. "He doesn't want a doctor, and he seems scared to death of law officers. Can you come out here alone, without any red lights or anything like that?"

"Of course. Keep him quiet until I can get there."

"How long, Rod?"

"No lights, no siren; I won't be able to push it much over eighty. Call it twenty minutes, okay?" He hung up.

Actually, Rod Poole was in the driveway in sixteen minutes.

By the time he arrived, Susan Knight and Johnelle Henderson had brought a light blanket from the house and had covered Homero Artiz. They had finished cleaning his facial wounds and had tried to talk with him. He seemed dazed and said little. They competently refused to let him try to sit up or walk away.

Efforts to elicit information about the attack that had been made on him had met stony silence.

When Rod Poole drove up, rocking the black Ford sedan to a halt and jumping quickly out to hurry over, Susan felt a pulse of reassurance. Tall, youthful, darkly good-looking, Rod Poole had been careful never to show her his brisk official side. He had always been lazily good-natured. Now, however, after eight months of dating, she was finally getting the first glimpse of his professional conduct; the quick, efficient air about him made her feel better at once.

Poole's eyes took in everything at once as he strode closer: the general surroundings, the battered Rambler and broken glass on the ground, Homero, Johnelle Henderson, and—last of all but most intensely—Susan. His eyes pierced her for an instant with a force she had never experienced before, even in their lovemaking. He was reassuring himself that she was all right.

"I'm fine," she said.

Moving his black-holstered revolver back out of the way, Poole squatted beside Homero. His fingers touched Homero's throat and then his rib cage. "Does this hurt?" He probed behind Homero's shoulder blades. "Does your back hurt?"

"I can sit up," Homero said.

Poole ignored this. "Turn your head from side to side. Any pain when you do that? Move your legs for me. That's it. Can you move your arms?"

Homero complied. "I am all right," he insisted. "I am not hurt."

"I can see that," Poole muttered. Then he put his hands under Homero's shoulders. "Okay. Do you want to sit up?"

"Rod?" Susan said. "Are you sure? Internal injuries—"

"He's been beaten." Poole's eyes were like glaciers. "If they had wanted him dead, he'd *be* dead. Most internal injuries would have already shown up some way."

Cautiously he helped Homero sit up. The Chicano's face drained from the movement and pain, but he nodded vigorously.

"I can stand," he insisted.

"Take it easy a minute," Poole said.

Homero's eyes flashed anger. "I am all right! They should not have sent for you, sir. I can stand!"

Poole studied Homero a moment, then stood. "All right. Go ahead. Get up."

"Rod?" Susan said again.

"Stay out of it," Poole said.

Homero struggled. He got to his feet, turned very pale, and sank dizzily to his knees.

"That settles that," Poole said, kneeling again. "I'm going to take you to the emergency room."

"No! I am not badly injured. I—"

"What's your name?"

"Homero Artiz. Please, sir." Homero's single eye—his right had puffed closed—stared in alarm at Poole's notebook and ballpoint. "It is of no consequence."

"You don't want to file a complaint?"

"No. No."

"What were you doing here when this happened?"

"I work part-time for Mr. and Mrs. Henderson."

"You were working here this morning?"

"Yes, sir."

"Were you working alone?"

Johnelle interjected, "My husband went to town, and I work in—"

"Let *him* answer," Pool snapped.

Homero said slowly, "Mr. Henderson went to order wire. I was here alone."

"What happened?"

"I do not know, sir."

Poole's head jerked up. "How was that again?"

"I do not know what happened. I was sitting beside my car, to have lunch. I had finished my sandwich and coffee, from the thermos. Then someone grabbed me. Someone hit me."

"How many were there?"

Homero's expression was veiled, stubborn. "I do not know, sir."

"Tell me what one of them looked like."

"Sir, I saw no faces."

"What did you see?" Poole's face was becoming like stone.

"Nothing, sir. It all happened so fast."

"How did they manage to sneak up so close?"

"Sir, if I knew that, I would have seen them."

"Did you hear anything before they hit you?"

"No, sir."

"Did you hear them drive in? Or do you think they walked?"

"Sir, I know nothing. I was having my coffee. I was attacked."

Rod Poole studied Homero intently. "Do you have any idea why they wanted to beat you up, Homero?"

"None, sir. I swear it!"

"Tell me about your enemies."

"I do not have any enemies, sir!"

Poole kept trying very patiently. Susan exchanged looks

with Johnelle Henderson. They both knew Homero Artiz had to be lying. Susan could tell that Johnelle had no more idea than she did why the worker would do so, unless it was sheer fright.

Finally Poole snapped his notebook closed. "Do you have a driver's license, Homero?"

Homero flinched. "It is in the car, sir. In the glove box."

"May I get it?"

"Of course, sir. It is in a plastic folder."

Rod Poole walked around the smashed Rambler, climbed in on the far side, and opened the glove box. His head bent as he examined something. Then he moved around, evidently looking at something else. He took a full minute or more. Then he came back around the car with the license in a folder.

"This your correct name, age, and address?"

"It is, sir."

"This is your Rambler?"

"It is, sir."

"Do you have the title?"

"It is at my home."

Poole made a note from the license and then handed it to Homero. "Do you have any *theory* as to why this was done to you?"

"Sir, I have no enemies. It must be someone who is crazy."

"It must be," Poole said heavily. "A party or parties unknown came here in some unknown way and approached you in some unknown manner and attacked you for unknown reasons, their number and appearance is unknown, and then they wrecked your car for similar unknown reasons, and left by unknown routing for parts unknown—at a time unknown. I'd say *something* is crazy here."

"It is the truth," Homero said quietly.

"Okay. Please walk to my car. I'll take you to the hospital just as soon as I have a word with the ladies here."

"Sir, please! I do not require medical care. I cannot afford it."

"I'm taking you to be checked, Homero. Sorry. That's SOP. I need a medical report for the paperwork I have to turn in."

"But I do not want a report written! I am not hurt!"

"Just wait in my car, sir, please."

Homero climbed back to his feet and wobbled toward

the cruiser. He went to the far side and painfully eased himself inside.

Rod Poole turned back to Susan and Johnelle Henderson. "What do either of you know about this?"

"I came home from lunch and found him on the ground," Johnelle said. "I really don't know any more than that. I heard the things you asked him and I saw what you were looking for. The only thing I can add is that I saw a car at the end of the road, leaving, as I drove in. But it was dusty and I didn't see much."

"What kind of a car?" Poole reopened the notebook.

"A Buick I *think*. I think it was brown, but I'm not too sure. I wasn't paying too much attention at that time because I didn't know it might be important."

"Did you notice the license plates?"

"No. I'm sorry."

"That's all right. The fact that you didn't notice probably means it was a state registration. How many people in the car?"

"Two, probably. Two men. The driver was wearing a hat—a baseball cap. A red baseball cap. That's all I noticed."

Poole scribbled. "Anything more? Anything at all?"

Johnelle frowned. "The car had those big tires. Fat ones. They were white sidewalls, I think."

Poole wrote again. "Anything more?"

"No. I'm sorry."

"Okay, tell me about Homero. Do you know of anyone who might be after him?"

"No. We don't know him that well. But I know he's a good worker, very hard-working, polite, punctual, dependable. I'm sure all the people he works for would tell you the same thing."

"Who are some of those other people?"

"I'm sorry. I don't know. I'm sure my husband would. He ought to be back soon."

"I'll come back later, then." Poole closed the notebook and frowned at Johnelle a moment.

"What is it?" she asked.

"We've met," Rod Poole said.

She flushed. "My son has a motorcycle. You—"

Light dawned on Poole's face. "Right! I remember now. He was out on the highway and the bike wasn't street-legal."

Johnelle Henderson winced with embarrassment and something more, a concern that showed a deep family nerve had been touched. "We've made him put the lights back on it. But he still isn't supposed to go off our road. If you ever see him out there again, I hope you'll stop him again, just as you did before."

Poole smiled. "I will if there's time. But maybe he won't get out there much more."

"One time is too often," Johnelle said firmly, the worry furrowing her brow. "We've told him and told him."

"Well," Poole said, "kids get a little wild at that age. Thanks for the information. I'll be back later to talk to your husband."

"Rod?" Susan said. "Do you believe Homero's story?"

"Hell no. He's lying from start to finish."

"Why?"

"I don't know. Scared, maybe, that he'll get worse if he tells us anything and we can't keep the guys locked up. Maybe he could have something of his own that he's afraid we'll find out about."

Johnelle Henderson said, "I find that hard to believe. He's a fine person."

Poole studied her face, and his eyes were hard again. "He even lied about lunch, Mrs. Henderson. His sandwiches are still in the sack, and that thermos of coffee hasn't been touched since it was filled to the brim this morning."

"Why?" Susan wondered aloud. "I don't understand why Homero would want to protect people who attacked him this way!"

"I don't know either, hon," Poole said. "But I sure aim to try to find out."

15

It was the Thursday of the same week, on the first day of July, that Robert Mancini received a brief telephone call from John Endicott at Timmons Corporation. The call came shortly before 5 P.M. Endicott asked for a meeting next week to discuss further Jules Trello's bulk-wine proposition.

"Has my letter and the accompanying memo reached you yet?" Robert asked.

"Yes, Bobby, it did. But we've all talked it over here, and we still think we need to give this some more discussion at your end. Will next Wednesday morning, the seventh, be all right?"

Robert did not argue the point. Whatever had to be done, it would be done in the meeting. He checked his calendar, and the meeting was set for 10 A.M. at the winery.

When he drove home more than two hours later, he was depressed about it. His options for heading off the proposal seemed limited, but he could not risk a confrontation on the matter. Either way, it appeared he would lose ground.

Trying to get his mind off the matter, he stopped first at a small winery in the northern reaches of the valley and visited a friend, Henry Barton, who made Pinot Noir and Barbera in limited quantities and under the strictest traditional controls. Then he stopped at a roadside cafe and had a sandwich and coffee. Dark was gathering when he finally drove into the mountains and reached his home. It was dark, silent, and lonely. He went through the house, turning on lights.

Opening a chilled bottle of Riesling, he propped up in front of the television set and tried to watch it for a while. But it was no good. Worries intruded, and the silent house whispered of his loneliness. He thought of calling Audra, but he could not risk another long-distance argument.

When he found himself thinking again of calling Barbara Turner, he heaved himself out of the easy chair and padded in his slippers out to the pigeon house.

As usual, the White Kings made a commotion at his arrival. Some of the fully mature males began throating their combat sounds and pecking at one another, as if in competition for his attention or the food they knew he would distribute. There was a lot of fluttering and moving around, and the sharp odor of pigeon excrement filled the screened little house. Two pigeons, almost fully grown, had been rejected by their mothers a few months earlier, and Robert had successfully raised them by hand, first with baby cereal in a medicine dropper and then by stuffing water-soaked grain into them with his fingers. These two fluttered mournfully, working their wing stubs in the baby recognition signal, and one of them flew over and perched on his left shoulder, trying desperately to peck food from his ear.

"All right, all right!" he chuckled, feeding the bird a few grains by hand just to reassure the creature that it still had its "mother."

Some of the water bowls were dry or dirty. He cleaned and refilled them. The bossiest males tried to fight over the bowls, at least until he strewed the grain around and gave them something better to argue about.

Standing still, he watched the eating and drinking begin. The birds accepted his presence, calming down. It was nice standing in the roosting house with the night beyond the screens and such a sense of life close around him. He felt a sensation of peace steal through him.

His father had kept both pigeons and rabbits. There had been no reason for either—certainly his father would have looked on the suggestion of eating any of the pets with the same horror that Robert felt at such a suggestion. It had been something to do, something that was fun and life-sustaining. Robert could remember many evenings with his father in a little house like this, or along the row of rabbit cages, listening to his father carry on monologues with the animals. It was silly, and his father had known it was silly, and so it was all right. A man needed things he could do which let the boy inside him continue to breathe.

Thinking about it, Robert experienced a keen sense of love and loss in terms of his father. He had been a great and gentle man. In a way, Robert would never get over his death. Whatever he was, his father had made him that way. Just as he sometimes felt distantly that he was carrying on for his father when he tasted a good wine he had made, so now, here, in an idle and possibly foolish pastime, he was also his father's son, continuing.

Robert had always wanted a son of his own. Audra had wanted children too . . . once. The final tests had never been made because they did not want to know for certain whose fault it was that their marriage was barren. But it had been a blow, too, like some of the other things.

Perhaps Audra could have moved away from the shadow of her father and the rest of her family, Robert thought, if she had had a child. If his own life continued to be inextricably bound up with the memory of a dead father who had always been benign, how much stronger must the feelings that Audra—or Jules—must get from a father who still lived, and had always driven them unmercifully?

He would go south this weekend. He would try.

Returning to the house much later, he saw that it was nearly 11 P.M., and time for television news. He poured himself another glass of wine and turned to the best station. He only half-watched. The house was very still and he was acutely aware of his isolation.

About ten minutes into the local segment of the news, the report showed a city hall meeting that had taken place about noon. As the camera swung around the room, showing spectators, Robert came to full attention. Briefly, the camera showed Barbara Turner at the press table, pretty, frowning, rapidly scrawling notes on a pad as a councilman spoke.

Something caught in Robert's throat. He had forgotten how lovely she was.

The report went on to something else. He sat there a minute, tingling as an idea swept over him. Then he got up and strode to the telephone table.

Her number, which he had gotten from Information several nights earlier and then not called, was on a notebook page.

If he thought rationally about it, of course, he would not dial the number now, either.

He dialed quickly. *Christ, what am I doing?*

She answered. "Hello?" And instantly he remembered the husky timbre of her voice, and knew how she must look. He felt better.

"This is Robert Mancini," he said. He had to clear his throat. "I hope I didn't wake you or something."

She paused a beat, but then sounded quietly pleased. "Hello. No, I wasn't busy."

"I got thinking after I had dialed, Hell, I'm probably getting her out of bed or something."

Her voice was husky and amused. "I was reading."

He was filled with gladness. "Not watching TV? You were just on TV. Let me be the hundredth to congratulate you. They showed a report on the council meeting, and there you were."

"Oh, lord, I hope I wasn't smoking!"

"As a matter of fact, you weren't. But why?"

"I'm trying to keep Jimmy from smoking, and if he saw me on TV with one in my mouth—!"

"You were working hard, and you looked very cool and professional."

"Thank goodness!"

Robert paused and his mouth began to go dry as he knew what he wanted to say next. He spoke around the idea. "Except for your TV appearance, I didn't really have anything in mind."

"That's all right. I'm glad you called."

"I just . . . wanted to talk to you."

"I understand." Her tone, which went far deeper than the words, seemed to show that she really did understand—and had accepted him in mysterious feminine ways he could not comprehend.

"Is your work going well?" he asked, feeling instantly like a fool. (Christ, how long had it been since he had tried to make small social talk with a woman like her?)

"I've increased my hours," she replied, "and Mike has me deluged with both spot news and features."

"That shows he likes you."

"I could stand for him to like me just a little bit less!"

"At least it shows acceptance, though."

"I suppose so."

He fumbled mentally. This was no good, no good at all.

He was saying stupid things. Sweat popped out on his body. "I think Mike must be a good editor. He seems to assign good stories."

"Yes. I've enjoyed working for him. He speaks highly of you, incidentally."

"Oh? That just shows we don't know each other very well."

"I'm not so sure of that. I want to thank you again for helping me stay in that meeting last Sunday. And thanks for calling me tonight. It was a nice surprise."

She was ending the conversation. He had to say what was on his mind, or not say it at all. He felt panic.

"Barbara," he said hoarsely, "I wonder if I could see you sometime."

There was silence on the line for a second or two, and he expected any of the many stock replies she might make: It wasn't a good idea; or, What business did you have in mind? or, I don't think I understand what you mean; or some other pretense at misunderstanding—innocence.

She chose none of the wiles. "I would like that," she said.

"I know it must sound pretty abrupt and out of left field." He was very happy and excited. "I thought we might have dinner some night soon. Or we might take a drive and have a good talk."

"Yes," she said.

"I have to be—out of town this weekend. But maybe the first of the week."

"That would be fine, Robert."

"I could call you the first of the week."

"Yes."

"That's great," he said. "That's just perfect. I'll call you the first of the week, then."

"Thank you for calling. Good night."

"Good night."

He hung up the telephone and walked back into the living room. The news was almost over. He felt confused: excited, guilty, eager, worried. A telephone call, he told himself, meant nothing. But he could not convince himself of this. He had taken a new step, and even as it filled him with uncertainty, he knew a new kind of anticipation. How could he be telling himself that he could renew his faltering marriage, and yet at the same time be so transformed by the bittersweet longing that came from the sound of another woman's voice? He did not know.

16

The Fourth of July weekend had dumped heavy traffic on all California's highways, and south of San Jose it got worse rather than better, as Robert Mancini had anticipated. It was very hot and hazy, the peak of Saturday afternoon heat and traffic, and Robert did not drive hard.

If the truth were known, he was not eager to complete the last two hours of his journey. He did not know what to expect from Audra, or from August Trello himself. The fact that so many members of the big family would be there only made the situation less attractive. But Robert knew that this was a trip he had to make, back to the huge hillside estate where Gus Trello ruled like a medieval baron over his family, his personal holdings of more than twelve hundred acres of vineyards, and the sprawling, two-headed giant known as Trello Industries and the August Trello Wine Company.

Robert Mancini's winery was of average size, or a trifle smaller, in comparison with most in the Napa-Sonoma-Mendocino country. It was a midget in comparison with the giant that had grown under the hand of Gus Trello. The Trello label could be found on no less than fourteen kinds of cheap wine, ranging from a mediocre "Burgundy" of Napa Valley co-operative grapes to several brightly colored berry-and-apple concoctions that no serious wine drinker would consider true wine at all. Its fermenting capacity was said to be more than twelve million gallons, with a capability of bottling forty thousand cases a day. The Trello label was known in every civilized nation of the world, and it was Gus Trello's often-quoted boast that he could make better wine from apples or pears than most vintners could produce from the finest grapes. "It's all chemistry," he had once told *Fortune* magazine; "My wine is the best in the world because I have more good chemists on my payroll."

It was the kind of nonsense that made some winemakers smile and others grit their teeth. No one was ever quite sure just how much of it Gus Trello really believed. However much one questioned Trello quality or seriousness, however, no one could question a colossus that could bottle more wine in a day than many wineries produced in a year. Only supergiants like E&J Gallo could look down their noses at the Trello capacity. The wine was produced in incredible quantities, and Gus Trello had found ways to build a world-wide system of distribution. Many might hate him; more envied or feared him.

It was not the kind of operation that Robert cared to join. For all its genius, it could not produce great or even good quality. Ph.D.s in chemistry might believe they could laboratory-control the profoundly complex changes that took place during fermentation, and it was all very well to say that the only real difference (on paper) between the juice of the Thompson Seedless and that of the Sauvignon Blanc was a handful of molecules that could be injected mechanically. For Robert, as for other dedicated wine-makers of the world, the truth of fine wine was more mystic than scientific. Nothing could reduce fine wine to formula. The noblest grape, given perfect conditions and lovingly looked after, might be crushed and started on its fermentation with the greatest care and precision, yet inexplicably produce only an ordinary vintage, as had been the case with the reds of the Bordeaux in 1959, a year first proclaimed the vintage of the century. Yet in another year, when conditions might appear hopeless, a few days or weeks of warmth at just the right time could start a vintage destined to be magnificent; such had been the situation in the Médoc in 1961.

Winemaking was not wholly a science, though man might use every tool of science and technology to help him in his maddening quest for perfection. Winemaking would always be partly a labor of love, done best in small quantities, with a few dedicated men keeping close watch over every step in the process.

This was Robert Mancini's view, and it was the one that had separated him from Gus Trello. Basically the same issue had contributed to the breakup with Jules at Schreck Brothers. And Robert knew that Gus Trello still harbored bitterness over both turns of events.

He had no choice but to visit now, and try to make peace. He owed it to Audra. He had to try to patch things up.

Driving off the highway and onto a well-paved two-lane road, he passed through flat fields that contained vines as far as the eye could see. After a little while he drove through a veritable city of huge steel tanks, like a refinery scene in New Jersey, but these were Trello wine fermenters. A little while later, he went through a small town, and then past two small wineries which had once been independent, but were now part of the Trello empire.

Thirty minutes later, in the hills, he reached a dirt-road turnoff. He followed it until he came to a steel gate in a high fence. This gate was open, but posted with a sign warning trespassers away. He turned in.

The private road narrowed, twisting through brush and rising woods. In a few minutes it led to another gate, this one of high iron-work in a ten-foot cyclone fence that extended out of sight both north and south. There was a small black building just inside the gate. Before Robert could touch his horn, a youthful guard, wearing a Trello Industries name badge, came out to greet him. After Robert identified himself, the guard went back to his shack and made a telephone call. He then returned and opened the gate most courteously.

Five minutes later, Robert reached August Trello's mansion.

Built of native stone, the house was four stories tall, fully one hundred yards wide, and fronted by an expanse of lawn and trees the equal of Mount Vernon. Stark gray in the late-afternoon light, it had shadows the color of blood . . . or wine. Severe rows of windows looked out vacantly. Trees formed a soft backdrop, and lesser outbuildings flanked it on both sides. As Robert drove slowly up the long driveway, he passed groundskeepers mowing, trimming and raking. Nearer the house, a handful of small children scampered and yelped on the lawn. A dozen cars, including Audra's, had been parked haphazardly all over the expanse of cobbled pavement in front.

Taking his overnight case from behind the front seat, Robert walked to the pillared front porch of the imposing structure. As he was about to reach for the doorbell, the door opened and a youthful, weak-faced man barged outside with a golf bag over his shoulder. He was wearing lemon slacks and tee shirt that appeared to have just come from the box, and his cleats hammered on the terrazzo tile. He was darker-haired than Jules Trello, and younger, but might otherwise have been a copy.

"Bob!" he grinned. "Bob Mancini! Great to see you, stud!"

"Hello, Gus," Robert said. "It's good to see you again."

"The name is Gus *Junior*," Gus Trello said with a mock show of horror. "My Christ, don't let the old man or anyone hear you take *his* name in vain when speaking of the black sheep of the family!"

Young Gus was easy to like. He could have counted his days of honest work on one hand, but like many who have given up any thought of being useful, he had done a fine job of making himself attractive. Robert nodded toward the golf clubs. "A little late to be going out, isn't it?"

"I played this morning," Gus Jr. said. "I was pushing the ball a little. I'm going out on dear old Dad's front acreage, there, and hit some shag balls. Want to join me?"

"I'd better check in," Robert said.

"Okay, stud," Gus Jr. grinned. "Here. Lemme help." He shoved the doorbell button in and out several times, he leaned inside and hollered, *"Somebody come, we got more company!"* He dodged back out. "I bet one of the servants will haul ass now, man."

"Hit the ball well," Robert said.

"I will—I hope. I've really been depressed lately, though. I've gone from plus four to plus eight this year. That's why I'm working so hard on the irons."

At that moment, a frightened-looking female servant appeared in the doorway. Gus Jr. went his way, whistling, and Robert was ushered inside. As the door closed, he was in a cavernous entry hall, all sound of the children and other activity outside completely shut off. The house was like a hotel, and the maid furthered this impression by taking him into a side living room, whispering that someone else would be along, and leaving him there by himself.

Somewhere a clock ticked. The house smelled dusty,

rank from tobacco smoke, distantly fetid with some animal rot.

The room, like all the many rooms in the Trello mansion, was furnished in heavy, dark furniture, with equally dark and heavy draperies at the tall, narrow windows. After Gus Trello had overseen the building of the house following World War II, he had hired interior designers with instructions to buy the finest, price being no object. Every room was crowded to overflowing with authentic Edwardian pieces such as Gus had perhaps yearned for in his own poverty-stricken childhood. The mansion was a museum of marvelous furniture and accessories from Britain, all of continental Europe, and the Far East. It was dusty in this room now, somewhat neglected, like a movie set long unused.

As Robert waited, he began to be aware of faint sounds of voices coming from beyond the windows on his right, the side wall of the house. The draperies were drawn tight, but he walked to them and parted the folds with his hand.

The window looked down across the side yard and over protecting shrubbery into the rear yard area. The large swimming pool, in the shape of a great teardrop, gleamed in the sunlight, surrounded by curved paving, a patio area dotted with colorful umbrella tables, and more heavy shrubbery, lawn and trees. There were a number of people swimming or sunning themselves. Robert recognized Audra at once, reclining in a deck chair; she wore a one-piece black swimming suit that was right for her figure. Jill Trello, wife of Frank, was nearby, talking idly with Dora, the wife of young Gus. Loretta, Audra's sister, sat on the edge of the pool, watching four younger adults play some kind of boisterous water tag. These had to be children's children or friends; Robert recognized none of them.

Audra appeared calm and well inside herself. She fit the scene very well. It had taken a series of shrewd maneuvers involving old, theretofore unsalable sherry to make Gus Trello unquestionably wealthy during the Second World War, but he had never been poor, not since his earliest years. The children had been raised to expect luxury and service in exchange for whatever hard duties their father imposed upon them. Robert wondered if any of his marital trouble might have begun to fester when Audra first realized that he might never be anywhere near as rich as her adored father.

"Robert?" a voice behind him said.

He turned. The man standing there was tall, painfully lanky, with the family's dusty hair, tightly curled. His bright, nervous eyes stared out of deep sockets and he had the air of a man about to fly to pieces from sheer nervous strain.

Robert crossed the room and extended his hand. "Frank, it's good to see you again."

Frank Trello gave his quick smile, which was more a nervous grimace. There was no humor in the man. "Gladys told me you had arrived. I'm sorry I can't stay long enough to visit, or show you around. But you know your way around. Welcome. I have to rush along."

Robert glanced at Frank's "uniform"—gray slacks and matching gray shirt with the sleeves half rolled. "Are you in production at one of the wineries today?"

Frank Trello's eyes snapped nervously. "We have eighteen thousand cases being bottled at Blue Creek this afternoon and an important test being run on a new white dessert wine we're market-checking. I had a few items to check with my father, and now I'm late getting back."

"Is Gus holding his own?" Robert asked.

Frank paused in the act of turning hurriedly toward the door. "I think so, yes. He isn't going to the plant much now. That's why I had to hurry over here to ask for some decisions."

"I suppose you're beginning to take charge now," Robert said.

Frank betrayed sincere surprise for an instant. "By no means. My father still makes all the decisions."

"I see."

"That's the way we all want it," Frank added. "I know I'm not capable of making some of these decisions."

"You'll have to, soon, won't you, Frank?"

Frank seemed not to hear. His eyelids snapped up and down several times as he scowled into some interior space filled with problems. "It's a delay factor in the decision-making process, driving back and forth. This illness has really upset the business routine."

"From what I understand, Frank, this illness is more than a business inconvenience."

Frank looked blank a moment, then nodded. "Oh. You mean the terminal aspect of it. Yes. We're all sad. Well, Robert, it's good to see you again. Maybe there will be time tomorrow for us to have a good talk. Like the old days, eh? Make yourself at home. Go on out and see the family. I think Audra is at the pool."

"I saw her," Robert said. "I'll head that way."

But Frank Trello was already in motion toward the door, his expression again betraying the fact that he was lost again in whatever maze of business problems currently beset him. He hurried out, and was gone.

Robert wondered if Frank Trello ever paused long enough to think about what he was doing at any given moment. Perhaps he was always so busy planning the next dozen moves in his chess-like life, fighting to avoid some terrible mistake, that he never really lived "now" at all. Did that kind of life make a man actually dead?

It was a shame and a waste, Robert thought. The Frank Trellos never enjoyed the cool of a sunrise or the velvet texture of a living leaf. Frank Trello, like his brother Jules, had been born running, and his father had drilled him to run faster. Frank's existence was built around the killing desire to prove himself worthy of his father. Jules, it seemed, had reacted differently, driving himself just as hard to demonstrate that he did not need his father at all.

Of the three sons, only Gus Jr. was different. August Trello had bullied, bossed and browbeaten his other two boys into patterns of conduct centered around achievement, a hard-driving ruthlessness to others and to self that admitted no limit. In this, the father's tactics had "worked": he had made them Trellos.

In young Gus, it had broken him. He had never tried in his life, except at self-indulgence, and probably never would. His brothers might kill themselves trying to prove they were worthy, and even perfect. Gus Jr. would die denying that he had ever given a damn.

The daughters and even daughters-in-law had been affected too, Robert knew. Perhaps he would never understand Audra because of this heritage.

Shaking himself mentally, he left the room and entered a hallway that led deeper into the great house. As he proceeded down the hallway past more vacant rooms, he almost collided with an elderly black man hurrying from a side corridor.

"Mr. Mancini!" the old man said, recovering from the bump and showing fine white teeth in a genuine grin. "Welcome, sir!"

"Cline," Robert said, shaking hands with Gus Trello's oldest and most trusted servant, "I thought you would have retired by now."

Cline chuckled and shook his head. "What would I *do?* Go visit my children? No, sir. I like it here a lot better."

"From what I see so far, Cline, you have your hands full with all the visitors."

"We have a houseful, sir, and that's a fact. And more coming, from what I've been told."

"The place smells like a damned train station. Has there been a fire?"

"No, sir. That's just all the cigarettes and such. And then Dora's pets, if you've noticed, sir."

Before Robert could ask what the servant meant, a door banged open a few paces down the corridor and someone came up from the basement. He was a rotund, pale-haired youth wearing cutoff Levi's and a faded UCLA tee shirt. Barefooted, he had a bottle of wine in one hand and a plastic bag of chipped ice in the other.

Seeing Cline, he grinned. "Hey, Cline, I couldn't carry any more. How about going down and getting a couple more bottles of this stuff and bringing them out by the pool? It's this sweet stuff in bin C, on the bottom shelves."

"Yes, sir," Cline said, his venerable black face a polite mask.

The boy loped down the hall away from them, and out of sight.

"Jim Henthorne, sir," Cline said in response to Robert's quizzical look. "Stella's young man, sir."

"Stella? I'm drawing a blank."

"Loretta's second husband's daughter by his first marriage, sir."

"It's getting complicated."

"Yes, sir."

Robert walked with Cline as far as the door to the basement. "What kind of wine is that he's sending you for, Cline?"

Cline's features betrayed nothing. "That would be Château La Tour-Blanche, sir."

"Jesus Christ! He's drinking Château La Tour-Blanche out of the bottle, with crushed ice, like soda pop?"

"Yes, sir."

"Jesus Christ!" Robert repeated, profoundly shocked. La Tour-Blanche was one of the great Sauternes of the world.

Depending on the vintage, the wine ranged in price from expensive to priceless. But beyond the price, it was an act of sheer stupid vandalism to treat any great wine so carelessly.

"Does old Gus know people are pillaging his cellars?"

"I imagine he does, sir, yes, sir."

"I can't imagine him standing for it."

"He's changed, sir."

"Nothing could break that old man, not even cancer."

Cline smiled sadly. "Not broken, sir. He can yell with the best of them, if he has a mind to. But he's . . . different."

Robert thought about it. He was still numbed by discovery that they were going through the great wines of Gus Trello's cellars. Should he say anything about it? Did Gus really realize what was being done?

"I had better go fetch two more bottles," Cline said, heading into the wooden staircase that headed downward.

Left alone again, Robert was not quite ready to go outside and face Audra and the others. He felt a great anger inside about the wine. He turned into the nearest room to try to cool off.

It was another of the seemingly endless series of living rooms. Like the other one Robert had visited, it was furnished darkly, massively. Purplish draperies made it dark. Along an inside wall was a dim, glass-fronted cabinet or display case of some kind. He caught a faint glint of dull gold.

It was then that he knew where he was, remembering an earlier time when he had stood in this room with a feeling of awe.

He approached the trophy cabinet, fumbled on the side of the case, and flicked a switch. Lights buzzed to bluish brilliance inside the shelves, bathing rows of tarnished old cups, trophies and plaques in cold light. Behind the trophies, pinned to blue velvet backing, were rows of blue and red competition ribbons. On a lower shelf stood several very old bottles of wine, each bearing the once-proud Trello label.

Robert scanned some of the engravings at random: *First, California Wine Show, 1936; Excellence Award, Berlin, 1937; Special Merit Award, London, 1935; Exceptional Merit, International Wine Festival, Paris, 1937; Grand Cru*

Extraordinaire, Bordeaux, 1939; Grand Prize Claret, New York, 1940.

They were all here, all the top awards won by August Trello Wine Company during that rare time between the end of Prohibition and the gloom of World War II. No one had made wines like Gus Trello in those years. He had been the first to convince the world that California wines could excel.

The old trophies, still lovingly kept in this seldom visited room, added to Robert's sense of gloom and depression. He wondered if old Gus ever felt regret about the way he had chosen to go, toward mass production and wealth.

He reminded himself, however, that this subject was closed to him. *I am here,* he reminded himself formally, *to pay my respects and prove to Audra that I care about her and her family. My motive is to try to begin salvaging our life together if that is still possible. Every other thought or feeling must be expunged.*

He left the room and went on down the long hall toward the back of the house, intent now on visiting poolside. As he neared the back, however, he was waylaid again by a woman's voice shrilling from a room off to his left:

"My goodness gwacious sakes! Has poopy puppy done do-dos again?"

Robert peered in. Sunlight from uncovered windows smote his eyes, and the sickly odor of fresh dog dung assailed his nostrils. The room was a sort of parlor, opening onto a tiny enclosed garden, but had been closed up tight. Most of the furniture was wicker. The carpet was a thick, richly colored oriental.

Two large black poodles had been leashed to the legs of chairs on the far side of the room. As Robert looked in, the two ungainly animals were leaping around in ectasies of excitement over the scolding they were getting from Dora Trello, a tall, dark-haired woman wearing a floor-length floral pool robe. Two dishes of water had been overturned on the carpet, and there was a fresh wet pile of dung nearby.

Dora waggled her finger at the frenzied pets. "You are naughty, *naughty* puppies! Mommy will spank if you keep being so naughty!"

Robert started to move away, but his movement caught Dora's eye and she whirled on him. "My God, Robert, hello! Have you seen Cline anywhere? We have a little problem here." She came across the room, a big woman gone very slightly to matronly fat, but still with the grace of a dancer. She brushed by Robert and poked her head into the hall. "CLINE!" she bellowed.

There was no response. She made a face. "Wouldn't you know it? They're never around when you need them. God-damned N double A CP has ruined them all. CLINE!"

She turned and swept back across the room to throw open windows. "Shit! And you can take that both ways! I don't suppose you've seen my darling husband around either, have you?"

"I saw Gus when I came in. He said he was going off to hit some golf shots."

Dora threw out her arms in a grandiloquent gesture that emphasized the exceptional size of her well-formed breasts. "Everybody has left me in the lurch! God! I'm going to have to change these babies' diet!"

"I think I know where Cline is," Robert said. "I think that carpet might be permanently stained if that mess isn't cleaned up right away."

Dora pointed to several other areas of the rug, and he saw for the first time that there were perhaps a dozen yellowed circular stains already on the carpet as mementos of earlier accidents. "The carpet is no big deal, but I hate it when they walk around and step in it. Then I have to wash it out of their paws and in between the pads and everything else. Yuk!"

The carpet, Robert thought, would have cost more than two thousand dollars even in the simpler time when it had been laid down. He started out to find Cline.

"Let him come to us, Robert," Dora said sharply. "CLINE!"

"I'll go on outside, then," Robert said.

Dora looked him frankly up and down. "At least tell me how you've been before you pull another of your vanishing acts."

"I plan to stay until tomorrow. And I've been fine, Dora. You?"

She grinned crookedly. "Always the gentleman. Hell, Robert, *I* know Audra has left you. Everybody knows it. Have you come to take her back, or to tell her to go to hell? I doubt that she'll leave the old man right now, you know. She's really pissed at you, and everybody is taking it hard about the cancer."

Robert formed his words carefully. It was never wise, he had learned, to be careless around Dora Trello. She loved verbal combat when she was a little drunk, and enjoyed her own witticisms in direct proportion to their cruelty. "How do you think Gus is, Dora?" he asked.

"My Gus," she countered, "or old Gus?"

"Well, both."

"My Gus is just the same, soft in the head and hard in the pants. You said he was going out to hit golf shots. Would you like to bet ten dollars that he's really out in the bushes with one of his own blond in-laws sitting on his face? As for old Gus—well, it's a mess, Robert. Really. They cut everything out of him they could, you know, but I guess it was just all over the place. They said he had six months. Of course nobody has even admitted out loud that he has cancer, so we all tippytoe around, you know that kind of bullshit, and he's starting to fail just a little . . . just the slightest little bit. I mean, he *knows*. And he gets morose and sad, and the other night, for Christ sake, he was talking about old times and he started to *cry*. It was just revolting, just really shitty, I mean everyone was embarrassed as hell and didn't know what to do, so we all pretended we didn't even notice."

The picture affected Robert strongly. The last thing he had imagined was Gus Trello weeping. He did not know what to say, so he didn't say anything.

Dora looked at him, studying his expression. Then, murmuring sympathy, she came across the room and threw her arms around his neck, pressing heavily against him. He was enveloped by her heavy musky scent and the odors of sun and oil and sweat.

"I'm sorry, baby," she murmured, leaning back to look moodily into his eyes. "I know this is all pretty shitty for you, too."

"I'll find Cline for you," Robert said.

He found Cline coming up from the basement and told him the bad news. The elderly servant walked with him to the kitchen area, where he filled a pan with hot suds and went back the way he had come. Robert did not return. He stood in the huge, hotel-equipped kitchen alone.

For the first time he was really uncertain that he was doing the right thing by coming here. He felt alien.

The feeling was not just because of Dora. She was eccentric, but Robert knew he would never truly understand the driven Frank Trello either, or the shattered young Gus. And now they and all the others were back, flocking in, making the old house really a hotel, because the old bull was dying.

Robert knew he must go out and face Audra now, and then face old Gus. He did not feel ready. But he could not delay any longer, pretending to refamiliarize himself with the terrain. Because the terrain had changed. Rooms were filled with dirty laundry and suitcases and playpens and overfilled ashtrays, empty bottles of ravished wine and even incontinent poodles. Nothing was the same any more. It was all out of control. There would be no familiarization; that would be like trying to feel at home in an airport.

It was, clearly, time to go outside.

He left the kitchen and went past a utility room, past a storage room, past a vacant playroom with a dusty ping-pong table in its center, past another living room with a grand piano in it, and past a silent screened porch. He reached a shadowy doorway that led him onto a patio, and beyond was a walk lined with sun-drenched forsythia, geraniums, roses, azaleas and chrysanthemums, all force-fed in a greenhouse somewhere to simultaneous vivid color. When the flowers faded, they could be discarded and replaced, just as people could bo.

He went down a few steps to a lower section of patio around some hedge, into sunlight again, and crossed a sunny lawn toward the pool area.

Frank Trello's slender blond wife, Jill, was on the diving board, the sun bright on her pale body. She dived cleanly and came up fast, as if frightened by her own daring, and stroked for the side. Near the ladder, a big young man, one of her sons, was tussling with a blond girl who was either his girlfriend or his wife; he was bullying her. Loretta and her latest husband were at a table sipping drinks, and with them was a much younger couple. Audra was still by herself, but nearby. Two small children played in a sand-box under the trees.

It was Loretta who first spotted Robert. She got quickly to her feet and walked to meet him. "Robert. How nice." The slight sharpness of feature that made Audra a memorable woman was exaggerated in Loretta, so that she was merely hatchet-faced. She had neglected her body, allowing it to go to fat that wobbled and waffled as she moved.

Robert was subjected to a round of introductions, including Tony Steele, her new husband, who was a small man with eyes Robert immediately disliked. Another young couple had appeared, and they all seemed to be related to Steele by his first marriage in some way.

As soon as he could, Robert moved away from them and to Audra, who had remained seated alone, watching.

"So you did come," she said.

"Yes."

"You just arrived?"

"A few minutes ago. I saw young Gus and Frank inside. And Dora."

Audra's mouth tightened. "Dora has been lying in wait for hours."

"Are you all right, Audra?"

Her eyes challenged him with subdued bitterness. "I feel very well, thank you."

Of course that had not really been the question, but before he could reply, Jill Trello came over, dripping, from the pool. She was, as usual, under a frigid control. "Robert. Hello. Welcome."

"Thank you," he said. "You look well, Jill."

"Thank you. You do too. It's been quite a long time."

"Yes, it has. But you certainly have a houseful."

"We've always all been close," Jill told him levelly, "even if some member of the family or other, or some consort of a member, strayed."

Robert tried his best to be friendly, smiling back at her. "As a consort, I hope I'm not intruding."

"I'm sure," she said, unyielding, "Father Trello will want to see you."

"That's all right, isn't it?"

"It isn't my house. Like everyone else, I take orders."

Robert's patience snapped. "I didn't come here after Frank's job, Jill. I don't want your husband's job."

"Then what *do* you want?"

"I came because I've been told old Gus is dying."

Loretta, perhaps sensing that an argument was building, came over. "Would you like me to tell my father you've arrived, Robert? He's just in the back garden."

Robert hesitated, glancing at Audra. He thought she might want to talk first.

Audra was colder than he had ever seen her. "Yes, Loretta," she said. "Do see if Daddy will see Robert now."

Loretta turned and padded off. Jill, after hesitating an instant, went after her in silence. Robert swung back around to his wife.

She said, "It wasn't really necessary for you to come, you know."

"I wanted to come. There are a lot of things about Gus that I admire. You know that."

Her chin tilted. "Even if you do consider yourself his superior?"

"Audra, I didn't come here to fight with you. You know what you just said isn't true. I came to see your father and I came to see you."

"You won't buy me back with a visit."

"I didn't think it was a matter of buying or selling. I've missed you."

"Have you? I find that very hard to believe."

"It's true. We need to talk. We've had so many misunderstandings—"

"It was very hard for me to leave and come here alone, Robert. But now I have, and I'm not going back with you tomorrow. Let's understand that right now."

"Audra," he said softly, struggling with himself, "what do you want me to say?"

Tears glistened in her eyes. "I don't want you to say anything. What *I* want to say is that I'm not going to spend the rest of my life alone. I've spent practically my entire adult life alone, waiting while you studied wine, or inspected fields, or made business trips, or worked overtime at your precious winery. I'm still young . . . I still have some time left. If I don't make a decision now, it might soon be too late."

"Too late?" He was puzzled by the phraseology.

"To find someone else."

"My God! Is that what you want? To find someone else?"

"If there's nothing left for us together, yes."

"I don't even know you," he said huskily. "You're not making sense to me. I look at you, and all I can see in your expression is some kind of . . . hate. Has it been that bad? I thought I understood you!"

"You don't even understand yourself," she replied, reasserting an icy control. "You probably really do think right now that you want us to get back together. But you've never needed me. You've always looked down on my whole family. You've never really cared about anything but your damned wine. And now you think you can visit with my father, and I'll swoon back into your arms. I *won't*. I won't go back to the way things were. Not if it kills me."

She still had a vast capacity for hurting him. He was angry and frightened simultaneously. He looked at her, seeing his wife and a stranger in the same flesh. Was it too late? Had it been over a long time, and was this only the officiating for the sake of formality? He did not know what he could say. The wetness of her eyes was at variance with the angry set of her jaw, showing her own tearing ambivalence.

She said, "I know this is costing you a lot, Robert. I want you to know that I understand just how much this effort is costing you. I'm sorry I can't swoon into your arms. But I'm beyond all that. I have to save myself now even if it means destroying everyone else in the world."

"We can patch it up, Audra. We can at least try."

"Only on *my* terms."

"What are your terms?"

"You have to show you care for me. You have to stop hiding inside yourself. You have to stop mistrusting your emotions and let them out, and really show me love. You have to do whatever I say you have to do to make me happy."

"Audra, I can't *make* you happy. No one can do that."

"You see? You're too selfish. You've never given anything of yourself to anyone else in your life."

"Are you sure," he asked, stung again, "that you aren't describing your own conduct now?"

"You see? It's impossible. Now that I'm away from you, I can see just how impossible it is."

"Audra—no."

She trembled then, and her control nearly broke. One tear slipped down her cheek. Angrily she brushed it away with her hand. "I don't know what I want. I don't know anything. I just know I can't go on." She turned and looked toward the far end of the pool area. "There's Loretta. You're being summoned. Go."

Robert saw Loretta well beyond the pool, standing at a white metal gate in the high shrubbery that formed a boundary between this area and another courtyard. She waved for him to come over.

Gus was, presumably, waiting.

"Excuse me, please," he said to this woman who had been his wife, and he walked away from her.

17

The rear courtyard was small, snugly enclosed by high shrubs. In its center was a free-form brick patio. Gus Trello was there, beside a small wrought-iron table. He wore baggy corduroy pants and heavy, high-topped work shoes and a faded-green flannel shirt with the sleeves rolled, and he was in a wheelchair.

The wheelchair, despite warnings about it, was such a shock to Robert that he did not at first see Fredricka Trello on a small metal bench nearby. It was not until Loretta had walked him quite close that he spied the tiny, gray-haired woman as she rose, smiling, and extended her hands to him.

"It is so good to see you again, Robert," she said, her brown eyes alive with genuine warmth. She was a tiny woman, weighing less than ninety pounds, but her hands were strong.

Robert kissed her on the cheek. "Hello, Mother Trello. You look fine."

"I am very happy you are here."

She was whispering, and as he glanced beyond her, Robert saw that Gus Trello had not raised his head from his chest. The old man was very still. "Is he asleep?"

"No, only resting."

It was Loretta who walked nearer the wheelchair. "Daddy, it's Robert. Here he is. Robert has come to see you."

Gus Trello raised his lionlike head and glared. If a great,

wounded animal were cornered, Robert thought, it would have eyes like this.

Robert moved forward and offered his hand. Trello accepted it. His grip was hard and unyielding, testing Robert's strength in turn. A thousand new lines spiderwebbed the old man's face, but the blunt jaw stuck out as stubbornly as ever and there was no hint of weakness or self-pity in the wide-set, slightly sagging eyes. There was yet an enormous force in the old man. Robert inadvertently glanced down at the wheelchair, with its gleaming knobs and handles, thinking that it looked almost obscene.

Trello caught the look. "They make me use it. It takes time to get back on your feet, eh?"

"I'm sure it does." Robert was already acutely uncomfortable, being drawn immediately into the maze of unspoken lies about the cancer. He added, "I know you'll be glad when you can get out of that gadget."

"Huh!" Trello grunted. "Trouble is, when I get out of this gadget, I get in a worse one. A box."

Both Loretta and Jill had stolen close, hovering to hear every word. Loretta moved forward, patting the old man's shoulder. "That isn't *true,* Daddy! You know it! You're getting better all the time," she added in that simpering way some women always adopt around the very sick. "You're fine—just fine." She patted him again.

Trello jerked away from her hand, almost tipping his chair. "Don't *pat* me, God damn you!"

Stricken, Loretta took a step back. "It's just that we're all so proud of your progress—"

"Shit and turds! Shit and turds! Don't try to tell me how I am! Do you not think I know how I am? How I feel?"

Loretta shakily extended her hand to touch him again, as if somehow she could claim reassurance—or affection— with a touch.

"Do not pat at me, I said! Do not touch me! You have never done a God-damned thing for me! You and Jules and Frank and Audra, you are all alike, parasites! Failures! Weaklings! Do not try to drag me down to be a weakling like you!"

Fredricka Trello sighed. "Ah, Gus—"

"Leave us," Trello interrupted with a grave dignity.

"But Gus—"

"Leave us!"

As he spoke, the old man spasmodically raised himself

half out of the chair. He gave every indication of being ready to rise and hit his aged wife if she did not obey. His eyes were red with tears of sheer fury. Fredricka Trello moved, obeying him. She took first Loretta's and then Jill's arm, and led them out of the courtyard.

They went out of sight.

"They think I am stupid man," Trello said. He got a large red bandana out of his hip pocket and loudly blew his nose. "Sit down here in front of me."

Robert sat on the bench. Hummingbirds moved like huge insects through flowering shrubs nearby. It was quiet. Trello glared at him, daring him to speak. Robert met his gaze but said nothing.

"I am dying," Trello said finally.

"The family believes you don't know that."

"A big game, eh? Pretend Gus Trello is not dying. Let us all come and wait, and walk around on tiptoes, patting him. But let us pretend he is not dying." Suddenly, like a wind-gusted cloud, the old man's expression changed from anger to bewilderment. He spread the fingers of his large hands and rubbed them lightly over his chest. "I feel like I am filled with broken glass."

"Gus, I'm sorry."

Trello cocked his head, and the belligerence was back. "You are sorry, eh? I would have thought you would enjoy it since you hate my guts. But you are right. You probably are sorrier for me than most of these weaklings."

"They love you, Gus. Maybe they haven't measured up to whatever you thought they ought to be, but—"

"Weaklings!" the old man snapped bitterly. "Frank: a coward, a big fool that has to ask permission to go to the bathroom, even. Jules: a liar, you can never believe his word, a cheater. Loretta: a fat sow that goes from man to man like a slut with a tin cup. Now even Audra: you work hard and you have trouble, so she comes home with snot in her nose. And my Gus, he is the worst of all: a playboy that wears silk underwear!"

His indignation at the end was so strong that Robert had to smile even as he winced.

"That is funny?" Trello demanded.

"No, Gus. It isn't really."

Trello straightened up in the wheelchair. "I come to this country with one suit and some candlesticks to sell so I can eat. I ride rails out to California. I begin. I *work*. And

Fredricka. That woman! She works like any two men! We get a start. We did not make much wine before Second World War, you know. It was fine wine, the best. *Everybody* get to know Gus Trello!"

Robert nodded dutifully. He had heard Gus tell the story before. He had told it repeatedly even before this illness, and probably even before age had begun to push his mind increasingly into the past while more recent memory faded in unimportant areas, so that he told the same old stories over and over.

"The wine was the best, Gus," Robert agreed.

"In Second World War you could sell anything," Trello added. "You could sell *anything* with alcohol in it! I had dessert wines, fortified wines, I had not been able to sell. When I saw I could sell them to the soldiers, I bought a lot more, resold it before anybody else was smart enough to know what was happening. That started making me rich, and that was all I needed. I worked all the time . . . *all* the time. Now I am big. I am *big* man. You think I got big with weakness, patting people, lying?"

"I know you didn't," Robert said.

"Worst," Trello added with dull anger, "is how pain comes. They all see it sometimes. So then they pat at me, pity me. God damn them! Gus Trello does not need pity of fools and weaklings!"

"Is the pain bad, Gus?"

"Sometimes. Yes. Sometimes. But I never tell them. They only try to guess. They want to fill me up with shots. Hypo, ch? Bullshit on hypo. No hypo. As long as I go without hypo, I can know some of what is going on."

Robert said nothing, although he was tempted. He wondered how much this man really knew of what was going on . . . the stink of cigarette smoke and dog shit in the house, the vandalism of his cellars. It seemed inconceivable that Gus Trello could know, and allow it. Yet perhaps he had no choice now, with the cancer eating his body away, and it did not matter to him. The loved ones had already swooped down, moving in tightening, ravenous circles, to devour his life.

"Audra," Trello said now, "I thought was little better. But now she has moved out of your house, eh?"

"She wanted to visit here awhile, Gus—"

"Shit and turds! Do not try to lie to me! She has left

you! Maybe she wants to get divorce and start being like Loretta, eh?"

"We're going to work it out. I—"

"And my fine crook son, Jules. With his fine new shit winery purchase he is so proud of, he calls to brag to me on the telephone about all the time, he has this plan for you to take his new shit wine and sell under your label, eh?"

Robert tingled. "How do you know that? Did Jules tell you?"

"If Jules had told me, I would not have believed it because all Jules does is lie. You think I am stupid? You think cancer is in my head? I am not stupid man. I have sources of information."

Yes, he had his sources. Robert knew it would be fruitless to try to find who the sources were, too. But it showed that Gus Trello was not finished yet. In earlier years it had been his boast that he knew more about every aspect of California wines, including day-to-day business, than any man alive. It might still be true. The telephone in Gus Trello's room might still be alive half every night with calls all over the country as well as to nations like France, Germany, Italy, Chile, Algeria, and even Brazil.

Robert admitted, "Jules made a proposition, yes."

"But you are not accepting it, eh?"

"That's right."

"Good. If my fine son Jules made the offer, it is crooked. Shun all deals from Jules. He only drags people down to perdition."

"Gus, did it ever occur to you that you're awfully hard on Jules? On all your own children?"

"Whose children *are* they, eh? Whose children are they?"

"All right. Forget it."

"I forget nothing! Never! I remember you, too. You have been stupid, too. You were stupid when I would have made you in charge of all my wineries, and you said no."

"Maybe I was. But that's a long time ago. I didn't come here to rehash old arguments."

Trello's chin sank toward his chest, and his voice softened. "We could have had all your valley, like I have all of this valley. We would today be bigger than Guild—maybe bigger than Gallo. You would not be running a winery that is not even in your own control sometimes. You would not carry around this worry that some parent company—what does that shit company make? *Biscuits?*—you would not burn in your belly with fear that a shit biscuit company might take over, throw you out."

"That won't happen. I don't know how you get so much information so fast, but I'm not here because of *my* troubles."

"You don't think maybe just a little bit that old Gus Trello will bail you out?"

"No, God damn it!"

Trello grunted, amused. "But what if biscuit company makes you go along with my fine crook son Jules, or get thrown out? You think the world will take care of you, give you a nice new winery again, say, 'Here, Mr. Mancini, you are nice man and you make nice wine, so here is a new winery.' You think that?"

"No," Robert replied, goaded. "But isn't that *my* business?"

Trello pointed a blunt finger at him. "You married my Audra. That makes you in this family. That makes it my business, eh?"

"It's the same old problem, Gus. You think you own people."

Trello counterattacked. "You sure don't own Audra, eh? She leaving you, eh?"

"This conversation," Robert said wearily, "is a quagmire. I'll deal with Audra. You can stay out of that, too."

"Ah! Sure! But listen. Audra is not like my wife, Fredricka. You know that? Fredricka is small but she is strong. She never weighs more than hundred pounds in her life. But she hoes grapes like a man, work harder than hell. Has four kids, three babies more lost. She is tough." Trello shook his head with admiration. "God damn. She is *tough*. She is like me. She is good match. Maybe too soft with kids, but good. But her daughters are not like her, they are weak. Loretta is a puppy dog. Her husband, her new one, has made lots of kids, but down deep he is queer. I know this. Don't look at me like that, I *know*. He is queer! But Loretta don't know, she is stupid. He pets her like puppy dog, so she says okay to anything. Now. Audra. She is weak, too. She is headstrong. What Audra needs is have man be tough on her. You should never have let her leave. You should beat shit out of her. Then you fuck her. Beat her, fuck her. Beat her, fuck her. You could still do that. You could still make a woman of her, maybe. What? You grin. Why? This is serious!"

"I was just thinking," Robert said, "that it's a good thing you retired from politics when you did."

"Huh!" Trello grunted in amusement. "Women's lib, eh? Women's libbers have stroke if they hear me talk about what it takes to make a woman strong, eh? Good. Get all women's libbers in Los Angeles Coliseum. I make speech, they all shit pants, drop dead from a stroke. Better. Listen. You want my Audra back again?"

"Gus, I don't know."

"Stupid answer."

"Honest answer!"

The old man squinted. "Explain."

"The Church's teaching is correct. I don't care how many people get divorces. We made promises. We have to try to work it out—"

"Okay, then!" Trello cut in. "I tell you what. You go back to your biscuit company, tell them to stick it in ass. You come back down here."

Robert stared, uncomprehending, then beginning unbelievably, to comprehend after all. "I can't do that, Gus. Christ!"

"Come down here," the old man urged. "Take over. I have board. But you run whole operations, eh? People say you never get a second chance, but that is bullshit, here is your second chance. You can be close, you can live here, even. That way you will get Audra back, too."

"I can't do that," Robert repeated gently, amazed. "Gus, I wouldn't last in your operation five minutes."

"Shit talk! Shit talk! You would like it! You would be rich! You would have Audra back! Two birds! One stone!"

Robert hesitated. He did not want to fight again. He did not want to hurt this old man. There was still power in him, and ruthlessness. He needed no more setbacks.

As if believing the hesitancy meant consideration, Gus Trello leaned forward, nearer, and the anger faded, leaving a naked vulnerability in his eyes. "I want my kids happy. Bad as they are, I want that. Frank can never be happy; he is stupid and weak. Jules can only be happy as a crook. Loretta only has her men. You can make Audra happy. You can be my son."

"Gus," Robert said slowly, "I wish I could. I mean that. I know how you feel. You probably don't think I do, but I do. I admire a lot of what you've done. You've fought your way up by yourself."

Trello sat up fiercely. "But you are going to make same mistake a second time? You are still God-damned fool?"

"I came here to patch up any old hard feelings, not start them up again!"

"Shit and turds!" Trello cried. "Your talk is all shit and turds in your own mouth!"

Robert stood. There was no sense in continuing it. There was too much pain in it for both of them now. He started to walk away.

"Come back!" Gus Trello yelled.

Robert turned as he neared the gate.

The old man's eyes sagged. "You are fool."

"Let's try to talk later, Gus. About something else."

"You do not chase success like me, is that it?" Trello demanded. "But you chase something else, eh? Just as bad, this dream of perfect wine. Just as bad, eh? It can kill your soul."

Then Trello leaned forward with an intensity that turned his face a ghastly white. *"Do not chase your goal so hard you lose everything else.* Remember I have told you this."

Thunderstruck, Robert stared at him a moment. The tone and the words together answered every question he had had in his mind since his arrival.

The old man knew all of it—the filth, the decadence, the greed and fear that had gathered around him. He knew how his home had become a hotel, and how it—and he—were being used. He knew how the circles were becoming tighter as the cancer gnawed his body.

He knew *all* of it—and it had not destroyed him.

Robert turned and walked back to the pool area. Both Jill and Loretta smiled at him as he walked toward them. He wondered if they had heard the old man shouting, and were pleased.

He stayed awhile. Audra was polite and icy, hurting him more than she could possibly have done with a frontal attack. After a time, Dora came out with her dogs. In an hour or so, someone wheeled Gus Trello in and he sat there on the sunny deck, hunched over in his chair, in his lumberjack shirt and workboots, scowling, saying nothing. Everyone worked hard at strenuous pool games to prove what a grand time they were having.

Shortly before nightfall, on the pretext of a call from his winery, Robert departed. No one saw him to the door.

As he drove away from the great mansion, crimson in the fading sunlight, he saw Audra in an upstairs window, watching. He gave no sign and neither did she. He drove straight home and arrived in the middle of the night.

18

Susan Knight noticed immediately on Monday that Robert Mancini seemed both subtly depressed and preoccupied, and she felt a strong tug of curiosity about his weekend visit to the Trello mansion. It was as likely, however, she told herself, that he was concerned about the meeting with John Endicott and E. Z. Simms, now only forty-eight hours away. In any case, there was no way she could ask directly.

It was hardly a routine week that was getting under way. A new vintage of Pinot Chardonnay, done now with both its oak mellowing and brief bottle rest, was to go on sale Friday, and the shipping department was a beehive as the green-stamped cartons, each containing twelve bottles, were loaded onto trucks for destinations across the country. At the same time, the cold-fermented Sauvignon Blanc—the same wine which the still unknown clumsy saboteur had almost damaged two months earlier—was now through this process. Tastings had shown it was of fine quality, and now a new series of steps would be started for it: drawn carefully from the tanks to leave sediment behind, it would be further chilled, centrifuged to remove all other impurities, and placed in 500-gallon French oak barrels for a minimum of six months prior to bottling. Only the uninitiated imagined that a winery was busy at restricted times of the year; the work continued in all months as various wines reached different processing steps, and each new action required many others in a domino effect.

Late in the morning, Susan met Robert in the production rooms, and thought the busy morning had restored some of his color. He had been in the midst of the activity, as she had, since 8 A.M., working in a different sector of the building.

"It's all going well," Robert told her. "Have you had any snags?"

"If you're thinking of our friendly old saboteur," Susan smiled, "he hasn't been in evidence. Everything is right on schedule, and this afternoon we'll start cleanup in the tanks we've emptied this morning."

Robert nodded. "It crossed my mind that this would be a fine time for trouble, if somebody was going to try to cause us any."

"Maybe the whole thing with the Sauvignon Blanc was some sort of prank—someone who got in by accident."

"You're forgetting that we've had information leaks. Our problem is still here. We have to stay awake. There are also some things you and I need to discuss to get ready for Wednesday's meeting. Can you have lunch here today?"

Susan was dismayed. "I told Rod I would drive into town and meet him, Robert. Maybe I could still catch him and change plans—"

Robert smiled. "We can meet after lunch. If the poor guy is actually getting you away from this place for an hour, I'm damned if I'll interfere."

"This time," Susan corrected him, "it isn't pleasure."

"Ho ho. You mean you plan to fight?"

"You remember what happened to Homero Artiz?"

Instantly Robert sobered. "Of course. Is there news?"

"All Rod would say on the phone is that he has made some more contacts, and has something to share with me. I'm afraid it's no breakthrough; he didn't sound that happy. But I'm anxious to hear what he does have."

Robert patted his shirt pocket for a cigarette that wasn't there, and scowled. "Homero is all right and back on the job. I know that much."

"Yes, but I'm afraid his car isn't. I talked to Ned Henderson yesterday. In addition to broken glass and lights and slashed tires, they had opened the hood and struck something through the radiator in a dozen places, ruining that, and then they broke all sorts of things with a hammer or something. Homero doesn't have the money to fix all that. Ned dragged the car over beside his toolshed and they covered it as well as they could with sheet plastic. It's just going to have to sit there."

"How is Homero getting around the valley to his jobs, then?"

Susan shook her head. "He found an old bicycle somewhere. Ned said it looks like a relic from 1920. He's riding that."

"Ah, that's terrible," Robert breathed in sincere regret. "I hope Rod has found out more than you think. In the meantime, I want you to ask Ned Henderson to have Homero contact us. We ought to be able to use him outside a few hours a week, whenever he has holes in his schedule."

"I'm sure he can use the money," Susan said, pleased.

"Have a good lunch. We'll talk later."

Susan left the winery shortly thereafter, and drove the short distance into the small tourist community where Rod Poole had agreed to meet her. There was a tiny but excellent Chinese restaurant on a side street, and Rod was standing in front, waiting, when she drove up.

His news was neither encouraging nor definitive. Two more attempts to persuade Homero Artiz to discuss his situation had drawn blank responses. The scanty description of the brown Buick seen by Johnelle Henderson near her vineyard had been included in Poole's reports, but was not sufficient for general circulation. There was no information in the records on any previous trouble Homero might be striving to hide, and a computer crosscheck did not show any pattern of remarkably similar incidents involving either Chicanos or Anglos. The Artiz family had a small but solid credit rating, having paid for their two hundred-dollar car in twelve payments, all on time, and now paying eleven twenty-five per month to Montgomery Ward for a portable television set.

The family lived in the poorest section of the city, along with hundreds of other families, mainly Chicanos. The two children were not of school age, but were cared for daily by a federally funded pre-kindergarten while Homero worked in the fields and Dolores Artiz waited tables in a small diner.

A few days ago, Dolores Artiz had taken a second job, four nights a week from six to ten, washing dishes in a

Mexican restaurant. Both her old employer and new supervisor said she was a good worker and very quiet.

Rod Poole had gone to see Dolores Artiz. He said she was a small and pretty woman, very frightened by his visit, but just as taciturn as her husband. She had no idea who might have attacked him. She had no idea why anyone would want to attack him. They had no enemies.

Poole had tried to press her. Her fear had visibly increased. She had begged him to forget the incident and leave her and her husband alone. It seemed clear that further pressure would only add to Dolores Artiz's misery.

"What are you going to do now?" Susan asked when Poole had finished his glum recital.

"I don't know," Poole admitted. "I've got a request out for a military service record, if any, and an FBI check. If both of those came up blank, that probably ends the effort as far as looking into Homero's background is concerned."

"What about that brown Buick Johnelle Henderson saw? Surely there must be something more you can do there!"

Poole slowly shook his head. "There are only a couple of things wrong with that line. Number one, we don't really have enough description; we can't start pulling over every recent-model brown Buick, now, can we. Number two, we have no concrete evidence whatsoever that the Buick even had anything to do with the attack. Number three—" Poole paused, and his face showed distaste. "Well, two is enough."

"Rod, what's number three?"

"Okay, number three. You know, we've got a fine department. We really have. We don't have as much money and equipment as we'd like, but every man in the department is good at his work, and motivated."

"But what," Susan insisted quietly, "is number three?"

"I've asked all the guys to watch for this car," Poole admitted. "But I just don't have any confidence that many of them have taken me seriously."

"Why?"

His eyes were opaque with bitterness. "When I worked in the LAPD, there used to be a saying I'd hear sometimes. If there was a stabbing, say, in a nice white neighborhood—people with money and social class—we'd get right on it. If the same crime took place in Watts, we'd investigate, but there wouldn't be so much excitement. Some of the guys would shrug at a stabbing or other kind of murder in a black district. 'Just another nigger deal,' they'd say. Well, I'm afraid there are a few guys around here who take the same attitude toward a Chicano being hurt or robbed or even killed."

Susan stared at him with a sense of outrage trickling through her. "Rod, that's ridiculous. That's so cynical it makes me sick!"

"Tell me about it," Poole said grimly. "You have a high crime rate in a ghetto, so you say that's just how ghettos are, so you don't work very hard to prevent the crime from getting even worse—so you have high crime rates in ghettos. It's a stupid damned attitude, a vicious cycle. But there it is, And we've got some of it around here, too."

During the talk, the food had been brought and they had disposed of as much of it as they wanted. The teacups were empty again, and a smiling waiter brought the check and two fortune cookies. Breaking the cookies and reading the fortune slips hidden inside was a ritual needed at this moment to distract both of them from a topic too troubling to continue.

Poole grinned ruefully as he read his slip: "You will have great joy with the one you love."

Susan made a face at him. "Don't count on it, buster."

"What does yours say?"

She read it: "A great stroke of luck."

"Great," Poole said.

"It's bound to come true. It doesn't say whether the luck will be good or bad."

Poole picked up the check and counted out a small tip to leave on the table.

"Rod?" Susan said.

"Yes?"

"Before we go," she said slowly, "there's one more thing I have to ask—one thing I wonder if you've considered."

"What's that?"

She did not really want to raise this question. As long as she had thought about it, however, it was a possibility despite its unpleasantness.

It had to be asked: "What if Homero is an illegal immigrant?"

Poole said nothing. His face hardened. He got up, helped her with her chair, and then led the way to the cash register. She waited while he paid the check, and then they went outside together. The day seemed to have become warmer and brighter while they were inside in the air-conditioned dimness.

They went to Susan's car and stood beside it.

"I was just thinking," Poole said, "in a general way, about a lot of the field workers and other common laborers we have in California. You know we have a law now that allows a wetback to turn himself in and possibly gain citizenship. The only trouble is, the illegal immigrant needs a certain amount of documentation—red tape and paperwork. I suppose for a Mexican, say, who had been in the country ten or fifteen years, with a good job, the procedure might work just great. But if they can find anything at all in your past that doesn't look just right, or your letters of recommendation aren't good enough, you can still be sent back to Mexico.

"That's the same fate that befalls people here illegally if they get caught," Poole added, looking off across the street somewhere. "They get shipped back in a truck or something. I've seen pictures. They're treated humanely, of course. But there they are, caged in trucks or buses, like criminals instead of what they are: poor people who tried the only thing they knew to try to find a better life."

As Susan studied him, understanding dawning, he turned slowly to meet her eyes. "As to your question inside a minute ago, I'm sorry. I didn't hear you. I guess I was preoccupied, thinking how I haven't had a single idea about Homero or his problem that I haven't already shared with you."

"I see," Susan replied quietly. "Well, it was a silly question anyway."

Stubbornly adhering to the law, Poole opened her curbside door for her, making her climb across the center console. She waved, started the engine, and drove to the corner for the turnaround that would take her back to the main road.

If Homero Artiz was, in addition to everything else, an illegal immigrant, then there might be little more that Rod Poole could do for him, she thought now. Illegal status seemed like a logical theory, explaining in part why Homero would fear the authorities. He might also—she had to face this, as she knew Rod Poole had done—be involved in something else that was illegal, something they had not yet guessed. Probing too deeply into the causes and perpetrators of his beating could end up by plunging him into deeper trouble than his attackers.

Susan knew she would not mention her theory to Rod Poole again. He was not a federal officer. His sense of fair play would allow him to justify squelching whatever suspicions he might have, as long as they were not thrown into his face too often. If this hindered investigation of the beating, so it had to be.

Reaching the corner, Susan turned around and drove back past the restaurant. At the next intersection she turned left, heading down the main street for the distant highway intersection. It was well past noon now, and cars lined the curbs. The tourist season was in full cry, and visitors filled the sidewalks. There were many small children, and people were flocking from shop to shop along the street, which was designed with many small shops to attract the tourist trade; many carried colorful shopping bags already crammed with souvenirs.

Needing some drugstore items, Susan was lucky enough to find a parking place directly in front of the store. Smiling, she thought of her fortune cookie and reminded herself to tell Rod that it had come true. She went into the store and shopped quickly.

Returning to the car, she restarted the engine and waited for a gap in the thin but steady traffic. As she did so, she watched the drive-in facility of the small bank almost directly across the street, because cars departing the exit ramp might turn into her path.

The car on the ramp was a blue Chevrolet, and it beat her into the first hole in traffic. She waited again, sharing time between her rearview mirror and the bank exit.

The car presently at the bank's side drive-in window, she noticed, was a brown sedan.

Then she tingled slightly.

The car was a brown Buick sedan, very dusty, coated with the kind of yellowish dust one got from vineyard roads.

There were two men in the front seat. The driver, just getting back some cash from the teller, wore a red baseball cap.

Impossible, Susan told herself.

She looked again.

Both men in the car appeared young. She could not see them very well, but the white-blond hair of the passenger was vaguely familiar. Where had she seen him before? She could not remember.

Of course the whole thing was ridiculous, and she knew it. Luck like *this* simply did not occur. It was a chance of— what?—one in a million? But she was still excited. She imagined what it would be like if she actually had a break like this, then failed to follow up. She *had to* follow up!

Hurriedly digging into her purse, she found a pencil and small notebook. The Buick was departing the exit ramp now, and as it turned in front of her, she copied down the license plate numbers. The Buick, with its two occupants, headed straight south toward the highway.

It crossed Susan's mind to try to follow them, but that was a little too melodramatic for her. As she looked across at the drive-in facility, however, she saw that no other car was in the drive right now. That gave her an idea that was almost equally wild—one she knew she would never follow up on unless she did so at once, before she had time to consider it.

Swinging into traffic, she cut left at the corner and entered the drive-in facility from the back. As she approached the drive-in window, she rummaged through her overstuffed billfold and found what she was looking for.

The girl in the drive-in window slid the metal tray out at her as Susan lowered her window.

"Hi, there!" the girl's voice said metallically through the loudspeaker.

"There was a car just here," Susan said. "A brown Buick. The driver was wearing a baseball cap. Will you please tell me who he was?"

The girl looked startled. She was very young. "You mean his name? Gosh. I can't do that!"

Susan held the small card up in front of the teller's glass wall. She had kept it in her billfold because Rod Poole had given it to her as a gag. Colored red, white, and blue, it appeared frighteningly official, even to a gold seal. Susan's name was engraved on the front. One had to look carefully to realize that the seal was a picture of Uncle Sam, and the fine print certified that she was a genuine Law-Abiding Citizen who paid taxes.

Susan waited only until she saw the young teller's eyes widen at the official appearance of the card, and then jerked it away before she could read any of the printing. "Miss, I'm in a hurry. Please give me that customer's name!"

The girl became flustered as she riffled pieces of paper. "Yes, sure. Gosh! Wait a minute . . . He has an account here, and he cashed a check for . . . let's see . . . twenty-five dollars." The poor child appeared relieved as she held up a check. "Here it is."

"Hold it to the glass," Susan ordered, "so I can copy."

The girl obeyed. Trying to look stern, Susan copied the name and address off the check. "Thanks," she said brusquely, and drove away.

A great stroke of luck, she thought, remembering the fortune cookie.

The moment she was back in her office at Robert Mancini Vineyards, she called the sheriff's office. Rod Poole was in.

"You again?" he said with mock irritation.

"Rod, I just saw the car."

"What?"

"The car. The brown Buick. I just saw it. Well, it *might* not be the car, but it could be. And there were two men in it, and the driver was wearing a red baseball cap."

"Hell's bells," Poole muttered. "Did you get a number?"

"Yes." She gave him the license-plate digits.

"Maybe it's nothing, honey, but I'll run a check on it. I'm ready to try anything. That's good work."

"I also got the name of the driver," Susan added.

"What?"

"I said—"

"I heard you. How did you get the guy's name?"

"Oh, God, don't ask. I probably broke a law or something."

"What?"

She was so pleased and excited that she dragged out the oldest grade-school joke. "Rod, you're beginning to sound like a light bulb. Take this down. Philip Dennison. 2221 Marlboro Lane. City. Do you want the telephone number?"

"What the hell did you *do?* Mug the guy?"

Feeling smug, she gave him the telephone number, also taken from the check.

"Good lord," Poole muttered. "How did you—no. I'm not going to ask again. Maybe you're right. Maybe I don't want to know. I'll check this through records and call you back."

"Anytime you need more help, dear, just let me know."

With a sound ominously like the growl of a bear, Poole hung up.

19

It was the same night about eight o'clock that Robert Mancini, having first made a nervous telephone call, drove into the city and found Barbara Turner's small home with no difficulty but butterflies everywhere.

"I thought maybe I could beg a cup of coffee," he had said lamely on the phone.

"That would be fine," Barbara Turner responded instantly. "Here?"

"That would be all right."

She hesitated, then added, "My son is here."

"That's fine."

She gave him directions.

It was a small house, probably rented, almost hidden behind evergreens that had been allowed to grow much too big. Lights glowed behind curtains, and when he reached the small front porch Robert could hear a radio or record player going, something fairly loud, with a vocalist and guitars. He pressed the doorbell, wondering if it would be heard.

It was. A slender boy opened the door and peered out at him. This, unquestionably, was her son. The resemblance was strong despite the boy's youth. He had dark hair and handsome eyes, and was dressed in jeans and an Elton John tee shirt.

"Yes?" the boy said over the musical racket.

"You must be Jimmy. My name is Robert Mancini. Is your mother—?"

At this moment Barbara appeared in the doorway behind her son. Her jeans were more faded than the boy's, and her tee shirt, pale pink, had no rock star on it. Smiling, she looked soft and lovely and relaxed. "Hi," she said. "Come in."

Robert stepped inside. The door led directly into a small living room. There was a couch and two chairs, some plank-and-brick bookshelves, a small television set that was dark, and a record player, the source of the music. Schoolbooks were strewn around the floor.

"Jimmy," Barbara Turner said, "this is Mr. Mancini."

Frowning slightly like someone trying to be older than his age, the boy extended a slim hand. "We were just introducing ourselves, Mom. How do you do, sir."

Robert shook hands with him. "I like your tee shirt, Jim."

Jimmy beamed. "Do you like Elton John?"

"I don't know a lot about him, but I know a superstar when I see one."

Barbara put her hands over her ears as if she were about to go mad. "Jimmy, please turn that thing down. Or *off!*"

"Aw," Jimmy murmured. But he slouched across the room and turned the volume down somewhat, making normal conversation possible.

"I think probably you ought to take your homework to your room," Barbara told him.

"I've just got another few minutes, Mom, and I can finish this record. Okay?"

Barbara sighed. "Okay." She turned to Robert. "Will you sit down?"

Robert sat on the couch facing the record player, and she took one of the chairs. He was intensely aware of her in this new setting—at home, softer, more relaxed, subtly different in her casual clothing. If anything, he liked her better than ever. Already, somehow, a tension was draining from him. He had been as nervous as a schoolboy, but now he was here and she was here and it was all right. It was where he wanted to be. He relaxed.

Jimmy came over and sat on the couch beside him. "Do you know Bernie Taupin?"

"I don't think I do," Robert admitted.

"Bernie Taupin is Elton John's lyricist. They're insepar-able pals. Elton John gives Bernie Taupin a lot of credit.

But Elton worked hard to get where he is. He has about six mansions, maybe more. You know, he started in a small combo, but right away he started moving up. Now there's nobody that can even touch him. When he made 'Goodbye Yellow Brick Road,' some critics said it wouldn't be a big hit. But he's the only person who has ever released a record and had it be number one on all the charts immediately."

"He sounds like quite a man," Robert said.

"Oh, he is. He's a good tennis player. He makes so much money, he doesn't even know how much money he makes. You know, when the Rolling Stones go on tour, they're so popular they charge twelve dollars a ticket, or even more. But Elton John won't rip people off. He could charge anything and the house would be filled. But he says he won't rip his fans off. He keeps ticket prices about six dollars, or something like that. That's the kind of man he is."

Robert grinned at Barbara, whose expression was amused and wearily tolerant. "This must be the headquarters for the Elton John Fan Club."

"No," Jimmy said. "The headquarters is in Woodland Hills, California."

"You're a member, then?"

"Sure!"

"Jimmy," Barbara said warningly, "finish that homework and head for the hills—your own room. Mr. Mancini and I have some things to discuss."

Jimmy nodded, but kept at it. "You're the man who owns the Mancini winery?"

"That's right."

"Well, I don't know much about wine. I haven't tasted much. But to hear my mom talk, you sure must make the best in the world."

Robert grinned again, and Barbara, possibly coloring, got to her feet. "I think maybe this has gone far enough. The coffee is ready, Bob, if you want to brave the kitchen for a while."

Robert nodded and also stood. He had not missed her calling him by his first name earlier, and now he liked the sound of the diminutive form when she was the one saying it. She started for the lighted doorway that evidently led to the kitchen, and he leaned over her son a moment.

"We'll talk more later, okay?" he said, and reached out to tousle the boy's hair.

Jimmy shrank back sharply. Then he seemed to realize

that he had moved with an abruptness that could offend. "I'm sorry, sir," he said. "I just . . . don't like strangers touching me."

"Okay," Robert said easily. "Fine." He turned for the kitchen door.

"It's just the way I am," Jimmy added. Then he grimaced. "Sort of weird."

"Listen, Jimmy. You're not weird. No one who likes Elton John can possibly be weird. Remember that."

The boy, whose face had shown a deeply troubled streak for a moment, responded with a wide grin. "I *will* remember *that!*"

Robert entered the kitchen, which was a small room with a breakfast nook at the rear. It had a neat, uncluttered look, and was comfortably old-fashioned. The windows around the breakfast nook were open, bringing in the cool night air and the scent of lilacs to mix with the rich aroma of the coffee on the stove.

Barbara was placing cups and saucers on the table where other utensils and a small plate of cookies had already been arranged. "If I hadn't gotten you out of there, you would have had to listen to an album-by-album account of Elton John's career."

"Well, he's a nice kid. I like him."

"But weird," she laughed.

"That's what he said, but I disagreed with him."

She had started for the stove, but stopped and turned. "Did he say he was weird?"

"Well, it was my fault, Barbara. I reached over to muss his hair. I forgot how kids today set their hair and everything else."

Barbara's face turned serious, some ghost trying to emerge. "And he pulled back from you. Wouldn't let you touch him."

"Sure, but no problem. Adults take kids too much for granted."

"It isn't just that with him. I wish it were just that. He was very friendly with you. I was astonished. And pleased, of course. I guess I had told him about interviewing you, so he was ready to like you. But he's really a very remote little boy most of the time. Very much a loner."

"With adults, or with kids?"

"Both." She stood there, the worry clear on her face.

"It's probably just a stage," Robert suggested.

"But you don't have children," she reminded him gently.

"Which makes me some expert, right? I'm sorry."

"No," she said quickly. *"I'm* sorry. That was a stupid thing to say."

"Forget it."

They looked at each other for a moment, and her eyes changed somehow. Robert was stabbed deep inside, and shaken. It was as if a great spark had leaped between them again, as he had felt in his office that first time, but much more vivid, striking him much more deeply and with far greater potency.

He managed a smile. "How about that coffee, lady?"

The spell broke and she laughed softly. "Before it boils away."

She poured the coffee and joined him at the table. Under the soft red light of the campy Coca-Cola fixture over the table, her face was softened and vulnerable. She wore little makeup, only lipstick, and watching her made him ache inside.

"You made your trip?" she said.

"Yes. I went down to visit my wife's father. You may have heard of him. Gus Trello."

"Of course," she nodded.

"I don't remember what I told you. Old Gus is dying of cancer. It wasn't a very happy visit."

"I read a story about him not long ago. It must be terrible for the family."

"It was a bizarre experience for me, I can tell you that."

She watched him very seriously, waiting. This, he recognized, was her way. She would not press him and she would not make idle conversation. She simply waited, interested, sympathetic.

Perhaps because he so wanted to communicate with her in any way, or perhaps because it was so much in his mind, he started, haltingly at first, to tell her about the visit. He glossed over Dora's gross language, and mentioned Audra only very briefly, saying nothing of their trouble. Before telling of the talk with Gus Trello, he found himself telling her about the old man's past, even paraphrasing some of his own oft-told yarns. He relaxed again, became involved in trying to recreate the scene for her, and told about the confrontation with the old man.

She was a very good listener, making him pause only once as she refilled the coffee cups. He found himself telling her not only what had happened, but of how he had felt when the enormous incongruity of yet another offer had finally dawned fully on his consciousness.

Finally, he explained about Gus's last words and what they had signified to him.

"That great, cruel, kind, lonely, surrounded old man," she said at last after he had finished.

"And if you show pity," Robert smiled, "he'll kill you."

"Does he really feel that way about his children?"

"He loves them, but trying to make them more than they could become has turned the love almost to hate."

Barbara sipped her coffee. Her fine hands moved with grace. "I think all this makes me understand Jules Trello a little bit."

"Well, Jules isn't all that bad."

"Oh, no," she argued with quiet firmness. "We'll have none of that, Mr. Mancini. I've done some more foraging in old files. I have some little idea of what Jules Trello did to you before you left Schreck Brothers. And there are enough hints between the lines of *other* things he did . . . before and after that. I stick to what I said at the meeting. Jules Trello is a very dangerous man. He fascinates me in a way. But I don't like him. He scares me."

"That about states my own view," Robert admitted. "We have a meeting at the winery Wednesday that Jules sort of brought on us."

She inclined her head, a silent signal of interest, and he was about to go on when the music in the living room was abruptly cut off. They both reacted, she glancing at her watch. It was almost nine o'clock.

"Bedtime!" she called.

Jimmy came into the kitchen, his schoolbooks in his arms. He had a slight frown on his face which showed he had been doing some deep thinking.

"I'm going, Mom, I'm going," he said.

"Yes, you are, young man," she replied. "Now."

Jimmy walked over to face Robert. "It was nice meeting you, sir."

"My pleasure, Jim. And I apologize for trying to mess up your hair."

The boy didn't blink. "Mr. Mancini, are you dating my mother?"

Barbara appeared so stunned she said nothing.

"Well," Robert replied awkwardly, "not exactly, Jim. I think you could say we're friends."

"Jimmy," Barbara said. "Bed."

"It's all right if you are," Jimmy said. "I just sort of wanted to know."

"Well, Jim, I think I was trying to be honest with you. Your mother and I are friends."

The boy's troubled frown deepened. "My father was killed in Vietnam."

"I know."

Barbara repeated warningly, "Jimmy."

"My father was a hero," Jimmy said. "We've got the medals. I don't think I could ever respect a man like I respect my father. I just thought, if you're dating my mother, you ought to know that. I was real little when he went overseas, but he wrote me a letter. I've still got it."

Barbara got to her feet. She was very pale. "Jimmy. Come on. To bed. *Now*." She grasped his shoulders.

The boy pulled away, his eyes never leaving Robert. "What my dad said was, he was going away, and he felt better knowing my mother had another man around the house. Me. I was the other man. That meant I was supposed to take care of her."

"Jimmy!" Barbara grasped the boy again and started propelling him toward the doorway. Some powerful complex of emotions had turned her sheet-white.

At the door, Jimmy pulled away from her for a few seconds, again facing Robert. "What I'm trying to say is, nobody can replace *him*. If you date my mother and try to get her to marry you or anything, then that's going to make us enemies."

This time Barbara got him through the door. Robert sat still, tasting his coffee. He heard their voices, hushed— she reprimanding, he arguing stubbornly—in an adjoining room. He could hear only the tones, not what was being said.

In a minute or two the conversation ceased. Robert heard bathwater running. Barbara did not immediately return to the kitchen. He was glad for the delay because he had been surprised by Jimmy's outburst—surprised and more than a little dismayed. Nothing was simple, not for anyone. He felt an intruder. But he knew rationally, too, that the greater tragedy was for a boy trying desperately to be a man, and live up to the dream of a child.

When Barbara returned, her face was splotched pink as if she had scrubbed it vigorously. She avoided his eyes as she sat down again.

"Robert, I'm terribly sorry about that."

"Don't be."

"It was just inexcusable. I don't know what—"

"Hold on," Robert said, covering her hand with his own. "Now it's my turn to say I just won't put up with something. Let's not lie to each other, all right? I didn't come here for a cup of coffee. Oh, sure, I wanted that. But you know I came to see you—to talk with you, to hear you, to look at you, to *be* with you. Jimmy is right on target. You know that and I know that."

Silent, she raised her amazing eyes to his, and the messages were all there: fear, concern, anguish . . . a very deep caring.

He said thickly, "I left out part of my visit to the Trello house. Audra is staying there. I guess you could say she's living there. I don't know if that means we're separated or not—I mean it's not a legal separation, and she might come back—I don't even know if she wants to come back and I don't know if I *want* her back. I'm a Catholic, you know, and I've always thought . . . in my own life . . . divorce was . . . unthinkable. But here I am. With you."

She watched him. He could detect the flicker of a pulse in her throat. The bathwater somewhere in the house had stopped, and it was very quiet. He could hear his own heartbeat.

Then, gently, she removed her hand from under his. "I think we need more coffee," she said, emotion husky in her voice. "And then I think we probably need to talk about something else."

He sat mute as she stood and went to the range. She came back with the coffee pot, nearly empty now. She equally divided the remaining coffee.

"You told Jimmy exactly the right thing," she said. "We're friends. With your background, and my background, and the way I feel, and the short time we've known each other— that's what we really are." She looked at him again. "I need a friend."

"Does that mean," he asked, "that we'll never be anything more?"

"How can I answer that?" She walked to the stove and

put the empty pot down with more clatter than was necessary, and remained with her back to him.

"I want to see you again. I don't want this to be an ending."

She turned, almost somber. "Then you shall see me again. That's up to you, isn't it?"

Before he could quite know what to say, she walked briskly back to the table and sat down again. With comic brusqueness, she pushed the cookie plate toward him. "Now eat some of these and shut up, will you?"

Grinning, Robert tasted a cookie. It was delicious. "You're a fantastic cook, lady."

"Go two blocks to the corner, turn left, and tell the man at the grocery. The credit is all his."

It was fine again. The moment had passed. They could talk some more.

20

It was late when Rod Poole called Susan Knight.

"Hey, Sherlock Holmes," he said. "Maybe we've got something here."

"Tell me," Susan said simply.

"Listen. I'll read the stuff I've collected. Philip Dennison. Age twenty-four. Drives a taxicab at night sometimes. No other visible means of support. The car checks to a David D. Arnstedt, 818 Mateo. Age is twenty-five."

"I think I'm going to go to sleep now," Susan said.

"They've both got rap sheets. Listen: 'Dennison, Philip Pryor. White male. DOB, et cetera. January 16, 1970, jailed for investigation of burglary, released; October 10, 1970, public drunk, fined fifty dollars; June 11, 1971, fighting, ten days county jail; November 2, 1972, suspected larceny of an auto, released; February 14, 1973, burglary, two years in state prison, paroled on January 15, 1974.' Now. The other guy. Ready?

" 'Arnstedt, David DeWayne: March 20, 1973, simple assault, thirty days in the county jail; January 16, 1974, investigation armed robbery, released; August 10, 1974, assault, charges dismissed for want of prosecution witness.' "

Susan sat down on the edge of her bed, unable to believe that she really had struck paydirt. "They *are* good suspects, then, Rod."

"I plan to do a lot more checking out, honey. I don't

161

know yct where it will lead—if anywhere. But I durn sure plan to find out."

Susan felt a surge of hope and excitement. "Rod, come over and we'll talk more about it . . . and celebrate. I told you that fortune cookie of mine was accurate. Maybe we could, uh, work on yours, too."

Poole hesitated, and then she could hear the grin in his voice. "Just like you, Sherlock. You give a man a lead and then try to take it back again."

"What does that mean, Rod? Come over here!"

"Huh-uh. You know I'm having to check on this deal on my own time. If it wasn't for *your* carping, I might have let it drop just like everybody else. But you've got me fascinated again now. So I'm here at work, still. I've got an hour or two. I aim to do some more digging."

"So you can't come over?" Susan said, not sure whether she was pleased by his enthusiasm or irritated and disappointed by his unavailability.

"I'll call you in a day or two," Poole said, and hung up.

Susan stared at the telephone, and then replaced it on the hook. She walked to the dresser mirror. She looked fetching, she thought, in her shorty nightgown.

"Damn," she murmured, and went to get a glass of milk.

21

July had brought intense summer heat to southern California. In an agricultural valley not far from the urban sprawl of Los Angeles, hot wind blew across the fertile, irrigated land. That this had once been desert, and now bloomed only because of massive irrigation, could be seen in the patches of land along the narrow highway where no water was used. Here the earth was barren sand, blowing, littered with tumbleweeds and bits of trash.

Along one stretch of the naked highway there was a kind of city. Shacks made of plywood, cardboard or tin extended in random disorder through a series of arroyos and burned-out gullies. Here and there clothing flapped on makeshift clotheslines, and dogs yapped as they ran in small packs from one place to another. The wind rattled tin flaps and hummed through cardboard walls.

Most of the shacks were deserted at this time. Only a few of the very old, and the smallest children, remained. Everyone else, from the age of about ten to sixty, had gone to the fields.

Within another few weeks, the shack city would be virtually deserted again, but not just for the daylight hours of labor. Most of the workers, predominantly Chicanos, would have begun a seemingly random migration northward in search of later crops to work and harvest. They would not feel homeless, because migratory work was the pattern of their lives, and the wealthy landowners to the north would provide them with cardboard or tarpaper shacks, too.

Near the highway, a small building stood out from the others. Once a frame gasoline station, it now had its windows boarded up and no signs in view. It was sturdier than anything else around, however, and was given a rather official appearance by the American flag cracking in the wind on a metal pole in front.

A battered pickup truck drove up to the frame building. Two young Chicano men got out and went inside.

After its days as a gas station, the building had once been used as a school. All interior partitions had been torn out, and blackboards installed along one wall. The other walls were yellow plaster, latticed with deep cracks, as was the ceiling. The concrete floor was gritty with sand blown in constantly through three opened windows on the west. The glare of the afternoon sun shone in on three ancient metal desks, one file cabinet, one 1950 Underwood typewriter on a rickety wooden stand. Papers on the desks were held down by rock paper-weights, as was perhaps the only item in the room that did not fit the pattern: on the top of the filing cabinet, a thick sheaf of wide, pale-lined sheets of paper—a computer printout.

A funeral-home calendar adorned one wall. Another contained a framed picture of The Sacred Heart, the kind many Catholic homes included decades ago. On the wall over the blackboards was a large cloth banner showing a bird of prey in an attacking dive; beneath it on the banner were the quilted words *WORKERS UNITED*. The colors were green, red and black.

As the two newcomers entered the room, a lone man turned from the blackboard where he had been studying columns of numbers and a tacked-on map of the wine country north of San Francisco. He was small and very slender, with dark skin, a sensitive mouth, hair that was prematurely gray, and eyes that seemed almost luminous. He wore the worker uniform: bluejeans, white shirt, heavy shoes, a straw hat. A small silver cross hung from a thin chain around his neck.

"Good," he said when he saw the two younger men. "I have been waiting."

Juan Lupé, the taller of the two, removed his straw hat in a signal of respect. "Our departure was delayed, Alfredo."

Alfredo Rodriques nodded, walked across the room, and shook hands both with Lupé and with his companion, whose name was Carlos Murnan. "Have there been any developments since our telephone talk?"

"The owners have not met again," Lupé replied. "They are worried but we see no signs of a strong organization."

"What of the workers?"

"You know the sentiments we have found. We left Rosario there, as you said, to continue the work."

Alfredo Rodriques nodded again, his signal of understanding. "Then we will proceed as planned."

Lupé hesitated, then said, "I repeat my cautions."

Carlos Murnan, the shorter lieutenant, betrayed impatient anger. "And I, Alfredo, counsel stronger measures than so far agreed upon!"

Rodriques lapsed into English for the first time with a slight, sad smile. "The trip did not bring you two any closer together."

"There is no guarantee of success there," Lupé said. "We are spread thin."

Murnan countered angrily, "We must strike now. Our brothers wait for us to come free them from their injustice!"

Rodriques studied the faces of the two young men, two of his most trusted aides. He felt a generation older, although the gap in years between them was less than a decade. Neither of them had been with him during the battle with the Trellos; they had earned his trust in later, but smaller, skirmishes. They did not really know—either of them—what an attempt to organize the valley might become.

Turning toward the map on the far wall, Rodriques walked closer to it, pretending to study details while he considered how to handle the division between his two associates.

He would not move without caution. He could not afford division within the ranks. In a decade of leading the field workers of this area, there had been those who said he was as soft as a woman, while others had said he was an iron-fisted tyrant. He had been jailed many times, had been beaten, shot at, denounced, once thrown from a speeding car by unknown kidnapers. Businessmen negotiating with him had angrily called him callous and unyielding, a machine. Yet he was the same Alfredo Rodriques who had been caught by television cameras as a child once handed him a flower, and he broke—bone-tired—and wept because the gesture so touched him.

There were those who pointed to the violence that sometimes followed the movement of Rodriques organizers into new areas; they said he gained nothing for his followers, and was a dangerous, egomaniacal fanatic. There were others who claimed with equal fervor that he was not only a great American but a contemporary saint. There was only one narrow area of general agreement about Alfredo Rodriques, and ironically this was one only whispered: He would not grow old; if one of his frightening fasts did not kill him, some external violence probably would.

Having considered his immediate problem—and given time to his two lieutenants to cool down—Rodriques now turned back to face them again.

Carlos Murnan flashed, "Strike now! Move at once! Show them we will not accept any more delay or we will crush them!"

Rodriques looked at Murnan in astonishment for an instant. Then he threw back his head and laughed. The laugh boomed richly out of his strong chest, echoing through the room. It was a genuine, spontaneous, wholehearted laugh, and he bent over, gasping for air, tears coming to his eyes.

Lupé and Murnan stared in shock.

"Forgive me," Rodriques finally managed, gasping as he wiped his eyes. "You sounded, Carlos, so much like a very old movie I saw on television only the other night. So fine! So angry! So certain!"

Murnan colored but stubbornly held his ground. "It is my belief."

Juan Lupé evidently thought he saw his opening and moved into it. "Caution is the key, Carlos. We should wait another year—"

"If Carlos sounds like an old motion picture," Rodriques cut in with a fiercely controlled anger that blew up out of nowhere, "then you, Juan, sound like a very old woman with shrunken dugs."

This time he did not let them reply, but went on at once. "You have made contacts in the valley. We know what the situation is. We have our people alerted in San Francisco. The vineyards will all be under great stress this year due to a predicted bountiful harvest and falling prices. We would be wiser, perhaps, to wait until prices and over-

planting have not already put the growers under such stress
—they might this season react more violently against our
demands than they would in better times. But we cannot
wait any longer. We have waited too long already."

Rodriques paused, seeing the combination of respect and
bafflement in both men's expressions. At times like this he
became almost like a parent to his followers. The role of
the parent was to counsel conservatism, caution. Yet sometimes, too, the parent had to teach boldness.

"You will return," he ordered. "Four more men will join
you from our San Francisco office. Accelerate the signing
of key local leaders as you find them, but do not open any
massive campaign for signatures. That will come later,
after we make our march there in force."

"When will the march come, Alfredo?" Murnan asked
hopefully.

"Soon. In August at the latest."

"Before the harvest, then."

"Of course, before any harvest."

"If we attempt to organize and block the grape harvest,"
Juan Lupé said slowly, more careful with his words now,
"the growers and winemakers will resist fiercely."

"Of course they will," Rodriques agreed. "But the threat
of spoiling the harvest is our weapon. The harvest also im-
plies a deadline for settlement."

Lupé almost spoke again, but thought better of it.

Rodriques felt a burst of compassion for him. He was
a good man, but his viewpoint had lost in today's brief col-
loquy, while Carlos Murnan's angrier approach had won.

Actually, although he valued both men very highly,
Rodriques trusted Juan Lupé the more. He could not say
it, of course, but there were times when he worried that
Carlos Murnan's evangelical fervor would get out of control; he had to be watched most closely.

And Rodriques sympathized with Lupé's fears. Rodriques
confronted the prospect of organizing the northern wine
country with considerable trepidation. It was as if he stood
before a great door, and beyond it raged a terrible fire. If
he opened the door in an effort to extinguish the flames,
they might consume him. But if he yielded to the fear and
remained where he now stood, the fire might eat its way
through the door and then be uncontrollable and catch and
consume him wherever he waited.

He was also more tired than anyone knew. The years

had begun to catch up with him far earlier than they would have with any man who had known a normal life. He was still, in years, a young man. But his body was old. Poverty as a child had made him small and thin, and then had come scarlet fever and, later, hepatitis. Field work and strike violence had broken, at one time or another, both his arms, his pelvis, and several ribs. He had never regained full strength after his latest fast, two full weeks of silent prayer with only a little water each day, and there were times when he felt a frightening vulnerability in his head as well, as if the physical debilitation would unexpectedly unhinge his mind.

He did not want this effort against the winegrowers and winemakers any more than did Juan Lupé. But it was necessary because the workers would never, otherwise, be treated fairly.

"We will proceed logically," he said now, smiling. "We will not make hasty or careless steps, and we will speak with moderation. In the meantime, your work is to contact the people there and formulate the lists."

"Is there anything more?" Carlos Murnan, satisfied, asked.

"Pray to the Virgin," Rodriques suggested.

The two men left, and in a moment Rodriques heard their truck start up and drive away. He was alone again. He made some notes for further demographic information he would buy from a northern California public-relations firm, and then studied the map some more as he put small X's along roads where he and his marchers could stop and hold press conferences for maximum exposure. He made a note to himself to make sure all his group leaders field-tested their Citizen's Band radios before they went north, and he thought about new ways to raise money, and about the advisability of an updated, computerized, attitudinal survey in some sections of the northern grape country to provide insights into the local Anglo thinking.

Having done all this, Rodriques then took some of his own advice. He knelt on the bare concrete floor and began to pray.

22

When Susan Knight walked into the Wednesday meeting with her armload of production reports, sales estimates and other paperwork, she was both excited and apprehensive. She was also very, very tired. Robert Mancini had waited until Tuesday noon to explain to her fully what plan he had concocted to head off the proposal for buying the poor-quality Elmhurst wine, and had taken no one else into his confidence. This had required the two of them to make all the studies necessary before the meeting, and that had taken most of the night.

The idea was solid, Susan thought, and ought to work. But she worried that Jim Young and even Mike DeFrates had not been briefed ahead of time; they would be surprised at best and probably angry as well, seeing that such secrecy could be interpreted as reflecting suspicions concerning their loyalty.

"I trust both of them," Robert had explained to Susan. "But anyone could let something slip. You and I can get the job done if we work hard enough, and security is more important this time than bruised feelings."

Susan hoped DeFrates and Young would see this logic after the fact of their surprise.

The weather had turned cool. Clouds obscured the sun. The meeting room seemed austere in the light of the gray sky. Nancy, Robert Mancini's secretary, was already at her place, as were a glaring Mike DeFrates and mild-eyed Jim

Young. John Endicott, puffing a cigar, stood near the gray windows with E. Z. Simms. On the table were three attaché cases, propped open, filled with Simms's latest computer projections and other data.

Because she had gotten home very late and was behind with her laundry, Susan was wearing a dress rather than the pantsuit style she usually preferred. Worse, from the standpoint of this meeting, the dress was decidedly feminine, with a hemline shorter than Susan preferred.

The moment Endicott turned to greet her, he took notice. He did what was designed to be a comic double take. "Allll right! I like that! Great legs!"

Ignoring his leer, Susan dumped her heavy load of papers on the table at her place and sat down immediately. She was afraid her anger had made her face red. "Good morning."

"E.Z."—Endicott grinned, nudging the smaller efficiency expert—"I foresee a great meeting today. When Susie shows her great legs, they must all be in a real friendly mood."

E. Z. Simms showed no amusement. He glanced at a new gold Pulsar watch. "I believe," he said primly, "it is time to commence." He turned to look around for Robert Mancini, and as if on cue, Robert walked through the door. He looked drawn, but he, too, had dressed uncharacteristically. His shirt was a brilliant lavender, open at the throat, and he wore no jacket.

"Gawwwd damn!" Endicott grinned. "Another precinct is heard from."

Robert shook hands with the two Timmons representatives, spoke to everyone else, and took his place at the head of the table. He shot Susan an extra glance and she nodded slightly, sliding toward him one sheaf of her papers, the summaries that she had finished personally typing only minutes earlier.

Robert glanced over them briefly and then looked up as Endicott and Simms moved to the table. "I think we can begin immediately. We have no special reports, John, and this extra meeting is at your request."

Endicott put his wet cigar in an ashtray in front of him, frowned at a small notebook, and ignored the lists of figures that E. Z. Simms was trying to slide under his elbow. "Yes. Well, as you all know, at the last meeting Jules Trello met with us and made two proposals. One was general, about grape prices this fall. The other was a proposal that Mancini Vineyards should buy some bulk wine he picked up with the Elmhurst Winery, and that we should bottle that wine and distribute it under the house wine label or some other."

Endicott paused, looking around. Susan saw that Robert was making his face a polite mask; Jim Young appeared cool and noncommittal; Mike DeFrates glared at Endicott steadily. E. Z. Simms had his head down as he fiddled with his printouts.

"Now I know," Endicott resumed, "that the preliminary reaction here was negative to Jules's idea. But frankly—we made no secret of this—E.Z. and I were a little intrigued by it. I'm speaking now of the second proposal, to buy and distribute the bulk wine."

Endicott glanced at his notes. "We checked further into the situation. What Jules Trello has for sale is enough wine to make about eight thousand cases of red wine and about fifty-five hundred cases of white. The red is a legal Cabernet, fifty-one per cent, and the white is partly Riesling and partly Chardonnay. Jules has assured us that all three of these wines are of high Elmhurst quality, no worry on that score.

"Now. Jules suggested an asking price of one hundred and fifty thousand dollars for the whole lot, delivered right to the doorstep outside here. We thought that was a fair price, assuming we planned to sell the Cabernet as Cabernet, and not some house wine, but we haggled with him. Jules is anxious to clear out those buildings, and frankly we bargained hard because we assured him that we weren't about to do anything that was financially risky, or that might hurt Mancini Vineyards in any way, shape or form."

Endicott paused dramatically. "Well, folks, what we got Jules Trello to accept as a potential offer—and he's no easy man to bargain with, as you know—is a flat price of one hundred twenty-five thousand dollars for that wine. A clear savings of twenty-five thousand from his original offer."

Mike DeFrates seemed unable to contain himself any longer. "That's a high price for a wine like that. Eighty per cent of the cost of a bottle of wine comes from production—cooperage, equipment, glass, labels, corks, distribution. Giving him almost a dollar a bottle, when it isn't even bottled, is way out of line."

E. Z. Simms cleared his throat. "Actually, the pre-bottle cost computes to about seventy-seven cents, not one dollar."

"I don't care if it—"

"Mike," Robert cut in quietly. "Let's hear it all and then talk, all right?"

Fuming, DeFrates subsided.

Endicott picked up smoothly. "Well, we did a little rudimentary figuring, and what we came up with was a return to the winery after selling this wine that's quite impressive. Using the most conservative estimates, we don't see any way you can fail to make a profit of at least a dollar a bottle. And this is low-cost wine that will sell fast, all of it, for all practical purposes, within the next ninety to one hundred days. That means we're looking here at a minimum extra profit of about one hundred and sixty-two thousand dollars before the first of November."

Endicott paused, expecting comment. He looked disappointed when he didn't get any. So far, Susan thought, it was going as anticipated. Pressure to add profits fast.

Endicott spread his big hands on the table. "Well, now, you can understand that when we had these figures, we were compelled to take the matter to our superiors on the Timmons board. And people, I want you to know that the board sat up and took notice! The board is very interested in this."

E. Z. Simms rustled some of his papers and said dryly, "There is great admiration for Robert Mancini Vineyards throughout the Timmons Corporation. No one would think of starting policy outside the parameters of local management wishes. However, in view of the clear statistics, the board wanted us to return to you with the facts. The consensus was that no thinking individual could turn down such an opportunity."

"People," Endicott resumed, "we should be candid with one another. Timmons Corporation is in a period of retrenchment and reexamination. Some companies under the umbrella have had setbacks. While Mancini Vineyards has consistently grown and shown profit, the general feeling upstairs is that the winery has not made as much profit as it might during this crucial time period for the general operation. For those reasons, the board has asked us to take a second hard look at this entire matter."

Simms chimed in again. "On the other matter, that of grape prices, it was also the clear consensus of the board that payment of quality bonuses, or taking any other action that might tend to elevate the general price structure, would not be in the company's best interests."

Susan felt a pulse of surprise at this, and saw that Robert, too, betrayed the feeling. They had been so intent on the wine-buying proposal, and so sure that any action of grape prices would be on the borderline if not actually illegal, that they had not prepared for this matter. She waited to see how Robert would react in words.

He did not make her wait. "On the pricing of grapes, are we to understand that the Timmons board is giving a direct instruction to us not to pay the premium-grape bonuses that we've offered every year we've been in existence?"

Endicott gave every indication of dismay. "Bobby! Timmons doesn't give *orders* to its sister firms! Our job as liaison officers is to convey the Timmons thinking to you. The last thing in our mind is to issue orders! Surely mature businessmen—" He remembered Susan and winked at her —"and businesswomen, I might add—can reason together and find the best policy without the need for high-pressure tactics."

Mike DeFrates blew up again. "I don't know why we're sitting here listening to this God-damned crap! We've always given bonuses and that's the only way to get the best grapes. And Bob told you the last time you were here: he doesn't want any part of a cheap Cabernet."

Jim Young chimed in, speaking for the first time since the session had opened: "Part of the concern is clear to any businessman. If this wine is substandard, it will possibly sell. But its poor quality could damage the label in the future. Disappointed buyers wouldn't come back for anything in our line."

Endicott smiled good-naturedly, as if humoring a child. "We considered that. Frankly, profits are long and the public's memory is short. Look at the oil companies if you don't believe that."

"We're not selling oil," Mike DeFrates growled, making Susan smile despite the tension.

"The regular Mancini label could be altered in some slight way to show that this wine is different," Endicott suggested. "Not much alteration—we're counting on product identification—but enough to avoid any possibility of damaging the other fine wines."

Jim Young asked, "Are you sure this wine would sell?" It seemed a curious question, coming from him as sales manager, and his tone was studiously neutral.

"It will sell," E. Z. Simms said. He rustled papers, unfolding a mammoth printout. "The computer's projections—"

It was Susan's turn to lose patience. "I'm sure the computer is accurate as ever, E.Z."

Simms appeared startled. "Of course it is."

For a few seconds no one spoke. The room was still. Susan waited, and then Robert began to make the move they had charted.

"I want to understand this," he said, frowning as if puzzled. "The concern here is in no way connected with wanting to help Jules Trello move his wine. Is that correct?"

"Certainly not!" Endicott said. "Jules's bad luck is our good luck. Our only concern is showing the maximum profit in this quarter!"

"Good," Robert said. He took one sheet off the top of the pile of typed summaries and passed the stack down the table. "As you can see, the whole question of buying Jules Trello's bulk wine is no longer an issue. All of us are sympathetic to Timmons's desire to make the maximum profit. We want to co-operate. With that in mind, I have just authorized immediate preparation of our entire stock of red and white house wines, normally held back for at least two months yet. These figures show the quantity we have in the warehouse, including all the red that Susan blended just prior to our last meeting."

He paused, and Susan saw that every other face in the room was slack with surprise.

He continued, "This is irregular. As all of you know, we like to put more bottle age on even our house-label wines, the cheapest we produce. Selling these wines now is a slight compromise. I don't like compromise. But I'm confident that this wine, even lacking several weeks of bottle aging, is infinitely superior to anything Jules has to sell to us in bulk.

"Further," Robert went on, "this wine can start shipment next week. The entire process will be simpler. The bottom row of figures on your sheet of paper shows the profit margin, and you can see that our profit with this transaction will exceed that which you outlined for a possible deal with Jules."

Susan maintained a straight face, but she wanted to jump up and down and laugh aloud. It was perfect and it was all true and there was no way to argue with it. Like Robert, she hated the prospect of releasing even the cheapest wines prior to the planned date. But she knew from experience that only a connoisseur might detect the difference, and few connoisseurs would be buying this wine. It was a compromise, but one eminently justified by the alternatives.

No one had spoken, and most heads were down as they studied the compact compilation of facts on Susan's summary sheet.

Robert added, "Susan has total inventory figures and anything else you might want more detail on."

It was Mike DeFrates who reacted first, and as Susan had feared, he was livid when he looked up. "This is going to screw up every production plan on the board."

"I know that," Robert said quietly. "I'm sorry about that, Mike. It can be done, and it's necessary."

"The wine won't be as good, going early!"

"I told you: it's a small compromise and I don't like it. But I've decided."

"Why," DeFrates demanded slowly, "was this kept a secret from me?"

Jim Young said, "It was a secret from me too, Mike. You aren't alone."

"I only made this decision yesterday," Robert replied grimly. "Of course I could have run around and let you know. I was damned busy. Furthermore, Mike, and Jim, we still don't know who might have leaked some information out of this winery earlier—"

"Are you saying," DeFrates yelled, "that I—"

"No, I'm not!" Robert cut in firmly. "The fewer offices involved in this, the less chance of some inadvertent comment that someone else might pick up."

"I should have been consulted! I should at least have been informed!"

Robert's face hardened. "Possibly you're right, Mike. I made the decision. If you don't like it, blame me. I stand by it."

DeFrates, red-faced, shot Susan a murderous look. She was stunned, and understood. DeFrates felt he had not been trusted, and had been embarrassed. *And he blames me.*

Endicott, his color more pale than it had been earlier, emerged from a quick, whispered conversation with E. Z.

Simms. "You've already started the, uh, procedure to get this wine shipped?"

"The order has just been given. Mike will start on it after lunch. It's not complicated."

"What about the Schreck Brothers-Elmhurst proposal?"

"Isn't that moot?" Robert countered. "You wanted profit in the quarter. Here it is, and more of it—and easier—than Jules's plan allowed."

Sweat glistened on Endicott's face. "Why not do both?"

"Sell our wine early and still go ahead and buy Jules's wine?"

"Yes. Sure. Why not? I don't see why it's now moot."

"The market won't absorb that much house wine from us. Buy and bottle Jules's wine now, and you've flooded the market to the detriment of the profit plan we just set up."

Endicott mopped his forehead with a handkerchief. "We have to study this."

"Meanwhile," Robert assured him calmly, "we'll go ahead."

E. Z. Simms said, "If you sell this house wine early, you're not really adding to profit. You're only moving the profit up earlier in the year."

"Not so," Robert said, playing another trump. "I've already ordered Susan and her assistants to start making plans for the addition of a new wine this fall. We're going to start producing a Beaujolais. We never have and I'd like to try it. As you know, that's a fruity wine that's consumed very young. It will fit nicely into our schedules, and there's an overabundance of Beaujolais grapes in the area."

Mike DeFrates, still seething, spoke again. "You should have cleared all that with me, too. I'm in charge of production."

"Mike," Robert snapped, "we'll discuss it later."

DeFrates subsided.

There were more questions. The discussion went on. After a while, it clearly became meaningless. Both Endicott and Simms appeared stunned, and by the time the meeting broke up, the color of Endicott's face and Simms's expression also betrayed anger as they began to see how they had been maneuvered out of a proposal that both must have worked hard to prepare. Mike DeFrates, too, was still angry; when the meeting ended, he strode out of the room without a word.

Endicott and Simms, Susan thought, would be heard

from again. And in thwarting them this time around, Robert had angered one of his most loyal associates. The victory, in the long run, might turn out to be a very tarnished one . . .

23

In the days immediately following Robert Mancini's gambit to avoid buying Jules Trello's bulk wine, an appearance of calm was everywhere in the valley. It was deceptive.

The news wire brought word that Alfredo Rodriques had intimated that he and some of his followers would be in the valley soon, without specifying what "soon" meant. More of his advance men had been seen in the area, quietly contacting field workers and handing out brochures about the need for agricultural unions. There was some consternation as a result, especially among growers also being increasingly concerned about continuing vague rumors of a likely plunge in grape prices in the fall.

Jules Trello was behind most of the price rumors, carefully planting them through third parties and with men he had manipulated before, such as Merlot-grower James Higgins. This was part of Jules's continuing plan to drive prices as low as possible and, at the same time, if possible, harden resistance to Rodriques' union.

The rumor effort was not one which Jules gave much time. He could not afford to give it much time. Word that his bulk-wine proposal had failed was a most serious blow, forcing him to scurry around anxiously, patching up a number of short-term notes and performing the kind of financial hocus-pocus that he knew better than most men. It was exhausting, nerve-straining work, and none of it did more than postpone his crisis showdown a few weeks. He would not be able to see even the most illusory light at the end of the tunnel until he disposed of the Elmhurst wine at a decent price.

Maintaining his usual outgoing and enthusiastic façade, Jules had a number of telephone conferences with John Endicott. He felt Endicott had let him down at the worst possible time, but still hoped something could be salvaged.

"You should have been ready for that trick he pulled," Jules told Endicott bitterly during one conversation.

"How could I?" Endicott countered angrily. "It was totally unexpected."

"You should have refused authorization."

"Jules, I keep telling you. This is very delicate. It isn't a matter of authorization. Timmons Corporation hasn't taken straight-out control of Mancini Vineyards . . . yet. And if I started doing some of the things you've suggested lately, we would never get it away from him. Some of the members of our board think that man walks on water. We have to be careful . . . go slowly."

"The grape prices," Jules said. "You have to insist there."

"I hope to."

"You *hope* to? You *have* to!"

"The goal," Endicott reminded him, "is to create a situation where Bobby gets so much on his high horse that he loses all his support. Then we'll have the stock showdown. You and I both know how that will turn out. Once he's out of there, a silent stockholder with a minority interest, then our other plans can go forward. But these things can't be rushed!"

"What am I supposed to do in the meantime?" Jules demanded shrilly. "Be calm while everything falls down around my ears?"

"Jules, your situation surely isn't that bad."

"Oh, no, of course not," Jules lied, getting himself together. "But I need to move this Elmhurst wine. Do you have any new ideas on that? Have you contacted the people I mentioned to you?"

"I'm afraid, Jules, no one appears very interested. Why don't you just take my advice and sell it to some winery back East for blending."

"I need more money than I could get that way!"

"Well, then, I don't know anything to suggest."

Jules knew he had to take some new and drastic action.

His own part of the larger plan shared with John Endicott and one or two others was for further expansion of the Schreck-Elmhurst holdings in the coming year. Then, with luck, he could locate a large corporation interested in expanding into the wine business, and he would sell enough shares to solve all his longer-term financial problems once and for all.

There was precedent for large corporate tie-ins with independent wine operations. Paul Masson was now owned by Seagram distillers; San Martin was controlled by the Southdown Land Co.; National Distillers had bought Almaden in 1967; Robert Mondavi was tied in with Ranier Breweries; Italian Swiss Colony was owned by Heublein; Souverain, by Pillsbury; Berringer Brothers, by Nestle, and so on.

But that was all in the future. Jules's immediate problem, remained the same: disposing of the Elmhurst wine.

After more days of stewing about the problem, he took a step he did not really want to take, one betraying his desperation.

Carmine D'Angelico controlled a worldwide distribution network for all kinds of goods. Operating out of Chicago, he was, it was said, one of the most powerful wholesalers in the world. It was whispered that he had close connections to many powerful mobsters. It was also said that he had done work for the CIA in both Europe and Southeast Asia. Many men feared him, and Jules was among them. But they had met a few times over the years, and Jules knew that D'Angelico also distributed wine on a worldwide basis.

When he placed the telephone call to Chicago, Jules felt a pang of deep apprehension. He had to be very careful. He imagined D'Angelico, squat, dark-browed, brutal, at his ornate desk, holding the telephone like a toothpick in his hairy paw. D'Angelico represented raw power in more than one form. But Jules had few options remaining.

"Carmine," he opened, smiling. "It's a real pleasure talking to you! Have we been introduced? It's a pleasure to be here talking to an old friend, let me assure you of that. Where am I?"

"Cut the comedy, Jules," D'Angelico's hoarse voice replied. "I'm busy. You have something to say?"

"I plan to come to Chicago soon, Carmine, and I wanted to talk to you."

"What about?"

"Well, two or three matters."

"Sorta talk for old times' sake?" D'Angelico's voice dripped sarcasm.

"Partly that—"

"Forget it. No time. If that's all you called for—"

"No, wait! Carmine, I have some very fine wine that I've been thinking of letting go. There's some Cabernet, some Chardonnay, and some Riesling. I need the warehouse space, Carmine, and I wondered if you might be interested in a purchase of this kind."

"I might be. What label?"

"It's in Elmhurst cooperage—"

"That dog label! Who's going to buy that shit after all the lawsuit publicity. Are you crazy, Trello? You're wasting my time."

"It could be bottled under any label," Jules said hastily. "And the price," he added desperately, "is right for you, Carmine."

"Yeah? How much?"

"I don't want to talk that part on the phone. Look. What if I fly to Chicago in the next day or two? We can sit down—"

"I leave tonight for France. Don't know how long I might be gone. We could talk when I get back, maybe."

"The sooner the better, Carmine. I need to move this wine to have the warehouse space."

"Is it good wine?" D'Angelico sounded suspicious.

"It's excellent," Jules lied. "Top drawer. When I come to see you, I'll bring a bottle or two along and you can judge for yourself."

"I might be interested," D'Angelico said. "I'll get in touch when I'm back from France, okay?"

"Yes," Jules said. "Fine."

The connection was broken. Jules wondered about the extent of the risk he was taking. If a man like Carmine D'Angelico ever learned that the wine was substandard— was not even real legal Cabernet—the reaction might be terrific. But Jules reminded himself that he had no choice. Driven, he had to proceed.

Jules Trello, however, was not the only person who felt a sense of deepening personal crisis. Although he believed his actions had taken immediate pressure off his situation *vis-à-vis* Timmons Corporation, Robert Mancini knew that nothing had been ultimately decided. And in addition, his growing relationship with Barbara Turner was a source of savagely mixed emotions.

He called her the night of the meeting, and found talking with her on the telephone almost as easy as being with her. They talked an hour. Two nights later, they met again at her home and for the first time were truly alone, because her son Jimmy was practicing for a school play. On both these occasions the talk was good, easy, and meaningful, but by tacit agreement they did not return to any reference that might test deeply into where they might be headed together, or why. And they did not touch.

Then, after other telephone calls, Robert suggested they might go out together. "We might drive," he said carefully. "Or we could find a steak house."

"I know that's impossible, Bob," she replied.

"Why is it impossible?" Of course he knew.

"We aren't going to play games now, are we? I wouldn't like that."

"There are places we could go together, Barbara."

"Yes," she said. "But we would both have one eye cocked at the door for every new arrival, worried we might see a familiar face."

"I don't think I would feel that way."

"Then you haven't thought seriously about it. Practically everyone knows you on sight, and my work is already beginning to make me a little well-known, too. There would be someone who recognized us. Then there would be gossip. You can't afford that."

"Why do you say *I* can't afford it? You have as much to lose as I do."

"No. That's not so. Most of the people I know, if they heard a rumor that you and I were seeing each other, would think. 'My God, how neat.' You're the personality. I'm the nobody. You could be harmed. I don't have a professional reputation to uphold the way you do. If rumors got started, I might be irritated. But if anything, my reputation would be perversely enhanced, like those women who claimed they slept with the President; *he* was the one damaged by the gossip, not they."

"I know that makes some sense even though it's stupid," Robert told her. "To put it another way, this is all on my terms. I'm only using you."

"Don't talk nonsense. Now let me make a suggestion. I have to work awhile tonight. What if you picked me up there, and we took a drive? Maybe we could have a sandwich at a drive-in somewhere, and then you could deposit me back."

Torn between guilt and pleasure, he followed the suggestion. They drove to Vallejo, where they ate in his car, and he hid the fact that she was *right:* he found himself glancing at other nearby vehicles, afraid of seeing a face he recognized . . . one that might recognize him. Despite this, however, it was a good evening, and a pattern had been set for later meetings.

Meanwhile, Rod Poole's investigation of the two men now identified as Phil Dennison and Dave Arnstedt was brought to at least a temporary halt.

"Why?" Susan demanded.

"There's no longer any question about it," Poole told her bleakly. "As long as I could ignore it, it was all right. But I can't ignore the obvious any longer. Homero Artiz is an illegal—a wetback."

"Does that mean he isn't entitled to protection from the law?"

Uncharacteristically, Poole responded angrily. "Get your head on straight, Susan! How can I try to arrest those two guys? I don't have anything else on them, and Homero will never testify against them because they'll shout for the federal boys, and he'll be sent back to Mexico in a cage!"

"Are you so sure now that they're the right suspects?"

"I've asked a lot of people a lot of questions. I've used some snitches. Dennison and Arnstedt have some kind of extortion racket going. I'd be willing to bet my life on it. With Homero, they're probably demanding hush money to prevent an anonymous tip to the Immigration boys. With other people, maybe the grounds for the blackmail is different. I want those two bastards. Bad. I intend to stay after them now. But until or unless Homero Artiz is willing to risk return to Mexico—which would be a disaster for him—I'm handcuffed as far as he is concerned."

"What you're saying," Susan replied after thinking about it, "is that Homero can either go on paying hush money forever, and getting beat up whenever they feel like it, or he can be deported."

"That's it, I'm afraid, honey."

"Rod, that doesn't give Homcro a very bright future, does it?"

Poole stared at her for a long minute, his eyes seeming to sag with weariness. "Honey, it doesn't give him any."

Part Two

to tousle the boy's hair.

Jimmy shrank back sharply. Then he seemed to realize

1

As July deepened toward August, unseasonable cool and cloudy conditions persisted. Although the cool snap had not yet continued long enough to cause genuine apprehension, growers began to discuss it and worry: a cool season could mean a very late maturing of the grapes, and if the harvest extended well into October, the rains might come, with results that could range from slight diminutions in quality and quantity to total disaster—unripened grapes rotting in muddy fields.

Throughout the wine country, the grapes were well set on the vines now, long clusters of small green berries packed snugly under broad green leaves which often hid them totally from casual view. Profound changes had already begun within the fruit. Early concentrations of tartaric and malic acids in the cell fluids, as high as 3 per cent, had begun to diminish, each plant using its photosynthetic capability to produce sucrose. Early growth of the berries had been due to cell division; now the long drama of ripening was under way and the fruit began to swell as the vine moved sugar from leaf to cluster.

Sugar content was still very low, and with the cool, cloudy weather it was proceeding more slowly than normal. Warmth and sun were needed if sugar levels—vital to fermentation—were to rise toward 20 per cent or even higher.

Many other variables still threatened the grapes, and many uncertainties lingered, as they did every year until

187

the last moment when it was finally time for picking, and the climax of everything, the crush.

The vines were susceptible to many exotic diseases, funguses and parasites. Even vigilant growers had been known to fall prey to some of these ailments, although preventive measures continued constantly. Technical and trade journals regularly reported entirely new maladies that had appeared in one area or another.

In addition, the vines were threatened by simpler but no less destructive concerns. Rodents, rabbits, birds and other creatures might cause serious damage. High winds might rip off leaves or entire stalks, not only decreasing the crop but damaging each vine's ability to ripen what fruit remained. Although summer rains were unusual in this valley, they had been known to occur in conjunction with prolonged haze and fog, which encouraged rot or berry cracking. Dry winds during periods of heat could damage fruit by tossing the leaves in such a way as to expose the fruit to sun scald.

So now in late July only the threat of frost was past. The wind machines—great fans or aircraft-type propellers mounted on platforms over vineyards and driven by powerful engines—were still, their blades turning only as casual breezes turned them, because there was no need to circulate great masses of air in attempts to prevent extreme cold from settling to the ground. And the vineyard heaters had been stored for another year. But nothing else was certain. Not yet, and not for a long time.

To Susan Knight, it was apparent that the valley was more tense than normal, and not only because of the weather. Although nothing more had been heard from Timmons Corporation or its representatives since the plan to buy Elmhurst wine was headed off, she shared with Robert Mancini a gut feeling that they had not heard the end of it, although neither of them could predict what form new difficulties might take. Only two nights earlier, for no apparent reason, a stack of wine-filled oak barrels had tumbled out of alignment in the secondary cooperage building, with five barrels bursting or leaking badly so that almost three hundred gallons of prime Pinot Noir were destroyed. It might have been a freak accident. It might also have been sabotage again.

Concerns, however, extended far beyond Robert Mancini Vineyards. More organizers for Alfredo Rodriques had been seen. There had even been a few small, disorganized rallies by Chicano field workers, and excitement was high among some of them as reports circulated that Alfredo himself would lead a march to the valley within a matter of days. And despite published statements by a number of winemakers that nothing could accurately be predicted about possible grape prices in the fall, rumors were rampant that prices on the top grapes were likely to be off as much as 40 per cent from the previous year.

"I don't know where the rumors are coming from," Susan told Ned and Johnelle Henderson. It was a hazy morning and she had stopped to visit briefly on her way to the winery, finding Johnelle just ready to leave the house for her own work.

"Everybody is saying it," Henderson told her as the three of them stood outside the house near her car. "Prices *are* going to be down. It's not a rumor, it's just a damned fact."

"Nobody can predict what the price levels will be just yet," Susan argued. "What if this cool weather persists? What if all the original crop estimates are off just a few percentage points? We can never be sure of anything, really, until the grapes start coming in to the crushers. That's when we *know*."

Henderson began to reply, but was interrupted by the appearance of Jamie Henderson from the back of the house. His hair unkempt and his clothes fashionably (for teen-agers) cruddy, he had a notebook in one hand a piece of toast in the other. He waved and walked over to his small motorcycle and straddled it.

"Jamie," Johnelle called sharply, "your helmet!"

"Do I have to?" he called despairingly.

"Get it," Ned Henderson said.

The boy slouched back into the house and emerged again quickly with the helmet. He jammed it on his head, started the bike, revved it a few times with a cornpopper sound that chased the morning quiet, and waved as he kicked it into gear.

Talk was impossible for a few moments until he had driven past them and well up the dirt road toward the highway.

"That bike," Johnelle murmured, "will be the death of me."

"Do you let him ride it to school? I thought he wasn't allowed on the highway."

"He rides it to the corner and chains it to the fence. Then he waits for the school bus. I could drive him to the corner, but oh, no."

Ned Henderson watched the bike go out of sight. His expression was worried, but Susan could not guess whether he was worried about his son or about their previous topic, to which he now reverted.

"When I planted my Pinot Chardonnay," he said darkly, "they were selling for eight hundred dollars a ton, maybe even higher. Since then I've seen prices drop to five hundred, four hundred, and down lower. All our calculations on repaying our loan and making a living at this were based on getting at least three hundred dollars a ton. I thought I was being as conservative as hell in figuring the prices would go that low. If prices go as low as some people say they will this fall, we can't make it."

Susan studied the deep worry in Henderson's face, and the concern etched in Johnelle's expression. She knew the kind of switch they were caught in. She said, "When prices were so high, Ned, it was a fool's paradise. But there are only so many winemakers; they have a total capacity. Now there are just more grapes planted than there is capacity. And prices have gone up for everything else in the process: labor, glass, chemicals, labels and printing, cork."

"It's the overplanting that's done it," Henderson replied. "Everyone and his brother plowed under truck farms and planted grapes."

"I know. Look at your own variety, Chardonnay. Do you know how many acres of Chardonnay were bearing in California less than ten years ago? About one thousand acres. And do you know how many are bearing today?"

"Twice that," Henderson guessed glumly.

"Ten times that," Susan told him.

"Shit," he said. "Excuse me."

"The people who raise the finest grapes will make it, Ned. Remember that."

Johnelle glanced at her watch. "I have to go. But before I do, maybe you can explain why all the rumors we hear are so negative. *No one* is saying that even the finest grapes will get a good price."

"Where are all these rumors coming from?"

"You haven't seen all the newspaper articles, and the

magazines? Everyone says we're overplanted, and prices will go way down. Then you have all these stories about slumping prices internationally, about old French wines about to be dumped on the market by speculators who lost their shirts. As Ned says, all the news we hear is bad."

Henderson nodded. "And the local talk is even worse. There was a guy here the other day from Schreck Brothers. A field supervisor. They finally got around to coming by to see what was wrong with my vines—the deal Robert Mancini and you helped me with long ago. I told them I hope to sell the grapes I get this year to you. He said you won't be paying quality bonuses any more, and the chances are that you won't buy my grapes at any price."

"I can tell you," Susan said sharply, "that that's a lie."

"You *are* going to pay quality bonuses?"

Susan remembered the talk about it in the last meeting with Endicott and Simms. "We haven't made an announcement, she said, realizing that it sounded lame. "Until we do, I think you can be sure our policy will be the same as always."

"That's funny," Henderson said. "I was upset about what the Schreck guy said, so when I was at your winery the other day, I happened to see Mr. Young. He said it was probably true."

Susan came to full alert. "Jim Young? Our sales manager?"

"That's the one."

"And he said *what?* I want to get this exactly right."

Henderson frowned. "I said I had heard the Mancini prices would be real low, and there wouldn't be any quality bonuses. He said . . . let me think . . . he said, 'Well, our prices will be low, and no one should count on a quality bonus.' Then he said, 'I'd say anyone with immature vines will be darned lucky if they sell their grapes at any price.'"

Susan was stunned. She found it hard to believe, but she knew that Henderson would not lie on something she could check so easily. There was no reason for him to lie at all. She said cautiously, "I think there's been a misunderstanding, Ned. I intend to check up on this."

Henderson sighed. "Well, I don't think I'm the only person he's told something like that. I've got an idea some folks wouldn't be so worried if the rumors were only coming from Schreck. This big meeting at the end of the week will probably bring up all the rumors from everybody."

"I didn't know about the meeting you're talking about," Susan said, startled for the second time.

"It hasn't been publicized or anything. It's all the growers, except the big co-op people."

"Where is this going to be, and when?"

"Friday night, in the old Moose Lodge downtown."

"I'm going to look into this, Ned," Susan said. "You've given me quite a bit to think about."

Johnelle looked at her watch again. "I've *got* to go."

"I do too," Susan said. She was anxious now to get to the winery and confront Jim Young with this. She knew, too, that Robert Mancini would be vitally interested not only in this aspect of the growing mystery of the rumors, but about Friday's upcoming meeting.

Johnelle Henderson got into her car and drove down the dirt road. Susan had a few more words with Henderson, and then followed. As she drove up the road slowly to avoid raising excessive dust, she saw the slender figure of Homero Artiz wobbling toward her on an ancient red bicycle.

Susan braked to a halt, got out of her car in the narrow, dusty road, and waved to him as he approached. He recognized her and came to a stop beside the car, straddling the rusty bike.

"Good morning, Homero," she said.

"Good morning, Miss Knight," he replied in his immaculate English. He was soaked with sweat from the long ride. A brown bag was strapped behind the seat, containing, she assumed, his lunch.

Susan studied his face. "You seem all over the effects of your accident."

Homero's face lighted in a brief smile. "Yes. I am fine again."

"Have you had any more talks with my friend Rod Poole?"

The mask slid over Homero's face. "Yes. But there is nothing for us to discuss. I know nothing."

Susan almost lost patience and blurted out what she and Rod Poole both now accepted as the probable truth. But she knew that if she did so, it might thrust such a direct challenge in Homero's face that he would panic—even run.

"Homero," she said slowly, "I really think you and I should have a talk sometime soon."

"That would be most pleasant, Miss Knight," he said with no expression.

Damn! There was no way to penetrate his façade short of direct confrontation. But how could she step back and forget it, knowing the kind of hell his life must be?

Irritated, she compromised. "You may hear from me soon, then, Homero."

"Have a nice day, Miss Knight," he said, and pedaled on past her car, wobbling from side to side.

Susan started her car again and drove toward the winery. She found herself driving faster than usual in her eagerness to get there and try to find some answers. Homero, she told herself, simply had to be ignored for the moment, if that was possible. Of primary importance was the misunderstanding . . . if that was what it had been . . . between Ned Henderson and Jim Young. Of almost equal significance was the fact of the growers' meeting scheduled for week's end.

When she reached the winery, Susan had not yet fully decided whether she would report directly to Robert Mancini, or first question Jim Young. As it turned out, the problem was taken out of her hands: the first person she ran into as she entered the office wing on the second floor was the slender sales manager.

"You look like a lady in a hurry," the slender Young smiled. "What's up, anyway?"

"Jim," she said, deciding, "could we have a word alone?"

"Of course," he agreed. "Come on into my office; it's closer than yours."

His office was not much more than a cubicle, and was jammed with sales reports, sales displays, and file cabinets full of correspondence. Jim Young's style was to be modishly dressed and cool in appearance at all times, but his office always looked like a cyclone had just blown through. In his years with Robert Mancini, he had always been a member of the inner circle, although his expertise was in the marketplace rather than in any areas closer to the actual production of fine wine. Susan knew that Robert Mancini trusted him implicitly, and forced herself to be very careful to avoid bruised feelings.

"Now," Young said, propping his feet on his desk. "What's up?"

"Jim, I just saw Ned Henderson, and I think he badly misunderstood something you must have said the other day. I thought I should let you know, although I think I straightened it out."

Young frowned. "What are you talking about?"

"Well, when Ned was over here one day recently, *something* that was said got all turned around after your conversation with him. He went home thinking there was no chance we would buy his grapes this fall, and got the impression that we had ruled out any possibility of paying premium-quality bonuses."

Young's eyes became coolly hostile. "You don't think a man with vines as immature as his stands a chance of a quality bonus, do you?"

"Probably not," Susan admitted. "But we have given him a verbal commitment to buy whatever grapes he matures, and if the weather is ideal, it's possible he could get a bonus, even though his quantity won't be very great."

"Possible," Young said. "Not likely."

"Granted."

"I was just trying to make the guy face his situation realistically. Wouldn't you say his chances of having high quality are pretty slim?"

"Of course," Susan granted, beginning to feel that she was being grilled, and realizing that Young must have said something far closer to Henderson's report than she had first suspected. "But we *do* intend to buy his grapes, Jim. And as far as *I* know, we do plan to pay bonuses for top quality, as usual."

"How can you say that?" Young shot back. "You were in that meeting. You heard John Endicott say we weren't to pay bonuses."

"You mean you *did* tell Ned Henderson that we won't pay bonuses? Oh, Jim! With all the wild rumors flying around about low prices, that was the worst thing you could possibly have said!"

"I don't think I spoke out of turn," Young snapped. "I was trying to give the guy a realistic picture."

"All the growers are terribly worried already! There have been a number of small meetings to allow them to discuss what they'll do to try to keep prices up. They're *upset*, Jim! There's a big meeting this Friday night. When we haven't made any announcement, as far as I know, about bonuses or prices, I think you were really badly mistaken to be saying things that might add fuel to the rumor fires."

Young's face stiffened and his feet swung off the top of the desk. He stood. "I think it's time we talked about this with Robert. Right now."

"Is that necessary? I was just trying to—"

"I'm God-damned tired of listening to insinuations. Maybe I'm just a flunky salesboy and you're a big-shot winemaker, but I'm not taking any more from you. We'll settle this right now."

Livid, Young barged out of his office, leaving Susan alone, shocked. She got up quickly and followed him, catching sight of his back as he turned the far corner of the hall and charged toward Robert's office.

Oh, great! she thought, following. *Now I've got a fight on my hands!*

Feeling shaky inside, she went through the reception area, past Nancy's startled expression, and into Robert's office. Young had left the door open, and was already leaning over Robert's desk, talking low and fast into Robert's look of surprise.

"I told Henderson what I think is the truth," Young was saying. "And I resent little Miss Fidget or anybody else going around behind my back and saying I didn't know what I was talking about!"

"Susan," Robert said crisply, "shut that door."

Susan obeyed, then turned back to face the desk.

"Now, what's this all about?" Robert asked her.

Struggling with a sudden urge to cry, Susan repeated the gist of her conversation with Ned Henderson, and explained what she had said to Jim Young. The sales manager glared silently through her recitation.

"I didn't mean to poke my nose in," she concluded. "I *thought* it was a misunderstanding."

"I'm sick of her throwing her weight around!" Young said.

"All right, that's enough," Robert said, his face stony.

Both of them faced him in silence.

"Jim," Robert said quietly, "no decision has been announced on quality bonuses. Our policy in the past has been to pay them."

"Endicott said—"

"Endicott does not run this winery."

"My impression—"

"Listen to me!" Robert said sharply.

Young subsided, his eyes sullen, his hands in fists at his sides.

"I think you're both overreacting," Robert said. "If there was any question, Susan, you should have consulted me. You're not Jim's supervisor, and I understand his resentment. Do you understand what I'm saying?"

"Yes, sir," Susan said, and the tears were closer.

"Jim," Robert added, "you were wrong to say what you did to Ned Henderson. I intend to buy his grapes. I intend to pay the best price. The question of quality bonuses and the eventual price level is not yet decided, and anything you've told anyone to the contrary was not only misleading; it could encourage rumors that can only hurt the whole industry."

"So you're telling me I should rescind what I said?"

Robert's eyes flashed with anger at the challenge in Young's tone. "I'm telling you—if you have to have it straight—to keep your damned mouth shut when you obviously don't know what you're talking about."

Young went pale. "Is there anything else?"

"That's all."

Young turned, shot Susan a look of pure hatred, and slammed out.

Thoroughly miserable, Susan went nearer the desk. "Robert, I'm sorry! I didn't think—"

"That's right," he cut in. "You didn't."

She stared at him. His anger seemed all out of proportion to the offense. "What he said was wrong—"

"Susan, there are people around here who might resent you just a little. Did you know that?"

The idea amazed her. "No," she admitted.

"You came in only a short time ago, and through a combination of circumstances moved right to the top. You're attractive, and you're still a very young woman. People like Jim Young—as wrong as they are—tend to resent your rapid advancement. I thought surely you had enough sensitivity to know that, and understand that you have to go gently with employees who have more seniority."

"I only thought of the problem."

"Well, all right. What's done is done. Jim was wrong. I'm glad we headed off any more rumors starting in our own house, at least. I just wish you had been more diplomatic."

"I will be in the future," she promised. "I just didn't *know*."

He was still angry with her and his expression showed it. "Is there anything else?"

"There's a meeting of the growers Friday night. I guess learning about that was partly behind my feeling of pressure about the rumors. Did you know about the Friday night meeting?"

"No. Tell me about it."

Susan did so. She added Ned Henderson's remarks about Schreck representatives spreading rumors of low prices to come. "The growers are more upset by the day. If they band together and try to put concerted pressure on the wineries, we could get into a really nasty situation."

Robert grimaced agreement. "I'll have to attend the meeting. With all the talk about Alfredo Rodriques coming, and now more rumors of the bottom falling out of prices, those growers are getting desperate. It's up to us to try to keep the record straight and the facts on the table."

"Robert, *will* prices fall disastrously low for the growers?"

"I can't believe they will." Glancing at the window and its view into the gray morning, he made another face. "If this weather stays on much longer, there won't *be* any harvest."

Susan hesitated, but then her curiosity got the better of her sense of caution. "And we are going to pay quality bonuses as usual—aren't we?"

Robert's eyes flashed with new anger. "That's what I intend. But we haven't announced it, and we probably won't. It would be suicidal to announce a policy in advance that our friends from Timmons could beat us over the head with."

"I see," she said uncertainly. "Of course—"

"And with all the other pressures we face," Robert added, "I want you to know that I resent pressure from you."

Numbed by the renewed attack on her, she could only stare at him. She saw his fatigue and the pent-up nerves. Despite these explanations for what she saw as his unreasonableness, she was cut deeply and could not respond.

"In the future," he told her, "report to me if you think there's a problem. Don't try to handle it yourself. And while I appreciate your advice on matters of policy, please don't try to force me to make policy, or announce it, before I see fit."

"Robert! I wasn't trying to throw my weight around! I didn't intend to make it seem like I was forcing policy on you! I thought we would pay bonuses as usual, and when I heard—"

"I think we've thrashed it out, Susan," he said with a note of finality.

She stared at him. Although she could summon any number of reasons why he was under pressure, and might be forgiven for reacting unfairly, she was shocked. She realized that she, too, was responding more personally and intensely than she should have. It was only a momentary flare-up—a misunderstanding—wasn't it?

But she could not speak. Her throat was full.

"That's all for now, Susan," Robert said more gently.

She had intended to speak with him about Homero Artiz —seek advice on whether to confront the young worker with her suspicions, and offer help. But she could not do that now. She had been dismissed. She turned and walked out of the office.

Hurrying to her lab, she tried again to make a mental list of all the reasons why Robert Mancini might explode unfairly. She knew in her own mind that she had done nothing really wrong. It was finished, and it should be quickly forgotten. She was overreacting terribly.

She had to put it out of her mind, she told herself as she entered the lab, finding it deserted. The thing to do now was get back on an even keel—think about Homero's problem, because this now was one she had to deal with, if it was to be dealt with at all. Everything else was out of her hands, and she was stupid to be so upset because of a moment's temper flare-up.

But once she was safely inside the lab, she locked the door behind her. Then, quite before she knew what was happening, she was leaning against the blending table, her face buried in a towel, crying.

2

Night fog clung low to the ground, and around the drive-in on the outskirts of Vallejo it painted silver shadows around the tall pole lights. Cars stood silent under the unreal illumination, their gleaming surfaces beaded with moisture. Carhops moved in and out of the central building, its flat roof bright, pulsing red and green from neon, and occasionally a car entered or departed. But it was too late for heavy business now and the mist was closing in, making every movement seem secretive.

Off to one side, parked against a railing that separated the drive-in from the bright white splotch of lights from a convenience grocery, Robert Mancini sat behind the wheel of his car. Barbara Turner was in the seat beside him. There were cups of coffee on the tray at his window, but they had long since turned cold.

"Still," Robert said wearily, "there was no excuse to blow up at her that way."

"Susan would understand," Barbara assured him.

"Tomorrow I'll call her in and try to make it right. Damn it, the more I think about it, the more I think it was Jim Young I should have really gone after. I don't know what got into him, making public statements like that."

"Did you ever—" Barbara began, and then thought better of it. "No."

"What?"

199

"Maybe I'd better not."

"Say it."

"All right." Barbara's expression was almost stern. "Did you ever consider the possibility that Jim Young could be your source of trouble?"

"You mean the one who leaked information? You mean the saboteur? No. That's just out of the question!"

"Well, all right."

"Jim is as loyal as the day is long! He's been with me almost from the first day out there. He even owns a small parcel of stock. No. There's no way he could be our trouble-maker."

"It was just a passing thought."

"It's impossible, Barbara. I feel sure of that. Whatever he may have said to some people, he thought he was doing the right thing—what would help us."

"I'm sure you're right," Barbara said, and smiled.

Robert watched some people in a nearby car flick their lights to get their tray picked up. The girl came obediently and the car backed out, the headlights briefly flashing across his face. He fought the impulse to duck.

"You definitely plan to attend the growers' meeting Friday night?" Barbara asked.

"Yes. I've called Tim Crocker. We'll go together."

"That means you probably won't have time to go south this weekend."

"I don't think I would have gone anyway."

"Your wife is still there with the family?"

The question was asked too casually. Robert knew that the topic was as painful for her now as it was for him. And yet they returned to it: the fact of Audra's presence, of his dilemma. "She's there," he said.

"You should go to see her if you can."

The statement made him unaccountably angry with her. "Why?"

Her eyes showed her compassion. "Bob. No games."

"Yes, you're right. I should go to see her again. But not for the reason you may think. I should have the courage to face what I think she's already faced. We should talk about—finishing it."

"But that isn't what you really want to do."

"It's what I want to do now. It's what I may not have the nerve to do."

Barbara said nothing, and she looked away from him now, her face betraying pain.

And this, too, goaded him. "I'm giving you nothing. We don't just hide from would-be gossips. Now we're even hiding from your own son. I can make decisions in my work. Why am I so paralyzed over *this?* Audra has made it clear—she won't go on."

"But she's ambivalent. She probably still loves you. If you think you can work it out, and if you want to work it out—"

"I've never had a relationship with her the way I do with you! Not even at first, when we both thought we were in love. It was always a tug of war. Old Gus was always in it somewhere. The tension went on and on and now it's broken." He thought about it, his mind tumbling over itself in painful convolutions. "And I didn't even want to talk about any of this with you tonight. I told myself we *wouldn't* talk about it. Already I'm dragging you into my problem, into everything, and that isn't fair to you. I'm using you—"

"You said that before. Now stop it! I mean it. You just make me mad. If I felt used, I wouldn't be here!"

"But what about Jimmy?"

The question stopped her for an instant. Since Robert's first visit to her home, on the times he had returned, or had gotten her son when he called on the telephone, the boy had retreated from him. There was a solemn hostility, a watchfulness, now. Perhaps sensing the emotion that had begun to skyrocket between them, the youthful "man of the house" somehow saw himself as a guardian, and Robert had become his unsworn but clearly stated enemy.

"Jimmy will adapt," Barbara said finally. "He's a good boy."

"Maybe he sees it more clearly than either of us. I'm older than you are. I'm not free. You should be meeting men your own age—men who wouldn't have to take you off to stupid drive-ins somewhere."

"Bob," she said sharply, "I told you to stop that."

"What do you want me to do?" he asked out of his agony. "What do you want me to try to talk about?"

Their eyes met. As her lips parted and she caught her breath, the answer was very, very clear in the dim, hazy light from the building nearby. Again, as it had happened before, he felt a raw shock, as if a great galvanic charge had leaped between them.

He smiled, shakily trying to talk his way around it. "A little car like this isn't designed for groping. There's all this machinery between the buckets. And we're not children, Barbara. It isn't like two kids. Touching you—holding you—isn't a tentative experiment that doesn't mean anything."

"You talk too much," she said, and with a sudden, incredible movement was partly across the center console, the gear shifter and everything else, and was slipping her arms around his neck.

Awkwardly, with a tearing hunger, he moved to meet her halfway. Her hair brushed against his face fragrantly, and then her eyes seemed to swallow him up at immensely close range as they widened, then closed, and his mouth found hers. With a tender urgency, her lips opened and he felt her teeth, and then entered her with his tongue. She shuddered nearer, responding with a desperate, longing strength. He felt his soul leap out of himself.

"You were right about one thing," she whispered in his ear, hugging closer after the long kiss.

"What?" he said, dazed.

"You said a kiss couldn't be a small thing. Not for us. You were right."

He tried to kiss her again, but she startled him by drawing back, moving away and to her own seat again with a hectic quickness. She was as shaken as he, and her breasts moved with tumultuous need.

"Flash your lights," she told him.

"What?"

"Flash your lights," and here she managed a breathless smile. "Summon the carhop. Have her take the tray away. And then take *me* away somewhere. I don't care where. I won't discuss it any more. Anywhere: a motel, your house, the end of a dirt road. I want you. I need you. Now."

3

At about the same time Robert Mancini was in Vallejo with Barbara Turner, Susan Knight visited the home of the Artiz family. She had persuaded herself that the day's earlier events could not be allowed to dissuade her from confronting Homero and his wife after a suppertime conversation with Rod Poole.

Poole had been glum but definite. He had indications that Homero was not the only worker of Mexican extraction being regularly visited by Phil Dennison and Dave Arnstedt. But Poole could not approach any of the additional presumed victims for fear of alerting Dennison and Arnstedt to the surveillance.

"Someone has to *confirm* what we suspect," he told Susan. "If I can just get that much, I have a plan to put those guys out of circulation for a while. Without that, I've had it."

"But Rod, you can't expect Homero to testify against them! He would be signing his own death warrant as far as staying in this country is concerned."

"Someone has to testify," Poole said. "If they don't, we're helpless. And sooner or later, someone will get worse than Homero got—just as, sooner or later, Homero will be discovered anyway when he misses some payments and Dennison and Arnstedt send an anonymous letter."

"Rod, should somebody see Homero and put the cards on the table?"

"Someone should. But *I* can't. I'm the law."

"Then *I* will," Susan decided.

"When?"

"Tonight. The sooner the better. Before I lose my nerve."

"Honey, are you up to it, after today?"

She had told him briefly about the conflict in Robert Mancini's office, and had not hidden the strength of her reactions. Now, however, she had had a few hours to consider it, and her natural resiliency had asserted itself. "I might have forgotten to be diplomatic, Rod, and I regret that Robert took it the way he did. I guess most of all I was shocked to realize that Jim Young . . . and possibly some others . . . resent me the way they evidently do. But I just have to put it out of my mind and do my job. I was *right* to ask Jim directly. If I had gone first to Robert, someone could have said I was tattletaling behind Jim's back."

"That's my girl," Poole grinned. "Will you let me know after you've had your talk with Homero?"

"Yes. I'll call you."

So Susan had sought out the Artiz house. Small, hidden by an unkempt hedge in a row of identical frame homes that were scarcely more than shacks on an alley, the home was composed of a single room with a corner walled off for the bath. The furniture was scanty—an ancient round dining table and clumsily repaired chairs, a couch covered by a loose blanket, a recliner chair with the stuffing coming out in great gray gobs where the fabric had been worn through, a portable television set, the beds for Homero and his wife, and for the two small children. The room was almost cold as the night chill penetrated, and Susan sat at the table with Homero and his wife, Dolores, while the children sat wide-eyed in front of the TV in the far corner.

Homero Artiz had not long been out of the shower. His skin was pink from scrubbing and his hair glistened wetly. Dolores, a very young-looking girl with chocolate eyes and long ebony hair, sat with workworn hands twisted together in nervousness.

"I know it's late," Susan told them. "But I wanted to speak with both of you at the same time if I possibly could."

"Dolores has just returned from her second job," Homero said grimly. "But whatever you wish to say, Miss Knight, if you will please tell us now, because we go to bed early in order that I can have an early start in the morning."

"Of course," Susan said nervously. "I know what I want to say might look like meddling, Homero. Believe me, I'm trying to help."

Homero and Dolores waited, watching her carefully.

"Those men who beat you up," Susan began. "They—"

"Again those men?" Homero broke in. "How many times do I have to tell you and others who ask? I know nothing! It is all a mystery to me! Can you not let this thing rest?"

Susan saw that there was no easy way to proceed, so, bracing herself inwardly, she plunged ahead. "We know those men have been blackmailing you, Homero. We have reason to believe that they're doing the same thing to others—perhaps to many of your friends. We want to stop them."

"Homero—"

"Silence," Homero snapped. To Susan he said, "I do not understand any of what you are saying."

"Those two men," Susan went on. "Their names are Phil Dennison and Dave Arnstedt."

At statement of the names, Homero's eyes narrowed sharply, betraying recognition. Dolores gasped and groped for his hand with her own. Their fear was all too clear, and Susan felt a stab of uncertainty that she was doing the right thing. But it was too late to turn back.

She added, "And there isn't any doubt why they're blackmailing you, Homero. You're in this country illegally."

"No!"

"If they turn your name in to the Immigration Service," Susan went on, hating this part of it, "you'll be arrested and sent back to Mexico. You and Dolores, here, and the children."

"No!"

Susan turned to Dolores, almost unable to face her wide, shock-filled eyes. "There's no other explanation. I'm not going to tell anyone. Why hide it any longer from me?"

Homero shot back bitterly, "Why come here and attack us with lies? We are honest people. All because of an accident—"

"It wasn't an accident, Homero! Admit it! I want to help you!"

Dolores put her hand over Homero's clenched fists. "She is right, my husband."

"Be still, woman! We—"

"It is true," Dolores told Susan with grave dignity. "It is as you say. We are not citizens and we have no papers. And we are not the only ones they take money from each week."

"Fool!" Homero said with an almost vicious force. "Can anyone learn the truth from you with a few random words?"

"It isn't a random guess, Homero," Susan told him. "The Hendersons respect and admire you. They want to help. I'm their friend, so I want to help, too. And Rod Poole's only motivation is to prevent this sort of thing from happening to others. We're all on your side. In investigating as best he could, Rod has found that the only explanation for everything is the one you've just admitted."

Homero looked up at her with eyes that were smoky with bitterness and humiliation. "So are we to testify against those men? And be sent back to Mexico?"

"*Someone* has to, Homero!"

"Then let it be someone else! Let us stay here in our new home and make a living for ourselves, and raise our children!"

"Even if that were possible, how do you know someone else wouldn't come along to blackmail or threaten you? How do you know the Immigration people wouldn't discover you anyway? Homero, Homero! Listen to what I'm trying to say to you! Your only hope is to turn Dennison and Arnstedt in, and look for a way to become a legal immigrant, not someone who always has to be hiding and fearing every knock on the door!"

"Do you know what chance I would have getting back into this country by legal means?" Homero asked her. "I need letters from businessmen—sponsors—in both countries. I would need a work record. I would need money—much money. And even after all that was together, if I could ever assemble it all, the papers would go to the government. Months would pass. Years. The papers would finally be lost. Even if this country would allow me to come back, Mexico would not allow me to get out. I know this. I know the story of others. If I go back home, I am doomed to stay there forever!"

"I don't believe that," Susan argued gently. "Arrangements are made every day—"

"Almost all are families who have been here many, many

years, and now have some money and a long record of employment. I do not have these things. The only way I could hope to be accepted would be to go back home, pretend I had never spent these few years here against the law, and hope to be allowed to enter your country on a quota. But it is as I have said. I do not have such powerful friends. I would die in Mexico, waiting, while some public servant held his hand out for one more bribe, saying that this last bribe would make everything all right!"

"If you were to make it possible to arrest Dennison and Arnstedt," Susan insisted, "it would be a very brave act. It would be recorded. The court would be on your side. The law would be on your side. Rod Poole and I know powerful people, and they know others. Mr. Mancini would work for you, I know."

For the first time, Homero showed some sign of wavering. He looked questioningly at Dolores, whose eyes mirrored her pain. "I brought you here for a better life. But we have this fear, those men coming here in the night, attacking me, demanding always more, looking at you with those looks as if their hands were already touching you—"

"It is all right, my husband," Dolores said.

"It is *not* all right! It is a hell! But if I do this thing, we may never have even this much again!"

Susan put her hand over Homero's and Dolores's locked hands on the tabletop. "You could sign a deposition, a sworn statement. Rod Poole could hold this a few days, give you time to get back to Mexico. Once you were there, and safe, he could arrest those two men, and have them punished. Then, at once, you can begin seeking legal entry. We'll help you. We'll never stop working on it until you've returned, free, with no reason to be afraid any more."

"You do not understand how hard it is," Homero said. "We may stay there for all our lives."

Dolores shook her head. "But we would be freeing our friends, my husband. Think of that. They would be freed, too, and would never again have to pay those two men. Think what that would mean to Raphael and—"

"No names!" Homero hissed.

"You see?" Susan said. "You all live in fear. Someone has to take the first step to break it!"

"Why should it be us? Why should we take this chance alone?"

"Because someone must."

Homero sat up straighter, his face a mask. "It is wrong to ask us to be the ones. We have no money, not even a way to get back to Mexico. We have a few things here that we now own. Would we leave them for thieves?"

"I know your car was wrecked," Susan told him, seeing the problem and a solution simultaneously. "Let Rod and me lend you enough money for another car, one that will take you back to Mexico so you can haul your belongings. You can pay me back—"

"We might never have enough to pay you back!"

"I know you would, and soon. Let me prove how sure I am about it by helping you find another car."

Homero stubbornly shook his head. "It is impossible."

"Homero," Dolores murmured.

"It is my decision," Homero told her sternly. "It is my life."

Dolores's eyes flashed. "Yes, my husband. But you are not always at home. You do not know everything. You do not know how this Phil, and this Dave"—she spoke their names like obscenities—"can come here, and you are at work, and they can look at me, talk about the need to raise our payments even higher . . . speak to me softly of how I might make the payments easier for us if I will just be . . . nice . . . to them a little while."

Homero's skin turned gray. His eyes became gashes in his face. "They did this?"

Dolores hung her head. "You cannot always know how they might visit here—try to touch me—and say it will go worse with all of us if I am not more friendly with them— let them—"

Homero's hand shot out and grasped his wife's long hair with savage quickness. He jerked her head up to peer into her tortured face. "They have done this?"

"Yes!" She hurled the word like a dagger.

"You did not tell me!"

"Why should I tell you? So you can seek them out and try to kill them, and yourself be killed? What can I do?"

Homero rose, hauling her painfully to her feet with him. "When they did these things, and said these things, did you—you did not—" He stopped, hanging on the words, his mouth twisted as it worked to speak the unspeakable.

Then he let go of her so suddenly that she cried out softly and sank to the floor at his feet. "No. Of course." His voice suddenly very soft, shook under the force of his emotion.

"You did not. I know this." He turned and looked blankly at Susan. "But they would keep coming back, continue . . . try to convince her, try to touch her, and one day she would be tired, perhaps sick and worried, and afraid, and that day they would come again, asking, touching . . . and she would not say no any more, she would have broken, and to have a moment of peace she would give in—"

"No!" Dolores cried brokenly at his feet.

Homero continued to look at Susan with a terrible calmness, a desolate certainty. "We are none of us saints. One day they would have their way. In everything. And what would I do? I would be old. Broken. Like a geld, powerless—afraid to speak for fear they would *yet* send us back."

Dolores began to sob. The children turned from the television at the sound of the raised voices and weeping, their small, round faces worried.

Homero took a deep, shuddering breath. "Tell your Rod Poole we will talk. I will accept your help. We will go back home."

"You'll never regret it, Homero," Susan said with intense emotion. "I promise you that."

"I pray you are correct about that, Miss Knight. I am very frightened."

4

The last week in July had brought peak tourist traffic to San Francisco, and noon-hour traffic was even heavier than usual around Union Square. A brisk wind coolly whipped the trees in the park, and flocks of blue pigeons stepped quickly to avoid hordes of pedestrians. Traffic—cars, taxis and buses—seemed to circle endlessly, disgorging customers for Gumps, I. Magnin, Macy's, Abercombie & Fitch, and other businesses. Near the St. Francis, a four-man marimba band played a curbside concert and periodically passed the hat. Near the center of the park there was a large crowd, and cloth banners vied with crudely painted placards as organizers of the meeting competed with their hecklers for attention from the media.

At the center of the circular throng, Alfredo Rodriques was packed in tightly by a handful of his aides, reporters, TV cameramen and photographers. A lot of jostling was going on. Portable TV lights sizzled brighter than the feeble sunlight. Cameras whirred and flashbulbs popped. Print reporters scribbled in notebooks while radiomen shoved blunt microphones at Rodriques' face. The wind was cool but Rodriques was sweating.

It was Thursday, the day before the scheduled meeting of growers in the valley.

"Trucks will carry us part of the journey," Rodriques was saying. "Our final leg, from the mouth of the valley, will be walked."

A reporter shoved a microphone closer, almost hitting him with it. "What kind of a reception do you expect when you arrive?"

"Since our mission is in peace, and we plan no disruption, we expect no trouble."

"Do you think this new activity on your part will make a lot of people angry up there?"

Rodriques paused a beat before replying. Over the heads of the close-in media people he could see the milling crowd spreading back into the park. His cloth banners mixed with the hand-scrawled signs of the hecklers: *Go Back to Mexico* and *Commie Rats* and *Wetback Union* and *Never!* Earlier, one of the cloth banners depicting the Virgin had been torn out of the grasp of two women and torn up by a half-dozen young bullies. The police, hanging back on the edges of the park, had moved in quickly to disperse the thugs, but not quickly enough to save the banner.

Rodriques' people had the sternest orders not to respond to any obscenities or challenges. Most of those here in the park with him had been through the Trello war with him, and were acquitting themselves properly—quietly. Still there was tension, a thick ambience that lay over the central section of the park. Violence was never so far away from any public demonstration that pressed any cause other than the flag or motherhood, and guns had struck down men in public life who had done less than Alfredo Rodriques to stir strong emotions.

There would be strong emotions in the valley, too. It was simply human nature.

Rodriques, however, replied to the reporter's question within the flickering of an eyelash: "Our cause is just and we seek no trouble. We have no reason to expect any angry reception."

"You leave San Francisco next week?"

"That's right. With our walking parts of the journey, we plan to arrive in the valley itself a week from next Monday."

"On August the tenth?"

"That is correct."

Several reporters called questions simultaneously, and Rodriques heard three of them simultaneously:

"How many people are you taking?" *and—*

"What are your specific goals in the valley?" *and also—*

"Do you have a local parade permit up there?"

"Local authorities in the valley know our intentions," Rodriques said, responding to the last question first. "The chief of police and the sheriff's department are in contact with our representatives on the scene. A parade permit will be issued."

More voices clamored, but Rodriques ignored them to answer the other questions he had already picked out.

"We expect to take sixty persons from San Francisco to the valley. Most of them are local workers—"

"Local San Francisco workers, you mean?" someone asked sharply.

"Men and women whose homes are in the valley," Rodriques corrected. "*Not* outside agitators. Once in the valley, we will begin an effort to enlist more local workers in our cause, signing petitions for the recognition of our union as a collective-bargaining agent. That is our first goal: achieving and demonstrating the solidarity of the field workers. Once that has been accomplished, we intend to seek an opening of discussions about common interests."

" 'Common interests' may sound pretty good to you," a lank-faced reporter for a local newspaper cut in, "but to my editor it will sound like doubletalk."

A reporter nearby, the bearded representative of an underground paper, showed a broad row of teeth. "Try working for a free press, Mack."

Rodriques ignored the byplay. "Our common interests include recognition of the field workers' union in contracts, bargaining with individual employers over the rights of their workers to wage standards, insurance, humane working conditions and overtime, as well as vacation benefits and retirement, and a discussion of the entire situation surrounding the unique problems of workers who may live in a migratory pattern during part of every year. I refer here especially to problems of educating the young."

A new voice asked, "Have you had contact with growers or vintners up there as yet?"

"Letters have gone out today to all growers and vintners in the area. The letter outlines our plans and goals."

"It's been said that unionizing the field workers will wreck the industry."

"We are reasonable people. Would we try to wreck an industry that supports us?"

"You'll drive prices up. You'll force little guys out. Then the powerful merged companies that remain will beat you just like they beat you down south during the Trello fight."

Rodriques ignored his pulse of anger. "We were not beaten by August Trello. The struggle continues."

"The fact remains that another union represents most of the field workers down there today."

Rodriques located the heckler, a graying reporter representing the Los Angeles *Times*. "Mr. Theimer, you know as well as I do that the Trello struggle is not over. You also know that the field workers today are receiving a better wage, and working under better conditions, than before the struggle began. How can you say we lost when this is true?"

"Are you saying," Theimer responded, "that it doesn't matter what union represents the field workers just as long as they get what they want?"

Again, no observer could have detected the pause before Rodriques' answer. But within his mind flashed a series of images: the first organization meetings and the first confrontation there on the winery road with both August Trello and his sons, Frank and Jules; the arrests; the night rallies; the beginning of the boycott; the cropduster airplane attack; the firing of known sympathizers, and the beatings; the three children found dead in a hit-run incident; the phony negotiations; the rigged elections; the moving in of the other union, the national one, the one whose president dined with Gus Trello and shared country club credentials with him; the pious statements; the affiliation of Trello workers with this second union, and the pathetic contract that finally emerged from the smoke-filled room. And finally the smiling, casual murmur from the scarcheeked representative of the other union as he and Rodriques happened to be standing near one another as the ultimate contract—with its defeat for Rodriques and victory for the national organization—was read to the gullible reporters: *"Tough luck, buddy, but we needed new member dues; we got a tough presidential election coming up, you know."*

All Rodriques said, however, was: "Our union better represents the field workers. Any union which betters their lives, however, is preferable to none."

"Is it true," a voice sang out at the back of the pack, "that you've become a rich man leading this union?"

Blind rage flashed. Rodriques whispered an ejaculation—*Jesus, Mary and Joseph!*—to ask for control. And in response came control at once, from God.

Thankful, Rodriques spoke quietly. "I have no wealth."

"You deny that you have a numbered Swiss bank account?"

Where did all the lies come from? "I deny it because it is untrue."

"You were quoted as saying you would continue this fight until the wine industry gave in, or you destroyed it. Any comment?"

"I did not say that."

"You deny reports you want to hit hard this summer to prove your clout, so you can run for Congress?"

"I do deny that. It is a lie."

"Do you deny you plan to run for Congress?"

"I have no political plans of any kind."

"There were mysterious fires during the Trello thing. Do you expect any mysterious fires in the valley?"

Again Rodriques had to fight his temper. "Our people do not destroy. We had nothing to do with any fires."

"What do you know about the fires?"

"Ask Mr. Trello about the fires."

"Are you trying to imply—"

"No."

The voices clamored again. Rodriques picked out a voice and replied, again mentally sending a brief prayer to his God to help him maintain calm. Minutes passed, and then more. The crowd, if anything, grew. Rodriques felt hemmed in, surrounded, trapped. The odors of tobacco and expended flashblubs mixed with the oily vapor of the hot cameras and the steamy floodlights. He smelled the rankness of his own sweat, and that of others.

The reporters could go on and on, he thought dully. They never seemed to tire. The questioning became a competition among them, to see who could get the next response, who could find a new angle, who could, perhaps, so infuriate the great Alfredo Rodriques that he would break and lash out blindly, destroying his image as a pacifist and a Christian. Now *that* would be a lead; that would be worth waiting around for.

Rodriques struggled not to resent them. It was their job, and they, like all men, were blindly scrambling after the dollar. They served their system. Because they knew he despised their system, and considered it evil, they worked extra hard on him. But they could not break him. They could not stop him, he thought. Only death could stop him.

"Do you deny saying you would demonstrate in the valley regardless of what concessions might be offered to you?"

"I deny it, yes. I have stated our goals."

"What do you say about reports that sixty-four per cent of your organizers are Communists?"

"I doubt it."

"You don't know?"

"They are Christians."

"If it were proven that they are Communists, would that bother you?"

"They are Christian men and women. That is what matters to me."

"Then you don't care if they're Communists or not."

"I didn't say that."

"Do you deny your union had a very large contribution from sources in Cuba?"

"That is not true."

The battering continued. Rodriques hung on, running on adrenalin now, or on the grace of his God. He was weak and slightly nauseated, and on the edges of his vision were dancing yellow sparks—pain sparks, he called them. More time passed. Police broke up a scuffle. Rodriques began to feel a feverish chill, and signaled to Juan Lupé's brother, Pedro, who handed him a paper cup of orange juice laced heavily with sugar. Rodriques sipped the sickening fluid, hoping the sugar would add to his strength.

He was not a well man. Only this morning, two doctors sympathetic to the cause had urged him not to take part in the valley effort. But Rodriques would continue. He did not really seriously entertain the notion that he might simply collapse and die. He had always known that one day he would be a martyr.

Another question came from the crowd: "You knew Jules Trello when he was with his father, isn't that right?"

"That is correct," Rodriques said.

"We have a UPI story today that quotes Jules Trello. He's up where you're going now, you know. The story says Trello says any demonstrator who steps on his property will be shot. It says your movement will die if it tries to fight the valley growers and winemakers."

Rodriques smiled faintly, almost truly amused. "I remember Jules Trello, and the statement is worthy of him."

"Do you plan to confront Jules Trello once you arrive?"

"We confront no one—and everyone. We have stated our goals."

Much later, when the meeting had finally broken up and Rodriques was safely in the back seat of an old Volkswagen, headed for the local headquarters, it was Carlos Murnan who brought up the subject of Jules Trello again. Murnan had come back to San Francisco especially to report and be at the press conference.

Now his eyes were like candle flames. "Did you hear what Jules Trello said about us, Alfredo? Son of a pig! We will see who is destroyed in this battle!"

"We will not fight anyone in the way you imagine," Rodriques replied sharply. "We will struggle for our cause. If you imagine you will start some personal vendetta in that valley, Carlos, you will return to the south."

Carlos Murnan showed slow shock. "Of course, Alfredo. I understand."

"We are not seeking revenge," Rodriques insisted, "and even less, violence. That is not our way."

"Yes, Alfredo."

"Remember it!"

"Yes."

But the outburst worried Rodriques perhaps more than all the pounding questions that had so wearied him . . . more than all the fears he harbored about the struggle that lay ahead. The feelings of men like Carlos Murnan were a simmering bomb, waiting a chance to explode. Rodriques feared such an explosion . . . knew it was only the force of his will that stood a chance of keeping the explosion from coming.

He was, he knew, beginning a journey on a tightrope over a chasm of fire. He felt a new and deeper chill of apprehension.

5

Once Homero Artiz's decision had been made, there was no argument that every action must be taken quickly, to eliminate any chance that his deposition-signing might leak back to Phil Dennison and Dave Arnstedt. They must not be warned that the net was closing around them, and Homero knew he must leave the valley quickly to avoid possible retaliation.

By Friday morning, the brief, secret court appearance had been made, and Homero's part-time employers notified at the last moment. After a painful discussion, Homero agreed to accept a loan of three hundred dollars from Susan Knight. The landlord had not been told as yet, but Dolores Artiz had already quietly packed the family's belongings.

All that remained was finding a car—an action necessarily postponed until Homero's last day of work on Thursday.

When Susan and Rod Poole reached the used-car lot in response to Homero's call, they found him standing in the middle of a field of cracked paving, surrounded by rusty junker automobiles. The car lot was festooned with small red-and-white banners, and a sign proclaimed that this was "Happy Sam's."

Homero, standing beside a rusty red 1955 Studebaker, was not alone. With him was a youthful salesman who introduced himself as Archie. In his mid-twenties, Archie wore red doubleknit flared slacks, white tee shirt with a

217

tiny alligator over the breast pocket, and white belt and loafers. His blond hair was modishly long, and a growing belly pooched over his belt.

"Any friends of old Homero's are friends of mine," he grinned, pumping Rod Poole's hand exuberantly. "When he said he wanted to get your opinion, I said, Why, sure! Great idea! We're proud of all our cars here!"

"I haven't seen a Studebaker for a long time," Rod Poole said, walking around the vehicle. Susan watched, staying out of it.

"Well," Archie replied, "like I said, it's an oldie, but it's a goodie. Homero knows. He drove around the block with me." He patted the front fender. "They don't make cars like this any more."

"I have explained that we plan a trip," Homero said. "I must be sure it will reach our destination." Homero was wholly turned in upon himself, gravely tense but under control. He was pale and his eyes were like old slate. Any watchful observer, Susan thought, would have seen instantly that he was either ill or in some terrible trouble.

Archie didn't notice. "Homero, old buddy, this car will go anyplace. It's a dandy. I'd take this car on the road myself."

Rod Poole completed his walkaround inspection looking grim. "Mind if I have a look under the hood?"

"Sure! Delighted." Archie gave Susan a ribald wink. "There's a little voyeur in all of us, huh?" He untwisted a piece of wire holding the hood closed and then raised the creaking cover.

Inside, the engine appeared to be a black mass of steel sunk in a mud-spattered cavity of wires and tubing. Poole bent to look more closely, poking at hoses and wiring.

"Nineteen and sixty Chevvie engine," Archie explained. "It makes a nice match with the Studebaker transmission, and it's a good engine to have worked on—if you ever need it—because you can always get parts."

Susan watched as Poole completed his brief examination under the hood. He walked, frowning, to the left front wheel. Squatting beside it, he grasped it at the top and rocked the car violently side-to-side.

"Front end is solid," the salesman said. "You know, I believe in progress, but by golly, these old kingpin front ends just last forever. I've got a nineteen and seventy Lincoln Continental over yonder with the ball-joint front end on it, you know, and by gosh I'll tell you the truth, it hasn't held up the way this old car has."

Poole walked to the driver's door and opened it. There was a creaking noise. He sat inside on upholstery that was mainly springs poking through shredded nylon seat covers.

"Get you some new covers for about twenty dollars," Archie said, "and it'll look real nice inside."

Poole's eyes were waxen. "Mind if we fire it up?"

"Key's in it, pahdnuh!"

He started the engine. To Susan it sounded amazingly quiet. He gunned the accelerator a few times and dark smoke gushed from the tailpipe.

"Been sitting too much," Archie said over the racket. "Get her out on the highway, blow her out, she'll be fine!"

Poole backed the car up a few feet, rocked it to a quick stop, and moved it forward, again hitting the brakes abruptly. The car continued to rock and sway, little hourglass streams of rust powder falling out of the fender wells. Poole cut the engine and got out scowling.

"See?" Archie beamed. "Sound as a dollar!"

"That might be an apt comparison," Poole said unsmilingly. "The clutch feels weak, the brakes are mushy, the front end is about half shot, and it wouldn't smoke like that if it didn't need some carburetor work."

Archie turned angrily toward Homero. "Old buddy, is this guy trying to sell you a new car or something?"

"He is a friend," Homero said quietly.

"Well, listen, I don't know if he's acting like your friend or not. He's going to mess this whole deal up for you, and I was going out of my way to give you a break on this fine old car."

Poole said, "The carburetor has to be fixed. He wouldn't get ten miles down the road before he got arrested for pollution."

Archie mopped his face with a moist handkerchief. "Friend, this little booger came in here wanting a car under five hundred bucks. This is the only car we have on the lot under five hundred. We're no fly-by-nights. We've been at this same location for more than three years. We're in business to stay. We don't deal in junkers. This is an old car, sure, but we wouldn't even be handling it if there was anything wrong with it."

Poole looked at Susan. "What do you think?"

"I'm not the expert. It's up to Homero—with your advice."

"Homero?" Poole said, turning.

"If it will go as far as we need to go," Homero said, his face unhappy but stoical, "it is sufficient."

"It ought to be okay if you don't push it hard." Poole looked back at Archie. "But that carb has to be fixed."

"Well, say," Archie frowned. "We're selling this old car as is."

"How much is that?"

"One ninety-nine ninety-five."

Poole raised his eyebrows. "I might have a try at the carb myself, Homero. I've got an idea that's all it is."

Homero looked at the car and then nodded. "Yes. I will take it."

Archie grinned. "That's great, old buddy! Come on over to the office and we'll sign the papers and get you on the way in your new car!"

Susan lagged behind Homero and the salesman for a word with Rod Poole: "I doubt that Homero has much cash other than the loan. This means he'll be going back with a hundred dollars to his name."

"I know it, damn it. But the car isn't too bad, everything considered, and he won't beat the price."

"I just wish he would take more money from us!"

"Well, we've been through that. We've just got to go ahead and cinch the case on those bastards that caused all this, and then get Homero back in again the right way."

Susan did not reply. They followed Homero and the salesman into a tiny metal building into which a desk and filing cabinet were stuffed. There was a faint sun in the sky, and a window air conditioner chugged away. The cubicle stank of cigars.

Archie quickly scrawled in some forms as they watched. Within a few minutes he pushed them across the desk to Homero. "Okay, pahdnuh, sign here and here and over here on this one, and we're in business."

Homero signed. While he did so, Archie punched numbers into a little calculator. Homero took out a worn billfold and looked expectant.

"Fine and dandy, good buddy," Archie smiled. "Just give me your check or cash now for two eighty and fifty cents, and she's all yours."

"How much?"

"Two eighty," Archie said blandly. "And fifty cents."

Rod Poole stiffened. "You said two hundred before."

"It's all on the papers there, fellah. The *car* is two hundred, but you've got these other costs, you know. There's the legal fee, and a title search. Then the notary, and change of registration, plus the pro-rated share on the tags, plus delivery and preparation charges."

"That's ridiculous!" Susan burst out.

"Haven't any of you ever bought a car before?" Archie asked.

Homero stood. "I will not pay this amount."

Archie stood too, his face clouding over in a remarkable imitation of outrage. "You just signed the papers, little buddy. Don't make me call a cop."

"Oh," Poole said softly, reaching for his wallet, "that won't be necessary."

"You stay out of this!" Archie snapped. "What is this? Some kind of con operation? I know a cop. I'm going to call him right now!" He reached toward the telephone.

Poole snapped open his wallet and held it in front of the salesman's eyes. Susan felt a burst of sheer hot pleasure as she saw Archie's mouth fall open.

"Well, now," he stammered, "just a—just a minute there, guy. I was just having some fun, here—"

Rod Poole reached out and grasped the front of Archie's shirt, pulling him halfway across the desk. "Take the man's two hundred dollars, *friend,* and give him a nickel change."

"Yes, sir! Yes, sir!" Archie made a ghastly attempt to laugh. "Gosh, just a little joke, eh?"

Poole said nothing more. The transaction was completed, and Archie, giggling and fawning, handed over the keys. Then he waved to them as they drove away, Homero in the smoking Studebaker, Susan and Poole behind him in the Firebird.

"The God-damned bastard," Poole said. "If we hadn't been there, he would have made it stick."

"How could he, Rod? Just because Homero is Chicano, and didn't read all the figures—"

"It wouldn't hold up in court, maybe, but how often would it get that far? The salesman pulls the trick, then he makes his demand. Then he calls some corrupt cop on the take. The ordinary customer caves in from sheer panic, and pays through the nose."

"I loved it when you showed him your badge."

"Yes," Poole said bitterly. "But I won't be there on the trip south. There will be others waiting to rip him off if they can, and then he'll reach the border, and barring a miracle, he'll run into civil servants, police, army officers—all sorts of Mexican officials corrupt enough to make Archie, back there, look like an angel." He turned to her, his face worried. "I don't know if we've done the right thing here."

"My God, don't say that now!"

"What if he gets arrested on the way, or at the border?" Poole paused a beat. "What if we can't get him back in?"

"We *have* to get him back in!"

Later in the afternoon, Poole was on duty. Susan, however, went back into town just in time to see the family climb into the old car. Its back seat and trunk were loaded with household possessions, mostly pots and pans and bedding. The rear end of the Studebaker sagged low. The children peered out of the back-seat clutter with huge, worried eyes.

Susan leaned through the passenger window to hug Dolores Artiz's shoulder. "We'll see you again—soon."

Dolores nodded and tried to smile. She looked at the small house that had been their home and then bent her head low to try to hide the tears from the children.

Herself almost overcome, Susan forced a bright smile for Homero, behind the wheel. "Write to me the moment you find a place to stay. We've already started writing letters and making calls. It won't be long, Homero. I know it."

Homero nodded soberly. "Thank you, Miss Knight, for all you have done. You will be repaid."

The thought that he was concerned about repaying her at a time like this was almost too much for her control. But Susan maintained her smile until Homero engaged the clutch, and the Studebaker wheezed slowly away and down the dirt alley, the children's faces peering back at her over the mounds of clothing and blankets in the rear window. At the corner, the car turned right and vanished. It was only then, for the second time in the space of less than a week, that Susan wept.

6

The old Moose Lodge, site of the Friday night meeting of the small, independent growers, was in an upstairs area of an old building in a depressed section of the city. A small stage stood at one end of the room with American and California flags flanking a lectern on a table. Bare electric light bulbs extended from a maze of wiring and plumbing in a high ceiling overhead. The bare wood floor was crammed with folding chairs facing the stage. The room was already crowded with more than forty men, and the air was smoky and warm. Bugs splatted on window screens while smaller ones that had gained entry buzzed around the lights.

Robert Mancini, with fellow winemaker Henry Barton, sat on the last row near the door to the stairs, observing. Both of them had called other winemakers, but it had been agreed that more than two observers might be resented. Robert and Barton were to report to their colleagues.

The meeting had been under way for more than thirty minutes. The present speaker at the front table was the fourth. A thin man whose glasses reflected coruscations of light as he moved, he was one of the grower-organizers of the meeting. His name was Overholter.

"With the field-worker union coming in the week after next," he said, his voice amplified by a portable system, "we need to know what our situation really is. I agree with that. But we didn't call a meeting to talk about Alfredo

Rodriques and his people, and talking about him is a mistake, as I see it, in this meeting. We're here to talk about prices and all these rumors. What we need to do first is collect information: go talk to the wineries, find out what their plans really are, and then see what sort of deals we might strike with the co-ops if it comes to that. There's no sense arguing about things we don't have any control over, and I don't see where we'll accomplish anything by losing our tempers just yet."

Henry Barton leaned closer to Robert's ear. "You were right. He's trying to keep it cool."

Robert whispered back, "I'm not sure some of them want it cool."

Barton, clearly worried, nodded agreement.

The mood of the crowd was tense—closed-in, nervous, on the edge of real anger. Fighting words had already been called from the floor, and the second speaker had talked about dumping his grapes rather than selling them below four hundred dollars per ton. While most of the small growers near Robert and Barton had nodded to them with no real hostility, others had sent them harder looks, challenges. The general mood was sullen if not outright hostile. Too much rumor had been in the air, and the growers represented were too much concerned about their futures to stand on ceremony. Robert had expected some of this, but the mood struck him as harsher than anticipated. He did not like this.

From the lectern, Overholter was continuing: "I would move, when the time is right in this meeting, that we set up six committees. Each will have an area of responsibility to collect information. We also set up a publicity committee to make sure everybody gets our message straight."

An elderly grower called from the floor: "I say we vote tonight on the idea of issuing a statement. We tell the world we won't accept prices that are below cost of production and a decent profit."

"Well, that might be all right," Overholter said cautiously. "It's an idea we would have to talk about and then vote on."

Another grower partway back in the hall rose to his feet. He was a big man in a bright plaid shirt, his hair cut in a burr. "What do we do after we collect all this stuff and make all these statements?" he asked as heads turned to identify him. "Hold more meetings right up until the day we start meeting in the poorhouse?"

Many of the men muttered angry agreement. Overholter looked more nervous. "We have to have the facts on our side before we can do anything. Once we have the facts, we can present a united front."

The grower in the plaid shirt remained on his feet. "You'll committee the thing to death. There's only one thing these people understand, and that's force."

"It's too early to talk about force," Overholter said. "What force do we have? We have to present the facts after we determine them —"

"Sure! We form committees while Rodriques comes in here and bleeds us dry."

Robert leaned toward Barton. "I don't recognize that guy from this angle."

"Higgins," Barton replied.

Robert sat back with a soft shock of recognition. Higgins was a Merlot grower who sold to Schreck Brothers. A year ago Higgins had hired a number of new field workers—Chicanos—to plant an additional ten acres of vineyard. There had been some sort of dispute—the facts had never come clear—and two of the workers had been injured when Higgins's pickup truck loaded with fertilizer ran their sedan off the road inside the vineyard. No charges were brought; it had been raining and Higgins swore his truck skidded. The workers and their friends left the area. It was said now that Higgins had no Chicanos in his employ.

Higgins had also been heard from in other ways. Robert could recall a number of angry letters to the editor signed by the man, and there had been stories once about a speech he made at a local rally of a splinter-group political party. Higgins was evidently one of those men perpetually angry about society, changes in the culture, big government, taxes, medicine, alleged corruption in high places, and any action he could envision even remotely as tending to hedge him in. Robert could remember one letter from Higgins which had told the local editor that automotive pollution controls were part of a plot to cut down American mobility and freedom.

He was showing now, however, that he was not a harmless crank. People in the room were listening to him.

"I don't know what the rest of you are going to do,"

Higgins said now. "But if you set up committees and pussyfoot around, you'll be doomed. I've talked to people. I *have* the information. Prices are going to drop out of sight, and people like Rodriques are going to be hitting us with pickets and everything else, trying to force our expenses way up. The only way you'll get anything done is to give the winemakers an ultimatum right here and now."

More voices were raised, many angry, most agreeing. Overholter, the spotlight shifted from his scheduled remarks, tried to get it back. "I don't know what kind of force you have in mind, James, but—"

"I'll tell you!" Higgins called back. "I've already made my move. Do you want to hear about it?"

"Let him talk!" someone called, and others joined in.

"What," Overholter asked despairingly, "did you do?"

"I grow mainly for Jules Trello. I went to him. I told him what I'd do if he didn't give me a written guarantee right here and now on what he'll pay for my grapes this fall. You want to know what he did? He gave me a letter." Higgins paused dramatically. "I *know* what *I'm* going to get paid this fall."

There was an uprush, a general hubbub. No single voice predominated as men talked to those nearest them in surprised reaction. Barton told Robert, "I don't like the way this is going."

Robert said nothing. The idea that prices could be set specifically this early in the season ran contrary to the way things had always been done, and the established way had a wisdom to it. It allowed open competitive bidding, within the framework of contracts if they existed: the best grapes drew the best prices, and the general price structure was dictated by the dynamics of the free marketplace. In their mood now, the small growers might stampede into set prices that stood just as good a chance of hurting them as the wineries. It was a bad idea.

Someone had gotten the floor and called to Higgins, "What price did you get this early?"

"I'm not saying what we agreed on," Higgins replied. "It might not be quite as good as last year, but we all know we won't see prices like last year's again. Let's just say I got a price I can live with."

Barton murmured, "If I know Jules, a low one."

Someone called to Higgins, "What did you tell Schreck

Brothers to get them to agree to it? You talked about using force."

"I didn't use any force," Higgins said. "But I told 'em I would if I had to. That was enough."

"What force?"

"All right. We're in the middle of the summer. Some of you have given your grapes their one midseason watering, but most of you haven't. I told Jules Trello that if I didn't get some kind of a guarantee, the watering could just go to hell.

"I told him," Higgins added over the growing uproar, "the grapes wouldn't get their water, and they'd just sit there, and there wouldn't *be* any harvest this fall!"

The room erupted into a babble of comment that made the earlier outburst seem tame by comparison. Excitement swept the crowd. At the front table, Overholter tried to regain attention. "We can't ruin our crops! What do we get paid if we have no grapes?"

A man who had not previously spoken rose to his feet. "That won't happen! Listen, if Higgins could make Jules Trello knuckle under with a solo threat, what's going to happen for the rest of us if we *all* make the threat together?"

"It's irresponsible!" Overholter replied. "We don't know that it would work, and if they call our bluff, we've committed ourselves to suicide!"

This started the general uproar again. There was disagreement, and Robert saw men arguing nearby, but the general tenor was favorable to the Higgins proposal. The idea was sweeping the meeting before other viewpoints had even been heard. Toward the front, where other individual arguments had broken out, Overholter huddled with two of the other meeting organizers. They were frowning and talking earnestly, obviously upset at this turn of events.

Barton told Robert, "I couldn't give a price guarantee right now! I don't even know if I would be setting the price high or low! If they start talking about not watering, they're starting a war they've got a fifty-fifty chance of losing!"

"I know," Robert said, and then the idea lanced through to him.

A fifty-fifty chance of losing.

Of course.

He understood.

The explanation for the reasons behind James Higgins's suggestion was suddenly as clear to him as if it was an idea of his own. Perhaps no one else in the room would accept it, even if he could have won a chance to try to explain it. But he knew Jules, better probably than any of them. In a flash, he saw the only explanation of why Jules had caved in to an obvious power maneuver by Higgins, a grower whom he already had locked in with a contract.

Jules could only gain by a grower revolt of the kind suggested.

Robert would have bet all he had that Higgins's price guarantee was very, very low. But faced with the rampant rumors of disaster, the grower had grabbed for it in desperation, willing to accept almost anything rather than more uncertainty. Perhaps—though this might be far-fetched—Jules had even subtly *encouraged* Higgins to advance this veritable extortion scheme during this meeting.

If there was a general grower revolt, Jules Trello would capitulate—at a comfortably low price. Because they did not really want to leave their vines unwatered, and because they were scared, the growers with contracts to him would accept.

He would thus be guaranteed low grape prices.

And the other wineries in the valley? The other growers? What if an impasse was reached here and there, and growers were left with no buyers? Couldn't Jules then move in with an even lower offer and get their grapes? Or do as some wineries did—take the grapes and pay whatever price he wished to pay long after the crush?

The more Robert thought swiftly about it, the more convinced he became that he had seen through the game. It was a wild, daring, and even dangerous scheme, the exact kind that would appeal to Jules. The only thing that could go wrong for Jules, really, was for all the other winemakers to capitulate with very high offers, and as Barton had just said, they simply could not afford to gamble high.

Jules himself could not easily lose. If other growers and winemakers might be ruined in the turmoil, Jules's thinking clearly would be that that was their problem, not his.

But even as Robert saw what he knew was the pattern, he knew he could not try to state it here or anywhere else. He saw it so clearly because *he knew Jules;* others did not, and would not understand how it was so typical of him.

Meanwhile, however, arguments continued through the

room. Overholter had made two vain attempts to restore order. James Higgins now had a cluster of excited growers around him on the floor, and was expanding on his proposal.

"We've got to head this off," Barton told Robert now.

"How?" Robert countered.

"I don't know, but we more or less represent all the others we talked to. Aren't we compelled to say *something?*"

Robert did not have time to consider this, in the general confusion, before Overholter managed to be heard over the address system. "If we'll just come back to order," the slender man pleaded, "maybe we can discuss this sensibly."

A man near the side of the room called over the lowering murmur: "I think facing up to the wineries with a watering threat is a lot better than forming committees while our grapes—and us, too—die on the vine."

"Christ," Barton muttered beside Robert.

James Higgins stood again. "I want to say just one more thing."

Overholter wearily nodded because he obviously had little choice.

This time Higgins turned to address the back of the room, and all had their first good look at his broad, stubborn, red and angry face. "We don't just face up to the wineries. We also face up to Rodriques and all his Mexicans. When they come in here, if they start trying to throw their weight around, we don't take anything off of them. If any of them try to march onto *my* land, I intend to protect it by whatever means necessary."

A roar of approval went up.

Robert winced inwardly. The men in this room had been subjected to a steady stream of anonymous rumor about prices, and the advent of Alfredo Rodriques, a largely unknown but feared force, was now imminent. They were frightened about their very livelihood, and the firebrand faction led by James Higgins was about to carry the day.

"I fail to see," Overholter said from the front, "why we have to talk about the Chicano field workers. That's not what this meeting was called for."

"They go together," Higgins boomed back. "We have to make the wineries give us fair prices on one end, and we have to make sure nobody forces our labor costs too high on the other. What ties them together," he added after a dramatic pause, "is that *we're* in the middle!"

Another grower, tall and bearded, jumped to his feet. "I say Jim Higgins is right. I say it's time we stopped messing around and started standing up for our rights! I want to say right here and now that I'm not going to water my vineyard until I get a price guarantee, and I'm not going to let any field workers browbeat me into anything. If any of those demonstrators come in here and try to come onto *my* land, I intend to beat the living hell out of them!"

About half the men in the room were left in silence by this statement, to be sure, but the other half cried agreement that added new shock with its violence. More people were on their feet. At the front, Overholter turned to his colleagues and spread his hands in frustrated helplessness.

"Robert," Barton said sharply, "we have to say something."

"What?" Robert demanded almost angrily, because he agreed but could not think of a proper tack.

"Something. Anything! If they go ahead with this, they'll turn the whole valley into an open battleground!"

Robert hesitated. He was still so numbed by seeing through Jules Trello's plot that he could not think of anything to say—anything he could say which would be *believed*—that might smooth the situation. More voices were being heard. Someone was urging caution and moderation, but three others were shouting him down. The excitement had grown, and was feeding upon itself.

They wanted some guarantee, Robert thought. Only their worry had allowed them to be stampeded this far. They had to have something they could believe.

Then, as suddenly as he had seen the Jules plot, he knew what he had to say.

There was simply no time to consider the possible ramifications. He was on his feet before he even knew exactly how he could express his idea.

Feeling like he was a character in a bad dream, he waved his hand for recognition.

Overholter shaded his eyes with a cupped hand. "Is that Mr. Mancini in the back asking to be recognized?"

Heads turned.

"This is a growers' meeting!" someone called.

"He shouldn't even be in here!" another voice chimed in.

Over the rumble, Overholter countered, "I told Mr. Mancini and Mr. Barton that it's a public meeting, and they could attend. I explained that before we opened.

Seems to me that their presence here shows the same concern about the situation that we all have."

"More like," Higgins boomed, "they're here to spy on us."

"Let the man have his say," someone else suggested to a rising, muted chorus of agreement.

Overholter took the decision to himself. "Do you want to come up here, Mr. Mancini?"

"I can say it from here," Robert called back.

"Let him have the floor!" a man nearby said.

"Order," Overholter said.

Robert waited, his pulse high, and the room began to still. He began: "No one has set prices for this fall. No one can, because no one knows what the crop will be. But I know that most of the rumors about the bottom falling out are just not supported by any facts. There could be a slump, but not a disaster. I think you've been misled by false rumors."

"Do you deny," James Higgins called, his voice loud in the silence, "that the wineries plan to cut prices to the bone because of the overplanting?"

"Compared to a few years ago," Robert replied, "the prices will be low. They may be below last year."

"That's doubletalk," Higgins said.

"We all want the best possible grapes," Robert replied, keeping a tight rein on his temper. "The wineries can't have the finest grapes if the growers aren't making a decent living at raising them. That's basic."

"It sounds," Higgins retorted, "like you're running a charity."

Robert allowed himself a thin smile. "No. If a man raises fine grapes and has good luck with them, I have to pay a premium if I want to get them away from the man who runs the winery down the road. We bid. That's supply and demand. But if a man raises poor grapes, I won't have them at any price. So I'm not pretending I'm a charitable institution. I'm just saying we need each other, and no one is out to cut your throat."

There were murmurs that this made sense, but Higgins was not through. "You people always have it all your way. Now it's our turn to put on some pressure!"

"Three years ago," Robert said, "I paid one thousand dollars a ton for peak Chardonnay. I didn't like paying it.

I had to pay it because that was what the market demanded. *I* sometimes feel like *you* hold all the cards."

"What do we do," Higgins fairly shouted back, "if this cool weather stays on, and we have heavy rot, and you winemakers offer fifty dollars a ton?"

"What do I do," Robert replied, "if my sales slump, and somebody dumps a few million cases of French wine on the open market below my cost of manufacture? We both take our chances, Higgins. That's what it's all about."

"We deserve some kind of guarantee!" Higgins cried with a passion that clearly came from the heart. "What are we supposed to do when everybody says we're wasting our time growing grapes we won't be able to sell for enough to pay our bills?"

A hush fell over the room. It was the crucial question, of course, and every man awaited Robert Mancini's answer. He had to reply now, and it had to be the right answer, one that would give them some assurance that their life work would not be extinguished by economic forces they did not comprehend.

By now Robert knew the assurance he could give. He also knew rather clearly how deep a personal risk it involved. But he had no choice. He had Jules to thank for this, he thought.

"No answers?" Higgins taunted him.

Overholter said sharply, "James, let the man answer."

"I have an answer," Robert told the men in the room. "It's only *my* answer. I can't speak for any other winery."

"An answer on pricing?" someone asked.

"On pricing, yes."

The room became so still that the buzzing of insects, and the sounds of voices outside in an alley, raised in some sort of disagreement, seemed preternaturally amplified.

"No one knows how the season is going to go," Robert told them. "No one has a certain figure on even such basic facts as how many acres will come into production this fall. Everything is educated guess. But I can personally guarantee that no one who deals with Robert Mancini Vineyards will have to accept disastrously low prices."

"That doesn't mean *anything!*" Higgins retorted.

"Listen to me," Robert said. He spoke slowly, to make sure they heard every word: "No one with grapes of the quality we want to buy will be asked to sell them at a price lower than ten per cent below last year's prices."

The silence became prolonged. Faces showed that he had not been clear, that they were struggling to understand the implications of what he had just said.

It was a man near Higgins who spoke. "You come in here and say you'll offer us something, and then you offer us prices ten per cent *below* last year?"

"I'm not setting a price," Robert said. "The figure of ten per cent below last year is a floor. I guarantee that the prices I pay will not go *below* that floor."

This time the words impacted. Voices buzzed quietly but intensely on all sides as growers turned to one another to react. They had come into the meeting thinking in terms of rumors which said prices would fall sixty, seventy, or even eighty per cent below the previous year's levels. The look on James Higgins's face showed that the floor offer was far above whatever he had accepted from Schreck.

Robert pressed his advantage. "Please understand that I am *not* saying I will pay prices *definitely* ten per cent below last year's. I may have to pay *higher* than that. The ten per cent figure is the *minimum* I'll pay—I guarantee it."

It was an unheard-of offer. It was unlikely that anyone in the room had seriously hoped for prices within ten per cent of the previous year. Robert had not wanted to make the statement, but it was hardly a ploy; his budget already allowed for prices ten per cent *higher* than last year's, although every projection showed that that much money would not be needed.

His problem would not be with the finances of the offer. It would be with the reaction he might get from Timmons Corporation when they learned he had pledged a minimum in this way.

"Will you put that guarantee in writing?" someone asked.

"I've made it here," Robert said. "I'll make the same announcement to the press. I don't see how I can make it any more definite than that."

Overholter was flushed with excitement. "That sounds good enough for me."

Higgins retorted, "What if nobody else goes along? What if it's a trick?"

Someone called back, "How can it be a trick?"

"What if nobody else goes along?"

"I can't speak for anyone else," Robert said. "This is my statement only. But I do know this much: the wineries haven't been starting these low-price rumors . . . at least the people I've talked with haven't known *how* the rumors got started. We don't want a bottom fall-out any more than any of you do."

Voices buzzed again, and then Henry Barton was on his feet beside Robert.

"Mr. Barton?" Overholter said.

"I'm a small operator," Barton said, and then had to clear his throat and begin again, louder. "I'm a small operator. What I do probably won't affect many of you. But I heard what Robert just said. I'll go along with it. I can live with that kind of floor. I make the same pledge."

Once more, voices rose in a hushed chorus of surprise. But the tone of the sound was different now, without the angry overtones heard earlier. Even James Higgins appeared dazed, uncertain of how to proceed.

Then new questions came, directed at Robert and Barton. But, again, the hostility had subsided. The small growers were filled with a subdued excitement now . . . a feeling mixed with new hope.

As he answered the questions as well as he could, Robert knew that he and Barton had perhaps taken the first steps toward heading off a confrontation of forces that could have wrecked the industry in the valley. At the same time, however, he was nagged by the recurring thought that Timmons Corporation was not going to like this one bit.

John Endicott had spoken out clearly against quality bonuses . . . had talked about getting grapes as cheaply as possible. This would sound like featherbedding to a man like Endicott, and perhaps to some of his superiors. The worry tugged and grew and stayed with Robert through the remainder of the meeting, and he finally stood in the room afterward, talking with Overholter and a few remaining growers, with a sinking sensation that he had perhaps averted one fight, but could have started a new one for himself.

"If we just find more co-operation like yours," Overholter told him warmly, "we can solve all our problems."

It was at this point that one of the growers who had already left the room suddenly burst back into it.

"Down in the alley!" he panted. "Somebody has had the hell beaten out of them!"

7

Robert followed Overholter and Barton down the rickety wooden stairs to the street level of the building. The grower who had alerted them to trouble in the alley beside the structure had run ahead, and plunged back into the dark mouth of the alley as they cleared the front door. Several other growers stood near cars along the curb, staring, and another man was in the street, talking excitedly to friends who had already started to drive away, then had stopped abruptly as they saw signs of the excitement. Robert saw still another bystander beside his pickup truck, a Citizen's Band radio microphone extended out through the window; he was talking fast over the air, probably summoning some sort of help.

The alley was very dark. Robert jostled against someone coming from the other direction, and heard more shouting behind him. He followed Barton past some trash cans and piles of litter, and then skidded to a halt near the intersection of another alley, where a small security light over a red steel door cast faint illumination on wet bricks.

A half-dozen shadowy figures stood in a ragged circle within the area of the light. As Overholter pushed closer, Robert and Barton followed him.

"Oh, good Lord!" Overholter groaned.

Robert elbowed through the men in order to see.

Two figures lay sprawled on the pavement, unconscious.

One man was on his side, crumpled up with his legs drawn under himself in a fetal position, while the other was flat on his back. Both appeared to be Chicanos, dressed in poor field-worker clothing. A pair of broken eyeglasses was on the pavement. The face of the worker which could be seen was a jolt to Robert: the closed eyes sunken pockets of dark-red fluid—blood—and more blood trickling from his mouth. His shirt had been half torn from his body.

The other man coughed wetly and rolled over. His face was worse than his companion's.

"Call the police," Overholter said huskily. "And an ambulance."

"They already did that," one of the growers said.

"What *happened?*"

No one spoke. The men looked furtively at one another.

Grim-faced, Overholter knelt beside one of the victims. He reached inside a pocket and withdrew the man's wallet. Opening it, he looked at a card in a transparent compartment, flinched, and held it up for Robert and Barton to see.

In the center of the identification card was the garish insignia of the Alfredo Rodriques organization.

"They were trying to climb the fire escape to listen in on the meeting," a man in the shadows said hoarsely. "Some of our guys caught them."

"And did *this?*" Overholter cried.

No one replied.

Overholter's face worked, ghastly in the slanting light. "I heard noises out here while the meeting was still on! Who was outside here? Who did this?"

For a moment no one spoke, and Robert thought they would maintain silence; they would not reveal the identity of the attackers if they knew it, and he imagined for a few seconds that they would say nothing at all.

Then, however, someone replied: "Someone saw some men running. Someone else came back here to investigate. That's all we know."

"Was it some of our group?" Overholter demanded.

"We don't know," the same man said. "No one saw anything clearly enough to say."

"It was just shadows," someone else said.

The men now here, Robert thought, had not done this. Nor would they. If they did know who the attackers had been, however, they would never reveal the faintest clue. One stood by one's own kind, rightly or wrongly. Whether it was true or not that the two Chicanos had been trying to spy on the growers' meeting might never be known for certain. Just as the growers, even if they abhorred this beating, would stand by their fellows if they had recognized them, so the Chicanos, evidently Rodriques organizers, would stand by their story . . . whatever it might be.

It was not merely a terrible factionalism born of the threat of a valleywide demonstration or strike. It was also, Robert thought, a kind of racism. And it demonstrated starkly that whatever might have happened upstairs, a frightening potential for disaster remained.

Sirens sounded in the distance. Overholter, shaken, walked with Robert and Barton back to the mouth of the alley where now more cars idled with lights and engines going, and more excited small-group conversations continued.

"It shouldn't have happened," Overholter rasped, his eyes reflecting quicksilver headlights. "If some of our people did this—!"

"It might have been someone else," Robert said, trying to spare Overholter some of his anguish.

Overholter did not reply. Around the next corner came a police car with lights flashing and siren loudly running down. Following close behind came a white ambulance. The two vehicles rocked to a halt beside cars already double-parked. Two policemen sprang out and ran toward the alley. White-clad technicians erupted from the side and back doors of the ambulance, withdrawing a stretcher.

"I'll talk to them," Overholter told Robert and Barton. "There's no need for you to stay."

"We will if you want us to," Robert said.

"No. You've done enough tonight." Overholter blinked rapidly several times, struggling to re-establish calmness. "I hope to contact you the first of the week, gentlemen: both of you. We have a little newsletter, and your guarantee should be made a special issue. Anything we can do to keep things calm—well, we're all in this together."

Robert and Barton walked to the car. Robert drove, and as they headed back into the valley, they discussed the meaning of the meeting and the actions they had taken, as well as the savage scene they had found in the alley afterward. Barton was subdued, worried. They agreed to make as many telephone calls as possible over the weekend, notifying their associates of what had transpired.

"I hope," Barton said, worried, when they sat in the driveway of his house on the valley floor, "people don't think we went off half-cocked."

"That's a risk we took," Robert pointed out.

Barton held out his hand. "I'll be in touch Monday, if not before."

The handshake was firm and meaningful. Their action together had cemented a friendship.

Once he was alone in the car and headed north on the empty highway, Robert asked himself if the decision he had made in his own mind following the beating discovery was a rational one. He could not be absolutely certain. He felt physically and emotionally drained. But if he was to take the next step that his instincts urged him to take, it should be taken tonight, and at once, despite fatigue and lateness of the hour.

Mentally he again reviewed the things that had been said, and his conclusions concerning them. He felt sure of his ground. The idea of confronting Jules Trello on this was not pleasant, but benefit might come from it.

It had to be done.

When he reached the road that led west to the remote hillside area where Jules had built his house, Robert turned off and went in that direction.

The road ran straight for a mile or two through vineyards, then began to curve and twist as it rose from the valley floor. Trees and rocky outcroppings replaced tended fields, and only every once in a while did the car headlights pick up a mailbox or a house set back in the dense vegetation. When Jules had built his new home five years earlier, he had selected a magnificent site, a high shelf midway up the mountain, and he had bulldozed a fine old acreage of Chenin Blanc to provide the space. His house, while not on the scale of his father's, was very grand indeed.

Set well back off the twisting mountain road, surrounded by woods, it was sternly traditional and very large. Three stories in its central wing, it extended outward, north and south, in lower sections. Brick, stone and redwood, it presented a long array of brightly lighted windows casting faint shadows down onto the enormous curved driveway serving a front porch with massive pillars as impressive as any seen in the Old South. Off to one side was a multiple-car garage area, but Jules's white Lincoln was parked in front.

Robert parked, walked to the front door, and pressed the door button. He could not hear the chimes inside. It was still, and a night bird called.

The door swung open, spilling light out of a massive, traditional foyer rich with oriental rugs and huge mirrors. Carole Trello peered out at Robert. She wore a floor-length white peignoir and gold mules, and had a glass of white wine in her hand. Her eyes widened when she recognized her caller.

"Oh, my goodness!" she murmured, smiling. "Is Baby *surprised!* Is it really *you*, Robert?"

"Is Jules home, Carole?"

Unsteadily she stepped back, gesturing airily for him to enter. "Goodness! What *fun!* Baby hasn't seen her nice Robert for *ever* so long!" Spilling a little wine from the carelessly held glass, she moved against him and tried to kiss him on the mouth. "Yum. Daddy is up in his office somewhere, ever so far away." Her eyes taunted him. "Are you sure you came to see *Daddy?*"

"It's important," Robert told her. For no good reason he felt a great anger toward her, which he tried, badly, to hide. Once at a family function, when she was very drunk and they were alone, Carole had forgotten—or neglected —her baby talk and pretense of stupidity. Some of her essential bitterness had spilled out. She was not a stupid woman, and deep within her was a simmering hatred of herself for the vacuous creature she played   out of fear, lack of confidence in herself, or as her ticket to continued comfort as Jules's possession. On that occasion, when the suffering woman underneath briefly surfaced, Robert had tried to become her friend. As if terrified at the prospect of anyone knowing her real self, Carole had instantly become seductive—very seriously so, and not merely with her usual playful act—thus quickly repelling him. Since that time she had never failed to throw up the sexual smokescreen the moment they were alone, for protection against any further threatening overtures toward revelation of her real self. It sickened Robert, and never failed to anger him.

"I understand," she said now, her laughing eyes somber beneath the mask, "that Audra has left poor Robert."

Robert pointed toward the elaborate intercom station imbedded in the wall. "Will you tell Jules I'm here, please?"

She sighed and went to the station. Her crimson-tipped, helpless hands flicked switches with the precision of a computer technician. A yellow light flashed at her.

"Daddy?" she cooed, bending nearer the microphone-speaker.

"Yes?" Jules's voice rasped back.

"Someone is here to see you. It's Robert."

"Who?" The tone said he had understood, but didn't quite believe.

"Robert, Daddy. Robert Mancini. He wants to see you."

"I'll be right down." The yellow light went out.

"Come into the living room," Carole said, breezily leading the way with a flourish of a long golden arm that rattled a dozen thin bracelets.

The living room was enormous, open two stories to a cathedral ceiling, with a great fireplace on one wall, a sunken, sumptuously carpeted area before it, and a wall of glass looking out onto a large lighted swimming pool and patio area. Tiki torches glowed brightly on a sloping lawn surrounded by tall trees and shrubbery.

Carole glided to one of the white leather couches near the fireplace and dropped onto it. It was a movement that combined the wanton and the carelessly graceful, and more of her wine spilled. She crossed her legs, allowing her gown to fall open to a point almost at her hip. Pretending unawareness of this, she held the wine glass high and waggled it. "Will nice Robert-Wobert give Baby more wine, please?"

He went to the corner bar and took the bottle of Fumé Blanc from its ice bucket. He was pouring the wine for Carole, ignoring the cat's leer of her eyes, when Jules strode in.

He was wearing a blue jumpsuit and house slippers, and reading glasses perched incongruously on the end of his nose. He grinned, donning his stranger act. "Robert! Long time no see! You're a sight for sore eyes! I know, because seeing you has made my eyes sore already!" He removed the reading glasses and slipped them into a pocket.

"Robert-Wobert was giving Baby more wine," Carole singsonged. "Wasn't that *nice?*"

Jules looked down at her. "Jesus Christ, cover yourself up."

"Daddy," Carole moued, "he's just *family!*"

Jules turned back to Robert. "Has something happened to my father?"

"Nothing like that, Jules. I'm sure you would hear sooner than I if there were any news like that."

"Not if Frank had his way," Jules grunted. Then he frowned and stared harder. "All right. What do you want?"

"I went to the meeting of the small growers tonight," Robert said.

"That doesn't concern me."

"That's where you're wrong, Jules. That's why I came by. I think this concerns all of us."

Jules put his hands on his hips and glared. "You know, I'm pretty busy, and I don't remember issuing you any invitations lately. Do you want to spit it out so I can get back to work?"

"Gladly," Robert said, and briefly explained what had been said at the meeting, and the action he and Barton had taken. As he told it, Jules looked first bored, then surprised, then incredulous and angry.

"I don't know what any other wineries may do," Robert concluded. "But I intend to stick to my pledge on that floor."

"Is that what you came here to tell me?" Jules demanded. "That you made a God-damned fool of yourself and took a big step toward bankrupting your business?"

Robert was conscious that his fists had balled. "Not really. What I wanted to say to you specifically is this: You don't seem to realize how incendiary the entire situation is; we all need to pull together to keep things cool."

"Are you trying to hint that I started any of those low-price stories? Because, if you are—"

"I'm not hinting at it, Jules. I know you've been the source of most of those rumors."

"You—!"

"You've also been tacitly encouraging hotheads like James Higgins," Robert added. "And I came here to try to show you how dangerous that course of action is—to tell you that you'd better cut it out right now. You might think you stand to cut a little bigger profit, but it could backfire on you and everyone else."

"Don't threaten me, you son of a bitch!"

"I'm not threatening you, Jules. I'm trying to make you

see how dangerous these games really are. That statement to the press about Alfredo Rodriques was stupid—"

"Stupid! You—"

"Stupid. There's no way statements like that can help the situation. All they can do is fan the flames. And this deal you made with Higgins, after his threat on watering, was just as bad. You *knew* he would start trying to instigate a valleywide grower rebellion along the same pattern."

Crouching, Jules Trello looked like a wild animal about to pounce. His tawny hair bristled, his lips had curled back, cords stood out like cables in his neck. "Now you listen to *me,* motherfucker. Don't come up here again with your sermons. Stay out of my business and stay out of my way. I had you pegged the first day I saw you sucking around my father, trying to use Audra to get in . . . take over. I'm sick of your holier-than-thou attitude. Even at long range, you make me want to puke. Get out. And don't come back."

Breathing shallowly, fighting the anger with all his strength, Robert moved toward the door and the foyer beyond. "I warned you, Jules. Don't bring destruction down on all of us. Stop the rumors. Stop some of your incessant maneuvering, in the name of God. This is far too serious."

"No wonder Audra left you," Jules sneered. "If your sermons get any worse, you ought to start wearing a Roman collar." Then Jules's eyes suddenly became crafty and pleasure-filled, which should have warned Robert that the next words would be filled with the finest kind of cruelty.

"Although," Jules added, smiling, "if you put on a Roman collar, I suppose you'd have to do a better job of hiding that nice new extracurricular cunt you picked up down there at the newspaper—"

Whatever he might have said next was lost. Robert's control flew to pieces. He turned back, and was down the three steps into the living room again before Jules could react. Robert's fist connected solidly on the point of his chin, with a solid, meaty shock that traveled all the way back into his shoulder. Jules was propelled backward, falling into a lamp table. Lamp, glass objects and table went flying. Carole leaped up and screamed. Jules plunged to the floor at her feet, his face a red smear.

Robert turned and stalked from the house. He started

his car in a frenzy of continuing anger and dawning regret. He pulled away from the house just as Jules appeared in the front door, with Carole being dragged helplessly as she clung to his arms, fighting with him.

Jules had something in his right hand. Seen in Robert's rearview mirror, it might have been a handgun.

Robert drove onto the hill road and descended with reckless speed. A deep and primitive chill spread through his body, replacing the heat of his anger, and then he found that he was almost helplessly shaky as reaction set in.

A gun? Yes, he thought. In that instant, Jules would have killed him. People died that way . . . including people ordinarily closer than he and Jules. The instant of passion was past now, and there would be no new attempt to use a gun. By now Jules was perhaps thanking his luck that such an attack had been averted.

But if the new outburst of rage would fade, the new and intensified hate would remain. The only good thing that had come from the meeting, Robert thought, was that Jules had had his warning.

The worst, on the other hand, had to be that Jules *knew*. He had obviously been referring to Barbara Turner. And if Jules knew, the word would spread; one could be sure of that, since the information could only harm Robert and Barbara both . . . and perhaps hurt Audra even more.

8

On Monday, August 3—one week before the scheduled march of Alfredo Rodriques' forces—word of the price floor offered by Robert Mancini and Henry Barton became general knowledge. A local radio reporter first heard of it and contacted Robert on Sunday, during an informal meeting with several other winemakers about the same information. By agreement, complete facts were given to the reporter, and he held up broadcast for almost twenty-four hours to allow other wineries to hear it first from Robert and Barton.

Shortly after the broadcast, Barbara Turner was on the telephone.

"I *know* you were swamped with work Saturday and Sunday," she said, her voice rich with intimate irony. "But we did talk on Mr. Bell's invention, didn't we? Or did I just imagine it?"

"I'm sorry, Barb," Robert told her seriously. "On Saturday I just couldn't let it out yet, even to you. And on Sunday I got mousetrapped into a deal with the radio station to allow us a few more hours for private discussions."

She sighed theatrically. "I could say something about gentlemen who take advantage of ladies, but I won't."

Her voice filled him with a memory of their lovemaking. They had not yet spoken directly of it since the night they had so urgently and blindly gone to a motel, and there discovered in each other something they had each imagined would never be theirs again. At that time they had made no promises; she had hushed him when he even tried to speak of the experience. Then had come the meeting, the pressure-packed weekend.

"I didn't tell you about it because I couldn't," he said now. "But there was another reason, too—something else that I have to tell you in person and not on the telephone."

"About the offer you made?" she asked. "Or—?"

"About . . . something else."

"I see." Once more she sounded amused, and enormously happy. "We seem to have business and pleasure getting mixed up here."

He could not refrain any longer, in fairness, from telling her about Jules Trello's angry remark. "I'd like to see you for lunch," he said.

"My deadline is two o'clock. Can we make it earlier?"

"Eleven?"

"Fine. Shall we meet?"

"Come here," he told her.

"Fine," she said, the smile in her voice. "But . . . Bob?"

"Yes?"

"You sound awfully grim. Is something very badly wrong?"

"I'll tell you when you get here, Barbara. All right?"

She said it was all right.

He had a full and hectic morning. There were production problems to iron out with Mike DeFrates, and a conference with Susan Knight about another blending. Susan told him about the Homero Artiz situation, up to date: the family was perhaps even now nearing the Mexican border. Robert dictated several letters to congressmen whom he knew well, and called a small Mexican winemaker of his acquaintance to tell him about the situation and solicit any help possible at that end. A little before eleven, Jim Young came in with some requested sales reports, and Robert had to be very gentle, recalling Young's flare-up at Susan Knight, when he found a pair of uncharacteristically sloppy mistakes in Young's shipping orders. Then Barbara Turner was late, and Robert had a chance to glance over the newspaper, seeing a small item that said police still had no leads in the mysterious beating of two labor union organizers for the Alfredo Rodriques group; the two men, the item said, were scheduled for release from the hospital on Monday.

For the sixth or seventh time in two days, he called the August Trello mansion long distance, and asked for Audra. It was Jill who answered this time, but she was as crisp and distant as Loretta had been on Saturday, and Frank on Sunday: Audra could not come to the telephone; yes, Audra would be told that he had called again.

Barbara Turner arrived at eleven-twenty.

She came in gaily, hugging her notebooks and purse, her eyes alive with a subdued excitement and pleasure. "I asked for an early appointment and then got hung up at the office. I'm sorry, Mr. Mancini." Her smile made mockery of her formality. In lavender, a color he had not seen on her before, she was somehow brilliant—elfin and exotic, girlish and womanlike—all at the same time.

Robert closed the door to the office. As he walked back past her chair on the way to the desk, she looked up at him expectantly. He knew she anticipated a touch or a kiss, some sign. He went stiffly past her and behind the protective desk again.

Her expression faded. "You were going to tell me about the price floor."

Hating the situation, Robert began at the beginning and explained all aspects of the grape-price situation. Although two winemakers had made it clear in strictest confidence that they disliked and mistrusted the kind of situation Robert and Barton had announced as their own policy for the fall, the others had endorsed it as a way of soothing tensions. Inadvertently, Robert had become a spokesman for the group. As he explained details to Barbara, suggesting other winemakers she might call for their own comments, he realized that he had put himself in the forefront of whatever conciliation efforts might follow. Whether he willed it or not, he had become a leader, and when the Rodriques forces arrived, he might be forced to continue in the same *ad hoc* role. It was not a prospect that pleased him.

Throughout the interview, however, the other matter nagged at him. He was both relieved and more tense when finally it was apparent that Barbara Turner had no questions. It was precisely noon.

"I have to rush," she told him, snapping the notebook closed. "I'm not quite used to deadline pressure yet. I'll need a miracle to get this written in time."

She did not need the turmoil of what else he had to tell

her, he thought; not when she faced a close deadline. And he welcomed a chance (coward's chance, he thought) to put off the telling a while longer.

"There's another matter," he said. "Can I see you this evening?"

"Yes," she said simply, without question.

"May I come by your house?"

"Jimmy will be there."

"That's all right, if we can talk alone."

She frowned slightly, sensing his tension. "Of course we can."

They agreed that he would meet her at 9 P.M.

After lunch, although full publication of the price-floor story would not come for a few hours yet, proof of the wide impact of the radio report came with a telephone call from John Endicott.

"Bobby, we've got this crazy news story up here in Portland," the Timmons vice president began. "It's *wild*. Gawwd damn!"

Robert braced himself. "What does it say, John?"

"It says you and some dingdong named Barton gave a bunch of growers some kind of fall price guarantee."

"That's right, John. We did."

"*What?* Gawwd damn! That's ridiculous! That's not good business! What the hell happened to make you do something like that?"

Robert outlined once more what had happened at the meeting and what his motivation had been in making his offer. He left mention of Jules Trello out of it.

"Listen, Bobby," Endicott told him then, "it won't work. It's a bad mistake. A real bad mistake, and I mean it! I'm already getting severe reaction up here from the higher-ups. I thought we had *sure* made it clear that every organization associated with Timmons was supposed to maximize profits this quarter. And then you come up with *this* deal! I don't know how I can justify it!"

"We did what we thought we had to do on the spot to prevent much more serious divisions and a potential for real disaster," Robert said. "I just explained that."

"Bobby, I can see how you could think that way, I sure can, believe me. But we've got this tight situation up here. I'm on your side all the way, like always. But this is going to put a lot of heat on both of us."

"The chances of prices being above the guarantee were

about a hundred per cent anyway," Robert countered. "With this weather, I don't really think we risked much at all. And the benefits—"

"Bobby, boy! You tied your own hands! Listen to me: I want you to retract that offer right away, before it gets any wider distribution."

"That's out of the question," Robert said sharply, surprised that Endicott would come so close to a direct order that he would have to challenge.

"Don't tell me it's out of the question, Bobby! Listen, I told you, I'm already getting heat from the big wheels up here. Now, if you know what's good for you, you'll rescind that guarantee, and fast."

Robert paused and took a deep breath. He had thought a crisis over final control here had been skirted with the early release of the house wine, and ducking of the question of authority concerning Jules Trello's bulk wine. Now, he thought, the issue of ultimate authority might be right back center stage again, and in a basically more angry situation.

He did not want such a confrontation. His attorneys had managed to pick up a few more loose shares of stock that were floating around in the market, but his math was still uncertain. If he forced Timmons Corporation to the wall— or they him—he had no assurance that he could win.

But he had known this at the moment he stood in the old Moose Lodge, hadn't he?

He had. Only this actual moment of the first step in confrontation was unexpected; he had imagined a letter, and a meeting in the board room.

"I can't retract my statement, John," he said. "It's the right thing to do, and it doesn't threaten us with real financial loss."

"Bobby, I've got to take this to the higher-ups."

"I understand."

"Do you want me to stall? Do you want to think about it till, say, six o'clock tonight?"

"No, John. I made up my mind the other night."

There was nothing more to be said and the call was terminated.

Other business kept the remainder of the afternoon busy. Shortly after six, he tried again for Audra, and again was refused contact by telephone. The evening paper carried a full, bannered account of the price-floor guarantee, and the telephone began ringing incessantly as friends and business associates called with varying reactions. When he left his empty house to head for the city and the longed-for, dreaded talk with Barbara about their discovery, he had to walk out with the phone ringing yet another time.

It was Jimmy Turner who met him at the door when he reached Barbara's home just at dark. The boy's mouth was turned down in a sulk.

"My mother is changing clothes," he told Robert. "She yelled for me to tell you she'll be right in."

Entering the house, Robert noticed a card table set up in a small space between the television set and a chair. Jimmy had set up the blueprints and pieces of a plastic sailing-ship model, and evidently had just begun gluing the keel to get started on the construction. Elton John was on the record player as usual.

As Robert walked over to look down at the model pieces spread all over the table, Jimmy turned the record player off.

"Tired of Elton John tonight?" Robert asked with surprise.

"No, sir," Jimmy said glumly.

"Why turn it off, then?"

"I just felt like it."

"I kind of liked that song that was playing."

"You say that," Jimmy replied sharply, "but it isn't true."

"Why would I say it if it isn't true, Jim?"

"Just to try to be nice to me. But I don't want you being nice to me."

Robert turned back to the model. "This is a dandy."

Jimmy said nothing.

"Going to be hard to build," Robert said.

Jimmy maintained his silence.

"I built a model something like this once," Robert said. "It was fine until I got to rigging all the lines and making the sails. Then it was the biggest mess I ever got myself into."

Jimmy plumped into a chair and started looking at a magazine.

"If you ever need any help on this," Robert told him patiently, "let me know. I sure learned a lot the hard way, by messing one of these up."

The boy looked up from the magazine, his eyes hard. "I

don't need any help from you, sir. Thank you just the same."

"Jimmy," Robert said, "I want to be friends."

"We can't be friends."

"Because I've been taking your mother out?"

"You're already married. I may be just a dumb kid, but I ain't *that* dumb."

It was a soft shock. "Sometimes people don't stay married, Jimmy. Sometimes they change and want to . . . be friends with someone else."

Jimmy's spiteful eyes were hard and angry. "We don't need you. We don't want you. You just mess up our life."

Robert tried to think of the right thing to say. Possibly there was no right thing. Still he tried to think of something, wishing everything could be different.

Barbara walked into the room, interrupting them. She had changed from whatever she had been wearing into a bottle-green knit-shorts suit and white tennis shoes that made her fine legs look trim and athletic. "Sorry. I had to unstick a garbage disposer and had grease and gunk all over me."

"Did you get it fixed?"

"I think it was a draw. It came unstuck and I came unglued simultaneously. Would you like some coffee?"

In the kitchen they sat with their coffee cups at the table. Barbara watched him, her happiness shining in her eyes, but the tension there, too. Again he had not touched her.

"What is it?" she asked directly, and at once.

He plunged in, telling her what Jules had said. He tried to gloss the exact words. Her face tense, she pressed and forced him to say exactly what Jules had said, and what had happened next.

"I don't know when we were seen," he told her, "or how. But if Jules knows, everyone will know. Jules will make sure of that. He never wanted me in the Trello family, and he'll delight in knowing the rumors are everywhere locally."

Barbara took a deep breath, her expression solemn. "I'm sorry, darling," she said.

"Don't say you're sorry," he replied quickly. "I'm the one who owes any apologies. You've done nothing wrong. I'm the one who came into this dragging unfinished business."

"But you're also the one with much to lose. I explained that to you before."

"Barb, let's not talk about guilt or loss. That won't get us anywhere."

"But this does change everything, doesn't it?"

He did not fully understand what she meant. He said, "I've been trying to call Audra. I have to talk to her now."

"What will you say?"

"I'll tell her she was right. It's over. Our lawyers can talk then."

"A divorce?"

"Yes, a divorce," he said angrily. "Of course. There can't be anything else now."

She studied his eyes with intense care. "Is that what you want?"

"There's no other solution. It's obvious."

"But is that what you *want?*"

"Yes."

"You're lying," she told him.

"I'm not lying."

"You are. You're still not sure. You still don't know. You spent your whole life thinking marriage was forever; you told me that. And now you can't change overnight, any more than she can. I think she is just as ambivalent as you are."

He reached for her hand. "Barb—"

She pulled away from him quickly, almost brusquely. "No. We have to be different now. We just can't continue as if nothing had happened. I just couldn't stand that."

"I don't understand what you mean," he admitted, trying to read her. "We're the same. We feel the same."

Her eyes glistened. "People knowing—people whispering and leering at us behind our backs. I thought that would be all right, too, but I see now that it isn't. That all makes everything we do sneaky . . . nasty."

"What are you telling me?" he demanded.

"Bob, you just have to . . . work things out. With your wife. I never thought I would be a bitch, but I discover I am a bitch . . . I *am*. We just can't see each other until we both know what the ground rules are going to be."

The words struck with the force of a sledgehammer. He had expected almost any other reaction. But as the surprise hit, he saw at the same time that she was right— exactly and intuitively right, without question. Something inside him wanted to strike her for being so damnably right in this.

"I've been trying to get Audra on the phone," he said, his voice husky with the complex of feelings that assailed him. "I'll contact her. I want a divorce. I'll work it out."

"If you really want that," Barbara insisted. "I'm not saying this to push you—to hurry you. You're not committed to anything with me. I made that clear from the start."

"I *am* committed to you!"

She stood, her eyes averted. "I think you'd better go. I have a big day tomorrow."

"Is that all we're going to say about it?" He was newly astonished.

She gave him a brief, grave smile. "Hey. What else is there?"

"Can I call you?" he asked miserably.

"Not for a while . . . okay?"

They faced each other across a space of four feet, a space that might as well—now—have been light years. A dozen things leaped into his mind to be said, but they were all incoherent. He ached with wanting her. She had given no ultimatums; she had said what she said only for her own self-preservation, and he knew this. He was, if he wanted it so at this instant, free of any obligation to her. He could walk out and never return, and there would be no hint of recrimination from her. She had faced the death of one man, and it had made her strong enough that she could now offer him even this.

He reached for her, and, before she could resist, pulled her close: their bodies brushed, her fragrant hair wisped across his lips. Then just as quickly he stepped away from her again.

"I love you," he told her. "I'll be back." He walked out of the room and out of the house.

9

Although it was very late when he finally knew exactly the things he had to say, Robert placed still another call to August Trello's mansion. Standing alone by his telephone in the darkened house, looking out at distant lights in the valley below, he listened to the other telephone ring a number of times. *It happens this way,* he thought: *not very dramatically; after more than twenty-five years.*

A male voice answered the Trello telephone: "Trello residence, good evening."

"Cline?" Robert said, recognizing the aged servant's voice. "This is Robert Mancini. I have to talk to Audra."

The servant paused a beat, and Robert distinctly heard the soft click that betrayed another instrument being picked up somewhere in the Trello house. Then Cline said, "I'm sorry, sir. My instructions are that Mizz Audra cannot answer any calls."

"All right," Robert said angrily. "Just give Audra this message, please. I'm coming down there tomorrow to see her. I intend to see her. This is a very important matter and I plan to stay there until I do see her. Do you understand? Will you please make that clear?"

It was Audra who replied on the extension. "That's all right, Cline. You can hang up."

"Yes, ma'am," Cline said meekly, and the line clicked as he discreetly lowered his receiver.

"Audra?" Robert said, his pulse thick in his throat.

"Yes?" Her voice had an arctic quality.

"I want to drive down there in the morning. We have to talk. I've been trying to call—"

"We have nothing to talk about now, Robert."

"No, that's where you're wrong. We have to settle some things."

"I've heard about your whore, Robert," she told him tonelessly. "If you want to talk about her, I'm certainly not interested, being a very conventional Trello, as you've often pointed out."

Robert's teeth gritted audibly, but he managed to keep his voice modulated. "Audra, you were the one who said it was impossible. I'm *home*. You walked out. Fine. You were right. We have to talk about this. We have to settle it."

"Settle it?" she repeated with a challenging lilt.

"We can't go on this way. We both know that. We—"

"Oh, but that's where you're wrong, Robert. Of course we can go on this way. As a matter of fact, for right now that's exactly what we're going to do."

He closed his eyes. The bitter, taunting quality of her voice rang in his ears, and he tried to cope with it and understand what she was saying. "We have to talk about a divorce," he said. "It's time. Maybe it's long past time."

"You even think you can end our marriage wholly on your terms," she responded. "But it isn't going to be that way. I'm not sure I've decided anything just yet. So don't waste your time coming down here. I know how you detest having to rub elbows with all the lower-class Trellos. And we have nothing to discuss at this time."

"Audra, I want a divorce."

"Oh you do, do you! And am I supposed to fall over myself getting to court to give you a divorce, just as I was always supposed to run to cater to every other whim? Am *I* supposed to hurry because you have a whore you want to legitimize? No. I won't talk with you. Don't try to force me. And I'm *not* going to rush into a divorce, Robert."

She paused then, venom dripping with every word, as she resumed.

"You've given me sufficient grounds. I know all about it from Jules. You've humiliated me. So now it's my turn. I'm going to *think* about it. I may think about it a long time. In the meantime, you're not free. If you want your whore, it's going to be adultery and everyone will *know* it's adultery. How terrible for your many admirers, Robert: Sir Lancelot has a flaw, after all!"

"Audra, Jesus Christ! You were the one who walked out. Now can't we at least have the decency—"

"Don't call me," Audra told him with savage sarcasm, "I'll call you." Then she hung up.

10

The crossing point between the United States and Mexico, on the road Homero Artiz had chosen, was also the place where a small, modern city met a ramshackle primitive village. On the American side, the wide streets were lined with cheap eating establishments, service stations, motels, and the inevitable insurance offices. A broad grass median between parallel streets on opposite sides of the border marked the international line, and in its center, straddling the north-south road, were the flag-decorated olive-drab sheds that marked the United States and Mexican checkpoints.

Homero and Dolores had been silent as he drove toward the border point, the two children solemnly poking their heads between them from the platform of bedding and other goods piled high in the back seat. Now the old Studebaker wheezed as Homero pulled away from a traffic light and started the last hundred yards.

"It would have been better at night," Dolores said now. "People drive back and forth more freely for shopping in the early evening, I think."

"We could not know the car would get too hot," Homero told her. "It had to be repaired. We have many miles yet to go."

"We could wait until this evening."

"Woman, it is already Tuesday morning. We have been

delayed too long. Besides," he added to reassure her, "we will have no trouble."

"We have no proper papers."

"It is is of no consequence."

Dolores frowned her worry, but did not reply. Homero whistled a tune to show her worries were groundless.

As a matter of fact, he was far more tense than he was willing to show. Although he knew the first checkpoints were a formality, open to allow normal commerce between the two communities facing each other across the border, he also knew there would be other stations farther inside Mexico. One would be the more serious customs station, where those seeking to go deeper into the country were thoroughly checked. And beyond that, at any point, might be an army checkpoint. Homero feared them in ascending order, because he believed he could get through the normal customs by telling the simple truth; the army checkpoints, however, were both more corrupt and more dangerous, and there a bribe probably would be sought.

Homero was in no condition to bribe anyone. Gasoline and repairs to the radiator had left him less than twenty dollars in his pocket. Half of this would be needed for a few more gallons of gasoline to allow them to reach the ocean village where Dolores' sister lived. They would be arriving virtually penniless at best.

Hiding this, too, from his wife and children, Homero put the Studebaker in low gear and eased up to the American side of the checkpoint behind a hulking Pontiac with tourists inside. The American customs agent waved the Pontiac through, glanced in at Homero and his family, and waved him on through as well. A few paces away, the Mexican gate was raised and the guards were waving traffic through with even less inspection.

Homero drove slowly under the raised gates, and they were back in Mexico. The old car bumped through a series of chuckholes, connecting rods and exhaust system rattling hollowly. A gaunt dog ran yipping across the street, and an old man pushing a fruit cart walked out from a curb as if no traffic were in sight. Homero turned right at the first street, following the sign, and they were plunged into a narrow, shabby canyon of decrepit buildings, streetside shops, packed sidewalks, and canvas-shaded peddlers' stands.

Dolores took a sharp breath, but said nothing.

The heat beat in on them. Homero knew it was illusion —that it was not really hotter on this side of the border. But he felt as if he could not get enough air. He had an impulse to shove down hard on the accelerator and ram through the cars and bicycles blocking the street ahead. He wanted to scream.

Patience, he told himself.

Rosita, the smaller child, began to cry. Dolores leaned over the seat, murmuring comfort.

Beyond the edge of the village to the southwest there was another checkpoint. Here the gates were down, and the border guards were more carefully inspecting a blue Volkswagen, containing two Americans, that had been stopped in the sparse hot shade of an overhanging roof. Homero pulled up behind the Volkswagen, and a plump guard with a waxed mustache walked self-importantly toward him.

"Good morning," the guard said, leaning to look in through the window.

"Good morning," Homero replied, also in Spanish.

"You have been visiting in the United States?"

"Yes, that is correct."

The guard glanced over the possessions piled high, the children, Dolores. "What is your destination, please?"

Homero gave him the name of the village.

"You are planning to take up residence there?"

"Yes, sir."

"Your papers, please."

Homero handed him the automobile registration, his driver's license, and the temporary insurance.

The guard looked them over. "Your other papers, please," he said impatiently. The blue Volkswagen had been waved through and two more cars were behind Homero now; the guard wanted to hurry him on his way.

"I have no other papers," Homero told him.

The guard scowled.

"Look," Homero said, "we have been working in the United States this long time."

"Wetbacking?"

"Yes, sir."

"Oh." The guard shrugged and signaled a colleague at the gate. He stepped back and waved Homero through.

Breathing again, Homero drove through and into the countryside.

"You see?" he told his wife. "We have no problem."

The country beyond the checkpoint was barren, strewn rocks and cactus and occasional heat-blasted trees in eroded ravines. Homero drove slowly, keeping a close watch on the temperature gauge, which now seemed willing to behave itself. After a long time, he stopped for gasoline and they all had a Coke. He drove on into intensifying afternoon heat, and the road he had chosen became gravel and then dirt.

It was a far cry from northern California, this land of his birth and childhood. Along the heat-shriveled roadway they met farmers and young boys plodding along, barefoot and carrying their hoes over their shoulders on the way from one field to the next. An old man tottered along, bearing a backload of sticks that reached three feet over his head. In a village, women stood with cans and urns around a community spigot in the square, and small children rolled and wrestled in the deep dust at the foot of steps leading into a white Spanish-style church more than four centuries old. In the country again, the road became more traveled, and paving resumed. A very old Ford truck, its back piled dangerously high with crated live chickens, passed with a toot of its horn. A green bus came from the opposite direction, and for an instant Homero and Dolores were looking into its crowded interior, where men and women sat, stood, hung to straps, jostling and weaving with the vehicle's motion. On top were suitcases and crates and a number of dogs strapped down with the other paraphernalia. They passed a little cemetery, very old, with the tombstones tilted and fallen down, and out in front of it a young woman stood wrapped in her colorful shawl, holding an infant. Now and then there was a little cornfield, but most of the land lay empty.

Homero drove for a long time without seeing another car or person. The children slept fitfully and Dolores also dozed.

She awakened with a start when Homero began braking. "What is it?"

Homero pointed ahead.

Five army trucks and a jeep were parked along the desolate stretch of road, two trucks and the jeep on one side, the others opposite them. Flags flew from masts on the trucks, cracking in the hot wind. There were soldiers in some of the trucks, and others up and down the road. They had rifles. Some of the noncoms and the one officer in view, now waving for Homero to pull in behind his jeep, carried automatic weapons.

"What do they want of us?" Dolores whimpered.

"It is all right, it is all right. It is just an army checkpoint."

Homero pulled in at the spot designated and shut off his engine. The officer, a captain, walked up to the car, a sergeant and a corporal following. Soldiers stood around idly, casting looks at Dolores.

"Your destination, sir," the captain, a young man, snapped.

Homero told him.

"Your papers."

Homero handed over what he had.

The young captain squinted at them and handed them back to the sergeant behind him. "A United States driver's license?"

"I have been a wetback," Homero said, willing to swallow his pride and use the verbal shortcut if it would get him through.

"I see." The captain frowned. He looked inside the car. "You have guns?"

"Guns? No, sir!"

The captain held out his hand. "Fifty dollars."

It was so direct and outrageous, after the other things that had happened to strip him of funds, that Homero barked a laugh.

Before he could speak, the captain blinked furiously. "Twenty dollars," he amended sternly.

"I have no money," Homero said.

The captain glanced into the car again, seeing the items in the back seat. "This is contraband."

"These are our home things!" Homero said. "This is a mockery! Let us go through, please!"

The captain took a step back and motioned to the soldiers. "Let him pass."

"My papers," Homero said. "That sergeant still has my papers."

"Twenty dollars," the captain said.

Homero got out of the car despite Dolores' attempt to hold him back. In the direct rays of the sun, standing in deep dust beside the broken asphalt road, he held his hand out to the captain. "Please. I have no money. We are poor. Give us our papers and let us go."

"Ten dollars."

Seething, Homero took out his billfold. He took out the bills that remained. "I have nine dollars."

The captain snatched the bills from his hand and shoved them into his pocket. "You said you had no money and then you have nine dollars. I think you are a liar." He scowled more deeply. "I think you have guns and contraband. Sergeant! Have the men search this car."

The sergeant barked an order. A half-dozen soldiers put down their rifles and approached the car. One of them opened the door on Dolores' side. She shrank back from his gaze.

"Dolores," Homero said shakily. "Get out of the car. Help the children out, too."

Dolores obeyed. She stood with the children in the tufted grass beside the ditch and watched as the soldiers started handing things out of the back seat. The pots and pans were placed on the dirt, along with the blankets and other bedding. The suitcases came out, and two men opened them and rummaged through. The pile of possessions began to grow as more was taken out and put on the roadside.

"This is wrong," Homero protested through set teeth. "We are poor people and we have done nothing wrong."

The captain ignored him and only looked off into the hot distance, as if greatly preoccupied or bored. Homero fought a wild impulse to leap at him. He knew what the penalty for this might be. The men might be army troops. They might also be a band of guerrillas only masquerading as army in order to shake down any who passed. It really made no difference. Whether they were outlaws or corrupt soldiers, any attack on their authority would have the same result: probable death.

Homero tasted bile as a soldier opened the trunk of the Studebaker and took out more blankets, another pasteboard suitcase, a paper bag of children's clothing, the electric coffee pot, a small radio, and finally, from the back where it had been packed most carefully of all, the portable television set.

"Ah!" the captain said. "Contraband." He barked another order. His corporal hustled to the rear of the car and picked up the TV set and the coffeemaker.

"What is he doing?" Homero asked unbelievingly.

The corporal walked to the nearest truck and handed up the two items.

"Is there anything more?" the captain called.

A soldier inside the car held up Homero's Timex watch, which had been hanging from a knob.

"Bring it," the captain said. The soldier complied. Into the officer's pocket went the watch.

Then he turned back to Homero. "You are partly blocking this highway. We will give you five minutes to pack these things and be gone."

"My papers," Homero said, fighting an angry urge to weep from sheer frustration.

The officer made a careless gesture, and the sergeant handed Homero the papers.

Homero's control broke as he and Dolores, with the children vainly trying to help, threw things back into the car. His breath sobbed from his lungs. No one would have been foolish enough to try to take a gun past a checkpoint, but he wished he had a gun now. He would have given everything for one gun and one bullet, and a clear line of sight on the captain's sneering face.

When the goods were packed, they got back into the car. The soldiers stood back, their dark faces impassive. The captain turned his back and looked grandly off toward the horizon. Homero backed away from the truck, engaged the gears, and creaked around it.

It was another three hours before they reached the village of Dolores' sister. There was a glad, tearful reunion between the women, and the children began at once exchanging stories and running around and around the tiny adobe house. Homero crept away, feeling like an animal that had been wounded and needed solitude to lick the wounds.

He found a place on a wall behind the hut. It was taller than the surrounding buildings, and because the settlement was on a hillside, he could look down to the vast blue of the Pacific.

Turning his eyes to the north, he could see the distant smudge that marked San Diego. By straining his vision, he saw—or imagined he could make out—the sprawl of the city's downtown buildings, and its harbor. It was a beautiful view over many miles and over centuries of progress.

It was also so close, yet so far. Homero wondered if he would ever get back.

Part Three

1

When the marchers of Alfredo Rodriques began their trek
northward into the valley, they were closely watched by
both the press and the general public. The man who was
destined to be among their most severe antagonists, however, was nowhere nearby. As the garish banners of Workers United neared the wine country, a fat commercial
jetliner was depositing Jules Trello in Chicago for his
crucial meeting with Carmine D'Angelico.

By transferring funds through several accounts to make
his personal finances appear more stable than they actually
were, and by a personal appearance before a bank board,
Jules had won a thirty-day extension on the deadline for
payment of his first Elmhurst note. A week of the extension had already passed, and it was vital to sell the bulk
wine to D'Angelico immediately. As a taxi took Jules
through the sweltering Chicago heat toward a hotel near
the Loop, he mentally re-examined his last telephone conversation with his quarry, and decided that there had been
no hint of his desperation in making the arrangements for
today's meeting. This was vital too, of course, because he
had to get a good price, not give the wine away.

His Accutron showed two fifty-eight local time when
Jules reached his hotel room and peeled off a sweaty coat
and shirt. Stretched out across the bed, he consulted a
leather-bound notebook and dialed the number of D'Angelico's local firm name, Pricewell Enterprises.

The switchboard operator put him through promptly to D'Angelico's office. The woman who answered there, after consulting notes or something, transferred the call to someone named Connie Livingston, D'Angelico's personal secretary. Jules announced that he had arrived late from San Francisco, but still hoped to see Mr. D'Angelico today.

"Mr. D'Angelico is in a meeting that's likely to run on quite some time now, Mr. Trello," Connie Livingston told him. She had a breathy, intimate voice.

"It's pretty important for me to conclude our business as soon as we can, to allow me to head west again," Jules told her. "I can stand by here at the hotel for your call back the moment he's free." This was pushing, all right, but it was important to show that he couldn't be left waiting indefinitely like some office errand boy.

"I'll certainly give Mr. D'Angelico your message, Mr. Trello. And possibly he'll see his way clear to get back to you sometime after four."

Jules wondered what the girl looked like, if her appearance was as tantalizing as her telephone voice. "I'll stand by, then," he told her.

"Of course, sir, if you prefer, I could reschedule you now for ten o'clock tomorrow morning."

"No, I'd rather see him today if at all possible."

"All right, then. But I know it won't be before an hour. At least that will give you time to relax a little after your flight. If you're like me, all you really want to do after a long airplane flight is just curl up in a nice hot bath and relax a while anyway."

"Well, by gosh, Connie, I might as well do that. I don't know a soul in Chicago and there's sure not anything else to do."

"Ah, that's really a shame, it really is." Was she smiling, having picked up the first hint from him? "I'll tell you what. You have your nice warm bath, and I'll call you back between four and five to tell you what Mr. D'Angelico said about meeting you."

Of course she was paid for having a sexy voice and a warm manner, Jules told himself as he showered and shaved. It was simply good PR.

Nevertheless, he realized that her voice had stirred him. He was far from home, and that almost always was a turn-on in itself. It had been a long time since he had felt much stirring of sexual interest. For whatever reason, with

Carole or anyone else, he simply couldn't function unless the relationship was either very, very new or very much a business proposition. Let a woman show any sign of emotional involvement, and he was finished instantly. He had thought about the chances of finding a prostitute here in Chicago, because with that kind of woman he always functioned very well indeed, there being absolutely no threat to him in such a cold transaction. But now he found himself wondering if by any wild chance he could use Connie Livingston instead.

It was a far-fetched daydream, but pleasing. He nurtured it, imagining what she looked like.

Probably five feet tall and two hundred pounds, he told himself.

At any rate, he would likely see her soon enough. He was ready for Carmine D'Angelico, and expected to get in yet today.

Since first contacting the wholesaler-shipper, Jules had tried to do more homework on D'Angelico and his domain. His research had uncovered scant new data. D'Angelico was a man of much mystery. He had his fingers in international shipping, in the wines of three continents, in Las Vegas hotels, in land development in Florida and New Mexico, in the manufacture of plastic toys for children. Many of these operations, as far as Jules had been able to determine, were quite small, and could not account for D'Angelico's reputed wealth and power.

Jules had concluded from his research that whispers about underworld connections must be true. He could not be certain. In his only previous business transaction with D'Angelico, both of them had been middle men for anonymous combines transferring title to a huge tract of land in south-central California. Within two years after Jules concluded his part of the sale of the land, a mammoth government project had sprung up nearby, and D'Angelico's buyers had reaped profits by selling tract homes in an area theretofore relatively worthless. It was possible, therefore, Jules believed, that the man's ties extended also to high places in government.

This was fine as long as the present wine transaction could be brought off with everyone happy. It did, however, give Jules some nervous qualms; he knew the red wine he hoped to sell was not only of poor quality, but not really the Cabernet he had advertised. He was taking a risk in trying to dump it on D'Angelico. The risk had to be faced because time was running out and no other prospective buyer was in sight with enough money to make it worthwhile for Jules.

Shortly after 4 P.M., the sultry-voiced Connie Livingston called back to say that D'Angelico could meet with him at five.

When he left the hotel for the short ride to Pricewell Enterprises, Jules carried with him a black attaché case containing two bottles of the unlabeled Elmhurst red. He had bottled these himself, using an old hand machine. The wine looked good in the bottle, ruby-colored and clear. When opened, it would emit a thin but satisfactory bouquet. It was only in the tasting that the wine would reveal itself, showing its poor pedigree in a thin, tart flavor with a slightly bitter acid aftertaste.

Jules had considered substituting some better Cabernet for the Elmhurst wine, but had rejected the ploy as far too risky. Carmine D'Angelico was no wine expert, but he knew his wines in a general way because their import and export, and wholesaling, were a part of his business. Jules wanted desperately to sell this wine, but nothing was worth the price he might pay if he tried to dupe D'Angelico, and then was caught at it.

The taxi deposited Jules in front of one of those tall glass cubes which had begun to transform Chicago into a miniature Park Avenue. The Lake Michigan breeze whipped flags in a nearby plaza. Jules entered the Pricewell Building, consulted a locater board, and entered an elevator which whisked him to the thirty-sixth floor.

The outer office on the executive floor was handsome but starkly utilitarian, with metal walls and plain tan desks. The first receptionist sent him down a hallway to a second, and the second sent for a secretary who led him through more corridors into a portion of the building where the walls were paneled and the beige carpet felt several inches thick. In this small waiting room, seated on a leather couch, and quite alone, Jules waited about five additional minutes.

A door opened into the room then, and a young woman came out. She was tall, Jules's height, with dark hair and a stunning figure. She moved like a model, and there was something very exotic about her.

"Mr. Trello?" She smiled. "I'm Connie Livingston."

"Of course you are," Jules grinned. "I knew that."

"Oh?" She appraised him frankly. "How did you know?"

"You look like your voice sounds—thank goodness."

"You're sweet. Will you follow me, please?"

Jules followed her down another corridor, enjoying the opportunity to examine her exceptionally nice legs. When they entered another office, much larger, with a huge desk and tasteful paintings on the walnut walls, he thought for a few seconds that it was D'Angelico's. Connie Livingston, however, gestured him to a couch and went behind the desk to sit down in a way that showed clearly this was her place.

"It will be just a few minutes," she assured him. "Would you like anything? Coffee? A highball?"

"Coffee," Jules smiled. "I want a clear head."

She pressed a button on an intercom. "Two coffees, Cynthia." She turned her startling eyes back to Jules. "I want you to know that I've enjoyed many of your wines. It's a pleasure for me to meet you in person."

"The pleasure is all mine," Jules said. "No kidding. I'm really glad to be here." He did his double take. "Where am I?"

Connie Livingston held crimson-taloned hands in front of her mouth and laughed. "You're *funny!*"

"Well, not really," Jules told her. "Nervous is more like it. I'm as nervous as a general in peacetime. I'm as nervous," he added, encouraged by her giggle, "as an eskimo in a steambath. I'll tell you one thing, though: when the going gets tough, the tough get going. Truman Capote."

"You *are* funny!" Connie Livingston beamed. "I think that's just grand. Here you are, a winemaker, at the hands of fate and the weather every year. And you have a sense of humor. That's wonderful."

"I need it," Jules assured her solemnly, "in my business."

"But the risks you're forced to take," she breathed, watching him. "The uncertainties!"

"There are times when only risk will bring results, Connie."

Her eyes were warm. "Of course."

The messages were going back and forth steadily. Jules, despite the tension he felt over the meeting with D'Angelico, was stimulated by this girl. He knew he had little time and he felt reckless.

"And speaking of risk," he said, "I'm going to risk rejection. I wonder if there's any chance you might go out with me tonight."

Connie Livingston smiled with obvious pleasure, then turned her full lips downward in a pout. "Raincheck?"

"I plan to go back to California tomorrow."

"Pooh," she said.

"So if you have another date," he added, "break it. Go out with me instead."

"That's sweet," she smiled. "I'll tell you what. Can I think about it while you're in with Mr. D'Angelico?"

"Of course," Jules told her. "If we finish here in time, we can go to dinner and a show. If my talks with your boss run later, we can meet after the business is over—whatever time that might be—for a nightcap."

A door opened. Another young woman entered with two cups of coffee on a small silver tray. As she was placing them on Connie Livingston's desk, a light flickered on the intercom. Connie picked up the telephone. "Yes, sir?" She listened, nodded, hung up.

"I'm afraid the coffee will have to wait," she sighed. "Mr. D'Angelico is ready for you now. Will you follow me, please?"

Jules got to his feet and picked up his attaché case containing the wine. His nerves were strung tight. He followed Connie Livingston out of her office and down the hall.

2

Carmine D'Angelico's office was long, narrow, and furnished entirely in dark shades and heavy textures: mahogany-colored shag carpet, deep walnut paneling, blood-red draperies which allowed no outside light whatsoever, black leather furniture, a large gray glass coffee table, bookcases of velvety ebony finish. D'Angelico's desk at the far end of the room dominated it: broad, very heavy, with ornate carving on the sides and edges.

With the exception of a small lamp turned low on a table in the corner near the door, the only illumination in the room came from a massive brass lamp on the edge of D'Angelico's desk. Its bright white chimney cast a pool of illumination over the paper-cluttered work surface, and shone upward into the face of Carmine D'Angelico himself.

He was a rather small man, so perfectly dressed in black suit, white shirt and dark-blue tie that he appeared like a window mannequin. This impression was heightened as Jules approached the desk by D'Angelico's eerie stillness. Not a finger moved, only his intense black eyes. He made no sign of rising to shake hands. The light showed an intense pallor of his skin, making of him a figure of charcoal slashes.

Connie Livingston said, "Mr. D'Angelico, this is Mr. Trello."

"We've met," D'Angelico said. "Sit down, Jules."

Connie said, "Will there be anything else now, sir?"

D'Angelico's eyes did not leave Jules's face. "Out," he told the girl.

She left, her movements silenced by the thick carpet. Jules heard the door close softly.

"So," D'Angelico said. He still had not moved except to blink his eyelids, and he seemed to radiate a chill. "Your plane was late but we meet now. Let's get to business."

"It's a real pleasure to be here," Jules cracked. "Where am I? Well, let's talk. A little talking never hurt anybody. Richard Nixon."

D'Angelico showed no sign he had heard. "You have this wine."

Jules swallowed and dropped the act. "Yes."

D'Angelico moved for the first time, picking up a gold pencil which he poised over a pad. "Cabernet Sauvignon?"

"Yes. I also have some Pinot Chardonnay and Riesling—"

"Is the Cabernet any good?"

"I brought two bottles with me if you would like to taste it—"

"Not yet, not yet. I don't know if I'm that interested. How much of this Cabernet have you got?"

"A little over eight thousand cases. It's still in bulk now, but it's ready to bottle, and that's how much it will make."

D'Angelico jotted the figure. "That's not very much. That's hardly worth messing with."

Jules tried to hide his astonishment, and a stab of greed. "It's a lot for me. We're not Gallo, you know."

"I know you're not," D'Angelico replied with a trace of sarcasm. "I'm just surprised you would come all this way to talk about this little amount of wine, that's all. What made me think you had more than that?"

"I don't know," Jules said nervously. "Maybe I didn't make it clear."

"Maybe you didn't," D'Angelico agreed. "The question is, is it worth my time messing with eight thousand cases."

"I suppose I could come up with more. We have a lot of wine in the Schreck inventory—"

"No, no Schreck wine that's already labeled or anything like that. What I'm looking for is good bulk wine that I can put whatever label I want on . . . with the understanding that whatever label goes on, the seller forgets he ever saw it. Do I make myself clear?"

Jules tried to summon a sick smile in the face of D'Angelico's saturnine expression. "I understand perfectly."

Whatever use Carmine D'Angelico had in mind for the wine was not, then, necessarily a legal one. It might be sales under a counterfeit label, or possibly blending with some other lesser bulk varietal. Jules had been given sufficient signal here and now that they were not discussing a normal transaction—that he was accepting a known risk if he proceeded. He understood this. But he had to proceed.

"Yes," he muttered nervously. "I do understand, as I said. Perfectly."

D'Angelico jotted a tiny checkmark on his pad. "How much white wine do you have?"

"Five thousand, five hundred cases. Also in bulk now, most of it. Most of it is Chardonnay. I estimate about a thousand cases of Grey Riesling."

"So you have thirteen thousand five hundred cases total."

"That's correct."

"If you sell me this wine," D'Angelico said casually, "your records will show that it was spoiled and destroyed."

Jules stifled his sharp intake of breath. The water was becoming deeper. Falsification of control and sales records would remove the last vestiges of legality from the transaction. Now he would be lying to the state of California, to the federal government inspectors, to the FDA and IRS.

This development hit him deeply with a new and growing fear. What if he were to get caught? It would be he who falsified and lied, not D'Angelico, who could always claim, if questioned, that he had not known anything of Jules's internal bookkeeping. And he would be the one punished, perhaps ruined.

Then Jules considered the other side. Was he not already on the brink of ruin if he couldn't sell the wine? Did he have *any* prospect besides this man who so blandly suggested breaking the law as a condition of the sale?

And there was one other matter, Jules thought suddenly. If the records were falsified—if it was so important that no accurate accounts were kept—then the income could never be traced. Whatever he got for the wine would be free and clear, *with no tax payment*.

It was an added dimension of possible gain, and counterbalanced Jules's nervousness.

"I'm sure I can handle the records to everyone's satisfaction," he said, amazed at the calm sound of his own voice.

"You're sure of that?" D'Angelico asked.

"Yes, I'm sure."

"Well, maybe I'm interested, then. You don't have as much wine as I hoped for, but you seem willing to co-operate."

Jules nodded eagerly, and then his own negotiating sagacity motivated him to counterattack. "My co-operation, of course, is dependent on our reaching a satisfactory price for the lot, and a cash down payment of one hundred thousand dollars against the total on or before the thirty-first of this month."

D'Angelico raised his eyebrows. "We would want all of it bottled, crated and on its way before the end of the month."

"Good God! I don't know if I could manage that!"

"If you're not ready to sell wine, why are you here taking my time?" D'Angelico tossed his pencil down in disgust.

"The wine is in the old Elmhurst cooperage," Jules explained. "You have to understand that I can't very well haul it over to my own line to process it. It has to be filtered and bottled there at Elmhurst. The machinery is old and some of it is probably broken down. I won't have many men I can put on the job, if we're to maintain security."

"Don't tell me your problems," D'Angelico shot back. "Assuming we can agree on a price, I want the wine ready for delivery in two weeks. Now, can you deliver or not? I'm a busy man."

"We can't even get labels printed that fast!"

"Don't worry about labels. Who said anything about printing labels? I can get the labels to you within a week. Come on, Trello. Let's not waste more time. Can you deliver, or do we call it a day?"

Jules squirmed. He did not know how he could bottle and label so quickly, using the skeleton force he would have to employ to work the old Elmhurst equipment. But he had to have this sale.

"I'll make the deadline some way," he said.

D'Angelico smiled coolly. "All right, then. Let's taste the wine. You said you have some in that case? What have you got?"

"I brought the Cabernet," Jules said, bending to open the case.

"Let's try it, then," D'Angelico said impatiently.

Feeling the sweat on his forehead, Jules produced one of the bottles and a caliper-type corkscrew. He extracted the cork and took his time wiping the mouth of the bottle, desperate for any extra moments he could give this thin, tart little wine to breathe and expand. Placing the bottle on the desk, he got out two plastic glasses.

"We really should let it breathe a few minutes," he said.

D'Angelico flicked a finger at the glasses. "Pour."

Jules obeyed. At least the wine managed to look good, very clear thanks to the extra filtration, and a ruby color. "If I had been sure you might be interested in the whites, I would have brought them, too. I can assure you they're very high quality. The Riesling has a very big nose, very pleasing fruit."

Ignoring him, D'Angelico picked up a glass of the bogus Cabernet. He held it to the light, inspecting it critically. He swirled the contents and sniffed rapidly, deeply, with his nose in the glass. An expression of distaste flickered over his face, and then he raised the glass to his lips.

Jules, forcing a smile, joined him.

The wine was bad, he discovered to his dismay—worse than it had seemed in the pipette drawn up out of a barrel. It was very thin and tart, with an unpleasant after-image of bitterness. D'Angelico, judging by his expression, was forming the same conclusions.

Jules licked his lips with gusto. "Well, it does need time to breathe, no question about that. Some youthful Cabernets are like that, as I'm sure you know. Give this little wine another few months in the bottle, and then let it breathe for an hour or so before drinking. Or better yet, decant it—"

"Nothing is going to help this wine, Jules," D'Angelico said, putting the glass down and wiping his lips with a handkerchief.

"You mean you don't like this little wine?" Jules asked, feigning astonishment.

"It's shit."

"Carmine! It's not a *fine* wine, but I think you're being too hard on it. I really do!"

"We won't debate that. You pretend what you want and

I'll know what I know. How much do you want for the stuff?"

The quick change of pace threw Jules for a loss. "For the red? You just said you didn't like it, and now you—"

"For all of it," D'Angelico cut in. "You said you have thirteen thousand, five hundred cases total. Okay. Eight thousand Cabernet, about forty-five hundred Chardonnay, about a thousand Riesling. One price, the whole thing."

Jules plunged into the attaché case for his notebook. "I have it broken down into a price for the red and prices on each of the whites."

"I don't want that. If I'm buying, I'm buying it all. Now you tell me a price per bottle or per case or in one chunk for the lot. That's the way I do business. I don't mess around."

"Let me figure just a minute or two."

D'Angelico smirked and leaned back in his chair.

The silence was oppressive. Jules rushed through some figures which made no sense to him whatsoever. This man went too fast for him—had him at a disadvantage, and knew it. Jules would have preferred to go more slowly, moving in on the negotiation a little at a time so he could feel his adversary out.

Now, however, there was no time for that, and he was under the added burden of knowing that D'Angelico recognized the poor quality of the red wine. He had to come up with a price that was high, to allow for bargaining, but not so high that his tactic was too obvious. What should this be?

Originally he had thought of brazenly asking for four dollars per bottle. He knew, with the little wine in front of him, that this was impossible. Should he ask three-fifty? He wanted to ask three-fifty, but knew he had no chance. He could ultimately go as low as twenty-two dollars a case and still be all right, but he hoped for much more. What figure to start with?

D'Angelico was waiting. The pencil drummed.

Jules looked up. "All right. Of course we have a differential between the red and the whites, and that's hard to figure, but I have a ballpark figure here that I think I could live with. That's for a single lump-sum payment for the entire shipment."

D'Angelico stared at him, unmoving again.

"Three dollars," Jules said.

"Three dollars for what?" D'Angelico spat.

"Three dollars a bottle," Jules said, trying not to quail. "Or let's say thirty-three fifty per case. I'm averaging, you see. That's a fantastic bargain on the Cabernet, three dollars."

"Ten cents," D'Angelico shot back at him.

"What?"

"Ten cents."

"I don't understand."

"You want three dollars? I offer ten cents."

"Ten *cents*? That's preposterous!"

"So is three dollars."

"Carmine, listen to reason! I can't *give* this wine away!"

"You have to bottle and cork," D'Angelico said coldly. "I supply the labels, but naturally you have to paste them. You have to put the bottles in plain pasteboard cartons, sealed. There's nothing more for you to do."

"What about delivery?" Jules asked, sparring for time to think. "Where do I deliver?"

"My trucks come pick up. You have no delivery costs whatsoever."

It was a sharp relief. This did make a difference. Jules felt a new eagerness to co-operate and get it settled. This man frightened him. "I didn't realize there would be no delivery."

"Figure it over," D'Angelico urged.

Jules busied himself with his pencil again, but as before, the figures were only a charade. He had asked for thirty-three fifty. He could go as low as twenty-two. Lack of delivery costs allowed him to shave that figure, but there was all the risk and the problem of getting it done so quickly. How low did he dare to go?

D'Angelico began drumming his pencil again.

Jules looked up. "I can go as low as twenty-five dollars a case."

D'Angelico put his hands flat on the top of the desk as if to shove himself to his feet.

"Twenty-four," Jules offered desperately. "I simply can't go lower!"

"I grow weary of this," D'Angelico said. "My top offer is ten dollars."

"Ten dollars!"

"My final offer. Take it or leave it. I'm a busy man."

Jules's brain spun through dismayed arithmetic. It was

less than half his minimum, below a third of what he had hoped. Adding bottling costs, it was a ridiculous price, one he truly could not afford.

"I want to sell the wine," he said thickly. "You know that. But there's a *limit*, Carmine! You must see that!"

D'Angelico pressed a button on an intercom and got to his feet. Even as he did so, the door at the back of the office opened and Connie Livingston glided in.

"Show Mr. Trello out." D'Angelico said without feeling.

"Can't we negotiate this?" Jules pleaded.

"Ten dollars." D'Angelico's eyes were ice. "I can stand on that offer until tomorrow at noon. After that, I'll have to take steps to find what I want to fill out this order somewhere else."

"Maybe there's some happy medium," Jules said weakly.

"Call me if you want to accept. Connie, after you've shown the gentleman out, come back in here." D'Angelico turned his back on Jules.

There was nothing to do but close the attaché case, stunned, and walk out behind the statuesque secretary. In a daze, Jules said nothing to her as she took him as far as the elevator lobby.

"I'm sorry it didn't go well," she said soberly, studying him.

"You heard?"

"Enough. And your expressions told me the rest, I think."

"I can't understand it. His offer is impossible. He——"

Her hand touched his arm, silencing him. "I have to get back. I'm sorry."

"We were going to talk about going out later," Jules said slowly.

She smiled with regret. "I guess it's impossible. Goodbye." She turned and walked away from him.

The ride back to the hotel was miserable, and then the blank walls of the room stared at him. At first, as evening came on and his shock began to fade, Jules felt only anger. But then this, too, passed, and he began frantically trying to see a way out.

Ten dollars a case meant $135,000, far below what he had hoped to get. But it would be cash, and there would be no costs for labels or delivery. There would be no taxes, either. Assuming that he used Schreck Brothers glass and cork, and hid the depletion of inventory into the next quarter, he might realize an immediate cash flow profit of . . . he calculated labor and incidentals . . . more than $125,000.

With this total he could stave off immediate disaster. By combining with one other account, he could pay the pressing Elmhurst note. This would in turn ease his credit problems elsewhere and allow new borrowing. Prices would be low on grapes, he was sure of that, and any new bottles and corks could be bought on credit. He could easily defer all grape payments for 120 days as well.

It was just possible, then, that he could squeeze through on D'Angelico's offer.

But it galled him. Carmine D'Angelico knew precisely how desperate he was, and was ripping him off in consequence. Even wine of the Elmhurst quality was worth more, in total, than ten dollars a case, and they both knew it. The whites actually raised the total value of the shipment.

There was, additionally, no place else to go. Placing the wine with an eastern blender would take far too long, even if a decent price could be agreed upon. It had come down to accepting D'Angelico's offer or accepting the likelihood of ruined credit and probable legal action.

This, of course, was unacceptable. Pacing the room as darkness fell, Jules was tantalized by how close he was to so many of his cherished goals. New actions against Robert Mancini were either in progress or pending; before too many months had passed, Jules might have the pleasure of seeing Robert out on the street again, where he belonged. The Elmhurst refurbishing would come, too, and all the other things. Jules's father would never see Thanksgiving, and although Jules savagely conceded the likelihood of Frank Trello taking over the empire's management, he still hoped for something . . . cash . . . in the will.

The personal debts, the business problems, and everything else were only temporary snags. If he could keep his head up just a little longer, everything would come back to him.

More minutes ticked away. Jules continued to pace, increasingly restless and depressed. In the morning, he thought, he would have to call and practically crawl. He would have to accept. In the meantime . . . ? He thought about Connie Livingston. He wondered what the best way would be to find a whore. Maybe that was what he needed: someone to take his mind entirely off his troubles for a few precious minutes.

Then the telephone rang, startling him. He snatched it up.

"Hi," a breathless feminine voice answered. It was she.

"I was thinking about you," he admitted.

"Ah. I've been thinking about you, too."

"Can you get away, after all?"

"Ah, Jules, you don't know how much I wish I could. It would be so much fun. But I'm calling on business, dear heart, I'm sorry to say."

His regret mixed with a sharp curiosity and wariness. "Business?"

"Mr. D'Angelico has had some calls since you talked. It now develops that he has to take the early morning jet to New York. So he asked me to call you and let you know that his offer has to expire at midnight tonight."

Jules gritted his teeth. The screws were being tightened. Despite his earlier tentative decision, he found it on the tip of his tongue to tell Connie Livingston what she could tell D'Angelico to do with his offer.

As he hesitated, however, she spoke again. "Mr. D'Angelico also asked me to tell you that he regrets having to change the deadline. To show you his continuing interest, he said to tell you that he is now willing to pay ten-fifty a case, if you want to call him before midnight and okay it verbally."

Jules felt a leap of renewed enthusiasm. It wasn't much, but perhaps D'Angelico had been sweating a little too!

"Give me the number where he can be reached tonight, if you have it," he said.

She gave him the local telephone number. She added breathily, "I hope it works out . . . Jules."

"I hope so," Jules replied, again responding to the promise of her voice. "And listen, Connie: are you sure you can't come over later?"

"Like I said, I am sorry. Good night."

Jules hung up the dead instrument. He walked to the hotel-room window and looked out over the alien lights of Chicago. Far below, busy traffic flowed with a nervous speed. Nearby, other tall spires stood glittering against a cloudy black sky, and as far as he could see were other lights, on a lower level, extending on and on. He thought he could make out the distant vacant black of the lake.

He was stabbed to the vitals by a loneliness so profound that he nearly wept. No one had ever treated him fairly. They were all against him, even his father and mother. No one had ever given him credit for how hard he had always tried. Now his father was dying and would be gone, and there could never be a moment when there was a word of encouragement from this man who above all others Jules had tried so much to please.

It was not fair . . . it was as if the world had conspired to bring him down and laugh at his efforts.

At least, however, he had this tiny chance. By selling to Carmine D'Angelico, he could buy time. Then, perhaps, everything would fall into place.

He turned from the window and walked to the telephone. Almost angrily he dialed the number Connie Livingston had given him.

"Yes?" It was D'Angelico himself who had answered.

"This is Jules Trello."

"All right." The words were dispensation to continue.

"I accept your offer of ten-fifty a case."

"Excellent. You've made a wise decision, Jules." There was no hint of emotion in D'Angelico's voice. "I'll have the labels delivered to you next week, addressed personal and for your eyes only. One of my managers will contact you within ten days to finalize arrangements for a pickup. Payment will be cash on delivery. Agreed?"

"Agreed," Jules said, swallowing.

"Excellent. Good night." The connection broke.

So there would be no written orders, and nothing on paper to seal the agreement. Jules knew this was as it must be, given whatever nefarious scheme D'Angelico had in mind for the wine. Even so, he was surprised that there had been no ceremony—nothing done on either side to seal the bargain.

Less than thirty minutes later, however, there was a quick rap on the room door. Surprised, Jules first opened it on the chain.

Connie Livingston stood there. She wore a raw-silk summer dress that clung to the lush contours of her body. The neckline was scooped, revealing the golden tops of her breasts.

"Hi," she said. "I got to come after all. Are you glad?"

With trembling hands, Jules unlatched the chain and ushered her inside. Her hair was perfect, her eyes glowed with pleasure, her lips were pink and wet as she smiled at him.

"Mr. D'Angelico asked me to come," she said.

"Oh," Jules said in sharp disappointment. "I thought—"

She handed him an envelope, thick brown paper and bulky.

Puzzled, he opened it. As he did so, he got a stronger shock. The envelope contained money—closely packed bills in large denominations.

"I think you'll find it's ten thousand," Connie Livingston told him. "To seal the bargain."

Jules looked woodenly from her eyes to the contents of the envelope and back again. "That was what he said? Was there—any other message?"

She touched her tongue to her lips. "Just this." She moved into his arms with a wanton eagerness, her body fully against him.

His mind spinning, Jules found her mouth. She responded hungrily, her hands first squeezing and tugging at his back, then flying to the buttons of his shirt. "Hurry," she whispered breathlessly. "Oh, *hurry!*"

In moments she was naked, golden and wildly alive in his arms. They staggered to the bed and fell across it, and in another few seconds Connie Livingston had pulled him atop her, had spread her legs, had helped him thrust inside.

"Just one more thing, darling," she whispered hotly in his ear.

"What?" Jules gasped, beside himself with the agony of pleasure she was giving him. "What? What?"

"Remember," she said, her splendid hips encapsulating him with a silken, erotic perfection, "Carmine treats his friends very well, and lives up to all his bargains. See that you live up to yours."

3

The arrival of Alfredo Rodriques' forces, as widely publicized and discussed as it had been, was not readily apparent to the throngs of August tourists, or even to those not vitally concerned with the local wine industry. There was a small, ragged parade. A headquarters was set up on the fringe of the city's Chicano quarter, and some press releases sent out. Two or three small groups of demonstrators appeared on highways, as if to establish their continuing presence in the public consciousness, but there was no real picketing or demonstrating; the demonstrators always seemed to be walking slowly somewhere else.

Thus, as mid-August neared, quiet lay over the surface of things, a low-key effort to get more field workers to sign Workers United pledge cards went on, and it became a waiting game.

The weather became more normal on August 12, and showed signs of staying that way.

"The grapes will come along fast now," Susan Knight told Robert Mancini with more optimism than she really felt. "We'll have harvest on some of the early varieties, within six weeks."

"We can hope so," Robert replied quietly. They had met in the winery conference room on a common mission: morning coffee.

Susan looked sharply at her employer, noting his pallor

285

and seeming preoccupation. "Doesn't the weather please you?"

He appeared startled by the question, but it failed to rouse him from his withdrawn mood. "Of course, Susan. I just have a lot on my mind today."

"I do too," she announced. "I had a letter from Homero."

Robert Mancini did warm to the conversation a bit at this. "Did he get back into Mexico safely?"

"Yes, and now that we have a letter so that we know for certain, Rod Poole can move on those thugs who were causing him all the trouble."

Robert nodded, evidently gratified, and stared into space.

His continuing state of funk troubled Susan. It was very unlike him. She was not sure whether she should make further effort to rouse him, but she definitely did not like the way he looked. She decided to make one more try. "I have Homero's letter here, if you want to read it."

Robert frowned as if concentrating on getting himself together. "Yes," he said simply.

She handed him the letter, and, as he read it, scanned it again herself beside him. She practically knew it by heart.

Homero's handwriting, like his English, appeared flawless after hard study of classical models:

DEAR MISS KNIGHT,

We have arrived at this address safely and in good health. I regret to tell you that we experienced some difficulty with the car, but had it repaired. In addition there was some difficulty with inspectors, with the result that we lost some of our goods.

We live with my wife's sister and her family. They are good people. I have work in a cannery. I have written all the letters as you suggested, and the priest in this village is giving me assistance.

We shall continue to live and work in this place until some decision comes on our letters. The priest says it is a very long and hard process. I have told him how you have helped us, and how you are working for us in the United States.

We are hopeful of hearing news from you. Each night we pray for your good health and happiness. If you have any more instructions for us to follow in the matter of our attempt to return to the United States, please write to us at this address.

Thank you for all you did. We hope we can see you again someday.

HOMERO ARTIZ

Robert read the letter with care, and then folded it neatly before handing it back. His face was grim and thoughtful.

"It's a sad little letter," Susan told him.

Robert nodded. "He sounds unhappy. Did you notice the way he said he hoped to see you again 'someday?' It sounds like he doesn't have a lot of hope."

"Robert, we have to get him back into the country!"

"I know, and we will. I talked with some people the other day. It's a lengthy process, yes. But things can be short-circuited at our end. The real problem is in Mexico."

"Is there anything we can do to help down there?"

"I just don't know. I have some letters out, trying to get the answer to that one."

They stood silent for a moment, holding their coffee cups.

"Robert," Susan said then, yielding to continuing impulse, "is there anything wrong that I could possibly help with?"

He smiled. "No, Susan. Thanks. I guess I'm just preoccupied about Alfredo Rodriques . . . and some other matters."

"Is it true that he's going to contact winemakers individually?"

"Yes, that's what I understand."

"For what purpose?"

"To explain his goals, I imagine."

"There was a rumor that some Chicanos were beaten up last night."

Robert frowned. "I heard that. What does your friend Rod say?"

"When the police answered the call, there was no one there. It was near a drive-in. There were several white high school boys around, but they said they didn't know anything. The police found some blood spots on the pavement, and confiscated some chains and tire tools from two of the boys."

"But no sign of the supposed victims?"

Susan shook her head. "It worries Rod more than if

he had found them. He believes there was a scene of some kind—probably some local Chicano boys and some local white boys, a name-calling match that escalated, with racial overtones."

"There's not much unusual about that, Susan."

"But we've had very little trouble of that kind, and this is the third report in as many days. And Rod says he believes the Chicano boys weren't there because adults responded to a CB radio call and came and picked them up."

"Why," Robert asked, "wouldn't they wait for the police? Wouldn't they gain by filing a complaint?"

"That's what worries Rod. He thinks the Rodriques thing is intensifying old hatreds, and he thinks the Rodriques organization has formed its own units to deal with trouble privately—outside the law."

"There was no sign of retaliation, was there?"

"No. But that's not the point. As Rod puts it, how can the law function if the victims try to take care of their own problems, and won't file complaints? The law won't even be aware of everything that's happening!"

Robert sipped his coffee and made what appeared to be a visible effort to concentrate on the conversation. Again she was puzzled by whatever was worrying him, but he spoke to the point: "Let's walk back to my office, Susan. Possibly we should call Rod and see if he has any new information."

She fell into step with him and went into the hall, but countered, "Rod won't be there. With the receipt of this letter from Homero, he's ready to close the trap on those two men. He's been working with an Immigration Service agent, and they hope to close in today or tomorrow."

"At least somebody will be off the street," Robert said. "For a few hours."

They went down the hallway, passing Jim Young's cubicle. Young was inside, fussing with paperwork.

"Word with you, Robert?" he called.

"In about ten or fifteen minutes," Robert told him. "Susan and I have a couple of matters, and then I'll get right back to you."

"Are you headed for your office?"

"Yes."

Young waved cheerily enough, his feud with Susan evidently forgotten, and she went on down the corridor with Robert feeling better about that.

"Jim is a good hand," Robert said, sensing her thoughts. "He would never bear a grudge a long time."

"I'm glad of that," Susan admitted as they turned into his office. "I feel like we have to have all our marbles together with everything else that's going on."

Robert went behind his desk and looked down distractedly at the uncommon amount of correspondence he had allowed to pile up. "I hope Rodriques moves along on contacting people. The longer this goes on, the more rumors will fly and the worse tensions can become. I'm not saying a settlement will be easy. A lot of people are dead set against *any* recognition of an agricultural union. We're behind most of the state in that regard, but troubles elsewhere haven't exactly heightened anybody's enthusiasm here."

"But more wineries have given at least tacit support to the price-floor idea," Susan pointed out. "That ought to dispel some of the worry."

"Yes. But a lot of the support is tacit, and I'm not sure I like the way I've just informally become the *ad hoc* spokesman. People expect me to lead now, because of an accident. How can I lead? How can I try to speak for anyone else? We have no real organization. And as far as Rodriques is concerned—"

The telephone blinked, interrupting him. "Excuse me," he said, and picked it up. "Robert Mancini."

Susan sat down and waited.

Robert's expression tensed. "Yes, Jed."

She remembered that one of Robert's friends within the Timmons organization was named Jed Witchley. Was this a call from him? Likely. She tensed, anticipating bad news; nothing but bad news had been associated with the Timmons name lately, she realized.

"I understand that," Robert said. "He called and made it clear. No, he said he would report it—" He stopped, interrupted.

Susan watched him. She saw his face change, darkening, as he listened.

"That's definite, then?" he said finally. "When will he call?"

He paused again, then said, "I see. Well, he made it clear enough, but my position is such that I have to stand on it."

Although she did not look directly at her employer now,

Susan felt her interest peaking . . . along with a sense of foreboding. The news, if she was any judge from one side of a conversation, was not good.

"I appreciate the warning," Robert said now, his tone somber. "There's nothing to do but see exactly how it's stated, and go from there.

"I know that, Jed. But I also know the situation here, and what's necessary to try to maintain some harmony with the growers. They're under pressure——" He stopped, again interrupted.

"Right," he said after a moment. "I will. And thanks again."

He hung up and looked at Susan with an additional worry in the lines around his eyes. "It seems we're going to get a call from Endicott."

"About the price floor," Susan said.

"Yes. Of course we already knew he didn't like it. Now my friend up there says some of the bureaucrats are having special closed meetings about it. Evidently Endicott has received instructions to call to ask for what E. Z. Simms would call 'on-site discussion' of the matter."

"Does that mean they'll order us not to stand behind your floor offer?"

"I can't think that. That would force the final showdown on stock control."

"Is there anything we should do to get ready?"

"We haven't even heard it officially yet, Susan. Just keep it under your hat. We'll wait for the call from Endicott and see what happens."

Susan took a deep breeath. "All right. I guess I'd better get back to work."

"You said the other day that you're about ready on the house white-blending plan?"

"I hope to have it today or tomorrow for your approval."

"I'll talk to you later," Robert replied, beginning to lapse back into his state of preoccupation.

Susan left his office and headed directly toward the lab. The meeting had taken much less than the ten or fifteen minutes Robert had told Jim Young they would be occupied, but she thought nothing of this. Her heels clicking on the tile of the lobby, she crossed into the hallway which led toward the lab. Here industrial carpet muffled all sound, and the doorways were closed and dark; the staff enologist, the cellarmaster and other specialists were occupied elsewhere this morning, and Susan's assistant had taken a few days off due to an illness in her family. The wing seemed deserted as she came to the door of the blending room adjacent to the chemistry lab.

The door was ajar a few inches.

This was very unusual. It was always locked when neither Susan nor some other member of the staff was using it.

Frowning, but suspecting nothing as yet, she swung the door open and felt for the familiar light switch on the wall. She flicked it and the lights sprang to brilliance.

A figure at the blending table—a man with his back to her—jumped with surprise even as she saw him and recognized that it was Jim Young. For a split second she understood nothing, and he did not move to face her.

"Jim?" she gasped. "What—?"

Something on his other side—on the table—made a clicking sound. Young hunched his shoulders, turning, jamming both hands into the pockets of his jacket. His eyes were at pinpoints from the bright light and he looked pale. He grimaced, assaying a smile. "So there you are," he said huskily.

"Jim, what do you want?" Susan demanded. "What are you doing in here?"

"I came looking for you."

"Looking for me here? Robert just told you that we were going to his office!"

Young appeared confused. "Oh yes, of course. I forgot. Well. You're here now. I wanted to ask about the plans for the Petite Sirah."

Susan stared at him, and finally her mind began to make linkages: Robert's statement that she would *not* be here in the lab, but in his office for several minutes; the lab lights being out, putting Young in furtive darkness; his obvious shock at her entry; the lame statement about the Petite Sirah, which had to be another clumsy lie because her latest report on the new wine was already in office circulation.

Then Susan saw something else.

On the table behind Young was her metal-covered blending book, containing her shorthand notations of blends attempted on the new lot of white house wine, along with inventory records and cooperage location charts.

Ice flooding through her arteries, Susan then *knew*.

She stepped to the wall telephone and punched the operator.

"What are you doing?" Young growled.

"Jim, stay right there," Susan warned. The girl at the switchboard answered. Susan snapped, "Mr. Mancini's office, hurry."

"What's this all about?" Young asked. "I just came down here to ask a couple of routine questions—"

Robert answered his telephone.

"Robert, Susan. Please come to the blending room. It's an emergency. Hurry." Susan slammed the telephone back into its cradle.

"What the hell did you do that for?" Young asked angrily. "Are you trying to make something out of nothing?"

"You didn't come here to ask about the Petite Sirah," Susan told him, her pulse thudding in her temples now. "I sent that report last week."

"I must have missed it. Is that some kind of transgression? Or are you insinuating—"

"Jim, you're lying. I walked past your office the other day and saw you reading that report!"

"You're crazy!"

"Am I?" Susan retorted, seeing the trapped look in his eyes now.

"I'm getting out of here," Young said. "I won't put up with any more hysteria." He started toward her because she was between him and the door now.

"Stop!" Susan said sharply, and, as Young kept coming at her, she grabbed at his arms, trying to repulse him physically.

"You bitch! Get out of my way!" Young shoved heavily. Susan was pushed away and against the wall beside the door. She *knew* now, and realized that her proof might be gone forever if Jim Young got out of the room before Robert Mancini could arrive. She looked around desperately for something—anything—to use as a weapon.

At that moment there was movement in the darkened hallway, and Robert stepped into the doorway. He took in Susan's position and Young's angry stance in an instant. "What's going on here?"

"Jesus!" Young exploded disgustedly, and started past Robert into the hall.

"Robert, don't let him leave!" Susan cried.

Robert hesitated, clearly baffled and uncertain. Young muttered another expletive and took another step, reaching the doorway itself. Susan, knowing it was her last opportunity, leaped after him and grabbed at his arm. He shouted and swung at her. She ducked and scooped her hand into his right-hand coat pocket. She felt papers there, wadded. She pulled them out. As she did so, Young saw what she had done and clutched at her paper-filled hand. The papers exploded apart and fluttered to the floor all around them.

Susan glanced down. "Look, Robert! Look what they are!"

They were pages torn from Susan's blending book.

Jim Young stared at the pages on the floor with the expression of a man reading his own death warrant. His face had gone colorless.

Robert Mancini, too, could only stare for a few seconds. As he raised his eyes to Jim Young's face, his expression reflected amazement and dawning realization.

"Jim?" he said unbelievingly. *"You?"*

"You don't understand," Young said hoarsely. "I can explain."

Robert's eyes swiveled to Susan.

"The lab was dark," she explained. "He was at the table when I turned the lights on. He must have thought there would be time."

"I never thought it was you," Robert told Young softly. "When we talked about our spy—our saboteur—you were one of the few who never entered my mind."

Young stared blankly. He raised a hand to brush at his face like a man who has walked into cobwebs. His hand shook. He appeared on the brink of tears.

"Oh, Jim," Susan burst out. *"Why?* Taking those pages would have been only a little puzzle—a small irritation. I could have reconstructed everything sooner or later. Why take such a chance?"

Young continued to stare a few seconds longer. Then, moving jerkily as a marionette, he turned and rushed out of the lab.

Robert did not move. He appeared to be in a trance.

"You have to stop him," Susan said. "You have to ask him *why*."

Robert jerked as if she had slapped him. Then, his expression hardening, he started for the door. "Stay here until I send for you," he snapped, and was gone.

Susan knelt to gather up the pages that had been torn from the book, but her fingers, icy from tension, were without feeling, and clumsy.

4

Jim Young, his face a mask of anger, was already taking things from his desk and throwing them into a briefcase when Robert walked in on him. A secretary in the next office was looking in, eyes wide, but Robert slammed the door in her face.

"I'll be out in five minutes," Young said bitterly. "You don't have to say anything."

"I want to know why," Robert said.

Young looked up sharply. "Do you have to ask, really?"

"Of course I have to ask! Are you crazy? We've been together in this business since we opened! I thought we were friends! Of *all* the people I might have suspected—"

"Save me the lecture." Young's voice was constricted by his anger.

"It's not a lecture! Jim, what the *hell* made you turn against me? Did you try to sabotage the wine? Did you start those leaks to the press, the rumors of trouble?"

"Of course I did. Are you so stupid you still don't see that? I did those things and I planned to do more."

"Is it money? Did you do it because someone paid you a lot of money? If you had problems, you should have told me. I thought we always leveled with each other."

"Yes, we leveled." Acid spilled out with Young's words. "And more and more it was DeFrates being moved up, Susan getting the delicate assignments—while good, stupid Jim sits in his broom-closet office and shuffles papers!"

"Christ, Jim! You've always done a great job. If I didn't talk to you very much, it was because yours was the one area I always thought was in such capable hands, I could just practically forget about it."

"There's no use talking about it. It's over and done with. I don't have much here. You can watch me pack. I'm only taking my personal items. You don't have to worry about that."

"Jim," Robert groaned. "Who the hell put you up to this? Tell me that."

"What makes you think someone put me up to it? Is it that I'm not smart enough to cause you any trouble on my own? Is that what you're saying? Is that it?"

"You did it for money," Robert shot back, beginning to get over the first numbing impulse of surprise, and seeing the logic now. "There's no other reason, no matter how bitter you had gotten without my realizing it." He paused and studied his former friend's white face. "Who was it? Based on the leakage of the Elmhurst information, I can guess, can't I. Was it Jules?"

"I'll never tell that and you know it."

"It was Jules," Robert concluded. "But I'll never understand why. Except for the Elmhurst information that helped him beat us to that purchase, what did you really do for him? Everything else was more a nuisance, given Susan's fast action on the fermenters when you cut them off. What good did any of it do Jules?"

Young dropped an onyx paperweight into the briefcase on top of some pictures and magazines, closed the case, slammed his desk drawers. His eyes as he looked up were like those of a dead man. "Will you call the police?"

It had not entered Robert's mind. For a few seconds he boggled. Then his answer came. "No. It would be a petty charge. I don't want to hurt you any more, and the publicity would be worse than the punishment for both of us."

"Always big, noble Bob," Young said. "Always putting the winery first. Christ, I don't know how you live with yourself, you're so perfect."

"Jim! God! We were *friends,* and I *still* don't understand what happened!"

Young picked up his briefcase. "All my keys are there on the desk."

Robert almost intercepted him as he started around the desk. None of the questions had been satisfactorily answered. Young was walking out—to where? Perhaps he had been motivated in part by buried rage and bitterness over real or imagined slights, but this could not be the whole story. What had he imagined he could gain by the acts of sabotage, like today's thwarted attempt to steal pages from Susan's records? Because Robert felt such an exquisite sense of personal betrayal, he had to have some answer, something he could understand.

The expression on Young's face, however, told him that any further attempt to delay his departure might result in an outburst of real violence. And that was all they needed, Robert thought with a rush of defeat: a fistfight that *would* bring the authorities in.

Young paused, glaring at him, awaiting a move.

"I can't believe it has come to this," Robert said, shaking his head. "But if that's the way it is, I'll get out of your way."

Jim Young showed some surprise at Robert's sudden defeated tone, and then his eyes glistened with tears. "You've always been good at maneuvering people, Robert. The worst part of it is that I believed you for so long."

"I never lied to you!"

"Sure. We were all in this together, one big, happy family. And we were all going to grow together, build together. I must have been really stupid to believe that story as long as I did."

"Jim, what did I ever do to double-cross you?"

"Did you ever imagine what it might be like," Young demanded, his face twisted, "to see somebody like Susan Knight come in, knowing nothing, and move almost at once nearer the center of decision-making than I *ever* had been? Did you ever imagine what it might be like to be stuck in the same little office, and be passed over, and have your wife always nagging you for more money, more social status—and finally have your wife *leave* you because you were small potatoes—and finally realize that there was never going to be any more responsibility, never a lot more money, never an operation really of your own— that you were always going to be just a scummy little salesman?"

Robert stared at this man who had been a friend, and the full import of the betrayal that Young must have imagined over the years began to dawn on him. It was a devastating feeling, far more shattering than Young's actual perfidy. *He really believes I only used him. He sees himself as a victim—thinks I forced him into this by refusing to recognize his real worth.*

"Jim," he said slowly, struggling for words, "I never meant to downgrade you. I honestly thought everything was all right with you."

Young's eyes burned. "Even when Irene left me?"

"I didn't know that had anything to do with your job—with money—"

"It doesn't matter now, God damn you! I'm getting out of here!"

Robert was still blocking the door. Young appeared again ready to attack him if he continued to block it.

There was nothing to do.

"I'm sorry, Jim," Robert said huskily. "I mean that." He stepped out of the way.

Young pressed past him and went out into the hallway. He walked quickly to the stairs and went down.

Robert, his heartbeat still too fast, went as far as the upstairs landing, with its tall windows looking down on the parking lots. He waited and watched Young walk to his car, get in, drive away.

Back in the anteroom to his own office, his secretary Nancy looked up with large eyes, whether at his appearance or through some knowledge from the lightning-fast office grapevine, he did not know or care.

"Mr. Young is no longer with us," he told her stonily. "Please notify Jennifer on the personnel desk. His salary will be prorated through the fifteenth and mailed to his home address along with his tax record and insurance termination papers. There will be no payment for accrued leave and no other termination payment of any kind. Tell Jack Hobson in sales that I want to see him in my office in thirty minutes. Please tell Mike DeFrates and Susan Knight that I want to see them in my office now. Call a locksmith. I want all office wing keys collected, the locks changed, and new keys issued on signature cards only."

Nancy did not look up as her pencil flew across her pad. "Yes sir," she said breathlessly.

Robert went into his office and closed the door harder than he had intended.

Going to his cabinetry, he took out a bottle of Zinfandel, opened it, and poured a glass. His hand shook as he drank it, and for once he wished for something stronger. He refilled the glass and carried it to the window that overlooked the inner courtyard. The sun-drenched old brick walls were covered with climbing ivy; roses were in full crimson bloom, and a slight breeze moved the leaves of the demonstration vines, heavy with maturing grapes now, along the brick walks. It was a time between tours, and no workmen were in view. The scene was medieval, bucolic . . . a scene of which, ordinarily, he would have been very proud.

His vision blurred as the full import of his betrayal swept over him. Any damage Jim Young might have done, or even planned to do, was of no great consequence. What mattered was the betrayal itself. In ordinary times, Robert thought, he could have handled the shock well enough. But the extent to which the revelation of Young's treachery had devastated him was proof of how thinly strung he was because of all his other problems. And still the single question drummed at him: *why?*

Young's explanation—jealousy and bitterness—was not quite enough. There had to be more. Robert believed firmly, based on the Elmhurst transaction if nothing else, that Jules Trello's fine hand was somewhere. But what had Jules been able to offer Young to encourage his perfidy?

Although he searched his mind, Robert could not find the answer.

He finished his second glass of wine. He felt better. He went to his desk and angrily pushed some papers around, waiting for Susan and Mike DeFrates.

His telephone blinked.

"Mancini," he snapped.

"Bobby," Endicott's voice crooned over a weak long-distance connection. "How are you today down there in God's country?"

"Fine, John."

"Hey, my friend. Gawwd damn! You sound like you're on your high horse! Didn't catch you at a bad time, did I? Dawdling that pretty Nancy girl on your knee, or something like that, maybe?"

"What do you want, John?"

"Well, Bobby, we've been having more talks about your price-floor deal down there."

Someone tapped on the door. Robert covered the receiver mouthpiece. "Come." The door opened and Susan Knight peeked in, Mike DeFrates behind her. DeFrates's face showed that he had been told at least part of it. Robert motioned them in and said into the telephone, "You told me you planned to solicit some more opinions from other Timmons executives."

Susan and DeFrates moved quietly to chairs, in response to Robert's gesture, and sat down. Susan was pale, and DeFrates's face was sweaty and about the color of a ripe persimmon.

On the telephone, Endicott told him: "It's about like I figured it would be, Bobby boy. Real resistance to your price idea there, real resistance. I called in hopes you might have taken my advice and given the matter some reconsideration."

"I explained my position."

"No change of heart?"

"It's not the heart that has to change; it's the situation. And that stands. So our position stands, too."

Endicott sighed audibly. "Then, I'm afraid we'll just have to have a little head-to-head down there. Management views this matter very seriously. *Very* seriously. Can you see your way clear to meet with E.Z. and me next Monday?"

"What time?"

"Say . . . ten o'clock?"

Robert angrily slashed a note on his calendar. "I'll set it up."

"I regret this," Endicott pontificated. "Co-operation—a spirit of giving and taking on both sides—usually accomplishes far more than any kind of confrontation. We still have every hope in the world of working out this misunderstanding to everyone's satisfaction, Bobby. I hope you feel the same way."

"Monday at ten," Robert said. He had to be careful because if he allowed himself any leeway, he might really lose his temper at this moment. "Is there anything more?"

"No, nothing more." Endicott sounded hesitant, baffled. "We can take a look at the whole thinking on both sides of this question then."

"Thank you for calling," Robert said.

Endicott listened in silence.

Robert hung up.

"Endicott," he told Susan and DeFrates. "We meet next Monday morning at ten to talk about the price-floor guarantee. It seems Timmons is very much against it."

"Bastards," Mike DeFrates rumbled. "That's all we need right now."

"Susan told you what just happened?"

"She told me. I can't quite believe it."

"It's true, I'm afraid." Then Robert briefly filled them in on his final scene with Young, struggling to make his tone unemotional. His voice shook slightly anyway.

Mike DeFrates balled his hands into big fists. "I would have punched him out."

Robert smiled. "Good thing you weren't there, then."

"I might go to his house tonight and punch him out!"

"Like hell you will. Now listen, Mike—".

"All right, all right. It was just an idea."

"We don't need any new trouble," Robert warned him.

"Why," Susan asked, "did he do it? You weren't able to pin him down?"

Robert had omitted Young's complaints about being passed over. They did not seem germane anyway. "I think it's clear enough that he had someone else paying him," he said wearily. "The thing that hurt us most, and complicated our lives, was the fall-through of the Elmhurst purchase and Jules Trello's subsequent request that we buy and market the Elmhurst wine. The first thing made us look stupid. The second created a little crisis with Timmons, which we managed to head off."

"Jim leaked the Elmhurst information," Susan said angrily. "To benefit Jules."

DeFrates leaned forward, his hands fists again. "Jim has been on Jules Trello's payroll?"

"That's my guess."

"I don't get it! Jules is a notorious tightwad when it comes to people who work for him. I can't see him paying Jim enough to make it worth his risk."

Susan chimed in, "And I don't see how Jules stood to gain that much. So he beat us to Elmhurst. Explain the cooling jackets that were turned off. Explain trying to steal my notebook pages."

Robert hesitated before answering because he was still working it out in his own mind. The pattern that had begun to emerge, however, made its own mad sense. "The cooling failure looked like bad management, in a way. It would have made us appear very disorganized and hapless if the wine had been ruined. The blending notes fall into the same category: our blending on the house white would have been delayed; we would have been scrambling around. We would have appeared disorganized, with labor problems and mismanagement."

"Are you suggesting," Susan said, "that *Jules* has been trying to cause trouble between us and the top dogs at Timmons Corporation?"

"It's a theory," Robert conceded. He knew it sounded far-fetched. Yet now that it was out on the table, he examined it and believed it more than ever. He added as he thought of it, "What might happen if we actually fell out with Timmons—had a showdown, and lost? The winery would be reorganized, if we lost. Someone like Jim Young might have stood to gain a lot if that happened?"

"But how would that help Jules Trello?"

DeFrates replied before Robert could. "You don't know Jules. He'd run from here to Miami Beach in his bare feet if he thought it would hurt Robert Mancini."

"But why? I know he *dislikes* Robert, but—"

" 'Dislike' ain't the word for it," DeFrates said.

Susan shook her head vigorously. "I just don't buy it. If Jules Trello is mixed up in this with Jim Young, there's something more that we haven't figured out yet. Jules has to see some way he would gain. He wouldn't do all this just for negative reasons, just to hurt Robert, no matter how much he might hate him."

"His father is dying," Robert suggested. "Maybe he fears old Gus will leave me something. Maybe he thinks he has to ruin me, if he possibly can, to head that off."

"I find that very hard to believe," Susan said flatly.

Robert leaned back in his chair and closed his eyes, listening to the pulse of a headache coming on. He considered the puzzle from various angles. His resiliency had begun to assert itself and he was thinking more clearly. The link between Jim Young and Jules Trello seemed solid. The reasons behind that link were more hazy. Susan, he thought, was right: they had not yet discovered everything they needed to know.

The discussion continued until Jack Hobson, the young sales assistant now to assume Jim Young's duties, appeared for his notification. From that point until midafternoon, Robert was engrossed in actions made necessary by the Young departure and the required reshuffling of other key people.

Shortly after 3 P.M., Susan Knight called from her lab.

"I thought it might cheer you up a little," she said. "I just talked with Rod. He pulled the noose closed on Dennison and Arnstedt a little while ago."

So engrossed in other things was Robert that for a minute the names did not register. He repeated them, drawing a blank.

"The two who were extorting money from Homero Artiz," Susan said.

"Of course. I remember the names now. That's good news, Susan. Very good."

"Rod was working with an Immigration agent, a man with Mexican ancestry of his own. Not only were they able to find two other families those two were blackmailing, but Dennison tried to extort money from the agent himself, thinking *he* was an illegal."

"I'm damned glad to hear it."

"Rod thinks they have a perfect case, and the judge hearing the arraignment was mad as a wet hen when he heard the sketchy details. The agent, it seems, made sure to have the arraignment before—"

"Let me guess," Robert smiled, remembering the name from newspaper accounts of various federal cases in the area. "Judge Gonzalvez?"

"As Rod would say," Susan replied with satisfaction, "ten-four."

"Now all we have to do is get Homero back up here— legally."

"I just hope there's time. We have to try to stay on top of it."

"We'll *make* time," Robert assured her.

Again he plunged into work, almost thankful for it. This way he did not have to think about the upcoming meeting with Endicott and Simms or about Barbara Turner.

He could not make the rumors stop flying about them; this damage to her had been done. Until he could somehow terminate his marriage—persuade Audra to co-operate in a termination that she had made the first step toward reaching—he had to respect Barbara's dicta concerning their relationship.

But it hurt. He was trying to give Audra a little time, attempting to maintain control of his emotions. Yet Jim Young's departure was exactly the kind of thing he most needed Barbara for, to discuss it with and get whatever insights she might have. His feelings about her were such that simply *telling* her would be enough, even if she said not a word in response. At least he could have been unburdened.

There was another side, too, to his longing. Without any egotism, he knew that she was as unhappy as he was. He had opened a door to her, and now it was closed again. Despite having her son with her, and in spite of her considerable strength, she was lonely now in a way she had not been lonely before, and this was of his doing. He had brought her pain when his desire was to shield her from it.

For the time being, he told himself almost angrily, there was nothing he could decently do but abide by her wishes. He might press himself upon her. If he succeeded, it would be at the loss of both her esteem and his own. Whatever happened, he could not take any action that might strip their relationship of *some* kind of dignity—at least what he vaguely saw as a dignity, and a rightness. He had to exercise a stern self-discipline because this was what she had asked of him, and he owed it to her as well as to his own self-esteem.

But this too hurt. Badly.

Shortly before 5 P.M., he was smoking one of his forbidden cigarettes when the telephone blinked. It had blinked a lot during the afternoon. Why he thought this time that it would be Barbara—unless because he had been brooding about her at the time—he would never know.

"Yes," he said expectantly, almost sure.

"Robert Wobert?" the teensy feminine voice said.

His insides fell. "Carole? What do you want?"

"Ooh my!" she murmured. "You sound *mad* at me!"

"Sorry," he corrected himself. "I was just surprised to hear from you." Then he had a very bad thought. "Is it Gus?"

"Jules asked me to call you," Carole's tiny voice almost whispered. "Can you come over to our house tonight about nine o'clock?"

It was the last thing he expected. For a second he remembered Jules with the gun in the doorway, and almost believed that the invitation was to allow him to finish the one-sided duel he had tried to finish before. But this was absurd.

Why, then?

Immediately an answer came: Jim Young's discovery

and dismissal. But that did not explain why Jules would react in this way, with an invitation.

"Carole," he said, "what does Jules have in mind?"

"Ooh," she murmured. "Baby doesn't know. Daddy said he twied to call you himself, but you were out. Can you come about nine?"

There was only one way to find out what Jules wanted. That was to do what he asked—go back to his house. Robert took only an instant to decide this, his curiosity overcoming any worry he might have.

"I'll be there," he said.

5

The Jim Young discovery continued to plague Robert Mancini as he drove from the city and a brief meeting with his lawyers toward Jules Trello's house that night. Robert's attorneys, however, had added to the things he could worry about: they had been unable to get any meaningful help in tracing unaccounted-for Mancini stock; there was a chance that some of this, too, was in control of Timmons Corporation.

"They could have a clear-cut control if they choose to vote the matter," Robert's senior attorney, named Klein, told him bluntly.

Passing the turnoff for Ned Henderson's vineyard, Robert saw the faint yellow gleam of the Henderson boy's motorcycle on the access road. It reminded him that he wanted to see Henderson to make sure he knew about Homero Artiz's safe arrival in Mexico and the subsequent arrest of his local tormentors. But this, like deep thought about the meeting with his lawyers, would have to wait. His present concentration needed to be focused on whatever Jules had awaiting his arrival.

Proceeding on northward, he found the hill road to the Trello house in gloom that had turned to night. The sun might still be shining on the Pacific, not so far away over the mountains, but the range had brought darkness to the valley even as the sky remained a deepening evening blue.

Jules had heard by now of Young's discovery, Robert

thought. This was the motivation for this meeting, unless there was something going on about old Gus which he was not aware of. He was anxious for the confrontation.

The big house was ablaze with light from top to bottom when he drove into the driveway. Although there were no cars in front, he caught a glimpse of Carole Trello's Corvette in the bricked side yard near the garages. Jules's car, he thought, was in the shadows beyond.

With a sense of gearing himself up for whatever might come, he walked to the front door and once more pressed the button. Memory of the last debacle here was fresh in his mind.

The night was still. He waited.

He was almost ready to press the button again when the door swung open and, in what seemed almost a replay, Carole Trello looked out at him. This time she wore a crimson housecoat, and did not appear surprised.

"You're prompt," she said with no sign of her baby-doll inflections. "Come in."

He entered, and she closed the door loudly behind him, then walked around in front to confront him with an impish smile. She wore no makeup and her hair was loose on her shoulders. He saw that she had been drinking.

"You're brave to come back after the last time," she told him.

"I'm too curious about what this is about to turn it down."

"Come along. I was just headed for the pool."

He followed her into the cavern-like living room and toward the open patio doors leading to the pool, which was lighted beneath the water.

"I'm sorry you had to wait for me to get the door, love," Carole told him over her shoulder. "We've had so much trouble with help lately. We don't have a single servant right now, and I was upstairs, just skinnying into my swimsuit." She paused at the patio doorway and cast him a look that was puzzling, one so charged with sexual innuendo that he thought it must be an intended parody. "If I had been sure it was you, I might have just run on down naked."

Robert smiled dutifully but said nothing. The tension she put between them was hardly new. It was irrelevant tonight.

She led him onto the patio. The pool gleamed like a big blue jewel. Only light from the house windows illuminated the grounds around it. The shrubs and trees made the large area feel closed in and secure. Robert looked around, but did not see Jules.

Carole walked to an umbrella table with pink-and-white metal chairs. She slipped her feet out of her slippers and began unbuttoning her housecoat. "If you want a drink, Robert, you know where the bar is."

"Where's Jules?"

"While you're mixing, I'll have a scotch on the rocks." She looked around. "I had a glass, where is it? Damn. Well, no matter."

Robert felt irritation growing. "Carole, will you please make sure Jules knows I'm here?"

She faced him across the patio, her eyes again alive with messages. She snicked open the last buttons of the housecoat and slipped it off. She wore the tiniest red bikini underneath. The little suit enhanced rather than concealed anything. Carole had maintained her body very well. Her waist was tiny, her belly flat, and no one had ever accused her of being underdeveloped. She was beautiful enough that Robert, despite himself, stared.

She dropped the housecoat onto the nearest chair and struck a model's pose. "You like?"

He smiled patiently. "The movies lost a star."

"But you've found me, love."

"Carole, where's Jules?"

She turned and executed a neat dive into the pool. As the water lapped against the sides in response to her entry, making millions of diamond reflections on the surface, she came up and pulled herself nimbly into a blue floating chair. The lights from the house gleamed on droplets of water covering her body. She crossed her legs.

"I'm sure you can find a suit in the cabana," she said. "Get into it. Join me."

"I didn't come here to swim, Carole. Now—"

"My goodness!" She made her eyes wicked. "What *did* you come here for? Skinny-dipping? Goody. Strip and come on. The water is fine." She paused. "Believe me, darling. The water is just *fine.*"

With amazement Robert felt a tremor of sexual arousal. He was angry at Jules's failure to show up immediately, and did not want Carole by any stretch of the imagination. But Carole as she was here, now, was the stuff of men's magazines, of pornographic fantasy. Long-legged, golden, heavy-breasted without sign of fat, she was a sex vision with the blue of the pool around her water-beaded body.

"You didn't tell Jules I'm here," he said. "Where is he? Can I go use the intercom?"

"Pooh," Carole smiled. "Jules isn't even here. We're *alone*, darling. Haven't you even figured that much out yet?"

Robert found it hard to believe. "He isn't here? Where is he?"

"Oh, at the winery, I suppose. I talked to him a little while ago and he said he wouldn't be home until awfully late." Then she turned on the baby act. "Ooh. We're awone at wast. Baby and Robert-Wobert. Is Wobert gwad?"

"Carole, Jesus Christ! Do you mean Jules didn't even ask me over here?"

She pouted. "Baby was wonesome—"

"Stop the God-damned act, Carole! This is ridiculous!"

Her face calmed and became almost cold. "Will you fix me a drink?"

"Did you invite me over her for *this* insanity?"

"Robert," she said with considerable dignity, "will you please fix me that drink, and I'll tell you?"

Disgusted and impatient, he strode into the house to the bar. He dropped two ice cubes into a short glass and splashed scotch over them, then walked back outside.

Carole beamed at him as he walked toward her. She had drawn the floating chair to the side of the pool. Her swimsuit, two dark ribbons, had been slung onto the decking.

"It was binding me," she moued, reaching for the glass. As she raised her arm, her breast was also lifted so that he stared at her large, erect nipple.

She saw his eyes. "You like?" she whispered.

The situation might be absurd, he thought—a segment from a very bad slapstick porn film—but it was no longer funny or even acceptable. He put the glass on the tiles and started for the house.

"Where are you going?" she called sharply.

"Carole, you're crazy. I'm going home."

"You don't have anything at home. And Jules told me you stopped seeing your girlfriend—" She stopped suddenly, her face registering the knowledge that she had let something slip.

Robert was on it instantly. "How does Jules know so

much about what I'm doing?" His mind leaped. *"Is he having someone watch me?"*

"Join me," she whimpered. "Get out of those silly clothes and join me here, in the pool. Don't you think I'm pretty?"

"Does Jules have a private detective on me or something?" Robert demanded. "Is that how he knew about her in the first place?" Then, as her face showed that he had struck a truth, he added, "Why is he doing *that?* What does he hope to gain?"

"Don't you think I'm pretty?" Carole asked. "Or are you like him—only able to function with a slut?" She held out her arms, her legs wantonly spreading. *"Come* to me, Robert! I've always wanted you. No one has to know. It will be like getting back at Jules, if you want to look at it that way—"

"Christ!" Robert said, heading for the house again. It was incredible; he could not believe it. But he did not know which was worse, the sudden awareness that Jules had been having him followed, or Carole's blind, clumsy attempts at seduction.

As he reached the patio doors, he heard a splash behind him, and then the sound of Carole's bare feet running on the pavement. He went into the house and was halfway across the big room when she caught him, her arms wet and clinging as she pulled him half around and fought to press her wet body against him.

"You'll love it," she panted, her eyes those of a trapped animal demanding submission or its own death. "I'm good. We can laugh at Jules behind his back. I've had lots of lovers and I know everything. I'll show you, darling—"

He caught her strong, slippery arms, forcing her back. She was strong. She seemed to slip, drop to her knees in front of him. He tried to step past her but she grabbed at his legs, being dragged.

"Just stay a few minutes," she panted. "Please." Her hands, like claws, flew to his crotch. "I want to suck you off."

Robert broke loose from her and went for the front door.

On her knees, the flagstone hurting her bare knees, Carole did not try again to go after him. She saw that she had lost. She slumped as he went out through the front door, slamming it behind him. She sobbed, feeling the sting of her nipples and the urgent wetness between her thighs.

She heard a car door. Then there was the sound of his

automobile engine starting. She heard the car drive away, tires squealing.

She was alone, nude, dripping on the tile floor. A puddle had already formed. She shuddered, chilled.

The silence of the great house mocked her.

Climbing unsteadily to her feet, she realized how drunk she was. She had needed a lot to drink for courage. But with his wife gone, with his new playmate gone, he should have been ready for her at last; she had convinced herself of this. No one was really faithful, she told herself; not in this day and age; the multiplicity of her own lovers proved it. She had been sure, once the drinks began to take effect, that this would be the night of nights when finally she and Robert Mancini would make love.

But everything had gone wrong. He was gone.

She rose to her feet, slicking her hands over her body to sluice off remaining water. She ached, she needed someone so badly.

But Robert was like Jules, she told herself. No better, no worse. What did they care what she needed? What did it matter to them what she might think or feel? She was an ornament, she was supposed to be stupid—they didn't care about her at all. No one did. Her husband was impotent, a brute, cruel to her, he understood nothing. She had never known a lover who valued her for herself. She had once seen one of those ghastly inflatable dolls that some sick variety of men must take to bed with them, and she now saw that she was like those dolls. A vastly improved model —she could move and gasp—but no more, no less.

How often had she reminded herself to talk baby talk, be stupid, lest Jules see a person standing before him, and reject her? But what had the acting gained for her? *This* kind of drinking to dull the pain? *This* kind of rejection by the one man in the world she had imagined could make her feel whole again, and a real woman?

When sex failed, when everything else failed, there was always one thing that sometimes helped purge the self-hate. Carol remembered it now. She rushed upstairs, threw on slacks and a tee shirt over her damp skin, found the keys to the Corvette, and went recklessly down the stairs again.

Driving had always provided release. She needed release now worse than she ever had in her life.

The Corvette's powerful engine leaped to life at the turn of the key. With a burst of hate and exultation she threw the gear selector into forward, making the Pirelli tires scream as she spun around in a tight circle. She stamped on it then, and the engine cried out its cry of sheer power. The Corvette fishtailed out of the parking area and down the curving driveway.

She could drive, she thought with fierce satisfaction. This, at least, she could do without anyone. She could *drive*.

At the end of the driveway, where it met the twisting road, she kicked in more power and swung onto the pavement in a controlled slide. She caught it just in time, swinging the wheel fully back the opposite direction to the stop, and aimed the long nose into the bright white of the headlights on asphalt, trees, brushy ditches, jutting rock.

She refused to yield to fear, making the Corvette hurtle through the first bad corner, and it was an almost sexual release, an orgasm of power and speed and control on the brink of total loss of control.

Down the twisting road she flew, alone, fenders brushing weeds first on one side, then on the other. The night cool rushing over the windshield brought tears to her eyes, but she blinked them away. Her hair whipped out behind her, tugging at her scalp, hurting her. She was tinglingly aware of every chilled pore. Her awareness flowed through her feet and fingers into the Corvette. The Corvette obeyed her.

She reached the bottom of the hill and forced the speedometer, against gusting spasms of fear, up past 75 on the flat, narrow road leading toward the highway. She almost overran the highway because of her speed and because it was empty, black in the night, and she was upon the stop sign almost before she could react.

Rocking the car to a halt for a moment, she was engulfed in a forward-flying cloud of dust raised by her own tires. With the dust were heat and fumes from the exhaust. She jammed her foot to the floor, fishtailing again as she entered the highway, heading south, rushing into fresh night chill.

Ahead were three cars, traveling slowly, bunched. She saw no one coming from the opposite direction. She had eased up on the accelerator slightly, but pressed it all the way down now. The transmission kicked into lower gear, the engine boomed, and she sailed around all three cars, seeing their tail- and headlights flash past, one set, two sets, three sets, and then she was back in the right lane again, the tach needle very high, the speedometer going past *80*. She allowed the transmission to upshift, but kept hammering on more power. The Corvette topped a slight rise, whooshing up on its springs and then settling again— *there!* a gust in her belly—and she guided the car around a sweeping curve, flashing past the headlights of some vehicle going the other direction.

The road was narrow here. The other car had seemed very close. Carole thought about death being inches away, and the thought was a powerful, a sexual, intoxicant.

In dying, she thought—if she were to hurl the Corvette into an oncoming car or truck—at the instant of impact, as metal crushed into her body and she was torn to pieces, literally, exploded—in that instant, she knew she would come. This made no sense but it was true. She knew it with bodily knowledge deeper and truer in this instance than her brain. She was one with the car, it was her body, vibrating, rushing, tires hot on the abrasive pavement, power surging through gear systems, metal pistons smashing up and down to the maniacal tune of winking spark plugs, chittering points, drinking the vaporized fuel, sucking in great greedy gulps of the moist night air, exploding it—

And her own body: the wind tearing at her hair, her face, her damp clothing, pulling at her every pore, lashing her like a thousand cool tongues. It was an ecstasy to go faster and faster, and this elegant car would go with her, be with her and do whatever she asked, and the faster it went, the faster it seemed ready to go.

On the empty highway, she reached a railroad crossing. The car became airborne, taking all control out of her hands, for a gut-sinking few seconds. Then it came down hard, almost flying out of her control, and she caught it, and her blurred vision showed the speedometer: *115*.

My God you don't really want to die.

Spasmodically she got off the accelerator. The car relaxed, slowing to *100, 90, 80, 70*. She breathed deep and fed in sufficient power to maintain this speed.

She wondered, continuing on, if she was really sane. She was not very drunk any more. She had wanted Robert Mancini so badly! With a lover like him, she could endure. Not only would she then have the joy of his lovemaking itself; she would also have the pleasure of knowing she was fooling Jules again, proving how stupid *he* was (when he thought *she* was the stupid one), but there would be the added pleasure of imagining Audra— cold, hateful Audra, who had never wanted her in the family: *See me, Audra, I'm fucking your husband. I've beaten you.*

But Robert had run from her. Rejected her. Now she had tried and it was worse than before, because at least before tonight she had had the expectation, and the dream. Now she had nothing but this crying need.

With a sob, she entrusted her steering wheel to the left hand, and with the right touched herself between the legs. She felt . . . moved . . . gently found that perfect place . . . began to press and stroke.

Her body began to respond.

The highway widened and became four lanes. She passed two slow-moving cars, but did not believe she was driving very fast. Dark vineyards flashed past on either side, distinguishable in the flit of her headlights. The wind pressed against her, her body dried, her mouth dried. Her hair flew backward, pulling at the roots, hurting her.

She loved being hurt during sex.

The speed of the car increased. The highway was empty again. She felt the vibration in the Corvette which signaled that now she was going very fast indeed once more, but she did not look down at the dials because she might see her own hand between her legs, and that would destroy the fantasy. Everything was going by faster and faster.

Then all at once something intruded on her vision at the right—on the edge of the road. A tiny light. Red. Small. On the edge of the road. Not another car—no way to know what it was—

Carole brought both hands to the wheel, her foot coming off the accelerator, and suddenly she was aware of what was happening and where she was, alone on the highway, going *very* fast—and the red light on the right edge of the road was upon her. The headlights flashed on something—movement—a motorcycle—someone on a motorcycle, no helmet, jeans, the flash of a white tee shirt.

The Corvette's tires screamed as Carole braked and swung the wheel to the left.

Too late.

There was a little clicking noise, a tinkle like glass, as something hit the right side of the car, and then it was gone and she was past it just that fast. She looked in the rearview mirror and was still so close that her own brakelights cast crimson on the stroboscopic instant that registered: a motorcycle half off the road, in the air, the driver airborn over the handlebars, arms and legs flung out like a comic aquatic diver.

She heard the crashing impact.

She closed her eyes for a second, then opened them. She had gone on several hundred yards, and the Corvette was under full control, and she could not see any other vehicle on the road. There were faint headlights far behind.

She had hit someone.

Stop. Go back. Help.

But she was drunk—she had been speeding—

No!

She grasped the wheel more firmly, continuing to slow down. The speedometer showed 55 as the car loafed. Ahead were the headlights of three or four oncoming cars now. Her own headlights seemed dim on the pavement. She had broken one of them. She remembered the tinkle of glass.

The cars were coming nearer. She was a mile, perhaps farther, from where it had happened. She did not know what shock had done to her perception of time. But she was stone sober now, shaking, and her mind frantically weighed possibilities . . . potentialities.

The first oncoming car passed. Then another. Two more.

She kept going.

Just ahead now was a turnoff that would lead her via the back road, the long road, home.

She could *not* go back now; it was too late. She had made her choice in those first instinctive seconds.

She took the back-road turn very slowly, and proceeded at thirty miles per hour. She had to get back home, examine the damage, hide the car. She had to pretend she had not been out at all tonight. She had to watch for the late television news . . . to see what had happpened.

Her insides felt pulverized. Her teeth chattered as she drove on, escaping.

6

At 9 P.M., Johnelle Henderson had urged her husband to drive to the access road "and bring that young man home, no ifs, ands or buts!"

At 9:30, Henderson was enjoying the TV show and said he would go in just a few minutes, but surely the kid would drag in on his own any minute.

"Ned, I wish you would go now. How many times do we have to tell that boy his curfew time?"

"If I have to go up there after him," Henderson retorted, "I'll take a layer off his hide before I bring him back here; I guarantee that much."

At 9:45, they both heard the sirens at the same moment. They looked at each other.

"That's right out at the end of our road!" Henderson said, coming to his feet.

"Oh, my God."

They ran to the car together. Henderson drove to the highway in less than one minute. The traffic was tied up, troopers were out directing it, and in the snarl of headlights and brakelights was the flicking, rotating illumination of an ambulance that was already at the scene.

Johnelle Henderson stayed in the car while her husband ran across the access road and climbed through the fence and went onto the highway. She saw his tension-twisted face, white in headlights, as he spoke with the trooper directing traffic. Then he went on across the highway, toward the activity around the ambulance, and she could not see him any more.

But then in a moment she knew, because she heard him scream.

7

When Susan Knight hurried into the emergency entrance
of the hospital a little after eleven o'clock, it was curiously
quiet: no rushing, no activity, the doors to the treatment
rooms ajar, a nurse quietly at work behind a corner desk-
reception counter. Then Susan saw Robert Mancini and
Rod Poole standing alone in the small alcove off to one
side.

She went to join them. As they turned, she saw the answer to her question in their faces.

"Is he all right?" she asked against everything their
faces were telling her. "Is Jamie hurt badly? Where arc
the Hendersons? What happened? *How* did it happen?"

Rod Poole rubbed his fingertips across his forehead as
if to extinguish some fact, or some memory. "I'm sorry,
babe. He's dead."

"Oh, God, no. Oh, my God." Susan closed her eyes and
almost fell.

Poole's strong hands caught her. "Okay. Okay, now."

"You can say that," she flashed. "Maybe little boys
getting killed is old stuff to *you!*"

Poole blanched and his mouth became a hard line as he
helped her to the nearest chair in the waiting room. "Sure,
babe," he muttered.

She sat down and covered her eyes with her hands.
She felt dizzy, and then something nudged her hands and
she looked up and it was Poole again, his face a mask—the

official face—and he was holding a tiny cup of water out to her.

"Thanks," she said, and drank it. She took a few deep breaths and saw both men watching her, and came back to herself.

"Rod, I'm sorry," she said. "My God. I don't know why I said that to you."

Poole shrugged. "Got to take it out on somebody."

"Rod, please forgive me."

His stern face creased into a smile. "Sure."

She turned to Robert Mancini. "Where are the Hendersons?"

"Ned is downstairs," Robert said. "He'll be back in a few minutes."

"The patrol has to ask these questions," Poole explained apologetically.

"And Johnelle?"

Robert Mancini lit a cigarette with a jerky motion. "She collapsed. They've given her something. She'll sleep till morning."

"But there will *be* a morning," Susan said with a shudder. "And she'll have to face it then."

"Everything was done that anybody could possibly do," Poole said quietly. "They had paramedics in the ambulance and they know what to do. Jamie was still alive when he got here, but he died in the elevator on the way up to surgery. They worked on him more than thirty minutes after that, trying to see if they—"

"I don't want to hear that!"

Poole looked at her. "I'm sorry."

"I'm jumping at you again. Rod, I don't want to jump at you that way! I'm just so upset. Of all the people for this to happen to—!"

"There aren't any right people for this to happen to," Poole told her.

"I know . . . I know." Susan made another attempt to pull herself together. "Robert, is Ned all right? I mean, is he holding together?"

Robert shook his head. "I don't know, Susan. I really don't."

"How did it happen?"

Robert Mancini's jaw set in anger. It was Poole who replied.

"He was out on the highway on that little bike," he said.

"Right where he wasn't supposed to be. No helmet, and his lights were probably so dim you wouldn't have been able to pick them up ten feet away. The car probably hit him before the driver even saw him."

"Is that what the driver said? Is it all Jamie's fault, then?"

"We don't have the driver."

"What do you mean, you don't have the driver?"

"The driver kept right on going."

"You mean it was a hit-and-run?"

Poole's forehead wrinkled. "There's the slightest chance that the driver didn't even know Jamie got knocked off the road. The kid could have swerved and lost control, and there might have been no impact whatsoever."

"I don't believe that," Susan said passionately. "You don't hit a motorcycle, or even run it off the highway, and not know it!"

"There's a bulletin out, but we don't have any witnesses. Nobody saw anything. Maybe someone will come forward with something when the story is on the radio and in the papers. But right now we don't have a thing."

Susan did not reply. She sat where she was, remembering the times she had seen the Hendersons' feisty, intelligent young son. She also remembered hints she had picked up casually that there was conflict in the family about Jamie's motorcycle, where and when he rode it, his use of a helmet. The Hendersons had been building their small vineyard for the future, and surely that future had had Jamie near its center. Both Ned and Johnelle, Susan thought, were strong people. But this heartbreak would test that strength.

Thinking of the hit-run driver who had caused the boy's death, she was filled with indignation. But she could not think of anything that might really help the parents, even capture of the driver-killer.

She watched Rod Poole and Robert Mancini. Robert paced aimlessly, his worry etched into lines of his face. She thought he looked very tired, and recalled the way he had been preoccupied even before the Jim Young discovery. It seemed a singularly inopportune time for more tragedy to brush his life. But then she saw the stupidity, born of emotion, that such a thought contained: was any time a good time for disaster?

Rod Poole stood silent, leaning against the wall. He was drawn in upon himself, controlled, private, showing nothing. This was his training, Susan thought. He had seen many such scenes. But she doubted that they would ever become routine for Rod. His sensitivity, often hidden behind a brusque, official exterior, was too great to allow him to become callous. However little he might know the family or the dead boy, he was feeling this too. Perhaps this was why she loved him.

Minutes passed. The silence pressed in.

Then a door from a stairwell opened. Ned Henderson entered the hall and started toward them. Susan rose, watching him with intense pity.

Henderson's hair stood on end as if he had been roused from deep sleep. He wore a faded cotton shirt and patched khaki trousers. There were light leather house slippers on his feet, and he wore no socks. His skin the color of wax, he returned her gaze with eyes that were light-colored and almost without focus.

"Thank you for coming," he said huskily.

Susan went into his arms, hugging him.

"It's okay," he said, giving her a terrible little smile as they separated. He turned to Poole. "I answered all their questions—signed the forms."

Poole nodded. "Do you want me to drive you home?"

Henderson seemed to think about it a long time, as if his mind had been slowed down by the shock. "No," he said finally. "Johnelle is upstairs. I'll . . . let me think . . . I'll go sit in the waiting room on her floor."

"You could sit in her room," Poole said carefully. "They might be able to put a cot in there for you or something, if that's what you think you want to do."

Henderson stared into space. Moments ticked away, and Susan was aware that they were all watching him with the same sympathetic acuity.

"I'll have to talk to the funeral home later," he said finally, no intonation in his voice. "I have a lot of arrangements to make."

Robert said, "We'll help in any way we can, Ned."

Henderson looked at him, clearly grateful. "I know that."

Again there was an awkward, prolonged silence.

Then Henderson said, "I shouldn't have let him have the cycle."

"You can't talk like that," Susan said.

"No." Henderson looked at her as if he had not seen

her before. "It was up to me. He wanted the bike. I could have said no. I could have put my foot down."

"Ned, don't blame yourself. My God."

"I kept telling him to wear the helmet, but he was at that age. He had to fight me about the helmet . . . you know?"

No one spoke. Henderson rubbed his fingers over his lips. His hand shook like he had palsy. He frowned at his hand, balled it, let it drop to his side. "Whoever hit him didn't stop."

"I know," Susan said.

Henderson took a deep breath. "Well, I don't know what to do, exactly. I mean . . . in what order. I spoke with the funeral-home man. I have to pick out a—a casket in the morning. All of that. Poor Johnelle. I don't know . . ."

Poole took his arm. "Let's go find your wife's floor and make the arrangements."

Henderson nodded and let Poole start leading him off, shuffling like a very old man. Then he seemed to think of something, and turned back to Susan and Robert. "Thank you for coming."

Susan filled up as she watched Poole take him on down the hallway toward the elevators. She turned to Robert. "I think I ought to stay here tonight. They don't have anyone."

"Yes," Robert said. "Will you call me early in the morning? I want to know what I need to do to help, and what the arrangements will be."

"I'll call you."

Robert nodded, awkwardly patted her on the shoulder, and turned to leave. Susan stood where she was until he had vanished beyond the emergency-entrance doors. Then she left the area, looking for the waiting room where she could spend the night. Rod would stay with her, she thought. It would be all right that way. She was numb.

8

Newspaper publicity of the hit-run killing of Jamie Henderson attracted a handful of the curious to his Saturday-morning funeral. The ceremony was very brief, and none of the curiosity-seekers joined the procession to the cemetery; behind the black hearse were only six cars.

A cloudy sky seemed to hang low over the hillside cemetery, with its view southward to an interstate highway and burgeoning residential development and northward toward the open crescent of the valley. A steady cool wind whipped evergreens and rustled through the taller trees around the central area of the cemetery where the hearse stopped and the few cars parked close behind.

The grave was on the side of a grassy knoll. A tent had been set up over it because of the threat of rain. Funeral-home attendants were just finishing the job of banking the grave with flowers brought from the church when the back doors of the hearse were opened.

Standing alone beside one of the cars, Susan Knight watched Robert Mancini and Rod Poole walk forward to join the other pall-bearers. Mike DeFrates was also serving, along with three men from the Hendersons' church. Susan saw them line up as instructed by the funeral director, a large and overweight man with a red face. There was that inevitable moment of clumsy waiting while an attendant released straps that held the coffin in place within the vehicle.

323

The small crowd—four women, two men, and a half-dozen of Jamie's former classmates—already ringed the gravesite. As the coffin was being rolled back out of the hearse, the minister and an assistant walked slowly from one of the cars toward the grave, the Hendersons beside them. Ned Henderson wore a dark-brown winter suit with old-fashioned cut and lapels; he appeared uncomfortable with the dark-blue tie, and the wind ruffled his overlong hair. Johnelle, in a black dress and hat, was steadied by his hand under her arm. Head down, she seemed to see nothing, and wobbled as she walked.

The coffin was lifted by the bearers, adjusted, straightened up. It seemed a very large coffin. The gray skylight glinted on bronze fittings. The minister, having accompanied the family to the grave, now returned to walk ahead of the coffin as it was taken forward.

Susan moved to the edge of the circle of mourners as the minister opened his book, his back to the coffin over the grave, and began reading Scripture. He was not a big man and his voice was tattered by the wind. Canvas flaps and fittings on the tent made continuous noise, along with the whipping of the trees and the distant roar of the highway.

Jamie Henderson's schoolfriends were clustered together on the far side of the circle from Susan, and she studied their faces. They appeared overly pink and scrubbed and solemn, the boys in their white shirts and ties and the two girls in dresses and hose. Susan saw them glance up occasionally, stealing covert looks at the Hendersons as if unsure of how they themselves should act or even feel. For some of them it was their first experience with death.

The minister finished his reading and led a prayer. He had been quite good at the church, talking about the dead boy's zest for life and the obligation of the living to continue their lives. His prayer was good, too: simple, basic, setting up no abstract heavenly conditions for salvation, and suggesting no phony consolations for the bereaved.

When the prayer was over he began a final, brief reading.

Susan took the time to examine the faces around her. She turned most intensely to the Hendersons. Ned kept his face down. His jaw pulsed as he fought to control his emotions. His eyes were vacant and determined. Beside him, Johnelle stared at the minister but seemed not to see him.

Her skin was the whitest white Susan had ever seen, her lips were parted, the rise and fall of her breast could be seen as labored and uneven. She was standing without support. She appeared on the brink of collapse.

In the two days since the accident, the driver of the death car, as the newspaper called it, had not come forward. Little else had been gotten from a continuing investigation.

The car evidently had broken a headlight in the accident. Scattered glass fragments at the scene were from a headlight, and appeared new. A driver had been found who claimed to have seen a car with one headlight approaching him south of the accident within a minute or two of the time it had taken place, but this driver had paid no attention to the kind of car he had met from the opposite direction.

Drivers who had been north of the accident location, including the first two on the scene only moments later, claimed to have been passed a mile or two up the road by a sports car of some kind. The car was not driving much over the speed limit when it passed them, they agreed, and all they could say about it was that it was low and open, perhaps a Jaguar, Corvette, MG, Triumph, Z car, or even a Toyota Celica with a slant roof.

One driver thought the car was dark-colored, the other thought it was yellow. One thought it was a sedan. The other said it was open.

"Jamie was out on the road at night, no helmet, with poor lights," Rod Poole had summarized for Susan the previous night. "There are no witnesses to say the car was speeding or anything else. If it hadn't become a hit-run case, the driver would have been released without charges."

"But the driver did run," Susan pointed out. "Why?"

"You don't always think straight at a time like that. Maybe he *was* speeding. Maybe he was even drunk. Maybe he just panicked. We'll probably never know."

"Surely there's some way to catch him!"

"How?"

"Look for new witnesses. Alert body shops that might be asked to repair front-end damage."

"Of course," Poole said. "Those things have already been set up. But the chances are very, very slim, Susan. The chances are, our driver will never be found."

Now, as the minister concluded the last prayer, Susan

thought how bitter it must be for the parents to suspect that the killer would never be known. She wondered if it was in their minds at this moment as the minister went to them, shook Ned's hand, and solemnly handed Johnelle the prayer book he had used. It was the same one, Susan saw, that had been in Jamie's hands before the coffin was closed at the church. It seemed ironic, Jamie with a prayer book. A cycle magazine or a spark-plug wrench probably would have been really more appropriate.

The minister signaled to the onlookers and they broke up, starting back toward the string of cars. The Hendersons turned and walked slowly back. They paused beside one of the cars, and Susan saw that Robert Mancini and Mike DeFrates had already moved to join them. Rod Poole was coming through the thin crowd to be at her side.

Together they walked to the others.

Ned Henderson's face was twisted and pale, and his wife was crying, her cheeks wet, yet trying to talk as if nothing were abnormal.

"But we want you to come by," she was telling Robert.

"Then we will," Robert told her. "Of course."

Johnelle turned to Susan. "I was just saying that we want all of you to come by the house on the way back through the valley. We have ever so much to eat—things people brought to us. We can have coffee, and . . ." Her voice simply trailed off.

Robert put his hand on Ned Henderson's shoulder. "Ned, I know nothing anyone can say will make any difference right now. We're awfully sorry."

Henderson mustered a stiff smile. "Thanks. I thought it all went very well, didn't you?"

So they took turns assuring one another that it had gone very well indeed, and meanwhile some of the cars were started, the hearse drove away.

"If it's all right, Ned," Robert told him, "I'm going to have a man come by your vineyard Monday morning. He can take a look around and do anything that needs to be done."

"I appreciate that," Henderson said. "But I intend to get back to work."

"Maybe that's the best thing."

Johnelle, removing her little black hat, said, "Ned will need the help, though. Jamie did do a few things, you know. And I'm going to be extra busy."

"Are you going back to work Monday?" Susan asked, surprised.

"Oh, not full time," Johnelle said, fixing her with dazed eyes. "Not full time for a while, anyway . . . until I've done this other thing."

"Other thing?" Susan said, when no one else spoke.

"Look for the man who was driving the car."

Susan boggled and looked up at Rod. He grimaced and then said gently, "Mrs. Henderson, I explained that everything that can be done is being done."

"Yes," she said softly. "But you and the patrol have many, many cases. Just this morning that boy was killed drag-racing. And you have the crimes and everything. I don't have any other cases, you see. I can work on this all day long, some days, and at nights, too."

Ned Henderson turned to her in the awkward silence. "Johnelle, we can't find that driver if the police can't."

"I can look," she told him firmly. "I have to look."

"There isn't any way you can do any good at it."

"Oh, yes there is. There might be. I have lots of places to look . . . lots of people to talk to and things to ask. I can put practically full time into it. I don't have distractions. I won't get discouraged or give up."

Poole said carefully, "We won't give up, Mrs. Henderson."

She smiled at him. "I know. But I won't either. I have to look, don't you see? Jamie was our boy."

Later, in the car driving away from the city, Susan told Robert, "It's a terrible thing. Searching for that driver will only keep her fixated on the accident. And it's such a hopeless search!"

"She won't be talked out of it," Robert replied. "And maybe, in a way, it's just as well."

"How can it be just as well?" Susan demanded, surprised.

"Susan, she has to do something."

Susan lapsed into silence at this. She had no answer for it. If Johnelle Henderson could work out her grief only in a futile search, then it was the thing she had to do. Susan saw this, but wished it could be otherwise. She remembered so vividly the bright promise of the couple only three months ago, in the spring.

They reached the Henderson house. Rod Poole's car was there, and four others. They went inside, where sandwiches were made, and cake cut, and coffee served. Everyone spoke quietly, with the result that everyone's voice sounded loud, and the house was filled with the mixed odors of the fresh coffee and the burial flowers that had been brought home.

At almost the exact time Susan Knight joined the others in the Henderson house after the funeral for the boy, less than fifteen miles away, Carole Trello gashed her finger on the broken headlight fitting of the Corvette, cried out in pain, and thrust her hand to her mouth to suck at the welling redness.

She was in the garage, quite alone. And frightened.

On reaching her house the night of the accident, she had found that the broken headlight did not prevent the fender door from closing over it, rotating it inward, when she turned the headlight switch to the *off* position. This had prevented immediate discovery by Jules or anyone else, and had given her some time.

There had been a black streak along the fender, a rubber mark perhaps made by a handlebar grip, but lighter fluid had removed this so that only an extremely careful eye might notice the tiny indentation in the plastic surface where the mark had been.

On Thursday, after learning that the motorcycle rider had been a boy—and that he had been killed—Carole had done absolutely nothing. It had taken a supreme effort of will to get out of bed at suppertime and play the baby doll for her husband. Fortunately, he was engrossed in some very vital project at the Elmhurst winery, work that took him back there each evening immediately after the meal and kept him there very late. Jules had, therefore, not noticed her emotional state.

On Friday she had seriously considered turning herself in. Even the newspapers quoted officers as saying the accident probably had been the boy's fault. So she had been wrong to run. She *wanted* to turn herself in, to take whatever medicine she had coming and try to assuage the guilt.

But she had been unable to work up her courage. It did not matter much about her own fate, but she knew what Jules's reaction would be. He would view himself as ruined. He would hate her. He would never look at her again.

And she would have to try to explain why she had run. She would have to lie about speeding, about having drunk so much. Then they would ask why she was out at all, and there would be no answer she could give. But *Robert* would know; he would put it together in time. Then he would hate her, too.

It was too late. She could not turn herself in now. She had to maintain her silence and cover her traces.

On Friday afternoon, then, she had driven into the nearest small town, visited an auto-supply store, and bought two new headlights, one with numbers identical to the intact lamp on the Corvette, one with identification from Jules's Lincoln. She had also bought some clear plastic floormats, a back-seat ice chest, and a little tool kit. With the exception of the tool kit, which she needed to change the headlight, everything else was smokescreen; she carried the extra items to the attic and hid them in a corner.

Changing the headlight was not as simple as she had thought.

The old lamp, or what remained of it, had come out easily enough, encouraging her. But impact had bent some small metal braces in the lamp fitting, and the new light would not seat properly. She had been frantically pressing on the fitting with her screwdriver, trying to make it fit, when her hand slipped and she cut herself.

Seeing that she was not bleeding too badly, she tried again now. The headlight would go into the hole all right, but she could not get the bolts that should hold it there to match properly. Sobbing with nervous frustration, she tried repeatedly without success.

Finally, knowing that her husband might be home at any moment, she pressed the new lamp into the fitting as well as she could. She walked around to the cockpit and turned the switch to close the doors over the headlights. A little motor whined. There was a clunking sound.

Walking back to the front, she saw that the right front door had not closed all the way. It was blocked about two inches from closure by the way the lamp did not seat properly. The door hung open that much, like a drooping eyelid.

Carole considered trying again, but her hand had started hurting and was dripping blood again. Closing up the tool kit, she stowed it behind the driver's seat, out of sight, and used a paper towel to wipe up the drops of her blood that had fallen to the paved floor of the garage. She would have to try another day when she was calmer and had more time. No one would notice in the meantime. She would not drive the car unless she absolutely had to. She would use the Volvo station wagon parked at the far end of the garage, as she had Friday afternoon when she went for the parts and tools.

Carole congratulated herself as she went into the house and found a bandage for her finger. She was holding together very well, and no one had to know. She would be fine.

But a part of her kept seeing the boy's figure on the edge of the road, kept remembering the slight impact and the view of him flying through the air, as she would never forget it, and she kept thinking, this part of herself, *I killed him I killed him I killed him*, and she kept fighting the impulse to claw at her own face and body.

9

When Robert Mancini walked into the winery Monday morning, it was with a feeling of being strung very tight. He did not look forward to the day's meeting with John Endicott and E. Z. Simms.

The brief weekend, following the burial of Jamie Henderson, had been almost as unpleasant as it had begun. His attorneys had no new information on the outstanding stock, but had pointed out that Timmons Corporation, if it held only 20 per cent of the shares that were not accounted for, clearly had control in a showdown. A few shares had appeared for sale, and Robert, digging deep into personal savings, had ordered purchase of these, though something told him that he was too late to salvage control . . . was indulging an almost Quixotic whim to do everything he might.

In another action just as dismaying, the lawyers had word informally that the firm representing Robert's wife had been in communication with her. It was understood, in that unnecessarily mysterious and oblique way that lawyers had with one another, that an action was to be filed seeking court recognition of their separation but not a divorce; if Robert's lawyers did not agree to a stipulated monthly allotment for Audra's support, a lawsuit would be drawn demanding same. Robert's counselors urged him to let them contest the matter to try to force Audra to file for divorce if she was to gain a penny. They explained that it was all maneuver at this point, and out of court.

The decision was a difficult one surrounded by areas of shadow. Robert, however, knew something that the attorneys didn't: Audra was in possession of information about his relationship with Barbara Turner; if he tried to force a divorce on his terms, he knew Audra was quite capable of filing a countersuit charging him with adultery, and putting Barbara's name into the matter in a way that even a friendly press could not simply ignore. Robert told the attorneys to negotiate whatever maintenance agreement Audra wished, and the attorneys threw up their hands.

When Barbara Turner called him on Sunday afternoon, they talked hungrily for almost an hour and then knew—each of them and at the same moment—that the agreement not to see one another simply had to be overlooked, if even for an hour. With a reckless eagerness he drove to her house and for the first time entered it in broad daylight. Her son was there. He was sullen and withdrawn. Robert and Barbara sat facing each other across the seemingly ten-mile width of the small living room, and talked until past five o'clock. When they parted, having not touched and not mentioned anything remotely connected with their personal plight, it was with no arrangement or implied promise to talk or see each other again.

Now that he had been warned accidentally by Carole Trello, Robert easily spotted Jules's private detective as he pulled away from Barbara Turner's house. A squat man with a genuine handlebar mustache, the detective was parked halfway up the block in his beige 1974 Chevrolet. As Robert approached him, the detective tried some kind of a ploy, starting to pull out in front of him, to precede him to the intersection. Something hot and angry broke inside Robert's skull. He swung his car into the left lane, got alongside the Chevrolet, and then whipped the wheel back to the right. He got a moment's glimpse of wide-shot eyes and the big mustache, and then he was past. The Chevrolet horn blared, the detective was sawing at his wheel, there was a satisfactory crunching sound, and as Robert looked in his rearview mirror from the corner, it was to see the Chevrolet halfway onto someone's lawn, and a hubcap rolling down the sidewalk.

Robert knew he had thrown off the surveillance only briefly, and that he had acted childishly. He felt good about it all the way home. Jules's motivation in ordering the watch on him was unclear, although it had borne results of the kind a Jules Trello might relish. From now on, Robert intended to do anything possible to make life miserable for the detective.

On the way to work this morning he had not spotted the Chevrolet or any other following vehicle.

There was little to do to make ready for the meeting, which would involve only himself and the two Timmons representatives this time. He had some coffee and read the mail and fidgeted. He went to his window and looked outside.

It was cool and cloudy again today, not a good day for the grapes in this season. Over the top of one of the buildings he could see a portion of the hillside vineyard, and was only slightly surprised to see Susan Knight and Mike DeFrates trudging uphill between the rows.

With time before the meeting, he thought a little hike of his own might settle his nerves. He left the office by the back door, went down the outside stairs, cut through the production building, and entered the sloping field of grapes.

The air was cooler, or seemed so, here at the foot of the hill. Up above his position he could see the distant figures of Susan Knight and Mike DeFrates as they stood beside one of the mature vines. Low-scudding wisps of cloud seemed practically touching their heads, although he knew this was an illusion. He started up to join them.

Powdery yellow soil worked into his shoes as he walked up. Flies buzzed, and the scent of the green leaves and ripening fruit surrounded him. He broke sweat and it felt good. There was not enough *work* in his life; everything was—to use his lawyer's term—maneuver. He realized that he had not been in the field for a long time, and had missed it.

Susan Knight and Mike DeFrates saw him coming, and waited for him. They stood between well-spaced rows of fully mature Cabernet vines. The mahogany-colored central stalks, twisting up out of the chalky soil, were as big around as Robert's upper arm, and their new growth extended gracefully on wires forming a T with the central supporting post. The vines had a strength and power to them, showing by their size and gnarled wood how they had endured.

They were among the finest old Cabernet Sauvignon vines in the area.

When Robert reached the side of Susan Knight and Mike DeFrates, panting a bit, he saw that Susan had a small instrument in her hands. It might have been mistaken for a weak microscope by a novice, but was in fact a wine tool known as a saccharimeter. By viewing the juice of a grape through its lens system, one could get a direct reading showing the percentage of sugar in the solution, a vital criterion in determining the ripeness of the fruit . . . and when it should be harvested.

"What is it this morning?" Robert greeted them.

"Good morning," Susan smiled. "So low you don't want to know."

Robert nodded. He had not really expected a very high Brix reading, and certainly nothing near the 22 they always hoped for in a grape ready to be harvested. Although sugar was a crucial element in deciding when to pick a grape for wine, it was not the only one. In 1974, destined to be recorded as a very fine year if not a great one, some fields had yielded grapes with a Brix as high as 28, and they had been superb. But other years had seen grapes held in the fields for just a bit more sugar formation—until, when they were picked, they had begun to dry, with resultant loss of overall quality. Each year was different, each was its own. Few pretended any more that California had identical vintages every year, because it simply was not true.

"We've had some warmth," Robert said now. "We'll have more. We'll be all right."

Mike DeFrates brushed dust from his hands. "I like to hear the boss-man sound that way."

Together, without consultation, they tested more grapes. The readings clearly showed that the harvest indeed might be very late, pressing close to the rainy season.

"We're due for some heat," Robert said, trying to sound positive again.

"We're not just staring at the rain if we go into October," DeFrates said. "The longer the harvest is delayed, the longer we're going to have all this hassle."

"Hassle?"

"With Rodriques. With growers sweating out prices."

Robert nodded, brought back to this. He had almost forgotten both problems in the aftermath of the Henderson boy's death and his own weekend of problems.

"Rodriques is going to Christian Brothers today," De-

Frates said. "He announced he'll also see Louis Martini and Tim Crocker."

"He's picking places where he thinks he'll get a good hearing," Robert observed.

"When will he be here?"

"I don't think it will be long."

They started back down out of the field, picking their way, examining the vines more for love than need; these fields were always carefully tended.

"Did you go by the Henderson place?" Robert asked Susan Knight.

"Yes," she said, frowning.

"And?"

"Ned was in the vineyard, working hard."

"Working it off," Robert said. "And Mrs. Henderson?"

"She had already left."

"To go to work?"

"To start her investigation."

It was bad news. "I wish she wouldn't go at it quite so hard. She *needs* to do it. But if she rushes through every hope that she's clinging to, and uncovers nothing—"

"I think she and Ned argued about it," Susan said. "I don't think he wants so much to do any of that today. But she was adamant. I think he's awfully worried about her."

They went on down through the field, reached the gate, and went through it into the courtyard behind the production building. The faint odor of fermenting wine mixed coolly with the scent of fresh leaves and fruit.

"Are you still on with Endicott and Simms after awhile?" Mike DeFrates asked.

"Yes," Robert said. "They haven't arrived yet."

DeFrates spat philosophically. "Glad that's one I can duck, anyway."

"I sort of wish I could."

"If you need somebody to punch them out—"

"Yes, Mike. Thanks, Mike."

DeFrates grinned grudgingly.

"Robert," Susan said, "I know you've got a lot on your mind, but could we talk just another minute about this Homero Artiz matter?"

"Why?" Robert asked. "Is there a new problem?"

"I got another letter from him," Susan said, worried. "He said he was working hard, and he's finishing up the last of the latest batch of paperwork—but he sounded so discouraged."

"It's going to take time, Susan." Robert was almost irritated with her for continuing to bring this up. He sympathized with Artiz's problem as much as anyone. But he had already written letters, made telephone calls. He felt confident that his friend in the wine business in Mexico was also working diligently on the matter. "Homero just has to be patient," he added. "And you do, too."

"I'm just afraid he'll be lost in an ocean of red tape. If there's *anything* more we should be doing, I just want to make sure we *do* it."

Robert led his two associates through the production building, out across the central courtyard, and into the original wing. "If you can think of something more to do, Susan, I'll do what I can."

"That's just it," Susan said as they climbed the stairs. "You've contacted congressmen, the Immigration authorities, everyone. They say it will take time. All right. But Homero says in his letter that he was told by some functionary down there that it might take *years*. That's the Mexican side of the problem, Robert! It shouldn't take years! Can you think of anyone else we could contact to try to hurry up the bureaucrats on *both* sides of the border?"

"I think you're hoping for a miracle," Robert said, leading the way into the office area. "The only person I can think of who might speed people up on *both* sides is the—" He stopped abruptly, taken by surprise by his own thought.

Susan, frowning, watched him. "Is the—*what?*"

Robert did not reply for a minute. The idea that had popped into his head was one of those ordinarily rejected at once as simply too outlandish, too bold. He would not have thought of it, he realized, if he was not so filled with impatience at all the other problems he faced. The prospect of really short-circuiting difficulties—*any* set of difficulties —was vastly appealing, no matter what outrageous steps were required.

Still thinking about it, he turned to look at Nancy, his secretary.

She told him, "Mr. Endicott called from town. He said they'll be just a little late, but they were leaving right then and expect to be here by ten-thirty."

Somehow the thought of Endicott and Simms, grinding

up the highway to join him in a meeting he did not want and even feared, helped crystallize Robert's resolve.

"Well, what the hell," he said. "Why not?"

"Why not *what?*" Susan asked.

"Okay," Robert said, feeling both reckless and pleased with himself. "We can *try* it. What can they do? Send out the FBI?"

"Robert," Susan said, puzzled and exasperated, "I don't know what you're talking about." She turned to DeFrates. "Do you know what he's talking about?"

"I never know what he's talking about," DeFrates said sourly.

Robert turned back to Nancy. "Remember when we sent the wine to Washington last year? The reception for the Governor at the White House?"

"I ought to," Nancy said fervently. "I had to help find your white tuxedo for you."

"We had that number," Robert told her. "Find that number." He paused and reconsidered. "Hell. Why not? Come on, Susan. Come on, Mike. I need your moral support on this one."

"What number do you mean?" Nancy asked, confused.

"Moral support on what?" Susan demanded.

"The number for the White House," Robert told Nancy.

"*What?*" Susan gasped.

Just doing something, for a change, rather than worrying, felt enormously good. Robert grinned. "If we're going to try to help Homero, let's try to help Homero. Let's not mess around. The man liked our wine. He may remember me. He may even *talk* to me, who knows? Put the call through, Nancy. Come on, you two. Let's put the responsiveness of the Executive Department to the supreme test."

He led them into his office. Mike DeFrates's mouth hung open. Susan Knight's eyes were like saucers. No one said a word.

Five minutes passed, and Robert began to think he was a little crazy to be doing this.

Then the telephone blinked.

Robert picked it up and gave his name.

A crisp, military voice told him, "One moment please, sir, for the President."

Robert leaned back in his chair, chilling from head to foot.

Well I'll be damned! he thought.

The familiar voice sounded over the line. It was a very good connection.

"Mr. President?" Robert said, aware of the sensation the words caused in the other two people in the room. "How are you, sir?"

10

Homero's problems in Mexico might soon be over.

Robert felt sure of this when he hung up the telephone, astounded at his own action and pleasantly surprised by the reaction of quick and keen interest his story had aroused in a man who had far more important things to worry about.

Any feeling of jubilation, however, was short-lived. John Endicott and E. Z. Simms arrived five minutes earlier than promised, and were ushered into Robert's office immediately.

"No calls, Nancy," Robert said as his secretary closed the door. Then he folded his hands on the top of his desk and waited, trying to show more confidence than was inside him. He was determined to make Endicott open the argument—if it was to become one—over the minimum-price guarantee.

Endicott took one of the chairs facing Robert's desk, his blunt fingertips resting lightly on the top of his thin attaché case. E. Z. Simms put a bulky case on each side of his own chair and popped open first the one, then the other. Both were jammed with notebooks and computer printout sheets, file folders and copies of memoranda. Robert also saw some news clippings.

"We saw some demonstrators on the highway," Endicott said. "Banners. Flags. *American* flags!"

"Were they Rodriques' people?" Robert asked.

"I'm sure they were." Endicott's lips curled in disgust. "They looked like it."

"Well, most of them are Mexican-Americans, then. That explains the flags."

"Not the American flag, sir!"

"Why not?"

"American citizens don't march around highways, disrupting normal activities. They never have!"

"That's an interesting patriotic observation, John."

Endicott looked up sharply. "You know damned good and well what I mean, Bobby. Those people aren't like us. They might have papers, but they're . . . different. Always will be."

Robert smiled thinly, knowing it might be foolish to argue about an item that the Endicotts of the world would never understand. But he could not wholly resist. "They haven't broken any laws, John. They have a right to walk down the road."

"Demonstrations stir people up," Endicott countered, his face a thundercloud. "You know that as well as I do. Aren't you angry about these outsiders coming in, agitating? It's *your* valley!"

"I get irritated. I'm also worried. Frankly, I wish they weren't here—that we didn't have this cloud over us, because I think I have a better idea than most people of how bad it could get. But they've got their rights, too. Some of them would say this is *their* valley."

"They didn't build its commerce," Endicott fumed. "They only want to tear down, and what would they put in our society's place? Nothing!" He paused, then gestured with a loosely closed fist. "Some people say demonstrations should be banned altogether—make it a law. Well, I know that's against the Constitution, and I don't say things have gotten bad enough yet to make us change the Constitution. But I'll tell you. I don't see what would be wrong with a law making them have their demonstrations privately, where people who didn't want to see them wouldn't be forced to see them. Ordinary citizens have rights, too!"

Simms, his grim face indicating probable agreement with this view, said nothing. Both men waited for Robert to react. He knew that he must not show them how invincibly wrong he thought their views really were.

"That may be," he said quietly. "However, I've got some

bad news I have to tell you that has nothing to do with the Workers United situation."

"On the prices?" Endicott demanded, leaning forward.

"Jim Young is no longer with us."

Endicott blinked. There was no initial show of genuine surprise in either him or in Simms, who did not change expression in any way.

Then, however, Endicott started backward with an overshow of reaction. "No longer with us? What do you mean? Is he sick?"

"He was terminated."

Endicott licked his lips, making a great exhibition of confusion. E. Z. Simms, giving a calculated demonstration of confusion that he would never have betrayed if he really were confused, asked, "You mean he resigned for a better position somewhere else?"

"I fired him."

"*Why?*"

"We have had some minor cases of information leaks, and at least two incidents of sabotage. The latest one was an attempt to steal blending records, and Jim was caught in the act."

"Good heavens!" Endicott murmured. "Why would a man like Jim Young do such a thing?"

Not, Robert noted, what were the incidents of sabotage, or who and where and when and by whom was Young caught. Robert felt his own suspicions beginning to harden. He hid this.

"We're at a loss to explain the motive," he lied. "Jim packed up and left at once. We've had no contact with him since. I'm afraid the case is closed and we'll probably never know what motivated him."

Simms spoke. "You do suspect, however, that someone was behind Jim's activities?"

"We aren't even sure of that assumption," Robert said, lying again.

"This is terrible," Endicott said. "I'm sure, however, that you moved promptly and properly."

"We have other good people in sales," Robert said. "There has already been a smooth transition."

"Yes," Endicott muttered. "Make a note of this, E. Z. We'll have to include it in our visitation report. I'm certainly sorry to hear it. Gawwd damn. I certainly am."

"I wanted to tell you about it, John. But I'm sure that isn't what *you* came to discuss."

Endicott scowled. "No, it certainly isn't. Actually, Bobby, we have two matters."

"One is the pricing situation. What's the other?"

"This entire thing with those Mexicans. As I started to talk about it before. Management is very concerned about the possible impact of these people and their efforts on Mancini harvesting, labor costs, pricing, the whole ball of wax."

It was not the subject Robert had expected to discuss, but he saw the obvious tie-in. He explained what he knew of Alfredo Rodriques' goals in the valley, and the few visits Rodriques had made thus far. "Rodriques hopes for a peaceful settlement, I think. If he wins recognition from a half dozen of the larger wineries, and one or two in the medium-sized, prestige class, like ourselves for instance, most of the others will fall into line. That's why we haven't had any direct confrontations yet. He's moving slowly."

Endicott nodded, saying that Timmons Corporation feared a wild-cat strike that might leave the mature grapes in the fields. Robert said everyone feared this, but no one would win from such a situation, including the field workers. Endicott agreed, but said the common desire to get the grapes harvested should not motivate any collapse in the face of Rodriques' demands. Robert said many of his Chicano workers probably would remain loyal to the winery in any case, but he certainly was in agreement that surrender by the wineries was no more of a solution than intransigence.

Timmons Corporation, Endicott said, would back Robert to the hilt in resisting "blackmail tactics." He said the corporation could send in labor-management advisory teams on request by the local management. Robert did not pick up this hint because he had read of a Timmons subsidiary's strike in Washington only a few months earlier, and the story had been graphic in detailing the old railroad methods used by the "advisors" to get the workers back into line.

When E. Z. Simms produced some clippings that mentioned grower James Higgins and his continuing outspoken bitterness against both the wineries and the field workers, Robert replied by frankly explaining his own concerns. He described Higgins and his actions at the growers' meeting.

In addition, Robert pointed out, the weather had again

turned cool. This meant late harvest, at least five weeks away, or late September, and probably October.

"I fail to see"—Endicott frowned—"how a late harvest affects the tensions we've been discussing."

"The later the harvest, the greater the risks. Cold. Rain. A freeze. We could lose a percentage of the crop, maybe a large percentage. That means that every day we run late, natural tensions increase, making tempers shorter. In addition, if we get into October, and the grapes start coming in, we're then really fighting the clock. In a normal harvest period, a wildcat strike would be very bad. But we might be able to delay a few days for negotiation. With a very late harvest, we just wouldn't have that sort of time."

"Meaning," Endicott said, "the late harvest makes you much more vulnerable."

"Yes."

"And gawwd damn, I bet that SOB Rodriques is counting on that!"

"I don't know about that part."

"I do, and I can see why this fellow Higgins is so bitter."

"Rodriques hasn't mentioned a strike yet."

"Yes, but it's implied!"

"It may well be," Robert conceded. "But I'm sure he would call for a general strike only as a last resort."

"If he strikes, I'd let those workers stay out until hell freezes over!"

"There's only one thing wrong with that, John. The vineyards would freeze over first."

Endicott scowled. "Which all goes to explain your thinking, I suppose, on that price-guarantee trial balloon you sent up?"

So here it was at last, in the open. Robert tried to show nothing. "If I hadn't made the statement when and where I did, things would be a lot worse right now. We would have growers refusing to water their fields, as well as Rodriques' people trooping up and down the roads."

Endicott nodded. "Yes, it got results. I can see that . . . appreciate that. It was a good stunt. Good publicity. The only thing we have to be assured of, internally and in strictest confidence, mind you, is that it was just good PR and not anything that's going to tie our hands here."

"It wasn't just PR," Robert told him. "I intend to honor the pledge I made. Several other wineries have also made the same pledge, you know."

"I know. But gawwd damn, what I'm saying is that we don't care what you *pledge*. We just want to be assured, in writing, that Mancini Vineyards will do like everyone else—grab the best, lowest prices you can get when the time actually comes."

"John, I intend to stand by that pledge I gave them."

Endicott's face twisted. "Well, I'm not saying *break* the pledge. What I'm saying is, that if the harvest is bigger than everybody can handle, and the bottom falls out on prices, you could honor your pledge to a few people. But what's to prevent you from discovering that a lot of the grapes are not quite the usual quality? That would knock prices back down. Costs down, profits up. That's all I'm saying."

Robert delayed his reply for a few seconds, wondering if Endicott himself could believe what he had just said. Was Endicott offering *him* a rationalization, or betraying the kind of weird thinking that an executive in Endicott's position sometimes himself had to believe?

Of course, Robert thought, it would work very nicely. The promised floor could be honored . . . with a few. Alleged lower quality would drive prices down for most growers. Something about acid or juice or even *botrytis* . . . something. The only thing in the world wrong with the scheme was that it was dishonest as hell.

"I intend to pay at or above the floor I guaranteed," Robert said.

"People at Timmons are very upset about that. I have to be candid with you on that point, Bobby. It looks like we have a situation where everyone else under the friendly Timmons umbrella is pulling on the oars together, to tighten belts and maximize profits, and you're down here pledging to send your profits right down the old tubes."

"John," Robert said, exasperated, "I didn't promise prices higher than last year's. My pledge is for a floor ten per cent *under* last year's level!"

"The price might go far below that. You need to maximize anywhere you can. If you get a break on the harvest, you have to grab it. All your other expenses are up, way up. E.Z., do you have the figures there?"

Simms pulled out a computer printout. "Glass," he said dryly, "is up sixty-two per cent. Cork, eighty per cent. Labor, fourteen per cent. Overall operating costs—" He stopped, shuffling the long, thin pages. "Operating . . . let's see, where is that figure . . ."

"Up nineteen per cent," Robert supplied for him.

Simms grunted, but kept frantically shuffling pages.

"Nineteen per cent," Robert repeated, getting more irritated.

"The computer figured it to four decimal places . . ."

"I'm not trying to run my own winery into the red," Robert said. "I haven't given all this effort to a company I intend to damage."

"Then, give us a confidential memorandum explaining how the price floor won't actually be operative," Endicott said.

"It *will* be operative."

"Bobby, I can assure you that top management doesn't like your idea . . . doesn't like it at all. I think I've made a real effort to make that clear to you."

"I've always had autonomy here," Robert said, his heartbeat picking up as he sensed that they were at the crux of the matter.

Endicott nodded solemnly. "That's the way Timmons likes to run things. You built this business. You should run it." His sagging eyes came up to meet Robert's. "Even if actual stock control may no longer be in your hands, but in Timmons's."

"What does that mean, John? That if I don't go along, Timmons will call for a vote of all stockholders on management here?"

"Gawwd damn," Endicott sighed. "That, Bobby, is the last thing we would *ever* want to do."

"But that's what you seem to be telling me: drop my floor guarantee, or face a stock fight for control."

"I certainly hope it doesn't come to that," Endicott said. "I mean that most sincerely. All we're trying to do is consult together, work out what's best for all of us. You can see that. Now in this case, the wisdom from the top says that this floor idea is harebrained. You're a big man. You know how to get around it—"

"John, I'm going to say this once more because you seem to be having a hell of a hard time hearing me. I will not back out on my offer to the growers. Period."

Endicott's cheeks puffed out. "Bobby, no one likes to be hard-hearted. But everyone has to co-operate."

Robert watched him, wondering what he was supposed

to say—indeed, what he could possibly say that might make any difference.

"There was a man in Chicago just a few years ago," Endicott said. "You probably know the name. Schwann. Schwann Shoes. Nice man. Good administrator. Well, sir. Jacob Schwann sold a controlling interest in his shoe factory to Timmons Corporation. Did Timmons move in, try to change things? No, sir. Schwann kept right on.

"Then, however, there were some fundamental differences of opinion, no need to trouble you with the details. In short, Timmons and Jacob Schwann came eyeball to eyeball.

"In a case like that, Bobby, Timmons Corporation is not impossible to deal with. Jacob Schwann was given the opportunity to buy back a controlling stock interest, so he could go his own way. Unfortunately, as I imagine usually happens, he was unable to raise the necessary two million in cash."

Endicott sighed heavily. "So today the Schwann Shoe Company is among the giants of the Midwest. And where is Jacob Schwann? Well, he has a comfortable home . . . his remaining stock takes care of that. But he has nothing to do with his own firm. He made a mistake. He was intransigent in a situation where he couldn't win.

"Don't *you* get in a situation like that, Bobby. Please. You make great wine. Gawwd damn. I like you. Reconsider this thing! It isn't worth the risk!"

There was a silence. Robert felt his pulse in his skull. Despite the earlier hints that somehow, at least in part, John Endicott and E. Z. Simms had been in contact with Jim Young about his dismissal (and activities prior to the dismissal?), it seemed now that Endicott did not want a confrontation. Endicott was trying his best to be decent . . . to persuade Robert not to risk a declared war with a corporate entity that thought it had the trump card.

Robert had been bracing himself for this moment, however, and did not hesitate long. More with a feeling of resignation than anything else, he spread his hands on the desk. "John—E.Z.—I'm standing on what I told those growers."

Endicott heaved a sigh which might or might not have been completely sincere. "You leave me no choice but to write a memorandum on this meeting, Bobby. The big boys are going to be very upset, some of them."

"I understand that," Robert said.

Endicott looked hard at him. "*Do* you understand that, Bobby?"

"Yes," Robert said.

Endicott stood heavily. "You'll hear from us soon . . . I'm afraid."

11

"Jules, we've got to take a short break. My fingers aren't functioning right, I'm so tired."

In the boarded-up basement of the Elmhurst winery, Jules Trello straightened his aching back and glared across the moving conveyor belt at Jim Young, who had just spoken. "We'll rest at midnight."

"Jules, *now*. For Christ's sake!"

Jules looked down the seeming unending line of filled bottles being transported past the labeling table on the broad conveyor belt. The two recent Mexican wetbacks at the far end—who spoke and read no English—continued to load unlabeled bottles on the conveyor, and to Jules's far left the other two Mexicans, also newcomers and equally illiterate, were taking the freshly labeled bottles off the belt and putting them in the unmarked cartons. Jules hated to pause for rest, but his own fatigue was extreme. Reaching out a dripping hand, he pulled the lever which shut down the makeshift assembly line.

Jim Young breathed weary relief in the sudden silence following the shutdown. He dried prune-like hands and reached for a cigarette.

Jules signaled the Mexicans at either end that they would rest five minutes. They grinned—the new ones always grinned because they were frightened—and sank to their haunches on the stone floor.

"Can we finish tonight?" Young asked, staring vacantly at all the bottles yet to be labeled.

"We *have* to finish tonight," Jules replied impatiently. "We're looking right down the gun barrel at our deadline."

"If you hadn't found that extra white wine, we would be finished already."

"The extra white means extra money, so shut up about it."

Young nodded and, like the Mexicans, simply sank to the floor for rest.

Jules looked over all the remaining bottles. It would take all night, but the cartons had to be ready for Carmine D'Angelico's trucks. Although Jules's hands were wrinkled and red from exposure to the fluid in the label-dipping trays, and his back and legs were afire with pain, there was no stopping now until it was done.

Discovery of Jim Young's actual role at Robert Mancini Vineyards had put a serious crimp in Jules's plans for continuing trouble-making. He consoled himself with the thought that events had now proceeded to the point where it was mainly in the hands of John Endicott anyway. And at last Young's dismissal had given Jules an intelligent worker in this illicit bottling endeavor.

The wine would be gone within another forty-eight hours. After that, Jules would have some financial breathing room. He could get back to his plans against Robert and to taking an active part in fighting Alfredo Rodriques. Sale of this wine would make all that possible again.

The gamble with this wine, however, had continued to enlarge into more frightening dimensions. Jules had known the risk he was taking in dealing with D'Angelico. But he was out of his element here. He had not fully perceived how far outside the law D'Angelico was taking him.

Not until the labels had arrived.

With a shrug of pain, he looked down at one of the labels floating in the tray, waiting to be pasted to an empty bottle of the Elmhurst "Cabernet." It was pale-blue and white, and it bore the name of a French winery, Château Lafornay. With its vintage date of 1966 and its official-looking phrases of *"Appellation Margaux Contrôlée"* and *"Mis en Bouteille au Château,"* it looked very authentic, but Jules felt a moment of panic as he thought of the possible consequences of the fraud.

12

Less than twenty-four hours after his meeting with John Endicott and E. Z. Simms, Robert Mancini was in a small restaurant on the outskirts of Portland, Oregon, as far from the sprawling Timmons Corporation headquarters as Jed Witchley and Paul Nietbaum could meet him during the working day.

The portly Witchley and youthful, modishly dressed Nietbaum came in almost furtively, glancing around as they shook hands and waited to be led to a corner booth.

"I never heard of this place, and don't expect to see anyone I know," Witchley said. "But I've still got those 007 jitters."

"I appreciate your meeting me at all," Robert said. "I've got an idea I may be *persona non grata* at Timmons today."

A waitress took them to their booth, in a section that was virtually deserted. It was still well before the normal lunch hour.

"Drinks, gentlemen?" the girl smiled.

Witchley hesitated, then shrugged. "What the hell. Martinis all around, gents? Yes. Three."

The girl went away. Nietbaum casually watched her legs.

"You're not exactly *persona non grata* yet," Witchley told Robert, reverting to the topic that had brought them here. "But I've already heard a little about your séance yesterday with my-gawd Endicott and the pewter computer.

350

I'll tell you what, my friend. You're in trouble and that's for durn sure."

"That's what I want to find out," Robert said. "How bad is it?"

"Real bad. At least five divisions of the company have lost heavily this year. That latest foreign wheat deal cost us a cool five million the last time the administration flip-flopped."

"On top of that," Nietbaum put in, "there were some stupid expansions last year. Don't quote me. I didn't say it." Then Nietbaum's stubborn jaw set. "Hell, go ahead and quote me. It's *true*. Big hunks and chunks of the company lost their asses. We've had wholesale changes in management, and the squeeze is on to make the new bosses look good. You've always been a sacred cow around Timmons, but even you aren't sacrosanct. Now your hassle on the bulk-wine proposal and this grape-price floor have drawn attention to you. Some of the new bosses are so paranoid and jittery they probably think you're doing it just to make them look bad."

"There are a lot of itchy tokuses on the top floor," Witchley said. "That's for durn sure."

"I'm not trying to hassle Timmons," Robert said. "I just know what's right for my company and the wine business down there."

"Well, sure," Nietbaum said. "Everyone knows that, if they're being rational. With all the head-chopping that's been going on, though, who's rational?"

"Endicott implied pretty strongly that the next step, if I don't recant, might be a full test on stock control . . . possibly a Timmons takeover."

Witchley puffed out his cheeks. "Well, shit."

"Is that possible?"

"Have you got the stock to control?"

"I don't know," Robert admitted.

"Then it's possible, for durn sure."

Nietbaum said, "I detect the fine hand of Jerry Bowen in here somewhere."

"Yeah," Witchley said glumly. "I wouldn't be surprised."

"Who is Bowen?" Robert asked.

Witchley sighed and folded his hands. "Jerome Bowen. Retired Air Force general. Called in by the top brass early this year to stop the flow of red tape. Strong feller. Dynamic. Throat-cutter. He's got most of the board behind him right now, and his big deal is moving management out of the offices here in Portland and into the subsidiaries, to run 'em directly and with a firm hand—his."

"I'm not a Timmons subsidiary," Robert said.

"Yet," Witchley added meaningfully.

"I won't be if I can control a vote."

"Yeah, but when I asked you a minute ago if you *could* control, you admitted you didn't know."

"Is that what might happen?" Robert asked. "A call for a vote, and if the numbers turn out wrong, out I go and in comes somebody from up above?"

"Yes," Witchley said. "Probably some asshole like Endicott."

"Or Simms," Nietbaum added.

"Or both," Witchley concluded.

"Does Endicott have this Bowen's ear?"

"Nobody has Bowen's ear. But I'd say Endicott is as close to the ruthless bastard as anybody."

"Maybe that's it, then," Robert said.

"That's what?" Witchley looked around. "Where are those drinks?"

"Maybe Endicott wants to play winemaker," Robert said. "That would explain a lot of things. If he forces me into a corner—and out—then he has a better job."

Witchley looked dubious. "Endicott is sort of a dummy."

"He's capable of it," Nietbaum argued.

"Yeah, I suppose he is."

By this time Robert had had another thought. "Is it possible that Endicott and/or Simms own any Mancini stock?"

Witchley's eyes widened. "Christ. I never thought of that. That would give him even more reason to want your chair."

"Some Timmons execs do have stock in companies under the umbrella," Nietbaum said.

"The company encourages it," Witchley added. "That's how they took over the roller-bearing company, remember? Schlasinger and Crock and Jermany had a shitcan full of stock, and when the vote came, they voted right down the old Timmons alley—and got rewarded with vice presidencies." He looked around again. "Where *is* that girl? I'm beginning to need that martini bad."

Robert was turning matters over in his mind with a

speed born of his mounting desperation. "Is there anyone at Timmons I ought to talk with about this?"

Witchley looked uncertain. "I can't think how it would help you."

"I hate everything being filtered through Endicott and Simms."

"I can see that, but I've looked over their memos very carefully. They're playing it right down the middle . . . on paper, at least. You couldn't convince anybody of anything, that I see."

"What about seeing this Bowen?"

"Oh, hell no! He'd eat your lunch. He's one of those spit-and-polish, send-it-through-channels guys. Going to see him, from his view, would be an admission that you have a weakness and can't stand on the record."

"I can't just sit back and wait for my eviction notice."

"Pick up any loose stock that's floating around," Witchley said grimly.

"That takes money."

"Shit, hock everything, but do it."

"I've been doing it already," Robert admitted.

"You've got stock. Your wife probably has some stock in her own name. Maybe you have friends with stock. Get it all lined up. That's the best hedge you've got—so much strength that they don't want to risk calling you. Because if they lose, then you'd be in the driver's seat, and that's for durn sure."

Robert thought about it. In his own mind there was no doubt that the coils were being closed around him. It was easy enough to look back from this vantage point and see that he had been a fool to sell so much stock in exchange for operating and expansion capital. But breast-beating would accomplish nothing. He had to deal with the given.

Audra did have some stock in her own name, he remembered—about five hundred shares. And somewhere in his memory was an inkling that old Gus might have bought some, too, when Mancini Vineyards first went public. He had to have those shares on his side, he thought. And he had to find new ways to raise money in order to be able to make discreet offers for others that might be floating on the market.

He had to go to Gus Trello's house again. He saw that.

With the situation as it stood between himself and Audra, it would be unpleasant at best. He had no recourse.

His two friends, however, were watching him, waiting for his reaction. He knew they did not have long, and he had not yet gotten all the information he had come for.

"What happens if I maintain my position," he asked, "and Timmons decides to see who has the most marbles?"

Witchley glanced at Nietbaum, deferring to the young lawyer on this.

"Simple," Nietbaum said. "The company sends you a registered letter that says in real neat legalese: 'Hey, Dad, I think we own your company now. We gonna have us a vote in sixty days.'"

"And then it's voted?"

"You better believe."

"And if I lose?"

"Then we got the roller-bearing company as a precedent. You're given another thirty days to spread your legs and enjoy it, or in come the new boss fellers. And out you go in the street, or wherever."

"Like old Schwann," Robert said, remembering.

"A classic case," Nietbaum said. "One of the first times our beloved firm showed its hidden fangs."

The girl was coming with the drinks on a tray now. Witchley looked thankful, and they said nothing more while she served. She gave them a pasted-on smile and went away again, promising that a waiter would be by shortly.

Witchley toyed with his swizzle stick. "A word of advice, Robert?"

"Sure," Robert said.

"Cool it," Witchley said. "Don't make waves. It's a real bad time. Go with Endicott. Roll with this punch. Take your time to try to pick up more stock. Fight 'em when *you're* ready."

"I can't. I gave my word to those growers."

"Well, giving your word is all fine and dandy, but you gonna lose your ass, mothuh, and that's for durn sure."

"Maybe not," Robert said. "Nobody can know for certain where some of the unaccounted-for stock is. Maybe I'll win if they force it to a showdown."

"Oh," Nietbaum said quietly, with regret, "from what I know, I think they're going to force it now."

"You can't fight city hall," Witchley added, "for durn sure."

"I'm not fighting city hall," Robert replied. "I'm just fighting Timmons Corporation . . . I think."

Witchley grimaced and picked up his martini glass. He raised it in a rueful salute. "Cheers," he said.

13

It was the noon hour, and virtually the entire office staff had left Robert Mancini Vineyards for lunch, when Susan Knight received the intercom call from Nancy, doubling on the switchboard and reception desk.

"Mr. Rodriques is here," Nancy said tautly, in a low voice.

"Oh, hell," Susan blurted in dismay. "Did you tell him Robert is out of town?"

"I did," Nancy replied in the same near-whisper, "but he's standing here in the office lobby and he says he'd like to speak to whoever is in charge."

"Well, that's Mike DeFrates."

"Mike went to the city a half hour ago."

"He doesn't want to see *me*. I'm not a boss around here."

"You're the closest thing to it," Nancy replied nervously. "I don't think I ought to just send him away. He has this package under his arm. He looks like he must want to talk to someone. He might think we're giving him a hard time if no one comes out."

Susan thought about it briefly. Handling Alfredo Rodriques properly, she knew, might be crucial to later relations with him. Nancy was right: someone had to see him.

"I'll be right there," Susan said.

When she reached the office lobby, she found Alfredo Rodriques seated on one of the mahogany-stained plank benches just inside the elevator doors from the first floor.

Her first impression was one of disappointment; Rodriques looked so very *ordinary*—much shorter than she had expected, and physically smaller in all respects. He wore a tan leisure suit, a worker's straw hat, a white shirt open at the throat. She noted a gold cross gleaming on a chain around his neck. Beside him on the bench was a thick brown envelope evidently stuffed with legal-sized papers of some kind.

Taking a deep breath, she walked up to the man. He rose, unsmiling, his quick eyes searching her with a wary intelligence. She introduced herself.

"I'm not really the person you want to see," she added, "but Mr. Mancini is out of town today, and Mr. DeFrates, our manager, left for the city just a little while ago."

"I am disappointed that I can't see Mr. Mancini this time," Rodriques told her with a slight, almost shy smile. "However, perhaps I can make an appointment for the first part of next week."

Intent on being a good host, Susan nodded agreement. "Why don't we go into Mr. Mancini's office and look at his desk calendar? I know he's eager to confer with you. Would you like some coffee?"

"Coffee would be good," Rodriques told her quietly.

"Nancy," Susan said, calling through the adjacent door, "could you please bring some coffee to Mr. Rodriques and me in Robert's office?"

Nancy got up quickly from the blinking switchboard and held up two fingers, obviously crossed. She hurried toward the conference room, where the coffee urn was located.

Susan led Rodriques into Robert's spacious, starkly decorated office. Feeling ill at ease, she showed the labor leader to a chair, then moved behind Robert's desk and sat in the unaccustomed position. Rodriques seemed to be waiting for her to speak again, so she looked for something to say.

"We've heard that you're visiting wineries and growers, Mr. Rodriques. I'm sure Mr. Mancini will regret missing you on your first visit." She looked over Robert's calendar. "It looks like he has some time open next Tuesday, September first."

Rodriques took a small black book from one of the breast pockets of his coat and glanced at several pages. "Perhaps at ten?"

"That looks fine. I suggested Tuesday because we do

tastings each Monday morning, and Mr. Mancini's schedule looks pretty busy in the afternoon. It might be best if you call us Monday, though, and verify this. He could have set something up that isn't written down here."

Rodriques used the stub of a pencil to write something in his book. "I will call Monday, then, but plan to be here Tuesday at ten."

"Good," Susan said. She also made a note.

Rodriques put the bulky brown envelope on the edge of the desk between them. "This package contains materials about Workers United. Included are outlines of our goals here in the valley."

"I'll see that Mr. Mancini gets them."

"It would be helpful if Mr. Mancini has studied the documents before our discussion."

Susan felt a stab of irritation at the calmly delivered directive. "I'm sure Mr. Mancini will look at your materials if he can possibly find time."

A faint smile, devoid of any malice, touched Rodriques' mouth. "I was not presuming to issue instructions, Miss Knight. I tend to speak too directly at times, and be misunderstood. I only intended to say that we have tried to provide helpful material here. Forgive me. I am a simple man."

Nancy returned with the coffees and supplies, making a reply from Susan unnecessary. She was glad for the interruption because she was beginning to realize that the last statement made by Alfredo Rodriques, at least, was not accurate. He was far from the simple man he appeared or professed to be.

Watching him stir a cube of sugar into his coffee, she studied his deft, economical movements and his facial expression. His hands were work-gnarled, but his fingers remained almost feminine in their delicacy. His eyes had a curious softness about them. Although there was a dark stubble of beard on his chin, his skin was very soft, like that of a child. His face in repose had a calmness and peace about it that was unnerving.

"You're visiting wineries today?" Susan asked after Nancy had gone.

"There had been a rally scheduled. It was postponed due to an unfortunate circumstance. I am visiting workers in the fields and seeing a few leaders as I can along the way."

"Mr. Mancini will regret having missed you this time."

Rodriques inclined his head. "Robert Mancini is one of the leaders I most want to see here before much more is undertaken."

"Mr. Mancini is not really a leader. There is no formal organization of winemakers in the area—"

"He is a leader, nevertheless," Rodriques corrected her gently. "His action in taking the first step with the growers was proof of that. Since that time, there is no doubt that many of the other winemakers have begun to look to him for leadership, for example. Some of those I have already visited have said as much openly."

"It's not a leadership he seeks," Susan said.

"Leadership does not always fall to the man or woman who runs after it. And you do not need to be uneasy, Miss Knight, that I have any intention of trying to entrap Mr. Mancini into the role of a spokesman for anyone else. I will not try to put him"—Rodriques paused and again displayed the slight, self-deprecating smile—"on the spot."

A subtle alarm system sounded in Susan's nervous system. Rodriques had again surprised her by articulating a feeling within her that she had not wholly become aware of until he spoke of it for her. She had seldom had the feeling that a stranger understood her so well . . . and, given their roles, it was not a pleasant sensation, although she had begun to sense that she could not really fear this man as an individual.

"Well," she said lamely, "I'm sure he'll want to see you Tuesday."

"Is there word of his father-in-law?" Rodriques asked.

"August Trello? Nothing recent that I know of."

Rodriques nodded. "I know August Trello well. And his sons, of course. It is a great tragedy that a man of such vigor should be struck down."

"Your relations with August Trello in the past were not exactly harmonious."

Again the slight smile. "A portion of my life is dedicated to organizing Trello Industries. You may know that I once spent several days in jail because of August Trello's charges against me."

"I know you aren't exactly friends."

"And so," this surprising man said, "you infer that my asking about his health is a cynical gesture, perhaps. But this is not so. I may despise what August Trello stands for.

He has brought many of us great pain. But I have seen him, spoken with him. I know his past and his work. He is a great man."

"Even though you hate him?" Susan replied, drawn out of herself to say what was really on her mind.

Rodriques' face set sternly. "I do not hate. There is no room for hate. All is a matter of justice."

Susan stared at him, trying vainly to read behind the repose of his features. Once more Rodriques caught her eyes with his own, and seemed to know her thoughts.

"Hate is a failure," he told her. "When hate enters, justice runs away."

"Is that why you've gone slowly here in the valley so far?"

"But we have not gone slowly. Each day more pledges are signed. Our strength grows."

"Perhaps," Susan amended, "I should have said, Is that how you've managed to keep your efforts quiet so far? You know, I think all of us have been frightened about real trouble. But so far there hasn't been any real trouble—"

"Oh, but that is where you are wrong," Rodriques cut in.

"One or two incidents," Susan conceded. "But nothing—"

"Of the nature of the so-called Trello War?" Rodriques said. "Perhaps. We are trying very hard to maintain a peace, Miss Knight. I know many good men—growers and winemakers—are also working to the same end. But the situation is not placid. It is very explosive, I am sorry to say."

Susan again studied his face, puzzled.

"The troubles have not been one-sided," Rodriques told her. "It is important for people to know this. We have had incidents here involving errors by employers, and we have, unfortunately, had errors by our own people."

"There's been nothing in the newspaper."

"None has been reported as yet. But it would be a terrible mistake to think our situation here is not dangerous. It is dangerous, Miss Knight. This is one thing I am trying to make clear to everyone I visit."

"Have you encountered a lot of personal resistance on your visits?"

"Nothing serious as yet." Rodriques' lips curled in the smile. "But that, I am afraid, will end later today."

Susan could not restrain her curiosity. "What happens later today?"

"I visit the Schreck Brothers Winery."

"To try to see Jules Trello?"

"Yes."

"He won't see you! You must know that!"

Rodriques shook his head wearily. "We can only go on so long, seeing those we believe will be receptive, or at least civil. The more stubborn must be confronted sooner or later." Rodriques' chest expanded in a deep breath, slowly exhaled. "It is time."

"Why run head-on into people like Jules at *this* time?" Susan demanded, concerned as well as puzzled. "You just finished saying there's tension already."

"Men like Jules Trello are the ones with whom we must do the most work, to convince them."

"You'll never convince Jules. You must know that."

Rodriques gave his little shrug. "We must try."

"Why confront each owner and grower individually? Can't you make your demands generally, and stay out of individual arguments?"

Rodriques spread his hands. "As you yourself have pointed out, there is no single organization to deal with. And what happens if we make general demands, and there is no agreement? Then are we not forced into the situation of a general strike, across the entire valley? No, Miss Knight. It is far better to deal with each man separately. Then perhaps there can be agreement with most . . . a concerted forceful effort only against those who will not consider discussion with us."

"So you'll deal with each winery and grower separately, one at a time," Susan said. "That will make this drag out forever."

"By no means. Already patterns have begun to emerge. We have hope for quick agreements between ourselves and several persons we have already met."

"If it's going well, then, why see Jules? That *won't* go well. You're just asking for trouble."

Rodriques' face hardened. "If there is trouble, it will be of Jules Trello's making."

"Would you like that?" Susan asked sharply. "Are you *sure* you wouldn't like to make an example of Jules?"

"Miss Knight, the situation is far too dangerous for that, I assure you!"

The flash of genuine anger showed the volatility of the man, and made Susan realize she had relaxed too much, had been far too candid. "I'm sorry," she said quickly. "That wasn't meant exactly as it sounded."

Rodriques' anger vanished as quickly as it had come. "Of course." He stood. "Now I must be on my way."

Susan walked with him to the door, feeling a growing urge to say something more. She felt a near compulsion to say it. "We're natural antagonists," she said finally. "I want you to know that I'm not in sympathy with a lot of the things you want done around here."

"Of course," Rodriques said quietly.

"I hope . . . somehow . . . we all get out of this . . . all right."

Rodriques smiled again, and his eyes held a gentle, warm light of genuine liking for her. He extended his hand. "Thank you for your kindness. We will meet again."

After he had gone, Susan stood in Robert Mancini's office for several minutes, pondering what, if anything, she should do. Finally her worry overcame her reticence and she went to the telephone and called Rod Poole.

Briefly she told him of Rodriques' plan to confront Jules Trello sometime later in the day.

"Great," Poole said bitterly. "Jules will squirt him with a fire hose, and then it will be Katy-bar-the-door."

"Can you go out there?"

"No way," Poole said flatly. "Until somebody breaks a law, we aren't getting near any of this. That decision was made on top, in conjunction with the city."

"What if Jules calls and says Rodriques is trespassing?"

"Then if Jules wants to sign the paper, I'll arrest Rodriques."

Susan sighed with exasperation. "Are you sure you couldn't just be out there in the Schreck neighborhood on your own? Just in case?"

"Number one, that would be against orders, and number two, I've got to go around this afternoon and requestion a few drivers who were on the road when Jamie Henderson was killed."

"Is there something new, Rod?"

"No. But the Hendersons, especially Mrs. Henderson, are going around on this private investigation of their own. They've interviewed everybody we have, and now we hear Mrs. Henderson has been visiting stores, garages, even junkyards, getting the names of anybody they can who might have bought a headlight for a Z car, a Jaguar, you name it—any car that might fit the general description of the one that hit and ran. So now," Poole added in disgust, "the sheriff is getting shook that the Hendersons might turn up something we missed, which would make us look stupid. So we're going over everything again."

"Rod, do you think you did miss something?"

"No. I think the Hendersons are crazy and wasting their time. But I follow orders."

"You can't blame them, Rod, I suppose."

Poole sighed. "Maybe not. I don't know."

"Well, about Alfredo Rodriques—"

"There's nothing we can do, honey. I advise you to forget it."

Susan thought about it more after she hung up. She decided regretfully that Rod Poole was right. It was unlikely that anything serious, in terms of lawbreaking, would transpire as a result of Rodriques' attempt to visit Schreck Brothers. But she also knew that it would be decidedly unpleasant. She wondered how it would go. She found herself wondering again why Alfredo Rodriques felt compelled to confront Jules Trello, surely his most obvious enemy, at this time. She sensed that there was more to Rodriques' motivations than he had told her.

14

Alfredo Rodriques had not completely explained the growing pressures he was under during his brief meeting with Susan Knight, nor had he been candid in stating why he was compelled to accelerate his original timetable in the valley. He was not pleased at the prospect of confronting Jules Trello, but he felt that he had little choice if he was to maintain control of his own people. But this too he had hidden.

Leaving the Robert Mancini winery, Rodriques walked to the gaudily painted Volkswagen microbus which was his mobile unit for the effort locally. Equipped with a heavy-duty suspension and a two-way radio, it had served him well in other campaigns. Memories of some of those strikes crowded back on Rodriques now as he climbed into the bus and faced the aide who had been waiting for him, Carlos Murnan.

"You return quickly, Alfredo," Murnan said, his eyes snapping to show how ready he was to lose his temper.

"Robert Mancini was not there. I spoke with an assistant."

"Did Mancini run to avoid you?" Murnan said. "If so—"

"No," Rodriques cut in to quiet down his overeager firebrand. "I was well treated. I return next Tuesday."

Murnan's features sagged as if he was disappointed. "Where do we go next? Do we at last go to meet Jules Trello?"

Rodriques started the bus and shifted into reverse to back from the parking spot. "Yes, Carlos," he said patiently. "We go to see Jules Trello."

"The pig will oink with fear when he sees us!"

"He is not a pig, Carlos. No man is a pig! And if you believe he will fear us, you are very much mistaken. Furthermore, *we* will not confront him. You will stay in the bus, as before. I will see him alone."

"I want very much to face this man, Alfredo."

"I know that, Carlos. You want it too much."

Murnan's dark eyes blazed. "Would you rob me of this chance to stand in the face of the man I most want to fight? Why would you do this to me?"

"Exactly for that reason! We are not going to see him to seek a fight. We will ask to explain our objectives, and hope for negotiation."

"You know that is impossible with a Trello!" Murnan said hotly. "This is the man who led the struggle against us in the south! He is our sworn enemy! He will try to destroy us! We must make it clear that we can destroy him if he resists us!"

Inwardly praying for calm against the repeated assaults of Murnan and his growing circle of supporters, Rodriques pulled onto the highway and drove north in light traffic. He waited to speak until he was sure he had himself well under control.

Finally he said, "Open warfare—with Jules Trello or anyone else—will destroy our chances of success. You know this, Carlos. I have explained it many times."

"There is no hope of accommodation with a Trello! We must show our strength and waste no more time in moving against him!"

"That is exactly what we will *not* do! We will try everything possible to avoid open warfare."

"Would you surrender to a Trello, then? Would you continue to walk on the tips of your toes? Are we to act as if we fear him?"

Jesus, Mary and Joseph! "No. But we will not seek a fight if it can be avoided. We will go as slowly as we must to avoid making enemies of those who might not be our enemies if we proceeded with caution."

"The harvest is less than six weeks away," Murnan argued. "After the grapes are harvested, they can afford to stall with us for a year. We must move with authority now."

"We are moving with as much speed as we dare, Carlos."

"Alfredo," Murnan said, modulating his tone in an attempt to be persuasive, "visiting Jules Trello today is a good sign. It shows our effort is being moved faster. But we must move faster yet! It is time to throw down the glove. We must pick a winery or a large grower and make our final demands, setting a quick deadline."

"And if the demands are not met?" Rodriques asked wearily, knowing the answer.

"Then it is high time we show our strength! We now have all the workers pledged to our support. We must attack that winery or grower that refuses to negotiate. We must close him down. This will prove to everyone else that we cannot be delayed much longer!"

"We must be responsible. It is not yet time for such actions. It would only close all minds to our just cause. We must strive for negotiation and restrain ourselves."

"We have been here more than two weeks now! What have we accomplished?"

"We have made great progress. There is hope for a peaceful solution. We must not endanger that."

"Time is on the side of the rich men," Murnan said bitterly. "They will let us proceed peacefully and slowly forever." Sarcasm and impatient anger dripped from his words like acid: "They will let us *negotiate* and exercise *caution* for ten thousand years. They will let us die with a promise of new compromise on our tongues. They understand only force."

"The time for force is not yet, Carlos."

"I believe delays only hurt us. We will lose our resolve, Alfredo! Think of the setbacks we have already suffered!"

It was true in part, Rodriques thought, driving, and it was very, very hard to answer Carlos Murnan's twisted logic. There *had* been serious setbacks, near disasters, which already had begun to form a division in his forces between the discouraged and the impetuous.

There had been a scuffle in a field six days ago, and two of his organizers had been slightly beaten up by other Chicano workers frightened of losing their jobs if the organizers were found there with them. A white foreman had slashed the tires of two other organizers' car a day later. There had been the near brush with real violence involving the two bands of teen-agers in a city drive-in.

Three days ago, a speeding pickup truck had swerved close to a small band of marchers on a side road. A fourteen-year-old boy had leaped to avoid being hit, and had broken his left leg in falling into the ditch. And on two occasions there had been attempts to break into the headquarters in town, the second time, cans of gasoline had been discovered in the alley where they had evidently been placed in anticipation of arson.

Meetings with growers and winemakers had been ragged at best. No one welcomed a concerted effort to organize field workers and push for a series of labor reforms that could only be costly. Many of the men Rodriques had met so far were obviously trying their best to be civilized, not only from essential decency but from worry over what might happen if the general situation deteriorated to open skirmishing. "No one wants another Trello War here," one grower had said frankly. But no one was going to concede a thing voluntarily.

Rodriques' followers knew this. His problem was in keeping them motivated without setting off a spark that could become a conflagration.

Increasingly, however, the firebrands like Carlos Murnan were becoming more restive. They were young . . . did not understand the long haul. They wanted action now, regardless of consequences. Each new incident deepened their impatience.

Rodriques' growing trouble in controlling them was symptomatic of changes in all parts of the revolutionary or near-revolutionary movement. There had been a time not so long ago when activists had an almost mystic belief in the wisdom of the body politic. "Demonstrate," the conventional activist wisdom had then said, "and dramatize your causes. And the people will respond once their attention has been drawn."

The late 1960s had killed this faith. Increasingly now the demonstrations were more violent, more explosions for their own sake than from any hope of winning public acceptance. And even worse, blind acts of violence had begun to appear with greater frequency: bombs left anonymously to kill unknown innocent bystanders, as if the perpetrators no longer had *any* individual wrongdoer in mind, but only wanted to strike out at random against anyone, doing anything to rupture the fabric of the society.

Rodriques knew these tendencies existed in his organization, too. Carlos Murnan had his followers. Rodriques had to keep them in line, or they might run ahead of him and create havoc and violence.

This, then, was why he was going to see Jules Trello today. The Carlos Murnans needed to see action, and feel the effort was moving forward. They had to be pacified somewhat to be kept in line.

Rodriques drove the remaining distance to the Schreck Brothers Winery in silence. As he turned in through the stone gates of the grounds, he felt his insides tightening. An older, no-nonsense commercial winery, Schreck Brothers consisted of one main building which conceded a little to tourist expectations by having pillars along its front porch. The remainder of the façade was brick and wood and without frills, however, and the production buildings on either side and to the back were steel paneling, and almost like factory construction. Lush vineyards extended in all directions.

"Wait here," Rodriques told Murnan, who frowned but obeyed.

Inside the main building, Rodriques entered a large, echoing central lobby with a circular information desk in its center. Two stories tall, the lobby had color pictures, internally illuminated, along the walls. Each picture showed some aspect of the winemaking process. It was an impressive entry for tourists, and there were about a dozen standing near the information desk now, waiting for the next tour. But Rodriques ignored them and walked at once to the side doorway which led to stairs, which in turn took him to the office wing one floor higher.

The receptionist at the end of the small, buff-tiled corridor smiled brightly. "Hi there! Can I help you?"

"I want to see Mr. Jules Trello, please. My name is Alfredo Rodriques."

The girl's eyes widened. "Just a minute, please." Scooping off her switchboard headset, she left her cubicle and vanished through a door.

Rodriques waited, his pulse thick in his ears.

After perhaps three minutes, the door opened. A uniformed plant guard came in. A middle-aged man with deep creases in his face, the guard wore a tan jacket that matched his trousers and paramilitary shirt, and he had a little badge on his chest which read, in tiny letters, *SCHRECK BROTHERS SECURITY*. The guard had no weapon in sight, and he looked grim and unhappy.

"Mr. Rodriques?" he said.

"Yes?"

The guard took him firmly by the arm. "Sorry, sir. My orders are to escort you off the property."

Rodriques had had worse surprises. He made no resistance as the guard walked him to the stairs and down them to the main lobby. Although he had expected to see Jules Trello, even if briefly, this prompt ejection was, Rodriques had to admit, as effective an answer as any.

The guard stolidly kept propelling Rodriques toward the front door . . . and the parking lot beyond, and Carlos Murnan.

"I will leave quietly," Rodriques told him. "You can let me go on from here alone."

"Sorry, sir. My orders are to see you into your car and off the property."

There was simply no point in arguing. The guard did not much like what he was doing, but was clearly dead set on carrying out his instructions to the letter. Rodriques accepted the realization that his attempt to pacify his firebrands was now in the process of backfiring.

The afternoon sun, obscured partly by clouds, was still bright after the few minutes inside the winery. Rodriques was almost to the microbus, the glum guard at his side, before he saw Carlos Murnan's expression clearly through the glare. Murnan was livid.

As the guard started Rodriques around the front of the Volkswagen, still clamped to his arm, Murnan came out of the passenger door. He rushed in front of the guard, crouching.

"Let him go, son of a pig!"

The guard stiffened. "Now just a minute, buddy—"

"Carlos," Rodriques snapped. "Get back in the car."

"This pig has his hands on you—"

"Carlos! *Do what I say!*"

Murnan glared at him. Rodriques did not flinch, but held the gaze. For a few seconds Murnan's anger was all directed away from the guard and toward Rodriques himself—source of his frustration, the one who was blocking his furious desire for overt action.

Rodriques breathed shallowly and deep.

It was Murnan who first looked away. With a muttered oath he flung himself back into the microbus.

Rodriques let the guard escort him right to the driver's side door. He climbed inside, closed the door, started the engine. The guard stood back, squinting against the sun and very ill at ease, while Rodriques drove away.

"He would not see you!" Murnan seethed. "He sent you away with a pig of a guard to attend you! Now will you agree it is time we made this Jules Trello our first major target, and struck him *now?*"

"We will do as I say!" Rodriques retorted sharply. "In the meantime, Carlos, you will keep quiet!"

The response was so much sharper than Rodriques' normal replies that Carlos Murnan stared, his eyes bulging, and actually lapsed into silence.

Alfredo Rodriques, however, knew that he had perhaps seen another bit of his control eroded. Carlos Murnan and all of the others like him—and they were growing in number daily as frustrations mounted—would not be held inactive much longer. The balance was becoming delicate. How much longer, Alfredo Rodriques wondered, could he maintain control?

15

On the last Saturday of August, three days after his meeting in Portland, Robert Mancini once more drove up the hill through ripening vineyards toward the home of a dying August Trello.

The old man had weakened, Cline had told Robert on the telephone. He had good days and bad. Amazed at the strength of his will, doctors said there was no accurate way to predict when the cancer might break him and end his daily struggles to rise, pretend nothing at all was wrong, and fight with everyone who came into his view. It might be days or it might be months, with the steady decline so slow that it was visible only in the longer haul.

It was midafternoon. The day's heat here was heavy and oppressive. Workers were in the vineyards, inspecting vines, checking stakes, applying chemicals. The harvest would be sooner here, perhaps in as little as three weeks.

In the north country the weather had turned hot on Thursday. People were again saying the harvest might come late in September. Robert thought not . . . wondered what his own situation would be in October when the grapes finally were ready. Alfredo Rodriques, whom he was to meet next Tuesday, might have a word on the success or failure of the harvest generally, he thought. And today's mission might go far in determining the personal fate of Robert Mancini *vis-à-vis* Timmons Corporation.

Robert parked his car among the dozen or so others

cluttering the front driveway. As before, there were small children on the sprawling lawn, and workers in the shrubbery and flowerbeds. A power mower was running somewhere.

As Robert walked toward the steps leading to the front door, the door opened and Frank Trello strode out. Wearing bib overalls, his rubber boots glistening near the knee with the pink froth of fermenting wine, Frank was so turned in upon himself, scowling with some new worry, that he did not see Robert for a moment. His eyes were sunken in their sockets and a tic danced at the corner of his left eye.

Coming down the steps, Frank broke into a jog as he headed for his pickup. He had always been running, Robert thought, fighting to prove his worth to a father who would never concede it. Only old Gus's death could have changed Frank's character, but it was probably too late now; Frank would continue running from long habit, still trying to prove himself, long after the target of his efforts was in the grave.

"Frank!" Robert called.

Frank stopped, saw Robert, and walked back. There was no hint of pleasure in his eyes. "You again, so soon?"

"I've come to see Audra, and of course, Gus. Are they inside?"

"I'm sure they are. Everyone is inside. Brothers, sisters, aunts, uncles, cousins. It's like a circus now."

"Cline said Gus is worse."

Frank blinked, surprised. "I was just with him, asking some questions. He's fine."

"What do the doctors say?"

"I don't know. I haven't had time to talk to them. We're running a hundred and twenty thousand gallons right now and that's just the start of it. I have to stay on the job, even if no one else does."

"What kind of wine is it?"

"Apple wine, over at Desert Grove. On Monday we start eighty thousand cases at Pine Hill, and we expect the grape crushing to begin before the middle of September. I'm running my head off."

Robert tried to look sympathetic. The logistics of the Trello operation were as complex as those of an army in the field. The combined capacities of Trello wineries exceeded *in three hours* the annual production of many fine wineries. Problems involved in such quantity production were of an order most winemakers could not begin to comprehend. Frank was carrying this load now, burdened further by the apparent belief that he was incapable of making even the most routine decisions without a trip here for angry, insulting orders. He was trapped in a pattern of self-defeat.

"It's too bad you don't have more help from young Gus," Robert said.

Frank's lip curled. "If I had more help from him, I couldn't get the job done."

"Maybe so," Robert conceded. "I just meant that you're carrying a big load alone now."

"There's no need to say things like that, Robert. I can hack it. I know what you really think of me, so don't pretend. It won't get you anything."

"I don't know what the hell you mean, Frank."

Frank Trello's face twisted. "I'm doing what you could have done, but you turned it down. I know you think this is a shit job, making shit wine. But somebody has to do it. We make an honest wine."

Dismayed, Robert put a hand on the other man's shoulder. "Frank, what you're doing is something I couldn't do. That doesn't mean I have to sneer at you, or you have to sneer at me. Mass-production wine is feasible here, and that's what old Gus chose to make. I couldn't have an operation like this in the north even if I wanted it."

"You won't have this one here, either," Frank retorted, shaking him off. "That will is ironclad. I have a good idea of the provisions. Your little visits up here won't change it any more than all these jaunts by Jules will."

It was news that Jules had been making the trek south, but Robert was not surprised. Perhaps Frank was correct in assuming that Jules's visits were motivated by avarice. "That's not what I have in mind in coming here, Frank."

"Good," Frank said, turning to walk toward his truck. "Because you really would be wasting your time. Believe me."

Robert walked to the front door of the house while Frank Trello was backing his truck from between some cars and driving away with a clash of angry gears. He had left the house door ajar, and Robert hesitated, then walked in.

The front hallway was a cacophony. A stereo set was playing upstairs at incredible volume. In some nearby ground-floor room, a television was blatting the sounds of a western movie, gunfire, hoofbeats, orchestra. Robert saw no one, and headed through a front parlor to the corridor beyond.

The alcove around the front telephone had been transformed into a cat feeding and watering station. Several small round bowls, blues and red and yellow plastic, had been overturned. A lanky Siamese sat on a table, watching a Persian rake its paws ritualistically through a mound of cat litter spilled from an overturned pan onto the carpet.

In the hallway beyond, Robert stepped over children's toys. The odor of Lysol had been added to the previous smells of stale tobacco, dust, and dog dung.

The TV set blared in the main living room, a great old hall complete with crossed swords over a mammoth fireplace and a suit of armor in one corner. The rug here had been rolled back. Five small children were wrestling around on the bare floor in front of the set. Another boy of about eight was riding the back of a couch as if it were a horse, and a girl of perhaps ten was finger-painting on a gateleg table nearby.

Another child, a towheaded little boy, reeled out of an adjoining room on a big red tricycle. He made straight for Robert, pedaling furiously.

"Gangway!" he cried, ringing the bell on the handlebars. "Peep peep!"

Robert got out of the way and the rider careened away and out of sight.

Deeper in the house, the room where Dora kept her poodles was still being used for them. The carpet was gone but the dogs remained leashed to the furniture. Several puddles and wet mounds of droppings decorated the gleaming wood. The legs of the chairs and tables had been reduced to splinters as the poodles, in an agony of boredom, chewed on them.

In still another room farther back, a radio was playing fast country rock at a volume which had been overwhelmed by all the greater noises. Inside, Dora Trello, in electric-pink shorts and halter, was dancing alone. Robert tried to slip by the door, but Dora spied him.

"Robert! My God! Will wonders never cease! Back already?"

"Dora," Robert said, his control slipping a little, "those

Goddamned dogs have ruined everything in the next room. Why don't you put them outside somewhere?"

"They *cry* when I put them outside, Robert. And what difference does it make? Everything around here will be part of a God-awful estate auction one day soon anyhow."

"Where's Audra?"

"Off in some corner, feeling sorry for herself as usual, I imagine."

"How is old Gus?"

"The clan hovers, waiting for the old bastard to kick off so we can read the will."

It was small wonder that young Gus drank, Robert thought, with this for a wife. After allowing himself the small outburst over the dogs, and having gained nothing by it, he struggled to stay calm. "I heard old Gus was weaker."

"He may be, but it's taking him a long enough time!"

"That's very inconsiderate of him."

"Did Jules come with you?"

"Of course he didn't. Is Audra—"

"Jules is coming this weekend sometime. Did you know that?"

"No."

"Oh, yes. As the heartbeat in the great patriarch falters, loyal son visits increasingly often, hoping the will is to favor him."

"I'll see you later, Dora."

"I'll holler if Jules arrives. I know how much you love each other, but you would enjoy the scene when he goes and sits at Daddy's knee and then slinks off again like the beaten cur he really is."

Robert's patience was not at its best today. He turned and walked away from her. He passed through the kitchen, and as he did so, he heard her turn the radio up again, much louder than before.

There was a large green plastic trash can at the back door of the hotel-sized kitchen. Bottles—empties—filled it. Robert glanced at them, jumbled together: a Trello peach wine; Château Palmer, 1964; Château Mouton-Rothschild, 1962; Coke; Pepsi; a 1958 La Tour; one of the great Heitz Cabernets; Diet Rite Cola; a fine old Moselle; 7-Up.

Robert did not probe into the debris. He did not want to find perhaps even older bottles, more priceless treasures that had been plundered. He felt slightly ill, and savagely angry.

Audra and Jill Trello were at one of the umbrella tables at poolside, while several youthful hangers-on splashed in the water. Jill saw Robert, first, and said something guardedly. Audra turned to peer at him, but did not gesture toward him.

He walked toward them. They both wore swimsuits, and it struck him that his wife was still a beautiful woman. He wondered why he had never enjoyed this fact when they were living together.

There was a bottle of red wine opened on the table between the women. They were sipping and snacking on a platter of cocktail crackers with cheese.

"Have you had lunch?" Jill asked, shading her eyes with a hand. "Join us." She produced another wine glass and a paper plate from a side table.

Robert sat down. Audra refused to look at him, her jaw set in the old angry line. He lifted the wine bottle to examine the label. It was a national brand Lambrusco that sold for around two dollars.

"If it's not good enough for you," Jill said, "feel free to go to the cellar for whatever you like. Everyone else does."

"I saw some of the empties in the kitchen. Can't you stop it, Jill?"

Her eyes flashed anger. "How? With a gun?"

"You can't just let them go through everything that way, like it was Coca-Cola."

"I've tried to stop them. They keep coming like soldier ants. What difference does it make? Either some of these college boys piss it down the drain or the rest of us fight over it later."

Robert compressed his lips, willing himself to silence. He poured some of the chilled Lambrusco and sipped it.

Jill made a move to leave. "I'll be back later, you two."

"No." Audra said sharply. "Stay."

"You have things to talk about."

"Stay! I want you to stay!"

Looking unhappy, Jill sat down again.

Audra turned to Robert. Her face was rigidly controlled, but her rage and bitterness were clear. "I have something for you before you leave," she said.

"What's that?" Robert asked, cautious.

"A file. A very interesting file. It's a series of reports from a private detective."

Robert put down his glass most carefully. "I wondered

why Jules hired him. I see now that it was to make sure you were spared nothing."

"Spared nothing? What an odd thought! Jules did me a great favor. I might have been stupid for lots longer without this file."

Robert stared at her, trying to penetrate the dancing hate in her eyes to see if there was anything else underneath—any pain, any other emotion he might identify with the woman who had been his wife. There was nothing. She was a stranger.

He said, "I'm sorry Jules had to hurt you this way, too."

"Jules is my brother. He loves me."

"You think that's why he hired a detective to watch me?"

"Of course."

"No, Audra. Jules hates *me*. Whatever feeling he might have for you is incidental."

Jill, showing increasing nervousness, again got to her feet. "I really think this is between the two of you—"

"No!" Audra flashed. "God damn you, you ice dolly, don't you see I can't handle this alone?"

Jill, her face stiffening into a mask, sat down once more.

Audra turned back to Robert with the same stern control. "I understand that the arrangements for separate maintenance are agreeable."

"I told my lawyers to accept whatever you want."

She licked her lips, straining now under a more furious burden of suppressed feeling. "Well, since reading the detective's reports, I think I've changed my mind. I want a divorce."

Robert did not speak. He was completely at a loss. Her turnabout had been too fast for any specific reaction on his part. He knew only the shock of it . . . and the first tracings of sharply conflicting emotions: relief and regret.

"Thank you," Audra said acidly, "for not leaping immediately into a song and dance of celebration."

"Audra, you know that's not how I feel."

"I know you have this girl." Tears brightened her eyes as she glared at him. "All right. I could make you suffer but I'm sick of it already. I won't be the wronged woman. I have more pride than that. You can have your divorce. I'll file for it. I assume," she added bitterly, "you won't contest?"

"I won't contest, Audra," he said quietly.

"I wonder what ever happened to all that Catholic caterwauling about marriage being forever?"

"I wanted it to work for us, Audra."

"One sniff of a wet cunt, and your philosophy didn't last long, did it?" Her voice mocked him. "The great Robert Mancini, so much purer and greater of heart than all the rest of us!"

He did not reply. So many conflicting emotions assailed him that he knew his reply would be incoherent . . . even a blind physical attack. The love and hate for this woman were still in equal proportions, he saw, and this, too, shocked him.

He knew they were finished now. While a part of him was sickened of her and himself, and felt intense relief that it was to be settled once and for all, another part of him knew that it would never wholly be over. Too much of their lives had been invested in one another. His destiny was with Barbara now, and he wanted it thus. But he saw what the nuns had meant—not knowing, certainly, the real wisdom behind the dogma when they articulated it: *marriage is forever*. Yes.

"I assume," Audra was saying stiffly, "our lawyers can work everything out."

"Yes," Robert said, reaching for his wine glass. His hand shook.

"I want a cash settlement. I don't want the house or anything else like that."

"Yes," he said, staring at the wine.

"And the property in San Francisco."

"Yes."

"I intend to keep the stocks that are already in my name. Of course you know that, I'm sure. I plan to go to New York. I still have my friends there. I think I'll try to find some kind of a job. I can still work. The people I know . . . I can help a publisher, or work in public relations."

Robert looked at her, seeing the pain. It was not the right time to say what he knew he now had to say, but there would never be a right time and it had to be said between them. "I'll agree to whatever you say, Audra. There's just one thing. The vineyard stock you have in your name. I want to buy that back from you."

She stiffened. "Why? Would it hurt you so much to know that a Trello owns stock in your winery?"

"No, nothing like that. I have a . . . there's a stock vote

coming up. I need to be sure I can control as much stock as possible."

"You should have thought of that before you went this far, shouldn't you?"

"I'll pay you considerably over the going price, Audra. Whatever you say."

She studied his face an instant, then shook her head. "No."

"Audra, I need that stock."

"No. I'll keep it. A woman in my position needs stock income. You can't have it, not at any price." Her eyes became hard and filled with a bitter pleasure. "And if you need the stock, you can come find me, wherever I am, and you can tell me why I should vote it your way, and then I can decide in terms of protecting my investment."

He did not reply at once as the dimensions of this new dilemma dawned on him. Her stock could become crucial, but there was no way in the world—now—of controlling it. The more he pleaded with her, the more perverse pleasure she could derive from withholding it from him. There was no way to convince her.

Audra said sharply, "Don't sit there looking like a martyr, Robert, please. It just makes me want to throw up."

His anger saved him and gave him control. "My attorneys will make an offer for your stock. I hope you'll reconsider."

"Will it hurt, darling, knowing that I have that stock? I hope so, because—"

"Audra, for the love of Christ!"

She stood quickly, spilling her glass of frothy pink wine over the top of the table. She ran toward the house.

Jill Trello stared at the spilled wine, then at Robert. For once her chilly veneer had been broken. She looked stricken. "I didn't want to stay, Robert."

"I know," he said.

"I think I'd better go after her."

He nodded.

Jill left the patio area. Robert sat alone, watching the sun begin to dry the cheap, fizzy little wine on the white tile tabletop. The people in the pool, none of whom he even knew, continued their lazy games and swimming. One boy kept trying to duck a girl and she kept squealing. Some time passed and Robert struggled to assimilate what had happened.

A few minutes later he was still alone at the table when

movement at the back garden gate caught his attention. He looked up to see Gus Trello manipulate his motorized wheelchair through the gate and into the patio entry.

Spying Robert, the old man pressed a button firmly, and the wheelchair hummed forward, approaching.

16

Gus Trello drove his chair up beside the table. He flipped a switch. The humming stopped and so did the chair's wheels. He snapped a lever backward. The wheels locked. He glowered at the pool play as if Robert were not there.

He had lost weight. His flannel shirt, the sleeves down despite the heat, hung on his bones, and the legs inside his corduroy trousers were wasted away. He was clean-shaven. There were new hollows in cheeks that once had been rounded.

Robert waited stubbornly for some sign of recognition.

"Someone," Trello said, "spilled wine."

"Lambrusco," Robert said.

"Huh! Somebody get mixed up, not steal the good wine?"

"Jill and Audra had this. Everyone doesn't raid your cellars."

Trello snorted again. "What difference, eh?" His chest heaved. "You put back great wine for grand occasion. The grand occasion turns out to be your funeral."

"You don't look quite dead to me, Gus."

Trello's fine teeth showed. "Not quite, eh? Is this what you came here to say? Give old Gus a compliment? Are you like everybody else, pat and kiss?"

"I came to see both you and Audra, but not to give compliments."

"Okay, what did you come for, then? You know Audra wants a divorce?"

Nothing escaped this man. "I know now. We just talked about it."

"So what are you going to do, eh?"

"We're going to get the divorce."

"Audra is stupid girl. She don't really want a divorce. Did you know that, or are you stupid too?"

"Life isn't as simple as you like to make it sound, Gus—"

"Bullshit! Bullshit! You want that girl? Okay! Do what I said! Go in now! Beat her! Fuck her! Take her home!" Trello looked hopeful. "You want me to lock door, keep everybody away so you can do it?"

"We're beyond that, Gus. Nothing would help. Your system might have worked for you—"

"My system works for all men, all women! Everything else is bullshit! A marriage is kept together by a man's muscle, his gut! You don't let a good vine grow wild. You don't be gentle, eh? You prune. You make grow the way you force it to grow. A woman is the same!"

"Gus, I'm sorry. It really is too late."

Trello looked at him for what seemed a long time. "Over?"

"I'm sorry, but yes."

The old man worked his chin forward and back, ruminating. Then he turned to stare at the pool again. "Jules comes tomorrow."

Robert accepted the change of topic. "Someone told me."

"He thinks maybe I will change my will or something. You think?"

"Maybe he just wants to see you. You're his father."

"Ha! That one never went to pot without taking plastic bag, putting it in, maybe he can sell for fertilizer! He thinks I will make him in charge of everything. Frank sees him with me, pees pants, he is so worried." He looked craftily at Robert. "Maybe you come back, same reason, eh?"

"I've never expected to inherit anything, Gus. Now with the marriage breaking up, I know I won't be welcome any more."

"I gave you a last chance, you dumb bunny, eh?"

"I know you did, Gus."

"Then what are you here for? What for you say you want to see me?"

"I've got a problem and it might be serious."

Trello made a snuffing noise through his nose. "*You* got

a problem, eh?" He rubbed fingertips over his chest. "*You* got a problem! You know what I say? Welcome to the club, eh? Welcome to club!"

Robert refused to be lured by the bait. "Do you own any stock in Mancini Vineyards, Gus?"

Trello's teeth clicked shut. "No."

"Someone—I don't remember who—made me think you did once."

"What I need stock in your shit and turds, eh? I own more stuff than you ever dream about! You think I am crazy, buying stock in teensy winery run by a big fool?"

It was the last blow. Nothing was to be accomplished by this visit. Robert poured the last of the Lambrusco and drank it. "Thanks for the visit, Gus."

"Wait a minute! Wait a minute! Not so fast! What trouble you got, eh?"

Robert met his eyes. "I imagine you already know a lot of it."

"I know you made a dumb-bunny offer to growers. I know those guys in Timmons Corporation don't like it. Is there more?"

Robert told him about the latest meeting with Endicott, and then about his trip to Portland and the takeover procedure outlined by Witchley and Nietbaum. Gus Trello listened, his head on his chest.

When Robert finished talking, the old man looked up at him with sad eyes. "You are one big fool, eh?"

"I had to make that price guarantee."

"Why? *Why?* What makes *you* the world's richest man? You think you are some savior? Some J. Paul Getty? You got a lot of Arab oil or something?"

"It won't cost that much, if anything, and those growers needed an assurance—"

"Shit and turds! Don't give me bleeding-heart talk, eh? You want advice for your trouble? Okay. Free. Here is advice. You won't follow my advice. You never will. But here it is, free. Take back your offer. Let prices fall where they will. Play along with big shots in Timmons, eh? Buy time. Maybe next year you get enough stock, force vote of your own."

"I can't do that, Gus."

"Then what do you do?"

"I'm buying all the loose stock I can."

"You got enough money?"

"As much as I've needed so far. The problem is finding stock at any price."

"So you thought maybe Gus Trello had some, help you out?"

Robert's anger pulsed. How this old man could get to him! "I was going to offer to buy it from you."

"Audra has stock?"

"Yes."

"Did she say she will sell to you?"

"No."

Trello snorted again, without mirth this time. "So. She gets a little revenge, eh? Make you sweat?"

"She said she won't sell it to me. What her intentions beyond that may be, I don't know."

"You are so—what do they say—cool," Trello sneered. "All the time, cool. You are so scared that shit runs down your leg, you act *cool*."

"What am I supposed to do, you son of a bitch? Roll on the ground?"

"And then you come here," Trello went on inexorably, sarcasm dripping, "and say you hope Gus Trello got some stock, maybe he will sell it to you or vote with you, eh? After you divorce my Audra! What makes you think I would help you if I could? What you ever do for Gus Trello?"

"If you had stock, you would have been well paid for it."

"What I need more money for? All I need now is casket and some flowers, right?"

"Right, Gus," Robert snapped back, control slipping again. "All you need is a casket and some flowers and all these fine people mourning you."

Gus Trello's head jerked back. He looked for an instant like he had been shot.

Robert was instantly filled with regret. "I'm sorry. I shouldn't have said that."

"This mess," Trello growled, "comes from you being a big shot. You couldn't work for Gus Trello, eh? You couldn't make cheap wine and lots of money. You had to make wine to rival the Bordeaux, the Burgundy, the Moselle, eh? Fine! Good! Now you got your fine winery and you got no wife and you got no money and you got no stock and it is shit and turds, eh? Whose fault is that? Is Gus Trello supposed to weep for you? You made a mistake. You live with it. Is nothing *I* can do."

"I know that," Robert said through set teeth. "I'm sorry to have bothered you." He started to stand.

"Unless I *want* to help you," Trello added.

Surprised, Robert looked down at him. "What?"

The old man's eyes were filled with craft. "I bet there is stock, eh? Somewhere. If enough money is offered, I bet stock comes to top to be skimmed. One million—two million—if enough money is out, I bet stock comes back."

Robert did not comprehend what he was saying. "I don't have that kind of money. You're talking about a transaction on a level that's beyond me."

"I always did!"

Robert started again to turn away.

"Wait, you dumb!" Trello barked. "You better wait, you Mr. High and Mighty, God damn!"

Robert looked at him again, waiting, puzzled.

Suddenly Gus Trello's face softened. "I love my family. I want my family happy. Even crook Jules. Even stupid Loretta. All. I am going to die soon. When, I don't know. Pretty soon now, I think. Okay. That is okay. But I want to think my family will be happy."

"They'll be happy, Gus," Robert said, baffled as to what he should say.

"Shut up, damn you! I am talking! Listen!

"Okay. Look at Audra. She is not happy. She needs a man. She thinks it is you. She wants you there, kid her, baby her, beat her, fuck her, all. She thinks she wants you, but you have to be the middle of her life, and she has to think *she* is the middle of *your* life. That is the way my Audra is.

"Audra don't want a divorce. Bullshit. Okay. Here is what I tell you. Go to her, now. Take her back. No divorce. Try again. Don't take no for answer, eh? Make her get back together. You can do it! Take her to Europe for a year again, eh? Second honeymoon. Visit wineries. Dance. See sights. Devote a year to my Audra. *Make her happy.*"

Gus Trello paused, a dribble of saliva on his chin. He looked keenly at Robert as if trying to will his reaction.

"For this," he added, "I give something in return. *Quid pro quo.* Legal term, eh? *Quid pro quo.* Good. You take Audra back, make her happy. I will get you your stock. I don't care what it costs. One million, two million, no matter. You take Audra. I save your winery." Trello paused, then slapped a hand on his own spare thigh. "What you say to that *quid pro quo,* eh?"

Numbed, Robert did not reply at once. It was, he saw, the essential kind of proposition that Gus Trello had made him once before, long ago, when the desire of Gus Trello was for him to manage Trello Industries.

Bend to my will and you will never have to worry again. *Give me your soul and I will give you everything you desire.*

It was so unexpected and bizarre that Robert almost barked laughter.

Then, however, he realized that it was also frighteningly tempting.

With the old man's help he could win Audra back. They had the years invested and she was still attractive. He could work on their marriage. They might be happy again one day. From an abstract moral point of view, this was even what he himself had been thinking he should do only weeks ago.

And if he took this course, the winery would be truly his again. There would be no test, no fear of Endicott or Simms, or of whatever new plots Jules might try. There would be almost unlimited power.

And what about Barbara Turner? The thought leaped up, unbidden, that she would find another man. She would be hurt for a while; they both would suffer. But they could get over it.

They could be *realistic,* in the terminology of the day.

Then, however, Robert had another vision: himself in Europe with Audra, trying, miserable. And he saw himself as fully a part of the Trello family, like Jules, like Frank, like young Gus, like Dora: locked in, imprisoned, another vulture in a legion of vultures, crippled by his surrender and pretending no surrender had taken place.

He had always said that his winery was his life.

If the ends justified the means, he should, in that case, accept this offer and consider it a windfall.

He was shaken by the impulse to accept. *Are we all so corrupt?* he thought, dazed.

Gus Trello was watching him, a gleam of triumph in his eyes.

"Well?" the old man said impatiently.

"I think you really want to help," Robert said huskily.

"Take it! Do what I say! It is best!"

Robert took one last look at the temptation, then breathed deeply. "No, Gus. I'm sorry."

Trello's face became mottled with anger. "There will not be another time! I will be dead! All your fine dreams will be shit and turds!"

Robert faced him, mentally seeing a door—the lid of a coffin—swing closed. This, he thought, was the last time he would ever see Gus Trello, and everything would end between them almost as it had begun, with rejection and with anger.

Gus Trello studied him. "You are one big fool," he said finally, and with two flicks of his fingers on switches, took off the wheelchair brake and reactivated the hummingbird motor. The wheelchair pivoted sharply, almost tipping, and then hummed off toward the gate of the courtyard from whence it had come.

17

Early Sunday morning, Jules Trello finished his instant coffee and walked impatiently to the kitchen intercom. He flicked the switch for the bedroom and said, "Baby?"

Carole's voice replied from a distance: "Yes, Daddy?"

"It's past seven. Hurry it up."

"Baby is hurrying," Carole pouted.

"I'm going on to get the car out. I'll be waiting outside."

"Oooh! Baby will huwwy *weal* fast!"

Muttering to himself, Jules left the house and walked to the garage, where he unlocked the outside switch box, pressed the button and watched the row of garage doors trundle up and out of sight. It was overcast overhead but the sun was beginning to break through, and the air was already warm. Another hot one, good for the grapes.

With the Elmhurst wine safely delivered, the unmarked trucks gone in the dead of night and unseen, Jules felt slightly more relaxed now, although his body still ached from the unaccustomed hard labor involved in the bottling and labeling. By now, he thought, the wine was probably out of California . . . perhaps out of the country. He did not really want to know. He had the money, and the immediate pressures in that regard had been eased.

Now, he thought, a dutiful trip to see the old man. Had to make sure there were no last-minute bitternesses that might remove whatever small sums or land parcels were in the will, and it was going to be interesting to see how

Audra had taken the detective's report. Then tomorrow, on Monday, Jules had to see a few friends just to make sure there was not going to be any wholesale caving-in to Alfredo Rodriques and his greasers . . . and possibly it was time for another call to John Endicott—goose him just a little.

Things seemed to be looking up.

Walking into the garage, Jules brushed by his wife's Corvette, noting the layer of road dust on its gleaming curved surfaces. Pay a small fortune for a playtoy, he thought, and let it gather dust in the garage.

The car probably needed driving, he thought. It was going to be a clear day. He could remove the top panels in moments and the trip south would give the car some needed exercise.

Walking to the driver's side, Jules found his key on his ring and got behind the wheel. He clicked the ignition on and watched the gas gauge swing up more than halfway. Then, knowing how Carole neglected everything mechanical, he decided to check the oil before starting the engine. He pulled the hood release and walked to the front of the car.

As he was about to lift the hood, he happened to notice the right-side headlight. The custom cover door was not fully closed. Muttering at incompetent mechanics, he poked a finger at the door. It did not budge. He went back around to the driver's side and flicked the lights on. Rewarded by the hum of the door motors, he went to the front again.

The headlight fixture, he saw at once, was not mounted properly. There seemed to be some pieces missing. This was strange. He turned and stared at the workbench, and opened the top drawer for a screwdriver with which he might tighten the mounting screws.

Inside the drawer, between tools, were two slender metal brackets, part of the headlight-mounting assembly. The drawer would not open all the way, and he reached back inside to see what was jamming it. His hand brought out a mashed cardboard carton which had contained a new headlight.

Jules did not know what to make of this. It was a real puzzle. He had not done any work on the Corvette. *Carole?* This seemed highly unlikely.

He stood thinking about the puzzle.

Then he had a thought that struck a chill to his bone marrow. Surely not, he told himself. Oh, no. *No.*

The trash container was nearby. He lifted the lid. Sunlight slanting through a window glittered on shards of broken glass and the gutted remains of the headlight.

Just be calm, he told himself. *Take it easy. Some logical explanation.*

Even though Carole was a moron where machinery was concerned, and asked mechanics to do things like empty the ashtrays for her, she obviously had been trying to change this headlight. She had not mentioned it to Jules and had even apparently made some attempt to hide it. If he had not elected to drive the car today—and check the oil—he might never have noticed.

But that didn't necessarily mean that there was a connection between this and the news stories Jules had read about the boy. No, no. No.

Jules examined the right-front fender of the Corvette. He found and traced with his fingertips the slight mar, running from near the headlight back almost to the door. Peering closely, he saw a touch of black, like a rubber burn, in the crease. On some instinct he bent closer to the fender, which was not dusty like the rest of the car, and his nostrils caught the faintest hint of lighter fluid or cleaning fluid—*whatever had been used to clean the rest of the rubber off the fender.*

He stood up, feeling like he had been struck with a sledgehammer.

In the bedroom, Carole was just picking her sunglasses and purse off the bed when he walked in. She was wearing a white pantsuit, and looked marvelous.

"Baby is ready, Daddy," she smiled. "Baby—"

Jules's opened palm cracked across her face, knocking her backward across the bed. Her purse went one way, her sunglasses another. "*No!*" she squealed.

"You God-damned stupid pig!" Jules shouted, swinging at her again but missing as she scrambled off the bed and put it between them. "You hit that boy! You killed that boy with your car, didn't you!"

"I didn't mean to!" Carole cried. "It was an accident!"

"But you ran! Jesus Christ, you hit and ran! Oh, you stupid—!" He walked right over the bed and caught her against the wall, lifting her off her feet. He raised his fist, wanting nothing more than to bludgeon her out of existence.

"No, Daddy!" Carole sobbed, tears streaming down her face. "No! *Please,* Daddy!"

Jules let go of her. She dropped to her knees, sobbing brokenly, clutching at his legs. "I didn't mean to, and it happened so fast. I was scared—I got mixed up—"

"You were drunk," Jules said, a sick realism beginning to replace his anger with a new, enormous dread. "I remember coming in late from Elmhurst that night. I smelled it on you. I had heard about the hit-run on the car radio and was going to tell you about it, but you pretended to be asleep."

Carole looked up at him, her cheeks blotchy and blackened by her running mascara. "I was so *afraid . . .*"

"You weren't really asleep," Jules said, his anger fading now, replaced by the sick thumping of his blood. "I knew that. But I didn't realize there was any real reason for you to be pretending."

"Please don't hit me again, Daddy! Please!"

"Does anyone know about the accident?" Jules demanded.

"No one saw me—"

"I mean, have you told anyone, you stupid cow?"

"No!"

"The headlight. Where did you get it?"

"I got it at a store, but I didn't give my name, and I bought a lot of other things."

Jules sat on the bed. "Jesus Christ, if this gets out it could ruin me."

"I didn't tell anyone, Daddy. No one saw me!"

Jules looked at her with a feeling that he might vomit. "You are so stupid."

"Yes," she hiccuped.

"You stupid fucking pig, I should kill you."

Her head lowered, and a drop of bright-red blood came off the tip of her nose, making a wide round spot on the thigh of her white pants. "Yes," she said almost inaudibly.

Jules took a shuddering breath. "It's done. There's nothing we can change now. If you turn yourself in now, it's probably negligent homicide. Christ, all my friends would be talking. We can't have that."

Carole raised her face to him. The mascara stained her cheeks, and a little stream of blood went from her left nostril to the corner of her mouth, where she licked it. "I would go to jail."

Jules held up a fist to her. He clenched it so tightly that he shook from head to toe. "God damn you, you slut, if that was all the damage, I'd turn you in just to get you out of my sight for a while!"

Her eyes widened and she quailed at the sight of the fist. She did not speak.

Jules fought for control. He had to think. He had to make the right moves. *Jesus Christ,* he thought, *this has to stay covered up.*

"I'll fix the headlight," he said, making his voice calm. "We'll drive the Corvette to Gus's, just as I planned. Change your clothes. Fix your face. I'll give you five minutes. If you take any longer, I'll make you wish it was *you* dead instead of that boy. God! How could you *be* so stupid? Don't I have enough trouble?"

This time she really did hurry. About ten minutes later, they left the house in the Corvette, with the side panels stowed, and drove south through the valley.

Jules drove at a moderate speed, much slower than usual for him. He felt naked and exposed. A patrol car went by, going the opposite way, and he watched it in his mirror, filled with nightmare apprehension that it would turn about, switch on its lights, follow him. *No one knows,* he reassured himself. *It's all right. Just don't panic.*

They proceeded on south. At one point, he noticed Carole suddenly stiffened, her hands becoming clutched fists of fear on her lap, and her right leg extended forward in an involuntary movement as if braking. Jules looked in his rearview mirror but saw nothing unusual, only a side road nearby, a grassy ditch, a fence line. There were not even any other cars very near.

He glanced at his wife's strained face, and then he understood.

"Was that the place?" he asked.

She turned to him, her eyes filled with horror, and nodded.

He had never seen quite such a stricken look on the face of any human being. For an instant he felt compassion. He reached across the shifter console and patted her hands.

"It's all right, Baby. Daddy is taking care of everything now."

Some three hours later, Susan Knight's Firebird passed the same place on the highway. It turned off and went up the Hendersons' vineyard road. Susan, driving, had Rod Poole beside her.

They reached the house. Ned Henderson walked out of the vegetable garden to greet them. The corn behind him was taller than the house. He was sweaty, dusty, and tired-looking, but he smiled as he shook hands with Poole.

"We were going on a picnic," Susan told him. "There's enough food for an army. We thought you and Johnelle might go along with us."

Ned Henderson brightened, then frowned. "I guess we can ask Johnelle." He led, limping slightly, to the back door of the house.

Johnelle Henderson, dressed as if for church, was inside at the kitchen table. She had road maps and county assessor charts spread before her, and was working with colored pencils and a list of names and rural route numbers.

"Honey," Henderson said gently, putting his hand on her shoulder, "they say they've got enough food for an army."

"And four bottles of Traminer," Susan added.

"Iced," Rod Poole put in.

"And even Rod can't drink that much Traminer."

A slight frown crossed Johnelle Henderson's pretty face. "Ned, you know I can't today."

"Let it go today," Henderson urged quietly. "It will be fun."

"No. You know I can't. I have so much to do."

"What is all that?" Susan asked, puzzled.

Johnelle pointed to the maps and listings. "We know the car had to be going south, and it wasn't seen by the ambulance, which entered the highway . . . here." She pointed to a red mark on the map. "Therefore, it had to turn off between the accident site—here—and this other red mark. I'm checking every road and every house. I'm visiting them all."

Ned Henderson met Susan's eyes. His own showed his pain and concern—not for his dead son now, but for his wife.

Rod Poole said slowly, "We asked a lot of questions, Mrs. Henderson. You know we're still working on it."

Johnelle's eyes flashed with anger. "Do you have charts like this?"

"No," Poole admitted.

"Have you questioned *everyone,* on *all* these roads?"

Poole's jaw set. "No."

"I am," Johnelle said. "I will."

Confrontation with obsession is seldom pretty, and for an instant there was an almost embarrassed silence.

"I see," Susan finally said.

"Honey," Ned Henderson urged, "let's try to forget it for one day, okay? We're both tired. A picnic—"

"You go on a picnic if you like!" Johnelle flared. "You forget Jamie if you want to!"

Henderson stepped back, looking like she had slapped him.

Rod Poole glowered, moving his weight from side to side, and Susan knew he was going to speak, and probably say something about the chances of this quest finding a thing.

"Rod," she said quickly, "come on."

"No, just a minute," he said, his jaw jutting out.

"Rod!" she said sharply.

The sound penetrated. He looked at her, surprised, and then slumped his shoulders. He turned toward the door and they went out, Henderson following them.

"That's how she is now," he said softly as they walked through the dusty yard toward the car. "She won't talk about anything else . . . won't do anything else."

"Maybe she'll get over it just anytime now," Susan said, not believing it.

"I hope so," Henderson said simply, his plain, earnest face twisted.

They stood by the Firebird a minute or two, talking inanely about the weather, with the instinct for leaving a place with normal social gestures even if nothing during the visit has been normal at all. Then Susan and Poole got in the car and backed around and waved and drove off, leaving Henderson limping back to the garden.

"She won't find anything," Poole said with dull anger.

"You can never convince her of that," Susan said.

"She's running herself down, ignoring her husband, letting everything else in the world go down the tubes for this stupid amateur detective work."

Susan, driving, said nothing.

Her silence seemed to make Poole angrier. "She's crazy!" he said finally. "Just—plain—*crazy!*"

"She may be," Susan agreed.

They reached the highway and turned north. About a mile farther on, they encountered a band of about forty Workers United demonstrators, hiking along the dusty roadside under the banners. Just as Susan's Firebird neared them, an ancient white Cadillac rattled down the highway from the opposite direction. The horn brayed and a beer can flew out of a back window, sailing over the heads of the marchers.

Susan glanced at Rod Poole.

"I didn't see it," he said bitterly. "This is my first day off in four weeks. I didn't see a thing."

They continued northward.

Shortly before 4 P.M., Robert Mancini drove up to Barbara Turner's house. Jimmy met him sullenly at the door. Barbara, still wearing her brief and fetching red skating dress, appeared apprehensive as she took him into the kitchen.

"I must be the world's oldest roller-rink groupie," she said, opening a bottle of Petite Sirah. "I started going to get Jimmy involved in something besides school and Elton John records, and now I'm roped into helping with the preschoolers every other Sunday. I know I look silly as hell in this."

"You don't," Robert said, frankly admiring her legs. "I think you could motivate *me* into taking up skating."

"Well, I'm sorry you had to call half the day before getting an answer."

"I am too, because I have something important to say."

She sat facing him, her eyes wary. "Something has happened."

He told her about his visit south, and how Audra had agreed to a divorce. As he did so, her large and expressive eyes changed, but he could not read them. When he finished talking, she did not speak for a while, and there was none of the radiance that he had half expected.

Finally she asked, "Are you all right?"

He understood then, and loved her more than ever. "I'm very much all right. Now I have something to say. When this is settled, will you—no, that's not quite right. I don't want you to take a long time thinking about this, lady, all right? I want a quick answer, and no hedging. Are you ready?"

She was very solemn. "I think so."

"All right. Mrs. Turner, will you do Mr. Mancini the very great honor of becoming his wife?"

Her lips hardly moved, and the reply was very soft. "Yes."

Neither of them moved. The clock ticked somewhere. Jimmy, wherever he was in the house, was quiet. Robert looked at her across the wine and wondered if he would ever have enough of simply watching her like this. She, in the red dress that really might have been a little silly on anyone else, was breathing very rapidly, and her color was high.

Finally she said, "I know I shouldn't be so happy. This is all going to be very painful for you. But I am happy. I feel like jumping and hollering. Does that make me a scheming woman?"

Robert put his hand over hers. "If so, you're the kind of scheming woman I want."

"And there won't have to be any more hiding."

"No. None."

"We can go out together in public? Have supper?"

"Yes."

"Go dancing?"

"I'm a terrible dancer."

"I don't believe you."

"It's true. I never really learned."

"I'll teach you, then. I'll make you a grand dancer."

"Are you a good dancer? Of course you are."

"With you I'll be the greatest. I'll be fantastic. Wait and see."

They looked at each other for another long time. The emotion was very strong in him, a gladness he would never have imagined he could experience.

"I love you very much," he said huskily.

"I love you," she replied.

"It's going to be . . . messy for a while. The divorce. And you know the situation I'm in at the winery."

"It will be all right."

"I might have to sell the house. I don't suppose you would ever want to live there anyway."

"I don't care. I could live anywhere with you. I could live on the moon with you."

He smiled. "The space suits might make things clumsy."

"No. I'd get right inside your suit with you and we'd only need one and it would be lovely."

"How long has it been since I've talked with anyone the way I talk with you?"

"You mean—silly?"

He looked down at her hand in his hand. "I wish I weren't bringing all this trouble along with me. I don't know how this is going to turn out. I've got to raise as much money as I can and pick up any stock that's around, but it still might not be enough. I could lose the winery. I've thought about it. If I do, I won't be broke. They'll have to buy me out. But there won't be enough to start a new operation."

"What will you do if it comes to that?" she asked, refusing to indulge in idle assurances or play any other games with him.

"I have forty acres up at the northern ridge," he said, admitting the thought that had been much in his mind. "We planted it in Cabernet and Zinfandel four years ago. It's a beautiful place. The vines are the best, and they're prospering. Because it's a thousand feet higher, it gets more sunlight, and the colder night air settles below it. It's going to be a fine vineyard. If everything else goes under, I've thought of living up there . . . building up there, a new home."

"If that's what you want to do, Bob, and you're asking, the answer is yes. It sounds beautiful."

"But you began seeing this man you thought was a big winemaker. What happens when he turns out to be a dirt farmer?"

She seized both his hands between hers and shook them with a fierce strength. "I don't *care*. I love you!"

There was a sound in the next room, and then an Elton John record began. Robert smiled at Barbara, and knew by her hesitant expression that they were both thinking the same general thing.

"I think we should," he told her.

"Now?"

"Yes."

She frowned. "Maybe we should let the idea dawn on him slowly—"

"He wants to be a man, Barb."

She heaved a sigh. "You're right." She stood, walked across the kitchen, and disappeared into the next room for a moment. She came back then, with her son behind her.

Jimmy was puzzled, that much was clear in his wrinkled forehead. He was barefooted and wearing only Levi's and a tee shirt with a ragged hole in its front. He faced Robert, however, with an almost military bearing. Barbara stood back, watching, with luminous eyes.

"Mom says you have something to say to me," Jimmy said.

"Jim," Robert said, surprised to find his throat dry, "you know that your mother and I like each other very much."

Jimmy's expression darkened. "Yes, sir."

"I think you also know that I haven't been living with my wife . . . that we've been talking about a divorce."

The boy scratched his head, shifted his weight from one bare foot to the other, and said nothing.

"I've asked your mother to marry me," Robert said gently. "We love each other. We think we'll be married in a few months, as soon as we can. In the meantime, we'll be seeing a lot of each other . . . your mother . . . you . . . me. I wanted to tell you myself, right away."

Jimmy's eyes narrowed with Robert's words, and he paled. He did not move a muscle. He stood staring, his face unreadable. Robert was aware that Barbara, off to the boy's side, was watching him with tense uncertainty.

Robert forced himself to smile. "Okay, Jim? I know it seems sudden. You'll have to get used to the idea. But we didn't want to con you. We wanted you to know at once."

Jimmy turned and stared at his mother. His lips drew back from his teeth as if he were feeling physical pain.

"I'm very happy, Jimmy," Barbara said softly. "Please be happy too?"

"*No*," Jimmy whispered, putting a lifetime of revulsion into the single word.

"We'll get to know each other," Robert told the boy. "It will take a while—I guess we'll both feel awkward, but it'll be okay. It will, Jim. Really."

Jimmy stared at him with genuine horror. "*No!* It *won't* be okay! You're not my father! You'll never be my father! I don't want you around here!" He stopped, looked at Barbara, flung his arms around, and started for the door to the living room. "Maybe *she* wants you around here, but I don't, and I never will, so just leave me alone!"

"Jimmy!" Barbara called sharply.

He vanished through the door. Elton John was abruptly extinguished to the accompaniment of a needle being hurled across a record. A door slammed.

"Oh, God," Barbara said.

"So much for my intelligence in handling kids," Robert

said glumly. "I guess you were right. We should have sneaked up on him with it, maybe."

"He's always taken that silly business about being the man of the house so seriously! Bob, I'm so sorry he acted that way! He'll be all right, really! Give him a little time!"

Robert took her in his arms and held her close. He felt her trembling. "Sure," he crooned. "Everything will be fine. Just give it a little time." But he wondered if he knew what he was talking about.

Part Four

1

On the first day of September, Alfredo Rodriques came back to Robert Mancini Vineyards for his appointed meeting. Susan Knight was having coffee down the hall when Robert Mancini came looking for her.

"You talked to him last week," Robert told her, "and I want a third party to witness our discussion. Will you join us?"

Susan followed her employer to his office, where she found Alfredo Rodriques waiting in a chair facing Robert's desk. Rodriques was dressed as before, although he looked, if anything, even slighter and more worn. He smiled and rose as Susan entered, and they shook hands.

"I wanted a witness to our talks," Robert told him, going behind the desk. "Do you have any objection?"

"None," Rodriques said.

Susan sat down quietly, her nerves tightening. She knew, as she suspected Rodriques did, that Robert Mancini carried as much weight with his opinion in the area right now as any individual. The session might be crucial.

"I appreciate your seeing me today," Rodriques said formally. "I know this is a most busy period for you."

Robert moved a few papers out of his way. He was being guarded and cautious, and it showed in his controlled features. "The Brix is coming up fast now. I hope we can be harvesting some early grapes within three weeks."

"That is good news."

"Yes. Others won't be ready until October, of course, as it appears now. But this warm spell is very helpful and encouraging."

"I hope," Rodriques said, "I will not require too much of your time."

"Would you like some coffee, Mr. Rodriques? Or a glass of wine?"

"Neither, thank you."

Robert folded his hands on his desk and waited for Rodriques to proceed.

"The nearing of the harvest closes the time interval that my organization has available to it for the most effective action," Rodriques said. "If you have read the materials I left with Miss Knight—"

"I have."

"Then you know clearly our goals here."

"The first step," Robert said, "is recognition, in contractual form, of your union's right to represent the workers."

"Yes. I have already visited a number of your colleagues to explain this. Among those I have seen are Korday, Christian Brothers, Louis Martini, Crocker Vineyards, Marcello, VanZandt—"

"I think," Robert said with a slight smile, "I've been kept informed of your visits, Mr. Rodriques."

"Yes, I am sure you have. Miss Knight was quick to point out to me that there is no single winemaker organization here. But you are widely recognized as a leader. This is because of your excellent general reputation as well as your action toward the growers on fall prices."

"I can only speak for my own organization within this winery when I talk with you, sir."

This had put the ball back in Rodriques' court, Susan thought with satisfaction. Robert was not being cajoled into thinking or acting like a leader or spokesman when he was not.

Rodriques smiled slightly, evidently getting the same point. "Yes, sir. On the other hand, let us be candid. The reception we get from a man of your stature may go far toward determining the ultimate fate of a program based on individual acceptance of union conracts, one by one."

So the ball was back to Robert. He did not blink. "Do you have some specific proposition for us, then?"

"You know that we have acquired signatures of field

workers petitioning for recognition as members of our group. At the present time we have more than three thousand such signatures on file. The lists are available for inspection at our headquarters. We are gaining more signatures each day."

"What percentage of the field workers do you think those names represent?"

"More than sixty per cent."

"And the other forty per cent?"

"Are being added."

Robert leaned back, watching Rodriques carefully. "I happen to know that some field workers have refused to sign. It would be dishonest to imply that you have total support. Some workers don't want any part of a union. They don't think they need it. They fear it."

"That is correct," Rodriques said calmly. "Some incidents that have been very unpleasant for my people have been instigated by other Chicano workers who wish we had never come here. There is no unanimity among the workers; there is no unanimity in any large group. Even among my union members there is sharp division about tactics that should be followed in the days and weeks ahead. I do not pretend to speak for a monolithic group."

The speech surprised Susan, and she saw that it had surprised Robert, too. She had promised herself to keep quiet, but had a question on the tip of her tongue.

Robert asked it for her: "If this is the case, how can you be pressing for recognition as the bargaining agent? It sounds to me like you need to get your own house in order."

Rodriques' dark face creased in a rueful smile. "There will never be a better time, or *any* time when we have unanimity. Any effort such as this is a series of compromises." His face became stern. "Further uncertainty and lack of obvious progress, from our standpoint, can be damaging."

"That sounds like a very risky thing for you to be admitting."

"No, sir. I try to speak the truth. My people need signs of some progress to remain motivated. Your side needs to start seeing that recognition of my union will not destroy the growers and vintners. The longer we shadow-box, the greater the tensions become . . . the graver become the risks of extremists on either side taking charge and causing truly serious difficulty."

"If you imply that some of us should sign whatever you put before us in order to avoid some unstated worse trouble," Robert countered, "it doesn't ring quite true to me. I don't know any winemaker or grower who likes the situation at present. You say you don't like it either. But let me remind you that you started it. Don't light the fuse on a bomb, and then suggest to me that I should be willing to throw myself on it for the general welfare."

Rodriques' face darkened. "No, sir. I did not start this. The situation has been here for generations: workers without a voice in their own destiny."

Robert appeared calm and in control, but he gave himself away to Susan at least by rummaging for a cigarette and lighting it before he replied. "If we start arguing points like that, Mr. Rodriques, we might be here a year. Neither of us wants that. What do you want from me?"

"I want you to sign a statement recognizing my organization."

"Has anyone signed such a statement yet?"

"No one."

"I won't be first."

"Why?"

"Frankly, Mr. Rodriques, I'm not that sure where I stand on some of the things you demand. The right of field workers to be represented at the bargaining table, yes. A decent wage—even medical insurance—yes. But let's not deceive each other. Recognition is not the last and final step. It's only the first step. Then come the demands. Then come the strikes. Then come the constant escalations of costs, featherbedding, all the rest of it. You ask me to be the first to sign a recognition statement. That's like asking me to put a gun to my own head."

"What would it take," Rodriques asked stonily, "to secure your signature to such a statement?"

Robert appeared ready for this. "Number one—a clear statement that membership in your union will not be required for employment. Number two—a no-strike agreement until December thirty-first."

Rodriques' eyes widened. He was flabbergasted. "You ask us to pull the teeth out of the watchdog's mouth!"

"No. I ask you to give in order to get. That's called a *quid pro quo*, Mr. Rodriques." Robert showed a small, grim smile as if he were remembering something. "Someone explained that to me recently."

Rodriques spread small hands. "What would we gain? Nothing!"

"You know that isn't true. You gain recognition. That's the vital step; everything else follows. I'm not like some of the people locally who think they can fight you indefinitely. I wish I thought we could. I hate the idea of your union or anyone else telling me how to run my business. But I see the handwriting on the wall. All right. I *know* that recognition means demands in January, if you do it my way . . . probably a strike. Maybe worse bitterness. It's coming. I see that. I worry about the situation right now. I worry about this harvest. I'm willing to recognize you. But only on these terms."

"I do not like these terms, sir."

"Neither do I! But I'm willing to grit my teeth and try to live with them, and if you're smart, you'll do the same."

"It is not enough," Rodriques said.

"It's never enough," Robert shot back. "That's my point."

Rodriques leaned forward, elbows on knees. Susan thought she saw genuine pain in his eyes. "I cannot suggest such an agreement to my people."

"I can't sign any more than that."

"I fear more serious crises!"

"If *I* didn't acutely fear the same thing, do you think I would even consider caving in to you like this?"

"You are not caving in. You would only make us helpless!"

It was Robert's turn to spread his hands.

Alfredo Rodriques glanced at Susan as if somehow hoping she might help. She saw his feeling of entrapment. He seemed under a very great pressure, more than his words had explained. She was puzzled and concerned.

To Robert, Rodriques said softly, "We will be forced to continue our efforts . . . perhaps broaden them."

"I've given this a lot of thought, Mr. Rodriques. I've talked with a lot of people. Take my advice and take what you can get."

"We must have immediate bargaining."

"Then you face nothing but a fight."

"We seek no fight."

"Of course you do. Your policy is one of confrontation."

"We only seek—"

"I know what you seek. I know what you want. I'm telling you what I think you may be able to get."

Rodriques' face set. "It is not enough."

"If the wine industry here tried to absorb all your demands in a year," Robert told him intently, "some of the growers might go under. Some of the smaller wineries might even fail. With the overplanting, we need more fermenting capacity, not less. Stand behind all your demands, wanting them all met now, and you can start a vicious cycle that leaves only a handful of big growers and a few large wineries, all of them powerful, all automated. Then your workers will be organized, and they'll be recognized, but *they won't have any jobs left.*"

Rodriques heaved a sigh. "We must press for our demands . . . or we must strike."

"And you'll sow bitterness that will take years to erase."

"Why do you stand so fast?" Rodriques demanded. "Your own operations will hardly be affected. Your programs for your workers already exceed every standard in any contract we have ever sought!"

"Mr. Rodriques, I'm telling you the kind of settlement you can reasonably hope to have signed now. I'm not just talking about myself. I know the people in this area and I'm talking about all of them."

"This kind of *quid pro quo* you mention—it is not justice."

"They seldom are. But they work."

"My people have waited too long."

"What will you do, then?" Robert pressed. "Try to lead a general strike, right at the time of harvest? There will be trouble. Some of those growers will bring in outside labor. Your people will be attacked. You'll have violence."

"There will be no violence on our side. I will control my people."

"How?"

"If necessary, I will stand before them. I will fast."

"You start one of your fasts," Robert countered, "and it will fan the flames higher. It will make evangelicals of your followers. That's the worst thing you could possibly do."

Rodriques nodded, his face solemn. "I know fasting will also make me a target of hate from the other side. I recognize that by fasting I might die."

"Is that what you want?" Robert asked sharply. "To be a martyr?"

"No, sir. No man seeks death."

Casting a despairing look at Susan, Robert turned back to Rodriques. "Take what you can get. It's a huge step forward. I can contact a dozen winemakers, and over half of them would sign the same agreement with me today."

"I cannot," Rodriques said.

"Then the trouble is just beginning. You know that."

Rodriques flushed and bright anger sparkled in his eyes. "I know it very well, sir!" He held out his right hand, the thumb and index finger almost touching. "I know that at times my control of some of my own people is *this* far from being lost. I know that every day I fight my own assistants to maintain order, and passive resistance only! I have to show them signs of progress. I have to give them hope, or they may run away and leave me standing behind."

"Sell them the kind of agreement I've suggested," Robert said. "God knows that will be hard enough to sell to my friends, too—but I think it can be done to avoid worse confrontation."

Rodriques breathed heavily and got to his feet. "I see we have nothing more to discuss at this time."

Robert appeared surprised at the sudden departure. "I'm assigning Miss Knight to maintain close contact with you. I will be available for more talks if you want them."

Standing, Alfredo Rodriques appeared smaller than ever, as if shrunken by some enormous psychic weight. "It is well. I thank you for your many kindnesses."

The two men did not shake hands. Rodriques bowed slightly to Susan and walked to the office door, Robert with him. They exchanged another few words in the outer lobby and then the union leader stepped into the elevator and was gone.

Robert came back into the office, frowning. "What did you think of him?"

"I had met him before," Susan said. "He's tough. But I had this feeling he was under more pressure today."

"I had the same feeling." Robert went to the windows and peered out at the sunny morning. He was silent for perhaps two minutes, and Susan saw that the session with Rodriques had left him worried and depressed.

When he turned back to her, however, his scowl was one of intent rather than passive preoccupation. "You're going to be on the go these next few days, checking fields. I want you to keep your eyes and ears open. Anything you hear or see about the demonstrations—about the mood of people generally—about anything—I want you to be sure to report it back to me. I think we have to stay abreast of events just as closely as possible."

It was a purposefully vague assignment, one Susan did not welcome.

That afternoon, however, when her duties took her to several small vineyards, she made it a point to listen carefully to the rumors and worry about the field-worker situation. She heard nothing that was new. When she pressed diplomatically here and there for opinion, she sensed that some growers might agree with Robert that a settlement might have to be reached sooner or later, and that they would welcome one sooner, if one was inevitable anyway.

It was the following day, however, that she was confronted by the depth of passion that lay beneath the generally controlled surface.

She was at a vineyard not far from Ned Henderson's, a Merlot field bordering a large acreage owned by James Higgins, who she knew was a minor supplier for Jules Trello as well as one of those who had almost started a no-watering insurrection in the face of reported low prices to be paid in the fall. Having finished her business in the field, she was walking alone back toward her car on the dusty side road when a large black Ford pickup trundled along and a burly, sweat-soaked man called a gruff greeting. This was Higgins himself.

"Hello, Mr. Higgins!"

"Checking them grapes?" Higgins grinned, bringing the Ford to a complete stop beside her.

"I just finished," Susan told him. She smiled, but wondered if it appeared as uncertain as it felt. She did not consider herself a shrinking violet, and yet she was distinctly uneasy. Higgins wore no shirt, and the sun beamed in on rolls of blackly hairy flesh over his powerful torso. The muscular arm resting so lightly on the doorsill was as big around as her thigh. She could smell his sweat and tobacco, the sharp odors rolling out of the truck's interior like the spoor of a wild animal's den. There was a tremendous aura of raw potential violence in James Higgins, held in check by the most slender threads.

"I'd better be hurrying along," Susan added.

"I heard Rodriques was over to your winery the other day."

"That's right."

Higgins eyed her. "I heard you been asking people what they think about settling with him."

"Well, it was just conversation, Mr. Higgins—"

"I'll tell you what I think. Would you like to hear?"

"Of course."

"Good. I feel this way about it. No son-of-a-bitching winery is going to steal my grapes, and no son-of-a-bitching wetback is going to steal my profits. If they try to come on my land or bother me, they're going to be damned sorry!"

"Well, maybe it won't come to that," Susan said, edging toward her car.

"It will," Higgins grunted. "You mark my words, it *will*. They'll push and shove and start trouble, and when they do, they'll be *sorry*. A lot of people feel just like I do. No Communist is going to take over my profits. You know the saying they used to have? 'Better dead than red.' Only some people turned it around—'Better red than dead.' I'm old-fashioned. I'm a caveman and I'm proud of it. I bought this land. I planted it. I've fought mold, mildew, leaf rot, frost, worms, rabbits, deer, dogs, birds, late rain, *no* rain, *botrytis*, fungus, twenty kinds of insects—you name it and I've fought it. Now I've got something. I earned it. I'm not giving any of it away to a bunch of weaseling little greasers talking about their fair share. Let the God-damned bastards earn their own share the way *I* did! Do you understand me?"

"I think I do, Mr. Higgins," Susan said.

"And there are more of us who think like I do than those greasers realize!" Higgins called after her as she got into her car.

My God, she thought, *I hope not.*

2

Robert Mancini believed that his interview with Alfredo Rodriques, as unsatisfactory as it had been in many ways, had been the best anyone could have expected. The fall harvest timetable had begun to grow short now, and the days following the meeting were packed with preparation, leaving little time for anything but the most casual contact with others in the business. He tentatively planned to see Timothy Crocker and a few other intimates at a country-club fish fry on Saturday, and mentally shelved this worry, as much as possible, until that time.

A part of Thursday, September 3, was devoted to his lawyers and broker. A few shares of Mancini stock had turned up and were purchased. A new and more complete inventory was being drawn up, trying to show where outstanding stock was probably held. Robert was arranging a personal loan, as large as he could swing, to allow for more stock purchases if they should become available. After a preliminary conference with Audra's attorneys about the kind of cash settlement she would require, Robert's legal advisers told him he could not afford to spend as much on stock as he stood ready to spend. He pointed out that he had no choice.

Given this activity, he had his problem with Timmons Corporation much on his mind.

Still, the registered letter early Friday was a numbing jolt.

He had it in the top drawer of his desk, along with an empty cigarette package, when Barbara Turner appeared a little before noon for a scheduled interview.

Imps were in her eyes as he escorted her into his office, closing the door.

"All right, *sir*," she said, turning before him to show off a new beige dress. "Recognizing that we must be proper, and conduct this survey about expectations for the size and quality of the grape crop for our illustrious evening newspaper, what do you think of my dress?" Then, twirling again, she really looked at him for the first time. His expression gave it away.

"Bob, what is it?" she said quickly.

He walked to the desk. "Well, Barbara, I hate to dump bad news on you, God damn it!"

"What is it?" she repeated.

He opened the desk drawer, took out the letter, and handed it to her. Sitting down while she read it, he hiked his feet onto the corner of the desk. He felt physically ill. He was irritated with himself for this. He had *known*. Why was the actual letter such a shock? Had he imagined it would not really come?

It was very quiet and Barbara's head was still bent over the letter and he knew she was either reading it a second time or trying to decide what to say to him. He hated this, too. He had never wanted to bring her trouble, and at this moment it seemed to him that he was bringing her nothing else.

He knew the letter practically by heart. It was not long but it was packed. Timmons Corporation, as probable major stockholder in Robert Mancini Vineyards, was calling for a vote of all voting stock to determine actual ownership and management control. A meeting of all stockholders was called for 9 A.M. on Monday, October 12, in the main dining room of the Timmons Corporation Executive Club in Portland, Oregon. Proxy information was enclosed.

Management of Robert Mancini Vineyards remained in the hands of Robert Mancini, founder and president, pending the vote tabulation. Messrs John C. Endicott and E. Z. Simms, Timmons vice president for Mancini operations and assistant executive controller, respectively, as members of the Mancini board, would commence on-site liaison work at the Mancini winery on or about September 21.

Further information concerning the meeting or questions relating thereto could be obtained from Armbruster & King, attorneys-at-law, Portland, representing Timmons Corporation, or from the undersigned, Jerome Bowen, chairman.

For the further information of stockholders who planned to vote by proxy, a proposed list of new officers and management personnel was attached.

Barbara Turner scanned the attached documents. "What does this mean, 'John C. Endicott, president, E. Z. Simms, vice president,' and then a blank space beside the words 'general manager'?"

Robert's lips felt stiff from the attempted smile. "I think it means Endicott and Simms will run the show if we lose the vote."

"And the blank space?"

"Maybe they'll ask me to be the general manager—work for them."

Barbara tossed the letter onto the desk between them. "Shit!"

"Such language!"

She looked like she might be ready to cry. "Come on, darling. Don't give me any brave acts. This is *me*."

"All right," he said quietly, dropping the act. "You see the letter. You know how I feel."

"Bob, I'm just sick."

"So am I."

"What are you going to do?"

"I knew it was coming. I'm already doing everything I know. We're trying to buy any stock we can find. I'm lining up my money to make it possible to bid high."

"How close is it going to be?"

He met her keen eyes. "They must not think it will be close at all, sending Endicott and Simms on down here that way."

"What does that mean, 'liaison purposes'?"

"It means they watch me so I don't steal anything, I imagine."

"Oh, damn. Oh, that really makes me *furious!*"

They discussed it. Robert explained as well as he could how foggy the stock-control situation had become. No one, clearly, owned anything like 51 per cent. His own percentage was higher than it had been in two years, thanks to recent acquisitions, but still was nowhere near absolute, certain control. No one believed Timmons held a clear majority either. But Timmons evidently guessed that the parcel it could vote was surely larger than Robert's.

"How much have you been able to buy back?" Barbara asked.

"Several hundred shares, actually."

"How much would you have to find to be *sure* you could win that vote?"

"That's a pipedream," Robert told her. "There's no way I could find that much stock lying around loose, and for sale."

"I'm just trying to understand," Barbara insisted. "How many shares would make you *sure?*"

Robert thought about the dismaying arithmetic. "Three thousand shares."

"At how much a share? I'm prying, but—"

He shrugged. "It's a matter of public record. This morning it was one hundred and sixty-two." He paused, seeing her frown as she tried to figure it. He added, "That's roughly half a million dollars."

"My God!"

"Don't worry about it, Barb. I won't be shelling out that kind of money. Number one, I don't have it. Number two, that much stock isn't on the market."

"It just isn't right for them to be able to come in here and just—take over," she said angrily. "I know! I know! That's the way it's done sometimes, and this is big business, little girl. But it makes me just *sick.*"

"Look," Robert said, speaking with greater calmness than he felt. "You've got an interview to conduct here, lady. And tonight, like it or not, you're going out with me. Did you ask Jim if he'll come along?"

"I did"—Barbara frowned—"and he said he didn't want to."

"I hope you didn't push him."

"You said not to, and I agree with that."

"Good. We'll go out by ourselves, then. He'll come around, given time."

Barbara leaned forward, frowning. "But Bob, what about this damned stock deal? You can't just pretend it isn't there!"

"I'm doing everything I can. What more can I do? Come on, lady reporter. Interview me. If you think I'm going to sit around all day, moping, I've got a lot of things to do, and so do you—including that dinner to-night."

She looked at him with eyes that showed the extent of her love. "We'll talk more about it later?"

"Sure," he said, and grinned at her.

As it turned out, there was something to celebrate, after all. Shortly before 4 P.M., a telephone call came from a senator who had been among the first to be contacted by Robert about the Homero Artiz situation in Mexico.

"What did you do?" the senator asked in his famous voice. "Threaten to sell all your wine to the Russians or something?"

"I don't know what you're talking about," Robert said.

"Good lord, man, somehow or other you've chopped two years' worth of red tape on both sides of the border. You *do* remember the Homero Artiz kid, don't you?"

"Of course," Robert said, quickening. "You mean something has developed?"

"Developed, printed, and hung in a frame over the mantel, my friend. I don't know who all you arm-twisted . . . I don't know if I even *want* to know . . . but I've had calls and letters today from the White House, Immigration, a U.S. district judge in San Diego, and the damned Mexican Embassy. Your friend Artiz has lots of help in high places. He's going to be able to re-enter the United States legally, on the citizenship track, before the end of this month."

Despite the weight of other worries, Robert felt quiet elation. He would enjoy telling Susan Knight and the Hendersons. "That's fast work, Senator."

"Fast? *Fast?* It's a damned miracle! Listen. If you always get results this fast, could you give me a hand on this trade legislation I've been trying to shove across the Hill for what seems like half my life?"

Robert hung up and called Susan Knight at once. She insisted on delivering the news to the Hendersons, and to Rod Poole, personally. Robert had the pleasure of telling Barbara.

As their evening progressed, he was very happy. But the news of Homero could not dispel the impact of the registered letter. He felt as he had once as a child, when he kept forgetting that he had to visit the dentist the following day, but then kept remembering again with a new surge of dread.

He was a big boy now, but this was no trip to the dentist, either. It seemed unbelievable, but it was happening; the cards were being played out; the web was tightening around him.

3

Although she was aware of growing tensions in the valley and certain that her husband worried not only about the general situation but his own crop as well, Johnelle Henderson remained single-mindedly dedicated to finding the hit-run driver who had killed her son.

A part of her whispered that it might be better to let it go . . . to allow the process of grief to begin eroding into regret. But she felt a personal responsibility for Jamie's death; if she had been more stern about his bike riding, she thought, or had gone on her own to bring him home that fatal night, everything could have been different: To expiate this guilt, she had to find the person who had driven the car.

She knew at times that this would not be viewed as rational by a bystander. She was not a bystander, and had to act on the basis of her feelings.

Her quest had first taken her to repair shops, garages, and even many area stores dealing in automotive supplies. Only after compiling an impossibly long list of accessory and headlight purchases, many of them anonymous, had she realized that she could not track her prey in this manner.

Therefore the map and the county charts, as well as rural-route addresses. It was her last strategy.

She had worked on this ploy for several days now. Her map was timed carefully and marked out. She knew within a minute or so the precise time of the accident that had killed her son. She knew within two minutes the time the police car, and then the ambulance, had entered the highway slightly over four miles to the south. Between the two times, no one proceeding north on the highway had noted a southbound car moving at a high rate of speed; those who had casually noticed a car with only one headlight did not think it had been speeding. The police and ambulance had not seen this car at all.

Johnelle's conclusion was that the death car had turned off the highway and onto a side road during the four-minute period between the accident and the entry of the emergency vehicles. In this distance of four miles, there were seven side roads, four to the west and three to the east. Her theory was that someone on one of the side roads might have seen the car, and would be able to furnish a better description of it, if she could just find that witness.

By picking the northernmost side road and visiting every house along its route for more than five miles, Johnelle had eliminated it as a possible source of witnesses. That work had taken two days. This morning she had checked the second road to the west, finding only seven houses; at three she had found no one home, and had them carefully noted for a call back in the evening; the other residents reported nothing.

It was time to begin checking the length of the first eastbound road. Johnelle knew that this road was more populated, and might take the rest of the day and a good portion of the weekend to complete.

It was four weeks now since Jamie's death. The trail was growing cold. Johnelle was tired, and her sense of defeat was growing. But she wouldn't stop.

Turning off the highway onto the narrow side road, she drove for several hundred yards, past an old truck farm on one side and a willow-choked ravine on the other, before she reached the first dwelling. It was an old frame house set back under the trees on the edge of the ravine, with dilapidated outbuildings and two junker automobiles rusting in a weed field. The front porch contained two derelict refrigerators and a porch swing.

Johnelle pulled into the gravel driveway and shut off her engine. The heat closed in around her, and silence punctuated only by the wind-stirred paddling of propellers, idle wind machines, in a vineyard beyond the ravine.

As she got out of the car, Johnelle saw a medium-sized white cur come out from under the front porch and start her way. The dog's tail was between its legs and it growled menacingly. She paused, chills coursing up her back. She was terrified of strange dogs. Was it true that dogs could smell an odor sent out by a person who was frightened? *Don't be afraid, he'll know it!* But she was afraid, and very tired.

"Nice doggie," she said. "Here, nice puppy."

The dog, head down but watching her, moved slowly forward. She held her hand out to him.

A voice came from the house, "I wouldn't do that, lady, 'less you want to lose some fingers."

Johnelle jerked her hand back and shaded her eyes with it. "Hello?" She could not see the person inside.

Then the front door opened and an old man limped out. He clapped his hands. "Here, boy!"

The dog loped over to him. He patted it, scolded it, and sent it back under the porch, then limped on over to confront Johnelle. He was skinny, in his eighties, toothless. A wad of chewing tobacco plumped one cheek.

"You lost?" he asked.

Johnelle's speech came readily after weary repetition. "My name is Johnelle Henderson, and I'm investigating a fatal accident out on the highway the night of August twelfth."

"Auto accident?" the old man asked with interest.

"A car hit a boy on a motorcycle."

"Huh! Well, I don't know nothing about that."

"It was a little past ten-thirty," Johnelle prodded.

"Are you one of them policewomen?" The codger looked her up and down with frank admiration. "Only one I ever seen was that Angie Dickinson on the TV."

"I'm an investigator," Johnelle said glibly. "Now try to remember. The night of this accident it was clear and warm. There was a county school meeting. It was the same night the President made his speech about China on TV just about suppertime."

The old man snorted. "I remember. Dumb speech, I thought. What's your opinion on China?"

"Were you here at the house later that night?"

"Yep." He grinned. "That was one of those few nights when I wasn't out with one of them chorus girls that are always trying to catch me."

"A car might have come down this road from the highway a little after ten-thirty. It would have had only one headlight. It could have been going fast. It would have been a little car—a sports car of some kind. Did you see anything like that?"

"Lady, by ten o'clock I'm in bed ever' night. I didn't see nothing, nor hear nothing."

Another dead end. "Is there anyone else living here who might have seen anything?"

"Nope, I live alone. Just me and old Spot, there. Say, would you like to come in outta that sun for a spell? I got home-brew beer."

Back in her car, Johnelle put a black X through the house on the surveyor's map, crossed it off her residential list, and started east again. The old man waved to her. She drove east almost a half mile before coming to the next house, a new one on about an acre of land. She found no one home and encircled the location on the map, indicating a call-back.

Within the next two hours she made five more stops for interviews and three other attempts where no one seemed to be at home. This effort took her to a point on the eastern hillside where her road dead-ended into another that twisted generally north and south through brush and rocks.

This was Gender Road, hardly a main thoroughfare but one which carried considerable traffic for its width and twisty nature. It went all the way south into the city and north for several miles, where it looped down hill and intersected the highway. Johnelle first took the southbound turn, and in the next hour or so talked to two more homeowners. They too were negative.

Returning to the Y, she proceeded north on Gender. She quickly came to a small A-frame house where the young woman who answered the door said no one had been home on the night of August 12. Johnelle then drove almost a half mile through dense woods, with mammoth stone outcroppings, before coming to other habitation. People moved here, and built here, for isolation, she realized. There was very little chance that anyone would have been watching the road.

Fighting new discouragement, she stopped at another house which was silent and deserted, then drove another few hundred yards and found a small brick ranch-style dwelling perched close to the paving. As she pulled up the steep, short driveway and locked her parking brake, she calculated that she was three miles from the highway, east of it, and then another two or more miles north again. It seemed hopeless.

Doggedly she rapped at the door. It was a nice little house, and very neat.

The woman who answered was nice-looking, too, plain but friendly. She told Johnelle that the family had been home that night; she remembered it because they had talked the next day about how they must have been watching the news when the fatal accident took place.

While the woman talked, a pretty teen-ager in hip-hugger shorts and bra was ironing in the doorway to the kitchen nearby. The girl looked to be sixteen or seventeen, and listened with interest, but said nothing.

"I'm sure some cars went by," the woman told Johnelle. "You'd be surprised at the traffic on this road sometimes. But Cindy, here, was the only one out and she was on a date somewhere, isn't that right, Cindy?"

"Yes, Momma," the girl murmured.

The woman shrugged. "The rest of us don't pay any mind to the cars."

"It was a small car," Johnelle repeated, ready to give up. "It would have had only one headlight—the other one was broken."

"Land, I wish we could help," the woman said sympathetically. "You poor thing, you look hot and pale. Would you like to come in for a minute? I've got some lemonade."

Perhaps it was the kindness that was the last straw. Johnelle broke and began to cry without making a sound.

"Aw!" the woman murmured. "Come in, dearie, and rest yourself!"

"I'm sorry," Johnelle choked. "No. Thank you. I have to get on—ask someone else."

Cindy, the girl at the doorway of the kitchen, came across the tiny living room with an expression of genuine concern. "It that car *that* important to you?"

"It was my son who was killed," Johnelle said.

Cindy frowned, hesitated, then stood up straighter. "I saw it," she said.

Johnelle chilled and stared at her. "What did you say?"

"I saw it," the girl said firmly, her eyes nervous.

"Cindy," her mother scolded, "you couldn't have! You weren't even around here! You were in town on a date!"

Cindy shook her head grimly. "I was right outside. Yes I *was*, Mother! Sometimes I—oh, crap, you'd find out sooner or later anyway—sometimes when Mark and I come back from a date it's early yet, and you and Daddy are just watching TV, so we turn out the lights and coast into the driveway and . . . sit there awhile."

"Sit there awhile?" her mother snapped. "Doing *what*, may I ask?"

"We just *sit* there, Mother!"

"Your father is going to hear about this!"

"Momma—!"

"Please," Johnelle cut in. "Cindy—you saw a car that night?"

"Yes. Just like I said."

"A small car," Johnelle prodded, going through her litany. "With only one headlight."

"Sure," Cindy said. "The right front headlight was broken."

Johnelle's heart quaked. "Yes." She had almost lost her voice. "The right front. Did you notice anything else?"

"Mark and I were just sitting out there," Cindy said solemnly, "sort of . . . you know, just messing around, you know. And it came up the road from the south. Its one headlight shone right on us for a second, which is why we noticed it. I didn't think anything about it being important—"

"Did you get a good look at the car?" Johnelle asked, shaking. "Did you see the license plate?"

"No, not really. I'm pretty sure it was a local tag, though."

"Did you see anything else?"

"Well, nothing much except the driver, a woman—"

"A woman!"

"Sure. The top was down, and you could see her hair blowing as she went by."

"She had long hair? A woman with long hair?"

"Uh-huh. Sort of blond, I think, but I wasn't paying that much attention. It was long, though, swirling out behind her."

Johnelle leaned against the doorjamb. Her knees had gone weak. It was not so much, but it was the first lead of any kind. The car had come this way. She could question others the entire length of Gender Road. And the driver was a woman . . . probably a local woman. It was so much more than she had had before.

"Was the car familiar?" Johnelle asked now, knowing that it was not really possible that any more information might be forthcoming. "It wasn't anyone you knew, was it?"

Cindy frowned, dubious. "No, I'm afraid not. But it was a Corvette. My Mark knows cars, and he commented on how he'd like to have a Vette like that someday. It was a Corvette with the top down, or maybe one of those T-tops, you know? The kind where you take the panels off? It was a dark color, either brown or dark red, a pretty new one." Cindy paused, frowned again, and took a deep breath. "A dark-colored Corvette, with the top down, and a woman driver—and she wasn't an old woman and she had long hair, probably blond, and the right front headlight was busted. Does that help at all, do you think?"

4

All during the remainder of the week following his meeting with Robert Mancini, Alfredo Rodriques had tried to calm his increasingly anxious, angry lieutenants. Meetings with two small vintners were promising, and Rodriques stressed his hopes in brief sessions with those of his aides who questioned him with growing obvious impatience at the headquarters in the city.

There were incidents. A handful of demonstrators, local workers acting on their own, appeared in front of the Van-Zandt winery, and a foreman had them arrested without consulting his employer. Although no charges were pressed and the workers were free within the hour, word spread rapidly. The tires on Rodriques' van were slashed during the night. A sign fronting the Korday vineyard was splashed with green paint, the Workers United color. A sheriff's deputy came to the headquarters to ask questions about the sign, and one of Rodriques' aides, a local worker named Hector Orrerra, became so abusive that the deputy nearly arrested him. A local detective cruiser appeared across the street from the headquarters and sat there, its two plainclothes occupants making notes on those who entered and departed, and using the radio. A rock thrown from an alley broke the cruiser's rear window. No one was caught. In a field fifteen miles away, white workers beat a Chicano with whom they had worked for several years;

the facts were clear, but the Chicano refused to name his assailant and no charges were brought.

By Saturday, September 12, when Alfredo Rodriques met with all his key aides in the secure back room of the headquarters, the situation had become fully pressurized. Rodriques was bone-weary and felt ill. He faced his men with the feeling of an animal trainer no longer sure he could handle the situation.

There were five men in the smoky, windowless room with Rodriques. He sat behind a card table, facing them.

Two were longtime assistants: Juan Lupé and Thomas Rosario. The ascetic Lupé and fat, balding Rosario had been with him since the Trello struggles in the south, and appeared to be the calmest men in the room. Seated side by side on a folding cot against the wall, they smoked cigarettes and waited without sign of emotion.

They would take orders, Rodriques thought. Their loyalty was not to be questioned. Although Juan Lupé had clearly indicated that he was leaning toward the more militant attitude of certain others here, he would bow to Rodriques' leadership.

Of the rotund Rosario, Rodriques had no doubt. Rosario was a dedicated practitioner of passive resistance and had often been severely tested. He would not fail now.

Two of the others looked—as they were—angry and impatient. One of these was the incendiary Carlos Murnan, who had become more outspoken with every passing day. Rodriques knew Murnan would press for stronger action, forcing some showdown, at once. It was likely that lean, youthful Jesús Cadz, a local worker who had become an intimate through ceaseless activity on behalf of the effort in the valley, might side with Murnan. Rodriques had seen them comparing notes only a few minutes before this session was called.

This left Hector Orrerra as a question mark in Rodriques' mind. An older man, usually reticent, he had moved into the inner circle when family illness forced another lieutenant to return to Los Angeles. Orrerra, about fifty, had come to Workers United from Seattle, where he had helped organize local workers there for another union. A hard worker, he had been in charge of gathering new membership signatures here, and had not yet stated an opinion about much of anything.

Knowing that he had to maintain his precarious control, Rodriques opened the meeting with a prayer. He petitioned Jesus Christ for wisdom, and asked that the Holy Spirit be sent among them to help them chart their future path. Raising his eyes slightly, he looked at the bowed heads of these men with him, men he truly loved, and asked God's blessing for them.

The prayer ended. Each man made the sign of the cross.

"We can be brief," Rodriques told them. "As I have told each of you individually, our reception at most of the wineries we have visited this week has been good. My suggestion—and you all know this as well—is that we continue as before, but with an increase in our public efforts. I plan a public call for a boycott of all northern California wines, effective immediately. Our supporters across the nation will be asked to demonstrate and hand out leaflets at all stores selling wines. This will have an immediate impact. Meanwhile, locally, we will call for a three-hour moratorium on all field and winery work for next Wednesday afternoon. We will mass our forces and march the length of the valley to prove our solidarity."

Rodriques paused, aware of Carlos Murnan's blazingly impatient eyes. "I believe," he resumed, "that these actions will prove our strength and bring about the signing of the first recognition contracts before the end of next week."

"How many contracts have we had signed *this* week?" Murnan asked.

"You know the answer to that," Rodriques said gently.

"None?" Murnan pressed angrily.

"Our reaction has been good. Many are on the brink of signing. With the actions I have outlined—"

"No, Alfredo!" Murnan cut in heatedly. "It is not enough!"

"Carlos, I knew when you walked in that you were eager for argument. State your position." Rodriques pretended more calm than he felt. Major decisions were the job of this group. He could be outvoted. It happened seldom, but there was precedent.

Carlos Murnan rose slowly to his feet and addressed the other men around him. "We have been here one month. In one more month the harvest may be done. This is the time of our greatest leverage. We must move faster."

Thomas Rosario raised his round face. "Alfredo has been

through many campaigns, Carlos. His advice has always been sound."

"We have accomplished nothing here!" Murnan retorted. *"Nothing!"*

Rosario replied calmly, "We have the workers pledged. We have shown our cause. We have opened negotiations."

"And in another month, while we peddle our papers and *talk,* they will have their harvest! And then our strength is gone for another year! I tell you, we must increase the pressure! We must strike hard, *now!"*

Hector Orrerra, who seldom spoke in these meetings, surprised perhaps everyone by speaking now. "What would you do, Carlos? Begin a general strike at once?"

In the momentary pause before Murnan replied, Rodriques almost hoped that his young firebrand would press for just such action. It was too early for this, and Juan Lupé was surely experienced enough to recognize it, as were Rosario and Orrerra. If Carlos Murnan pushed too hard, he would defeat his own cause.

Murnan, however, was not a fool, and had obviously done his planning.

"A general strike may be two weeks away," he conceded.

"Then what do you propose? What better than the things Alfredo has outlined?"

"Pick a winery," Carlos Murnan said, his eyes bright. "Focus our efforts upon it. Make the others see what we will do if we are not heeded at once."

"With a strike?" Orrerra asked.

"Not at once. First with a demonstration."

Jesús Cadz looked more interested. "What kind?"

"Remember what was done at the Henkerle Vineyards in the south? I urge that we select a winery here, and do the same as proof of our power to disrupt if we are not given serious attention at once."

Every man in the room, including Alfredo Rodriques, was startled by the suggestion. They all knew what had been done by another group at Henkerle. It had drawn widespread publicity, and had been effective.

Rodriques, however, remembered more than that. "Much public opinion was turned against the workers who did that to Henkerle, Carlos."

"Damn public opinion, Alfredo! It is not public opinion

we struggle against here! It is the wineries and the growers! Let them feel our power!"

"It means trespassing on private property. Have you, then, no more respect for the law?"

Carlos Murnan smiled. "Did you not just suggest a secondary boycott? Are we to honor one law, but not some other of *your* choosing?"

"Trespassing means possible violence," said Thomas Rosario, frowning. "And mass arrests."

"Can they arrest thousands of us? Can they continually shuttle their cars from one winery to another? What do they do after their jails are full?"

Juan Lupé spoke after a moment of silence. "Who would be the target for this effort, in your opinion, Carlos? A winery that Alfredo believes is friendly to us? In that case, would we not drive a friend away?"

"There is an obvious target," Murnan retorted. "There is one man in this area who will never surrender until we force him to his knees. There is one winery that has no friends of ours within it, so no one will be alienated." He paused dramatically. "All of you know who that man is, and the name of his winery."

"Jules Trello," Jesús Cadz said with angry relish.

"Jules Trello," Murnan echoed. "Schreck Brothers."

Cadz looked up, his eyes excited. "I like this. I have ached to see a blow struck. What better place? What better time?"

"What of Alfredo's plans?" Juan Lupé asked quietly, dismaying Rodriques with the sudden certainty that he was leaning toward the firebrand position. "Do we ignore Alfredo's experience? His judgment?"

"We do as Alfredo suggested," Murnan said. "This movement against Jules Trello is in addition, our acceleration of effort—our first blow toward victory."

"I like this," Jesús Cadz said quietly.

"Rosario?" Murnan challenged. "What of you?"

Rosario shot Rodriques a quick glance that showed his worry and hesitance to speak. "I fear that any such confrontation will lead to violence. There will be arrests—beatings. You would open the door to a furnace. You may not be able to close that door again. Choosing Schreck Brothers only makes sure that the fire will be blazing indeed."

"You do not support my motion, then?"

Rosario looked up at Murnan. "I was not aware that it was a motion, Carlos," he said. "Are we, then, to outvote our leader?"

"Alfredo has always allowed the Holy Spirit to work through a group," Murnan replied. "He has never issued orders that his most trusted advisers could not alter, with counsel and discussion." Murnan turned to Rodriques. "Is this not so, Alfredo?"

So the test had come. Rodriques mentally composed an ejaculation before speaking. He needed God's help now. He felt that he stood, with these men, on the brink of an abyss.

"It is so," he replied quietly. "If most of you wish to endorse this movement against Schreck Brothers Winery, then I will not forbid it. It is your struggle as well as mine. We stand together."

"You see?" Carlos Murnan said triumphantly.

"Nevertheless," Rodriques added quickly, "I must speak what I believe on this matter."

Every man, even the impatient Murnan, fell silent, watching him.

"Our goals are just," Rodriques told them, wishing he had more and better words to express what he felt. "We have come here in peace, and have come far—much farther, Carlos, than you in your present anger probably realize. I believe that within another week, if we follow my course, we will have the first agreements signed.

"After the first, the others will follow. Only a few will stand against us. If we must then take sterner action against those few, then it is the will of God.

"To move as you suggest now, however, is a mistake in my view. We will trespass on private property. The law will be against us. You are right in saying that Jules Trello is a sworn enemy. But by moving against a sworn and strong enemy, we invite the strongest possible countermoves —violence, as Thomas has said. I have a great fear that this action may begin a series of events destined to make us more enemies than friends, and solidify opposition rather than crumble it."

Rodriques took a deep breath, then continued: "The time is not ripe for this, my friends. It will be a terrible blunder. Be patient just a little longer, I beg you."

No one spoke for several seconds.

Then Carlos Murnan said regretfully, "We must vote, Alfredo."

Rodriques nodded. He did not know how this vote would come out. It was going to be close. He had no choice but to go around the room, now.

"Does anyone else wish to speak?" he asked, delaying.

The men watched him, their expressions worried and tense, ready.

"Carlos, your motion is to do the things I have outlined, but in addition to move against Jules Trello, as you outlined."

"Immediately," Carlos Murnan scowled.

"Immediately?"

"On Monday. The day after tomorrow."

No one commented on this amendment. It meant their minds were made up, and timing meant little to them.

"Very well," Rodriques said. "I assume, Carlos, you vote yes for your own motion?" He allowed himself a smile, although there was no pleasure in it.

"I vote yes," Murnan said.

"Jesús?"

"Yes," Jesús Cadz said.

"Thomas?"

"No!" Rosario said with force.

And so now, with Alfredo's vote, it would be two–two. The issue would be decided by Juan Lupé, an old and trusted friend who nevertheless seemed to be leaning toward Murnan's position, and by Hector Orrerra, who was an unknown quantity.

"Juan?" Rodriques said.

"Yes," Lupé replied, refusing to look at him.

Orrerra could make it a tie, a loss for Carlos Murnan.

"Hector?"

Orrerra licked his lips and then squared his shoulders.

"Yes," he said.

Carlos Murnan's explosive exhalation was sign of his triumph. For an instant, everyone began talking excitedly at once. Everyone, that is, but Rodriques and Thomas Rosario.

They looked at one another. Rosario's expression was bitter, resigned. In his eyes was the knowledge that Alfredo Rodriques shared with him: they had stepped onto a tightrope. They had to cooperate now. Their group had to show unanimity. Alfredo Rodriqués had to lead this effort, and Rosario had to aid him, if they were to maintain even a semblance of influence.

A pendulum had swung. They were committed.

5

On Monday morning, Jules Trello drove from home to the Elmhurst property, where he found his contractor, Adam Knotts, already supervising a crew of workmen. The morning was warm and windless. Jules was sweating as he stepped from his car and confronted Knotts on the broken pavement of the interior courtyard in front of the ancient stone mission building. The sound of hammers echoed from inside, and already a pile of rotted timbers and other trash had begun to grow outside the front windows.

"You understand that the work down below must come first," Jules told Knotts.

The contractor, a big man with a ready smile and thinning yellow hair, removed his baseball cap and mopped his forehead on his arm. "Yes sir, I'm having it done just like you said. We'll have all that old planking and those rotten pallets out of there by midnight, and tomorrow we'll start putting in the new flooring."

"The new barrels and tanks start coming by the end of the week," Jules reminded him.

"We'll be ready, Mr. Trello. Count on it."

"You can have the back doors knocked out and enlarged?"

"Oh, yes, sir."

"It doesn't look to me like you have very many men on the job. At the rate I'm paying you for this work, you don't have to have a skeleton crew."

Knotts grinned. "There's only so much room to work down in those cellars, Mr. Trello. But don't worry. We have a dozen more men coming tomorrow."

"All right," Jules said gruffly. "Just so you're sure." Then he turned on his grin. "Always make sure you have enough help. Richard Nixon. And never send a boy to do a man's work. Raquel Welch."

Knotts chuckled and put a heavy, friendly hand on Jules's shoulder. "I'll make sure, Mr. Trello! You're a card!"

It never hurt, Jules thought as he drove away, to make friends with the help. Knotts had held out for a 20 per cent retainer in advance on reconstruction of Elmhurst winery, but he wasn't going to get any more until after the first of the year, although of course he didn't know that yet. A little friendly feeling might ease the blow.

Driving out of the gates of the old winery, Jules glanced at the metal frame standard, already set in fresh concrete, which would soon hold the new sign he had on order: *ELMHURST WINERY, Founded 1908; Jules Trello, Prop.* Robert Mancini would have kittens every time he passed it . . . if he was in business to be passing it at all.

Despite the shock of learning that his wife had been the driver in the hit-run accident, Jules now drove toward Schreck Brothers with a general feeling of contentment. There was no way Carole could be caught, so it was just a matter of memory fading generally. No great harm had been done, and Carole, although she had been stupid, probably really hadn't been to blame.

On almost all other fronts, sale of the Elmhurst wine to Carmine D'Angelico had eased tensions. Debts were not pressing in as closely now. With the wine safely gone in D'Angelico's unmarked trucks there was nothing to fear.

It took no stretch of the imagination to know that the Elmhurst wine with its French labels, was by now almost certainly on the high seas. Jules imagined that the trucks had unloaded to a small vessel somewhere at night, and a subsequent transfer had been made far from shore. Perhaps—probably—his wine was not the only bogus French wine in the ultimate shipment. The ship would proceed through the Panama Canal and into the Gulf of Mexico, and the plain cartons would be labeled with markers identical to those on each bottle inside the carton. The ship would later unload somewhere in the South or perhaps on the East Coast, and wine bought at less than one dollar per bottle would be available for retail in the nine-to eleven-dollar bracket. A tidy profit for D'Angelico, especially considering that it was probably his ship and his distributorship handling the wine . . . as well as anything else that might be aboard.

Jules did not, however, begrudge D'Angelico his profit. Jules had made enough to get by. Now, with things also going so nicely against Robert Mancini, he felt that his father might live long enough, after all, to be forced to realize who was the real genius of the family.

Jules's sense of all being well began to fade when he drove into the Schreck parking area. There were more cars than usual—a lot more, and many seemed to be very old. He saw some small brown children playing in the shade of a camper pickup. Chicanos. He did not like the looks of this. What did he have? A caravan of poor people and college kids intent on tasting everything in sight, and buying nothing?

Jules hurried into the office wing of the plant, avoiding the main visitors' foyer. He found Pernell Redman, his manager, rushing up and down the office hall, wringing his hands.

"Jules! My God, I've been trying to locate you everywhere!"

"What's happening?" Jules demanded. "What's gone wrong?"

"Did you see all the cars? Did you see the mob downstairs?"

"I came in the side way. What's *happening?*"

"Field workers," Redman said bleakly. "Dozens of them. Maybe over a hundred, I don't know. They're all over the place down there!"

"God damn it," Jules snapped, "I left orders to throw any trespassers the hell off!"

"We couldn't do that," Redman said miserably. "At least not before getting your opinion—"

"I've given my opinion before! Jesus Christ! I don't want any of those dirty sons of a bitches picketing on this property, and we've got every right to throw them out!"

"That's just it. They're not picketing."

"Then what the hell are they doing?"

"The sign out in front says public tours and tasting, nine

to three daily. They insist that they're here to tour and taste."

Jules froze, understanding—remembering another winery once, in the south, where others had used this trick.

They were counting on their subterfuge and his worry about public opinion to tie his hands.

They were here as tourists, they pretended. If he threw them out, they would create adverse publicity. They would say it was racism. So he was supposed to welcome them, grin and take it. And they would come back again and again and again, shuffling through, smiling, drinking the wine, so cluttering the tour that other, legitimate visitors would see the mob and be discouraged and go elsewhere.

"I won't have it," Jules snapped.

"What can we do?" Redman asked.

Jules started for the door that led downstairs. "I'll by God show you what we can do!"

He plunged down the circular staircase and through a downstairs door leading to a hallway. Overchilled air conditioning struck icy fingers into his sweaty clothing as he reached another door, one leading into the central public foyer. He heard the rumble of voices and shuffling of feet before he jerked the door open, but he was hardly prepared for the scene that greeted him.

The central foyer was a great circular area more than a hundred feet in diameter and open to the roof high above. Ordinarily, at the peak of the tourist season, there were twenty to thirty people standing around, waiting for the next tour to begin at the central information desk.

Today Jules could not even see the central desk. More than a hundred persons jammed the area—women, children, infants in mothers' arms, men wearing the shabby clothing of field workers. The vast majority were Chicanos.

Near Jules's position were four white adults, two couples, middle-aged. Wearing colorful tourist togs and strung with cameras and souvenir bags, they were frowning at the large crowd. Jules edged closer to them in time to hear one of the women say, "I didn't count on anything like this."

One of the men nodded agreement. "No sense staying. Let's go up the road to Korday."

"*I* don't want to be shoved through in a mob like this," the other woman said.

The four of them started edging away from Jules and toward the exit doors.

Restraining an impulse to try to bring them back, Jules started working his way toward the central desk, still masked from his view. The general situation was of far greater importance than any single group. If he did not get rid of the Chicano demonstrators—whatever pose they were striking —his tours would be wrecked, he would be forced to close to the public.

Seething, he smiled through gritted teeth as he pressed past people. Some of the field workers recognized him and grinned broadly.

Jules neared the information desk, where he saw two of his girls being besieged for information brochures. At this point, Pernell Redman, hurrying behind him, caught his arm.

"Let go," Jules snapped.

"Jules, don't do anything we might regret. Don't lose your cool, because that's what they *want*."

Jules tore free of his manager's imploring hands and got to the information desk railing. One of the young women broke off from the visitors and came over to him. She was harried and upset.

"Mr. Trello," she whispered urgently, "what do we *do?*"

"What do they want?"

"They say they want to tour—taste the wines."

"Do they have a leader?"

The girl glanced around nervously, then inclined her head toward a youthful, dark-skinned man not far away in a group of several others. "He did the talking when they came in."

"Keep passing out brochures. I'll take care of this."

Pressing along the railing, Jules reached the man the young woman had singled out. The youth was with another man his own age and three women, one holding an infant in her arms. They were smiling and talking in swift Spanish as Jules touched the leader's arm.

The youth turned, fixing Jules with startling jade eyes. "Yes, sir?"

"What's your name?" Jules demanded.

"I am Jesús Cadz."

"You're the boss here?"

"Sir, I am here with my friends to see your fine winery. There is no leader."

"It won't do, Cadz. I'm Jules Trello. This is my place. I'm telling you one time only: get these people out of here."

"Sir, I do not know most of these people. Are you saying we cannot take a tour today?"

Jules was shriveling under the arrogant smiles of the Chicanos standing nearest and listening in. "You can't tour today or any day, you little bastard. Now get out."

Cadz frowned and made a show of being confused. "This is not a place open to the public, sir? The sign does not make of it a public accommodation?"

"It does not."

Cadz took out a small notebook with a blue cover. "Please be kind enough, sir, to state the exact reason we are being asked to leave. I want to make sure I represent your position accurately to the United States District Attorney."

"We can't take all you people on tours even if we wanted to, you little son of a bitch. Now are you going to get out?"

Cadz smiled. "If it is only a matter of your being busy, sir, we are willing to wait all day."

Jules balled his fists and for a blinding instant wanted only to smash the smile from Cadz's face. It was almost as if he could already feel the marvelous impact of his fist on those white teeth, caving them in.

Pernell Redman shouldered up beside Jules, breathing hard, and this somehow broke the moment. Jules struggled for control. Violence would ruin the winery's reputation and give the workers an issue in the press. No real visitors would come, fearing trouble, and then the workers would have won a point.

Shaking inside, Jules backed away from Cadz and his group, who stared after him. A different idea rushed into his mind. He felt a rush of pleasure. He knew what to do.

Brushing Redman aside, he climbed over the information desk railing and stepped up onto a three-step platform that the guides sometimes used for vantage when addressing a large group. As he did so, all eyes turned toward him. By effort of will, he drove the anger from his expression and managed a smile as he spread his arms.

"As you can see," he began, and voices hushed as his voice carried, "we have a very large crowd this morning. The first tour will begin at once. Now, I'm afraid a lot of you are going to have to wait awhile for another tour. To be fair, I'm going to move through the crowd now and select the people for the first tour sort of at random."

Climbing off the platform, he nodded to one of the

guides. "Judy, go on over by the door to the production area. I'll send the people for the first tour over to you."

As the young woman obeyed, Jules moved into the crowd, going swiftly, smiling all the time as he tapped people lightly and told them to go join the pretty girl at the far door. By the time he had circled the area, twenty-one persons had been split out of the crowd to go stand with Judy across the open hallway at the far end.

All twenty-one were Caucasians.

There were no whites remaining in the central foyer crowd.

Jules made his way back to the information desk and mounted the platform again. He smiled down at the sea of brown faces. "That makes up the first tour. If the rest of you will be patient, the next tour will be organized in"— he glanced at his watch—"in a little over four hours."

There was an instant of almost perfect silence.

Across the room, from the white group, a woman's voice called sharply, "Mr. Trello!"

Jules turned and identified a tall, blond young woman who had stepped out of the group. She wore a rather plain gray dress and stout brown shoes, but she was pretty nevertheless.

Jules walked over to her, aware that the other whites were listening intently.

The girl's hazel eyes were angry. "None of those Chicano citizens can join this tour?"

"This tour is filled," Jules smiled. "Now if you and the others here will just follow Judy—"

"Mr. Trello, my friends here are Chicanos. Why can't some of them go on this tour now?"

The bitch! A bleeding heart, turning against her own kind.

Despite the fresh burst of anger, Jules managed another PR smile to the other whites. "Just follow Judy, please. I'll have a word with this young lady, and she'll join you in a moment. Judy?"

Judy the guide caught the sharp cue. Beginning her smiling pitch, she swung the heavy oak doors wide, inviting the tourists through. They filed after her, and within moments the heavy doors swung closed, leaving only Jules and the blond woman standing in the broad hallway just off the foyer.

Many in the foyer crowd were watching, but from a discreet distance.

In a voice that would not carry to the others, the woman said, "I insist on the rights of my Chicano friends."

"You whore," Jules retorted shakily, half under his breath. "Does it make you feel righteous to run with that pack of jackals? Does that brown cock really turn you on?"

The blonde paled visibly.

This gave Jules his inspiration.

Smiling, he began softly and swiftly cursing her. He proceeded from profanities to obscenities, and carefully watched for her reaction to each epithet. The sexual references made shock register in her remarkably wide and transparent eyes, and he took his cue from this to intensify the verbal attack. He began to tell her what he thought were her sexual preferences, with men, women, and in groups.

The words seemed to hit the young woman with enormous impact. Her pallor increased. A hand, trembling, stole across her breast as if to protect her from Jules's onslaught. She took a slight step backward.

Jules moved with her, still smiling. He reached deep into his considerable experience, both in reality and pornographic fantasy. He hit upon a positive inspiration—he could so judge it by her gasp of real pain—with a suggestion about her possible liking for large animals. He began to elaborate upon this, almost enjoying himself as each word hit her like a fist. He was using the vilest gutter language.

Quite suddenly, as Jules began describing a certain act that would require the services of several other persons to perform, the woman's lips parted. Her eyes rolled back. She began to shake violently. Then she collapsed softly, without a sound, to the marble floor.

Startled, Jules stepped back from her.

Cadz, the Chicano leader, rushed forward. "What have you done to Sister Grace?" he cried shrilly.

"You call her your sister?" Jules sneered, misunderstanding. He looked down at her. Her fall had thrown her skirt high on shapely thighs. "That isn't what I would call her."

Cadz knelt beside the unconscious woman. He looked up at Jules. "Sister Grace is a nun of the Catholic Church."

As Jules reeled under this information, several other men moved up anxiously, pushing close.

One of them, a rotund youth, pushed his forefinger angrily against Jules's chest. "You go too far, Mr. Trello! We taught your father and we can teach you—"

The boy got no farther. It was not enough, Jules thought in a flash, that they invaded his property, that they wanted to hound him, that they were vermin. Now they enlisted women of his own church—*nuns*—and tricked him into insulting them, and then issued threats.

Jules's fist moved less than ten inches. He got his weight behind it, however, and it doubled the boy over in agonized loss of breath.

The others nearby gasped and started at Jules.

"*No!*" Jesús Cadz cried sharply, jumping to his feet.

"Get out," Jules told him. "You have two minutes." He was shaking with his anger. "I'm going for my security guards now. In two minutes I'll tell them to use *any means necessary* to clear this building."

Cadz heaved a deep, shuddering breath, evidently struggling with his own emotions. "If we do not, sir? What will your guards do?"

"We have tear gas, by God, and clubs. We'll use that or guns, if we have to!"

The blond nun—if she was a nun—moaned and began dizzily trying to sit up. Cadz bent again to help her, and other hands joined in. Cadz let the others help her unsteadily to her feet. They drew her away toward the crowd a dozen paces distant, watching with a combination of fear and anger.

"We will leave now," Cadz told Jules. "But we will come back."

"When you do, cocksucker, be ready for what I have waiting for you."

6

Susan Knight was deep in the cooperage area, a bung removed from a barrel of Pinot Noir, thoughtfully tasting and recording her impressions, when Robert Mancini and Mike DeFrates came down the high-stacked aisle of dark-colored barrels to confront her. It was almost noon and she was chilled from staying overlong in the cavernlike controlled temperature of 55 degrees.

The expression on Robert Mancini's face chilled her more deeply.

"I don't think I can *take* any more bad news just yet!" she said impulsively.

"Well, it may not be that bad," Robert told her. "But it's bad enough."

Susan looked at the two men, seeing their worry. Although she and Mike DeFrates had known generally about the growing problem with Timmons Corporation, it had been early this morning before Robert Mancini called the two of them into his office and quietly laid it all out for them with complete candor.

In another week, he had told them, John Endicott and E. Z. Simms would be on the grounds more or less permanently, and would be given office space. He explained details of his stock predicament, and showed them the Timmons letter.

"This letter came last week!" Susan pointed out. "Why

did you carry this around alone all weekend? Why didn't you tell us at once?"

Robert's smile had been thin and mirthless. "There was no sense spoiling your weekend."

DeFrates had said, "You sure do know how to spoil a Monday morning."

They had then discussed it in detail. Robert had explained his efforts to buy unaccounted-for stock, and gave a frank if bleak estimate of his position *vis-à-vis* Timmons. DeFrates stormed up and down the office, turning the air blue, finally getting so livid that he almost made the situation momentarily funny. Robert then outlined his plan for which employees should be informed, and how. A general announcement would not be made, although questions would be answered truthfully. Every effort would be made to put a happy face on things. There was no sense, Robert said, in everyone getting upset and losing efficiency when he still had hope of finding a stock bundle that might turn the tide.

Since the meeting a few hours earlier, Susan had felt like a sleepwalker going about her tasks. Now, seeing Robert's and DeFrates's faces, she knew something new— or additional—had gone wrong.

"What is it?"

"There's been trouble over at Schreck Brothers," Robert told her.

"Thank God *that's* what it is! I thought you were going to have more bad news about our situation here!"

"It might affect us here. It could affect everyone. From what we know so far, the field workers tried a sit-in type demonstration inside the winery, and Jules knocked a couple of people down, then brought out his staff of extra security guards."

"Oh, no! A general free-for-all?"

Robert shook his head. "The workers cleared out, evidently. The radio says a couple of workers were hurt. Tim Crocker called, and he hadn't heard it that way. He's on the way over to Schreck now to try to get the facts straight."

"What happens now?" Susan demanded.

"If this means a general effort to paralyze the wineries, we get ready for damned serious trouble. But we don't know that yet. We have to wait until we hear from Tim. He promised to call me as soon as he's seen Jules."

"What do we do in the meantime?"

"That," Robert said, "is what we need to talk about. Can you come up to the office?"

Susan replaced the bung in the Pinot Noir barrel, stowed her equipment, and followed the two men out of the cooperage, through production, and into the administration building. On all sides, amazingly, everything seemed to be going normally. Production was being given the final preparations for the hectic activity of the crush, now probably less than a month away. In the offices, employees went about their routine duties calmly, unaware of the cloud over their future existence. The sun was bright on high windows in the lobby loft.

Susan was struck by a sensation like she was in a bad dream. On the outside, superficially, everything was going wonderfully now. While the inside of every situation seemed ready to go to ruin.

Only Sunday she had talked with several other winemakers. Worry about the harvest had begun to subside sharply. It would still be late, it was true. But the recent warmth and sun had begun to bring the grapes on to a mature magnificence. As if trying to make up for giving them worries earlier, the grapes were now doing amazing things. In a few of the very warmest regions, some Pinot Chardonnay destined for use in Champagne had already been picked at a Brix of 18. In several areas the Pinot Noir was past 20, and continuing to improve. If the weather held, and the grapes continued to mature, they might harvest much of the Pinot Noir at sugar levels far better than the desired 22. A vineyard expert had told Susan Sunday that they might, in certain areas, be able to hold this grape until its skin was very soft, and the Brix equaled the level of some Pinot Noir in the remarkable year of 1974, an astounding 28.

The harvest would be late, yes. But it might go down as one of the greatest if present trends continued.

Given this knowledge and the businesslike activity around her, Susan continued to be assailed by the sensation that she was living in two dimensions at once: reality and nightmare. The threat of a takeover by Timmons Corporation was quite enough to preoccupy her every moment. If the effort by Workers United was about to become a prairie fire, it might be more than any of them could cope with.

Robert told his secretary to be sure to put through any call from Timothy Crocker, and then the three of them closeted themselves in his office. Robert fished around for a forbidden cigarette, found an empty package, and disgustedly tossed it into the wastebasket. Mike DeFrates silently offered him a Marlboro. Robert scowled at the pack and then shook his head. "I don't smoke," he said.

"So what happens now?" DeFrates asked.

"Maybe nothing," Robert said, rubbing his forehead as if he had a headache. "Or possibly escalation against all the rest of us."

Susan strained to concentrate on *this* problem, and not the other. She said, "Somehow it surprises me that they tried to go into Schreck Brothers. It's the worst target in terms of winning anything. And I just didn't get the feeling when we talked to Alfredo Rodriques that *he* was ready for a step like this."

"He might not have been," Robert said.

"I don't understand."

"He pressed very hard, here and some other places, for an agreement. He was *very* active all last week, a marked increase in his personal visits. What would account for that?"

DeFrates said, "His plan had it set up that way."

"Or," Robert suggested thoughtfully, "his own people were getting impatient."

"What do you mean by that?" DeFrates asked.

"A leader like Rodriques is the leader only as long as the followers *allow* him to lead. There's always pressure in that kind of organization. Some want to go faster, some slower. Some want confrontation, some are saying the whole effort should be abandoned."

"Yes," Susan agreed, puzzled. "But Alfredo Rodriques has always been able to hold the elements together."

"I think that may be what he was doing with all his personal diplomacy last week."

"Meaning?"

"He was under more pressure than he let on. He was hunting for a settlement here—anywhere—to hold up and show as real progress. He needed a sign to keep his followers from losing their patience and going ahead faster than he personally might want to go."

"Then you think Rodriques might not even have approved this sit-in, or whatever it was, at Schreck?"

"Oh, no. I think he must have approved it. But I'm guessing that he approved it only because he had to, to keep on being the leader. If your troops all start up a hill, and you want to be the captain, I think you'd damned well better get out in front of them whether you approve the tactic secretly or not."

"Why wouldn't Rodriques approve?" DeFrates demanded. "He stared this thing. He never showed any hesitancy to get tough before."

"I've thought about that," Robert replied. "When he was with us, he spoke of incidents . . . pressures. I think he knows better than any of us how flammable the whole situation may be. He wanted to go slow, but to get his people to go slow, he had to show them more progress than he could come up with."

"So what now?" Susan asked.

"Now he's boxed, I think. They've taken a new step. They got chased off with their tails between their legs. They can't just let that lie there. It's a defeat. They have to get back at Jules. The fight . . . as they used to say in the old days . . . is joined."

"But Jules will never give in!" Susan said. "And if what you say is right, neither can Rodriques!"

"Right." Robert looked grim.

Susan studied his expression. There were new lines in his face. He looked suddenly very, very tired. A rush of compassion arose in her. No one spoke, and all at once she was angry.

"It's not right," she said. "It's just not fair!"

"What's not fair?" DeFrates asked, surprised.

"We're sitting here talking about this damned strike, and every time I stop thinking about that even for *a second,* I'm right back thinking about the other thing! I mean, a week from today, that stupid John Endicott and that creepy little E. Z. Simms are going to come mincing in here, with their pukey little memos and computer printouts, and start throwing their weight around! It just makes me sick. I can't even think straight about this strike. Why should I even care what happens to Jules Trello? Here we are, practically staring at a complete . . . whole . . . *awful* change in Robert Mancini Vineyards, and we're talking about a bunch of strikers somewhere else!"

Robert Mancini's expression softened. "We'll get around Timmons yet."

"How can I count on it?" Susan cried.

"Trust me. If we *can* win, we *will.*"

"You built this old winery back from a ruin! Who was it that experimented with all the different kinds of oak, and started using so much Nevers, and practically fathered a whole new trend in the quality wine business here? Who showed everyone else how to use the centrifuge, and the computer, and was right in the lead with cool fermentation? If it hadn't been for you and a few others with you, we'd all still be making jug wine up here, and seeing our profits drop out of sight as all those new irrigated vineyards start producing farther south. Our house table wine is superior to any European *vin ordinaire* ever produced. We've got Pinot Noir and Cabernet and Zinfandel and Johannisberg Riesling down below that I'd stack up against any wine in the world! And now you've *done* all this, and we sit here worrying about a strike while maybe we're about to be taken over by a bunch of damned airplane and baby-bed manufacturers! It just makes me sick!"

Mike DeFrates grinned with appreciation. "So what do you say we fly to Portland and kick some asses, okay?"

"If I thought it would do any good—!" Susan began.

"It wouldn't," Robert said quickly, smiling despite the tension. "Look. We haven't lost any votes yet. I've got some pretty high-powered attorneys and a broker who's fast on his feet. They're working on this. I'm working on this. What we have to do right now is take one thing at a—"

The telephone winked and he picked it up. "Yes?"

He nodded. "Okay, Tim. I have Mike DeFrates and Susan Knight with me. I'm going to put you on the amplifier so they can hear you too. Okay?"

Evidently Tim Crocker had no objection. Robert pressed two buttons on a small, ivory-colored device beside his telephone and leaned back in his chair. "All right, Tim. You hear me okay?"

From a small loudspeaker Crocker's familiar voice replied, showing a hint of strain. "Fine, Bob."

"You saw Jules?"

"Yes. He's having some new signs painted that say, 'Tours to private parties only.' He says the gate guards will decide who is a private party and who isn't."

Robert grimaced. "Were people hurt over there earlier?"

"I don't think so. Jules hit a man. He says if they come back, that's just the start of it."

"Oh, hell," Susan murmured.

"What?" Crocker's amplified voice said.

Robert said, "Jules is tooling up for a fight, then."

"He's hiring thirty new plant guards. A security outfit in Napa will supply them, and they'll start duty at six in the morning. In the meantime, he's issuing guns to the security people and he's had all the big fire hoses hooked to the building hydrants."

"Did you try to talk to him?"

"I tried," Crocker replied dryly. "Then I went out and had a chat with my Buick. It paid more attention."

"Would it help if more people tried?"

"You know Jules. He's gearing up for a fight. I'll spare you the quotes, but he says if you're not with him you're against him, and if you won't stand and fight for your property now, you're a—well, I said I'd spare you the details."

"What about Rodriques' side?"

"You mean you haven't heard the latest?"

Susan tensed and saw Robert and DeFrates do the same.

"Maybe not," Robert said. "What is it?"

"They've just finished a big meeting at the Workers United headquarters, according to the radio. They voted to start a major effort against Schreck, starting tomorrow. Pickets, secondary boycott, called for his field workers to call in sick, the whole works."

"Christ," Robert said.

"That's about all the good news I have at the moment, Bob."

"Tim, thanks. I'll get back to you."

"Yes, I think we'd better stay in close touch."

"I'll call you." Robert broke the connection and turned to Susan and Defrates. "I'm going to make some more calls, and then after Jules has an hour or two more to settle down, I'm going to go over there and try to talk to him."

DeFrates said, "You heard how much good Crocker did. And Jules hates your ass."

"Well, I'm going to try, anyway. Somebody has to cool him if possible. Meanwhile, Susan, I want you to go to the city and try to see Rodriques."

"Me?" Susan said in astonishment. "Why? What can I *say?*"

"Just try to make sure he understands what a hothead Jules really is. Tell him that a lot of us want to keep this thing from blowing up, and will help if we possibly can. Try to get a reading on what his mood is. Maybe it will help if we just try some Kissinger-type shuttle diplomacy here . . . at least keep some lines of communication open."

"I'm no good at that sort of thing," Susan protested. "Why can't Mike do it?"

DeFrates grinned. "Because I'd lose my temper and punch somebody."

"Bullshit," Susan said.

"Mike is half right," Robert told her. "Also, you've talked with Rodriques twice, once alone, once with me. Maybe he'll see you. I doubt that he would see Mike."

"I'll try it," Susan said. "But I don't like it."

"There's been little that any of us has liked lately," Robert said. Then he showed his slight smile. "What's that cliché saying Jules always uses? 'When the going gets tough, et cetera.' Okay. Let's get going."

7

When Robert walked into the restaurant in the city that night at 8 P.M., Barbara Turner and Jimmy were standing in the vestibule, waiting for him. Barbara was dressed for an "occasion," a new lavender dress, medium heels, and even a tiny hat that might have looked silly, Robert thought, on anyone else. Her son wore tan slacks, white shirt and brown tie, and looked as sullen as she appeared happy.

"I'm late," Robert said apologetically.

"No," she smiled. "We were early."

"It's been quite a day." Robert reached out and squeezed Jimmy's shoulder. "It's great you came, Jim."

The boy kept his head down. "She made me."

Robert was determined that their first real public date was going to be an occasion no matter what pressures might be building elsewhere. "I'm glad you came even if your mom did have to make you. Come on. Let's see if this man has a table for us."

The restaurant, specializing in French cuisine, was by far the most elaborate in the city. Damask covered the walls, and dim illumination came from heavy iron chandeliers high in a beamed ceiling, and from candles on each white-linened table. The sprawling room was about half filled. A phalanx of tuxedo-clad waiters stood alert nearby as the maître d' led Robert and "his family" to their place.

Seating himself across the table from Barbara, with Jimmy on his right between them, Robert glanced over the pewter table setting and tried a second time to rouse the boy. "Have you eaten here before, Jim?"

"No, sir," Jimmy said, his head down.

"I think you'll like it. The food is excellent."

Jimmy looked up without expression. "I'm more a hamburger-type person really."

"If that's really what you want after looking at the menu, I imagine it could be arranged."

Jimmy looked around, withdrawn and silent.

Barbara, obviously tense over her son's continuing hostility but trying to ignore it, smiled brightly. "Did the meeting go all right?"

"There were eight of us there," Robert told her. "It was short notice to get many people together. Except for comparing notes and crossing fingers, there wasn't a lot we could do."

"Did we have a reporter there?"

"Yes. A young fellow with dark hair."

"Glasses?"

"Yes. He smoked a lot."

Barbara nodded recognition. "That's Paul Freyer. He's good."

"We gave him a statement about how eight area winemakers met to discuss the Workers United effort, pledged to meet with the workers anytime new initiatives promised any chance of more intensive negotiations, et cetera."

"And deplored violence?"

Robert winced. "And deplored violence. It wasn't much of a statement, but what could we say or do?"

"You had to try to say something after that little fracas at Schreck this morning. I'm glad you did."

A waiter interrupted them politely, standing until Robert noticed him. "Will you have cocktails before ordering, sir?"

"Good," Robert said. "Barbara?"

"A martini," she said, "straight up, with a twist."

"Two," Robert agreed. "Jim? Something?"

The boy looked embarrassed. "I don't know what I could have."

"May I suggest a kiddy cocktail, sir?" the waiter asked.

Jimmy's face colored. "No!"

Robert exchanged glances with Barbara as he understood. He said, "I think I'm going to change my mind about that martini. Do you have the Lillet aperitif vermouth?"

"Yes, sir," the waiter said.

"Fine. A bottle of that, very well chilled. And three glasses."

Jimmy looked up sharply, interested.

"Yes, sir," the waiter said.

"All right?" Robert asked Barbara.

"Yes."

Robert reverted to the topic. "I tried to see Jules this afternoon, after I hoped he had cooled down. He sent word out that he didn't have time to see me."

"That's just great," Barbara grimaced. "Did Susan Knight do any better with Alfredo?"

"Well, she saw him. He was polite. He told her they were going to mount a continuing effort against Jules, as an object lesson. Susan said he didn't give the impression of being very happy about it. That doesn't surprise me."

"If he wasn't happy, it would tend to support your belief that he's being forced to take stronger steps mainly to keep his own troops in line."

"I just don't think there's much doubt about it. He's accepting steps that he knows are dangerous, because he believes that his people will run off and act on their own if he doesn't yield somewhat to their pressure."

"And if they go off without Alfredo, they'll really get into trouble."

"They may anyway."

Barbara got a cigarette from her purse and he lighted it for her. She exhaled smoke and then asked, "You knew the state police have been alerted?"

"Hell, no! When? By whom?"

"The county contacted the Governor's office an hour or two ago. He agreed to put about a hundred troopers on special alert. He's not sending them into the area yet, but the wire story said he wanted to make sure he was, quote, ready for any contingency, unquote."

It was bad news, and Robert did not reply at once. Special police might be needed at some point, but if they were, it would signal a more complete breakdown in law and order than anything they had witnessed so far. Alerting special forces might be tactically wise, but announcing the alert was not wise at all, in his view. It could only increase worries and make people consider the situation nervously. There had been times when alerting extra law-enforcement officers had so exacerbated tensions that the stated need for force became a self-fulfilling prophecy.

"I wish the Governor hadn't been quite so quick on the trigger," he admitted finally.

"The Governor," Barbara pointed out, "has an election coming up."

In another few minutes the waiter brought the chilled vermouth and glasses to the table. Robert was aware that Jimmy watched with covert interest as the cork was removed and the bottle presented to Robert. He poured a half glass for Barbara, then a half glass which he put in front of the boy before pouring his own glass.

"Can I drink this?" Jimmy asked, looking from Robert to his mother and back again.

"An aperitif is designed to enhance the appetite," Robert told him. "The sophisticated drinker sips it very slowly and never overindulges. I have an idea that I won't have any more than this single glass; we can take the rest home with us in a brown bag."

Jimmy blinked at him. "But this is mine . . . the same as you guys are drinking?"

"If you want it," Robert told him. He raised his glass and sipped it very lightly by way of example.

Jimmy raised the glass gingerly. He touched the rim to his lips and let a few drops of the liquid touch his tongue. He winced, but tried to hide the reaction.

To cover his possible embarrassment, Robert raised his glass. "A toast. To peace. To the harvest. To the future."

Jimmy joined them in raising his glass.

"And to Elton John," he blurted.

Robert kept a straight face. "And to Elton John."

Frowning studiously, Jimmy touched the glass to his lips again. The level did not go down a drop. He replaced the glass on the table, but now looked around with more interest, and much more cheerfully.

Although the menu included more exotic items, they shortly agreed on *coq au vin* for all. As Robert glanced at the wine list, Barbara asked with mock innocence if the restaurant's cellar included a certain Gallo product. Robert ordered a Mancini Estate Bottled Pinot Chardonnay because it was quite the best of his own wines on the list, and pretended he hadn't heard her jibe.

While they waited for the food, and then while they ate, Robert told Barbara the few bits of news he had to report on his own continuing attempt to secure additional stock. He told her about the shocked, angry reactions of Susan Knight and Mike DeFrates when he had finally given them the full details of his predicament that morning, and they discussed the feelings of employees who had been loyal, and would feel even more shock if the vote next month turned out badly.

Robert tried to be positive. Twice, in addition, he made another attempt to draw Jimmy more actively into the conversation. The boy did not seem so sullen or withdrawn, but replied in monosyllables. He was making fairly good work of his supper.

Once during the meal Robert was vaguely aware that a group of five persons at a nearby table had been watching him as he glanced their way. A second time, one of the women, distinguished-looking and beautifully dressed, might have been staring, but looked away quickly as he almost met her eye by accident. He paid no attention at the time, being intent on Barbara and her son.

They talked about the harvest, nearer now with every passing day. Jimmy seemed to perk up when Robert spoke of the gondolas being tipped to dump tons of fresh grapes into the stemmer-crushers.

"I've never seen that," he volunteered. "I bet that's something."

"We'll have to get you out to the winery when we're in the crush," Robert told him. "I think you'll really enjoy it."

Jimmy seemed to remember that he was supposed to be hostile. He looked down at the wreckage of his meal. "I'll probably be too busy in school."

"We crush Saturdays and Sundays," Robert told him easily. "You can make it. Then maybe we can drive on out to my house. I've got quite a flock of pigeons out there, you know. I never get to fly them much. If I could get somebody like you to help me, maybe we could start giving them more exercise."

"Do they carry messages?" Jimmy asked.

"They haven't. But they could. If I took them a few miles down the road, they'd fly home. Maybe we could experiment with flying them even longer distances after the grapes have been harvested."

"Yes," Jimmy said, interest clear in his eyes. "It wouldn't be very good for them to land in some field and start eating somebody's grapes, would it?"

"It wouldn't be good for the grapes, and it wouldn't be good for our pigeons if the growers had a shotgun handy."

Jimmy grinned. "I bet!"

The waiter hovered. "Dessert, sir?"

"Jim?"

Jimmy remembered his act again. "Oh . . . I dunno."

Robert looked at Barbara. She made a wry face. "I'm stuffed . . . but whatever you decide."

Robert took a deep breath. He felt one of the few positive surges of feeling he had experienced all day. He was making some headway with Jimmy.

"The baked Alaska," he told the waiter.

"The small or the large, sir?"

"The large. We've got something to celebrate, right?"

"You're going to make us all fat!" Barbara said.

"Well, tomorrow we can diet, right, Jim?"

Jimmy smiled but said nothing. The remoteness was in him again.

Robert felt a small pang. It was going to be a long process, and a delicate one. He would never replace a dead war hero who occupied the center of Jimmy's memory . . . nor did he have the temerity to wish to do so. But he had always wanted a son. He wanted very badly to win Jimmy over. It would be perhaps a longer effort than he had first realized.

At least, however, he told himself, there are some signs of progress. When Barbara asked a question about how many kinds of grapes would be crushed, over what period of time, and how much wine would result, he tried to make his reply interesting for both of them. There was nothing he liked to talk about more.

The baked Alaska came, and it was a triumph. It was after 10 P.M. when they left the table, groaning to one another. Robert went to the bar to have the remaining vermouth put in a small sack, and when he returned to the lobby he found Barbara alone. Jimmy had gone off to the restroom.

"He had a good time," she said, her love shining in her eyes. "Thank you."

"Hell, lady," he said gruffly. "Thank *you*."

"I was afraid he would notice those people at the next table gawking at us, but he didn't, thank goodness."

"I *thought* I saw them looking our way a couple of times. I didn't know them. Did you?"

"No. But they must have recognized you from your pictures." Barbara sighed grimly. "I suppose they were gossiping about the story tonight."

Robert drew a blank. "About Schreck, you mean?" Then he saw by her expression that he was mistaken. "About what? I haven't seen the paper. Is there something about Mancini Vineyards?"

Barbara compressed her lips. "Oh, Bob," she said regretfully, like someone who had just committed a *faux pas*.

"What is it?"

She seemed to steel herself, and faced him squarely. "There was a small item. We didn't play it up, but news like that has to be printed, I guess, when the people are prominent. Your wife filed for the divorce today."

It was not a surprise, of course, but it hit him with a quick, unpleasant impact. The glances from the people at the adjacent table were now explained. They had seen the story—had probably gossiped about how quickly Robert Mancini began displaying his new woman.

"I'm sorry, Barb," he said quietly. "I don't give a damn myself, but I've subjected you to—"

"To an evening I'll never forget," she told him sharply, "because it was so wonderful. Now will you please shut up, Mr. Cuckoo? I'm *much* too full of chicken and wine and baked Alaska to have any kind of argument!"

He might have kissed her right then, but Jimmy interrupted.

8

Jules Trello saw the news story about the divorce late that night when he finally got to the newspaper, but his pleasure in finally getting Robert Mancini out of the family was diluted sharply by worry over the day's earlier events —and vanished entirely when he saw a different item on the following page.

AGENTS JAIL
SHIP CAPTAIN,
SEIZE WINE

NEW ORLEANS (AP)—Agents of the U.S. government arrested a merchant ship captain and seven members of his crew Monday, and impounded the cargo of the ship, the *U.S.S. Holmes*.

Included in the seized cargo were 40,000 cases of wine.

Preliminary details were sketchy, but one source said the wine, produce of France according to labels and shipping papers, is actually from another part of the world.

An agent from the U.S. Bureau of Alcohol, Tobacco and Firearms said the ship was boarded and searched, and the arrests made, as it prepared to dock in New Orleans.

Another source said the action was taken as a follow-up to a tip from an informer.

Names of the captain and crew, as well as details of the investigation, were being withheld pending formal charges.

There was no more to the story, but it was quite sufficient to send a chill through Jules from his scalp to his toes. Tossing the paper down after reading the item twice with a mounting sense of horror, he looked at his watch and rushed into the next room of the house where Carole, bikini-clad, was mixing herself a drink.

He hurried to the television console and flipped it on, turning to the best news station.

"What is it, Daddy?" Carole moued.

"Shut up, shut up."

The item came halfway through the newscast, and added only one more element. A broad investigation, the announcer said, was being conducted on both sides of the Atlantic.

Jules stared at the rest of the news, trying to confuse Carole about which item he had really been interested in. He felt sick at his stomach.

He simply had no doubt that the Elmhurst wine was part of the cargo that had been seized. Along with other bogus French wine, it had been almost ready for unloading in New Orleans as genuine French, high-quality import wine when it had been intercepted.

The château label Jules had put on his bottles was for a château that did not exist. Tracers into France would reveal that the shipping manifests, no matter how cleverly done, were falsified.

There had been a weak link somewhere—a turncoat who informed to the U.S. Government, probably because he or she was in deep trouble on some other charge.

What Jules did not know, however, was how deep Carmine D'Angelico's trouble might be personally. And how much possibility was there that part of the illegal shipment could be traced back here?

When the telephone rang even as Jules was thinking of this, he jumped to answer it. One of those instinctive sensations of prescience made his voice quake.

"Jules Trello here."

"Jules." The voice was unmistakable, distant—strained,

with traffic noise in the background. "You know who this is? Answer yes or no."

Jules swallowed thickly. "Yes."

"You know what happened?"

"Not very much—yes."

"It cannot be traced. People may ask questions, but there is no proof. You know nothing. Do you understand me?"

"Yes," Jules said hoarsely.

"I'm telling several people this same thing, so listen. No one must break. One man did. He's dead. Don't let anyone bluff you. Don't get panicky. We are *all right*. Do you understand?"

"Yes," Jules repeated with a feeling that he might choke. "But—"

There was a click, and then a dial tone.

9

On Tuesday, September 15, the day after the abortive tour occupation of Schreck Brothers Winery, scattered absenteeism among field workers was the only real sign that any kind of labor problem existed.

On Wednesday, Workers United escalated.

More than two hundred field workers assembled before dawn in a roadside park approximately two miles south of the Schreck grounds. A Catholic priest offered Mass on a picnic table and distributed Communion under the glaring white illumination of portable floodlights operated by television newsmen. After Mass there were no speeches, no exhortation. All the plans had been outlined earlier, and all the words said.

Shortly after 7 A.M., the demonstrators, now numbering about two hundred and fifty, formed a long, ragged procession four adults wide and moved to the edge of the highway. The sun peered over the eastern mountain range now, hazy in the rising morning heat. Fiercely colored banners were unfurled and hung limp from standards. In the hands of other demonstrators, quickly painted cardboard placards appeared.

The line started north, keeping on the grassy shoulder of the road.

Although some normal traffic tooled by, drivers gawking with curiosity or ill-concealed irritation, the road was emptier than normal except for the traffic directly related to the procession. A sheriff's cruiser, rack-mounted red lights flashing on top, trundled along the shoulder at the head of the line. A second unit, also flashing, brought up the rear. Cars belonging to three television stations followed, with a Chevvie van operated by a radio station's mobile news unit behind them, and two carloads of reporters even farther back. A city policeman on a three-wheeler trailed behind the press, not because it was his proper jurisdiction but because the sheriff had radioed the city for some help in preventing someone from running into the media from the rear.

Alfredo Rodriques walked at the head of the column, Carlos Murnan on his left, Thomas Rosario on his right. Rodriques was already sweating heavily and he felt dizzy and lightheaded from his fast, which was now twenty-four hours old. He had told no one of the fast. It was a matter between him and his God—a sacrifice offered to purify himself for the test he feared was ahead.

The presence of Rosario on his right helped Rodriques spiritually. He knew Rosario wanted no more of this than he did. The time was wrong and the target was definitely wrong, and, worse, the feeling—the ambience—was terribly wrong. During Mass there had been a sense of impatience, of inattention, even of latent hatred. These feelings surrounded Rodriques now, boiled up from his people behind him, mixed with the heat and dust of the air, saturated his wet pores. He was not frightened but he was very, very worried.

He had, however, absolutely no choice. It was clear that the majority would strike with or without him. He had spoken his mind and had been politely heard, then ignored. His job now was to remain as nominal leader, and pray to God he could exert enough influence to keep the day from becoming the kind of horror his instincts whispered it was to become.

The line of marchers toiled on northward. They began filing past fields of grapes, bursting with near ripeness. White field workers near a truck in the vineyard paused in their work and stared.

Carlos Murnan saw them and raised a hand in greeting. "Join us!" he called shrilly.

One of the whites raised his own hand slowly, the middle finger extended upward.

They kept going. Rodriques fought his lightheadedness,

showing nothing. In the distance now could be seen the roofs of the Schreck winery, and from the people behind him Rodriques could feel the tension, like a red, penetrating, radiating force, as it built. The procession was silent, only the shuffling of feet and labored breathing.

Another sheriff's cruiser, lights blinking, pulled alongside the head of the column. It remained in the traffic lane but reduced its speed to that of the marchers. Then it eased a few yards ahead and stopped. The door was opened.

As Rodriques started by, he recognized both men inside. At the wheel was Deputy Rod Poole, grim-faced and alert. The heavier, older man who had opened the right-hand door was Sheriff Buckingham Colby.

Colby removed aviator-type sunglasses and tucked them into his breast pocket. His brown uniform was neat, but wide sweat rings stained the areas around his armpits. His face was red and he looked hot, worried, and determined.

"Mr. Rodriques," he said, "will you get in the cruiser a minute, please?"

Carlos Murnan flashed, "Is Alfredo under arrest?"

"No," Colby grated. "I just want to talk a minute—"

"We are free men! You cannot interfere with our lawful—"

"Carlos," Rodriques said softly, actually embarrassed. He stepped across to the door of the car. "I wish to walk with the people. Will you drive along slowly, so no one will mistake what is happening?"

Colby nodded almost angrily. "Neither of us wants any misunderstandings. That's why we need to talk a minute. Get in."

Rodriques climbed into the dusty back seat of the cruiser, which was littered with maps and report folders. Colby closed the door quickly, evidently trying to preserve anything that might be left of the car's air conditioning. The interior stank of stale cigar smoke.

The sheriff leaned over the back seat to face Rodriques. "Nobody wants any trouble today. There are two or three things I have to say."

"I think I understand," Rodriques said quietly. He almost pitied the sheriff. This man was as trapped as he. They might not understand one another very well, but Colby had gone out of his way to try to be fair from the beginning of the effort in the valley. He would try to be fair now, Rodriques thought, even if both of them sensed that they were on collision course.

Colby held up a pudgy index finger. "One. If you try to enter Schreck property, you're guilty of trespassing. I don't want to arrest you or anybody else, but Mr. Trello has already made it clear that if we don't protect his property, he and his own guards will. If you step foot across his property line, you'll be arrested right then and there."

"All right," Rodriques said, giving the sheriff nothing more than indication that the words had been heard.

"Two," Colby said. "You are not to block their drives or their roads. If you do, you'll be arrested for disturbing the peace. Mr. Trello has made it real clear that he'll sign complaints for that, too."

Despite his unwillingness even to be here at this time, Rodriques could not restrain a sense of being hemmed in, and a resultant flush of anger. "Are you saying, sir, that we can do nothing but walk idly by this property? Is there nothing the law would allow us to do to show our cause and our dedication to it?"

Colby's thick lips compressed in anger. "Don't give me any dialectic, Mr. Rodriques. I'm just telling you what the facts are, not starting a God-damned debate."

"Very well," Rodriques said, seeing more clearly than ever the pressure the sheriff was under.

"Three," Colby said darkly. "I happen to know that Mr. Trello was in court in the city at seven o'clock this morning, trying to get a restraining order against you and your people even appearing on the highway out here by his property. The judge refused to issue that order. But I know that judge and what was said, because I've just been given a full report on the radio. If your people do *anything* that's out of line, and give the judge reason, he'll slap an order on you that restrains you from getting within two hundred yards of the Schreck property line."

Rodriques accepted this additional blow. It was not unexpected. The lines were being drawn very clearly, as in a childhood game where the bigger boy puts a toe trench in the dust, and dares the other to cross it.

And they were going to cross it. There was no way this could be avoided. Once a sequence of events was begun, the sequence had to be followed. The sheriff was much too late with his warnings, if *ever* there had been a time when they might have had a restraining effect.

"I thank you for your effort to make things clear, Rodriques said.

"We're not taking sides," Colby stressed, frowning.

"May I rejoin my followers now?"

"Stop the car, Rod."

Rodriques got out of the cruiser and rejoined Carlos Murnan and Thomas Rosario at the head of the column, which had by now gotten within a hundred yards of the gates to the Schreck winery. Inside the grounds, a handful of employee cars were in the lot, and two trucks were being loaded at a dock.

"What did the sheriff say?" Carlos Murnan demanded.

Rodriques told him.

"We will not be frightened!" Murnan snapped.

"Ah, Carlos, if the issue were fear, it would be simple enough. But no one is without fear, on either side. And I still believe this is not the time . . . or the place . . . for the action anticipated."

"We have voted. We go forward." Murnan's jaw jutted stubbornly.

"We will be arrested," Rodriques said. "We will only be forced to act even more strongly, or relent and appear as losers."

"They will not dare arrest us for peaceful demonstration!"

Thirty minutes later, they were arrested.

Television cameras whirred and reporters and photographers jostled one another for better position as the procession's head reached the Schreck gate. Sheriff Colby stood by his cruiser, watching. Rodriques saw four other patrol cars off to one side of a Schreck building, indicating that reinforcements for the law were close by, but out of sight pending possible need.

Without hesitation, Carlos Murnan strode through the Schreck gate and onto the private property. Rodriques, with a despairing glance at Rosario, followed.

The entire column, its tail many hundreds of feet back down the highway, seemed to pick up its pace as more demonstrators, holding their four-abreast ranks, walked across the invisible line that separated the public right-of-way land owned by Jules Trello.

At the front porch of the main Schreck building, a door opened. Jules Trello and two plant guards appeared, walking stiffly to the top of the steps. Even at that distance,

Rodriques could see Trello's glare of outrage and anticipation.

From his patrol car Sheriff Colby produced a portable bullhorn. He raised it and his lips moved. His metallic, amplified voice echoed over the parking lot, now beginning to fill with field workers, as more continued to file in.

"You are trespassing. Leave the property immediately or you will be arrested."

The demonstrators kept coming in.

Colby turned to his car and gave his deputy a signal. The deputy picked up a microphone and spoke into it.

From behind the Schreck buildings appeared five city police cars, three on the right and two on the left, followed by several Civil Defense jeeps, followed by four large National Guard-type open trucks. As the vehicles trundled around the buildings toward Rodriques and his people, he saw that they contained dozens of uniformed city policemen and highway patrol troopers.

In the distance came the sound of sirens.

Buckingham Colby walked through the milling, docile crowd of demonstrators and grimly took Rodriques' arm. "You are under arrest, sir. You and your followers please start boarding the trucks, or my men will be forced to use whatever means necessary to put you there."

Carlos Murnan rushed over, eyes ablaze. "We will not be taken so easily! Say the word, Alfredo, and I know our people will fight!"

"God, Carlos," Alfredo Rodriques muttered in dismay, "have you forgotten even *this?* If we use the ways of violence, *what have we left?*"

Murnan flushed, and stepped back. Rodriques brushed past him and the sheriff to walk toward the nearest truck, watched by a dozen patrolmen.

Rodriques climbed aboard. After a moment, others began to follow. Within minutes the truck was packed. It backed around in the lot and left the property, and headed south again, toward the city.

By 10 A.M., they had been arraigned in the county court and had been released on individual bonds by the surety company Alfredo Rodriques always had standing by at such times. By ten-thirty, most of the frustrated marchers had straggled back to the headquarters on the edge of the city's

Chicano section, and were waiting outside while a brief, fierce meeting took place within.

Rodriques again argued for moderation.

Carlos Murnan led the argument on the other side, for return to Schreck immediately after lunch.

"This time we will not cross the property line," he said hotly, "but we will lie in front of cars and trucks trying to enter or leave. We will stage a vigil around the clock. We will send some of our number to stand day and night in front of the home of Jules Trello—and the home of his every foreman."

The other aides muttered approval.

Rodriques felt little strength remaining. Never had a fast sapped him this rapidly. The morning had been a disaster, and now he was wilted by certainty that the afternoon was about to be assured of being even worse. Desperate, he cast about for some alternative.

"Think about this for one hour before a vote," he said.

"What good will that do?" Murnan asked.

"I have an idea," Rodriques said. "Give me an hour before we vote."

"An hour will make no difference!"

"Will you give me the hour?" Rodriques demanded with grave dignity.

Murnan colored. "Of course, Alfredo."

"I will take the van. I will be back before noon."

"Shall I accompany you? Or another driver, perhaps?"

"No," Rodriques said. "This time it is better that I go alone."

"You do not intend to tell us your mission?"

"When I return."

He picked the van keys off the front desk and went outside, going around the building to where the van was parked in the shade, and had been since the previous night. He unlocked the door and climbed behind the wheel.

The pattern of continuing escalation had begun now, and the pattern had to be broken soon or not at all. He intended to drive with all possible speed to Robert Mancini Vineyards. Of all the winemakers, Robert Mancini was the one with whom there was the best hope.

If necessary, Rodriques had decided, he would amend the agreement papers in his pockets to provide Robert Mancini with precisely the kind of no-strike guarantee he had earlier mentioned. Rodriques did not like it, but his premonition demanded action before worse things began. He had to get an agreement signed with someone *now*. He would give up as much as he must to be able to come back here to this headquarters in an hour or so and brandish a signed agreement—a sign of *progress*.

Perhaps, with God's grace, it would be enough to shunt the building rage and delay further confrontation that could only end in disaster.

So thinking, Rodriques put the ignition key in the ignition and turned it.

There was, rather than the sound of the starter, a little high-pitched whine. Then the inside of the truck seemed to light up brightly, and as the stunned Alfredo Rodriques was thrown violently forward by the force of the explosion, he knew what had happened.

A bomb in the van—

Rodriques' whole being was overwhelmed by the enormity of the sound of the explosion. Somehow he found himself being thrown *out of* the van, and although he was flying through the air . . . it seemed . . . his retinas had a split second to record the brilliant orange of flame and a tremendous gush of smoke and dust.

He also had time for the most fleeting sense of loss. *Now,* he thought, *they will go mad and will forget all I have taught them.*

Then Alfredo Rodriques knew nothing at all.

10

Word of the bombing of Alfredo Rodriques' mobile head-quarters reached Robert Mancini within twenty minutes.

"The way I get it," the city policeman said on the telephone, "not all the explosives went off, or something like that. He was thrown out of the vehicle through the door, which he hadn't closed yet."

"Then he's alive," Robert snapped.

"He's in emergency at City Hospital right now."

"What's his condition?"

"Nobody knows yet. The ambulance driver told a buddy of mine that he was unconscious—he'd been thrown against the wall of the building—but he didn't seem to be bleeding much and there was no sign he had been burned. But these drivers don't always know. The guy could be broken into a hundred pieces inside."

"And what's happening at the headquarters?" Robert asked, not sure he wanted to hear this.

"The fire department put out the fire. Five units of police officers responded to help the two already on the scene. There was a lot of panic, and then some of the workers started throwing rocks at the black-and-whites. Three or four people were arrested. There's a big meeting going on in the street right now. My buddies there say it looks like everybody is going back out to Schreck."

"Christ," Robert muttered. "Okay, Charley. Thanks a lot."

Within the next five minutes, even before Susan Knight and Mike DeFrates reached his office, there were three more calls. Henry Barton, the small winemaker who had first sided with Robert on the fall price guarantees, wanted to make sure Robert had been informed; Barton said most of his Chicano employees had walked off their jobs the moment someone heard it on the radio. Then Timothy Crocker called; Robert urged him to go to Schreck Brothers once more to plead with Jules for calm. "I'm sure he didn't have anything to do with the bombing; that had to have been some nut. Make him understand that he has to let the law deal with that crowd if they roar back out to his place again."

Crocker said dubiously that he would try. A moment after he hung up, one of the county commissioners was on the line to say that the Governor had been notified about the latest development and had activated the one hundred state police who had been on standby; they would be ready for duty within three hours. In addition, the commissioner said, the Governor was ordering two local National Guard units to report to the downtown armory immediately for possible riot-control work.

"Tell our key people what's going on," Robert told DeFrates when he and Susan Knight had been briefed. "I don't think anything will happen here just yet, but make sure you're on top of it if anything does. Susan and I had better get to that hospital. I want to see for myself how Rodriques is, and if I can possibly talk to him, maybe we can work together to try to calm things down again."

"What makes you think Rodriques will want to calm anything down?" DeFrates asked bluntly. "He's just been bombed."

Robert shook his head. "Mike, I'm convinced that Rodriques doesn't want a riot any more than he wanted to be bombed. Extremists on both sides are taking control, and we've got to stop them somehow."

Susan Knight asked soberly, "Is there really any chance that Alfredo Rodriques could exert influence from a hospital bed?"

"I don't know," Robert replied. "First let's get there—and hope we find him alive."

It was a warm, cloudless day. The scene along the highway on the trip to the city was almost crazily normal, with the exception of more patrol cars than usual; in front of

several wineries, traffic was heavy as visitors, perhaps unaware of what had happened, created small jam-ups entering and leaving vineyards which conducted regular tours.
Robert saw white workers in many fields, but few Chicanos. It could mean that the wildcat strike was spreading,
and along ethnic lines.

He drove hard, but with a feeling of mounting frustration. He recognized that his individual effort might be
worse than futile. Under the circumstances, however, he
could not sit at his desk and do nothing.

Expecting a throng of field workers at the hospital, he
was startled to find none at all. The emergency area was
deserted and orderly. A lone city police car was parked
nearby, but the officers were not in the emergency-treat-
ment area.

"We're looking for Alfredo Rodriques," Robert told the
nurse at the desk.

"He's now on the third floor," the woman told him with
a glance at Susan. "But there will be no visitors."

Susan broke in anxiously, "What's his condition?"

"If you're from the press, please see Media Information
on the second floor."

"We're not reporters," Robert said impatiently.

The nurse eyed him stonily. "My instructions are to give
no information."

Fuming, Robert led the way to the elevators, and to the
third floor. As they left the elevator on 3, they came face-
to-face with a pair of city policemen and a lone field
worker, an older man, who appeared to be in earnest conversation in the waiting area.

One of the policemen was vaguely familiar, and nodded
in recognition. "Morning, sir."

"How is he?"

"Well, sir, he's still unconscious. They've taken X-rays
and all, and they don't think he has a skull fracture or
anything like that."

"Was he burned?"

"A little on his arms, I think. It looks like he has a couple
of cracked ribs. The doctor said, though, he'd been awfully
lucky."

The Chicano man added, "If he regains consciousness
soon, the blow to the head will not have been too serious.
The doctor said we must now wait."

Robert extended his hand, introducing himself and then Susan.

"Thomas Rosario," the older man said.

"Mr. Rosario, were you there when this happened?"

"I was inside the building. I heard the explosion and ran out."

"He was alone?"

"Yes. He was going on some errand." Rosario paused, frowned, and seemed to consider his next words. "I can tell you this because I know your treatment of Alfredo was courteous when he spoke with you. It had been decided to return to Schreck Brothers, in greater force, and at once. I believe Alfredo was leaving to try to arrange some sort of truce, to prevent new trouble."

"No ideas on who put the bomb in the van?"

"The vehicle was locked and under watch." Rosario winced. "The boy who was supposed to watch the van from dawn until noon was not there. He had slipped away with a girl to join the march against Schreck."

"What is your understanding of the situation with the other workers now?"

Rosario's eyes were stone. "They have begun already moving back toward the scene of this morning's arrests. The angriest leaders are now in charge."

"I take it that you don't approve."

"I follow Alfredo," Rosario said with quiet dignity.

"There's no way you could head them off?"

"I have no voice now. The voice they hear is revenge, anger. I am not sure even Alfredo could stop them."

Robert frowned at Susan. "If he came to, and we could speak with him—"

"That's impossible, sir," the friendly officer said. "Our orders are that no one goes past this point."

"You're a little late to be protecting him, aren't you?" Robert shot back.

The policeman's face froze. "We follow orders, sir."

"Hell, I'm sorry," Robert said, disgusted with himself. "I know you're doing your job. Everybody is a little tight right now."

The officer's expression did not change. He had taken enough on his own today. "Yes, sir."

Robert made some quick decisons. "Susan, I want you to stay here. I'm going to make one more try to see Jules. Maybe between us, Tim and I can keep him restrained. At least I can get the sheriff to make a bullhorn announcement out there that Rodriques is all right. I'll call you here later for any news."

"Remember you're stranding me here," Susan said, frowning. "And I don't really see what I can accomplish."

"All right," Robert conceded, "I'm grasping at straws right now. You can keep me informed on what the situation is here, and that might be important. Maybe it's good just to *have* someone here, to show that everybody hasn't polarized. If Rodriques comes to, and he or Mr. Rosario need some help of any kind, you'll be here to try to provide it."

Susan looked unhappy. "Are you sure you're not just leaving me here to keep me out of the situation at Schreck?"

Robert had to smile. "Don't start calling me a chauvinist now, Susan. I've got enough trouble."

Leaving the hospital, he drove rapidly, alone now, across the city and to the main highway leading north into the agricultural portion of the valley. As he passed the city limits, he noticed the traffic begin to thicken and slow. Within another few minutes he saw flashing red lights ahead, and as the traffic eased closer, was dismayed to see what was happening.

The side of the highway was clotted with marchers.

City police cars were out, directing traffic. The marchers were staying to the shoulder, but even so their sheer numbers created such a spectacle that every driver slowed to a crawl in order to stare at them.

There were not just a few dozen this time. As Robert came up beside the stragglers at the back of the line, he was unable to see forward far enough to see the head of the column. Men were walking, but so were women and small children, hundreds of them. Almost all were Chicano field workers, but Robert saw a sprinkling of white supporters, including some housewives and even a few men in business suits, and as he moved on up the incredible line in the creeping traffic he saw, in a small park, numbers of cars parking and disgorging more white supporters who moved to the edge of the road and mingled with the procession.

Banners flew at scattered places along the column, and there were a few crude signs on cardboard that he did not read. What astounded him was the sheer number of the marchers.

THE WINEMAKERS / 473

There were hundreds, perhaps even thousands, and he saw more leaving cars to join them here and there, or standing on the shoulder waiting for the main body to pass so that they could fall in at the back. It was all quiet, orderly, purposeful. The bulk of the crowd, however, had a sense of a tidal wave about it.

As his car finally reached the head of the column, traffic speeded up. Robert kept pace, seeing the marchers dwindle in size in his rearview mirror. He glanced at his watch and did some mental calculations. If they walked all the way to Schreck, as they evidently intended to do, it would take several hours. When they arrived, it would be a fantastic scene—one filled with danger. But at least, he thought hopefully, the decision to march all the way might provide a few hours' breathing time.

On this point he was wrong.

Only a few miles farther north, he again saw flashing lights, and patrolmen in the road directing traffic wide of a vineyard-road turnoff. As he approached, he saw men standing in the vineyard not far from the highway. There were lawmen in the crowd of about twenty, and a cruiser, and a white city ambulance.

One of the two officers in the roadway just ahead of him was Rod Poole. It was one of the few pieces of good luck Robert had encountered so far this day. He waved at Poole and gestured that he wanted to pull to the shoulder. The deputy nodded, stepped aside to direct the cars behind him wider, and signaled for Robert to pull in behind his own cruiser on the side.

Robert parked and got out to walk to Poole's side. Poole was sweating in the intense, dusty heat. Exhaust fumes hung heavily over the baking pavement as cars inched around. Poole gestured angrily at a Renault that pulled almost to a complete halt to allow the occupants to gawk, thus stopping the long line of traffic piling up farther south.

"Move it!" Poole bawled, jerking his arm.

The Renault driver responded nervously, flipping around the blocked point to accelerate northward. Cars from that direction, headed south, were being hurried along by another deputy standing on the far side of the median.

"What happened?" Robert asked.

Poole did not look at him, concentrating on directing the traffic. "Fight in the field. Couple guys hurt."

"Can I go see?" Robert asked.

Poole ignored him, calling to a Pacer driver, "Come on! Please! Move on around there!"

Robert walked back off the pavement and around his car, stepping onto the hot dirt of the narrow vineyard-entry road. Gravel crunched under his shoe soles and dust puffed up as he strode rapidly back into the vineyard. The grapes were Pinot Chardonnay, and he saw two small gondolas, bright yellow, parked near a small tractor that had hauled them in. Picking baskets were strewn around the grass and some green grapes had already been dumped from boxes into the gondolas. Without thinking about it, Robert knew these grapes were for Champagne, and could be picked this early, at a Brix of about 18, because of this intended use.

The scene deeper into the vineyard was in a small grassy area just off the dirt road. Another gondola, more heavily loaded, sat there. More boxes were on the ground. Nearby were several opened lunch boxes, some with papers and wrappers strewn around on the grass beside them as if lunch had been suddenly interrupted. About a dozen workers stood in a sullen group not far from the lunch area, while five other workers—Chicanos—stood nearer the huge white ambulance. Four sheriff's deputies stood midway between the groups. Ambulance attendants were just sliding a stretcher into the back of the vehicle. The dark-skinned man on the stretcher was unconscious. Bright red had splattered the white sheet covering him. There was at least one other stretcher already inside, and Robert saw a paramedic moving around rapidly, moving overhead tubing.

As he moved closer, Robert saw an injured worker still on the ground near the deputies. The boy—he was hardly more than that—was sitting up, holding a white cloth to his face. The cloth was speckled red.

"Anybody want to say what happened here?" one of the deputies demanded of the two groups of workers.

No one spoke. The whites, banded together, watched with silent anger. The Chicanos glared back at them with no less hostility.

"Who started it?" the same deputy asked. He was heavy-set, a bluish shadow of stubble on his jaw in the sunlight.

Again no one spoke.

The deputy's chest heaved. "All right. Who's in charge of this crew?"

After a few seconds' delay, a lanky, red-haired man took a step forward. "I'm the crew boss."

"What's your name?"

"Wilson." The foreman's eyes shifted nervously.

"Okay, Wilson. What happened?"

"I don't know."

"You'd better know!" the deputy flared, pointing a finger. "It's *your* ass that's going to jail unless we get some answers!"

"Are you on *their* side as usual?" Wilson shot back.

"What happened?"

For a moment Wilson did not reply, and, as the ambulance attendants came back to help the third injured man to his feet, taking him to the ambulance between them, Robert thought it was an impasse.

Then, however, Wilson changed his mind. "We was getting ready for lunch. *That* bunch"—He shot a baleful look at the Chicanos—"said they was through for the day. We're doin' this field flat rate. I told them they'd finish what they started on because I counted on 'em and we'd lose a day if they left now."

The deputy waited, grim-faced, and when Wilson added nothing, he shook his head in disgust. "So you beat them up. Is that it?"

Wilson looked toward the man being loaded into the back of the ambulance. "That son of a bitch pulled a knife."

One of the Chicanos said sharply, "It is a lie!"

Wilson pointed to the ground nearby. "There the knife is!"

The deputy walked heavily over and picked up an open switch-blade. He turned to the Chicano who had spoken. "You deny this was used by your friend back there?"

The man shot back angrily, "Do you see anyone who has been cut by a knife? Georgio took out that knife only after these men began beating us!"

"You signed up to work, you greaser!" the red-haired foreman snapped.

"Alfredo's life has almost been lost! We will work no more with any Anglos until we have orders from Alfredo!"

The foreman took a step forward, fists balled.

"Now *hold it*," the deputy said.

Wilson obeyed instantly. The deputy's hand had gone to the prominent handle of his service revolver.

"You people," the deputy said, turning to the Chicanos. "Are you going to work or not?"

"No, sir," the spokesman said. "There will be no more work here from us this day."

"Then get off the property. Walk straight out this road. Now."

The Chicanos stared at him.

"Get moving," the deputy said. "And *keep* moving."

The ambulance's back door slammed. The attendants walked to the front.

"Our companions," the Chicano spokesman said.

"They're going to the hospital."

"We would go with them."

"That ambulance isn't a bus. Get moving. How you get to the hospital is your problem."

After a moment, the Chicano spokesman made up his mind. With a slight signal to his fellows, he turned and started past Robert to the road. The group walked rapidly for the highway.

Wilson confronted the deputy. "You're letting them *go?* You're not arresting them?"

"What would the charge be? Assaulting your fists with their faces?"

"All right!" Wilson flared. "We'll take care of them ourselves!"

"You'll take care of nothing but your own business, Wilson! You stay put. I've got a few more questions I want to ask."

The ambulance started and backed around awkwardly in the grassy restricted space. Robert had heard enough. He stepped out of the cumbersome vehicle's path and then turned to follow it up the dusty road.

It was only one more sign, but perhaps a significant one. The fight had already begun to spread along ethnic fault lines. It had to be stopped. The constant escalation had to be reversed. Whether anyone willed it or not, Jules Trello was the key.

Back in his car, Robert saluted the harried Rod Poole and swung out into the traffic again. There was no sign of the marchers. They were hours away, he thought, and at least he could be thankful that nothing yet threatened the momentary calm at Jules's winery itself.

On that he was mistaken.

This was apparent immediately when he neared Schreck Brothers less than fifteen minutes later.

He was still two miles from the winery entrance when

he encountered the first cars parked along the road. The parked vehicles were scattered at first, and he saw a few workers walking north from them like fans leaving vehicles to trek to a distant football stadium.

Within a few hundred feet, the line of parked cars became solid: a few recent-model cars, a few pickups, but mostly decrepit old sedans, parked parallel or at angles on the shoulder. And the crowd of people walking in the direction of Schreck was heavier now.

Again the traffic slowed, and once more Robert could see men in the road ahead, near the Schreck gates. He could see the roofs of the winery buildings now, but nothing more.

It was clear that while the bulk of demonstrators were marching, probably by necessity, those with transportation were already hurrying to the scene. The few hours of grace that he had imagined they had were rapidly becoming only a theory.

Nearer the Schreck gates the crowd on the side of the road swelled. Several police cars and highway patrol units were parked toward the front of the winery parking lot. Hundreds of demonstrators milled about on the broad paved driveway between the road and the Schreck fence. Barricades made of sawhorses had been stretched across the fence line on the pavement, and two more police cars and a sheriff's unit were parked there. Robert saw both law officers and uniformed winery guards.

Policemen were trying to keep a path open the width of a car from the highway to the gates. Robert turned in and moved slowly, assailed by a sense of claustrophobia as the crowd pressed close on all sides. A few fists pounded on his car's fenders, like shotgun reports inside. A policeman bawled orders and warnings, and the crowd moved back a bit, letting Robert nudge his car on up to the gate.

A Schreck guard came around the barricade. He had a billy club in his hand and he looked scared. "Sorry, sir. No entry."

"God damn it, Jack," Robert snapped, "you know me. You worked here when I owned part of the place."

"I've got my orders, Mr. Mancini. Sorry, sir."

"I've got to see Jules. Is Mr. Crocker still in there?"

"Yes, sir, he and Mr. Trello are meeting now, I think."

"Well, I've got new information," Robert lied. "Let me in."

The guard frowned with uncertainty and walked back to the sawhorses for a brief conference with a man Robert recognized as Sheriff Buckingham Colby. The heavier lawman listened, then walked over to Robert's car.

"What kind of information do you have, Mr. Mancini?"

"I said that to get in," Robert admitted. "I'm here for the same reason Tim Crocker is here—to try to get Jules calmed down and figure out something we might do to calm things generally."

Colby scowled. "I don't know if you can accomplish anything." He scratched his head.

Someone behind Robert's car began pounding his hands on the back fender.

"Quit that!" Colby bawled, and went to the back of the car for a minute.

When he came back, he looked in worriedly at Robert. "Okay. You can go in. I don't know what you can accomplish, but it's your funeral."

The sheriff walked back to the barricade. He and two of the Schreck guards pulled two sawhorses aside, letting Robert draw his small car past them.

With a feeling of relief to be out of the threatening, pressing crowd, Robert drove across the mostly empty parking lot to the front entrance of the main building. He parked beside the steps and went inside.

11

Jules Trello's receptionist appeared frightened, but she was game. "I'm sorry, Mr. Mancini," she said, hanging up the telephone. "Mr. Trello can't see you today."

Robert knew the office layout as well as his own. Without a word, he went past the woman's desk and opened the door into the area beyond.

"Wait!" she squeaked. "You can't do that!"

Robert kept right on going, through the small foyer and into the corridor beyond, past accounting and sales, across the catwalk into the next section of the building, and down another hall. The woman chased after him, protesting, but he paid no attention. When he reached Jules's door, he pushed it open and barged in.

Jules Trello stood by the windows, looking out at the distant spectacle on his doorstep. Timothy Crocker was in a chair beside Jules's ornate desk. Both men turned sharply as Robert entered.

"Get out of here!" Jules said loudly. "I left instructions—"

His receptionist came in behind Robert. "I'm sorry, Mr. Trello—I *tried* to stop him—"

Jules ignored her, his angry eyes on Robert. "Do you get out or do I have you thrown out?"

"I've just been to the hospital," Robert told both men. "Rodriques is still out cold, but they don't think he's badly hurt, after all. I came here to see if there's anything we can do to help."

"Help?" Jules echoed sarcastically. "Help *me*? That's a turnaround, isn't it?" He gestured toward the scene beyond his window. "And isn't it just a little late?"

"Maybe there's still some way to cool this off," Robert said.

"Yes, and the Governor has that way coming in an hour or two! We'll put so much force out here, those bastards will have to back down!"

"Maybe there's another way," Robert said.

"I told you to get out of here!"

"Jules, we don't have to like each other to work together long enough to prevent a hell of a lot of senseless bloodshed here!"

Timothy Crocker got to his feet. "I say, Jules. Let him try to help, if he can. That's what all of us are interested in—keeping this thing from going the rest of the way it's obviously headed."

"Who can stop it now?" Jules flared. "Look out there! Go talk to those people if you want to stop trouble! Do you think *I* caused any of this?"

"Yes," Crocker replied with a flash of anger of his own. "But let me tell you this: if you don't listen to whatever Bob may have to say now, I'll guarantee you that I'll *personally* make sure everyone knows that you turned your back on an offer of help. That will make you responsible for whatever may happen next."

For a few seconds, Robert thought Jules was going to throw both of them out. The receptionist still stood there, petrified.

Then, however, Jules let his shoulders slump. "All right, Phyllis. You can leave us."

The woman blinked. "Shall I call security, sir?"

"Did I say to call security?" Jules barked so loudly she jumped. "Don't you think security has enough on its hands already? Jesus Christ! Get back to your desk!"

The door closed quietly behind the frightened woman.

Surprisingly, then, Jules put on his Rotary Club grin. It was an amazing, an instant transformation. He looked boyish and almost jaunty. "All right, Robert, old sport. Let's hear it. And don't tell me you're glad to be here. I don't even know where we are. If there's one thing I hate, it's a fight. Cassius Clay." Jules chuckled at his little joke;

he was one of the few men in the world, perhaps, who continued to refuse to call Ali by his chosen name.

"I don't think force is going to prevent a fight," Robert said. "I just came from the city. There are over a thousand marchers on the way here. There may be twenty-five hundred by now, or even more. People are joining as the column moves along. They'll be here by four or five o'clock."

Jules went gray, but straightened like a martinet. "All-out war, right? Fine. I know what my father would do, and I can handle a situation better than he can. I'll call the Governor directly." He started toward his desk.

"What will that accomplish?" Robert demanded.

"It will protect my property!"

"Okay," Robert said. "Fine. But let's take a minute first to talk about anything any of us might do to stop the fight before it goes any further."

Jules reached for the telephone. "It's a little late for that."

Crocker asked, "Do you have an idea, Bob?"

"I don't think Rodriques wants this any more than we do."

"Shit!" Jules said.

"This isn't his way. Maybe, if we could give him *any* kind of concession to tell his followers, they could still be stopped."

"Cave in?" Jules said. "I don't operate that way."

"If Rodriques has regained consciousness, you could talk to him on the phone."

"I'm not signing any contract! Hell will freeze over! I—"

"You could agree to meet with him and talk about it! Even *that* might be enough to give him a wedge."

Jules shook his head. "I'll never talk with him."

"Let me call the hospital," Robert urged, knowing clearly how slender their remaining hopes now were. "Susan Knight is there. She can tell me what the situation is. Agreeing to talks doesn't have to mean anything, Jules. It's a tactic. I can make that clear to Rodriques. If he's conscious now, maybe he can use it. Maybe even *that* word would be enough for some leverage."

"They'd say I collapsed," Jules replied bitterly.

Tim Crocker spoke up. "They might say you took a brave step to avoid people getting hurt or killed."

"Don't give me bullshit rhetoric! Those are trespassers

out there right now! They're across my property line! If I had my way, the police would already be using their tear gas!"

"Jules," Robert pleaded, "let me call. Give us this one last chance. What the hell can anyone lose? All you'd say was that you were willing to stand in the same room with the man and listen to his speech. If those workers out there take it as a sign of victory—and quiet down, and let us have our harvest—are you going to complain about what *they* think when we all know how much *our* side has gained?"

Jules stared at him, his face devoid of expression. Robert dared not say more. He was ad libbing furiously, searching for any crack in the wall of mistrust on both sides. By offering Jules a way of rationalizing a telephone call as a possible trick on Rodriques, he was playing his last card in an attempt to establish communications any way he might.

Crocker said, "A call doesn't take five minutes, Jules."

Jules expelled his breath loudly. He shoved the telephone toward Robert. "Call," he said.

12

Alfredo Rodriques was conscious.

When the two dim figures came quietly into his hospital room, however, he kept his eyes closed and gave them no sign.

Rodriques was dazed, filled with pain and weakness, and more deeply lanced by a feeling of utter failure than at any time in his life. All he wanted at this moment was to lie very still, peering at the darkness of his own closed eyelids. He willed himself very still, refusing to respond to any stimulus.

When the voices began whispering, he knew at once who his visitors were. The male voice was that of Rosario, and the female was Susan Knight, the woman he had twice met at Robert Mancini Vineyards.

Poor Rosario, Rodriques thought. A dedicated man of peace, one of the few whom Rodriques had ever met who would never, under any circumstances, mete out violence. Rosario had remained by his side. No one else had remained. Well, it was theirs now. The bomb had given Rodriques his one unassailable excuse for opting out. He could not take part in a frontal attack on Schreck Brothers Winery, but he could not prevent it. By staying here and doing nothing, he could never be blamed for whatever took place. And so poor Rosario, Rodriques thought bitterly, and with real regret: for remaining faithful.

And poor Susan Knight, he thought: well-meaning, helpless little Anglo, could never truly understand any of it.

"Alfredo?" Rosario's husky voice.

Rodriques did not respond.

A hand rested on his shoulder, shaking him ever so lightly. *"Alfredo?"*

Rodriques remained still, breathing evenly, filled with disgust at his own pretense.

The two of them whispered.

"It is no use, Miss Knight. You see?"

"But the doctor said there's no indication of serious concussion. All the tests were negative."

"He sleeps."

"We have to arouse him. If we could just get him on the telephone, once he heard that Jules Trello was willing to talk, there must be *some* way we could get word to your friends."

"Yes," Rosario said with regret in his tone. "But is it only a way of tricking ourselves? Is there really hope?"

"You know them better than I do. If Alfredo *himself* contacted them, and said he was opening negotiations with Jules Trello, wouldn't it be enough to make them disperse while awaiting the outcome?"

There was a long pause, and Rodriques, safe behind his eyelids, pondered this new and interesting information. He wondered if there was any chance whatsoever that Jules Trello meant to begin sincere negotiations. He thought not. It was—he reminded himself—too late anyway. It was out of both their hands.

Rosario finally answered Susan Knight's question. "I do not know if even this could halt the march now, Miss Knight."

There was another period of silence, and Rodriques knew they were looking down at him. He kept his face serene.

No, he thought with infinite weariness, there was no way to prevent the violence now. Nothing short of a real breakthrough could do that, and he no longer knew whether he had the moral leadership to convince his followers even if he were to have such a breakthrough in hand.

He had lost everything in this brief struggle. It had been a blunder to come here so late in the year . . . so near the harvest. It had been a mistake to come, thinking he could control his young firebrands, when his own health was so precarious. Although he had worked hard here, he knew objectively that he had not worked hours quite so long or arduous as those he had put in during other, earlier struggles. He was not well. His physical weakness, combined with the peculiarly scattered and stubborn local resistance, plus the presence of Jules Trello on one side and men like Carlos Murnan on the other, had been his downfall.

He had simply lost control.

Now, although a part of him urged him to open his eyes and listen to these two standing by his bed—and try again—he was ruled both by his grieving despair and by a growing cold political conviction: *If he tried now to turn the tide, and failed, he could never be leader again.*

And so, in this way, the bomb had saved him. All he had to do was remain quiet, safe behind his eyelids. No one could ever say he had led into a debacle. No one could ever say he had failed his duty to counsel peace.

By remaining quiet, he would be safe to lead another day.

The thought of what was happening now . . . what would almost certainly happen in the hours ahead . . . filled his belly with a bitter fire. Was it not his duty (a part of himself questioned) to *try,* even in the face of sure failure?

His political mind replied immediately: the cause needed leadership over many months, many years. He was serving the higher good (his pragmatic self argued) by staying out of this battle in order to return with his authority nominally intact.

After there was a battle, his political self added craftily, people on both sides would have been hurt. Perhaps everyone would be more willing to listen to a quiet voice of reason and compromise.

Ah, God! he thought with such force that it was almost an outcry. *How corrupt you are now, Alfredo! So this is what comes from the years of talking humility, and learning to love your sense of power!*

But he did not stir, and the voices talked a while longer, earnestly worried, and then they went out of the room and he was alone again. He opened his eyes cautiously, assured himself that he was alone, and lay quiet, studying the tiles of the white ceiling and listening to his pain, of which there was more than one kind.

13

Between 4 and 5 P.M., all the marchers from the city reached the area surrounding Schreck Brothers. The crowd, grown to terrifying proportions, was variously estimated at three to five thousand. As they continued to press in, the front-gate area overflowed, and then they spilled back over the shoulders of the highway for two hundred yards in both directions, and began to fill the highway itself. Despite all that police, sheriff's deputies and patrolmen could do, all traffic halted on the highway and an incredible traffic jam began backing up for miles in both directions, north and south.

The throng was curiously orderly. Constantly milling, beginning to fill every bit of ground with trash and litter, it emitted a continuous dull rumble—the sound of talking voices—which could be heard in the remotest corner of the Schreck compound. But no one tried to climb a fence anywhere, and none of those near the barricades attempted to go through them.

Inside the fences, the Schreck grounds had been transformed into something resembling a military camp under siege. More than three hundred uniformed National Guardsmen, armed to the teeth, had been brought in trucks just before the highway clogged permanently. Between thirty and forty police cars were lined up in neat precision along the front row of the parking lot. The patrol cars, military jeeps and trucks mixed with ordinary vehicles in

486

a scene of mass confusion. An olive-drab helicopter chuttered continually overhead in the dying rays of the sun. In a tent near the front entrance of the main building a communications center connected those on the main grounds with others in the air, in cars elsewhere outside the perimeter, and at the scattered vineyard gates around Schreck's surrounding two hundred acres.

Robert Mancini and Timothy Crocker, like Jules and his employees, were now captives inside the main building. New attempts to contact Alfredo Rodriques failed as Susan reported he remained mysteriously unconscious. Doctors said they were now getting worried about hidden brain damage, but would not act for a while yet, because the brain was still a strange mechanism with powers to heal itself.

A little after five o'clock, Sheriff Buckingham Colby and a Guard colonel named Tinsley jointly addressed the crowd beyond the fences. They first tried to plead, and, when that did no good, took a harder line. Tinsley said the demonstration was an unlawful assembly, and ordered them to disperse. There was no visible reaction.

By 5:30 P.M., a judge in the city had issued a temporary restraining order which banned further demonstrations as a health hazard and menace to public safety. This ruling was transmitted to the crowd. There was absolutely no effect.

At a little before 6:00, two young field workers tried to scale the wall about seventy-five yards south of the main gates. As troopers rushed toward the spot, the workers' own companions hauled them down and pulled them roughly back into the anonymity of the throng.

A new element was reported beginning to show itself shortly after 6 P.M. On the edges and fringes of the crowd, young white males, many high-schoolers, had drifted in. City police detained, searched and arrested four of these almost the moment they appeared. The police confiscated two sets of brass knuckles, three switchblades, and two small-caliber Saturday-night specials.

A strategy session was held from 6:30 to 6:45. It was impossible to try to take everyone into custody. There were not enough officers to get the job done, and no place to put prisoners in this number anyway. The Governor was sending in two thousand more Guardsmen, but they would not arrive before midnight. A suggestion to try to arrest the field workers' leaders was briefly examined and rejected on the grounds that it might spark worse violence.

At 6:50, Colonel Tinsley ordered the crowd—again—to disperse. Again there was no response.

More white youths had moved in here and there, remaining in tight, hostile, mutual-protection groups. A scattering of older white males was also detected, and they were not the types to inspire confidence.

At 7:00, Robert Mancini again talked to Susan Knight at the hospital. "Susan, for Christ's sake, you've got to get through to Rodriques if there's any way to rouse him! There just isn't any more time left. Some of the demonstrators are making torches and bonfires. These Guardsmen are nervous as cats, and Jules is back to yelling that it's time to charge with the tear gas."

"I'll try," Susan said. "If he isn't conscious, there's nothing *anyone* can do!"

"Go sit in his room. Keep trying."

"I will. I can't promise anything."

"No one can. I'll call you in his room, on that number, if anything breaks loose."

"I'll probably know before you can call," Susan told him. "They have continuous news from a reporter out there. He's probably on the roof of the very building you're in. I got a nurse to go buy me a little transistor portable, and I've got the earphone in my other ear right now."

Robert hung up, unaccountably furious about the radio reporter somewhere above him on the roof. Was it, he wondered, just a great assignment to the reporter—a chance for some journalistic prize? If all the varying ambitions, prides, and hates of this cauldron were ever separated again and catalogued, it might fill a book the size of a dictionary.

At 7:22, much too soon for anyone to hear a response from the latest attempt to rouse Alfredo Rodriques, there was a scuffle between a dozen white youths and twice as many Chicano workers. Guardsmen and police rushed from the barricades into the highway to break it up. Two whites and three field workers were down when the melee was terminated, and the officers, in the center of a gaping hole in the throng, signaled for reinforcements. Another dozen Guardsmen, their rifles held for riot control, moved from behind the sawhorses and parked cars.

Something then happened. No one would ever be able to state exactly what it was. All at once a portion of the crowd surged at the soldiers, and someone was gashed by a bayonet. Fights broke out. A warning shot was fired. From behind the barricades someone threw a canister of tear gas. As it snaked into the mob, trailing its hissing white tail of fumes, someone picked it up and threw it right back again. It hit among the police and guards at the gate, scattering them momentarily.

The moment was enough. Seeing the barricades virtually unmanned, a hundred men in the front of the crowd surged forward. There was a great outcry, and the crowd—from front to rear—began to surge ahead. A voice roared over a bullhorn to hold fire. More tear gas exploded. The sawhorses went down or were swept away. The officers out on the road were swallowed up, simply seeming to vanish in the tidal wave of humanity flooding toward the gates. A dozen—a hundred—and then many more workers ran through the police lines, scattering. The police, troopers and soldiers began to fall back, using tear gas again and firing in the air. But the front line had been breached and the battle was joined.

14

Her transistor radio turned off for the moment, Susan cautiously opend the door of Alfredo Rodriques' hospital room. Thomas Rosario, seated beside the still figure in the bed, looked up. A single dim light shadowed his face, but his expression was somber, indicating no change.

Susan walked to the bedside. Alfredo Rodriques lay quiet, his face serene, eyes shut. He was breathing very softly, and his color appeared good.

Rosario said softly, "He is the same. I would have come for you if there was any change."

"The workers have broken through the Schreck gates," Susan said. "The police couldn't hold them."

Rosario flinched back. "They are fighting on the grounds?"

Susan hesitated, then took out her small transistor radio. "I'll keep it low," she said, and flicked the off-on switch.

The announcer's excited voice, raspy through the tiny speaker, was caught in midsentence: "—*and now appear to have the barricades back in place, but what a scene it is inside the fences! Clouds of tear gas drift over the parking lots, and the flashing red and blue lights of police and emergency units glint through the haze. The shadow of the mountains is over the entire area, so it's difficult to make out everything that's taking place around the buildings, but from my vantage point on the main structure I can see National Guardsmen trying to drive back a group of about fifty workers who are pelting them with rocks."*

Rosario wrung his hands. "This is the worst possible thing."

"Listen," Susan urged.

"Hundreds of workers flooded through the barricades before police reinforcements, with heavy use of tear gas, managed to re-establish a line. It looks like as many people are inside the grounds as remain outside, and the noise is tremendous—maybe you can hear it over my voice. Police have fallen back to form a solid cordon in front of the main building, the one I'm on, but there is fighting all over the grounds. Off to my left I can see Guardsmen advancing on a group of several hundred, it appears, who are fighting with sticks. There! There! A new wave of tear gas has just been launched at the workers trying to batter down the doors of the production building, ladies and gentlemen, and they are falling back. Now it appears that more demonstrators are attacking the front barricades, and I can see men running in the vineyards on both sides of the main compound—"

Susan flicked the radio off. "Robert asked me to make one more try to arouse Alfredo—if there's any chance of waking him—"

"Even Alfredo could do nothing now," Rosario said, sadly shaking his head. "It is too late. Carlos Murnan and Juan Lupé have had their way."

"If Alfredo were awake, he would try," Susan said forcefully. "Maybe he couldn't stop it. But even his presence out there might have calmed some of the workers."

Rosario's eyes flared with unaccountable anger. "Do not expect miracles now. They have taken it from his hands. It is as well that he is unconscious, and does not yet have to know."

"He would never talk that way," Susan retorted. "He's a fighter."

"How many lost causes must one man undertake? You would ask too much!"

"When he became the leader, Thomas, he accepted the risk. Now please move over a little. I'm going to try one more time to talk to him. This time maybe I can wake him."

Rosario grudgingly moved his chair to one side. Susan

leaned against the bed. As she bent close to Rodriques' face to speak, he opened his eyes.

It was a shock. His eyes were fully aware at once, with no sign of confusion. Susan stood up, her heart pounding wildly.

Rodriques said huskily, "You are right, Miss Knight. A leader tries to lead."

"You were awake," Susan said.

"Yes."

Meeting the man's calm gaze, Susan resisted the impulse to ask how much he had heard. Her intuition told her that he had heard all—or almost all—of what had been said, including the radio broadcast. She looked sharply into his amazing eyes, and saw complete control of his faculties there.

Rosario, excitedly on his feet beside her, bent closer. "You are not badly injured, Alfredo. It is a miracle!"

Rodriques struggled to sit up. Susan almost urged him not to make the effort, but something restrained her. Rosario, perhaps having followed Rodriques' lead so long, had no such compunction. He helped the man get himself in a seated position, and patted pillows in behind his back.

Rodriques leaned against the pillows, his face suddenly pale. Sweat filmed his forehead. He rubbed gently across his lower chest, where the loose-fitting hospital gown allowed the heavy taping to show on the sides. "I have hurt some ribs, I think."

"The doctor will want you to remain still," Susan said. "But you can talk. We can patch a telephone line into a mobile PA speaker. You can talk to the strikers at Schreck."

Rodriques tossed back the sheet, ignoring the fact that the movement briefly revealed skinny legs and shrunken genitals as he hung his legs over the side of the bed. "I will do better. Can you get me there at once?"

"My God, you can't just walk out of the hospital like that!"

Rodriques ignored her and with grave dignity raised an arm to Rosario. "Help me, Thomas."

"I don't even have my car," Susan remembered aloud. She was torn between concern for him and a mounting excitement: if he appeared on the scene, after being in the bombing, it might be exactly the shock treatment that could turn the tide. But he would be risking his life.

Rosario helped Rodriques to stand beside the bed. The

labor leader swayed slightly, hanging on to his aide. His smile was meant to be encouraging, but out of the ghastly pallor of his face, was anything else.

"Is your car here, Thomas?" he asked.

"Yes, Alfredo." Rosario paused, frowned, said it: "Are you sure you can do this? Are you able?"

"I must."

Susan said, "They won't let you leave! There's a nurse's station just down the hall, and there are two policemen there."

"Then we must find another way out," Rodriques told her. He shrugged off Rosario's supporting arm now, and stood alone. His color looked better. He set his jaw. "I must *try*. You yourself said this. You were right."

"If you get halfway out there and collapse—and die—you'll just end up making things worse. You can talk on the telephone—"

"Miss Knight, I have been lying here acting like a big fool and a coward! I am going!"

Susan met his eyes again and swallowed with effort. "There's a stairway to the left outside the door. If we can get you down the stairs, Thomas could pull his car around in the alley. I know the stairs lead out that way."

Rodriques nodded. "Thomas. Go bring your car to this back door she speaks of. Do you know the way?"

"I can go down the stairs now to see it," Rosario said grimly. "I will have the car there in two or three minutes."

"Go then." Rodriques looked back at Susan. "Will you help me dress?"

Rosario went to the room door. It winked light in from the hall as he passed through the opening and was gone. Susan accepted the situation for what it was; she went to the small metal closet against the far wall and found Rodriques' trousers and shirt on a hanger. She tossed them to him.

"Is my underwear there? My socks?"

Frantically Susan began opening and closing the metal drawers. They all seemed to be empty. "I can't find them—"

"No matter." With a pale grin of triumph over pain, Rodriques stood erect after stepping into the pants. He zipped and buckled them, then tossed the hospital gown onto the bed. His upper torso appeared very dark against the stark white of the broad adhesive bindings. He was as thin as a boy.

He slipped his shirt over his head. "My shoes?"

Again Susan looked frantically. Any instant, she thought, a doctor or nurse was going to walk in and end this whole fantastic attempt. She was unable to find the shoes, either. "I know I'm just looking in the wrong places, but where could they have hidden them?"

"No matter," Rodriques smiled, limping toward the door in his bare feet. "We must hurry."

Susan brushed past him to be first into the hall. The corridor was empty, although the candy and snack cart operated by a volunteer stood unattended about five doors down. Farther away, the nurses' station was a bright splotch of more intense light, but it seemed to be quiet.

On Susan's left, the stairway exit door loomed invitingly only the width of a single additional room away.

Rodriques padded into the doorway behind her and she took his arm, hurrying him to the exit door. She swung it open and let him go through first. Without his shoes, he was shorter than she. It seemed unbelievable that this small man could bear such responsibility. She let the exit door swing closed behind her and followed Rodriques quickly down the stairs.

They reached the first floor without incident. A small red sign pointed to a steel-jacketed door: *OUTSIDE.* Rodriques pushed against the heavy door and paled again from the effort. Susan shoved it open for him and followed him out onto a metal porch in the alley. It was hot and dusty and half dark, and just as they let the steel door close behind them, a battered old green Plymouth sedan trundled up from the left. It rocked to a halt at the foot of the metal steps and Rosario jumped out from behind the wheel to run around and open the passenger side for Rodriques. He dropped into the front seat with a gasp of half-stifled agony.

Susan reached for the back-door handle.

"No," Rosario said quickly. "You know the way better. Please drive."

Susan paused only a second or two. The Plymouth was at least ten years old, a straight shift, and it was rocking badly at idle. She swallowed hard; she would just have to manhandle it and hope it held up, because there was no time to learn its eccentricities.

She nodded and ran around to slide behind the cracked green plastic steering wheel. Rosario's rear door slammed.

Rodriques leaned back against the side glass of the car on his side, eyes momentarily closed.

Susan depressed the clutch, put the gear selector in low, and let the clutch out. The engine stalled. Gritting her teeth, she started the motor again and fed it much more gas. The Plymouth jerked away from the doorway, down the alley and to the parking lot exit.

By the time she was across the corner of the city between the hospital and the main valley road, she had the hang of it. The front end shimmied wildly as she turned onto the highway and watched the speedometer move up past 50.

"We may not be able to get very close," Rosario said anxiously, leaning over the seat to peer ahead.

"I'm going to take a shortcut up here," Susan told him. "It's a back road, and then two dirt roads. I know them all from inspecting fields and visiting growers. We can skip all the traffic that way, I'm sure." She paused and thought about it, passing a slower-moving car. "The one road back in to Schreck is rough. I just hope this car can take it."

"Miss Knight," Rosario said with offended dignity, "this car can take anything. I maintain it myself."

Rodriques surprised them both by chuckling. "I would never try to live as a mechanic if I were you, Thomas."

"I'm sorry about the jouncing," Susan told him. "There don't seem to be any shock absorbers left underneath us."

"Hurry," Rodriques urged. "Maybe I can do something . . . I do not know."

"Just seeing you there may be enough. We're all ready to try anything."

"I was too, Miss Knight, just before the bomb exploded. This move had been voted. I was preparing to come to your winery, to see if Robert Mancini might still sign an agreement recognizing us."

Susan glanced at him, trying to hide her surprise. "That recognition was contingent on a no-strike agreement through the rest of the year."

Rodriques nodded, his eyes on the road ahead. "It is a mistake, that kind of clause. It only postpones the inevitable bargaining. But if that is necessary to begin a move toward reconciliation, I will now accept it."

Susan did not reply. She felt a burst of elation followed closely by a bittersweet sense of irony. It could signal a breakthrough . . . but perhaps the events at Schreck

Brothers today had already gone too far, making such compromise impossible for most. The abstract problem of signing an agreement seemed very distant right now, when they were racing to try to stop a riot already in progress. She wondered how often wisdom came after the crucial mistake had been made. Of course the answer was: all too often.

She made the first back-road turnoff in eight minutes. The transistor radio had been forgotten in the hospital room, and the Plymouth's panel had only a rusty hole where a radio had once been, so she drove in an agony of ignorance about what was taking place ahead. She pushed the old car harder on the side road, whooshing over rises and bottoming out on every dip. The underside crashed and clattered, but she gritted her teeth and kept her foot down, reaching the first dirt road north again in four minutes flat.

This one forced her to slow down. It was simply impossible to hold the car on the road otherwise. Still, the Plymouth left an immense plume of yellow dust behind as they carreened along as fast as she dared.

"How much farther?" Rosario asked nervously.

Susan turned on the headlights against the encroaching gloom, but they didn't seem to help at all. "Five or ten minutes," she said, fighting the bucking wheel.

In less time than that they approached the next intersection, the one she knew led to a road off to the west which would parallel Schreck's farthest south boundary. As the Plymouth jarred over a dirt rise, almost becoming airborne, she saw a sheriff's car parked in the way a few hundred yards ahead. Its red light rotated slowly on top.

The brakes acted like they had never had linings as she stood on the pedal to bring the Plymouth to a skidding halt. Dust flew forward around the windows, blinding them all for an instant.

The sheriff's car was parked across the Schreck entry road. As Susan opened her door to jump out, a deputy she recognized got out of the cruiser and started toward the Plymouth. He had not yet recognized her.

"This road is closed," he said brusquely. "Move along."

"Jerry," Susan said, "it's me."

The deputy walked closer, squinting. Then recognition lit his face and he seemed to relax at the same time he glanced toward the Plymouth and became puzzled. "What in the world are you doing out here, Susan? And in this junker?"

"Jerry, I've got Alfredo Rodriques in this car. I'm bringing him from the hospital."

"Jayzus," the deputy muttered with surprise. "What's the deal?"

"If I can get him inside, he can talk to the workers. He wants them to stop—get out of there. There's a chance he can persuade them."

The deputy looked blank for an instant. Then his expression tightened as he made decisions. "Okay, I'll tell you what. I'll move my unit to let you pass. I'll radio the side gate up there about three miles that you're coming. Rod's up there some damned where. He or somebody else will get in front of you and lead you in through the south vineyard road."

"Okay, Jerry. Good." Susan ran back to the Plymouth, which had stalled again. It smelled hot and the gauge was all the way to the top. She cranked and cranked before getting it to fire. By this time, the deputy had gotten his car backed out of the way and could be seen through his windshield, talking fast into a microphone.

Figuring the sturdy old Plymouth engine didn't have far to go anyway, Susan spared it not at all as she shot the clutch, pulling onto the bumpy side road. The surface was the worst yet, and they were all over the interior of the car as she drove on the ragged edge of loss of control.

It was not good to think of what the pounding must be doing to Alfredo Rodriques, hanging on, gray-faced, in the seat beside her. She tried to think of nothing but getting him there. After that, it was in his hands, or the hands of the gods.

They swept around a number of bumpy dirt curves, then were able to go faster as they flashed alongside a neatly fenced field of what looked like Chardonnay. Ahead, Susan saw more flashing lights, and someone in the roadway swinging a flashlight. As the Plymouth pounded closer, she saw that the gate off to the right had been swung wide open, and a second cruiser was inside, brake lights pulsing.

It was not the only illumination nearby. They were less than two miles from the Schreck compound now, and although the western sky over the blue-black mountains remained pale yellow, the illumination nearer at hand could be seen clearly—a garish crimson reflection off rising palls of black smoke.

Something was on fire at Jules Trello's winery.

15

Following the squad car, Susan wheeled the Plymouth in through the south vineyard. As they neared the buildings, she could see that it was a small outbuilding some thirty yards from the main compound that was aflame. Men were shooting foam and spray into the boiling smoke, while behind them, nearer the main entrance, Guardsmen were picking up demonstrators who had thrown themselves passively to the ground, forcing their captors to drag them bodily to waiting trucks. A handful of rioters were pelting the firefighters with rocks, and even as Susan got a glimpse of the scene, she saw two tear-gas canisters arc through the air and explode among the rock-throwers, scattering them.

She had no time to see more. The cruiser ahead cut sharply right through a wire gate being held open by a policeman, and they clattered down a short gravel driveway that led behind one of the hulking cooperage buildings. The car ahead cut sharp left again at the far end, and when Susan followed she found herself pulling in behind the main structure.

The driver of the cruiser ahead jumped out and ran to a back door, beginning to hammer on it. Susan got out and rushed around to help Rosario with Alfredo Rodriques. The sharp bite of the riot gas was in the air, mixed with acrid smoke, and although they could see nothing here, the roar of voices and hissing of flames were incessant and frighteningly near.

Rodriques was soaked with sweat and seemed very weak as they helped him from the car. His eyes lighted with excitement and resolve as they started toward the back door, where the deputy was still hammering, however, and he seemed to reach inside himself for strength. He began walking firmly, his head coming up.

"Can we get in this way?" he asked.

As if to answer the question, the back door swung open and someone stepped out onto the small porch. Susan felt a flood of relief as she recognized Rod Poole.

Seeing her at the same time, he rushed down to her side. "What are you doing here?" he demanded. "It's touch and go out there—half the people who broke through have dropped to the ground, but the other half are running crazy."

Alfredo Rodriques grasped Poole's arm. "Get me inside, and to the front where I can see."

"You're supposed to be in the hospital!"

"Rod," Susan snapped, "do what he says."

His face tense, Poole took one of Rodriques' arms and virtually propelled him up the steps and inside. Susan and Rosario hurried after them. As they entered a cavernous rear hallway, she heard someone slam the door shut behind them.

The smell of smoke and tear gas was stronger here, paradoxically mixed with the distant sweetness of fermentation. There was no time for other impressions as she caught only a glimpse of Poole hurrying Rodriques through a doorway at the far end of the hall, and again she followed.

They burst out into the main tour foyer. It was the scene of helter-skelter confusion—Guardsmen, police, deputies, state patrolmen, a portable transceiver set up on the central information desk with cables strung across the floor to it and a soldier frantically talking into a microphone. A group of people had clustered near the front doors and windows which provided a view of the area out front. It was toward this group that Poole hustled Rodriques, and as the men turned, Susan recognized Jules Trello, Timothy Crocker, and Robert Mancini among them.

"Hasn't he done enough?" Jules was demanding hotly as

she moved close enough to hear. "Arrest him, God damn it!"

"Just a minute," Poole said, holding onto Rodriques. "If he thinks he can help, he ought to be allowed to try."

Jules was beside himself. Sooty sweat streaked his face. His eyes bulged with a wild anger. He was trembling. "He caused all of this! I won't have him in here! If you won't arrest him, by God—" He started forward as if to attack Rodriques.

Poole stepped in front of the labor leader, but it was not necessary. Robert Mancini and Timothy Crocker, moving as one, grabbed Jules's arms and held him back. He struggled, spewing obscenities.

Sheriff Colby rushed over. "Rodriques, if you think you can do anything, tell me what it is."

Rodriques, his pallor intensified, did not flinch. "Let me see what is beyond these doors—"

"Your God-damned riot is beyond these doors!" Jules shouted.

Colby nodded solemnly. "Come here." Taking Rodriques' arm, he led the little man toward the plate-glass windows.

Susan saw her own opportunity to view the scene, and edged after them.

Beyond the glass was the front porch of the main building, and then the steps down into the square between the building and parking lot. On the stairs of the massive porch, dozens of Guardsmen crouched, their rifles at ready. Out in the yard perhaps two-dozen paces ahead of them, a ragged line of city policemen stood with legs spread, touching foot to foot on each side, facing the crowd.

It was a broken mob, some of them standing silent, others jeering, a few rushing forward in futile, faked attacks, then quickly scurrying back as an angry policeman raised a club. Behind this constantly moving row of men were more rioters, but they were standing almost quietly, watching their fellows try to confront the massed force between them and the building.

Farther back, workers were running. At one point Susan could see a half dozen or so actually grappling with some police, and to their left was a band rapidly dismantling a rock garden for more missiles to launch at the firefighters at the nearby storage building. A jeep had been overturned; it rested on its side in the middle of the vacant part of the parking lot.

The back area of the riot scene was a melee of individual fights and chases, police, Guardsmen and rioters running in all directions. This was also the area where hundreds had simply dropped to the earth, unmoving, and it was the continuing attempt to load these demonstrators into trucks that was drawing the attacks of the more active participants.

The barricades were up again, and a huge crowd remained beyond them, extending back into the blocked highway. There were cars as far as the eye could see both north and south, headlights glittering in the growing darkness.

As Susan took it all in, a rock sailed unexpectedly into the men crouching on the porch just beyond the window. She saw one of the men stagger sideways and start to fall. His fellows supported him and yelled for help. Others rushed over.

Alfredo Rodriques turned from the windows and retreated to the place where Jules, Robert, Timothy Crocker, and several lawmen were clustered. Again Susan moved in to hear.

"It is some of my oldest followers," Rodriques said. He appeared truly shocked, even dazed. "It is the long hate for the name Trello. I did not count on this. I thought they would never do some of these things—"

"Are you going to make us a speech now?" Jules demanded harshly. "God damn you, this is all your fault—"

"Mr. Trello," Sheriff Colby said sharply, "let's hear if the man has any ideas."

"I have an idea, yes," Rodriques said quickly. He turned around. "Thomas?"

Thomas Rosario was still beside Susan. "Here, Alfredo," he said.

"We will go onto the porch," Rodriques told him. He turned to Colby. "Do you have a microphone that can be turned very loud?"

"I've got a bullhorn that you could hear in the city," Colby said.

"Good. If I can use that."

Rosario pointed out, "It is so dark, Alfredo, they will not all see you."

"I can solve that," Colby said instantly. "We'll get a couple men out to those cars, and have them turn the spotlights right on the doorway. When you go out there you'll be lit up like a Christmas tree."

"Yes," Rodriques said. He took a deep breath and touched hands to damaged ribs. "Quickly, please."

Colby turned to snap orders. Men ran in obedience. The portable bullhorn was brought over. Colby showed Rodriques how to use it.

Robert Mancini walked to Susan's side. "I don't know how you managed it, but we're going to owe you a lot if this works."

"That's right," Susan told him. "I think I permanently damaged my back in that damned old Plymouth."

Robert, not understanding, of course, looked sharply concerned. "What?"

"Nothing. Just a *very* small joke."

Jules Trello had been watching them from a distance beyond earshot; normal conversation could not carry against the roar of the crowd outside. Now, as if her smile was a red flag, he raged over to face her. "You're the meddler who brought that Communist in here. I'm going to file charges on you when this is over!"

Sheriff Colby had stepped close enough to hear this, and interceded angrily. "Jules, nobody is going to file any charges, least of all against this young woman. If Rodriques can get those people out of here, we can consider ourselves damned lucky."

"*Out* of here?" Jules said, his face appearing stunned. "No! No one is leaving here under their own power! They're all trespassers! I want every one of them arrested!"

The front windows erupted in silvery light as a spotlight was shone onto it. Immediately, even as it moved to the glass of the doors, a second bright spot joined it, dancing.

Colby said heavily, "I'd like to arrest every man jack of them too. That's the law. But right now I'll settle for getting them off this property—and getting this thing disbanded. If you have any sense—"

"I don't *have* any sense!" Jules screamed. "All *I* have is this property that they've entered! And a building they set on fire—"

"That was an accident—a torch—"

"And *my* grounds they've wrecked, *my* windows they've broken, *my* fields they've trampled, *my* plant they've tried to storm! And now you say to let them go off to rest so they can do it another day?"

More spotlights danced, wavered, held on the front windows. It was brilliantly lighted, the reflections blinding. The light shone on Jules's face, showing the depths of his near-hysteria. It was a brief, shocking moment for Susan. She was seeing the hate that had existed in this man for everything Alfredo Rodriques stood for since the long siege against August Trello Wine Company.

Colby saw it, too, and he spoke gruffly, stern control in his tone. "Jules, I have to handle this the best way I can. I've got the colonel over there, and Captain Mardeen from the patrol. They'll back me up. If Rodriques can get those people to back out of here, we're going to damned well let them go."

"*No!*"

"We'll file charges against everyone we recognize. But we can't ask them to stop fighting and just walk into the trucks. There's no way they'll stop that way." Colby heaved a deep breath. "I'm telling Rodriques that now."

"It isn't *right!*" Jules yelled. He whirled on Robert. "You bleeding hearts may think this will gain something, but it only tells them we can't defend ourselves! It's an open invitation to do it again!"

Robert and Timothy Crocker began talking earnestly to Jules, trying to calm him. The sheriff had walked to Alfredo Rodriques' side, and was in similar deep conversation with him. Rodriques nodded, his face a study in determination. Rosario was at his side, holding the portable bullhorn. The sheriff patted Rodriques lightly on the shoulder and said something to one of the officers at the doors. The door was swung open.

Susan, halfway between Rodriques and Jules Trello, saw Jules's quick, darting movement out of the corner of her eye. Whether she acted to protect Rodriques, or was simply in the way, she would never fully know.

Jules was coming at Rodriques like an open-field tackler, hate in his eyes. Rodriques, facing the brilliance of the spotlights in the doorway, did not see him.

"No—!" Susan cried, and got in Jules's way.

He hit her with shattering impact, throwing her down and crashing on top of her with numbing force. A bright-yellow pain lanced through her arm and she tasted something salty, her own blood. Jules kneed her savagely, unintentionally, fighting to get untangled and to his feet again. Men ran from all directions, grabbing at both of them. Dazed, in pain, Susan saw him pulled away, struggling. They held onto him. He was yelling.

Rod Poole was holding her in his arms on the floor.

"Christ," he groaned, "you didn't have to do that—I was about to grab him—!"

Susan looked at him with blurry vision. The pain was very bad and she was choking on her own blood. She raised her hand to her mouth—or tried to—and sobbed with the resulting agony.

"Oh, shit, your arm is broken!" Poole said. "Help! Somebody give me a hand here! Oh, hell, Susan, you've cut the hell out of the inside of your mouth—"

Alfredo Rodriques bent over her. "Are you badly hurt? Is there anything I can do?" His expression showed extreme concern.

Susan waved the arm she had use of. Gagging on blood, she found a word. "Go," she managed thickly. She waved toward the door. "Please—go!"

Rodriques understood. His face set. He turned, signaled to Rosario, and strode into the brilliance of the spotlights.

Someone had joined Rod Poole and Robert Mancini at Susan's side. He had a cool, wet cloth, and he pressed it to her mouth. It felt good, but the pain in her arm was rising and pulsing through her in excruciating waves now, so that reality seemed to pulse brightly, then fade, then pulse again. The rhythm, she realized, was really that of her pulse.

"Hang in there, babe," Poole said hoarsely. "We'll get you fixed up in a minute."

Outside, beyond the blinding silvery glare, came Rodriques' voice, amplified a thousand times: *"Stop! This is Alfredo! I call upon you to stop and move back at once to the road!"*

Susan did not hear any more. The pain pulsed and faded and PULSED and faded and *PULSED* again, and she fainted.

16

"I think it was ridiculous," Susan Knight told the two men the next morning as she signed out of the hospital. "I didn't have a concussion; I *told* the doctor I didn't."

Robert Mancini and Rod Poole, both unshaven and red-eyed, looked worse than she did, in her opinion, despite the two stitches in her lower lip and the cast and sling on her arm. Now they stared at her with such disbelief and obvious solicitude that she laughed at them.

She added, "The two of you look like *you* should have spent the night in here, instead of me."

"Sure," Poole said. "You know more than any doctor."

"And grouchy, too," Susan teased him.

"I'm ready to sleep about twenty hours," he admitted.

"Good. You can go to bed and Robert can drive me to work."

"You're not going to work," Robert said.

"Oh, yes I am!"

"I think that blow knocked the sense out of you. You're going home for more rest."

"Robert," Susan said in dismay, "there are tests to run. I have more equipment to double-check. We have a harvest coming up."

"I'm well aware we have a harvest, Susan," Robert said patiently. "You're going to get some more rest."

506

"I've only got a couple of days to update some lab records! You just know that E. Z. Simms will start right in next Monday, wanting to go through everybody's books."

"E. Z. Simms," Robert replied testily, "can go to hell. And you're going home to bed if I have to have Rod break your other arm."

Susan sighed with disgust and joined the two men in walking down the hospital corridor toward the outside doors. She thought of another good sally, but restrained herself. She knew it would accomplish nothing, and the truth of the matter was that she did feel a certain relief. Her headache continued to nag her. A few hours' sleep, she thought, would be welcome.

She knew that there would be no such respite for Robert Mancini. Two meetings were scheduled yet this morning, one with Alfredo Rodriques, who had refused to return to the hospital, and another with a number of growers and winemakers at Mancini vineyards. Before the day was out, if all went well, perhaps as many as a dozen agreements would be signed, recognizing Workers United as bargaining agent for the field workers.

Susan had been fully briefed on events that followed her loss of consciousness at Schreck Brothers the previous night. Alfredo Rodriques had been recognized at once by all those close to the main building, and the cry had spread back into the crowd, *"Alfredo! Alfredo!"* Over much of the throng, a hush had fallen. Only a few tiny bands of diehards had continued to struggle.

Alfredo Rodriques' speech had been short and moving. He told the crowd that forcible entry onto another man's property was not the way of Workers United. He said blood had already flowed, and would be much worse unless the demonstration and violence were halted immediately.

Worse than even injury or death, he told a throng now eerily silent, was the loss of honor for all those who refused to follow the way of peaceful protest. Those who thought they could win by violence, he said, had always been consumed by violence.

He urged everyone to leave the Schreck property at once. He ordered the marchers to start back toward the city or their homes wherever they might be. He asked this, he said, as their leader; those who did not obey at once, he added, were no longer his followers.

Tomorrow, he said, he would announce new plans. He

believed he would also be able to announce real progress. He urged everyone to stop fighting and leave. Now.

Perhaps a dozen workers, in three groups, continued harassing the firefighters. One youth cried something unintelligible and hurled himself at a policeman at the barricades.

Everywhere else, however, the sight of a supposedly badly injured Alfredo Rodriques, urging them to retreat, had a miraculous effect on the workers.

Most of those who had been fighting stopped at once, and, arms at their sides, started walking toward the main gates. Police and Guardsmen, alerted ahead of time, stood by to let them pass. The lie-down demonstrators rose quietly and began filing out. The crowd at and beyond the gates began to mill, and then break up, becoming a loose assembly of people turning to walk south with their fellows, headed back toward the city.

Rodriques stood in the glare of the spotlights, watching, and he wept.

Within an hour the grounds contained no more demonstrators. The last of the crowd was moving south. The highway, although choked, was open again to slow-moving traffic. The fire in the storage building had been extinguished, and a real fire-department unit was spraying smoking embers. In the light of emergency units and searchlights, trash blew across the sprawling grounds and parking lots, and workers were already beginning to clear away some of the debris.

Jules Trello had been relieved, but livid, demanding mass arrests. He was ignored because such arrests were impossible.

This morning, Susan had just learned, four-dozen Chicano representatives of the Rodriques organization—after carefully notifying the city and county, as well as Jules Trello, of their intentions, had driven to the gates of Schreck Brothers. There they offered to work free to help clean up the last of the debris, replant new vines where any had been damaged, rebuild the despoiled garden, and do any other work they might be asked to do.

Jules Trello had given them five minutes to leave the scene or be arrested. They left at once, without argument.

"Will the meetings today really end the conflict?" Susan asked now as they neared the bright hospital exit doors.

"Oh, no," Robert said. "Some, like Jules, will never give

in. It will go on and on. And Rodriques is right, in a way, that these agreements don't really settle anything. It's just a bad bargain that most of us, I think, will accept to complete this year's harvest in relative peace."

"After the no-strike agreement ends next January—?"

"There will be strikes. It's going to take years to resolve all of it. Possibly we'll never have times like the past . . . nothing may ever be the same again." Robert's face showed his weary regret. There was a resolve there, too. Susan read his expression and thought she understood: No one would like the agreements, but all had to accept them as the best temporary solution. They were not breaking the back of the conflict; they were declaring an armistice.

Rod Poole held the door for Susan and she stepped outside. As she did so, she noticed a sudden slight smile on his face. Robert Mancini, too, following her out, looked brighter, expectant.

"We do have one nice surprise this morning, anyway," he said.

Susan stared at him, not understanding for a moment. As she did so, two figures moved from a nearby slat bench against the building and headed toward her. It was a warm, lovely morning, and the two had been sitting in the sunlight; she had not given them so much as a glance until they now came closer.

She turned to look directly at them and her heart jolted as she recognized them.

They looked tired, too, and wore poor clothing. But their smiles were broad.

With a glad cry, Susan ran forward and hugged the small man with her one good arm. He seemed startled, but laughed as she turned and hugged his wife, too. Homero and Dolores Artiz were both grinning even more widely now, and their eyes had the brightness of tears.

"You're back!" Susan gasped, stepping back to stare at them, still not wholly able to believe it. "So *soon?*" Then she had a bad thought. "Is it—permanent? It isn't just a— a visit?"

"We have come back to stay," Homero Artiz replied in his impeccable English. "The regulations—the requirements—all seemed to fall away before us."

"That's wonderful!" Susan said, seeing new lines in Homero's face, thinking Dolores had lost weight. "But when did you get in? How long did it take to drive back?

Where are the children? Where are you staying?" She turned to Robert and Rod Poole. "I can't go home now! We have to help Homero and Dolores find a new house!"

"We are staying with friends," Homero said. "We will look for a house or apartment, but we are so glad to be back here again, a day or two will not matter."

"And you just got back?"

"Very late last night."

Dolores added, "When we arrived, we learned of the trouble. It had already ended . . . the demonstration of last night."

"And then we heard of your injury," Homero said. "We came here at once, but you were asleep. We talked with Mr. Mancini, and Mr. Poole."

"So we came back this morning," Dolores resumed. "We wanted to see you at once, and we hope it is not an, uh, appo—" She frowned and looked at Homero.

"An imposition," he supplied.

"Yes," Dolores said happily. "We have much to tell you, but most of all we must tell you that never, the officials have told us, has anyone moved through the procedures as rapidly as we have just done. There was surprise everywhere we went, and they said, 'This cannot be so,' but then they looked for our papers, and they were there!" Dolores clapped her hands like a child.

Homero moved about lightly on his feet like a natural dancer. He could not stand still, and, like Dolores filled with excitement, chattered like a magpie.

Susan beamed at them, loving them for their exuberance, and she saw Rod Poole and Robert Mancini grinning, too. It crossed her mind, even in the pleasure and surprise of the moment, that Robert had to be crushingly fatigued, and still faced not only the day's work but the specter of imminent takeover by Timmons Corporation. She had seen the news item about his divorce being filed, as well, and a part of her thought how ironic it was that in this moment of happiness there should be so much sorrow coexisting with it, as in another compartment separated from the "now" only by tissue-thin walls. How often did great happiness and equal sadness coexist in a moment like this?

17

The first five recognition agreements between representatives of the valley's wine industry and Alfredo Rodriques were signed on the day following the Schreck Brothers riot. Robert Mancini was the first to sign. On the next day, more than a dozen more contracts, stipulating nothing more than recognition and a no-strike pledge, were concluded.

With his immediate part in negotiations completed, Robert Mancini returned to the struggle to try to maintain control of his winery. Although a handful of stock certificates were in the Friday mail from his broker, the news was not generally good. Although inventory showed that Robert either owned or could definitely control 32.5 per cent of the stock, no other large bloc had surfaced, leading his lawyers to the gloomy conclusion that Timmons Corporation had to be sitting on at least as much strength, and probably more.

Legal maneuvers might delay any stock vote for as much as ninety days, and the attorneys were working with other experts to lay strategy for such a fight. Robert knew, however, that it would be empty tactics to fight for such a delay unless he had some hope of picking up strength in the interim. He delayed approval of actually beginning a legal battle designed to halt the vote for the time being.

Across the valley, others were busy. Some early grapes were now being harvested for blending purposes, although

Robert and most of the other quality winemakers were holding off and did not anticipate major activity for another two weeks yet.

Excitement had begun to run very high among some experts about the year's crop. Early cool weather had contributed to slow maturation, but now the weather was ideal; sugar and acid appeared very good, and so far there was no sign of *botrytis*. There was a general belief that the harvest might be the best of the decade, and perhaps one of the all-time greats—*if* luck with the weather held up through the next crucial fourteen days or so.

Homero Artiz and his family moved into a small house, a better one than the one they had vacated earlier, thanks to a continuing half-time job agreement with Timothy Crocker. Although onlookers were amazed that he found any time left after his long workdays, Homero immediately began a new personal project: contacting other Chicanos whom he knew were in the area illegally, and trying to help them find advice for making application to remain permanently, on the citizenship track. Someone in the Alfredo Rodriques organization heard of Homero's efforts the first weekend he worked on it, and by Monday, September 21—the day when John Endicott and E. Z. Simms strolled into Robert Mancini Vineyards and asked a startled secretary to show them to their offices—Homero had a lawyer working with him part-time to advise illegal immigrants.

Word spread quietly about the same time that two or more agents of the Bureau of Alcohol, Tobacco and Firearms were in the area. They had visited three wineries thus far, asking general questions about past vintages, wineries that had closed in recent months, and shipping methods.

The presence of agents created continuing interest because most vintners immediately made their own logical jump, connecting the agents' presence with occasional new stories in the press about an ongoing investigation on both sides of the Atlantic concerning bogus French wines confiscated at New Orleans. In the Bordeaux, one small shipper was under arrest, his warehouses under padlock, and in New Orleans the ship captain had been indicted for fraud. Speculation had it that there was some clue somewhere which pointed to northern California as the real source of the confiscated wine, although this was a conclusion drawn from imagination more than anything any news story reported. The governments of both the United States and France were playing this one close to the vest.

For Jules Trello, presence of the agents was a severe worry. He had, however, doctored his Schreck books to cover any shortages of glass and cork, and work on the old Elmhurst facility had progressed to the point where no one would ever find any evidence of the bottling he had done. There were no records to incriminate him.

He imagined he was as free and clear on this score as he was on Carole's hit-run accident.

Unknown to him, events were taking place that could prove him wrong on both counts.

Johnelle Henderson was continuing her single-minded, compulsive probe. From the bureau of auto registration she had a list of every late-model Corvette in a three-county area. She was concentrating first on the local county, and had already investigated a dozen persons who seemed to own the right model sports car. So far, being very careful, she had not gotten near an accusation, and had eliminated most of those on her list.

She had five names left to check, including that of Mrs. Jules Trello.

Ned Henderson urged her for perhaps the hundredth time to give it up, begin assuming normal activity again—start living again.

"You can't succeed," he told his wife, pain clear in his eyes.

"I will," she said.

"You're going to lose your job. You're giving up everything else for this, and it's wrecking our lives. He's dead, Johnelle! He's *dead!* Let him go! We have to go on living!"

Johnelle refused, and on the evening of September 23, when she got home very late, and he again begged her to desist, they had a savage argument about it.

By sheer chance, their argument took place on the same evening that Carole Trello received a jolting blow of her own.

Because Schreck Brothers was picking grapes on a 24-hour-a-day schedule, Jules was not at home although it was midevening. Carole was watching television when the door chimes sounded, and she remained in front of the set while the maid answered.

The black girl came in and announced that Carole had a visitor.

"Who is it?" Carole demanded, putting her drink on the glass table beside her.

"She didn't give me her name, ma'am. She said it was important to speak to you personally."

Sighing irritably, Carole dismissed the girl and strode to the front door. Salespersons were very unusual in the country, but not out of the question. She felt angry about being interrupted, and was prepared to be nasty if it was a salesperson, some stupid charity worker, or a political meddler of some kind.

The moment Carole saw the young woman on the porch, however, she had a good idea that she was none of those she had categorized as nuisances.

For one thing, the young woman was very beautiful.

For another, her silken dress, tiny sandals, and purse were obviously not only in exquisite taste, but patently expensive. And the dark eyes that met Carole's were quick with intelligence, appraising her just as frankly as she was making her own appraisal.

"Mrs. Trello?" the woman said. She had a husky voice —the kind, Carole thought absently, that many men would love.

"Yes?" Carole said, giving nothing.

"My name is Connie Livingston. I have something to leave for your husband, and I wanted just a minute or two of your time."

Despite her certainty to the contrary, Carole snapped, "Look. If this is some kind of a sales gimmick—"

"I can assure you that it isn't," Connie Livingston said with no trace of a smile. "I'm a friend of your husband, and this is important."

Was there the slightest possible odd inflection in the word "friend"? Carole did not know—knew she might have imagined it. Instantly, however, there was a hot bitterness in the pit of her stomach and a corresponding coldness in her bloodstream. Of course it was impossible, she told herself: Jules didn't . . . he was unable to function . . .

Carole, however, had never lived more than inches from an abyss of despair. She had always known how slender her hold on her husband really was. The childish act, the baby talk, the pretense at stupidity—all were ploys she used because they pleased him . . . acts she hated at the same time they denigrated her and made her hate herself for employing them. Her nightmare was that Jules would find someone else whose act was more fascinating, who might stir him in a way she no longer could. If that happened, she would be discarded . . . finished.

And something whispered deep inside her that this stunning young woman was more than a friend.

Carole's intense curiosity—and fear—overcame her caution. With a gesture she knew was almost brusque, she signaled Connie Livingston to follow her inside.

In the living room, the young woman sat on one of the leather couches, crossing sleek legs. She looked around with pleasure, completely at ease.

"You have a lovely home," Connie Livingston said.

"You have something to say to me?" Carole demanded. "You have something for my husband?"

Connie Livingston smiled again and opened her purse, taking out a normally sized white envelope. It appeared to contain a letter. She handed it to Carole. "This is a very important message from a business associate. It's vital that you hand this to Mr. Trello at your earliest opportunity, when you're alone."

Carole looked at the envelope. It was an ordinary dimestore envelope of the kind in her own desk, and it had no marks of any kind on the outside. She turned it over. It was sealed.

She looked back into the eyes of Connie Livingston.

"All I really have to say, Mrs. Trello," the woman said, "is what I've already told you. This is a most important message. It's highly confidential. Please see that Jules gets it as soon as possible, and when you're alone."

Carole had not missed the fact of the "Jules." It seared her. With complete certainty of a kind that defied logic, she *knew*. This woman and her husband. The knowledge was as sure as any she had ever known, and she was sick at her stomach with the knowing.

"Why not deliver this yourself at the winery?" she demanded hoarsely.

"I'm in the area only this evening. I knew it would be safe with you."

"Where are you from?" Carole asked. "How do you know Jules?"

Connie Livingston's smile was serene, with the selfassurance and coolness of a consummate whore. "I'm from Chicago. We met there."

"On the trip he made last month?"

"Yes." Connie Livingston closed her purse and rose to her feet. "Well, thank you for seeing me. I did need just this minute to impress on you that this is a most important —and confidential—business matter." She smiled again as if trying to be friendly, but it failed. "I'm just a messenger, you see."

It was the final mistake, if Carole had needed another to make her sure beyond any doubt that this woman and her husband . . . that the two of them . . . in Chicago, while she was here . . . had . . . Her mind recoiled from the truth.

Somehow she walked to the door with the woman. There was meaningless talk about the weather. The woman walked away, going to a sleek Lincoln and entering the passenger side. A man, faceless, was behind the wheel, and the car started at once and glided away, vanishing in the roadway.

The letter in her hand, Carole returned to the living room. Why a letter had been delivered, and what that might mean, were far from her immediate thoughts. She knew. She *knew*. It had all been in Connie Livingston's eyes: she had held Jules in her arms; she had crooned her pleasure in his ear; she had taken him inside herself, thrilling him, having from him the reaction that Carole had not been able to get for months now . . . *years* now.

Jules had lied to her. Perhaps—and this was a new thought—Connie Livingston had just lied to her too. Perhaps there had been no business in Chicago. Perhaps it had been merely a tryst—a way of cheating her, preparing the way to throw her aside.

At this point Carole again became aware of the envelope in her hands. She had to know what it contained.

Without more thought, her fingers became claws and tore it open.

There was a single sheet of ordinary bond paper inside. There was no return address, no salutation, no signature. The message was typed on the middle of the page in an anonymous IBM typewriter face:

> *Investigators are in your area now.*
> *Nothing can be proved. You may be told there is evidence. This will be a trick. Say nothing. If there are any records, destroy them at once.*
> *More than your own well-being is at stake. Others depend on you.*

The bearer of this letter reached your wife and entered your home without difficulty. Remember that. If any person fails now, another visitor with different intentions could reach your loved ones just as easily. The bearer of this letter does not know the contents.

Carole read the letter carefully, puzzled and frightened, twice. She retained her certainty about the relationship between Jules and Connie Livingston, but now it was not the only issue. She did not understand what the letter was about. It was clear, however, that Jules was in very serious trouble.

She paced the floor and tried to decide what to do. She *wanted* to meet Jules openly when he returned, tell him what had happened, what she had surmised, and what she had done in opening the letter. Then, she thought briefly, she would demand a full explanation, and help him shoulder whatever this burden really was.

But she could not. She had never been able to confront an issue squarely with this man who was her husband. Desire it as she might, she could not begin now. She was simply incapable of it.

With trembling fingers she put the letter in a fresh envelope, licked it, and sealed it. She waited for her husband to come home.

It was after midnight when she heard his car. He tramped in, dirty, tired, soaked with sweat, irritable. He was muttering something to himself as he crossed the living room, and started violently when he saw her.

"You're still up?" he said without pleasure.

She rose, a tumult within her, and handed him the envelope.

He frowned. "What's this?"

"A woman named Connie Livingston delivered it to the door."

If any further confirmation had been needed, she had it in the way Jules violently jumped at the sound of the name. "Who?" he said, collecting himself.

"A woman from Chicago," Carole said, so intent on holding herself in that she forgot her baby talk. "She said you were a business associate. She said this is an important, confidential letter."

His face a cloud, Jules walked away from her, his back

fully to her. She watched him, and heard the envelope rip open. His head bent and there was total silence as he read.

"Now, Carole thought, *he will turn and tell me truthfully what this is. Then he will explain it to me so I can share it with him.*

Jules finally turned. His lips turned in a crooked smile. "Silly," he muttered.

"A problem?" she said.

"It's a sort of business chain letter," he said, crumpling it and shoving it into his jacket pocket. "Nonsense, really." His chuckle had a hollow ring. "Anyone who would think that's important is an idiot! I've got far more important things to worry about right now!"

Carole eyed him. She would find out, she thought. He was in trouble and she would learn what it was all about. And then she would be able to stand by him whether he willed it or not, and not even a Connie Livingston could share him any more.

This was vital for her security . . . even her existence. She had so long deferred to this man, submerging herself in his desires, that she had no identity outside of him.

But for now, existence demanded subterfuge. She hid her tumult.

"Odd," Jules told her, "that they'd send some secretary to deliver it, though. I guess chain letters are against the law and they couldn't risk the mail."

Her heart quaked, thinking that he could imagine she was this stupid. But she fought back resentment as well as intelligence.

She donned her brainless smile. "Is Daddy hungwy?"

"As a matter of fact," Jules said, "Daddy could eat a horse."

"Ooh!" Carole preened and giggled. "Baby will fix Daddy a sandwich and coffee and cookies!"

"You're a good baby," Jules told her, patting her backside as she walked by him.

18

A flood of "helpful suggestions" began issuing from the offices of John Endicott and E. Z. Simms within twenty-four hours of their arrival, and by Thursday of their first week, the two Timmons representatives had succeeded in creating turmoil throughout Robert Mancini Vineyards.

Meetings, formal and informal, were unending. On Tuesday, September 22, Endicott proposed a new national advertising campaign and changes in warehousing to provide for automated barrel-handling two years hence. Simms suggested eliminating more than a dozen telephone connections and drew up a memorandum showing how employees could double up on the remaining instruments. A woman with four years' experience in the sales department interpreted one of Simms's remarks to indicate that her job was expendable, and reported this to Robert Mancini in tears.

On the next day, Wednesday, Susan Knight clashed sharply with Simms when he told her the lab records were inadequate. Robert spent three hours arguing with Endicott about the winery's participation in employee insurance programs and retirement benefits. By afternoon, Simms had laid out a plan to enlarge the rather simple computer system, designed only to monitor production procedures, to include a new bookkeeping system. Employees throughout the winery reported to work at a given time and left when their hours were over, and there was no time clock; both Timmons experts suggested that this should be stopped at once, and time clocks installed for everyone, including office personnel. Simms produced a plastic-covered board which would allow every person in the office wing, including Robert, to write a notation in crayon whenever he or she left the office for any reason.

"He's driving us all nuts!" DeFrates raged to Robert on Thursday morning. "Now the crazy so-and-so wants a weekly report from me on everything that took place in production! Pretty soon I'll have so many forms to fill out, I won't have time to do my job."

"Ignore Simms's suggestions," Robert said, smiling to hide his growing irritation and resentment.

"He keeps coming back at me!"

"Just ignore him, Mike. Smile and say yes and then go right on the way you were."

DeFrates walked up and down the office, fists balled, his face a study in perplexity. "I'm afraid I'll lose my cool and bust him right in the mouth."

"Try not to," Robert urged mildly. "Our company insurance doesn't cover bridgework, and a memo on that could be his next suggestion."

Beneath his façade, Robert was stewing. He viewed his role now, in part, as peacemaker. The role was leaving him little time for anything else. In four days, Endicott and Simms had turned the place upside down. It was a portent . . . unless the Timmons takeover could be avoided in the stock showdown.

"Bobby," Endicott said Thursday noon, "it isn't that we're trying to rock the boat. Believe me, that's the last thing on our mind. But gawwd damn! Everything we notice, someone seems to resent our helpfulness."

"Maybe you're trying to move too fast," Robert replied, struggling as usual to act as peacemaker. "After all, John, you're coming in here with the idea of taking over the winery. Do you really think I—or anyone else—is going to *like* what you're doing?"

Endicott's florid face twisted in a good show of dismay. "Bobby! Gracious goodness! Please don't misunderstand our role here for a *minute!* Yes, there's going to be a stock vote. I regret that. I sincerely regret it, believe me! But gawwd damn, we don't know how that's going to go, now, do we? I view our role as *advisory*. As *helpful*. You know, we're sending back daily reports to the big brass. The way I see it, your response to our suggestions is going to go far toward helping them decide, up there, what ought to be done around here in terms of management in the future."

"In other words," Robert said, "if we all start taking orders like little lambs, maybe we'll be allowed to stay on if I lose the stock vote?"

"That's the worst interpretation you could place on my words, Bobby! I'm disheartened to think we don't know each other better than that!"

By the slenderest margin, Robert held onto his self-control. He even managed a smile, and listened while Endicott listed several new ideas he and Simms had cooked up to streamline the operation.

An hour or two later, in another of the seemingly endless brief meetings, Simms joined Endicott, and the two of them moved into an area that brought Susan Knight out of her chair with outrage.

"These French barrels from the Nevers Forest," Simms said, scowling over purchase orders. "That's a question I'd like your opinion on too, Susan."

Robert saw Susan tense visibly. He had given her several pep talks, however, and she made a loyal try at being calm. "What about them, E.Z.?"

"They're expensive . . . *very* expensive."

"Yes," Susan said, obviously fighting mad underneath.

Simms held up the purchase order. "I strongly advise canceling this order."

"We need them for this year's wine!" Susan snapped.

Robert added quickly, "They're already in the cooperage building, E.Z. The order can't be canceled."

"Nonsense." Simms got out of his chair, walked to the window, peered out, turned, bounced up and down on the toes of his tiny shoes. "You can still return them. Payment hasn't been made, has it? If so, I find no such record in the—"

"Payment hasn't been made yet," Robert said. "But it will be made."

"Those barrels are just too expensive!"

To head off Susan's angry retort, Robert said, "We get a better price than most wineries now using Nevers oak. That's because we were the first to use them in large quantities and we get a preferential rate."

Simms's eyes widened. "*I'll* say you use a lot of them."

He shuffled the armload of papers. "This order says three thousand new barrels. And they cost three hundred dollars apiece."

Endicott jumped. "Gawwd damn!"

"Three hundred dollars times three thousand barrels is nine hundred thousand dollars," Simms added.

"Gawwd *damn!*" Endicott said.

"It's a big annual outlay," Robert conceded. "But it assures us that our wines that require exposure to oak always get it in good barrels. We sell our old barrels to two other vineyards."

"You mean," Endicott said quickly, "that you give away the old barrels before they're used up?"

"We sell them," Robert replied patiently, "for better than half the original price. We do so because we want fresh oak constantly being phased in. Elmhurst—that old winery we almost bought this spring—tried to use its barrels too many times; some of them soured. That's one of the reasons they finally went out of business."

"There's less expensive oak," Simms said with the bulldog expression of a man prepared for an argument.

"Oh, yes," Robert conceded.

"Why use oak at all?" Endicott put in. "I know it *looks* good, but beyond PR, how much good does it really do?"

This was a little too much for Susan, and she answered before Robert would pre-empt her. "For many wines," she said heatedly, "exposure to fine oak, and in small barrels to give maximum exposure, is one of the factors that smooths the wine and gives it distinction. The great wines of France—and they're the standard of the world—have always tended to have oaky overtones in the finished flavor. That's what people have learned to identify as top quality."

"Well," Simms said thoughtfully, "if a little flavor of oak is all you get from these barrels, there ought to be some other way to get it." He thought about it and then brightened. "How about an additive?"

Susan paled. "An additive!"

"Sure. Like food coloring. You could buy some imitation oak flavor and just squirt some in every batch. Now I *know*," Simms added quickly, "that the idea might first sound strange to a purist. But we're talking about nearly a million bucks a year here. Think of how much more profit could be realized if the wine could be stored in glass, say, or plastic, and then shoot in a little flavoring agent right there at the end."

"If that's all you know about wine," Susan said, "what are you *doing* here?"

Simms's face splotched. "I've been doing my homework, chickie. I'm not exactly a dummy. For example. Even some other kinds of European oak are cheaper than these doozies *you've* been buying. Limousin oak, for example." He paused dramatically, not knowing he had mispronounced the word. "That's a little cheaper. And Yugoslavian oak is lots cheaper. And then you get to American oak. Arkansas oak. Now, there's a bargain! You can buy Arkansas oak barrels for about fifty dollars a barrel. Fifty as opposed to three hundred. Six for one! What's wrong with good old American oak?"

"Arkansas oak has uses," Susan retorted. "But it gives *too much* oak flavor."

"Well, then, keep the wine in it a shorter time!"

"It's not that simple," Susan replied. "Nevers oak, Limousin, Yugoslavian, American—each has its uses. We use redwood, too, you know; it's neutral. And we *do* hold some wines in Fiberglas on special occasions. What you're talking about here is an art that men have been learning and modifying, through trial and error, for centuries! You can't just look at the checkbook and write off generations of taste and experience!"

"I'm just trying to tell you what good management would do," Simms replied stiffly.

John Endicott leaned forward toward Robert. "The crux of the matter, though, is the flavor of oak?"

"That's an oversimplification, but—all right. Yes."

Endicott inclined his head toward Susan, his eyes never leaving Robert. "I guess you tend to agree with her?"

"Yes."

"What would you think if we really pressed you to return those barrels?"

Robert's temper slipped. "Until there's a stock vote, I own this place. If you were to push me too hard, I'd have you thrown out on that highway."

Endicott stiffened. "That's clear enough. But my opinion is that if the customers are so all-fired anxious to have the taste of oak, you could damned well tape a twig to each bottle and let them chew on it."

This one was so outrageous that no one replied, although Robert knew very well that there were commercial winemakers in California who might have grinned at Endicott's hyperbole, and explained that they were operating on just such a philosophy. There was no way to explain to Endicott and Simms why many things were done as they were done here. The way to excellence was not the cheapest way; the relationship between excellence and retail price was not always as direct as it should have been, in justice. There were ways to market inferior wine as fine stuff, and turn a bigger profit. Robert could not very well try to explain his own refusal to do the same, not to two businessmen who prided themselves on being hard-headed realists. "Realism" today meant joining the outlook of the pack, and saying mediocre was good enough. "Realists" considered those who adhered to a stern personal code as elitists, and sneered at them.

After another few minutes, then, the oak debate temporarily abated. Simms came out with a new idea for plastic corks.

A little later, when they were alone, Susan burst out to Robert, "I don't know how much more of this I can stand!"

"Do what Mike does," Robert suggested. "Fantasize punching them in the mouth."

"Robert, this isn't very funny, you know!"

He turned sharply. "I know."

She was instantly stricken. "I'm sorry. Good God, that was a *stupid* thing for me to say."

"Forget it. I'm a little tired myself."

"I know it's really none of my business, but are you making *any* progress on heading this thing off?"

"It's *your* business," Robert told her quietly. "No, listen. This is important. It *is* your business. We didn't make the progress we've made here with people who punched a clock from nine to five and didn't give a damn. You have every right to know where we stand because you've made a contribution, and your caring has made a difference. I just wish," he added after a rueful pause, "I had better news for you."

"There's no way you could just buy stock from Timmons?"

"If it went high enough. At some point, I suppose, stock would surface. But we're talking about too much money."

"How much would you have to raise to be able to buy some more?"

Robert hesitated before replying, although he did not know why. He had mentally reviewed the math of this sort of desperate last-ditch effort often enough.

"To make a dent," he said firmly, "about eight hundred thousand dollars. To be reasonably sure of surfacing plenty of stock, and buying it fast, a million, two."

"Shit."

"Don't worry so much," he said, trying to cheer her. "I don't have anything like that amount to spend, but I haven't given up hope yet."

"Robert, what will you do . . ." Susan's face twisted as if she hated even the words—". . . if it doesn't go . . . right?"

"Well, I still have my portion of stock. I would try to sell most of that, I think. One of these days possibly one of the little boutique wineries will go up for sale. I might be able to swing that. And in the meantime I have forty acres in the hills. You remember when I took you up there once and showed it to you. Korday is going to harvest the grapes that make this year—" He paused, consulting his calendar watch—"good lord!—today, as a matter of fact. And starting next year that acreage will be in full production. I could live up there, work it."

"Alone?" Susan blurted.

This time he did not hesitate. It was time people knew. "No. Not alone. My wife's divorce action is going forward. I'm not contesting it in any way. When that has been finalized, if my luck holds, I intend to marry Barbara Turner."

Susan's mouth dropped open. "The reporter?"

"The same. I hope you approve?"

"Yes! I *do* approve! I don't know her well, Robert, but she's just a lovely person. I—I'm really glad for you!"

"It's all happened this summer, since the separation," he told her. "We met just about the time Audra left me . . . not long after." It seemed important to establish this.

"I'm just so happy for you, Robert," Susan said. "I really am."

"So you see everything isn't glum," he added. "And I've got lots of motivation for doing my damnedest."

"Will Barbara be out here again soon? I want to congratulate her."

"I don't know," Robert admitted. "I'm trying to discourage her visiting here right now, frankly, because I think she might outdo you and Mike DeFrates both in nose-punching impulses if she really saw what was going on at the moment. I'll be seeing her, of course. Sunday I think we'll drive up to the acreage and see how Korday's people did with their picking, and maybe have a picnic. She has a son, Jimmy. He's a great kid. He'll enjoy that."

Susan glanced out the window. "It ought to be a marvelous day for an outing. At least the weather isn't double-crossing us!"

This prediction, however, turned out to be short-lived. Friday dawned cooler, with high clouds skidding in over the mountains from the Pacific. The radio issued a revised forecast calling for rain by the first of the week.

Again John Endicott made an effort to be "helpful" as a result of this abrupt change in the forecast.

"I admit I don't know everything about this business just yet," he said, striding up and down the conference room. "But aren't you taking a hell of a chance, not planning to harvest more this weekend and as early as possible next week?"

"We're going to start harvesting what we can tomorrow," Robert reiterated. "But most of the grapes around the winery just aren't quite where we want them yet."

"You said yourself you *could* harvest them!"

"*Could*," Robert repeated.

"If it starts raining, half your crop is lost. How is that going to look to the big boys in Portland?"

"Frankly, John, I don't worry about how it might look to the 'big boys in Portland.' Most of the grapes close in to the winery aren't quite ready yet."

"Korday is picking. Martini is picking. Crocker is picking."

"All of them are in areas that are just a few degree days warmer than we are every year."

"But," Endicott insisted, "you said yourself that you *could* pick. You said the Brix is a shade over twenty-one."

"I want it well past twenty-two. I'm still hoping for twenty-four—even twenty-six on the Cabernet Sauvignon."

"When everyone else is willing to accept the usual standard," Endicott growled, "and work to beat the rain. Is there any chance, here, Bobby, that you're *trying* to make as much trouble as you can in view of the changeover we both know is coming?"

The suggestion struck so deep into him that he went cold instead of hot. The resulting burst of anger almost froze him in a control he had not known he possessed. "I'll overlook that, John."

Endicott would not let it go. Frowning, he pointed a finger. "I think I deserve an answer."

"If this is my last vintage here," Robert told him slowly, "I want it to be the very best of all. I want those grapes so soft, so full of sugar, that the wine is immense, bursting with fruit, with the kind of potential that will last twenty years or more. I've taken this kind of chance before."

"Yes, and in 1975 it didn't pay off! You lost a quarter of your crop. Tractors were stuck in the mud. Grapes rotted out there!"

"There were other years when it did work. And some of the 1975 grapes were of a beautiful—a unique—quality."

"I'll never understand you dreamers. To me, every grape out there is an investment. Grab the return! Don't gamble on something only a few thousand elitists in the entire world could recognize even if you got lucky and produced it!"

"That's what separates you and me," Robert told him.

"I'll have to report this!" Endicott fumed. "Gawwd damn! I just can't understand all this!" He left the room muttering to himself.

As a result of this exchange, Robert's first impulse was to allow all the grapes to remain where they were, running a total risk. But after an hour or so of thinking about it, he knew that this would be as much a direct reaction to Endicott as immediate harvest of everything in sight would have been. He had to maintain control . . . react as he normally would.

There were contract fields somewhat to the south, and these were in very slightly warmer mini-climate zones. Tests in recent days had shown these nearly ripe, and everything stood at ready around the winery. In a normal year he would have considered harvesting these grapes now, if a final check showed they were mature enough.

He would do the same now.

Within thirty minutes, he and Susan Knight had begun visits to a half-dozen vineyards along the highway to the south. They found the grapes consistently on the lower edge of acceptability. Leaving one of the last of these fields, they decided to stop by Ned Henderson's because it was on the way home, and his crop, though relatively small, would be picked with the rest.

As they turned in at the vineyard road Susan said, "I never pass this spot without thinking of Jamie."

"I know," Robert agreed soberly. "I just wish I thought they were starting to get over it . . . even a little bit."

"Johnelle is still searching for that driver."

"Oh, hell."

"It's true. Rod keeps getting telephone calls from people she's questioned. She won't give it up."

"Maybe the harvest of their own grapes will jar her out of it just a little," Robert suggested, knowing how vain a hope it was.

"Look," Susan said suddenly. "There's Ned, out in the field."

Henderson was out in the center of his vineyard, hatless, obviously taking samples with a saccharimeter. Robert pulled up on the edge of the driveway so they could cut directly between the rows to join him.

As he got out, a raindrop spattered onto his forehead. He saw Susan flinch from another one and peer up worriedly at the growing sodden clouds. "It looks like we could have a cloudburst anytime, Robert!"

"We'd better not."

A few more heavy drops spatted onto them and the powdery earth as they moved between heavily laden young vines to join Ned Henderson. He looked nervously optimistic as he brushed the pulp of a tested grape from his palm.

"What is it?" Susan asked.

"Twenty-one," Henderson said.

Robert made the decision that had been building since before his latest trip to the fields. "We'll start harvesting Monday, Ned."

"Great!"

"I've got an idea the crews will want to pick Smith and Maxwell, and then come by and catch you late in the afternoon."

Henderson's grin split his face. "I'm ready! Listen: I've started worrying about this weather!"

"It can't rain," Robert smiled. "I intend to leave our Cabernet and Pinot Noir out at least another ten days."

"Well, I'm ready to get mine picked! How much do you think I've got here?"

Robert scanned the acreage with a practiced eye. He knew Henderson was probably counting on an optimistic yield, but he knew rather closely what was really here. He opted for honesty. "Between fifteen and twenty tons."

Henderson's face fell. "I was hoping for more."

"It could run a little higher," Robert conceded, "but these vines are young, and you pruned well. That means a little less fruit, but very high quality. Your grapes will be segregated, and three people will evaluate them. If you deserve a quality bonus, you'll be paid one."

"I didn't even know about a quality bonus."

"It's a long-standing policy we have, but we don't exactly advertise it. Especially this year."

"I've heard prices so far are higher than anyone thought."

"They'll drop a little, in all likelihood, but it doesn't look now like anyone will be paid as low as that infamous 'floor' I mentioned a while back."

It was an obvious irony. Much of the controversy with Schreck and with Timmons Corporation had been over the price floor, announced in the face of Jules's rumors of catastrophically low prices. Now the early reports indicated that the crop would not be as bountiful as early optimists had forecast. Prices were likely to equal the previous year's, or surpass them.

"What do you think you'll be paying?" Henderson asked now.

"Between three and four hundred."

"That *is* high!"

"I'm only buying the best, you know."

Henderson grinned and looked around the vineyard. "And these *are* the best," he said softly.

"You've done a good job," Robert agreed, respecting his pride, wholly understanding it.

"With guys like Homero helping, and you people advising, how could I miss?"

Susan said perhaps too casually, "I'm sure Johnelle will be pleased."

A shadow chased across Henderson's face. "I hope so."

"Is she home?"

"No."

"Oh. At work."

"She's still out . . . looking."

"I'm sorry, Ned," Susan said simply.

Henderson's face reflected his worry for an instant, but then his spirit reasserted itself. He smiled again, the boy

coming out. "We'll be okay. Listen! Just keep it from raining until about November, and we'll all have it made!"

In the car, driving back to the winery, Robert and Susan
made plans for the early phase of the harvest. Details remained to be worked out, but it would go smoothly, with
the smoothness of previous practice and planning. As they
neared Robert Mancini Vineyards, driving past fields
where other wineries had crews already out and picking the
crop, there was time briefly to revert to the Hendersons'
problem.

"I *hope* the harvest gets her off dead center and back
to living," Susan said. "She can't just go on forever, chasing
someone she can't hope to catch."

"It would be ironic," Robert replied, "if she did catch
him."

"That's impossible," Susan said emphatically. "Rod said
so."

They did not pursue the matter. Entering the winery, they
walked toward Robert's office, where their initial plans for
the work to begin on Monday would be hammered into a
work schedule.

At the door to his office, however, Nancy intercepted
them.

"There's someone to see you," she said. "I showed him
on into the office."

This was unusual. Robert looked sharply at her. "Who is
it?"

Nancy handed him a card. "He's Andrew Webb of the
FBI."

19

FBI agents, in Robert's imagination, were supposed to stand over six feet tall, be in the prime of their youth, and have physiques like that of tight ends in the NFL. Andrew Webb did not fit the pattern.

The man who turned from the gray windows to shake hands was in his fifties and gray-haired. If he had once been robust, time had shrunk him, and now his neat but inexpensive dark summer suit hung loosely on a lank frame. He wore bifocals, and the hand he extended had a tremor like that of palsy.

"Mr. Mancini?" he said politely. His handshake was firm and his demeanor quietly respectful as Robert introduced Susan.

"The girl gave you my card?" he asked.

"Yes. What can we do for you?"

"We're conducting an investigation in this area, sir, and I would like to have just a few minutes of your time."

Robert knew that it must relate to the bogus French wine scandal, although he was surprised that the FBI was involved. He turned to Susan. "We'll postpone the planning for a little while, Susan. I'll call you."

"Actually, sir," Webb interrupted, "I also wanted to visit with Miss Knight, and if we could talk together, the three of us, it might save time."

Susan appraised the agent with an expression that was

friendly but apprehensive. "Have I messed up my income tax again?"

Webb grinned. "Nothing like that, Miss Knight."

Robert suggested that they sit down. Webb and Susan took chairs facing the desk, and Robert moved behind it. He felt a keen curiosity as to what this was about.

"Now, then," he said.

Webb's hands showed their disconcerting tremor as he took a notebook from a black attaché case. "I imagine, Mr. Mancini, that you have some acquaintance with what the press had published about the French wine case that another agency opened in New Orleans not long ago."

"In a general way," Robert said.

"All right. Our discussion here is in confidence. Agreed?"

Robert nodded.

"Agreed," Susan said.

Webb ticked off a checkmark on the notebook page facing him. He was very deliberate and careful, a pro doing his job. "The investigation of one aspect of the case has moved into this area for a variety of reasons that I won't detail for you at this time. Several associates from the Bureau of Alcohol, Tobacco and Firearms are also working here. We're looking for the origin of part of the wine seized in New Orleans."

"Part?" Susan said.

Webb looked at her for a moment. "Much of it has already been traced to Chile, and arrests have been made there. Due to peculiarities in the case and our relations with Chile, that hasn't been announced yet."

Robert hid his surprise. "But some of it came from this area?"

"We have reason to believe so, yes. The labels were printed in South Bend, Indiana, and the glass is American manufacture. Characteristics of some of the red wines and some of the whites in the seized cargo are believed to be definitely California, and our experts believe they show earmarks of this particular section."

"Wouldn't anyone on the ship confess?" Susan asked.

"I doubt that more than one or two of them know where any of the wine came from. There were two transfers on the high seas. No, ma'am. I'm afraid we have to try to locate the source by investigating here."

"How is that possible?" Susan insisted. "I'm sure that anyone who had any ideas would have already reported it.

It's in our interests to maintain the integrity of our wines, you know."

Webb smiled. "That's a policy question, and a little out of my bailiwick. I'm here because the Bureau has reason to believe that we have a case of fraud across interstate lines, and there may be connections here with organized crime. That means I ask the questions. I don't make judgments on them."

Robert fished for a cigarette and found one. "What can we do to help?"

Webb frowned at his notes. "Have either of you observed, or heard of anyone else observing, large movements of bulk wine out of an inventory in any unusual manner?"

Both Robert and Susan shook their heads in the negative.

"Have either of you observed or heard of anyone else observing truck movements of any unusual type, especially, say, at night?"

Susan shook her head again.

"I'm afraid not," Robert said.

"Have any wineries closed their doors and liquidated stores of wine in an unusual manner, to your knowledge?"

"No," Susan said.

Robert thought fleetingly of Elmhurst and its cooperage. But of course that wine, poor stuff, was still in the cellars over there. So he shook his head *no*.

Webb did not seem disappointed. He continued through his list of questions. He wanted to know about bankruptcies or burglaries, and about unusual profits that might have been noticed. He asked a number of sharp questions about various methods of controlling and keeping records of inventories. Although he seemed to know a lot about the way bottles and corks were shipped into a winery, he asked more detailed questions about shipping procedures. He had a series of hypothetical questions about the likely vintage of a Cabernet that might recently have been bottled for quick sale.

As the questioning progressed, Robert quite forgot the agent's palsied tremor. The queries were sharp and to the point, never hurried. Robert could see the man drawing a complete picture of the problems that an illegal bottler would face, and ways he might use to get around them.

"Now," Webb said, several pages of notes later, "is there any unusual activity, rumor, or report of any nature that might bear on this matter which we haven't discussed, but which you might want to mention at this time? Understand that rumors are okay. No one is going to be accused. Not on that basis. We're looking for any and all leads we might find."

"I can't think of anything," Susan said, frowning.

"Nor can I," Robert said.

Webb closed his notebook and lifted his attaché case off the floor to his lap. "All right, thank you. Now, there's just one more matter." He appeared slightly embarrassed. "You understand that there's nothing we can afford to overlook, even if it seems a little far-fetched."

Robert met Susan's quizzical glance with one of his own.

Flushing slightly, Webb removed what was obviously a newspaper-wrapped bottle from the attaché case. "Every winemaker and expert we've spoken with has agreed that a discriminating palette can often identify wines. Would you say that's true?" He began unwrapping the newspaper from the bottle.

"It's true generally," Robert said, beginning to guess what was to come next. "But if you're thinking anyone could taste that illegal wine, and give you a guess as to where, specifically, it's from, I'd say the odds are on the order of a million to one against it."

Webb nodded soberly. "I'm sure that's true, Mr. Mancini. Still, my supervisors believe that winemakers do taste a lot of wines, including those of their competitors. If the wine *is* from this area, there's always a chance that someone might recognize it. I've even been told that there are people around this business who can taste a wine and give an educated guess as to the field it was grown in, the grapes, I mean." Webb allowed himself to show his skepticism of this sort of miracle.

"Your supervisor is right," Robert told him. "I have a fairly good tongue, but Miss Knight, here, has made identifications in blind tastings that would curl your hair."

Webb looked more interested as he struggled with a corkscrew. "I'll be interested in your reaction too, then, Miss Knight."

"Here," Robert said, gently taking the bottle from him to extract the cork before he demolished it.

He was interested in the wine he was opening. This was a bottle, with an obviously phony Bordeaux label, of the wine that had created furor in both the United States and France. And now he knew that the furor included Chile, too, land of those leathery red wines that one day might achieve status in the wine world. As he drew the cork, he was keenly aware of everything about it: initial bouquet, quality of the stopper itself, color as evident through the dark glass. He did not expect to recognize the wine, but the problem fascinated him.

Although Webb, true government agent prepared for anything, produced paper cups from his attaché case, Susan quietly took three wine glasses from the credenza behind Robert's desk, and it was into these that the wine was poured.

"You understand," Webb told them, "we're interested in any observations you might make." For the first time he produced a small cassette tape recorder and placed it, running, on the edge of the desk.

Robert handed Susan her glass, moved one nearer the edge for Webb, and lifted his own. He felt a slight pressure from the tape machine.

"The wine appears a little thin," he said, holding the glass to the light. "Somewhat off color, on the blue side. Susan?"

Susan frowned at her own glass. "If it's Cabernet, it's very early Cabernet. The bouquet—well, it lacks any bottle bouquet. It probably isn't older than a 1973 or 1974. It has a slight bite, rather acidy and immature. Unpleasant."

Neither of them had yet tasted the wine.

"I think it's a blend," Robert said thoughtfully. "Probably with a poor Zinfandel, and possibly some Petite Sirah. The Sirah might explain the bright color."

They tasted the wine.

As it touched Robert's tongue, and he let it slide back toward the rear of his mouth, there was a sharp, slightly bitter sensation. His impression of its being thin was more than justified, and there was another taste—very distinctive—a quality of sourness that might have come from soured oak. There was also an aftertaste, as if seeds had been crushed in the wine's making.

It was at this point that Robert's taste buds and memory coalesced in an instant that froze time. Something stirred and then stood up in his mind, and he was transported.

He was questioning Susan Knight after her visit to the Elmhurst winery. She was telling him that the red wine there was sour, thin . . . with the aftertaste of crushed seeds.

"If we buy the winery," Robert had said, *"the wine won't do us any good?"*

"It might be used in blending," Susan had suggested dubiously.

"If what you say is true, I doubt the blending possibility. Chances are that we would have to pour it out. The barrels must have soured."

This wine—Robert tasted it carefully again—was not precisely as Susan had described it then. Its chemistry had been subtly altered by a reblending. But it could not be mistaken; it fit her description too well.

He looked at Susan. She was staring back at him with great, shocked eyes. There was no question. Her expression betrayed the accuracy of his guess. *This was the Elmhurst wine.*

The implications were stunning. Jules had somehow dumped the Elmhurst wine—the very wine he had been so desperate to unload, and had even tried to sell here. He had somehow sold it to the people who planned the phony French wine transaction, and he must have known what he was getting into, at least in a general way, because the sale could not possibly have been made through legitimate channels.

Jules had done this.

He was the one these agents were after.

"Well," Webb said, placing his glass gently on the edge of the table virtually untouched, "do you have more remarks for the tape?"

Susan was still staring at Robert, perhaps uncertain, at least so shocked that she was waiting for his lead.

"It's pretty bad wine," Robert managed, clearing his throat. "I think that's about all we can say about it."

Webb turned to Susan. "Miss Knight?"

She started violently. "No. Nothing."

Webb turned off the tape recorder. "Well, then, do either of you have any theory of where generally this wine might have come from?"

"No," Robert said, making a decision under pressure. "It could be from around here, but I'd like to think it isn't."

Webb eyed him closely. "Would you like to elaborate on that, sir?"

Had he picked up the signs of pressure? Robert felt sweat on his face. "I just mean that it's poor. And we like to think the people here have more integrity."

The agent seemed to relax slightly. "Well, I suppose it's a long shot at best. Anything more, Miss Knight?"

"No," Susan said huskily.

The agent began collecting things. "I'll leave the remainder of the bottle for you to dispose of, if you will, sir. I have more. If you happen to think of anything later, you have my card. That number is for someone who can always contact me."

Robert stood stiffly, a smile that felt silly pasted on his face. "Of course we want to help any way we can. It seems like you have a pretty hopeless job here."

"Oh, we'll find them eventually," Webb said cheerfully, snapping the locks on his attaché case. "Someone will talk, or something new will turn up, or we'll just keep asking questions, and one day we'll run into someone who gives us a new lead."

Robert's mind was whirling. Somehow he got through the rest of it, and finally the agent shook hands again, and left the office.

Robert stood in the anteroom until he was sure the man had not only gotten onto the elevator, but had left it on the first floor.

Then he walked back into his office.

"Robert!" Susan said intensely. "Do you know what that wine *was?*"

"Elmhurst?"

"Yes! It's so distinctive, you recognized it from my description!"

"We could be wrong." Robert took her shoulders and grasped her tightly for added emphasis. "We didn't say anything to Webb, and we're not saying anything to anyone—*anyone*—*ever.*"

"But my God, Robert! After all the things he's done to *you?* This whole mess is his doing! He hates you! Now he's broken every law in the books—thrown a shadow of scandal over the whole industry—"

"We don't know," Robert told her. "We only suspect."

"*I* know! I—"

"Susan, I know a couple of things. I know that if that counterfeit Bordeaux were ever traced here, it would create a scandal that would set the whole California industry back for years. I know that if anyone *is* going to be caught, he's going to be ruined—finished. And *I'm* not going to be the one to bring that on anybody."

"And I know there's an old man named Gus Trello, and he's dying of cancer. I know what a blow like this would do to him. He doesn't deserve that. Whatever he may have done himself, he doesn't deserve this."

Susan stared at him with huge, mystified eyes. "What can we do, then? If you're right, can we just—say nothing?"

"That's *exactly* what we're going to do," Robert told her. "Nothing. All we have is a suspicion, no matter how sure we think we may be. I don't want to be any more certain. I don't want to know. We've got to keep quiet, to *everyone*."

"Are you *sure*?"

"Yes. Maybe he didn't really know what he was getting into. Maybe he did. Whatever the story is, old Gus doesn't deserve it. Even Carole doesn't deserve it. It's not our business. We keep quiet."

"All right," Susan said with a shudder. "I think we may be wrong. But—all right."

In a little while Robert was left alone with the astounding aftershocks of the discovery. He imagined Jules and the torment he must be going through. He remembered what the agent had said so very casually, with such great certainty: *"Oh, we'll find them eventually . . . One day we'll run into someone who gives us a new lead."*

20

For Jules Trello, however, time had run out regardless of Robert Mancini's decision.

By noon on Saturday, Johnelle Henderson was down to the last two names of her list of Corvette owners, and the name on top was that of Mrs. Jules Trello.

Pulling into the driveway in front of the sprawling Trello house, Johnelle had an impulse to turn around and leave at once. It was not the first time she had felt this, but it came more strongly now. She was out of her depth among the very rich. They would think her a fool. Like all the others on her crossed-off list, they might answer her questions, puzzled and finally angered that she could even ask them about their activities on the night of the accident.

Johnelle had come too far now, however, to turn back. With a sense of dread and nervousness, she pulled up in front of the huge house, got out, and walked onto the front porch. She pressed the door-chime button.

Two more names, she thought. Then she would have done everything she could imagine. She would be beaten. The real driver of the fatal Corvette, she had begun to be convinced, was probably in a place like San Francisco, far from any possibility of being located. It had been vain ever to imagine that luck would make the driver a local resident.

Although she intended to force herself through the last name on her now tiny list, she had begun to face the probability of failure, and its consequences. She had to put it out of her mind soon now. She had to try to live again. As the initial shock continued to fade, she had also begun to realize how bizarre the entire search had been, how strangely motivated. But only the effort of searching had purged her, allowing her now to face the fact of never knowing.

The door opened. A black maid peered out at her. "Yes?"

"Is Mrs. Trello home, please?" Johnelle asked.

The maid's eyes were hostile. "Who is calling, please?"

"My name is Johnelle Henderson."

"One moment, please," the maid began, "and I'll see—"

She got no farther. A shadow moved behind her in the hall, and a striking blond woman—Carole Trello—appeared beside her. "I'll handle this," Carole said.

The maid nodded and went away.

Carole Trello wore a tiny pink swimsuit that revealed all the contours of her lush, deeply tanned body. She had a highball glass in one hand and a cigarette in the other. "Yes?"

"My name is Johnelle Henderson," Johnelle repeated. "I'm investigating an accident, and if you would answer a few questions for me it might be very helpful."

Ordinarily, it was necessary at this point to reveal that the accident had killed her son. Then, under the guise of asking the Corvette owner about other such owners of their acquaintance, Johnelle managed to learn what the interviewee had been doing on the night in question. It was not always possible after such an interview to verify the suspect's story, but in a surprising number of cases it was— it was amazing how seldom people seemed to be alone for extended periods—and in the unverifiable situations, Johnelle had to be content with her intuitive reading of the person's veracity because it was the best thing she had.

Carole Trello, however, did not ask the usual questions about what accident it might have been, or why Johnelle was asking questions. She looked at Johnelle with a gaze so piercing, so loaded with some deep feeling, that something profoundly primitive was stirred in Johnelle's heart. *My God,* she thought.

"Come in," Carole said.

Feeling weak, Johnelle followed her into the living room. It was, she noticed vaguely, so expensive and large that ordinarily she would have felt overwhelmed and subdued by it. Now, however, she could only concentrate on the beautiful woman who sat opposite her on the couch.

"An accident?" Carole said, and quickly downed a heavy portion of her drink.

"My son was killed," Johnelle said. "On a motorcycle."

"How did you find me?"

The shock was so severe that Johnelle's vision blurred. "Find you?"

"How did you identify me?" Carole Trello's face twisted. "It was an accident! You have to believe that! I didn't know what I was doing, running away. But it was his fault. He swerved right in front of me!"

Johnelle was aware of the beating of her heart, like an engine running wild, about to explode. Staring at this rich, beautiful woman—here in her costly house—she felt a wave of nausea followed quickly by a burst of hate that became almost instantaneously something else—a kind of awe and disbelief.

This was the end of the quest, the moment she had dreamed of, driven herself in hopes of experiencing.

It was nothing like she had imagined. She could not identify how she did feel, but it was not anything like the emotions she had expected.

"You should have stopped," she heard herself say huskily. "You should have tried to help."

Tears appeared in Carole Trello's large eyes and streamed down her face, dropping onto her bare brown thighs. The tears flooded out of her, and yet she made no sound, did not so much as tremble.

"I'm sorry," she said. "I wanted to stop. I was afraid. I'm so sorry."

"He was just a little boy."

"I know that. Oh, Jesus, don't you know I *know* that?"

It was nothing like the dreamed-of consummation. Johnelle found that she could not look at this woman with genuine hate. Horror, yes. And some revulsion. But she was amazed that another emotion was stirred, too: a deep pity.

She tried to deny this. Her voice, as she heard it, cracked with tension and bitterness. "You're going to be arrested. You're going to be punished for what you did."

Carole Trello twisted her hands together, rocking forward and backward in a paroxysm of despair. "I was driving, and I had been going fast, but I wasn't going very fast then, I swear it. His lights were so dim—how could anyone see those dim lights? And he was on the pavement, not the shoulder, like the newspapers said. And he swerved out. I tried to miss him but it was too late—I just brushed him, for a second I think I thought he was all right, and then I saw him in the mirror and I was going on and I was so scared, just too *scared*." She drew a shuddering breath as the tears continued to stream, destroying her face. "I fixed the car. I read about how he died. I wanted to call—to say I did it. But I didn't. And then every night I go to bed and I think about it, see that tiny little red light on the back of his cycle, and feel that brush, when we touched, and he's dead, I know he's dead, I did it but I didn't mean to, and what can I do? What can I *do?*"

It was all wrong, Johnelle realized with new horror. Whatever this woman might be and whatever she might have done, Johnelle could only see that her grief and pain were exquisite. It should not be this way. The death driver should be cruel, thoughtless . . . and then it would have been so easy.

Johnelle said slowly, struggling for the words, "I have to tell the sheriff. You have to pay. I've looked and looked for you. You have to be *known*."

"Please don't tell them!"

"I must," Johnelle said, astonished that an option could even be imagined.

With an awful, grotesque movement, Carole Trello threw herself onto her knees in front of Johnelle. She raised her tear-streaked face, plucking with icy fingers at Johnelle's skirt. "Please! Please! Just let me—" She hesitated, then clutched more frantically—"please just let me do it myself! Will you do that much? Just let me go in on my own—admit it!"

"But *I* have to go tell them," Johnelle said without thought.

"Why? Why? Why can't I go admit it? Why can't I be left that much?"

It was on the tip of Johnelle's tongue to say, *Because this is the way I imagined it*. This amazed her. Nothing was as she had imagined it. Why should this be?

She said slowly, "You'll go in to the sheriff's office? Now? Admit it?"

"I'll call my husband. I have to have him go with me."

"And then you'll go? And tell them everything?"

"Yes! I swear to God! Yes!"

It crossed Johnelle's mind that there might be a trick. But then she recoiled from this possibility because there could be no trick. She had found her quarry. There was no mistake. There was no way out for Carole Trello. What difference did it make how the truth came out?

"I'll wait until six o'clock tonight," Johnelle heard herself say. "They'll call me to tell me when you turn yourself in." Then, amazed at herself, she added, "Will that be enough time?"

"Yes!" Carole Trello sobbed. She fumbled with Johnelle's hands, wet now with tears, trying horribly to kiss them. "Thank you! Thank you!"

Shuddering, Johnelle pulled away. "Six o'clock, then," she said, and bolted blindly for the front door.

Carole Trello remained crumpled on the floor in front of the couch. Her eyes were closed and she was racked by new sobs. She heard the car start and drive away, and she realized that there was a mad similarity between this experience and the one the very night when Robert Mancini had driven away, and then she had gone to the car, and driven fast, and seen the motorcycle and driver too late.

She managed to get herself to her feet. She had to think now. She had to call Jules. The hiding was over and she was lost. He had to help her.

Going to the telephone, she realized how deathly still the house had become. If her maid had heard any of it, she was staying silently back out of sight, perhaps listening now with acute, wise and hating eyes. The maid had always hated her. The maid would be secretly pleased.

Trembling violently, Carole called the winery. The switchboard said Jules was in a meeting. Carole screamed that it was an emergency. Jules responded quickly when the operator evidently told him how his wife sounded.

"What happened?" he asked tautly.

"Oh, Jesus, support me this time, Jules. Be my husband, *please,* darling—"

"Carole! What are you hysterical about? What happened?"

"They know, Jules. About the accident. The boy's mother was just here. She knows everything. I have to go turn myself in—"

"Wait a minute! Wait a minute! Christ! What are you talking about?"

"Come *home!*" Carole wailed. "I need you! I've been caught!"

There was the slightest pause, and then Jules said thickly, "I'll be there in twenty minutes."

He was there in ten.

Carole rose silently from the couch as he rushed into the room. He looked wild—hair on end, eyes wide, mouth agape.

"What happened?" he demanded. "Who was here? What did you admit?"

Carole sobbed and tried to move into his arms. "It was horrible. The boy's mother—"

Jules shoved her roughly away from him. "Talk sense, God damn it!"

Carole choked for air and managed to tell him what had taken place. As she did so, Jules began pacing, periodically tugging at his own hair in sheer frustration.

"You were stupid!" he said finally. "They didn't have any proof and then you confessed! You were an idiot!"

"I had to! She knew it anyway!"

"But she had no proof, you dumb whore! Now—Jesus Christ, what can we do . . . I have to think of something—"

"I'm going in, like I promised," Carole said. "I'm going to confess."

"And ruin my reputation?" Jules replied. "Have everyone know I'm married to a drunken cow?"

"Yes!" Carole screamed back at him. "And you're going with me—you're going to stand by me—"

"That would mean admitting I *knew* about it! Are you crazy? If you go in, you go in alone! Oh, I'll hire lawyers . . . Jesus, I think you still might be able to beat it, or get off with a suspended sentence . . ."

But his rejection had sprung something loose inside Carole. She realized only an instant before she spoke that she was going to have her husband with her this time . . . this one time. Because she had a weapon, and knew in the moment that she was willing to use it if she must.

"You'll go with me," she said, a strange sense of calm descending over her.

"Never!"

"You will," Carole told him. "Because I know about that woman, Connie Livingston. I also know about the letter she brought. I know what the letter *meant.*"

Jules turned to her. "What is it . . . you think you know?"

"The letter said to keep still. I wondered about what, but I figured it out. It's the Elmhurst wine. All that work," she went on, seeing the impact of her words on his expression, "all those nights at Elmhurst. I didn't understand it. But then I realized all of it. You sold that wine, and it was the wine they confiscated in New Orleans, and Connie Livingston works for the man you sold it to, and he was telling you to be quiet."

"You're crazy," he said, dodging her eyes. "You don't know what you're talking about."

"I *know!*" she flung back at him. "And I know you fucked her in Chicago—fucked her and fucked her when you never make love to me, you say you can't, and now you're going into the city with me, Jules, because if you don't, if you don't stand by me, I'll tell everything!"

Jules took two steps toward her. She expected to be hit. Her insides cringing, she somehow found a strength she had not known existed in her: she faced him without flinching.

His eyes, red-rimmed, seethed. But he did not raise his hand—and this, in a way, was more terrifying than a blow.

"All right," he said softly. "I'll go to the city with you."

"Yes," she said, and assayed a smile. "Baby—"

"And I want you to understand that you're right about Connie, too," Jules added in the same quiet, venom-filled tone.

"I know as much as I want to know."

He held her with his eyes, and they were hungry for her pain. "I did fuck her. We came together every time. She's more of a woman than you ever dreamed of being. I don't have a problem. You're the problem. You always have been."

"No," she whispered.

"Go get dressed," he told her in the same voice, his eyes now gone dead to her. "I'll go with you. I'll pay your price. But don't ever expect me to touch you or talk to you or have anything to do with you again."

It was too much. Carole felt her strength breaking. She reached out her hand. "Daddy—"

"Get ready," Jules said, turning away from her, and adding with an infinite scorn, "cunt."

Carole walked out of the room. Her legs were without feeling. Was she weeping? She did not know. Where was the maid? It did not matter. Everything was blurred, disintegrated. She did not know how she got up the stairs.

Her own bedroom. Like a zombie she stripped off the swimsuit. Its two pieces fell to the carpet. She had thought he would like the suit. She had imagined this scene, her removing it, he responding . . .

She stumbled into the bathroom and confronted herself in the large mirror. The brilliant lights on either side of the mirror showed her the havoc of her face, and the cruelty of the brilliance showed, too, the lines of age beginning to encroach around her eyes, her mouth. As she stared in a moment of utter despairing objectivity, it seemed that more years extended before her, stripping the last of her beauty, and she saw the bone structure beneath the skin.

She stared at the skull of her face and saw her own death.

She had been caught. She had revealed her secret to Jules—had used her ultimate weapon. His hate for her was fully revealed. There was nothing ahead but the revelations, the scandal, the hate, the aging, and being alone.

She was crying again as she rummaged through drawers of the bathroom, searching. She knew what she had to do. It was so difficult. She first found an electric shaver, but that was no good at all. Her regular razor was a Trac II. She felt a few seconds of hysterical amusement as she thought what a terrible thing it was for suicides, this Trac II blade with no real exposed edges.

Kneeling in front of the bottom cabinet, she removed several unused bottles of bubble bath, placing them on the tile to get at the back of the shelves. There was a real safety razor somewhere, she knew it. She rummaged, a little portion of her consciousness flitting about some of the vain fantasies she had harbored once about the large, ornate glass jars of bubble bath . . . bathing with Jules, bathing with Robert . . . with some other man who could make her feel *whole*.

She found the old safety razor. She opened it and there was an old two-edged blade inside, rusty, with hair stubble and petrified lather clinging to the edges.

She stood, her vision clearing, her entire body going cold. She held the flimsy blade between the fingers of her right hand and poised it over her left wrist. It was such an awkward thing to do. It would hurt. She was afraid.

Taking a breath, she stabbed at the inside of her wrist with the blade. The blade bit but slid off. Blood oozed from the nick. It hurt. The pain maddened her. She slashed again, again hesitating, making only one ugly gash that seemed hardly to bleed at all. She gritted her teeth so hard they made cracking sounds and prayed to God and slashed again, truly slashing, and deeply.

Red fountained out of a wound that opened under the keen edge like a laughing mouth. The blood splashed onto the basin and the tile and the fronts of the cabinets and her legs. It was hot on her legs.

Sobbing, she transferred the blade and slashed well into her right wrist. More blood spurted.

Dropping the blade, she turned and fell against the bathtub. Red shot everywhere. It was hideous, it was making such a mess. She swung her gaping wrists over the tub and let them dangle out of sight. She caught a glimpse of gushing red against white porcelain, but then she squeezed her eyes shut and collapsed against the tub, kicking over several of the bottles of bubble bath, shattering them.

Downstairs, Jules heard the shattering of glass. He cursed and went on mixing a drink. But then some instinct warned him. He put down the glass and ran for the steps.

He thought she would be having a tantrum, hurling things.

"Carole?" he called angrily, walking into her bedroom.

There was no sound. He walked to the bathroom door. It was closed. He listened. There was no movement on the other side.

"Carole?"

With no response, his concern suddenly magnified a thousand times. He shoved against the door. Something blocked it. He shoved harder and the object moved enough to let him stick his head through the crack.

The thing that had blocked the door was Carole's nude left leg. She was collapsed over the side of the tub, and the interior was splashed red everywhere.

"Jesus Christ!" Jules screamed, hurling the door open.

He fell to his knees beside her, grabbing her into his arms. Her eyes remained closed. Her arms flopped horribly, splashing blood all over his face. He stretched her out on the floor, and he was screaming, and he grabbed the nearest thing—a towel—and tried to press it against one of her gashed wrists. It soaked in an instant.

Memory stirred from somewhere, and he moved the towel, wrapping it around her arm. Sobbing, he twisted it tight and cast around for something—anything—to use for leverage. There was a brush set on the counter. He thrust the handle of the brush into the knot he had made and twisted it around and around, violently, squeezing her arm. The flow of blood from this wrist slowed and almost stopped, and still shouting he knew not what, he began frenziedly tying another towel on the remaining arm.

The black maid appeared in the doorway and cried out.

"Call the hospital," Jules choked, using the brush handle for a second lever. "Tell them I'm coming. Call the patrol and tell them to meet me—give me an escort."

The maid leaned weakly against the door facing, her eyes glazed.

"Move!" Jules screamed at her. "Run! Do what I tell you!"

She responded then, rushing out of the bedroom. Jules, choked by his own sobs of fear, scooped his nude wife up in his arms and ran with her down the stairs and out of the house to the car.

21

At four-fifteen, Jules called the Henderson home. Johnelle Henderson answered.

"This is Jules Trello. May I come by to talk with you and your husband?"

"Mr. Trello?" Johnelle sounded puzzled and wary. "About—?"

"About my wife. About the accident."

There was a pause, then Johnelle said quietly, "We're at home."

"I'll be there in just a few minutes."

Jules drove with extreme caution on the way north from the city to the Henderson vineyard. His nervous system had been taken beyond its limits, and only the most strenuous self-control kept the shaking in check. The mental image of the blood, and the feel of Carole's seemingly lifeless body, nude in his arms, kept coming back over him in waves of sickness.

Partway to the vineyard, he was passed by a sheriff's car going very fast. He watched it rocket on out of sight over a distant rise in the highway. Another accident, he thought dully. More death.

He had to salvage whatever he could now. It was in his hands, and the try had to be made. It might be too late to prevent scandal. But all his life he had been confronted by situations apt to destroy him; he had never given up and he would not give up now.

He felt strangely at peace, without real feeling, as he turned off the road to the Henderson vineyard. He even noticed with a kind of automatic caring that the grapes in their field looked good, and would be a fine addition next year when the contract came into force. The planning, corner-cutting portion of his brain even tried to calculate what sort of prices he would be paying a year hence. He realized this train of thought consciously, and felt a wave of self-hatred.

The Henderson car was parked by the house and no other was in view. A few pigeons fluttered from the sparse, parched lawn to the flat roof as he slammed his car door and walked to the front porch.

Ned Henderson, his forehead furrowed with concern, opened the door and invited him in. It was a small living room. Johnelle sat on the couch, very pale. A free-standing divider closed off the view into the kitchen. It was quiet as Ned Henderson indicated a chair for Jules, and went to sit at his wife's side.

Jules locked his hands in front of his knees. "My wife tried to kill herself this afternoon."

Ned Henderson flinched.

"She cut her wrists with an old razor blade," Jules said, surprised at how small and controlled his own voice sounded in the quiet room. "I took her to the hospital. They gave her a lot of blood. She'll be all right now. They have her asleep." He felt tears on his face.

"Mr. Trello," Ned Henderson said slowly, "Johnelle told me what happened . . . earlier today, I mean. We didn't expect this. I'm sorry."

Johnelle said fervently, "We're both very sorry."

As shaken as he was, Jules saw, with that careful part of his mind, that he had their sympathy. His cunning whispered that this would help, perhaps greatly. It was as if he was watching himself perform.

He said, "Carole can't turn herself in now."

The Hendersons stared mutely.

"I know," Jules resumed, "that nothing can ever make up for the loss of your son. Nothing can ever compensate you."

"We had to know who did it," Johnelle said.

Jules stared at his hands, still stained under the nails by blood. "I'm here to ask you to let me try to make amends in the only way I know. It's very little. It's the only thing I know to offer. I want to try to—to indemnify, in some way."

Ned Henderson frowned. "Indemnify?"

"I know it doesn't really help," Jules said. A part of him shattered, meant this more than anything he had ever said in his life. The other part, untouched, applauded his cunning. "I want to pay you. I want to give you twenty thousand dollars."

"That won't help," Henderson said hotly.

"I know it won't help. I just want to give it to you. It's a way of saying how really, really sorry both Carole and I are. I want to give you the money in cash. It will . . . help you. You can pay off a lot of things. You can . . . try to get your feet back on the ground. It's the only thing we can really do now, don't you see? We want to do it to try to make up for some of our guilt!"

Bravo! a part of him said: *no one could ever say it's a bribe!* And at the same time, the rest of him meant it sincerely, precisely as he was saying it, with no strings attached . . . as a way of expiation, even of trying to help the wife who had almost killed herself, and in so doing had stunned him with the knowledge that he did not want life without her.

He added hoarsely, "Please let us give this to you."

"We can't take your money!"

"Make it a trade," Jules said, "if it would make you feel any better. Consider it a bargain."

Both the Hendersons looked at him, and then their eyes changed as they began to understand.

"But she has to admit it," Johnelle said. "Or we have to tell it. You do see that."

"Hasn't she suffered enough?" Jules countered. "What can arresting her, dragging her through a trial, possibly accomplish? She almost died today!"

Ned Henderson balled his fists. "Our boy *did* die!"

"Let us give you this money," Jules pleaded. "It's all we can do. No one has to know—not about the money, not about the wreck. Carole will never be the same. If she were to go to trial, it would probably be a suspended sentence anyway, and why put her through all that? Let me give you this money. It will make so many things so much easier for you. And let my wife live with her guilt."

"A bribe, in other words," Ned Henderson said angrily.

Johnelle put a hand on his knee. "Ned."

"No. That's what it is, isn't it, Mr. Trello? You pay us the money, and we keep quiet?"

"It's not a bribe," Jules insisted. "It's just the best way of settling the matter for all of us. I know it may sound harsh, but I beg you to think about it. It's best for everyone!"

"How could you even think we would consider it?"

Jules stared at them, and his nerves were so shredded, they looked so earnest and vulnerable, that he was sincerely and deeply touched again. He felt a tear slide down his cheek. There was no act in the crying; he was on a very ragged edge and not wholly in control. But he also knew that the tear wouldn't hurt, once it had happened.

"The money is yours," he said thickly.

"Our silence in exchange?"

"Call it," Jules said, remembering something his father had often said, "a *quid pro quo.*"

"But it *is* a bargain—a bribe," Henderson snapped.

"If you want to call it that, yes. Call it what you want. I'm here to protect Carole. I'm here to try to help you."

Ned Henderson put his palms on his knees and straightened up. He glanced at his wife, who appeared frightened. "I think that should be enough," he said. He paused and raised his voice. "Rod?"

There was movement at the edge of the divider between the living room and kitchen. A deputy sheriff, his face a study in grimness, walked into the room.

"I'm sorry," Ned Henderson told the shocked Jules. "We thought it might be something like this. We didn't know about your wife—but we just thought it might be something like you've just done. So we prepared for it."

Jules stood, the massive nature of his calamity beginning to dawn.

"I'm sorry," Johnelle Henderson told him soberly. "I really am."

"I was—trying to help," Jules said. "Trying to—make amends."

Ned Henderson bunched his lips and slowly shook his head.

Jules turned in mounting panic to the deputy. "It certainly wasn't a bribe—not anything like that!"

Rod Poole took his arm. "Mr. Trello, I'm sorry to say that I'm taking you downtown."

22

Knowing that Robert Mancini would be thrown completely off his stride by the headlines in Sunday morning's newspaper, Barbara Turner called him at once.

"You've seen it?" she asked at once.

His voice sounded hollow. "Yes."

"Bob, if you want to call off our drive to the hills today, I'll certainly understand."

"No," he said, his voice firmer, although evidence of his numbed state was still clear enough. "There's nothing I can do, really. I'll pick you and Jimmy up at ten, just as we planned."

"You're sure?"

"Yes. I'll want to go by the winery. Alfredo Rodriques is out of the hospital, and he asked if he could meet me there to pick up a copy of the agreement. I might try to call old Gus, too . . . I don't know about that. I have to think about that. But I think we should go ahead with our plans."

Troubled, Barbara nevertheless agreed. She did not expect it to be the happy occasion they had tried to plan it to be. She knew Robert well enough to understand that he could not take a light view of Jules Trello's disgrace, no matter how strained their relationship might have been.

The newspaper had all of it: the hit-run story, Carole Trello's attempted suicide, Jules's attempt to give the Hendersons money. Jules had already been charged with attempted obstruction of justice as well as being an accessory

554

after the fact of Carole's charge, likely to be manslaughter. Jules was free on bond. Carole, the story said, would be released by the hospital on Monday and charged at that time.

The ugliness of the situation affected Barbara herself, but her training as a journalist, as well as her comparative remoteness from Jules, allowed her to handle it emotionally. She knew that Robert would be much harder hit.

It came as a special kind of irritation, then, when Jimmy announced that he had no intention of accompanying them on the trip to the hillside vineyard.

"But Bob is counting on you to go!" Barbara protested.

Jimmy was on one of his sullen streaks. "I want to go skating." He refused to look at her.

"I want you to go with us."

"Are you going to force me to?"

"No," she snapped angrily now. "A man Bob knew very well is the one in that big mess all over the front page. Bob will need people around him today who can act cheerful. If you're going to act like a little brat instead of a man, *go* skating!"

It was a very sharp exchange for them, perhaps the sharpest she had ever spoken to him. He appeared startled, but if he wavered, he did not act upon any change of heart. He left the house silently, and when Robert arrived a little before ten, Barbara had to tell him that her son had elected another way to spend the day.

Robert looked haggard. His jaw set at the news. He nodded. "You still want to go?"

"Of course," she told him. "If *you* do."

They went to his car and drove in almost total silence to the winery. Up and down the roads, crews were harvesting. It was cool again today, and cloudy. A few stray raindrops hit the windshield on the way, but not enough to require the wipers.

"Will your crews be out tomorrow?" she asked at one point.

"In some fields," he said. "Not near the buildings."

"How much longer will you wait?"

"Another week, perhaps ten days."

"Is that a big risk, with the weather this way?"

"Of course," he said, as if surprised she had to ask.

Barbara lapsed into silence again after that. To him, she saw, all the crucial parts of making wine were inextricably bound up with risk. The vines were planted at risk, grown at risk, matured at risk. Even if all went well, there was never a way to know what small changes would take place in hugely complex molecules even after fermentation was completed, and the wine rested in the darkness of oak. Seen in this way, Robert's sales of stocks over the years to provide additional operating capital was only another risk like all the others. He had always lived with uncertainty, knowing he might lose the next time.

In this, Barbara thought, there was a bond between him and men like Jules Trello. Whatever Jules had done, or tried to do—however deep Jules's hate might run—they understood each other at this level. It might explain in part why news of Jules's disaster had so dampened Robert's mood.

Another aspect of Robert's feelings was revealed shortly after they arrived at the vineyards. They found Alfredo Rodriques waiting for them alone in a Volkswagen, the lone car in the sprawling, tree-shaded parking lot. Rodriques looked paler than usual, but more relaxed. They talked for a few minutes about the weather and the harvest.

Then Rodriques said guardedly, "Jules Trello, I see, has trouble with the law."

"Yes," Robert said.

"You take no pleasure from this," Rodriques observed.

"I don't like to see anyone in that kind of trouble. Jules and I were members of the same family for a long time."

"Yes," Rodriques said. "The family of August Trello."

"I hate this for that old man."

"He has not been a kind man. I happen to know that he has not tried to help you in your own present difficulties. He is often selfish."

Robert looked quickly at Rodriques, squinting as if trying to read the expression that went with the words. "Gus is also a great man."

Rodriques sighed. "Yes. In his way."

"I'll get your copy of the agreement."

While Robert was getting the paper, Barbara remained with Rodriques on the front steps of the main building. She congratulated him on the progress his union had made. He smiled sadly and told her that it was a struggle that would not be ended for many years, and would yet hold suffering for many persons on both sides.

"Is it worth it?" she asked bluntly.

"Of course," he said. His expression very much resembled the one Robert had given her when she asked about risk.

At this point Robert returned with the agreement copy.

Rodriques took it and put it in a pocket. He studied Robert's face. "You have talked with Jules this morning?"

Robert shook his head. "There's no way I can approach him. He would interpret it as gloating. All I can do is stay away."

Rodriques sighed. "Yes. It is so." He extended his hand. "I will talk to you soon, Mr. Mancini."

Barbara stood at Robert's side while they watched the Volkswagen trundle down the driveway and move south, out of sight, on the highway.

"Do you mind waiting just another few minutes?" Robert asked her then. "I really think I'd better call Gus."

"I'll wait here," Barbara told him.

Robert again went into the deserted building.

Waiting, Barbara mulled the problem of Jules Trello, and the tangled ways it related to Robert, and to a dying old man in the south. She wondered—knowing Robert's earlier suspicions of some links between them—what the reaction of John Endicott and E. Z. Simms would be to Jules's downfall.

Watching the clouds move overhead, she thought again, as she often had, about Robert's dilemma with Timmons Corporation. As she did so on this occasion, a new thought occurred to her.

She paused and examined it.

It was, on the surface, outlandish. But she would do anything in her power to help this man now.

Was there really any chance her idea might actually succeed, and change the course of events?

She was still thinking about it when Robert came back, looking no happier.

"Did you get through to him?" she asked.

"No, I talked to Frank. They haven't told him yet. They'll have to. Frank says," Robert added, displeasure in his voice, "that Gus seems no better and no worse. Frank says the news will be a shock, but it won't hurt him any."

"Frank sounds like he would make a wonderful robot."

Robert stared into the cloudy distance a moment, then seemed to remember their plans today. He made an evident effort to shake his mood, smiling at her. "Let's head for the hills and try to talk about something else."

Every instinct in Barbara's personality motivated her to make the drive pleasant for him. She chattered about everything imaginable, and by the time they drove out of a brief little rainshower on the way up the dirt road to the highest elevations, it seemed that she had begun to succeed. Her new idea was still in the back of her mind, being examined. For now, however, her job was to cheer Robert up.

Robert's motives, if Barbara could have known them, were remarkably similar. On the drive north, and then into the mountains, he reminded himself that he had already given her sufficient burdens. Jules's situation, atop everything else, had shaken him. He felt a little depressed that Jimmy had refused to come along, and knew that it had probably been more a revolt than Barbara had been willing to admit. Now, however, was the time to put trouble out of mind for a while if that was possible.

They neared the forty-acre vineyard. Robert drove slowly the last half mile because the road was little more than a track scoured out by a bulldozer to allow the planting trucks in a few years earlier. The Korday vehicles, here recently for picking, had knocked down brush and weeds, but the going was still rough. For the last hundred yards or so, he had to drop the car's transmission selector in the *L* range.

The car emerged from the brush-lined pathway onto an open grassy area near trees. The ground sloped very sharply from left to right, so that Robert had difficulty getting his door to stand open against gravity long enough for him to climb out. He walked around the car and helped Barbara out. She smiled, the slight, moist wind moving her hair.

"It's warmer up here!" she said.

Robert took her hand and walked with her into the vineyard, which rolled uphill away from them.

The crumbled earth was not soggy, but the light rain that had fallen earlier had darkened the soil and made it adhere to their shoes. Moisture clung in glistening beads to broad leaves of the young vines. Footprints and tractor marks crisscrossed the ground, and the vines, although they had been carefully picked, appeared depleted and somehow diminished with stems broken and hanging limply here and there.

Robert examined some of the vines, then raised his eyes over the rough landscape. Studded with boulders, it rolled to his right into a small decline, then vaulted lumpily upward to a horizon high against the misty, shifting sky. To the left, more broken rock jutted between the vines, and farther off to one side the hill ran downward steeply into grass and then the end of the cleared area, where pines stood silent, shady.

"I know a vineyard exists to be picked," Robert admitted, "but it always strikes me as just a little sad to visit at this time."

Barbara gave him a puzzled smile. "Sad?"

"The vines look so much smaller—more vulnerable. Without the fruit they aren't the same. They look . . ." He groped for a word.

"Ravished," she said.

"Yes." He turned to her with surprise. "You understand that, too."

Shading her eyes with a cupped hand, she looked over the vineyard. "Yes. Very well."

"When the vines are older, it's different. They're gnarled and tough. They're like old fighters, showing their scars. It isn't so evident then, the picking."

"We'll see this vineyard get old like that."

The thought gladdened him. "Do you like this vineyard?"

"I love it."

He led her deeper into the field. The faint, rich odors of earth and leaves enveloped them. On the ground were a few fallen grapes. He tasted them and let her taste, too. They walked on, downhill now, toward the stand of pines and grass.

Robert pointed it out for her. "We can grade a good road up this far. You see?" He pointed to the distant car. "The road can come right up the edge of the vineyard to this spot." He hesitated, knowing both the joy and sadness, of the next statement, but then he said it: "We can build a home here."

Barbara moved away from him, walking closer to the pine grove.

He followed her, saying, "The drive to town won't be so bad."

She turned to him, her eyes betraying messages that were not in her words. "And will we have a tractor?"

"If you want a tractor, we'll have two. Do you have a weakness for tractors, lady?"

"I might have a weakness for a man on a tractor."

He took her into his arms and squeezed tight, filled with a feeling that he wanted to press his love through her very skin and inside her. She clung, returning her own strength.

"We won't exactly be poor, you know," he told her.

"I know," she whispered.

"It won't be hard to find a buyer for the house below. I've already had some feelers about it . . . since the divorce story was in the paper. And as soon as I sell my stock—"

"Don't say that yet! You haven't lost yet!"

"We have to face it, lady. The chances are very good that I will."

She broke away from him and moved in among the pines, her hips moving with natural grace. "It will be a lovely place for a house."

Robert followed her again, going purposefully to a place where a slab of volcanic rock jutted out of the needle-softened earth. He made a conscious effort to be light-hearted.

"The living room," he said, standing on the slab. He pointed toward the vineyard and the uphill slope to the sky. "And this will be our front-window view."

Barbara turned all the way around, looking back into the trees. "And we'll have woods behind us, and off to this side we can look down the mountain."

"In the winter you can see the valley floor from here."

"Jimmy will love it up here."

"I wish he had come."

"He'll come the next time."

They were both silent for a little while, trying to get over the dimming effect of her son and his continued reluctance to accept things as they had become.

Robert made a more strenuous effort after the silence had gone on too long. "Jimmy," he said, "will work his tail off."

"Yes!"

"He has to learn how to plant, how to treat diseases of the vines, the way to read the grapes and know what they need next."

"He'll be a fiend for work!"

Robert nodded. "I think we need to start making plans for this house right away."

"All right," she said, turning around again. "The driveway will come up this way?"

So it would be a game. "Yes," he said. "With the garage on that side over there."

"Can we put the garage in without digging up trees?"

"Oh, I think so."

"Good, then. And will we have flowers in front?"

"If you plant them, lady."

"I'll plant them. And in the back we can have shade-loving things. And window boxes. Would window boxes be too corny?"

"Window boxes would be ideal."

"I'm not the most domestic thing in the world, you know. I might forget to water my window boxes."

"Jimmy can do it. He has free time between three and four in the morning."

She laughed. "Perfect!"

"Poor Jimmy," Robert said. "This will teach him not to stay home."

She walked closer to him, suddenly serious. "Bob?"

"Yes?"

"If we do . . . move here. If you have to give up the winery. Please don't get bitter."

"I won't."

"Do you promise?"

"Promise!"

She smiled briefly and turned to walk away from him again, turning this way and that, hands behind her back like a young girl promenading. Aware that he was watching, she stopped a dozen paces away from him and pointed to the ground she stood on. "What is this?"

He understood. "Well, I'm not sure. How about the kitchen?"

"Yes," she said, savoring the word. "The kitchen."

Watching him, she moved again, a little farther away. Against the background of the woods she was very beautiful, and he felt a lump start in his throat.

"Now?" she asked, stopping again, teasing him.

"A bedroom," he said.

"Ours?"

"I don't think so. I think ours would be . . . let me think . . ."

"All right," she said, moving slightly nearer some of the trees, into a little hollowed-out spot between two pines, where the carpet of needles was brownish green and very deep. "More over here, then."

"Yes," he told her.

"With the fine back view."

"Yes."

Her eyes changed then. "And will you make love to me in this bedroom?"

"I certainly hope so."

"I didn't mean *then*," she said.

He watched her.

She said, "I mean now."

The rush of desire constricted his throat, but he felt compelled to make a joke of it. "Don't you worry about the neighbors?"

"I've closed the curtains," she told him. Then she reached to her hip and snicked a zipper. She stepped out of the skirt. She wore no slip and her fine legs gleamed as she kicked off her shoes, bent briefly, laid the skirt out carefully on the pine needles.

"You see?" she said. "I've turned down the bed."

With a single movement, her eyes not leaving his face, she slipped her panties down off her legs and stepped out of them. She crouched, then reclined on the skirt, one leg bent.

"Of course," she called to him, "you might be such an old poop that you prefer staying over there in the living room by yourself, watching TV. *Do* you"—and here her breath caught—"watch a lot of late TV?"

He walked over to her. He knelt beside her, touching her thigh, marveling at the texture of her skin. She breathed sharply, her hips moving ever so slightly in a convulsive response.

"No TV," he said.

Her hands flew to her blouse, opening it to him. He stretched beside her and their legs intertwined. She squeezed him with a fierce passion as their mouths joined. Then she broke away, pulling back.

"Did you turn off that stupid TV?" she whispered in his ear, her tongue darting. "Did you lock the front door? Did you put the cat out? Did you remember to take out the trash? Did you—" She gasped as he moved over her, and entered.

23

It was well after dark as Robert Mancini drove back to his home on the hillside that night, and he was startled to see lights behind the glass foyer windows. He knew he had left only the security lights set, as usual, to come on with dusk.

Depressed about the charges against Jules and Carole Trello, profoundly worried about the fate of the winery, and nagged by all the other tatters of lives that seemed to be tugging about him, he had approached his house nevertheless with a sense of acceptance and a deep joy after the day with Barbara. He had been pondering, not very deeply or wisely, how so often the greatest happiness and greatest sadness seemed to strike almost simultaneously into a person's life. But the lights in his house jerked him out of the thoughtful mood, and he drove into his driveway watchfully, puzzled.

There was a yellow Plymouth sedan in the driveway, but no one in sight. He parked behind the car, a rental with a small company sticker on the rear window. He walked into the house.

In the lighted living room he found Audra seated on the leather couch, a small pile of plastic-wrapped clothes and personal items beside her. She wore beige slacks and a white blouse, very plain, and she did not have a drink in her hand.

"Audra?" he said, really surprised now.

She smiled thinly but calmly. She was wearing her hair more simply and had very little makeup, and although she was very pale, she seemed fully in control and with a new air about her which was almost . . . he groped for the word to fit the impression . . . *placid*.

"The same," she said quietly. "I hope you don't mind, Robert. I came because of Jules's trouble. There were a few things I wanted to pick up."

Robert sat facing her across the coffee table, conscious of the old need to gear up for a struggle. "I'm sorry I wasn't here when you arrived."

"I've been here quite a long time this evening. It was almost nice . . . looking around, thinking." She turned her head to look around the room, the same slight smile on her lips. There was very little tension in her, it seemed.

"Well," Robert said slowly, "it's rough about Jules and Carole. I just hope they can . . . you know, get through it."

"They will, don't you think?"

"Audra, how did Gus take it?"

"He cried, and that was awful. But then he lost his temper and started swearing and yelling." Her eyes glistened for a moment, but she shook her head and smiled again. "He's all right."

"I had heard you were in New York."

"Yes. I came back for a few days, and then this happened."

"Do you plan to stay awhile, until something is settled on the charges?"

"No, Robert. And I didn't come here to talk about Jules, or even about my father."

Robert took a slow, deep breath, watching her. He still could not pinpoint the new placidity within her. This was a new aspect of her personality that he did not know how to face. She had not attacked him; there seemed no bitterness in her. He did not understand, and was more wary than ever. He said nothing.

"I'll be going back to New York," Audra told him. "I may stay tomorrow—here, that is—and then go back south long enough to see everyone for a few hours. But then I'm going back East. I remembered these last few things in our storage room. I hope you don't mind."

"Audra, this is all yours. That part is settled. You know I'm just camping here until the new owner closes out the paperwork. I intended to put anything personal of yours into secure storage anyway—"

"I know. I know." She grimaced slightly, but as if amused with the situation in a rueful way. "We don't have to apologize to one another any more, do we?"

"No."

She brightened, sitting up straighter. "I'm going to be all right, Robert."

"I'm glad of that."

"I mean really."

"Yes."

She reached into her large tan purse and drew out a small manila envelope. "I had my lawyers take care of this." She handed the envelope to him. "I'll maintain ownership of my stocks, as I told you earlier. But you have here the necessary papers to allow you to vote my shares any way you wish."

Numbed by surprise, he stared from the bulky little envelope to her face. "I don't know what to say."

She stood. "Then don't say anything. I don't want to spend all my energy hating any more, Robert. That's it, you see. And I want you to keep your winery if you possibly can. I want you to be happy."

"Audra, I—"

She smiled and moved nearer, putting a cool fingertip across his lips. "You already said you were speechless. Leave it at that."

He stared at her. She was lovelier than he had seen her in many years. There was an inner strength in her now. He sensed somehow that it was not fully developed, but already she was in control, not happy, but intent on *becoming* so.

"Daddy will die," she said softly, without inflection. "So I don't delude myself that we won't see each other again. But we'll never see each other again like this . . . alone. And certainly not in this house."

There was an aching in Robert's throat. "Audra, I'm sorry everything turned out the way it did for us."

She turned and looked around the room again, just for an instant, her eyes bright. "It is a beautiful home, isn't it? We were happy here once." Then she laughed softly, ruefully. "However!"

Robert cast about for the right thing to say, and there was nothing. "We won't know about the winery for a while yet. Your stock will help. But if we still lose, I'm sure your investment will be safe—"

"I don't think I'm going to be civilized a lot longer," she cut in, her voice almost breaking. "So I'd better be on my way." Clumsily she picked up her plastic-wrapped packages. One, containing a coat, slipped to the floor. Robert hastily gathered it up for her, bumping against her. There was an awkward instant again and then she turned toward the doorway, letting him carry the package for her.

Outside in the reflected dull light from the entryway she loaded the plastic bags in the back seat of the rental car. She slammed the door with too much force, turned to look up at Robert a moment, and then thrust out her hand. "Goodbye, Robert."

He took her hand. It was trembling and cold. "Audra, I don't know what I'm supposed to say—what I can say—but—"

She moved nearer and her lips brushed his cheek. She was crying. "God bless."

She fled around the car, got behind the wheel, started the engine. He stood rooted. He saw her hand flick whitely in a little wave, and then the car pulled away. She maneuvered the narrow driveway very manfully, and the taillights flared for a second at the road, and then the car turned and accelerated and was gone.

24

When Susan Knight walked into the winery on Tuesday, two days after news of Jules and Carole Trello's charges had been made public, she had little expectation of seeing Jules at the scheduled noon luncheon in the city, and no idea whatsoever that the day would end in the beginning of a desperate gamble to prevent the impending takeover of Robert Mancini Vineyards.

She was struck, rather, by a sense of familiarity, pleasure, sharp regret, and irony. The building was redolent with the heavy, sweetish odors of fermentation, odors she knew and loved as the most exciting time of the year. But she knew, too, that this might be the last such season for her here, where she had been so happy.

The Pinot Chardonnay had been picked Monday at Ned Henderson's and a number of other larger vineyards a few miles south. The crush was well under way: dumped by bunches from the gondolas into the stemmer-crusher, the grapes were stirred by mechanical paddles, partly crushed, pulled from their stems, and pressed through holes in the outer walls of the stainless-steel cylinder.

From this point, after other treatment as gentle as a massage, the grape skins were removed and the pure golden juice and pulp sluiced through treatment with sulfur dioxide to eliminate undesirable organisms. Within six hours of crushing, the slightly settled, treated, and chilled *must*, in jacketed fermentation tanks that would hold the temperature at 54 degrees, was inoculated with the purest strain of wine yeast. The process, continuing batch after batch, from tank to tank, would not complete its primary stages for a full six weeks. Racking and ion exchanging would follow late in November, with storage in oak to follow. Next summer the wine would undergo further tests, be centrifuged, and bottled. After the bottle rest it would be offered for sale more than eighteen months from now.

Susan proceeded directly to the production area, where she found both Mike DeFrates and his assistant working with Robert Mancini along the line. As they always did when working with this stage of the business, all three men looked hectic but happy.

"Some of the grapes coming in this morning are at twenty-four," Robert told her with a significant look.

"That's great!" she exclaimed.

"The sugar is leaping," he added. "It's going to give us a really fine wine, and the fruit is tremendous—a very big nose."

"They're still saying rain," Susan reminded him.

Robert nodded. Were there new lines in his face? "We'll keep holding off closer to the winery anyway. I want to take the gamble all the way."

Susan studied his expression, seeing the care as well as the pleasurable tension. She knew and understood his motivation to make this vintage the very best. It might be their last together. Growing within her, however, was the belief that they had begun to press their luck on the weather now; she knew the sugar in virtually all the grapes was high enough to allow for a very good harvest at once.

"How much longer do you think we can risk it?" she asked.

"Until early next week."

She was startled. It was to be a *very* long risk. But she said nothing. He knew the magnitude of the gamble better than she. If he wanted to take it, she would support him.

"Our friends from Portland," Robert added, "don't like the idea much."

"I didn't imagine they would."

Robert smiled faintly. "Surprisingly, they didn't put up the fight I quite anticipated."

On Monday, both John Endicott and E. Z. Simms had been much quieter. There had been only one sharp exchange when Endicott learned inadvertently that the vineyard was to pay quality bonuses, as it had every year in the past. Robert had stood his ground, however, and Endicott had backed off, muttering only that the matter would be reported.

Susan had her own theory about the Timmons representatives' sudden quieter mood. She was well aware of Robert's suspicions that there was a relationship somehow between them and Jules Trello; the Elmhurst transaction and subsequent bulk-wine offer had tended to support this idea. Now Jules was in serious trouble, and obviously preoccupied with it. Susan believed that Endicott and Simms no longer had quite the certain future they might have had before the Saturday arrests. She was not able to judge exactly how Endicott and Simms tied in with Jules, but their subdued behavior yesterday bolstered her belief that they did.

Thinking of this, she reminded Robert now, "We have the noon luncheon of the people who want to talk about forming the new vintners' association."

Robert mopped his forearm over his mouth. "I'm going to let you go to that one, Susan."

"*By myself?*" Susan asked.

Robert grinned. "Aren't you a big girl now?"

"Well—*yes,*" she said. "But I can't—what if they want to vote on something?"

Turning with a hose in his hands, Mike DeFrates growled, "Abstain."

"Why aren't *you* going?" Susan shot at him.

DeFrates turned a valve on the hose, flushing it into the floor drain. "Work!"

"I don't think it will get to a voting stage in one meeting," Robert said. "If it does, you know our policies. We support the idea of the association. Go, and play it by ear."

"Do you suppose Jules will be there?"

"I wouldn't guess either way."

"He's supposed to be master of ceremonies, until a meeting chairman is elected."

"I know. Ordinarily it's the kind of thing Jules would love. Now it's just the opposite." Robert's face twisted with sympathy. "Can you imagine the prospect of going to a session like that? Facing all your friends?"

The phrase "all your friends" struck Susan forcibly. How many friends did Jules Trello really have? A friend was one who knew a person well. Certainly Jules had acquaintances who liked him. But friends? Until this moment she had never really had any insight into the loneliness the man might really feel.

She felt a stronger curiosity about whether Jules would be there at all, and if so, whether he would play any part. "I'll represent us as best I can," she told Robert.

"Don't worry. If you don't know how to vote on something, you can always point out that you're just a woman, and can't possibly be expected to understand such matters."

"Mike," Susan said. "Give me that hose and stand back out of the way!"

It was the only genuine moment of laughter of the morning. For the remainder of the time, they were all much too busy to make more jokes.

Nevertheless, Susan was still in a better humor than she had known earlier, even when she left the winery and began the brief drive to the city for the vintners' meeting. There was hope yet, she told herself. No stock vote involving any amount of publicly owned stock was absolutely a sure thing. She had an almost primitive belief in ultimate justice, which she recognized as naïve but clung to because she sensed that without it she would be prey to a poisoning bitterness. Things *would* work out, she tried to assure herself.

On the drive to town, she studied the gray clouds milling overhead and noticed that nearly every other winemaker was harvesting at full pace. Trucks and tractor-drawn gondolas were everywhere; many vineyards had already been stripped of their fruit, and many others were now being picked. She felt a renewed tug of worry about Robert's gamble—another full week of hoping heavy rains would hold off.

If there was anyone anywhere with a bloc of stock that was yet uncommitted, she thought, it was conceivable that the outcome of this final wager on the weather could be a swaying factor. If the stockholder was aware of the situation, and knowledgeable, and if it rained and the black grapes went to ruin, would the stockholder then vote with Timmons? Contrarily, if the gamble paid off in grapes of extraordinary quality, would the same stockholder vote to keep Robert Mancini in charge?

Susan realized how far afield from reality such speculation was taking her, and it dismayed her. This was the kind of thing that happened under tension; everything could be seen in the focus of the impending central crisis; every decision might be warped by it.

And then she had another thought: was Robert delaying so long, taking such a great risk, to prove to himself that he was *not* afraid?

She tried to put this, too, out of her mind.

The meeting, at a relatively new motel which had a large conference room, already showed signs of high attendance when she arrived five minutes early. The lobby outside the room was packed with men—and a few women —she knew. One of those she spied was Barbara Turner, and, breaking away from some other friends, she walked to the reporter's side.

Barbara Turner shook hands pleasurably. "I wondered if you remembered me."

"I think I would now," Susan said, adding, "Robert told me."

Barbara showed a slight blush which was anything but tough and journalistic. "I'm glad he did. I hope you approve?"

"Very much so."

"You don't think it's wrong for him?"

Susan studied the slightly older woman's handsome face and saw that her concern was real, and that the question was sincere.

Barbara added, "I want very much for everything to go right for him."

"I think you might be the best thing that ever happened to him," Susan said frankly.

"My God," Barbara replied fervently, "I hope so."

Susan was struck by how different it was, talking to this woman instead of Audra Mancini. Audra had always been icily proper, but the suspicion—almost the hate—had always been just behind the eyes. Robert deserved a woman who was caring, she thought. She felt so glad that he had found such a woman now that she almost blurted out the sentiment.

"There's another reason I'm glad we happened to meet

here," Barbara Turner told her now. "I intended to come by the vineyard this afternoon to try to catch you."

"Me?" Susan said, surprised.

"I think I have an idea," Barbara said. "It may be crazy. I'd like to try it on someone."

"We could sit over here," Susan suggested, pointing to a nearby couch.

Even as Barbara turned, however, one of the winemakers appeared in the dining-room doorway, now filled with milling people. "Let's get started, everyone!" he said loudly, jovially. "Lots of words to spout so we can get back fast to that crush that's going on out there!"

Barbara said, "I'll come by the winery about four. How would that be?"

"Fine," Susan said. "I'll be there."

"Is there somewhere we'll be able to talk alone?"

This puzzled Susan. "My lab, I suppose."

"I don't even want Robert to know we're meeting. I think you'll see why when I get there. He might think I have a spring loose."

Susan was feeling pangs of a thoroughly whetted curiosity by now, but almost everyone else had spilled out of the lobby and into the dining room. They had to follow.

Once inside, they found chairs at one of the rear tables with two men from Flint Ridge and a woman who was an enologist for Belleville Wine Cellars. Only a few persons remained on their feet, and waiters were already serving at the front of the room and along the head table on the stage.

By craning her neck, Susan managed to answer her first question about Jules Trello. He was there, third from the center on the left. In the bright overhead lights, his sandy hair shone. His red sportcoat and wine-colored tie looked natty, and he was smiling at the man on his left, Timothy Crocker, and evidently holding a quite normal conversation.

Inside, Susan thought, he had to be cringing. She was sure he would not participate. She felt a certain kind of admiration for him in coming. That had taken a brand of courage in itself.

The meal was served, and the others at the table engaged in general idle conversation, making it impossible to continue any meaningful talk, one-to-one, with Barbara Turner. Susan speculated about what Barbara might want to talk about, but simply drew a blank. She ate quickly, like the others, and took part in the chitchat.

No one at their late-served table was quite finished with dessert when there was the tinkling of a spoon on a glass up at the front table, and she turned along with every other head in the room. She got a start. It was Jules Trello behind the lighted lectern, looking youthful, a crooked, wry smile on his face.

"Well, listen, folks," he said, his voice strong over the PA system, "if you're not finished eating, I guess you can do one of two things. You can ignore me and keep right on, in which case I ain't responsible, or you can quit now while you're still ahead and hope the jokes are better than the pudding."

There was a little ripple through the crowd, and Susan saw more uneasy glances exchanged. Clearly she was not the only one thinking of Jules's trouble . . . wondering how he could possibly speak.

Jules Trello, however, showed no sign of discomfort. Gawking this way and that, tugging with an index finger at his collar as if it were too tight, he tossed a quip *sotto voce* to the head table, and the people who heard it doubled over with laughter. His grin beamed. Hiking his elbows in the air, he leaned over the lectern to be closer to the microphone, the crooked grin broadening.

He looked not only at ease; he looked cocky.

"I was going to say," he said, "that a funny thing happened to me on the way to this meeting today. The only thing is, the really funny thing that happened was to that durn chicken I just et. Did you notice that chicken? Man, if all the chickens in northern California were laid end to end, I think it would happen in this motel's dining room."

Through the ripple of laughter, he tugged at his collar and made a face and bobbed up and down and took a sip of water, made a face like it was poison, and reached for his wine glass. This drew a burst of applause.

"Seriously," he said, "I'm glad to be here today." He did a double take. "Where am I? No. I'm not here to give you a bunch of bull. It's going to cost you four dollars a pound. Well, we're all here today to start a new organization. I think it's time we got organized. That's a famous historical quote. General Custer at the Little Big Horn. No. Really. We all know we've got a great future behind us."

Amazed, Susan watched as the little sandy-haired man bobbed, waved, rolled his eyes like Eddie Cantor, and milked the laugh with more foolishness. When it began to diminish, he perched practically on top of the lectern again. "And I'll tell you something else!" he said so loudly that the microphone overmodulated, breaking up his words. "We've got an even greater future ahead of us—*all* of us!"

There was a whoop somewhere in the hall, and then an enormous instant thunder clap of applause. Without having any clear idea why, Susan knew she would be applauding too if it were not for the cast on her arm. She felt a deep, shuddering chill.

He was *so* cocky, so corny, so much the silly, strutting, *macho* entertainer, defying them not to love him, that in this moment—given this single moment and this setting and this role for him—most of them had to respond. The applause rolled through the room. The looks on most of the faces nearby were filled with an intense, almost angry admiration.

Jules waved his arms, pleading for silence. "So it's about time to get down to the vote. Well, before we do, there's one more thing I want to do before you vote, and get my fanny off of here and back where I belong, on the sidelines. I've done it before sometimes, and I know a lot of you think it's old-fashioned and cornball, and all of that stuff, but by gosh we've all been through a lot." He paused meaningfully. "All of us have. And we ain't outta the woods yet. But I want to tell you. I never, in my whole life, had more faith—more of a belief—that we ought to stand together in song."

Almost without breath, Jules leaned even closer to the microphone. His voice rasped off-key, with intense feeling, "Oh, beautiful . . . for spacious skies . . . for amber waves of grain . . ."

Voices joined. Susan was bowled over. She could not believe it. She could not comprehend it. No one was this full of bravado—this capable of taking charge in the face of adversity.

But she realized, with another little chill, Jules Trello was doing it—making it work. Riots, arrests, disgrace— nothing, he was *showing* them—could hold him down.

In this moment, Susan saw more of Jules than she had ever seen before, and she saw something in addition. Even if the federal agents ultimately tracked him down, *that* would not be the end of this man, either. Whatever he might be, he had been through more than one crucible. His spirit might be warped, but it had the flinty glaze of the indomitable.

25

John Endicott was waiting for Susan when she returned to the winery.

"Just a little confab," he told her with his best smile. "Any objections?"

"I'm delighted, Mr. Endicott," Susan said sweetly.

Endicott chuckled at this sign of good humor and led her into his new office. It had been a storage room for accounting and payroll, but new carpet and ceiling, contemporary office furniture, painting, and a rather nice abstract print on the long wall had turned it into a surprisingly tasteful headquarters. A credenza behind the long black desk hid all the memoranda and reports, and stacked metal baskets held the work presently occupying Endicott's attention. He was an organized man, and much more intelligent, Susan suspected, than his normal bluff manner suggested. She believed that much of this was a ploy to make others underestimate him, and thus be easier for him to manage.

Which was what Susan promptly did.

"Sit down, sit down." Endicott smiled, holding a comfortable padded chair for her. "I understand you took in that vintner meeting in town over the noon hour."

"That's right," Susan said. "It was well attended, but no real voting was done."

"Well, that's fine anyway. Was another meeting scheduled?"

"Yes, but after the last of the crush."

"Next week or the week after?"

"No, actually the first week in November. Not that very many people will be crushing even next week. But there's all the cleanup and close control activity."

Endicott rocked in his swivel chair. "Yes, indeed. They held the meeting mercifully short?"

Susan relaxed, confident that he was only curious. "I'm sure they all wanted to get back to work. Just as I did."

"I've never understood the tremendous rush once the picking and the crush get under way," Endicott said. "Oh, I know the grapes won't stay in absolutely top condition very long, but most of these fellows act like it's a matter of life and death to get everything done today."

"When the weather is good," Susan pointed out, "you have to take full advantage of it."

Endicott looked dubious. "Would you call this such good weather?"

"Well, it isn't raining like it could be tomorrow," Susan said.

And then saw she had been mousetrapped.

"Yes," Endicott sighed, "it could rain tomorrow. As a matter of fact, I've just talked with the weather bureau and they say a fifty per cent chance of *heavy* rain tomorrow. Since you brought it up, Susan, why do you suppose Bobby refuses to harvest all these grapes?"

"He believes they'll continue to improve for another week," Susan said stiffly.

"Well, they certainly won't if it rains, as you just pointed out!"

"Robert has more experience with grapes—and with weather here—than either of us does, Mr. Endicott. I certainly can't quarrel with any judgment he might make."

Endicott smiled at her, nodding. "You're loyal. I like that. E. Z. and I have both commented on your loyalty and fine work. Many times. *Many* times we've discussed it among ourselves, and with others in Portland. We value you, Susan. I want you to know that."

Susan's face felt stiff and hot. She was very angry with him for trapping her into seeming agreement with his known position that the grapes should be picked at once. Now his transparent flattery assumed she was an idiot . . . an assumption that was, perhaps, partly justified by her conduct since she had entered his office.

She told herself to stop talking with her emotions and use her head. "Thank you, Mr. Endicott."

"It's certainly premature," Endicott told her smoothly, "to talk about the future. I know and admire your loyalty to Bobby. But since you are such a special person, I do want you to know . . . that if the vote goes in such a way that there is a management transfer, you're certainly very high in our planning for all contingencies.

"You know," he said, fondling a cigar, "Timmons Corporation prides itself on advancing womenfolk. We have a woman on our board. I think it's safe to say that your future with Robert Mancini Vineyards—or with Timco Wines, as the case may be—is limitless."

"Timco Wines?" Susan snapped. "Is that going to be the new name if you win in the stock voting?"

"It's been considered," Endicott said. "Of course, in honor of Robert Mancini's noted contribution to development here, there will always be a high-quality line of wines bearing that name too, unless Bobby himself objects for some reason."

"You seem very sure of winning the vote," Susan said carefully.

"Timmons Corporation seldom goes into a situation without thorough research, Susan. That's the beauty of the operation. From top to bottom, *planning*." Endicott paused, made a great pretext of pondering his next remark, then visibly relaxed. "I think I can tell you this. I would never say it to Bobby, because, frankly, it would sound to him like we were facing him with a situation that's cut and dried. But our computers show only about twelve per cent of the entire stock unaccounted for. Much of that is scattered to the winds—some possibly even lost, or forgotten in bank vaults, because the most strenuous efforts have failed to turn up the owners. And candidly, Susan, poor Bobby would have to scour up just about *all* of that to have a chance against what Timmons knows it controls, one way or the other."

Susan watched him. She knew that she was being told this in order for the word to be taken to Robert—to signal him to give up his continuing efforts to find additional certificates, and begin to accept directions with greater equanimity. She had been tricked, then oiled, and now used. She did not trust herself to say something immediately.

"You can help us," Endicott told her, switching to a frontal attack.

"How?" she asked.

"Talk to him," Endicott said earnestly. "Try to convince him to harvest these grapes! He respects your judgment. The good Lord knows I don't want more conflict here. But you and I both know that this risk he's running is just too severe."

"I can't convince Robert Mancini of anything, Mr. Endicott. *He* still owns this vineyard."

Endicott sighed heavily with apparent regret. "Yes . . . but I wish there were some way to convince him that he's making a mistake here, one likely to cut his own profits as well as ours."

"I certainly can't help you," Susan said stiffly.

"Like this quality bonus thing," Endicott went on, as if ruminating. "Sincerely motivated, but making a terrible impression in Portland. We're *all* in trouble over that one."

Susan bit her tongue to keep from replying.

There was, after all, nothing she could say without losing her temper now. Perhaps Endicott was able to manipulate most people in his employ with tactics such as these. But she was not in his employ. Nor would she ever be. Only the thought that she might somehow help Robert by appearing to be neutral kept her from saying so.

Endicott sighed heavily. "Well, Susan, thank you for talking with me, anyway. You know, this is a loyal gang of people around here. Gawwd damn, I just hope we can inspire the same kind of loyalty in the years ahead . . . you and E.Z. and me."

Susan managed to get out without saying anything obscene. She wondered briefly if Endicott had tried the same tactic with Mike DeFrates, and then knew that of course he had not; he still had all his front teeth.

"It was sickening!" she fumed to Barbara Turner when they met in the lab shortly after 4 P.M. "They're running around, manipulating people, and God knows how many people are falling for it! They can't even wait another month! They've got to be playing all their nasty little power games even before the vote!"

Barbara Turner set her mouth grimly. "That's what I wanted to talk to you about—the vote, and how it looks from your vantage point."

"My vantage point is awfully damned limited, Barbara, but I can tell you what Endicott told me during that session."

"Do."

Susan did, adding glumly, "I believe he told that very straight, too. It's the kind of information he wouldn't have to lie about. He wanted Robert to hear about it and know it was accurate, so he would lose his motivation."

"Is there anything," Barbara asked, "that would be certain to turn things around?"

Susan looked at her. "Only an awful, awful lot of money."

Barbara nodded. "This idea I have. It's probably got one chance in a thousand. I'd like to tell you what it is."

"I'll try anything," Susan said.

Barbara briefly explained what she had in mind. As she did so, Susan listened with mounting dismay.

"I don't think we would have a chance, Barbara. Not a chance!"

"We've got to do something," Barbara said. "We have to try to help in some way. Can you think of any other idea?"

"No," Susan admitted.

"Are you sure this wouldn't work?" Barbara demanded.

"I don't *think* it would."

"But are you sure there's absolutely *no* chance?"

Susan met Barbara's eyes. What, after all, did they really have to lose? If they didn't make the attempt, wouldn't they both always wonder . . . just a little?

"Hell," Susan breathed. "There might be one chance—a small one."

"Then I'm going to try it," Barbara said.

"Correction," Susan said. *"We're* going to try it."

Barbara smiled for the first time since her arrival. "Oh, great. Tonight?"

"What will you tell Robert?"

"Nothing! If we fail, maybe he'll never have to know."
Susan took a breath. "Tonight, then. Why not?"

26

On Wednesday, the last day of September, very little went right for Robert Mancini. He started the day more irritable than usual because he had not been able to see Barbara Turner Tuesday night, thanks to some "confidential assignment" for her newspaper. Then Wednesday morning Susan Knight came in an hour late, looking like she had been up all night on a bender. Then it rained a tenth of an inch, and even before a late afternoon wind began blowing, drying the grapes and preventing any major damage, Susan added insult to injury by being preternaturally cheerful.

"What are you being so cheerful about?" he asked her finally on the morning of the next day, the first day of October.

She turned like a child caught with her hand in the jar. "It isn't raining," she told him.

Word from his lawyers and broker was bad. The beehive activity of winemaking was an added irritant, a reminder of impending loss. He tried very hard to concentrate on his work. He would not, he kept telling himself, either go to pieces or allow bitterness to take over.

Mike DeFrates was a consolation. He had a bitter argument with E. Z. Simms about hiring practices at midmorning Thursday, and if Robert had not intervened, might have hit the smaller man. Later, Robert got DeFrates alone in his office for a brief consultation.

"Mike," he said meaningfully, "cool it. I mean it!"

"I'm going to knock that mother down before this is over," DeFrates fumed.

"Don't take it so personally."

"Personally?" DeFrates exploded. *"Personally!* Jesus Christ and little grasshoppers, that's what working here *is all about!* If I'm not going to take it personally, what the hell am I doing here?"

"We aren't the only people who care, Mike."

"I know," DeFrates muttered. "But shit."

"I've told you. We're still in charge . . . for a while yet, anyway. Just ignore Endicott and Simms."

"That's like telling me to ignore a turd in my under-wear!"

Robert laughed and banged him on the shoulder. "Get to work."

DeFrates morosely left the office, leaving streaks of mud and *must* on the carpet.

Robert walked over and picked up the chunks of mud. The carpet showed other marks, older scars from work boots, including his own. He wondered if E. Z. Simms would rip up the gray shag and install tan industrial carpet, and post signs about wiping your feet.

It was becoming so much harder than he had ever imagined it would be.

The telephone rang. "Robert Mancini?" a familiar voice said.

"Speaking."

"This is Tim Crocker. Your voice didn't sound like you for a minute there."

Robert cleared his throat of some of the emotion. "What's on your mind, Tim?"

"Listen, I just had a call from this fellow E. Z. Simms. Said he and that other liaison type—what's his name—?"

"Endicott."

"Yes, Endicott—he said they want to have lunch with me to talk about future plans for co-operation between our companies."

Robert said nothing. It was a new small blow that they couldn't even wait until the voting had made things official.

"Are you there, Bob?"

"Yes."

"Well, listen. The call kind of puzzled me, you know?

Simms started giving me all this business about plans for co-operative field work between Mancini Vineyards and Schreck Brothers, and how a third winery could come in. Pooled work force, and so forth. What kind of a deal are you cooking up there, buddy? And what's the status of this guy Simms? Why is it coming from him and Endicott?"

"You know what my situation is in relationship with Timmons," Robert said.

"Sure, but it isn't all that serious, is it? I mean, I've just assumed it was an internal hassle." Crocker paused and then his voice tightened. "Jesus, it isn't *serious,* is it?"

"I'm afraid it is, Tim."

"You don't mean these fuckers are going to . . . Bob, you surely didn't let so much stock go that there's a real problem of control."

"I'm afraid it looks like I did, Tim."

Crocker's surprise and dismay were shown by the silence on the line.

Robert added with effort, "It looks like I may be through here."

"Bob I don't know what to say, man."

"There isn't much anyone can say."

There was another pause. Then Crocker added, "I told Simms I had to check my calendar. Wanted to call you first. I'll call him back and tell him to shove it in his ear."

"No, don't do that."

"Why?"

"In the first place, you may have to live with these people. Listen to what they have to say. Also, it occurs to me that they're starting to come out in the open with something I've only strongly suspected: a solid link between them and Jules. So meet with them. See what their proposal is."

"If we could show Jules was mixed up in this, would it help?"

"I don't know," Robert admitted. "But if I had evidence, I might go to Portland and see if I couldn't raise a little storm of protest. I have some friends up there yet. If it looked like there was some hidden scheme here . . ." He left it unfinished because it was so indefinite.

"I'll meet with them, then," Crocker said tautly. "But Bob, why didn't you let a guy know? All this time you were in the middle of the negotiations with Rodriques and everything else, shouldn't you have been working on this problem of your own?"

"I've been doing all I can, Tim. Believe me."

Crocker's sigh of disgust was audible. "Okay. I'll get back to you. And listen." He paused again.

"Yes?" Robert said.

"I'm sorry, man. Really sorry."

Robert hung up. He walked to the windows and looked out at the gray day. It would be sentimental, he assured himself, to imagine that he would be losing friends like Crocker. He would continue to see them. But he did regret the change in status between them. A man defined himself in terms of his work. He already felt diminished.

The sky overhead was growing darker. He watched the clouds. *Just hold off a few more days!* he thought fervently. *Let us get that Pinot Noir and Cabernet next week!*

Was he crazy, praying to clouds?

About eleven-thirty, Endicott and Simms left the building, evidently headed for their lunch with Tim Crocker. Due to the weather, only a handful of visitors was in the winery at this hour. Robert took a land chart from his desk and spread it before him, noting the lands owned or under contract to his vineyard, those of Schreck Brothers, and those of Tim Crocker. He saw that they formed a rough crescent extending through the midsection of the finest mini-climate zone.

The three wineries, in a loose coalition, would become the most potent single producer-grower in the area, he saw. Jules's fields and winery, on the edge of the best land, would have its position enhanced by the association. But the others might have better practical use of the Schreck bulk-wine capacity too, in poor quality years.

Robert saw how it might work . . . how it might be part of the dream behind all the scheming that had and was taking place.

Jules, after all, had never been merely a schemer after empty revenge. This might be the pattern through which he expected solid financial gain, as well as added power and prestige.

Robert was trying to think of some way to approach the Timmons board with this vague evidence when Susan Knight, her color high, poked her head in the door. "Busy?" she asked brightly.

"Come in," Robert said, folding the map.

She entered, cup in hand. "I'm looking for a place to hide a few minutes."

"This is as good a place as any. I've been doing a little hiding myself."

Susan did not take a chair, but walked around the office as if there was too much nervous energy in her to allow quiet.

"Has something gone wrong?" Robert asked, watching her closely.

She turned to him, her eyes electric with excitement. "Me? No! I'm fine!"

He felt new tremors of irritation with her. She seemed particularly bursting with some combination of worry and hope and tension. He attributed it to the crush. But was it this easy for her to forget their predicament?

"Sure everything is all right?" he said.

"Fine!"

"This is an odd time for a coffee break, isn't it? It's time for lunch."

Susan walked to the door, which she had left ajar, and glanced into the reception area for a moment. "Well, Robert, I'm a very odd person."

"Susan," he said, losing patience, "what the hell is going on? The last time somebody acted this way to me, I was ten years old. It was a surprise birthday party."

She glanced into the tiny foyer again. Sounds—the elevator door opening—penetrated. She stiffened, then turned to him. "You have company," she said.

Robert walked partway across the office and peered past her into the crack between door and frame. He saw that the elevator doors were open, and a middle-aged man in chauffeur's uniform had stepped out. Behind him—Robert's shock was extreme—was a small, thin, older man in a gleaming metal wheelchair: Gus Trello.

Beside Gus Trello as he wheeled into the reception area was Barbara Turner.

"What the hell—?" Robert breathed.

Gus Trello had not yet seen him through the door. The old man wheeled his chair squarely in front of Nancy at the desk. Trello had two objects across his skinny legs: a very old, bulky leather briefcase, and, on top of that, a brown paper bag which he clutched securely.

Robert started for the door, hearing Nancy's murmured greeting.

As he swung the door wide, he heard Gus Trello saying, "I look for Robert Mancini."

27

For Susan Knight, it was an event she would never forget in any detail.

Facing the old man in the doorway of his office, Robert Mancini was slack-faced with surprise. Gus Trello, spying him, whirled his chair smartly from Nancy's desk.

"You are in, eh? Are you too important to see Gus Trello?"

"Of course not," Robert said, finding his voice. Then, as if dazed, he stood in the way.

Trello pressed the button of his chair and whirred toward him. He was going to run right over him.

"Robert!" Susan said.

Robert stepped back just in time, and Gus Trello drove into his office, calling over his shoulder to the chauffeur, "You wait out there, eh? Good!"

Barbara Turner followed him in past the stationary Robert. She told the old man dryly, "If you're trying to give me orders to stay outside, I'm afraid you're going to be disappointed."

Trello turned the chair near Robert's desk and shot her a look that was bright with rueful respect. "I am not a fool. I only boss people that will take orders. You and this one" —he shot Susan a wry glance—"are like mules!"

Robert walked to his desk and stood behind it. "What the hell is going *on* here?"

Trello glared at him. The old man's color was awful, a splotchy gray, and it seemed to Susan that he had wasted away slightly even in the hours since she had last seen him. But his eyes were incredibly alive: expectant, angry, happy, indomitable. He clutched his briefcase and brown bag with a stubborn strength, as she had seen his son clutch the edges of the lectern at the vintners' meeting. In his mortality he was magnificent.

"You think you know everything, eh?" he asked Robert. "You think maybe you are too good to come right out, ask for help?"

"What are you talking about?" Robert shot back.

"Robert, be quiet," Susan said, a fear gusting through her that a wrong word would spoil it.

"*You* shut up," Trello told her sharply, his eyes filled with liking. "I know you got no practice shutting up, but you *try,* eh?"

"Yes, sir," Susan breathed, smiling despite her tension.

Trello glared at Barbara.

She said, "I'm not saying a word."

Trello grunted as if he didn't believe it. He swiveled back to Robert. "You told me your trouble. Only you never said it was as bad as it was. You made it sound bad, yes. But not that you would lose this place if you did not find help. Why was that? Too proud, maybe?"

"I made it as clear as I could," Robert said, obviously mystified. "I couldn't beg."

"You are my son-in-law! Who says a son-in-law cannot beg?"

"Gus, I'm not your son-in-law any more."

"Shit and turds! Don't give me shit and turds! Once a son-in-law, always a son-in-law! You think I got time to break in a new son-in-law? You think I care what you and Audra do? You and me, we are the same. We understand each other!" The old man's eyes narrowed. "Maybe we are too much alike, even, eh?"

Robert slowly sank into his chair, pale, his eyes at pinpoints. He said softly, "I don't know what you're doing here. At this moment I'd have to say we don't understand each other at all. Are you going to explain?"

"Always I explain!" Trello sighed. "Everybody is stupid!"

Robert's jaw set again, giving warning of possible harsh words. Before he could speak, however, Trello raised his right hand in a gesture of weary reconciliation, grasping his sack and briefcase with his other arm.

"Okay," he grunted. "I thought you were in trouble, but I thought, 'Well, it is good for him. He is too arrogant, too stubborn. Let him sweat, eh? He will fight his way out and maybe he will get humble, a little.' Eh? But the other night, I am in my house. It is late. I am in my room, alone, with TV. My family is out at pool, in game room, running around in cellar for anything left, dogs shitting, everything. Eh? Okay.

"Then comes Cline. He says two ladies to see me." Trello swept a sarcastic, admiring glance at Susan and Barbara. "*These* two. Come to see Gus Trello."

Robert stared at Barbara, then at Susan, in mute surprise. Susan flushed with a hot pleasure, but said nothing. Barbara remained standing near the old man's wheelchair, her eyes fondly on his face.

"I say bullshit!" Trello resumed. "I say, 'You think I am going to see my son-in-law's so-called girl winemaker and his new girlfriend? Bullshit!' So I tell Cline to send them away."

Trello paused, coughed wetly, fumbled for a bandana which he dabbed at liver-colored lips. His pallor worsened.

"Do you want a drink of water?" Robert asked quickly.

"Water?" the old man yelled. "After whole life of wine, do I now drink water? Water has germs! Water kills! Keep quiet!"

Without a word, Barbara poured some chilled water from Robert's desk carafe into a paper cup. She handed it to Trello.

"Thank you," he said meekly, and drank it.

"Now," he resumed more strongly, handing back the cup. "I send these two girls my message, eh? Okay. Next thing I know, here come two girls right into my bedroom! Cline is running after, saying, 'No! No! You cannot go in there!' Jill is running, 'No! No! You have to get out, he is sick man!' " Trello snorted laughter. "I start turn on my chair, drive away. *This* one"—he pointed at Susan—"grabs chair! Wheels skid on rug! I am trapped! Then *this* one"— indicating Barbara—"says to me, 'Mr. Trello, is stuff we came long ways to tell you, and you are going to listen.' "

Trello rolled his eyes. "My God! They are crazy, I think! Are they going to kill me?"

Robert swung around toward Susan. "You two went down there?"

"Yes," Susan said. "Tuesday night."

Robert turned back to Trello. "I didn't send them, Gus."

"Ha! Listen! Nobody sends two girls like this *anywhere*, eh?" The old man sighed. "They are tough girls, you know it? How come you got two of the world's toughest girls on your side? I don't think you deserve them, you know? I should have had sons like these two."

Barbara smiled at him softly, with love. "We would never have put up with your tantrums."

"Ah," Trello said gently, "maybe not. Maybe is what I needed—someone tough." He sighed again. "Frank has worked hard. Jules has worked hard. But Frank needs a boss, he cannot make up his own mind. And Jules . . . aagh! Jules is bull in china shop. But okay. My will is set up. Everybody will get something. Frank will run company, but with board to boss him. Jules will get some stock. Money, plenty. The business will go on. Old fox is gone, but business goes on, right?" He glared at Robert.

"You don't look gone yet," Robert told him.

"Bullshit! What do you know how far gone I am? Shut up!

"Now. These girls tell me your whole deal, the predicament. I have thought about it. But before I tell you what I have decided, there is something else to do, so maybe—for once—you will understand something, eh? Probably not, probably you will not understand. But maybe."

Still glaring, Trello began unwrapping the brown paper bag, removing folded pieces of newspaper and dropping them to the floor. "You got corkscrew? Glasses? Decanter?" He removed from the wrapping a dark, very old bottle of wine, carefully continuing to hold it in the position it had been since his entry.

Susan went to the credenza. Because her cast and sling made her awkward, Barbara helped her put the glasses and corkscrew and crystal decanter on the edge of Robert's desk.

Trello handed the bottle to Robert with tender hands, not varying its position. "You open. Be careful with old cork."

Robert looked at the label. His eyes narrowed. He nodded for Susan to watch him as he opened the bottle, and she moved closer.

The label was old-fashioned. Across the top it simply said *AUGUST TRELLO,* none of the trimmings of the modern corporate entity. Susan had never seen this label except in a picture book of California wine history.

It was a 1941 Cabernet Sauvignon, the California claret that had won more international prizes than any wine ever produced in this country. A legendary wine, produced in a very small quantity, it was said to have had uniquely fine qualities, was perhaps the single wine above all others that had shown the way to excellence for Californians.

The cork was old and crusty, but Robert extracted it expertly. He handed it to Gus Trello, who sniffed it and nodded.

"Yes," he said. "This bottle and one more, I hide from the vultures. People talk about twenty-year wines. But this is a wine that will last a hundred years, if any is around to try it."

Robert stood with the bottle cradled in his hands, his expression expectant, awed. "I didn't know there was any left in the world."

"Decant it! Now! A wine this old does not stand up to the air very long! We got to decant because it has lots of sediment, from its age. We did not run stuff through filters and centrifuges, all that, then. We *fined,* the old way. Decant! Quickly!"

Robert held the decanter and bottle to the window light and slowly began pouring the contents into the crystal container. Susan could see that the wine had indeed thrown a great deal of sediment, but Robert's careful pouring kept it suspended in the bottle, like a gray cloud, while the wine entering the crystal decanter was sparkling-clear, the deepest, loveliest red.

There was total silence as he finished the decanting, stopping when the sediment cloud had reached the very neck of the bottle. He put the bottle on the edge of the desk.

"Pour!" Trello grunted. "Quickly!"

Robert poured some of the wine gently into the four glasses before him. As he did so, the first of the bottle bouquet reached Susan's nostrils: rich, complex, incredibly robust and magnificent. She understood Robert's earlier expression of awe; it had reached him at that moment.

Trello reached for one of the glasses, savored the bouquet, and looked at each of them. "Take," he said. "Drink."

Susan reached for her glass as did the others. She inhaled, then slowly tasted.

She experienced a profound feeling that was almost religious. She had never experienced a wine that even approached the complexity and perfection of this. A deep, mysterious, ebony taste of great age and dignity was underlaid by a trace of fruit, and as she let the fluid trickle down her throat, it was warming, leaving a perfectly clean, dry, immaculate effect. She had tasted nearly all the *grand cru* wines of the world. But nothing quite approached this.

It had been very big, very hard, very acid in its youth. It had to have been so to grow thus in the bottle. But now its long wait was ended. From a sunny vineyard somewhere in the south, from vines planted long before she was born, the wine had begun, and was nurtured, racked, watched after, wedded to the finest oak. It had slept a while then, maturing as it slept, and had been a young giant when placed in the bottle. Its long wait for this moment—its years of growth and change and development—had begun too before her own birth.

No man could have predicted a bottle of wine such as this. Any of a million unpredictable accidents would have made it something less—a single day of too much or too little sun, a few raindrops, a single crushed seed, a stray yeast spore, a jostling, a change in a few molecules in the dark cellar. But the tiny *possibility* of this miracle would not have existed at all if every loving step had not been taken to assure conditions as ideal as man could make them.

An accident—yes. But only an enormous love and care by Gus Trello had made the accident a possibility.

Now it was here and it was whole. It was perfect.

No one had spoken. The glasses were partially emptied. Susan held her glass carefully by the stem, aware that the heat of her hands could be deadly. The wine was very old, exceedingly fragile. Within minutes it would decay, and be something less.

"Gus," Robert said finally, his voice husky with feeling, "it's simply magnificent."

The old man nodded, and his voice, too, was quiet. "So what do you think you will do if you lose this winery, eh?"

"I have some other land not connected with this. I'll raise grapes."

"I asked you to be my manager. You said no. I asked you to work with me. You said no. Now you will lose your winery. Do you think you made a mistake in not coming in with Gus Trello?"

"I've made many mistakes," Robert said, his expression betraying his perplexity. "But I suppose what I've always wanted to do was make a wine as great as this one. I can't regret trying."

Trello's head sank to his chest. "I wanted you to sample this wine. No one else would understand it. This Susan girl is smart, but even she is not understanding it right now like you do, eh?"

Robert put his glass on the desk. "Any man who made a wine that approached this one, Gus, was a success in life."

Trello snorted. "I made this wine. All. I loved fine wine like this. But then it was not enough, eh? Money. I wanted more. Big family. Big dreams. So I go another way— cheaper wines. Easier. Quicker. I was not stupid like you. I was smart. Hurry the wine. Make more of it. More fields. More plants. More. More. So there was not any more Gus Trello wine like this one."

In Robert's eyes was the pain of compassion. "Some of your wines today are good, honest wines, Gus."

"Bullshit! My wines today are nothing! I wanted success . . . money. So I got my success, and you know what it is? My success is shit and turds . . . shit and turds."

Susan waited, tears in her eyes. She did not know exactly what Gus Trello planned for this meeting. She had not been prepared for this. But then she realized that she could not have prepared anyway. In this instant, the old man stood naked before them in his success and in his failure.

Barbara moved closer to him and put her hand on his shoulder. He started as if he had been stung, but then smiled and put his hand over hers for a few seconds. He raised his head and his chin jutted. "I liked you, Robert, because I saw you were like me, a mule. Do not ever stop being stubborn. You have been more my son than my sons. Just like these girls are more my daughters than my daughters. Do not be like old Gus Trello, eh? Make fine wine. Do not end up with shit for your life."

He turned to Susan. "Fill the glasses. The wine is dying."

Susan silently obeyed.

Trello, however, did not reach for his glass just yet. He began unbuckling the straps of the antique briefcase. His eyes glinted, showing a resurgence of his spirit.

"When you came to me for help, you mentioned stock. I thought, 'Let him fight hard, be scared. Maybe he will learn some humility.' I did not see it was such a fight as these girls have explained to me. I had some of your stock, Robert. I knew my son Jules had some, too. I planned to make you fight your own fight. You were a mule; you did not tell me clearly that you could not win without this other stock."

Trello opened the flaps of the case, then rested his bony hands on it for another moment. "I went to Jules last night. Jules, my son, the big crook, eh? I think he had a plan for turning his own life more to shit, by voting this stock against you. But I have some weapons too, eh? Do you think my son Jules will hold this stock and use it against you if he knows I will change my will against him? Ha! I may be sick. I can still make most people do what I want!"

With this, the old man tipped up the briefcase.

Onto Robert's desk spilled dozens—hundreds—of stock certificates.

"My shares," Trello said. "Jules's shares. Yours. I think this will be enough to make Timmons Corporation shove up ass, eh?"

Robert Mancini had gone a ghastly white as the certificates tumbled onto his desk. Now he raised a shocked face to the old man's. His lips opened, but he appeared incapable of speech.

Trello raised his hand. "Make good wine. This is all I ask." He grimaced. "I guess is one thing I can ask and you will do, eh?"

Robert licked his lips. His voice when he spoke was hoarse. "Gus—hell, you've just saved it for me!"

Trello raised his wine glass to his lips, tasted, and made a face. "It is already fading." He put the glass down again, squared his shoulders, and glared at each of them in turn. "Maybe I will have a *quid pro quo,* eh?"

Susan exchanged glances with Barbara, and chilled. Was it a mirage?

"What do you want?" Robert asked cautiously.

"Take me through your winery," the old man said, a challenge in his eye. "Show me how you make your wine. I think you will never make a wine as good as this one of mine, but I would like to see how you intend to try!"

28

A little later, with Gus Trello busily driving his wheelchair on ahead somewhere, Susan and Robert were explaining the centrifuge to Barbara Turner when John Endicott and E. Z. Simms appeared on the catwalk overhead. Endicott waved to them, and both men started down.

Susan looked at Robert, knowing that they were both thinking the same thing: Endicott and Simms did not yet know what had happened to them.

"Oh, please," Susan said. "Can I?"

Robert grinned. "Go."

Susan walked forward to meet the two men at the foot of the metal stairs.

"We just had an interesting lunch with a mutual friend, Susan," Endicott told her. "Tim Crocker."

"I have something to tell you," Susan said.

Something in her expression seemed to freeze them.

"Do you remember telling me," she asked, "how much stock Robert woud have to have to win a vote?"

"Yes," Endicott frowned. "Of course that was confidential—"

"You were counting on Jules Trello's stock, weren't you."

"Well, now, that's an impertinent question, and—"

"You were," Susan snapped. "But I have some news for you. You'd better run to your computers, both of you, and start refiguring. Jules won't be voting that stock for Timmons. Robert has that stock now. He has another four thousand shares of the unaccounted-for certificates, also."

Endicott raised shaking fingers to his mouth. Simms, his eyes bulging, opened his lips to reply.

"I think," Susan added, "that means a switch of about fifteen per cent, total. I think it means there won't *be* any vote, because you've just lost, and you don't even need the computer to know it."

John Endicott turned to E. Z. Simms. They stared at each other.

"Surprised, Mr. Endicott?" Susan asked. "Surprised, Mr. Simms?"

Then, as they turned back to her in their shock, she could not resist.

The grin hurt her face.

"Gawwd *damn!*" she told him.

29

Each day the weather threatened. Over the weekend there were light showers. Fog masked the northern reaches of the valley, bringing with it traces of *botrytis*. The winemakers rushed against time and weather, making their harvest.

A few vineyards waited, and gambled. But not many.

On the seventh day of October, the black grapes showed a Brix over 24. The grape skins were velvety soft. The picking began, all by hand at Robert Mancini Vineyards, for extra care.

Shortly before noon, the first gondolas, bright yellow in the fading light, were pulled into the winery production area. Lifting clamps were attached to the sides of the first gondola.

Robert Mancini stood watching the work, along with Barbara Turner and her son Jimmy. Susan Knight and Mike DeFrates stood nearby.

The lifting winch clattered and the gondola began to be raised on one side, to be tipped into the stemmer-crusher. On the top of the great mass of deep-purple Cabernet grapes, clusters began to shift and tumble, so fragile that even this broke some skins. Juice glistened on the mound of ripeness.

Mike DeFrates caught Robert's eye, grinned, and held up a fist in triumph.

The gondola was tipped farther. The grapes began to

tumble out in a purple avalanche. In the fields more gondolas were coming now.

"It's going to make great wine," Robert told Barbara
and her son.

"Maybe the best ever?" Jimmy asked, squinting.

"Of course," Robert said, as if surprised. Then he put
a hand on the boy's shoulder, pointing as he explained
operations. Jimmy watched and listened, forgetting to be
aloof, caught up in the sound and excitement.

The grapes plunged, tumbled, cascaded down into the
stemmer-crusher. The machinery did its work. Juice—hundreds of gallons of rich, foamy, brilliant dark juice thick
with battered skins and oozing pulp—sluiced toward the
first great sterilized vat. This was as it had been for men
who made wine through the ages: the end of one kind of
waiting, and one kind of climax, yet the beginning of something new and profoundly different and yet the same.

As the first tank filled, Robert Mancini conferred with
Jimmy. The boy nodded eagerly. Robert patted him on the
back and walked around the tank building, to reappear
moments later on a catwalk up on top, where the juice
continued to pour down. Robert was carrying a five-gallon
drum which Susan Knight, instantly recognizing, smiled to
see.

Robert signaled Jimmy to join him. The boy climbed
up the metal ladder and stood with him on the top. There
was a round manhole in the top of the tank, and they
could look down into it, seeing swirling, frothy pink foam
on top of the *must*.

Robert pried the lid off the metal container he had carried. He spoke to Jimmy. The boy reached his hand into
the container and brought up a handful of the pure, cream-
colored yeast. He held his hand over the tank opening and
spread his fingers, letting the yeast meet the *must*, and the
wine was born.